HORROR IN PARADISE

HORROR IN PARADISE

Grim and Uncanny Tales from Hawaii and the South Seas

Selected and Edited by
A. GROVE DAY
and
BACIL F. KIRTLEY

MUTUAL PUBLISHING

First Edition

Printed in Australia

Acknowledgments

"The Puzzle of the Ninety-Eight" from *The Blue of Capricorn* by Eugene Burdick. Copyright 1961 by Eugene Burdick. Reprinted by permission of Houghton Mifflin Company.

"The Honolulu Martyrdom" from *Shoal of Time* by Gavan Daws. Copyright 1968 by Gavan Daws. Reprinted by permission of the University of Hawaii Press.

"Bully Hayes and Ben Pease" from *Slavers of the South Seas* by Thomas Dunbabin. Copyright 1935 by Thomas Dunbabin. Reprinted by permission of Angus & Robertson.

"The Marchers of the Night" by Mary Pukui and Martha Beckwith. From *Kepelino's Traditions of Hawaii,* edited by Martha Warren Beckwith (Honolulu: Bernice P. Bishop Museum, 1932). Reprinted by permission of the Museum.

"The Girl in the Red Gauze Blouse" by Marjorie Sinclair. Reprinted by permission of the author from *Hapa,* No. 3, Fall, 1983. Copyright 1983.

"Over the Reef" by Robert Dean Frisbie from *The Book of Puka-Puka,* copyright renewed 1957 by Florence Frisbie Hebenstreit. Reprinted by permission of Mrs. Hebenstreit.

ISBN 0-935180-23-0

Library of Congress Catalog No. 86-060370

DEDICATED
to the memory of my dead wife,
JOAN,
who read thousands of pages
of Pacific narratives
helping me look for suitable accounts

BACIL F. KIRTLEY

Foreword

The islands of the Pacific have been a favored region for legend and romance ever since the early eighteenth century, when Jonathan Swift invented the tales of Lemuel Gulliver. But when the great explorers filled in the map with charted islands in place of mythical kingdoms and writhing leviathans, a shelf of "true" literature began to accumulate.

Ever since the ancient era of our cave-dwelling ancestors, listeners have shivered with delight when hearing stories of terrifying events while sitting in safety around the evening fire. Today, the popularity of horror tales and films repeats the instinctive joy of viewing another's distress while comfortably at home. Horror fiction is a marketable type along with romance, sci fi and fantasy, westerns, sea stories, and detective yarns.

We have chosen, however, except for the opening short story, to collect here a volume of narratives of actual events—as true, that is, as truth is possible with messages from the uncanny world. Horror of a crude and obvious sort, of course, can be found in your daily newspaper; but few such episodes are worth preserving as literature, lacking as they do the shivery appeal of whisperings and tellings. We have sought not only stories of sorcery and the supernatural, but also classic narratives of man's inhumanity and desperate survival by beach and ocean, in jungle or city highrise. Often the true accounts of what has happened in the island world of Oceania rival in suspense or allure even the most imaginative yarns of South Sea fiction.

The selections that follow draw upon supernatural folklore, reports of sprites and phantoms, visions and fancies. Here are tales of the kahuna cult of Hawaii and the witch doctors of New Guinea, ghosts on high isles and reef-decked atolls, diabolism and fatal tabus. Here are the misadventures of beachcombers and yachtsmen, and buccaneers like Bully Hayes and Ben Pease. Here are the wars of island tribesmen and the beleagured defenders of Wake Island in World War II. Here are the survivors of an attack on a ship by an enraged whale, or the sun-parched occupants of open boats on the vast world of water. Here prowl phantom animals and here march the menacing giants of the nighttime. Here the sudden "cauld grue" of fear brings a copper taste to the tongue and a conviction of the existence of things that must not be.

The arrangement of the stories comprises a reverse chronology based on the date of the incidents they present. Starting with more recent events and exploring into the past, the reader, besides encountering memorable tales, may find it easy to make something of a historical excursion into the Pacific past as well. The range in time runs from the 1980s back to the ancient years before Captain Cook's ships sighted the Hawaiian group. The boundaries of "paradise," for our purposes, extend across the Pacific from Juan Fernández in the east to the Carolines in the west and encompass the island areas of Polynesia, Melanesia, and Micronesia.

We have aimed to present herein a variety of episodes and personalities. The collection, we feel, reflects occurrences, or aspects of life and character, that will evoke for the reader pretty much the seamy side of Pacific life as it was, in spirit as well as in fact.

A. G. D.
B. F. K.

University of Hawaii

Contents

HORROR IN PARADISE

Marjorie Sinclair

The Girl in the Red Gauze Blouse

Marjorie Sinclair is the author of two important novels: *Kona* (1947) and *The Wild Wind* (1950). These reflect life in Hawaii just before and after Pearl Harbor. She has also published poetry, biography, and translations of poetry from China, Japan, and Polynesia.

Mrs. Sinclair, educated at Mills College, first came to Hawaii in 1935. She married the late Gregg M. Sinclair, president of the University. After his death in 1976 she married Leon Edel, author and educator. In the islands she is well known for her "ghost stories," of which "The Girl in the Red Gauze Blouse" is an outstanding example.

> The lives of children are
> Dangerous to their parents . . .
> *Louis Simpson*

1

ON Tuesdays and Saturdays I always go to visit Tommy, my small son. He lives in a special school where children with his kinds of problems are trained. It is six blocks from our house. I always walk, even in the driving wind and rain. I really prefer to walk in wind and rain. They prepare me.

When I went this morning, I noticed a girl ahead of me. I don't often pay particular attention to casual persons—especially on the way to Tommy's. This girl, however, walked with a kind of arrogance which was almost a stately dance. Her brown hair fell to the waist; straight and shining, rippling slightly as she moved. She wore tight blue jeans and a red gauze blouse which was torn over one shoulder. On her feet were rubber zori. Her heels were cracked and dirty. Her appearance was quite typical of many girls in Honolulu, but her manner marked her. It was the swagger—with a touch of anger. She might indeed, three or four generations ago, have been a young chiefess, used to having her wishes granted immediately.

When the girl reached Tommy's school, she paused at the walk leading to the front door. I waited. I did not want to have to face her. I never wanted to see anybody before going to Tommy. Besides, my feelings for some unexplained reason ran strong. It was as if she had said something rude or had done something which inflamed me. My attitude was quite senseless and a little frightening. I had never even seen her before! And to have it happen before visiting Tommy—just seeing him was enough disturbance for any day.

I was relieved when she started on her way again. I turned up the walk to the thick glass doors of the school. At the entrance I looked back to see where she had gone. She was nowhere in sight. It was a quite sudden disappearance, especially as I could see a good two or three blocks down the street. I took a deep breath and opened the door.

Tommy stood, as usual, in a corner of his airy bedroom. His arms, tightly held to his side, seemed thinner than I remembered. His small face was pale, his eyes and mouth pulled in like an old woman's. He looked shriveled and unwell. He had never been a rosy, plump child; he was thin from babyhood, and his skin had a dry-leaf pallor. I sat on the floor in front of him and spoke his name quietly over and over again. Occasionally when I did this, his lips would tremble or his fingers reach very slightly in my direction. Out of some dark place inside came a vague impulse to touch someone—his mother, if he understood I was his mother. Or what a mother was. At least he had an impulse—I had touched something in him. You may imagine how I waited for these moments.

Today, however, he remained impassive. He looked at me for three or four minutes. He looked—but it was more as if I wasn't there. Finally he turned to the window. I could see only his back. Above him tinkled the wind chimes I had bought for his birthday. I asked him to listen to the music. His back stiffened. I stood up and went to his small rocking chair. He loved the chair and would rock for hours on end, so they told me. I began to rock. It was comforting. Just the movement soothed fear and anxiety. Finally I tiptoed from the room. His teacher always laughed at me for tiptoeing. But I had no desire to disturb Tommy—wherever he was in his dark place.

In the hall the teacher was waiting for me. She said he had spoken some words during the week. His appetite was not good, but he hadn't lost weight. "He's coming along nicely" were always her parting words.

I left the school in my usual devastated condition. Inevitably I went home from these meetings to prepare a miserable dinner for Tom and myself and to spend the evening drinking wine in front of the TV. Tom almost never asked about Tommy. I imagine my mood told him all he could bear. He seldom went to see the little boy; and he would never go with me. We had not yet been able to talk in any direct way about our child, to ask why we should have had such a little boy—to discuss the meaning of Tommy in our lives. The doctors and teachers tried to encourage us about him. But whenever we attempted to talk, we both became angry. It had been this way for almost three years—Tommy would soon be five.

I had not found the courage to tell Tom what I now recognized as a truth—that Tommy would never be more than he was. It is a truth of the kind that one is horrified to reveal—one runs away from it. At times now, the child no longer seemed pathetic to me. He was simply a sad grotesque little human being, a creature which shouldn't have been born. At moments I hated him. I hated him because I had created him—I had given birth to a distorted, unnatural creature. The child's existence both accused and imprisoned me. One has a right, I said defiantly to myself, to hate one's own creation, especially when it is unnatural and so frighteningly sad. Furthermore, the hate filled me with guilt. I told myself over and over that I was a mother without feeling to hate a damaged little boy who was flesh of my flesh. Flesh of my flesh, those ancient words appalled me . . . How much Tom and I had wanted to have little Tommy!

A few days after I saw the girl in the red gauze blouse—her image remained in my mind—I had a dream about Tommy. One of the strangest and most frightening dreams I ever had. He was a Hawaiian child. Of course in actuality he was part Hawaiian—from Tom. And I had much wanted a Hawaiian child. In the dream he was a brown-skinned little boy whose head had grown to a monstrous size. He had to hold it up with his small hands. Like an overripe melon. Tommy lived on a sandy beach where low-growing trees shaded him from the hot sun. Naupaka and other shrubs grew lushly along the edge of the sand. Tides pushed up, leaving ragged lines of coral rubble from the sea. This little landscape was very sharp and clear like a miniature painting. Between the shrubs and the coral rubble Tommy had a very small spot to sleep, but it was hard for him to find a place for his monstrous head. In the shifting fashion of dreams, we were suddenly high on the lava slope of the mountain behind the beach. There were scrubby trees, and many people were milling about. Tommy was walking among them when suddenly he cried out. I rushed to him. His great head had broken like an egg, and the blood drifted out like a piece of red gauze. I screamed and woke up. I couldn't stop trembling, and Tom shook me gently. I told him I had a dream but couldn't talk about it. He put his arms around me and pulled my head onto his shoulders . . . He let me cry there softly and stroked my hair. I kissed his cheek in relief and gratitude.

For a while after this dream I could not bring myself to see Tommy. The large head of the dream reminded me by contrast of his babyhood, when everyone had admired the shape of his head and the beautiful proportion of his little body, the long slenderness of his fingers. This was before we knew about his trouble. I remembered the feel of that little head in my hand and how deeply and tenderly I loved him. I loved him even more because he seemed so frail.

There was another reason I loved him in this special way. He had something I didn't, I couldn't have. Something I wanted more than anything. He had a share of his father's Hawaiian blood. I was one of those persons who romantically yearn for the purity and directness of a people close to the grass and earth, to the sea and mountain. I had grown up in miles of pavement and apartments. And I came to Hawaii to escape from those drab stretches of cement, steel, glass. I longed for mountain areas where I could be lost in the foliage of forests, hearing only the birds, the wind, and the water. It was, I thought, almost magic that I should meet Tom and marry him. He had a big sprawling family which welcomed me. I felt at home in a world which had always been, I thought, beyond my reach. Then came the baby. The baby established me, I was part of this world I wanted. I had given my flesh to it.

My flesh—in horrible distortion. The dream of the monstrous head lingered. I relived it every day; I saw the head break, I saw red float out. And I wondered why the dream had in this oblique fashion connected Tommy with that handsome girl in the red gauze blouse.

2

Gary, a friend of Tom's, invited us one Sunday to go out on his catamaran. I packed a lunch and we sailed out of the yacht harbor on a blue-green sea. I settled myself comfortably on the trampoline and let the men handle the boat. Gary sailed expertly through the reef channel and out into the open choppy water. The men talked. I watched the vaporous clouds and the green mountains. The wind stroked my arms and legs. I was sleepy and closed my eyes.

When I awoke I saw the girl leaning against the mast, her long hair moving in the wind like seaweed in the water. I wondered if I had somehow missed the fact the Gary had brought a friend. The girl was handsome—a straight nose, full lips, and fine tan skin. Her eyes, a dark brown, bulged slightly and seemed fixed on a far-off place. Then I saw her blouse. It was red gauze. I told myself in panic that I must still be asleep. Yet I saw her very clearly, and I could hear Gary and Tom talking and the water rushing along the side of the boat. I could even feel the warmth of the sun on my body. Suddenly the men swung the boom to change tack.

The movement did not disturb the girl—the boom seemed to pass right through her. Her gauze blouse hovered like a brilliant flame. I pounded my hand lightly on the trampoline to make sure I felt the rough texture of the fabric. I pressed my cheeks and forehead. I was awake and everything was real. She remained there against the mast, motionless, her eyes fixed. I got up on my knees and started to move toward her. Gary saw me and shouted, "What about lunch?"

Mechanically I reached for the lunch basket and opened it. When I looked again at the mast, the girl was gone. A moment of anxiety struck me—was she a warning? Was Tommy ill? Then I scolded myself. I didn't believe in such things; I didn't believe in apparitions or omens. Tom shouted, "What are you waiting for?" I unpacked the sushi and barbecued chicken. The men moved toward me on the trampoline. Tom looked at my face. "Something wrong?"

"Yes," I said and tried to smile. "I saw a ghost."

"That's possible," Gary said. "You're not the first one. This boat has its own ghost—it was here when I bought it."

"What kind of ghost?" My breath faltered.

"I'm not sure. I never saw it. Somebody said a girl. There was some kind of accident with the first owner."

I forced myself to pass the chicken around and to pour the wine in paper cups. I told myself to be calm. But the rest of the trip was agony—a kind of nightmare in broad daylight and on the blue of the sea.

The next day Tommy's teacher called. She told me he wouldn't eat. The doctor had said that they might have to force-feed him. "But we don't know if he will stand it. He is quite rigid and unyielding, yet at the same time passive." I told his teacher I would come.

He was lying on his bed. His pale face made his eyes and hair seem even darker. He was utterly listless and took no notice of my presence. There was not even the usual stiffening. I touched his hand. He seemed to have traveled beyond human hope into a hibernating animal world. Perhaps it was a relief to him. I wished suddenly—with horror—that he could die. My mouth went dry and chalky. It was the first time I had admitted the idea of his death. But I knew it had lain dormant in a recess of my brain. Death would be release. For the child—for Tom, for me. But death cannot be made to come. His little heart was young and strong. He might try to starve himself. But medicine would cope with this small organism. I shocked myself—Tommy an organism. I trembled and tears flooded my eyes. The teacher patted me on the shoulder. "They go through all kinds of stages."

I knelt by the bed and stroked his forehead. It seemed cold. He looked at me—his eyes were empty, almost like eyes which are all pupil, a dark hole.

The teacher said, "We have recently found him curled up under his bed or in a closet, like a little animal in a lair."

"I don't want him to go to a hospital," I said. "I hope you can take care of him here."

"He's no care. He just lies here and submits to anything we do for him—except eating. Most of his stiffness and stubbornness have gone."

"Maybe he is wiser than we are."

The teacher was puzzled and faintly shocked at something she didn't want to grasp in my words.

I walked from the school into the hot July sun. I felt all shriveled up. It was as if my body had never carried the child lying on that bed. As if I were an aged woman carrying only death in me. I had given birth to death. If only he could die. And then, intruding on my despair, coming down the street, I saw the girl in the red gauze blouse. She was walking with a boyfriend and they held hands.

I watched as she went alone into Tommy's school. The friend waited near the front steps. In about five minutes she returned. She was smiling. Her smile seemed to me strange and somehow sinister. He took her arm. I followed them.

Her arrogance was still in her fine vigorous form. I had a fantasy of the two young people having a whole stream of beautiful children with dark hair and sturdy bodies. The children would grow naturally and comfortably. I remembered how her apparition had leaned against the mast of Gary's catamaran. Like a sign, an omen. But—of what? I told myself that I made too much of an illusion—it was all in my imagination. This ordinary Hawaiian girl was no chiefess, no ghost. In spite of the noble arrogance of her carriage.

I followed the young couple almost as if I had been bidden. Tommy was pushed out of my mind. They continued to hold hands. Now and again they stopped to kiss lightly. I could see that she dominated him, that he was enslaved. She would make him miserable ultimately. She would always blossom elegantly and arrogantly. She was a chiefess—yes, that I would have to admit. She would always have her way. I hated her for what she would do to him. He was a fine-looking young man, slender with black curling hair. Tommy might have grown up to be like him.

At the edge of the neighborhood shopping mall, they turned into McDonald's restaurant. I followed. They laughed, drank cokes, ate their hamburgers slowly. Two tables away I had a hamburger and coffee. I gulped the hot drink, not touching the sandwich. My mind cleared. I stood up and without putting the trash in the bin walked out the door. I could feel their attention upon me. But in my mind's eye I could see Tommy lying quiet and cold upon his bed.

The moment in the fast-food place was a turning point of sorts. It was a moment of the everyday, of the usual human round of morning, noon, and night. I thought if Tommy weren't sick, he and I could sit together at McDonald's. For him it would be a treat—as it was for all the children in the restaurant, and for the girl in the red blouse and her boyfriend. We would sit on the plastic chairs at the plastic tables and gaze at plastic ferns hanging over planter boxes; we would eat hamburgers and french fries; we would be ordinary people—a mother and her small son—having a little treat. Everyday people just like everyone else. Why should I hate a little boy who couldn't be like everyone else—who couldn't do the simplest small thing? He could only curl up like an animal in a lair. The girl—that beautiful proud tall young woman—would know, I thought, what I couldn't know. She was close to grass and sea and mountain. She could reach him—because of her long dark hair, her tan skin, her whole self which, though proud, would yield to a little boy who had Tommy's need.

Sometimes it was comforting to think of Tommy as a small animal. A creature wild and delicate, and yet responsive to words and touch. Once I broke through Tom's barrier about the child to tell him, thinking it might help. He said I was on dangerous ground. "An animal can respond," he said. "Tommy can't. Just stay with what he is. We must learn to accept him—and after a while forget him."

I hated such a reasonable approach to Tommy. It was cold and negative, as if he had no existence. Therefore I had no existence—not even as a mother. Tommy remained a part of my flesh—as if he were an arm or a foot. I know this was an absurd notion. But it was real. I remembered his baby head in my hand—now at times the monstrous dream head. There were other dreams, when his head was a boat shaped like a scallop shell which drifted on sea and in air and passed right through my body as if I were a wraith.

That was why the coffee and hamburger had become important—and even the girl in the red blouse. They were real and concrete. I saw the girl occasionally as I walked to Tommy's, sometimes with and sometimes without her friend. Her appearance continued to fascinate me—her carriage and her languor. I felt certain she must have chiefly blood. She reminded me of the portrait of the great chiefess Liliha, leaning on the shoulder of her husband Boki. Both of them had the romantic, noble-savage grace an English artist had imagined in the early nineteenth century. The girl seemed almost a reincarnation.

I speculated about why she appeared so frequently in our neighborhood. But whenever I tried to draw a fantasy around the fact, I stopped myself. There was too much fantasy in my life already.

I formed the habit after visiting Tommy of eating a hamburger. She had started that, and I was grateful she had given me this odd touchstone. This strange comfort. She reminded me of how things actually are, how one eats and sleeps and grieves over a child like Tommy. So I ate the hamburger and watched whenever she came in, which she often did. And I envied her. I envied the stream of vigorous children latent in her body. How one dislikes a person whom one envies!

One day when I went to visit Tommy, the teacher said that the new aide, Lani, was with him. "She's very good with Tommy. You might like to watch them for a few minutes before you go in."

I went to his closed door, which had a small window for observation. I looked in. Tommy was seated on a mat on the floor. His head was bent over. Across from him sat a young woman in a pale blue uniform. Her head, the hair in a neat bun, was bent too. They both examined a pile of blocks lying between them. She pointed at one. Slowly Tommy put out his hand, his first finger pointing. With a darting movement he touched the block and then pulled back. She took his hand and guided it again toward the block. She spoke. His hand remained above the block, suspended awkwardly. She seemed to be coaxing him. Slowly he lowered his fingers. He touched the block with a fingertip. "Good!" I could hear her say. She looked up, and I saw her face. The girl in blue was the girl in the red gauze blouse.

My first impluse was to rush into the room and snatch Tommy away. But I didn't. I didn't really want to. I continued to observe. Tommy stood up. He kicked at the blocks — his face impassive as it usually was, with the small lips pulled tight. Lani said something. He kicked again and began to walk over the blocks. One turned under his feet and he fell. She was quick to lift him up and take him on her lap. He did not cry. She held his head as I had once held it, cushioned tenderly in her hand. He lay quietly in her arms. His head was beautiful: the dark eyes, the dark curly hair, the skin that no longer seemed to have a pallor. Lani must have had him out in the sun. He was hers. He belonged to her, I was convinced. A wave of hate spread like a chill through my body. She had possessed him so easily, so comfortably. I couldn't do it. I never could!

I walked away, out the door of the school and straight to McDonald's. I ate a hamburger. It was delicious. I listened to the people around me speaking their little bits of gossip. I watched the children squirming in chairs too large for them, munching on buns. The spasm of hate disappeared. I was happy.

At home Tom asked, "How is Tommy?"

"Fine. He's just fine."

Yao Shen

Emma de Fries and Queen Emma of Hawaii

A series of esoteric exchanges in recent years between a full-blooded Chinese woman and a part-Hawaiian counterpart is narrated by a former University of Hawaii professor to whom manifestations appeared on the fifteenth floor of a Honolulu apartment house.

Yao Shen (1912–1985), born in Chekiang, China, earned a bachelor's degree in English at Yenching University, Peiping, in 1935. Coming to the United States on a graduate scholarship, she received a master's degree at Mills College and an Ed. D. at the University of Michigan. She served at that institution as a professor until coming to the Manoa campus of the University of Hawaii in 1962. There she taught and carried on research in linguistics until her retirement as a professor of English in 1977. She taught at a dozen other centers in America and abroad, and published nearly one hundred professional papers.

Her one excursion into personal revelations concerning the spirit world was circulated under the pseudonym of "Shin Ling," meaning "heart" and "spirit."

I FIRST met these two distinguished ladies when Emma Alexandria K. de Fries came to bless the Contessa apartment house, a thirty-seven-floor highrise on South King Street, Honolulu, on September 24, 1971. The Contessa had been recently constructed on land that included a Hawaiian churchyard and a cemetery, from which the bones had been cleared away. The builders had held an elaborate groundbreaking ceremony that began with a blessing of the site by the minister of Kawaiahao Church, which owns the land, first in Hawaiian and then in English. He was followed by a Japanese Shinto priest, who blessed the four directions. A Chinese lion dance and firecrackers concluded the event.

During construction, however, more bones were found, so the minister gave another blessing, and the bones were re-interred according to his specifications. Later I was pleased to learn that he too was buying an apartment at the Contessa; but, then, after undergoing lung surgery, he decided not to live there. After moving to my own apartment in May, 1971, I learned something that was even more distressing: the Contessa was haunted. People claimed to be seeing ghosts, and soon strange things began to happen to me.

One mid-morning in June, for example, as I was walking along the Contessa side of King Street on my way to the nearby University of Hawaii, I saw a dark, neatly dressed lady standing at the intersection of Kahoaloha Lane, where there was a pedestrian walk but no traffic light. She appeared to be waiting for traffic to clear so that she could cross; and, thinking it easier for drivers of cars to see two people walking together than one in the pedestrian walk, I joined her with a smile. She too was Oriental, but she did not respond; and while in the walk she lingered behind me singing. Before we got to the other side of the street, she told me to go back to China, my homeland. She continued in this vein for a very long block until we got to the bus stop at the corner of King Street and University Avenue. By that time, I was so upset that I did not know whether to go on to the campus or to return to my apartment. When I tried to walk away from the bus stop, she was right behind me. And when I turned and walked back, she did the same. People waiting on the benches watched us, until the bus arrived and I got on. From the bus, I could see her sauntering away, and I noticed that she carried nothing in her hand, such as a purse or a bag. I was still so shaken that I resolved from then on to walk only on the Contessa side of King Street and leave the other side to her.

But it did not work. Early one morning three months later I noticed another strange person, this time with rather dark skin, crossing Dole Street against the light as cars from all four directions stopped and waited. There were bits of dried grass on the person's left ankle; and again nothing in the person's hands. From behind, I could not tell if it was a male or a female, but I concluded that, whichever it was, the person must have slept the night on the ground. Then it seemed gradually to take on the shape of a woman, who, while I was waiting to cross with the signal, had reached the other side of the street, where she turned around, stared at me, and waited. I crossed over with the crowd that had been waiting for the light, and then she, too, seemed to be following me. I stopped; she stopped. On the campus I paused to look at a long flight of steps in front of Bachman Annex; she did the same. I turned around to look at her; she stood still and looked at me. She appeared to want me to do something for her but said nothing. Since I did not know what else to do, I walked on; she followed, close behind—until I quickly turned onto a crowded pedestrian walk where I was able to lose her.

Back at the Contessa, a noise that had been building up was now deafening. It sounded as if tons of bricks and mortar were ceaselessly being poured down the rubbish chute outside my door from the building's topmost floor, day and night. And when I perceived that other residents of the building heard nothing, I understood that something must be wrong with me, or with my apartment, and that I must do something about it at once.

Since I did not understand Hawaiian customs, I assumed that all the appropriate measures had been taken to ensure a peaceful life at the Contessa; and now I did not know what more could be done. As I worried and fretted and sought uncertainly for a solution, I developed acute hypertension. One day when my physician and I were talking in my apartment, the seven floor-to-ceiling glass windows and doors rattled and banged so loudly they seemed about to shatter—but only for me, because he heard nothing. At this point, he recommended Emma de Fries, a *huna nui,* or high priestess (one with deep wisdom of the spirit), whom he knew to have taken care of similar problems after more orthodox treatments failed.

When she asked me about myself over the telephone next morning, I told her that I had come from mainland China in

1936 and to Honolulu in 1962; that I was a traditional Chinese constantly remembering heaven, earth, and my ancestors; and that I lived close to the Invisible. Every now and then, since childhood, I said, I had seen a white-robed guardian angel, who at times would speak to me. Immediately sensing the state I was in, Emma assured me that she would be at the Contessa that afternoon. I told her I would meet her by the Contessa and she could not miss me; I always wear my short hair straight, and a Chinese dress—in the style of 1936.

As I waited, a car pulled up with a large woman in a red gown at the wheel. Bound around her head were two strands of small cowrie shells, and her eyes looked very strange. I was seized with the feeling that one has when meeting a close relative not seen for some time, and that I had a million things to tell her. When she got out of her car, I noticed that below her long voluminous red gown she was also wearing red *tabis* (mitten socks) and *zoris* (thongs) with black velvet straps. The two ends of a wide red band around her neck hung down past her knees. When I looked up, her eyes were still funny. Plainly funny.

As we walked into the building, Emma told me that she knew of the problem at the Contessa: a small one which could be easily taken care of, she said. The bones that were disturbed during construction belonged to three people who were not happy with the blessing they had received. In the lobby she noted the structure of the building, and as I lingered with her I could feel all around her a strong outpouring of warmth. Heavy and tall, she looked like the old pictures one sees of Hawaiians of special importance. But her eyes were different from those of any human face that I had seen in all my sixty years. They appeared to have merged into one single eye which had grown in size to cover her face from temple to temple, eyebrow to cheek. "There is nothing wrong with your place," she said, as soon as we reached the entrance to my apartment on the fifteenth floor, "but I'll bless it anyway."

"Please do not," I replied. "I don't want you to bless my place only. I want you to bless the entire site. If you bless the site, my home will be included, the home of everyone else, and our common domain. My father always said, 'No amount of wealth can make me feel rich, if all around me are poor relatives.' How can I be happy in my own home, if I'm surrounded by unhappiness?"

"All right," said she, "I'll bless the site, *then* your place."

So I proudly ushered her onto my lanai, where she paused for a long moment, slowly surveying the city, and sky, and sea from Punchbowl to Diamond Head. "You see, the three people are unhappy, because the bones of each one are not together."

"I don't blame them," said I. "I wouldn't like to have one arm of mine on mainland China and the rest of me here."

"Exactly," said Emma. Extending toward the sky her left hand, as the hand nearer to her heart, and her right hand downward, as if touching the three spirits one by one, she blessed them gently and reassuringly in a voice as warm as that of the brightly shining sun. "In a little while we will all be one," she said in such a way that I thought I had never before known grace. She paused for another long moment, then smiled, turning toward me very slowly but with evident satisfaction: "Everything is fine now. They are happy. Now let's see the rest of your place."

The blessing seemed an instant miracle. Nobody followed me again, nor was I disturbed by any more racket in my ears. In fact, it has seemed so quiet since then that I sometimes actually wish for noise, just to be certain other people are living here.

Emma gave my home a most detailed blessing, moving slowly and quietly from room to room, pausing with deliberate looks into the distant sky, scrutinizing carefully each corner of every room, touching all major items of furniture, silently verbalizing her blessings and following each of them with a smile. She would lay her great hand on walls, counters, and those appliances that have wires or pipes connected to the ground, at the same time waiting and listening but not moving on until satisfaction beamed over her face, permeating the air with a mother's gentle assurance. While we were moving around my bedroom, she looked at the closet and asked what was in it. "May I have a look?"

"Of course," said I and opened the doors. "Look anywhere. Nothing but clothes."

But pointing toward one corner, "What's in that?" she asked.

"My footlocker. I store my mainland winter clothes in it."

"Something else too. What?"

Then I recalled. "Oh, some scrolls that I don't want to get damp."

"Scrolls!" Emma looked at me sternly, "You mean scrolls which the Chinese people respect and you chuck away in a dark corner like that? Hang them up! Don't you Chinese people always have a place in your home where you keep a scroll hanging? A place for respect?"

"Yes," said I. "In this apartment the place would be above the altar table in my living room facing Diamond Head."

"Then hang the scrolls there."

I promised I would.

After Emma finished blessing my apartment, I told her about the two women who followed me. She was interested to know if they were haoles (Caucasians) or if they had darker skin on the order of hers and mine. She herself, she said, was one-eighth Chinese on her mother's side. As we talked, it seemed to me that the air was full of reluctance for us to break up, though we both knew she had to catch a plane soon for the island of Kauai. I later learned that she was going there to attend her brother's funeral. When we said goodbye, I noticed her eyes were no longer so strange.

Since that first meeting, Emma has visited me quite often, frequently noting that my home was full of "such warmth." We usually sit across my dining table, she facing out toward Waikiki, and chat about things of the spirit. Soon I began to call her "Auntie" because of my growing affection for her.

One day I showed her a clipping from a recent issue of *Fate* magazine (Vol. 25, No. 6, June, 1972, page 82), that identified her as the great-great-granddaughter of *ka huna nui* (the chief *huna*) of King Kamehameha the Great. It quoted her story about "a beautiful woman dressed in white" who appeared out of nowhere to halt the progress of her half-Hawaiian and half-Caucasian grandpa, Howard de Fries, on his way to gather mountain apples. Then a boulder that almost certainly would have killed him thundered across the path ahead, but when he turned around to thank the lady for saving his life, she was nowhere to be seen.

"Every word in it is true," Auntie Emma said.

During another visit I asked her to get in touch with the three spirits who had been disturbed by the building of the Contessa and to tell them that they would be welcome at my place any time. "I'm a traditional Chinese," I said. "We always share our home with others."

She smiled. "They are not here any more. They have moved on. Don't worry about them."

Everything was going along just fine. When Auntie Emma again came to call, I told her that I had silently promised the first woman who had followed me that I would not walk on "her" side of the street. But now I wondered if it would be all right for me to do so. Not that I had to. I just wanted to know if it would be all right.

"Of course, walk anywhere," she answered firmly. "There is no evil around you."

And then, still walking on the Contessa side of the street a few days later, I saw two little Oriental girls of not more than five years old waiting at the Kahoaloha Lane crossing. Each had the most beautiful shiny smooth hair hanging below her waist. Each carried the largest size Philippine tote-bag. Their tiny hands clutched two or three of the largest University-of-Hawaii spiral notebooks, hugging them closely to their light pink sweaters. I thought I ought to cross in the pedestrian walk with them for the same reason I had earlier crossed the street with the woman who told me to go back to China. I asked the girls if they did not want me to help them. They looked at me shyly, giggled, and chatter-boxed with each other. I decided to mind my own business and walked on, but I could not forget the girls. So I turned back and crossed with them. Skipping and chatterboxing, they happily went ahead. But when they reached the push-button that allows pedestrians to change the traffic light, they stopped, pushed it, and waited to re-cross the street. It made me feel very strange indeed, having just gone out of my way to help them and now discovering they wanted to go back again. They turned around to look at me, talked to each other some more, re-crossed the street when the signal turned green, and disappeared into the morning crowd.

When I asked Auntie Emma if they were somehow related to the two women who followed me, she thought for a moment and said, "Who else would they be?"

"They came to walk me to the other side of the street to let me know that I could walk on their side of the street?" I continued.

Auntie Emma said, "What could be more obvious?"

One morning, remembering the person who had followed me onto the campus, I thought of how we both had stopped and looked at a long steep flight of steps in front of Bachman Annex. But when I got to this point, I discovered that there were no such steps and never had been, for the building has only a ground floor. And I wished I could have remembered the words I thought I had seen on a big gold sign at their top.

When Auntie Emma telephoned early in June, she asked me as usual how I was.

"Great, great, great!" said I. "Finals are over. Grades just got turned in. And I'm going to spend all summer doing nothing but decorating this place of mine until it's exactly the toy box my heart desires. Just great! Remember, you always say 'Do something for yourself'? I'm going to do it good and thorough. And! Next time when you come, those scrolls that were in my footlocker will be hung up, just as you said. Isn't that great?"

She did not say anything for a moment, then she said, "Are you really so fine?"

I assured her that I was. There was no response at the other end of the line. So I went on, "Don't you worry about me. I'm sitting on top of the world. Life is like one endless bed of roses." Then I began to wonder. Why she had asked?

"Last night I dreamed I was boiling some lemon grass to give you a bath," she said. "I just wondered what happened to you."

At last I recalled a recent minor siege of shingles. My left leg, from knee to toe, had been covered with marks. "But I'm fine now," I said. "I still have all sorts of black marks on my left leg, my foot, and all of my toes, but they don't bother me. When they itch, I try to forget it. That's all."

Nevertheless, Auntie Emma soon arrived with a quart of lemon grass tea. I was to drink one glass the first thing in the morning and one glass the last thing before bed. "Are you going to drink it?" she asked.

"Sure," I answered. "It's just like Chinese herb medicine. My maternal uncles were herb doctors. I'm used to it. You are one-eighth Chinese; I'm sure you've seen Chinese herbs in Chinatown."

I faithfully followed her directions. After one day, the itch was gone. At the end of the third day, all the black marks except for the first real bad one had disappeared. My doctor was delighted and amazed.

On December 7, her birthday, Auntie Emma came over again and said, "During deep meditation, your white-robed angel came to me in a radiant light to tell me you are my spiritual daughter. It has happened three times now." And with this new relationship so well established, she began to confide in me more deeply.

"When I was five years old, we were living on Lemon Street in Waikiki," she said. "And late one afternoon when I was sitting in my grandfather's lap on our lanai I noticed a certain tall man going by. His clothes were loose and flurry, and he seemed different from the other people, very different. I looked at him and looked at him. It seemed as if he did not have any substance—as if he was sort of airy. I followed him with my eyes as he went by, and I felt very strange. At the same time, a loud wailing rose out of the house next door; and the following day we learned that the father had passed on—at about the same time I had seen the tall man."

Later, when Auntie Emma was nine and living in Aiea, she was sitting one early morning on a bench under a guava tree on the big lawn in front of her house, when she saw behind her right shoulder a lady in white with flowing white hair, impressively white. She had two huge eyes that were very, very different from ordinary eyes. Instead of having pupils, they were full of radiance. Oh, they were so beautiful, Auntie Emma recalled. "What's your name?" asked the strange lady.

"Emma," she answered.

"But you are really Alexandria," said the lady.

"Yes," Auntie Emma replied, although she always knew that her grandfather had named her after Hawaii's Queen Emma.

Entranced by the strange white-haired lady's eyes, "Your eyes are so beautiful," she said.

"Do you want to touch them?" the lady asked.

"Yes," answered Auntie Emma, reaching up and touching them with the first three fingers of her right hand, and feeling a tingling sensation in the tips of her three fingers. Looking at her fingers, she could find nothing different. She rubbed them with her right thumb. The tingling feeling did not go away. Then she turned to look back at the lady again, but the lady was gone.

Still feeling a strangeness, she turned to look over her left shoulder—and there was a white robed *man*. His hair too was long and flowing but black. His eyes too were very big, without pupils but full of radiance. Oh, they were so beautiful. The man asked, "What's your name?"

"Emma," she answered.

"But you are really Alexandria, aren't you?"

"Yes," she replied. She realized then that her own name was supposed to be Alexandria. This was what they were telling her.

During this conversation the man's black hair gradually turned white, and it became just like that of the lady, impressively white.

"The same person!" I interrupted Auntie Emma to say. "The same person!" I repeated.

"Yes," she said. "You see, they can be either man or woman." Then she went on with her story.

"You have beautiful eyes. May I touch them?" she asked the man, and he told her she might.

So she reached up and touched them with the first three fingers of her left hand and took her hand away. Again she felt a tingling in the tips of her fingers. And again she looked but could find nothing different. She rubbed them with her left thumb. The tingling did not go away. She turned around to look again at the man, but he was gone.

Earlier in her story, as Auntie Emma told of the first apparition, it seemed to me that the oval face of Hawaii's Queen

Emma gradually superimposed itself over Auntie Emma's round one, Queen Emma's slender neck over Auntie Emma's full neck, and her angular shoulders over Auntie Emma's ample ones. Above a low wide round dark yoke, the queen's neck was bare, and her dark hair was piled neat and high, as in the pictures one sees of her. This clear image of the stately queen remained without motion for six or seven seconds. Then it gradually faded away; the top of her face, which appeared first, disappeared last.

While Auntie Emma was telling me about the second apparition, I again felt an intense presence, but different from that which I felt when the queen appeared. This presence began immediately in front of me and moved across the dining table to Auntie Emma and up over her bosom to her face, where I saw that single eye again, covering the part between temple and temple, eyebrow and cheek. Once again she looked the way she did at the very first; but in a few seconds the presence faded away, and Auntie Emma's eyes returned to normal.

When I was unable to keep the experience to myself any longer, and interrupted to say I had seen the queen, Auntie Emma looked at me squarely for a long moment. I had known she was named after the queen and had been for many years a hostess at Queen Emma's Summer Palace, which has been restored as a museum. Now quietly and contemplatively she said, "Many people have told me I'm her re-birth."

Then she continued with her story.

After touching the eyes of the two apparitions, she gazed at the tips of all six tingling fingers. There was nothing different about them that she could see. She rubbed them with her thumbs again and again. Then she brought her hands together with the ends of the three fingers of one hand touching those of the other. And as if from some magnetic attraction, her hands stuck together. She tried to separate them but could not. She pulled and pulled and pulled but could not pull them apart. Finally, with great effort, she managed to do so. She looked at the tips of the fingers again—still nothing different to be seen. Again she rubbed the three fingers on each hand with their respective thumbs—still the tingling was there. Then, with her fingers, she stroked her eyes a few times. When she stopped and opened her eyes, everything she saw appeared nearer and clearer.

She got up and walked back to the house, where her grandfather was standing on the lanai. "Emma!" he demanded. "Where have you been?"

And when she said nothing, he told her that her eyes looked different.

Before she left the Contessa that day, Auntie Emma, who says she's approaching seventy, broke into a big smile. "All my life people have told me I would have a Chinese daughter," she continued. "I always wondered how that was going to be. The day after your doctor told me about you, I said to my sister Marion, 'My Chinese daughter has come.'"

A week or so later, I told Auntie Emma over the telephone that the more I thought about Queen Emma appearing at my home, the more honored I felt. "Imagine! Hawaiian royalty condescending to visit my humble shack, when I'm a total Chinese without a single drop of Hawaiian blood or a solitary Hawaiian cell in me."

"That's right," Auntie Emma's voice said at the other end of the line. "In this life." A long pause. "In one of your previous births you were a Hawaiian." Then she went on, "Did you not say that you felt something telling you that you were moving away from Ann Arbor before you came out here? Did you not say that you felt something telling you that you were moving out of your former apartment in Honolulu before you settled at the Contessa? There must be a meaning behind all this."

In trying to sense out this meaning, I recalled the Chinese concept of the relation of heaven, earth, and the individual: a person completes one life cycle when he reaches sixty, and a new cycle begins at sixty-one. At sixty, after wandering for thirty-five years from one rented apartment to another in the United States, I had at last bought a permanent residence. But it was not until I had come to know Emma de Fries—as kahuna, auntie, mother, and queen—that I was made to feel at home, and ready for a new cycle to begin.

Eugene Burdick

The Puzzle of the Ninety-Eight

Born in Iowa in 1918, Eugene Burdick went as a child to California. After high school he worked as a clerk, ditchdigger, and truck driver until he had saved $150, enough to enable him to enter Stanford University. He was graduated in 1941 and soon thereafter was married, taken into the Navy, and sent to Guadalcanal. As a gunnery officer aboard various ships, he spent twenty-six months in the Pacific.

With a Rhodes scholarship at Oxford, Burdick won a Ph.D. degree and while a professor of political science at the University of California at Berkeley published his first novel, *The Ninth Wave* (1956). Thereafter he gained celebrity as co-author of *The Ugly American* with William Lederer (1958) and *Fail-Safe* with Harvey Wheeler (1962). "The Puzzle of the Ninety-Eight" is taken from *The Blue of Capricorn,* a collection of factual and fictional writings about the Pacific (1961). Burdick died in 1965 of a heart attack during a tennis match.

THIS story is nine-tenths true. The ninety-eight died, and they died in the circumstances which I depict. These facts are as accurate as the records of a military court-martial can make them. But no court-martial knows what goes on in the minds of ninety-eight men who lived the most isolated life of any prisoners of World War II. That must be the task of imagination.

Wake Island is a V-shaped atoll which rises about twelve feet above the water. The land above water is tiny, no more than two and a half square miles. It is also miserable—coral rubble and sand so porous that it will hold no fresh water. Few plants can live on such land, but the morning-glory vine, a shrub called desert magnolia, and a dwarf Buka tree supply patches of green color.

The open end of the V-shaped atoll is closed by a barrier reef. The great sea waves rage at the reef incessantly, and their booming can be heard over the entire atoll.

Wake is one of the most solitary islands in the world. It is no part of a friendly archipelago. The closest islands, and they are tiny, are far distant. It is thousands of miles from ports like Honolulu or Tokyo. There are no signs of Pacific peoples there, and there is nothing to stay a person—no water or vegetation or shelter. The water around Wake is an endless reach of virgin waves. They surge against Wake and then go on for thousands of miles more before touching land. It is lonely beyond the telling.

The waters immediately around the atoll and within the lagoon are magnificent. On the lee side of the island the water is utterly pellucid. One can see the details of a brain coral at a depth of over a hundred feet. In the lagoon and about the reef there is an abundance of barracuda, yellow tuna, mackerel, shark, and giant ray. On land the only living indigenous creatures are great swarms of birds, a multitude of small land crabs, and that is all. Rats have escaped from ships wrecked on the reefs of Wake and have grown huge and sleek. These living creatures, all of them, play an important part in the story.

Wake would be valueless, uninhabited, bleak and forgotten except for one thing: the airplane. Its very loneliness, its isolation in the midst of empty ocean, made it an invaluable piece of land. It provided a place where planes, to and from Asia, could land and fuel. It was also a place where the military apparatus of the United States could put an advanced outpost—not a strong outpost, for it was too small for that, but a sort of military eye to sweep the emptiness. It was an outpost that was necessarily without muscle. Even the mechanical ingenuity of Americans could do little with such a tiny area.

On the morning of December 8, 1941, Wake Island (it is across the international date line and in Pearl Harbor it was the morning of December 7) bustled with activity. A total of 516 servicemen and 1,216 civilians were at work. An airstrip had been laid out and was in primitive operating condition. The three small islands of the atoll, Peale, Wilkes, and Wake itself, were jammed with dumps of ammunition, gasoline, unmounted guns, big water distilleries, small mountains of food. A Marine squadron of twelve F4-F wildcat fighters had just been flown into the island. The Pan American plane, the China Clipper, was at anchor in the lagoon. There was no aircraft detection apparatus of any kind on the island.

At 11:58, eighteen Japanese two-engine bombers, hidden by clouds and unheard because of the booming surf, barreled down on the island in power dives, dropped fragmentation bombs, made a long graceful curve in the sky, and came back to strafe.

It was the beginning of a short, bloody, and ferocious battle. On Christmas Eve, Colonel Devereux did what few Marines have ever been called upon to do. He left his command post with a white bag tied to a broom handle and began negotiations for the surrender of Wake. There was no humiliation in the surrender. The defenders had fought well. The Marine fliers, working under unbelievable difficulties and overwhelming odds, feverishly cannibalized each plane as it was destroyed, until their last plane was literally a mechanical mongrel made up of the parts of six other planes. Then it, too, was lost. The ground defenders fought off one Japanese assault force. The civilians tried to enlist in one or another of the Armed Forces, but were turned down for their own good. If they stayed civilians they would be treated as noncombatants. With a fine disregard for international law the civilians "attached" themselves to various units. They hauled ammunition, set up guns, fired them, dug trenches, fought fires, repaired planes, and died. But none of this could turn aside the inevitable. When the Japanese returned they returned in numbers so vast that the issue was never in doubt.

With the surrender, the Japanese faced a difficult choice. They were determined to build Wake into one link of a powerful chain of fortified islands from which they could continue their strikes eastward. The hundreds of Americans on the islands were merely a hindrance to this, and the Japanese decided to evacuate them as soon as possible. However, they also wished to use the equipment which the Americans had installed on the island. It was intricate and strange machinery. They needed American help to maintain it and they knew that.

The Japanese made a fateful choice. All of the American military personnel was to be evacuated and most of the civilians. The evacuees were sent to Shanghai and most of them survived the war. But one hundred Americans stayed behind.

Not one of the hundred selected Americans was alive after October 7, 1943. Two of them died ordinary deaths. One succumbed to septicemia and was buried. Another, a confirmed alcoholic, displayed great ingenuity in stealing liquor from the Japanese. The third time he was caught he was ordered to apologize and to agree never to steal alcohol again. With the strange lunatic courage of the absolute alcoholic, he looked his captors in the eye and refused. The next moment he was beheaded.

The remaining ninety-eight Americans were to die in one of the most eerie, lemminglike, mysterious, and courageous episodes of that or any other war. Or perhaps it was simple madness.

The Japanese, aided by the captive Americans, began an amazing fortification of Wake. Almost literally they dug deep into the coral and then pulled it over themselves. They built hundreds of coral and concrete pillboxes, underground magazines, and carefully dispersed command posts. Most of these were "bombproof" and were connected to one another by a complex pattern of tunnels and trenches.

Above ground they laid down a fantastic array of defenses. The entire length of the oceanside of the atoll was protected by huge tank traps. Seaward of the traps was a system of slit trenches with steel and concrete pillboxes scattered among them. At the very edge of the sea there was a low hummock of barbed-wire entanglements with land mines placed underneath them. The raised parts of the island bristled with cleverly concealed guns of every description. Anything that could be damaged was buried. Every jeep had its own revetment, every barrel of fuel was buried deep. The island was one vast honeycomb which housed 4,500 Japanese and their ninety-eight American helpers.

They busily dredged the channel between Wilkes and Wake to permit submarines and ships to enter the lagoon. They started to dredge a turning basin for submarines off Wilkes and a channel which would allow submarines to come alongside shoreside quays for replenishing and repairs.

But the Japanese had made a terrible strategic miscalculation. Their vast row of defenses, aimed at Australia and all of Oceania, was stopped short. Midway remained in American hands. Kwajalein and Eniwetok became available to American forces. Also American cruisers could lie safely out of range and lob shells onto the island. Wake became a "milk run." Cruisers and battleships returning to Pearl Harbor emptied their magazines on the island. Task forces going west used Wake as a practice target, but were given careful instructions not to hinder the dredging of the submarine turning basin—it would be valuable when the Americans repossessed the island. In any case the American air cover over Wake was so intense that no Japanese sub could use the basin. In the midst of a holocaust of bombs and shells the dredge working the turning basin operated with perfect immunity. Carrier planes, and later land-based planes, were almost constantly overhead. It soon became impossible to reinforce or supply Wake by surface vessels. Instead of being a redoubt in a massive defense line, Wake had become an isolated and tortured island, under continuous siege.

The last attempt at surface reinforcement came in 1943. The *Suwa Maru* of ten thousand tons came to Wake with supplies. A patrolling American submarine torpedoed her twice just as she came to her moorings. In desperation, her skipper ran her onto the reef, where her rusty carcass can be seen today. Now for long months and then years the empty horizon around Wake was broken only by hostile ships which came in quietly but brazenly, lobbed in their devastating bombardments, and then vanished.

The ninety-eight Americans were, under the circumstances, given remarkably good treatment. The Japanese, knowing that they were essential for the maintenance of the island's intricate communication and distilling systems, gave them better rations than the Japanese soldiers received. Even so, the ninety-eight lived in a queer and dreamlike world. In those scattered hours when it was possible to be above ground they worked for the Japanese to repair bomb and shell damage. At night they crowded back into their two shelters and talked. They were all highly skilled craftsmen, and it is safe to assume that their intelligence was a cut or two above average.

What do men do in such utter isolation? They talk, they conspire, they form cliques, they engage in irritable arguments, and they exchange rumors. Indeed, rumors become the staff of their psychic life. This is true of all prisons and concentration camps. But most prisoners, by one means or another, have a contact with the outside world. Even in the most closely guarded of Nazi concentration camps, there were clandestine radios and fairly accurate reports of what was happening on the "outside." Guards could be bribed for information, the progress of the war could be charted, escape committees could be formed, hope could be nourished. But on Wake there was not the slightest possibility of contact with the outside. The Americans did not speak Japanese, and the Japanese themselves had only the most meager radio contact with Japan. There was also the stunning and always present realization that they were surrounded by hundreds of miles of open sea. The Pacific, the sheer immense bulk of water, was their most efficient guard, kept them in the most perfect isolation. The Japanese knew this too, and the actual guard maintained over the prisoners was slight.

There is no other group of prisoners I know of during World War II which lived in such complete physical and psychological isolation. Anything that the ninety-eight "knew" must be manufactured from whole cloth.

Psychological and social anarchy cannot be endured for long. We can assume that at some point the ninety-eight men, consciously or unconsciously, formed themselves into some sort of social hierarchy. Natural leaders emerged; some men became identified as comics; others became chronic complainers; some withdrew into themselves. But one thing is certain, the group could feed only on itself. Slowly it began to manufacture a "reality" about the outside world. Some men more imaginative and persuasive and glib than the others made guesses as to what was happening outside. Just as in primitive societies the unknown is made known by oracles, so the ninety-eight invented a mythology. As it was passed from man to man it lost the quality of myth; it became a form of reality. When it was repeated back to the original oracles they also believed it. All of them believed for a simple reason: in such awesome isolation man must have something to believe, or go mad.

The tiny world of Wake became increasingly bizarre. The water distillers still worked, and rainwater was carefully gathered, but food soon came into short supply. The Japanese made heroic efforts to supply the island. Surface ships being out of the question, they attempted to send in food by submarine. These supply submarines made a hazardous and slow passage from Japan. In daylight hours they submerged and stopped their engines. At night they came to the surface and went ahead at full speed. They carried a curious cargo. Hundred-pound bags of rice were surrounded by crude latex rubber and made into a waterproof and floatable package. Hundreds of these were strapped to the open decks of the submarines.

When a submarine arrived off Wake, it was still in mortal danger. American submarines constantly patrolled the island, and the chances of being detected were high. To surface during the day, even for a few moments, was to commit suicide. The Japanese submarines and the garrison developed a peculiar technique. At a prearranged time, chosen so that the tide would be favorable and the night at its blackest, the submarine would surface for a few moments. Lining the windward edge of the reef would be hundreds of Japanese soldiers, peering into the darkness. When the submarine surfaced, picked men ran down the decks, cutting the bindings which held the rice bags to the submarine. The submarine skipper then gave a single guarded flash of an Aldis lamp toward the shore. Then he closed his hatches and submerged. As the submarine sank, the rice bags floated from her decks and bobbed on the water.

For the Japanese lining the reef, it was a desperate time. Quite beyond their control their very life was bobbing about in the dark water. The Japanese soldiers, their eyes sharpened by hunger, studied each of the unending procession of waves. There would be a tormented period when they did not know whether tide and wind were favoring them. Then, with luck, the heavy yellow packages would come surging up onto the reef. The soldiers were too desperate to cheer. They fought the bundles free of the surf and trotted them to a central storehouse. The next morning, every foot of the periphery of the island would be searched to see that no bags had been missed. Occasionally, the tides would play a cruel trick, and in the morning they would see a dozen of the bags that had worked around into the lee of the island. They might sit there for days, only a hundred yards offshore, but the Japanese did not dare to put a boat into the water. At night, the more skillful swimmers would venture into the dark waters to try to retrieve the bags. Occasionally, they were successful. Sometimes the swimmers merely disappeared forever into the ocean.

The ninety-eight Americans were aware of a successful submarine delivery only because of the sudden spurt of optimism and good cheer among their captors. Admiral Sakaibara, the officer-in-charge of the island, was too orderly a man to permit an increase in rations. He had some inkling of how far the food had to be stretched. The Americans began to feel the pinch. Their food rations were cut. Ribs began to show on men who had always been fat; thin men became gaunt. When food was divided they gathered and watched quietly, only their burning eyes revealing their intensity.

Very soon, however, even the submarine trips became too hazardous. They were discontinued and the island was on its own. Everyone, including the Americans, now realized that they had to subsist on their accumulated stores plus whatever food the island and its surrounding waters could supply. There commenced one of the most ingenious and thorough efforts ever made to find and husband food. Rat hunting, for example, became an organized activity. The orderly Japanese records indicate that they caught and devoured over 54,000 rats. The thousands of birds on the island were carefully stalked, slaughtered, and eaten. Every crevice, however small, was searched to see if it might contain bird eggs. Land crabs were hunted with a ruthless intensity.

By the end of 1944, there was not a single bird, rat or crab left on the island.

Nothing was wasted. The Japanese discovered that the leaves of the morning-glory vines were edible, and the island was soon bare of these. Too late there was the realization that the very thoroughness of the search was a mistake. By killing *all* of the birds and eating *all* of their eggs they had assured that no new generations of birds or eggs would appear. By killing *all* of the rats they assured that no new rats would appear. By eating *all* of the morning-glory vines they assured that no future vines would grow. It was a bitter discovery. It was also irreversible.

Their wits sharpened by desperation, the Japanese set about to build truck gardens. But how does one build a garden on an island which has no soil? The Japanese extracted the soil from their own bodies. They carefully gathered the night soil, their own excrement, mixed it with sand, and dumped it into great boxes made of brass and iron. This compost was then planted with tomato and squash and melon seeds which came in by submarine. Never were gardens so carefully tended and so carefully watched. The precious water, now in short supply, was sluiced over the plants by the helmetful. Full captains were given formal responsibility for guarding the tiny plots. Occasionally during a strafing, spray bullets would tear into the gardens, tearing plants to pieces, spraying excrement over the containing walls. After a raid each plot was carefully surveyed and salvageable vines were replanted. Bits of scattered excrement were gathered and returned to the plot. Hopelessly shattered plants were used in soup.

The Japanese were used to eating seaweed, and the reef and lagoon were denuded of edible seaweed to the depth that the Japanese could dive.

At first the fish along the reef and inside the lagoon were caught in abundance. But the Japanese made a crucial mistake. They used hand grenades, which could be thrown into a school of fish, and the explosion stunned the fish long enough for them to be gathered. The Japanese did not know, however, that the explosion also killed the billions of fish eggs that accumulated invisibly in the crevices of the reef and lagoon. After a short while, the fish were also exterminated and there were no new generations to replace them.

The ninety-eight Americans watched all of this with a horrified fascination. At some point in 1943, they began to realize that the bombings and the disruption of the island life were making their skills unnecessary. They spent less and less time doing useful work. More and more they talked and watched and returned to their talking. They were torn between hoping that the Japanese would find food in which they would share and satisfaction in seeing their captors grow weaker. For a time they speculated on whether the Americans would reinvade before all of them starved or whether the island would merely be bypassed. Such ambiguity became impossible. They came to the conclusion, and no man dared or wished to oppose it, that the invasion would occur first. In so hermetic an isolation, with hunger beginning to make tempers sharp and rationality difficult, they all sensed that their survival depended on unanimity. A minority view, even a well-considered minority view, was impossible. Those that doubted were silent, and finally even they came to share the view.

The disruption of Wake continued. Once the entire garrison had been tightly bound together by an elaborate communication system. It was gradually destroyed. Now little clots of Japanese soldiers huddled around their gardens, stared hollow-eyed at the ocean, dragged themselves to cover when American planes approached. Once, when soldiers had died, their bodies had been cremated and the ashes returned to Japan. Now they were carefully buried beneath the garden to add nourishment to the soil. There was also a time when the various groups of men had visited with one another. Now this called for too great an expenditure of energy. They beat out signals to one another by banging wrenches against empty CO_2 bottles. Where once the island had teemed with busy men, it now became more roomy. The Japanese were beginning to die from hunger. Eventually half of them starved to death—over two thousand bodies went beneath the garden plots to enrich them. By day the survivors did a minimum amount of repair work. By night they slept. The certainty of doom became a vapor in the air. The private diaries which the Japanese kept were long messages of farewell, written by men who were certain of their death.

But somehow the Americans lived. Not well, but they lived. They grew thinner. Their desperation grew sharper.

The weird life around them drove them into an ever more intense solidarity. They were called upon to do almost no work and knew they were expendable. Their boredom, their ignorance, their shared desperation, their proximity, their gossip made them oddly identical. Rumors became more important than food, were hashed and rehashed, reexamined from different points of view, taken as rumor at first, but quickly hardened into "facts." There was still a hierarchy among them, but what they thought, the inside of their minds, came to be strangely similar.

They discussed the possibility of capturing one of the boats and trying to escape by night. They debated it endlessly and then one day were given their answer. Three of the stronger Japanese ventured out in the boat to do some fishing. The boat was heavily camouflaged and looked like nothing so much as a piece of drifting seaweed. However, it was no farther than a few hundred yards from the shore when a Corsair came hurtling over the horizon, drew a pinpoint bead on the boat, and strafed it. All three Japanese were killed; the boat sank. The Americans knew that other boats were buried about, and it would probably be easy to steal one, but they knew they would be strafed before they could escape.

They talked again. They racked their brains for solutions. But now the months of isolation, the awareness of the vastness of the ocean about them, and a growing irrationality because of the inadequate diet had reduced their perceptiveness. They dared not even argue among themselves any more. Each man sensed that an argument, an act of selfishness, a misunderstanding might set them at one another's throats, snarling like hyenas. They whispered gently to one another.

At one point a B-24 bomber bombed Wake and then came in low and slow for a strafing attack. By now long experience and a diminishing supply of ammunition made the

Japanese antiaircraft gunners extremely accurate. They waited and then at the plane's lowest elevation opened fire. The plane was mortally damaged, made a slow burning circle in the sky and finally crash-landed at the edge of Wilkes. The Japanese commanding officer made a decision. The fliers were tried and then killed, and parts of their bodies were eaten in a *Bushido* ritual. Only the heart, liver and lights were eaten by the Japanese. There were those among them who would have willingly eaten the entire bodies, but they were not given the chance. After the ceremony the remains were given a ceremonial burial.

On the day of October 6, 1943, the tension grew greater, stretching the nerves and rationality of the ninety-eight men to the very limit.

That day American planes, clearly flying from carriers, made a savage raid on Wake. The dive bombers picked their targets at leisure and then dived. The fighter planes shrieked up and down the atoll, shooting at anything that moved or was above the surface. A chance incendiary set one of the buried fuel dumps on fire so that the very coral itself seemed to be burning with an inexhaustible flame.

The Americans peered up at the attacking planes, torn between pride in the bombing and fear of death.

That night the ninety-eight began another, and the last, of their long whispered and very intense conversations. They knew only four facts for certain. First, the fighter planes had stayed so long over the target that the task force from which they came could not be far over the horizon. Secondly, the Japanese were rapidly weakening. Hundreds hung at the edge of starvation. Third, the ninety-eight were now starting to show the signs of malnutrition, and starvation was probably not far away for them. Fourth, they knew that the only feasible location for a landing was on the lee side of the island, with the best stretch being at the channel that separated Wake from Wilkes Island. This is all that the ninety-eight could have known. All other facts were denied to them. The Pacific, unending and silent, told them nothing and allowed nothing to be told.

Sometime during the night of October 6, in their low-pitched but deadly serious conversation, these four facts fused into a common agreement: they were to be rescued the next morning, at the juncture of Wilkes and Wake, by an American task force. So identical had the ninety-eight become, so smooth their method of communication, that their unanimity was as solid as a fused granite boulder. Not a man doubted that the task force would reach them.

The emaciated men now began to act with an incredible deadly efficiency. They called to the guards who, unsuspectingly, opened the doors and looked in. They were seized by the throat by powerful hands and strangled. Their bodies were thrown into the barracks and the ninety-eight began to move across Wake.

With an eerie quality, almost a ghostliness, they flitted past the innumerable dugouts and posts. When a Japanese head did appear and question them, the closest man would simply reach out, and with a strength of desperation, choke the questioner to death. In an area which was so crowded with persons, the passage of skilled and trained Marines would have been a miracle. Also, every Japanese on the island had become sensitive to even the smallest sound in the coral: it might be a rat or a land crab. Contrary to popular belief, starving men do not sleep a deep exhausted sleep. They sleep lightly, restlessly, nervously. But the ninety-eight filtered past dugouts, around command posts, past sentries, by a manned radar station, and finally came to the last pillbox which overlooked the channel between Wake and Wilkes. Quietly, without a word, they made a vicious silent assault on the pillbox. They captured it and killed every occupant without raising an alarm. Then they waited, gazing out over the ocean with utter confidence for the arrival of the dawn and the American task force.

Dawn came, pink and soft, and then passed into the brassy light of early morning. The sea was empty. Still the ninety-eight did not lose confidence. No one panicked. No one proposed doing anything except precisely what they were doing.

It was at this moment that the Japanese discovered what had happened. They quickly organized several companies into search parties, fully armed and carrying hand grenades. They searched Peale and found nothing. Then they started, in a line abreast, to sweep down Wake. They searched every dugout, every shell hole, behind every rock. As the Japanese skirmish line got to the narrow end of Wake, it grew denser and denser. The Americans waited unperturbed. Between them they had six guns and a small amount of ammunition. They looked out to sea calmly, and then back at the approaching Japanese. There was no hysteria, no whining, no defection.

The ninety-eight prepared to resist the hundreds of fully armed Japanese. They fought with their six guns, rocks, sticks, and some with their bare hands. It was short, bloody, and final. In a half hour, fifty of the ninety-eight had been killed.

The forty-eight Americans that were left stood in the welter of blood and bits of flesh, dazed by the explosion of hand grenades, but curiously calm. As the Japanese surrounded them they still looked out over the ocean, still hopeful that deliverance would come.

It did not. Prodded by bayonets and rifle butts, the remaining forty-eight formed two lines and marched back up Wake. They were taken to the north shore. There they were given shovels and ordered to dig their collective grave. They did this calmly and without protest or remorse. Occasionally one of the Americans would stand up, wipe sweat from his forehead, and gaze confidently out at the horizon. The Japanese watched in puzzlement as the Americans quietly went about their last mortal task. When the grave was dug, the Japanese were still suspicious. They bound the Americans hand and foot and then backed cautiously away from them. The Americans gazed impassively at the Japanese, uncomprehending. Then they looked again at the blue encircling Pacific, scanned it as they had scanned it for years. They smiled at one another with confidence, sharing some secret which was denied their captors. They had passed some psychological point of no return and now were ready for whatever consequences followed.

At a command from a Japanese officer, machine guns began to chatter and rifles to crack. The forty-eight were smashed back into the grave by a solid hail of bullets. A few moments later not one of them was alive. The Japanese covered them over with sand and coral.

In 1946, Admiral Sakaibara and Lieutenant Commander Tachibana and fourteen others were sentenced to hang by the military commission which was convened on Kwajalein to investigate the circumstances of the deaths of the ninety-eight. This was done.

Clifford Gessler

Phantoms and Physicians on Tepuka

Born in Milton Junction, Wisconsin, in 1893, Clifford Gessler, journalist and poet, served from 1924 to 1934 as telegraph and literary editor of the *Honolulu Star-Bulletin.* Seeking a change, he joined the Mangarevan Expedition of the Bernice P. Bishop Museum and in 1934 sailed to the Tuamotu group on the ninety-foot sampan *Islander.* He and Kenneth P. Emory ("Keneti") were the only outsiders on the atoll of Tepuka Maruia (the place of the puka tree) from May 15 to July 29, 1934, and closely shared the lives of the Polynesian inhabitants. Two uncanny selections are taken from his 1937 volume, *Road My Body Goes.*

Gessler then went on the cutter *Tiare Tahiti,* by way of Vahitahi and several other islands, to Papeete, where he spent some time as a penniless beachcomber. His later adventures, wandering among the Tuamotu, Austral, and Society groups, are told in *The Leaning Wind (1943).*

GHOSTS

SOME time in the night of our first day on the island, I was awakened by a sound as of pebbles thrown against the side of the house. It was not a loud sound, but a definite one, and the pauses between were as of someone listening.

My first thought was that an early-rising pig or chicken had wandered against the house, but the beam of an electric torch, flashed into the darkness, revealed no living thing.

"Somebody is playing tricks," I concluded, though in view of the absence of cover for such a trickster to hide near the house, and the known reluctance of Tuamotuans to venture out at night without a light, this explanation was slightly lame.

"It was without doubt a spirit," said our neighbors next morning.

Such stone-throwing ghosts are common in the Tuamotu, the more so in the "civilized" iron-roofed islands where they can make more noise. All the islands are haunted; the imagination of the Polynesian has peopled his darkness, often with shapes of fear. The spirits of the newly dead wander abroad, seeking literally whom they may devour. This latter propensity of the nocturnal apparitions was less emphasized at Tepuka, and there may have been some connection of this omission with the contention, plausible enough, of the people of that island that they had never been cannibals. On the former man-eating islands, such as Vahitahi and Hao, it is a natural transition, as Stevenson pointed out long ago, from the eating of the dead by the living to the eating of the living by the dead, and a certain kind of spirit is therefore as greatly feared as the werewolves and vampires of medieval Europe. Nevertheless, the haunted darkness of the coconut groves was regarded with extreme caution by our friends and neighbors; nor would they sleep at night without a light in the house: a dim and smoky lantern, turned low, or if, as often happened, oil failed, a wedge of copra burning, propped upon a stone.

Our friends, however, were not alarmed on our behalf. It seemed, or so I understood, that the pebble-tossing spirits were not especially harmful. The visitation of the night might be interpreted as a favorable omen rather than otherwise, signifying that the island spirits recognized our presence and were making us welcome. Moreover, the white man usually is immune from the attacks of the powers of Polynesian darkness. How else explain his recklessness in violating native custom, in sleeping without a light, in eating under a roof, in transgressing any number of prohibitions that have grown up in the half-light of remembered experience in these haunted lands?

I had occasion to observe this fear of the beings of darkness later when at her request I accompanied the daughter of Maru on an errand to the house of a relative, somewhat remote from the main village. Temata led me along the road that leads to the cemetery, but struck away from it into the forest before we reached that point. She was taking no unnecessary chances.

Among the trees, however, she showed increasing alarm. Every large bush, every oddly shaped shadow, caused her to clutch at me in fear. In the gloomiest portion of the wood, an ominous shape appeared suddenly out of the blackness and lurched across our path—a figure of more than human size, it seemed, and of scarcely human shape, with a great antlered head nodding through the gloom.

My companion, in terror, buried her face in my shoulder; I could feel her whole body quivering with fright.

"Let there be life!" said the apparition, and Temata burst out laughing with relief. She had recognized the voice of one of her own living relatives.

Our "ghost" was only an honest citizen of Tepuka who had been bold enough, or forced by necessity, to go out at night alone, and the oddity of shape was merely the effect, in the darkness, of the burden he carried on his shoulders.

On the way back, as we hurried over the stony paths that her bare feet knew so well and mine so poorly, I told her that she was safe with me, for the spirits had no power over a white man. She seemed to accept this, but I think she remembered it, not without a trace of malice, at a later time, when, the spirits having apparently punished me for some trespass, she said, "It serves you right!"

Others told us that the dead rise at night and walk about the village, "in their habit as they lived," indistinguishable from the living, except as they are recognized for individuals who have long since departed this world. For that reason, the road that leads past the small and relatively new cemetery of Tepuka is avoided at night. Nor, we gathered, is this return confined to the dead there interred, whose demise scarcely can antedate the last hurricane. The more ancient dead, it seems, arise from the sea and visit the scenes of their former life.

Surrounded by an atmosphere of such beliefs, one easily slips into the feeling that, after all, anything might be possible. In a spirit half serious, half humorous, I walked out, on a fine evening, down the forbidden street. Far to the left, toward the lagoon shore, lights gleamed through the trees from the houses clustered there. A brighter light moved a torch fisherman, probably, emboldened by hunger to venture abroad at night. If so, he was the only torch fisherman I saw in my time on the island. The early moon cast dense black shadows on the white sand of the road; the forest on either side was dark, and its clumps of pandanus and tournefortia resembled not at all their daylight aspect. It was easy to understand how the mind of the native could populate that darkness with menacing shapes.

The cemetery, however, looked harmless enough: a bare, low-walled quadrangle, lately weeded and swept, in which the few graves, with their wooden crosses, their withered wreaths, seemed lost and lonely in the expanse of moonlight. I walked slowly past; no vampire figure arose. At the end of the road, I sat for a while on the stone curbing, looking out at the sea which rustled softly on the reef. It was a peaceful spot: one could be alone here with the sea and sky, the hard clean stony land, and whatever spirits might be awake.

The evening meeting would be over by now; the dance would be beginning at the house of Maukiri. I walked back slowly through the sand of the road, pausing to sit for a few minutes on the cemetery wall. Perhaps it was the moonlight, perhaps my Western unbelief—but the enclosure of the dead gave up no visible spirit, emitted no ghostly sound. I was to remember, with a question, that moonlight vigil when, long afterward, the *tahunga* shook his head, saying, "You have walked too near a grave." But that evening, as I slid down from the wall and continued my way toward the lighted houses, I thought only of Walter de la Mare's traveler who knocked at the moonlit door, and nobody answered; how, as he turned to go, "Tell them I came," he said, and how "the silence surged softly backward, when the plunging hoofs were gone."

I WALK TOO NEAR A GRAVE

I HAD begun to think that the Dangerous Islands—with the exception of Reao—were a more healthful environment than many more civilized places.

And then, it seems, I walked too near a grave!

It started with that tiny eruption, like a heat blister, on the back of the little finger of my left hand. We never could trace the source of it to any known injury. Perhaps a sliver from a mat; one of the small thorns that arm the edges of pandanus leaves; these are but random guesses. Perhaps some decaying sea growth in the partly enclosed warm water of the lagoon, where we swam, generated a poison. Now my whole body was afire with it.

On my return from Tepoto, Keneti and I opened the infected area with a sterilized pair of scissors and treated it with such medicines as we had. Next day the entire hand was swollen as far as the wrist, and the finger itself was larger than a thumb.

Keneti was plainly worried.

"We're not getting anywhere with this. If the *Vaite* were here I'd send you back to Papeete aboard her. I'd be afraid to risk you on the *Tiare Tahiti;* we couldn't treat the wound properly, and it would be hard to keep sea water out of it. All the natives say sea water is bad for these things."

But the *Vaite* was far away. There was no available contact with civilization; no communication. Even had there been a ship available, I might have reached hospitals and physicians too late. We must depend on our own meager resources, and those of the natives.

The natives! There was a thought.

"We're just groping around in the dark, trying to treat this infection with civilized remedies," Keneti concluded. "Our treatment not only isn't curing it; it seems to be making it worse.

"It's a native infection. The natives undoubtedly know a lot more about it than we do, and if it were my own hand, I'd have them treat it with their own medicines. They've had hundreds of years of experience with the few native diseases there are. Likely enough this kind of infection isn't known to civilized doctors at all."

"What do you do for this illness?" I asked Tauria, who was in the house at the time.

"A tobacco poultice," was his suggestion.

I had chewed tobacco just once. My mind flashed back from that coral island to the grassy violet-starred bank of a little river in Wisconsin; my father nodding in an afternoon nap over his fishing-pole; the sample plug of Battle-Ax that had been tossed on the doorstep, brought furtively from my pocket. I hadn't repeated that experiment. However, if I didn't chew now, Tauria would, for he was eager to try the remedy. So I reduced to pulp a sufficient quantity of the acrid Tahitian "twist" and bound it upon the injury.

The tobacco didn't make it worse, but it didn't improve it, either.

"Tauria is only a young man," Keneti reflected. "If I were you, I would consult Paunu. He is a tahunga; he probably knows just what to do in cases like this."

Paunu displayed professional interest.

"It is an *uruaitu,*" he diagnosed, using a word long vanished from the language of daily speech, "a ghost-head."

"A ghost-head," he repeated. "Who has had cause to work sorcery upon you?"

"As far as I know, I have done nobody any wrong."

"Temata has cast a spell on you," suggested Roki, who did not like the daughter of Maru. I recalled the grievance that young woman cherished against me, proceeding from that fateful joke of weeks ago.

It was unfortunate that my blunder had been directed toward Temata, who was of a peculiarly sensitive and proud disposition. Others of my friends might have overlooked or forgiven such a slight, having compassion for my ignorance. But Temata had already a rather difficult time of it at Tepuka. Of alien birth though of Tepuka ancestry, with a smattering of foreign ways derived from residence at Fakahina and in Tahiti, and deficient thereby in the fundamental art of a Tepuka woman: the making of hats and mats—she had developed a deep-seated inferiority complex and a correspondingly active defense mechanism which caused her to be stigmatized by the native sons and daughters of her ancestral island as "*teoteo,*" which might be translated "uppity" or "big-feeling."

Paunu turned to Temae, grandfather or great-uncle of the suspect: "Has Temata worked witchcraft against Pari?"

"Nonsense!" scoffed Temae. "Temata does not know witchcraft."

"What then could be the cause?" I queried.

"You must have committed some sacrilege without knowing of it, and a spirit has entered your finger. Perhaps you have walked too near a grave."

"Perhaps so," I agreed. I did not tell them of the time when, having heard that the spirits of the ancestors arise on moonlight nights and walk along the road that passes the tiny cemetery, I had gone there and sat on the stone wall of the House of the Dead for the time it takes to smoke a pandanus-leaf cigarette, and no spirit had appeared.

"Will you invoke the spirits for me?" I asked Paunu.

"I will do so if it becomes clearly necessary," he promisea. "But first let us see what can be done with medicines. My daughters will go to the forest and pluck herbs. We may be able to cure this illness by natural means."

Roki and Tauhoa talked of island medicine as they gathered the young leaf buds of the karauri and the flower buds of the piupiu and crushed these things upon a stone. Roki chewed a bit of the green leaf of a young coconut tree, spat it upon the mixture, and bound the poultice upon the finger with a strip of cloth torn from a clean pareu, relating meanwhile their previous cures.

"The first time Pini the son of Maono went to Fakahina, he came home very ill. He could not eat. We made medicine and in one day he was well."

It appeared, however, that the medical skill of Paunu's daughters was not equal to my case. Next day the pain and swelling had reached the shoulder; the arm was paralyzed and I shivered with fever. Keneti was visibly alarmed.

"Paunu," I insisted, "you will have to make magic."

Now Paunu, although a sorcerer of sorts, is also a prominent member of the church of the Sacred Heart, and he was clearly reluctant to traffic with the ancestral spirits by means of the ancient magic, except as a last resort. These things, he would have explained if I had persisted, were things of Satan. Still, if it became necessary to fight demon with demon, he assured me he would do so.

"Go first," he counseled, "to Toriu. He and his wife Tinaia, daughter of Temae, know the *rakau nati.* You have seen this medicine used. Did not Noere the Younger break his leg when he fell over a canoe? The leg was treated with that medicine, and now Noere walks about and plays marbles with the other boys in the street. Go to Toriu and Tinaia, and try that medicine. If it fails, I will invoke the gods."

Toriu and Tinaia gravely inspected the infection.

"There can be no doubt," they agreed, "that the *rakau nati* is needed. We will come tonight and treat your illness."

Just after dark they came, Toriu bearing a half coconut shell filled with a reddish, thick liquid, shot with pale gleams of gold.

"The root and bark of the karauri and of the horahora," Toriu explained, when asked, but there may have been other and secret ingredients, for the concoction had a strange, muddy consistency and a thick, earthy smell. The horahora, however, is a plant of known virtues: in Hawaii, where it is called noni, it is used even in this day of modern surgery to reduce fractures and sprains.

Tinaia washed the whole hand carefully, and applied the red medicine with a white feather. Red and white are colors pleasing to the gods; to use a black feather would have been gross malpractice, by island standards.

Toriu cut the ends off a bud coconut, a little larger than those the children use for juggling, and placed the truncated nut under my arm to block the circulation and check the spread of the infection.

"Hold it there all night," he ordered. "It will keep the evil spirit from climbing farther up your body."

They remained long in the house that night, turning over the pages of back-number magazines, and marveling at pictures of strange things in the white men's country. Among those pictures were scenes of hospital operating-rooms, in a play then popular in America, where white-robed surgeons wearing inhuman-looking masks wielded sterilized instruments over sufferers like myself.

"White medicine men," I explained. "The masks are to keep away the evil spirits that cause illness, which in the white men's language are called 'bacteria.'"

Toriu understood. He understood the white robes, too, from his viewpoint, and approved. He and the white medicine men had a good deal in common; though they would give different reasons for it.

The pain dulled; whether from the effect of Toriu's medicine, which was cool and soothing with a curious drawing sensation, or merely from nerve fatigue, I do not know. I must have been still somewhat feverish, perhaps delirious. I lay quietly on the mat and closed my eyes.

"Will he recover?" asked Keneti.

"It is hard to say," Toriu replied cautiously. "A native can recover from the ghost-head; a white man—we do not know. We have never before treated a white man. They are not accustomed to our diseases, as we are not accustomed to theirs. We die of colds, which to the white men are a slight thing. They sneeze and cough, as do we, but they wipe their noses with handkerchiefs and go about their work. As for us, our lungs fill and we die."

"If you had come to us sooner," said Tinaia, "it would have been better. The evil spirit had already reached the armpit before we began treatment. It is under the left shoulder; it is near the heart. If the evil spirit reaches the heart, there is no hope."

Paunu, who had been listening, got up, with a strange expression on his face, and went out into the haunted night.

In the languor that crept over me as the pain subsided, I lay listening to their talk with an odd detachment, as if they were speaking of someone else. Looking back upon it now, it seems strange that I was not terrified. We were utterly isolated. It had taken the *Tiare Tahiti* three weeks to reach us, and it might take as long to get back to any port where there were physicians of our own race. The natives said it would be fatal to travel, in my condition. There was no way of calling help. Only the herbs and incantations of these islanders, and what sturdiness of constitution I might have, stood between me and a miserable death. Yet, strangely, I felt no fear, but only a mild curiosity and a sense of peace. It was good, I reflected dreamily, to lie on these cool mats, with these kind people watching over me.

By one of those curious twists of psychology which magnify trivial occasions in memory, the date July 24 has stood out in my mind since on the night of that date a boy of ten years or so, in his bed in a Wisconsin village, reflected sadly that the summer vacation was half gone and he hadn't done many of the things he wanted to do. That boy, playing at "savage" in backyards and pastures and woodlots, would have derived a curious compensation if he could have looked ahead and seen himself on July 24 of a much later year in his house of leaves on a coral island, even though disabled and in pain. Part of the celebrated "lure" of far and primitive places no doubt is a response to the boy in man; in such surroundings, among childlike peoples, he regains the play-world of his childhood. Where the pursuits at which he played as a boy are the serious vocations of adults, he finds a satisfaction of some instinct as old as the childhood of his own race.

However this may be, on that day, the second of Toriu and Tinaia's treatment, the infected hand felt slightly better, and the general symptoms less pronounced. Old Temae, who had seen many such cases in his long life, predicted that it would be far advanced toward recovery in a few more days.

"This illness is well known," he explained. "It occurs oftener on the sole of the foot, but it may attack any part of the body. On the foot, it often develops from a stone bruise."

Day by day Toriu and Tinaia came and washed the hand, and painted each day a smaller area with the medicine, which left a stain like dried blood.

"We are forcing the evil spirit down into the spot where it entered," Toriu explained.

Whatever the merits of that theory, the results justified the practice. Soreness and swelling receded as the treatment continued. By the third day, the infection had been localized. It rose—true to its name—from the base of the finger in the semblance of a ghostly skull, a high hard dome of pain.

"It is time for the poultice," declared Toriu with some satisfaction. He prepared it as Roki and Tauhoa had done, from the same herbs, and bound it with a strip of red cloth.

"Do not burn the dressings, or throw them away carelessly," Tinaia warned. "Put them in this coconut shell, and I will dispose of them fittingly. It is not well to anger the gods further."

She meant that she would bury them in the ground or throw them into the sea; the practice differs in different countries and with individual medicine-makers.

The poultice was cool and soothing.

"On Monday, in the middle of the day, the swelling will break," Tinaia predicted. "Keep it covered until then, and don't let anyone see it."

Visitors came and squatted beside me, and caressed the other hand: Maukiri and her daughters, urging me to come to their home to stay, that they might comfort me; Temae, who himself knows sorcery; Ngohe, mumbling words of sympathy; Tukua the chief's daughter; Roki and Tioma, fragrant with scented coconut oil; Tauhoa, always practical and helpful, rolling up a bundle of my clothes to wash. Teuri, a frightened expression on his long, serious face, crossed himself with pious precaution before passing the doorway of this house into which "Satan" seemed to have entered.

The child Riua sat at my feet, in silent sympathy. Teuringa-iti came with her sweetheart Maono the son of Maono, bringing a great basket of drinking-nuts. Paniroro, who had returned on the *Tiare* with us from Tepoto, talked of the lands she had visited. Paniroro was a traveled woman; she had been to Fakahina, that port which draws so many of the young people from the two islands, and to farther Fakarava, capital of the Tuamotu.

"This," as she pointed out to Tinaia an advertisement in one of our magazines, "is a coloring for the lips, and this for the cheeks. I have seen a white woman, the wife of the administrator, use them so"—indicating in pantomime the application of rouge and lipstick. "The white women's faces are pale, and they paint their lips and faces, for they have not the natural color of the human skin, as we have."

She had a child with her—a pretty little curly-haired girl—who, she said, was half American, a quarter Chinese and a quarter Tuamotuan; and showed us pictures of the child's parents, whom Bob recognized as friends of his in one of the more westerly islands.

"It was Tiki, the first man, who brought illness and death into the world," said Paunu, who followed my progress closely. "Tiki made Ahuone, the first woman, out of a heap of sand, and their daughter was Hina. When Hina was grown, she was very beautiful, and Tiki made her his second wife. But Ahuone found it out, and Hina was ashamed and fled to the moon. Then Tiki, in his grief, gave himself death, and since his time all men must die."

"But, Paunu, was there no way of undoing the curse of death?"

"Alas! There was none. Maui tried to win back eternal life for man. He wrestled with Tiki at the bottom of the sea, and tried to take out his own internal organs and exchange them for those of Tiki. If he could do that, he thought, he could conquer death, for Tiki's organs were still immortal; Tiki had created death only by an act of will. But Maui's brothers followed him and interrupted him with ill-timed questions, so that he failed.

"So mankind was still troubled with decay and death. But Tama saved man many troubles."

"Who was Tama?"

"He was the son of Tané, lord of the sky. Our ancestors prayed to him to cure wounds, to heal the bites of eels and sharks, and bruises from falling out of trees. He was called the God Who Makes to Live.

"You understand, of course, that all these things are but heathen tales, and things of Satan."

"Yes," I replied, "but it seems to me rather significant that this Tuamotuan savior was called Tama, which means the Son, and that he was the son of Tané, the creator of all things good and beautiful . . . and that the name of Tané means Man. For the Christian scriptures, as you know, speak of the Savior as the Son of Man, who is the Light, the Way and the Life."

"It may be so. It is a deep study. But it is true that our ancestors believed Tama healed the sick. When people are very ill, as you have been, their spirits sometimes leave their bodies and wander into the Great Darkness. It was Tama, our fathers believed, who led such spirits back into the bodies, and the sick people then recovered."

"Did they always recover?"

"Sometimes the spirit refused to go back into the body. Then the body died, but the spirit lived, and Tama led it to the spirit-world. If the spirit ate the fruit offered by demons in the Darkness, Tama was powerless to save. The demons, in great boats, chased such souls and threw them into a frightful place; the same, no doubt, as the hell of which the priests have told us."

"If the spirits of the dead are teachers, as I have heard, why then do the people fear them?"

"They do not fear that kind of spirit. But a man has more than one spirit within him. One spirit remains in the body when it is buried, and that is the one that is feared. Such spirits come out of the graves at night, hold parties, and even go fishing. It is very dangerous to meet them."

There was more of this. And day by day the visitors came.

The elders sat on the floor and chanted. My adopted grandmother Teuringa was the liveliest of the lot, grunting and moving her stiff limbs in an ancient dance as if recalling long-past amorous encounters of her youth. Tinaia, holding her pet pig in her lap, joined in the rousing chants.

So the days passed, in a hut woven of palm leaves and thatched with the leaves of the pandanus, floored with pebbles; under treatment by a mixture of herb doctor and pagan magician, a thousand miles from a hospital, but surrounded by kind and loving friends, who sorrowed at my discomfort and grieved for my imminent departure.

Practically the whole village called. Only Temata the daughter of Maru did not come near.

"It is proof," charged Roki, "that she has caused this illness by witchcraft."

"Tell her," I suggested, "that I myself am a sorcerer and that I will make Hawaiian magic, which is stronger than the magic of Tepuka, to bring trouble upon her worse than mine."

Tukua, Temata's cousin, who was sitting in the doorway, appeared startled.

"Temata has made no magic," she protested. "Temata doesn't know witchcraft."

That evening Tukua returned, bringing Temata, who seemed ill at ease. Other visitors watched her narrowly as she entered and squatted near my mat. Temata looked around at them defiantly, then turned to me, saying defiantly: "It serves you right!"

Monday came, and my nurse Tinaia remarked with satisfaction the fulfillment of her prediction. The infected spot, when she unwrapped it, resembled nothing so much as a miniature volcano in eruption. The next treatment, she indicated, was a poultice of soap—red soap, by which she meant the harsh yellow laundry soap that comes in long bars in the schooners from Tahiti. Keneti exhibited a cake of a widely advertised American brand which is much redder, with a strong antiseptic odor. Tinaia was visibly pleased.

"It smells of the spirit-world," she commented with delight, as she observed its redness and sniffed its medicinal aroma. Surely the gods would now be favorable. She shaved off thin flakes of it and laid them gently on the infected area.

By this time I was feeling much better and had begun to stir around the house and even to walk out into the street. Temata passed, on her way to the well. I had been waiting for this occasion to try a little experiment.

Pouring a few drops of alcohol on a ball of cotton, I touched a match to it and stood in the doorway, tossing the burning cotton up and down on the palm of my well hand, and chanting what I could remember of a Hawaiian prayer which in ancient times was chanted, with proper accompanying ceremonies, to bring retribution upon one guilty of black sorcery.

> "The fire burns,
> fire of the dense darkness . . .
> Fire is in the heavens,
> decay, maggots, corruption,
> death is in the heavens!
> O Kane, o Lono, o Ku,
> breathe death upon the sorcerer
> and upon him who procured the token of death. . . ."

The divergent dialects of the Polynesian language have enough words in common to enable a Tuamotuan to grasp something of the import of such an invocation. Temata was alarmed. She ran toward me, scooping up sand, as she ran, to throw upon the flame.

I chanted on, waving the burning cotton out of reach.

Hurling another handful of sand, she walked away, more uneasy, I knew, than she was willing to admit. The sorcery of Hawaii is famous throughout the Polynesian countries.

"Will she die today?" asked Roki, in awe.

"She will not die," I reassured her. "I have not made the spell complete. I only wanted to frighten her, because in my illness she mocked me. If I had taken a lock of her hair and burned it with the magic fire that does not burn my hand, then she might indeed die."

"She deserves to," said Roki severely. "She is a woman without kindness."

Next day Toriu bent a long yellow-white fiber of coconut husk into a noose and twisted it gently but firmly deep down in the infected place; then, with a sudden sharp movement, drew it out, removing the "core" of the infection.

"In three days you will be well," he promised.

He continued to apply the soap dressing for a day or two; then announced that it was time for the final medicine. This was a fine charcoal, made by burning coconut shells in a fire of husks. He dusted this dry dressing carefully into and over the wound.

"Let this powder remain. Don't bandage the finger with a cloth."

The following day he came for the final treatment. His little son played on the floor with his pet pig as Toriu dressed the wound.

"A fine boy," I said, making conversation. "What is his name?"

"His name is Rino. I have a daughter, too," he added, "a grown-up daughter, fourteen years old."

"I have met your daughter Temaru. She is very beautiful."

I refrained from adding that she also had many lice.

"Do you want her?" inquired Toriu hospitably. "If so, I will send her to you tonight."

"You are indeed kind," I answered. "But I am still weak from my illness, and the boat cannot be held any longer. Now that I am well, we must sail at once."

A week later, at Vahitahi, two natives led me to a small house at the farther side of the village.

"This is the house of Hinao. He is very ill."

There lay Schenck, who had warned me three months before—now propped up in a vast bed, against a pile of pillows, his emaciated features, uncut hair, and drooping mustache suggesting a ghost come back from the Great Darkness. Beside him lay a cane, with which it was his custom, when needing attention at night, to batter on the sheet of corrugated iron that closed in one side of his house, to summon the other white visitor on the island, Ua, to his aid.

"Have you any quinine?" he inquired. "There's none on the island. I'm having a recurrence of that fever I caught in Fiji."

Quinine was brought from the cutter. Hinao, as they called Schenck there, had lost twenty-six pounds and had been unable to retain solid food for two weeks, but in three days more he was able to ride in the handcart which is used to transport copra to the landing and corpses to the cemetery. We put him aboard the copra schooner for Papeete, in care of the bishop of French Oceania, who was returning there from Mangareva.

"Never eat fish cooked," the bishop was saying as the sailors dragged the whaleboat off the reef.

His Grace had been a resident priest at our own island of Tepuka Maruia, and had been so long in the service that he had acquired a native palate.

"Never cook fish. Never put salt on it, or lime juice or lemon juice. Eat it fresh from the sea, as the good God made it. Only then can you appreciate the subtle distinctions between the flavors of the various fishes that He, in His wisdom, has provided."

Gavan Daws

The Honolulu Martyrdom

The efforts of the citizens of the Territory of Hawaii to obtain the status of statehood for the islands were seriously threatened in the early 1930's. Although an integral part of the United States, the territory was judged to be a creation of the Congress, which could legally discriminate against the residents. A shocking demonstration of this position was the aftermath of a crime of violence — the so-called "Massie Case."

Headlines in September, 1931, blazoned the charge that a band of Honolulu hoodlums had assaulted the wife of a young naval officer. At the trial of the indicted youths, the jury was so baffled by uncertainties in the evidence that it was unable to agree on a verdict. While a second trial was pending, one of the defendants was taken and killed by a party made up of the naval officer, his mother-in-law, and two Navy enlisted men. The four were tried and found guilty of manslaughter, but a sentence of ten years' imprisonment pronounced upon them was commuted by the governor to one hour.

Lurid treatment of the case in the nation's newspapers resulted in an investigation of law enforcement in Hawaii and some laxity and inefficiency was corrected. The threat of having Hawaii ruled under a commission form of government in which the Army and Navy would have some powers was averted, but for years the echoes of the case blackened the repute of the Territory, and Hawaii did not achieve full membership in the American Union until 1959.

Gavan Daws, born in Australia in 1933, came to study and teach at the University of Hawaii in 1958. He is author not only of *Shoal of Time: A History of the Hawaiian Islands* (1968), from which "The Honolulu Martyrdom" is taken, but also *Holy Man: Father Damien of Molokai* (1973) and *A Dream of Islands (1980).* For some years Dr. Daws has held the chair of Pacific History at the Australian National University.

IN ALL the careful social calculations being made at the islands during the twenties and thirties, one large group of men was usually discounted: the members of the United States armed forces who manned the naval base at Pearl Harbor and the army posts strung out from Fort Ruger at Diamond Head to Schofield Barracks on the central plain of Oahu. The servicemen could not be ignored altogether—there were too many of them for that. But neither could they be assimilated—again, there were too many of them. So they were tolerated, but only just.

Pearl Harbor became the home of the Pacific fleet, and Schofield Barracks was the biggest army post in the United States. Even in the years of disarmament after World War One, between fifteen and twenty thousand men were stationed in Hawaii. These figures made the armed services big business in the islands, and especially at Honolulu. The building of a dry dock at Pearl Harbor alone involved a payroll of sixty thousand dollars a month for almost ten years (a period that included a fresh start after the first pourings of concrete collapsed). Walter Dillingham's Honolulu Dredging and Construction Company and his Oahu Railroad and Land Company did well out of the development of the harbor, an undertaking second in cost only to the Panama Canal, according to one estimate; and all sorts of smaller businessmen—taxi operators, barbers, tattoo artists, nightclub owners, and brothel keepers—made a killing whenever the fleet came back from maneuvers or the enlisted men of Schofield came into town with their pay.

For the most part, however, the serviceman's money was more welcome than the serviceman himself. A surprising number of soldiers and sailors married local girls in Hawaii—thousands of them over the years—and this showed acceptance of a sort, but a feeling of estrangement between the two communities, military and civilian, persisted just the same. The question resolved itself into a matter of ingroups and outgroups, and the dividing line between servicemen and residents could not have been more clearly marked.

This game of ingroups and outgroups had been played for a long time at the islands, and a man's perception of the game depended upon his place in it. On the plantations—and in the armed services, for that matter—everything was in the open, with rank and occupation displayed for all to see. But there were other versions of the game in which definitions were more subtle, so much so, in fact, that they might escape an uninstructed observer. Someone unfamiliar with Chinatown, for example, might miss the point that more than one dialect of Chinese was spoken there, that the two main groups of Chinese immigrants, the Punti and the Hakka, had not much time for each other, and that community organizations such as the United Chinese Society papered over differences among other groupings based on family, clan, village, district, and provincial loyalties—all jealously preserved, and set aside only for compelling reasons. Someone unfamiliar with the Japanese might not understand that most of them came from the southern prefectures of Japan, and that they wanted themselves distinguished at all costs from the minority of migrants who came from the Ryukyu Islands, the Okinawans. A Korean did not want to be mistaken either for a Chinese or a Japanese, and his country's unhappy history made his point for him, if anybody took the trouble to find out about it. Chinese, Japanese, and Koreans alike took their various positions seriously, especially in relation to those late arrivals, the Filipinos, among whom, in turn, there were divisions—between Tagalog, Visayan, and Ilocano.

People who lived in Hawaii for any length of time could not help becoming aware of what the local game involved, and with practice they became skillful players. For most the skill was purely mechanical, simply a matter of carrying in the mind not one stereotype but several. But even these people developed a talent for manipulating stereotypes that very few mainland Americans had. This was demonstrated every day, in conversation. Out of the welter of languages and dialects spoken at the islands an expressive pidgin emerged, and a conscientious island dweller made a point of using the correct version whenever he spoke to someone who looked different from himself. Even white men and women took it up, because it got better results than the historic expedient of raising the voice and speaking slowly and clearly in perfect English on the assumption that not even the stupidest alien could fail to understand.

The serviceman, and especially the career officer, was a different case. An enlisted man from Pearl Harbor or Schofield, using up his liberty passes at the brothels of Hell's Half Acre or Tin Can Alley on the west side of Honolulu, might gradually come to appreciate the subtle differences between one kind of local girl and another, but his superior was likely to take a simpler and sterner view of the social situation in Hawaii. An officer who was also a Southerner, for example, would have his own sense of rank and station and his own sense of the fitness of things, and he might be unable to see Hawaiians as anything but exotic Negroes, Orientals as little brown men indistinguishable one from the other, and "local boys," especially those of mixed blood, as the embodiment of all that was worst in human nature.

So in actuality many different games were being played at the islands. White residents—most of them, anyway—observed local conventions without any intention of committing themselves to localism, but even this small concession was likely to be beyond a naval officer in whose considered view a local boy had broken the rules just by being born.

Once in a great while the rules were shattered, and then terrible things happened. In 1928 a deranged Japanese youth named Myles Fukunaga kidnapped the ten-year-old son of F. W. Jamieson, a white businessman, because Jamieson's firm, Hawaiian Trust, was about to evict Fukunaga's parents and their seven children from their rented home at Honolulu. Fukunaga demanded ransom, got it, and then strangled the boy. For a moment Honolulu seemed to be on the brink either of lynch law or racial war. The moment passed almost before it was perceived. Fukunaga was tried, convicted, and hanged not as a representative of his race, but as a sad and solitary criminal.

Fukunaga's crime was unsettling enough, but one way or another it could be put out of sight. This was impossible when, three years later, Thalia Massie, the twenty-year-old wife of Thomas Hedges Massie, a submarine lieutenant stationed at Pearl Harbor, told a story which—if it was true—meant that every rule of life at the islands had been broken. And once her story became known, the polite conventions and limited agreements that made it possible for men of different races to live together more or less comfortably were rendered meaningless.

On the night of Saturday, September 12, 1931, Mrs. Massie and her husband went with some of their friends to the Ala Wai Inn, a restaurant overlooking the drainage canal that marked the boundary of Waikiki. The Inn was done up like a Japanese teahouse with a dance floor downstairs. It was popular with the junior officers of Pearl Harbor; they liked to take a table on Saturday nights, do some talking and dancing, and have a drink or two (usually of okolehao, Hawaii's potent answer to Prohibition, a liquor distilled from mashed ti root, sold illegally and drunk openly everywhere at the islands). Thalia Massie was at the Ala Wai Inn under protest. After four years as a Navy wife she still did not like dancing or drinking, she did not like crowds, and she did not like most of her husband's submariner friends. Late in the evening she had an argument with one of them and slapped his face, and then she went outside, by herself.

The Hawaiian orchestra usually packed up for the night at twelve o'clock, but this time someone paid for another hour of music. Lieutenant Massie looked here and there at the Inn for his wife between midnight and one o'clock, but the dance came to an end and she was still missing. She had wandered away from the Inn, down John Ena Road toward Ala Moana, a road which ran along the water from Waikiki past a shantytown toward Honolulu. At about one o'clock she staggered out onto Ala Moana and hailed a car driven by a man named Eustace Bellinger. Her jaw was broken, her face was bruised, her lips were swollen, and she could hardly make herself understood. She asked Bellinger if he and his friends were white, and then she told them that she had been beaten up by five or six Hawaiian boys. She did not want to call the police, and Bellinger drove her home to Manoa valley.

Lieutenant Massie left the Ala Wai Inn when it closed. He thought that perhaps his wife had gone home with some Navy people who lived in Manoa, and he tried their place. Mrs. Massie was not there, so he used their telephone to call his own house. His wife answered. "Come home at once," she said. "Something awful has happened." Massie found her crying, and it was some time before she could tell him what had happened—the Hawaiians who forced her into their car on John Ena Road had beaten her, taken her to Ala Moana, raped her, so she said, and left her there. Massie called the police just before two o'clock.

The police were already looking for a carload of local boys. Between midnight and one o'clock a Hawaiian woman named Agnes Peeples and her husband, a white man, were driving through the intersection of King Street and Liliha Street, some miles away from the Ala Wai Inn on the other side of Honolulu, when another car came through the intersection and nearly collided with them. Both cars stopped; Mrs. Peeples got out, and one of the passengers in the other car, a Hawaiian named Joseph Kahahawai, got out too. They exchanged words, and then they exchanged blows. Mrs. Peeples took the number of the other car and went straight to the police. A radio description was being broadcast when Lieutenant Massie telephoned to say that his wife had been assaulted.

Massie took his wife to the emergency hospital to find out if she was badly injured. While they were there a police car, with its radio turned up loud, broadcast the details of the fight between Agnes Peeples and Joe Kahahawai. The number of the car, 58–895, and its make, a Ford phaeton with a cloth top, were mentioned several times, and then some added information came over the air: the driver of the car, a young Japanese named Horace Ida, had been picked up for questioning. After Mrs. Massie was examined, she went to the police station to tell her story once again, in detail, and this time she was able to give the police a description of the car in which she had been abducted. It was a Ford tourer, she said, and its number was 58–805. Horace Ida was brought into the room, and she asked him some questions. He did not say much. Later he told the police the names of the others who had been in the car with him: Joe Kahahawai, the Hawaiian who hit Agnes Peeples; Henry Chang, a Chinese-Hawaiian; David Takai, a Japanese; and Benny Ahakuelo, a Hawaiian. The police arrested all but Ahakuelo on Sunday morning and took them to the Massies' house in

Manoa. Mrs. Massie was sure Chang had assaulted her, but she could not identify any of the others with certainty. Benny Ahakuelo was arrested later the same day. By that time Mrs. Massie was in Queen's Hospital under the care of her own doctor, and Ahakuelo, Chang, and Takai were brought there. She said she could not identify Ahakuelo. The five young men, telling their stories to the police separately, said they had been driving around in Ida's car the night before. They had spent some time at a dance in Waikiki, and some time at a party in Nuuanu valley. They had nothing to do with the attack on Mrs. Massie.

The English language newspapers at Honolulu were sure the police had the right men. The *Advertiser* called them "fiends" who had kidnapped and maltreated a "white woman of refinement and culture," a "young married woman of the highest character." (The *Advertiser,* as a matter of fact, gave its readers their choice of sexual shocks on the day the first news of the assault on Mrs. Massie was released. Its front page carried wire-service stories about the evangelist Aimee McPherson, who had eloped with her voice teacher; a "society love tangle" on the American mainland; a duel over a "German beauty;" a kidnapping that turned out to be a "love hoax;" and the adventures of a "white queen of the jungle.")

Mrs. Massie's name was not printed, but within a few days the five suspects were identified in the press. The two Japanese, Horace Ida and David Takai, had never been in trouble with the police, but the other three had. Joe Kahahawai had been jailed earlier in 1931 for assault and battery. Henry Chang and Benny Ahakuelo were convicted in 1929 of attempted rape, and they served some months in prison before they were paroled. This clinched the case against them, so a good many people thought.

While the prosecutor's office was preparing its case, the suspects were tried in the newspapers; in fact "local boys" as a group were tried. Every stock character in the drama of outraged sexual morality made an appearance in the letters-to-the-editor column—"Indignant Citizen," "Vigilante," "Mother Of Three Daughters," and all the rest. Every imaginable act of lust was discussed and every imaginable punishment was considered—whipping, sterilization, emasculation. As the *Advertiser* said, the "gangsters" of Hawaii deserved nothing less; they were beasts at once primitive and degenerate, less civilized than the aboriginal blacks of Australia or New Guinea.

Mrs. Massie's mother, Grace Hubbard Bell Fortescue, arrived at Honolulu before the trial began. Lieutenant Massie had sent her a hasty telegram, and she took the first ship to the islands. As soon as Mrs. Fortescue heard her overwrought daughter's story, she began to worry that Thalia might be pregnant—a terrible prospect. Mrs. Fortescue arranged for an examination and an operation. The results showed no sign of pregnancy.

Among the interested parties in the case was Rear Admiral Yates Stirling, Commandant of the Fourteenth Naval District, which included Pearl Harbor. Stirling was an officer, a gentleman, and a Southerner. He had spent part of his career fighting revolutionaries in the Philippines and Chinese warlords on the Yangtze River, and he found little to impress him in the East. Hawaii, where not only Filipinos and Chinese but Japanese and native Hawaiians lived in what seemed to him disgusting closeness to white men and women, impressed him even less. He had nothing but scorn for "enthusiastic priests of the melting-pot cult," and even on the most beautiful Hawaiian day he could not get the "sordid people" of the islands out of his mind for more than a few minutes at a time. Now that the local boys had shown their true sexual colors, Stirling was caught between two duties: his responsibility as an officer serving the United States government, and his responsibility to his private code of honor. His first inclination, as he said, was to "seize the brutes and string them up on trees." But he realized that the law must take its course, "slow and exasperating" though it was bound to be.

When the case finally came to trial in November, 1931, the selection of a jury took two days. The difficulties were obvious. White jurors, haoles, might find the defendants guilty because of their race; Oriental or Hawaiian jurors might do the opposite. The Navy had a special interest in the verdict, too, and the Navy was one of the best customers of Honolulu's businessmen. If a juror worked for a firm that did business with the Navy, how would he vote? In the end a jury was chosen consisting of six white men, one Portuguese, two Japanese, two Chinese, and one Hawaiian.

The case for the prosecution was shaky, to say the least. The defendants had undergone a thorough physical examination when they were arrested, and their bodies and the clothes they were wearing that night showed no sign that they had had sexual intercourse. Neither, for that matter, did Mrs. Massie's body or her clothes show that she had been raped. That she had been beaten was clear; but beyond that very little was clear, even though her story of what happened after she left the Ala Wai Inn got more and more detailed the more often she told it. In court she identified four of the five defendants, more than she had managed to do before, but of course they were the only suspects she was ever shown, and she had never been asked to identify them in a lineup. She also got four of the five digits in the number of Ida's car correct, but again she had the help of the police in this. Her beads and cigarettes and other belongings were found in a clearing off the Ala Moana, and tire marks from Ida's car were found there too, but this did not mean much either, because some of the detectives assigned to the case had driven Ida's car to the spot to conduct their searches. The defense leaned heavily on the element of time. It was unlikely that five men could have raped Mrs. Massie a total of six times, as she said they did, *when* she said they did, and then driven to the other side of town in time to get into a near collision at the corner of King and Liliha Streets when this was known to have happened. To be sure, no other suspects had come to light, but then the police were not looking for other suspects.

The jury stayed out from the afternoon of Wednesday, December 2, until the afternoon of Saturday, December 5, when sounds of fighting were heard in the jury room. The foreman came out to say that they could not agree. Judge Alva E. Steadman told them to try again, but at ten o'clock on Sunday night the foreman sent out a note saying that the jury found it impossible to reach a verdict. Steadman declared a mistrial. A new trial would have to be arranged, and in the meantime Ida, Kahahawai, Chang, Ahakuelo, and Takai were freed on bail.

As Admiral Stirling heard it, "The vote of the jury began and remained to the end, seven for not guilty and five for guilty, the exact proportion of yellow and brown to whites on the jury." In Stirling's view the mistrial was a plain miscarriage of justice. The defendants were not men "who might be given the benefit of a reasonable doubt." Stirling was sure he spoke for most good Navy men. They were under discipline, but all the same the admiral "half suspected" that he would hear any day that one or more of the defendants had been found "swinging from trees by the neck" in Nuuanu valley. Stirling was half right in his half suspicions. Six days after the court case ended some men from the submarine base found Horace Ida in downtown Honolulu, bundled him into their car, drove over the Nuuanu Pali to windward Oahu, took their leather belts, and beat and kicked him unconscious.

Mrs. Fortescue was brooding over the unsatisfactory verdict too. She had rented a house in Manoa valley, and Thalia was living with her while Lieutenant Massie was on sea duty. The Navy assigned a guard to watch the house at night: Machinist's Mate Albert O. Jones, whose job at the submarine base was to train the boxing team. Jones had two pistols, a .45 service automatic and a .32 automatic he bought himself. Mrs. Fortescue also bought a gun, a .32 revolver. All over town, in fact, white women, and especially Navy wives, were taking out licenses for pistols. Mrs. Fortescue, however, had something special in mind when she armed herself. She wanted to get a confession from one of the beasts who—she was sure—had raped her daughter.

She did not take long to work out a plan. The five defendants still had to report each day to the Judiciary Building in downtown Honolulu. Mrs. Fortescue spent a morning there, watching them come and go one by one. She took her son-in-law into her confidence, and then told Jones what she proposed to do. Jones got a member of his boxing team, Fireman First Class Edward J. Lord, to join in the plot. Mrs. Fortescue made up a document meant to look like a summons. Part of it was handwritten, the rest was clipped arbitrarily from a newspaper headline: "Life Is A Mysterious And Exciting Affair, And Anything Can Be A Thrill If You Know How To Look For It And What To Do With Opportunity When It Comes." That night Mrs. Fortescue studied a photograph of Joseph Kahahawai's "brutal, repulsive black face," so that she would recognize him instantly when she saw him.

The next morning, Friday, January 8, 1932, Lieutenant Massie and Edward Lord drove to the Judiciary Building, in a rented Buick; Mrs. Fortescue and Albert Jones followed in Massie's Durant roadster. When Kahahawai came out of the courthouse, Jones waved the summons at him, pushed him into the Buick, and climbed in after him. Massie drove back to Manoa valley, with Mrs. Fortescue and Lord following in the other car. At Mrs. Fortescue's house Jones and Massie threatened Kahahawai with terrible things if he did not admit that he was a rapist. Massie, as good a Southern gentleman as Admiral Stirling, had been sexually humiliated, and Mrs. Fortescue, herself a Southern gentlewoman, was proud to see her son-in-law, "small, erect, dominating," striking terror into the heart of the dark-skinned Kahahawai. She looked away for a second (so she said later), and while her back was turned a pistol went off. She looked again to see Kahahawai on the floor, shot through the chest. Within a few minutes he was dead. The men stripped the bloodied body and put it in the bathtub, and tried to think what to do next.

Kahahawai's cousin, Edward Ulii, had been at the Judiciary Building when Kahahawai was taken away in Massie's Buick. Ulii heard something about a summons, but he noticed that the car did not go in the direction of the police station. Ulii went to the police himself, and a radio call was put out for the Buick. Less than half an hour later Detective George Harbottle (who had worked on the Massie case), saw the car heading along Waialae Avenue to the east of Honolulu, with Mrs. Fortescue at the wheel and the rear-window shade pulled down. Harbottle went after it. Some miles out of town he passed the Buick, got out of his car, and signaled Mrs. Fortescue to stop. She would not. Harbottle fired two shots and gave chase again. Not far from Hanauma Bay he forced the Buick to the side of the road. He put Mrs. Fortescue, Massie, and Lord under arrest, opened the back door of their car, and saw a white bundle tied with rope. A human leg was sticking out from under the covering, and it was cold. Kahahawai was on his way to being thrown in the sea.

The three were taken back to Honolulu in a police wagon, with the body of Kahahawai in a wicker basket at their feet, still tied in its covering of canvas and bed sheets. Albert Jones was found at the Massies' house, drunk, with the fake summons and a spent .32 shell in his pocket. He was arrested, and all four of the conspirators were charged with first-degree murder. Mrs. Fortescue was aghast. "But it wasn't murder!" she wrote later in a magazine article entitled "The Honolulu Martyrdom," which cast herself and her family in the role of martyrs. "We had not broken the law. We were trying to aid the law. Without a confession we knew there was no chance of clearing the slime deliberately smeared on a girl's character." Perhaps; but Kahahawai had not confessed, and now he was dead. And if his body had been thrown in the sea nothing would have been known about the cause of his death, and that was a question the law was bound to be interested in.

"People who take the law into their own hands always make a mess of it," said the *Honolulu Star-Bulletin.* Mrs. Fortescue could only agree. "Now, of course," she told a reporter not long after the killing, "I realize we bungled dreadfully, although at the time I thought we were being careful." But what about the unwritten law? Would that excuse Mrs. Fortescue and Thomas Massie their lack of expertise? They could argue that without the rape case there would have been no killing, and even though there was no conviction in the rape case surely there was incitement enough—after all, as Admiral Stirling said, Americans, and especially Southerners, could not be expected to take the violation of their women lightly.

Griffith Wight of the prosecutor's office was in a difficult position. When he was pressing the case against Kahahawai and his friends for the rape of Thalia Massie he had the support of a good part of the white community. Now he had to convince a grand jury that the respectable white killers of Kahahawai should be brought to trial for kidnapping and murder, and he knew it was asking too much to expect the people who had demanded justice a few weeks earlier to speak in the same firm voice this time. At first the twenty-one grand jurors, most of them white men, reported against indictment. Judge Albert M. Cristy refused to accept their report and sent them back to reconsider their responsibilities. Their next report contained an indictment for second-degree murder.

Mrs. Fortescue, looking for the best attorney possible, settled on Clarence Darrow, easily the most celebrated criminal lawyer in the United States. Darrow was seventy-five years old, in poor health, and long past his best as an advocate; but the weight of his reputation was impressive, and in the limited legal circles of the territory it might be decisive. Darrow looked into the case, professed himself interested in the psychology of a "crime that was not a crime," agreed to defend all four of the accused, and took ship for the islands in March.

Darrow's adversary, John C. Kelley of the prosecutor's office, was a tough and energetic man in his early forties, not easily overawed by reputation; indeed he had something of a name in the territory as a local Darrow. The selection of a jury began on April 4, and as the two men and their juniors went through the ritual of challenges it began to look as if local experience might mean more than a little. Of the twenty-six venire men, only nine were white, and the twelve who survived the attorneys' challenges made up the usual mixed bag of haoles, Chinese, Portuguese, and Hawaiians.

Once the hearing of evidence got under way, lines formed overnight outside the courthouse, and a place in line near the door was worth fifty dollars in the morning. The best people were willing to pay the price. Their presence gave the proceedings a kind of grisly chic, and the social reporters of the English language newspapers were careful to note who sat where. Almost to a woman the best people were for Mrs. Fortescue; the rest, the locals, were less committed to the idea that an "honor killing" was no crime.

Massie, as the aggrieved husband, took the responsibility for the killing (although Admiral Stirling liked to think Mrs.

Fortescue pulled the trigger out of mother love, and years later Albert Jones said he fired the shot). Massie testified that he was able to remember everything except what happened just before and after the pistol went off. Then, to show why Kahahawai was kidnapped in the first place, Darrow had Thalia Massie tell, all over again, what happened on the night of September 12. Putting the two stories together, Darrow argued that Massie killed Kahahawai in a temporary fit of insanity.

From the first it was clear that Darrow was uneasy with jurors whose faces he could not fathom. No one could play on a jury's emotions better than he—his towering reputation had been made that way.—but a Honolulu jury was an unfamiliar instrument. Would Hawaiians and Orientals be able to understand that a white man tortured by strain might crack and commit a crime and then have no knowledge of it? The case for the defense hung on that single point.

Darrow retained two psychiatrists, "alienists" as they were called then, to testify that Massie was insane when the shot was fired. One talked about ambulatory automatisms caused by psychological strain; the other talked about changes in the function of the suprarenal glands that might bring on chemical or shock insanity. Kelley also had two specialists, and they said—in their own technical language—that Massie was sane. Most people in the courtroom, and probably the twelve men in the jury box, simply let the big words go by.

Darrow's summation took almost four and a half hours. It was a classic performance (and, as it happened, Darrow's last—he never took another courtroom case). "At times," wrote a reporter, his voice was "as soft as a woman's. At others, it was like thunder that could be heard a block away. He was eloquent. He was dramatic. He was impressive in his rages, as his 225-pound body crouched and bent and his long, lean arms thrashed through the air. Now and then he brushed away a tear when dwelling upon some tragic part of the evidence." Darrow had never been unwilling to subordinate strict legalism to the higher law of humanity, and in the past he had often carried juries with him. But this time as he rang the changes on passion and pain, base lust and mother love, he found it hard going. "When I gazed into those dark faces," he said later, "I could see the deep mysteries of the Orient were there. My ideas and words were not registering." Mrs. Fortescue saw the same thing. "The stoical Oriental faces betrayed no emotion. Ethnologically and traditionally, white and yellow and brown are races apart. How could such a plea appeal to the six men to whom the white man's code is a mystery?"

Kelley talked about love too. He observed that the dead man's parents were in the courtroom. Had Mrs. Fortescue lost a son, or Thalia Massie a husband? No. "But where," asked Kelley, "is Joseph Kahahawai?" Then he talked about law—which, he said, Darrow had neglected to do. The "code of the white man," whatever that was, should not be allowed to usurp the place of the law. The four defendants conspired to kidnap Kahahawai. Kidnapping was a felony. Kahahawai was killed as a result of the kidnapping, and the law called that felony murder.

Judge Charles S. Davis gave his charge to the jury on April 27, the eighteenth day of the trial. They reached their verdict after forty-eight hours. All four defendants were found guilty of manslaughter, and leniency was recommended. On May 4 they were sentenced to ten years at hard labor in Oahu Prison.

They did not go to jail. Under the protection of the high sheriff they left the courtroom and walked across King Street to Iolani Palace, where the governor of the territory, Lawrence M. Judd, had his offices. Darrow went inside with them. Ten minutes later Judd announced that he had commuted the sentences from ten years to one hour, to be served in the custody of the high sheriff.

Robert Lee Eskridge

Wandering Spirits of Manga Reva

Robert Lee Eskridge, artist and author born in 1891, roved around the world and spent years in Hawaii and the South Pacific. His book *Manga Reva* (1931) is a valuable account of native life and a source for the bizarre story of Father Honoré Laval.

This Catholic priest went in 1834 as a missionary of the Society of Picpus to Manga Reva in the Gambier group. Laval obtained dominance over the chief and began a compulsive building program that lasted more than thirty years. A native police force was organized, which enforced the dictates of the apostle. People were hauled from neighboring islands to slave away, cutting stone blocks and erecting a spreading, 3,400-seat cathedral; churches; a monastery; and a nunnery (in which were immured young Polynesian maidens forcibly enlisted into convent life). As the buildings spread, the people died. A visit from his bishop finally put an end to Laval's dominance in 1871, and the jungle began reclaiming his monuments.

Eskridge fully shared the companionship of latter-day dwellers in the Gambiers, and narrates more than one tale of island phantoms.

THE three little islands, named Makaroa, Kamaka, and Manoui, are fairy kingdoms of some unhappy prince or of an exiled princess. Then the countless little motus scattered along the reef hold that sudden untenanted feeling I received from each and every island in the group. Some one had just left—but who? The answer came in a series of impressions and adventures which I narrate just as they occurred to me, without change or exaggeration.

My house [at Rikitea, the capital] was at nighttime shared by others of less substantial mold than myself. And as for the gardens, no one save myself ever went into them at night alone.

Even in the daytime, what with the wildness of the foliage and the ruined and gutted porches on one side of the house—two rooms only were habitable—and the hidden windows back of high unpruned oleander trees, the place had a slightly unsavory atmosphere.

At one side of the house ran a path from the main road to the beach. Parallel to this and some little distance from the house curved the old war canal. Used in the cannibal days as a canal up which the war canoes glided to a large inland harbor, it has now become a clogged and useless channel. The inland harbor is a taro swamp, and very gay it is with great heart-shaped shiny dark green leaves rising out of the swamp morass. A thin stream flows from the mountain down through the swamp, and so to the end of the canal which near my house empties itself into the lagoon. At high tide the waters from the lagoon run upstream. So one has the impression that the little stream can not make up its mind which way it wants to flow and tries both.

I locked up all the house except the two rooms in which I intended to live. In one I painted and slept, the other was used as a kitchen. They were not connected but were accessible from the same porch. The ancient path led right past this porch to the beach. This was, so the natives told me later, one of the oldest thoroughfares on the island. In cannibal days the war canoes stopped at the end of the path before entering the canal and unloaded, so I was told, such prisoners as had been captured in battle, either dead or alive. The preparations for the feast—of which the central dish was euphemistically called "long pig"—then took place in what was my back yard.

Once at high tide Tom, who had been browsing on the shell-littered beach, called me out to him. A storm had washed away much of the loose sand and shells that ordinarily were not touched by the tide. Four or five inches below the top of the bank was a thick layer of ashes and the usual remains of a big fire. Several human bones lay mixed with the débris.

Then Tom pointed to a dark brown object that at first glance had the appearance of a large round stone, the color of old ivory. I walked around it, and there, grinning at me, was the skull of a boy or young man of perhaps sixteen years of age, judging from the shape and size of the head and from the teeth.

"Well, he was long pig. That's certain!" said Tom, "and I wonder how he felt about it."

"And still feels about it!" said I, with a faint but unsuccessful effort at being facetious.

"Let's put him in the cook-house, so the boys won't take him," said Tom, practically, and picked him up.

That evening Tom and I sat discussing our beliefs about the other world.

"You know, Bob," said Tom, "you tell me things exist, but how do you know?"

As this was the hundredth time Tom had put the question to me I was growing a little restless, and answered peevishly, "Well, what do you demand to prove to you that there is another world?"

"Only to see something, actually to see something with my own eyes! I have felt slighted by Parquitala. Here I've been on the island for five years and he doesn't think I'm worth cultivating! He never looked me over."

"If he had, Tom, you would have demanded his visiting card before you would have recognized him as a bonafide *tupapau!*"

"Perhaps your're right. Perhaps it's in myself, whatever it is that keeps me from seeing them. yet things have happened to me here, strange things that I can't explain any other way. The first one occurred on my first Christmas Eve on the island. The girl and the family had all gone to midnight mass at the cathedral, and I was lying down on the grass near the end of your path, listening to the quiet movement of the tide. It sounded like music at times. Suddenly about three feet over my head a thing, a black thing about as big as a cat, flew past like a shot. I was so startled I couldn't move, and lay there motionless. Again it passed me, so close I could almost have touched it. Like a cat curled up asleep it seemed, and it moved through the air just as a fish moves through water. It flew upward to the top of the purau tree on your place, and vanished. I am absolutely convinced that it was not a bird. It had no wings."

"Well, if you don't call that 'seeing something,' just what would you call it?" I asked a trifle maliciously, and next moment regretted it. For Tom's face took on such a look of bewilderment and struggle that it was hard to look at him.

"That's just it! That's just the trouble," he burst out. "I seemed to see it. I'm sure I did see it. If it had been something I recognized, I would never doubt it for an instant. But—*could* I have seen such a thing? Didn't my eyes play some kind of trick on me?" He paused for an instant, and then went on more slowly. "You see, Bob, you can believe in these things without being afraid you are—well—going cuckoo. But for me, I live here with the natives, but I'm American after all. And if I give up everything my own people believe, and get to believing all the superstitions they have here, what will happen to me? The fact is, old man, I don't dare believe these things, and yet I can't get away from them!" His distress was so evident, and his dilemma so real, that I found no answer, and coaxed him back to the subject of what he had experienced.

"Two more things occurred. I was walking out to the farm on a bit of open road that winds through the valley before you get to the girl's land, when slowly trotting toward me I saw an enormous black dog. He passed quite close to me, and I saw him as plainly as I see you. And yet I know that *there is no such dog* on the whole island of Manga Reva, or any of the other islands of the Gambier. The natives of course insist that it was 'The Black Dog of Manga Reva,' *ure ere ere, te Manga Reva.*"

"But what is that?" I interrupted.

"Well," said Tom, "I haven't been able to find out exactly whose ghost he is, though some say he was once a high priest. At all events he is a friendly and goodnatured *tupapau* who is rather often seen both here and on the island of Marutea.

"But to continue with my experiences. One time I had had a fight with Pindini, the girl, and walked over to the farm and put up for the night in the little *ni'au* shack I had built there. In the middle of the night the sound of heavy footsteps approached, and coming close to the shack stopped beside the door. I waited a while. Then the same heavy steps returned the way they had come. I got up and went out. The moon, though low on the horizon, shed light enough to see distinctly everything in the little valley. There are no high trees and you can see for at least a mile in every direction. But not a sign of anybody was there.

"Next night the girl, feeling lonesome, came out with the dog. We made up as we always do, though I always swear the last fight will be the final one. We had gone to sleep, when I was wakened by the same footsteps approaching just as I heard them the night before. I hadn't said a word to her about them, so her reactions were genuinely her own. She raised herself on her elbow as the steps came closer, and her eyes were wide with fear as she pressed closer to me, whispering, '*Tupapau!*' The dog never moved, but every hair on his back was standing straight in the air and he barely whimpered, so frightened was he. The thing did exactly what it had done the night before. This time I jumped up, Pindini clutching me and begging me not to go, and ran out before the steps started away, when they seemed to come from just outside the shack. But again nobody was in sight anywhere. And the strangest thing was that I heard the steps start again and go heavily away even as I stood staring at emptiness.

"I forgot to mention, though I don't know whether it had any connection with the event or not, that shortly before I heard the footsteps the first time I had dug up some human bones not far back from the shack in a spot I had picked for my onion patch."

So Tom described the few experiences which he could not explain by any other means than the supernatural. However, he felt far more than he ever saw, and the thing that puzzled him most was—where did this haunted feeling come from, and what created it? Was it suggestion, or was there really some occult explanation? Ever since my arrival on the island and the experience that occurred to me on my first night there, when I sensed the strangeness that lay about me, Tom had turned to me in his perplexity, and had been avidly interested in what would happen next.

That first night I slept on my porch. The house was in such disorder that I preferred the moonlight and the heady perfume of the masses of oleander and frangipani that flourished riotously in the garden. I later learned that no native will ever sleep in the tropical moonlight, and even more decided about such matters are those white men who have gone native. Tom said he could never do it, as the house was odd enough at night even with the door shut, without asking the ghosts in by leaving it open! However, ghosts and the thought of them were far from my tired body and mind, on that first night spent in The Forgotten Islands in my new home.

My first intimation that all was not as it usually is was a sound of voices about me early in the morning. I sat up, and still the low flow of some unknown language continued. I got up and finally located the voices near the end of the path which terminated at the beach. I walked down the path with the voices all about me talking in a low steady stream. They seemed at times to come from just beside my head, yet look as I would in the silver moonlight I could see no living thing. Puzzled and unable to discover any explanation I finally returned to the porch and slumbered fitfully till the sun rose. . . .

It was perhaps two weeks after I had been installed in the plum-colored *fare* that the second visit of the *tupapaus* occurred. It was about five in the afternoon and I had finished my evening tea. The sun had already set behind a bank of cloud, so that it was fast growing dark. All my neighbors were evidently assembled in their cookhouses enjoying the evening *kai kai,* cold breadfruit and fish, for I met no one as I left the garden. Yo and Soniosa had departed their separate ways hours before, and would turn up I knew when they were good and ready to do so.

Walking across the bridge over the canal I passed on down the road in the opposite direction from the cathedral, past the tiny Protestant church that looked like an overgrown child's toy play-house. Even the Protestant preacher, an easygoing, sweet-natured fat Tahitian, was at supper with his brood, as the gleam of a lamp shone through the bamboo slats of his cookhouse under the deep shadow of the breadfruit trees. Through the strangely patterned trees the lagoon slowly changed color. The orange light died from the tops of the coco-palms, then touched the peaks of the twin and distant islands of Akena and Akamaru, where it rested for a second, and vanished.

The fantastic pandanus trees, with their foliage looking like a harvest of tails from green parrots, turned to black silhouettes against the now violet lagoon. Deeper blue became the sky high over the coco-palms, and slowly the perfumes of night were diffused throughout the new chilly air. The stone houses, though I knew them to have been long empty, looked darkly tenanted. I walked past a little faster. Gardens of houses long since deserted bloomed extravagantly behind tall hedges, with roses, frangipani, and hibiscus. Orange trees loaded with fruit climbed the hill back of me. One lone tree, heavily laden with oranges, clung as it seemed desperately to the top of a great gray rock which somehow caught my attention.

I became dimly conscious at that moment that someone was walking down the shadowed road toward me. Peering as well as I could in the dim light, I made out before it reached me the figure of an elderly Chinese in soft dark clothes. He was baldheaded and very dignified in his carriage. In one hand he held, at an unmistakably Chinese angle, a long pipe, which as he came nearer I saw to be unlighted.

"*Ia ora na oe* (good evening to you)," I wished him as he came opposite me.

He gave no sign of having heard me, but passed on as unseeing as a carved effigy in a procession.

I was puzzled and perhaps a trifle hurt. I had caused so much attention on my arrival that I expected more in consequence, and no native on the island but had questions to ask me, especially if he got me away from the others and alone.

So I stood puzzled in the gloom, when slowly, the same way he had come, the aged Chinese passed again. This time I was determined not to be ignored, so as he approached I gave him "*Bon soir, Monsieur,*" in French, on a note of insistence.

This time his head slowly turned, then his body, and he quietly advanced toward me, fixing me with the most extraordinary eyes I have ever seen. I cannot tell you what they were like, except that they were very dark, very piercing, and yet in some strange way entirely impersonal. They gazed at me as living eyes might gaze from a mask, for his face never varied a hair's breadth, nor did he utter a sound. For a space of time that seemed unbelievably long he stood close to me, holding me almost hypnotized by his look. Then, still with the same expressionless face, he turned and continued on his way, his pipe still held at the same imperturbable angle.

Oddly enough, I was not in any way put out by his gaze. On the contrary, I was conscious of a sense of well being, combined a little with the puzzled feeling a fish must have when yanked into a foreign element. Especially I felt curiously young beside this aged figure.

For a moment I stood in a sort of daze. Then I shook myself and turned to look after my strange companion. Although he had had time to take no more than a dozen steps he was gone as completely as though he had been a figure in my imagination. The road was empty, and it seemed to have grown chill very suddenly.

As I returned home the natives, like the village folk in a stage play, were out chatting over the day's happenings. Guitars and mandolins were being strummed, while Tahitian *hymenes,* soft and full-throated, formed an undertone to the conversation. This time I lacked neither regard nor verbal interest. Like the feudal prince I passed, nodding graciously to the assembled villagers. Not until a week or so later did I speak of my reserved friend to Tom. He and I were smoking our cigarettes and passing in review the affairs of the day when the old Chinese came to my mind.

"Where is the old Chinese who smokes a long pipe? I saw him some days ago," I asked.

"What old Chinese do you mean?" countered Tom. "There is no old Chinese on these islands. There are Ah Soy and Chin who run their miserable stores, and never have even rice to sell as they haven't the money to buy when the schooner comes. But they are not old and neither of them has a long pipe."

"I've seen them both, and it was neither. But I certainly saw this old bird, as plainly as I see you!" I insisted a little hotly.

"No, you didn't, old boy, as there isn't such a person to see!"

We would have argued half the night if Tom hadn't suddenly been struck by some idea. He stopped in the middle of a word, his jaw still open in surprise and his eyes filled with a sudden and wild speculation.

"By God," he said, half to himself, "it couldn't be he!"

"Who are you talking about?" I asked rather peevishly. "I tell you he came right up to me."

"Come over to the house with me right away, and we'll ask the girl's father Utato. He will know whether or not it is the one I think it is. Yes. Wait . . . "

By now my feelings were ruffled. First I had been made distinctly uncomfortable by an odd old gentleman, and now Tom doubted my story. Nevertheless I went. . . .

Tom in his slow halting way told in Tahitian my story of the meeting with the old Chinese. Hardly had the last words escaped his lips when an effect, electrical in its suddenness, took place in the room. In the light of the kerosene lamp the eyes of Utato seemed to grow larger and took on the expression of one who has seen something that isn't there. Pindini's smile ceased. She leaned forward, looking at me with all the ancient belief in her ancestors' gods written on her face. Touching her rosary the picturesque but stupid Tiare mumbled to herself.

Suddenly Utato, in an odd jerky voice, cried out:

"Parquitala!"

"Yes," said Tom. "I thought it was he, but I wanted to be sure."

By this time the porch was full of natives, coming from I don't know where, and the liquid name Utato had just uttered was repeated from mouth to mouth. A hypnotic influence seemed to possess us all. I found myself reenacting the scene, just how I stood when he passed me, and how he looked at me when he turned. All this I pantomimed to the cries of "*Aue, aue!*"

Then the spell was broken. Everyone started to talk at once, about Parquitala and when he had last been seen.

"Remember, Mytea?" said Utato. "We were playing cards one night and suddenly a shadowy form appeared at the door of the hut, smiled at us, and as quietly disappeared. It was the figure of a French gendarme that no one had seen before, nor have any of us seen him since."

My curiosity by now knew no limits. "But who is Parquitala?"

"Don't you know?" came from every throat. Tom finally quieted them, and told me the story of Parquitala.

Before Laval, fired with the mad flames of religious fanaticism, had started his holocaust of idol-breaking, there stood in the lovely Valley of Ititouiti at the foot of Mount Duff an altar dedicated to Parquitala. A small marae it had been, and not listed among the nine great maraes of the islands. No one clearly remembered why it was called Parquitala's altar. It was said that in the dim and ancient days of cannibalism a high priest had lived called Parquitala, who tended three grotesque gods on the altar that later was to bear his name. He had been, so old rumor relates, a great soldier, a mighty warrior, as well as a powerful magician. That he must have been a man of powerful personality is certain, as only three names stand out high above the countless others that have passed in The Forgotten Isles: Maputeoa, Laval, and Parquitala.

Now when Laval and his men were winding their way down the steep path that leads to the valley where Parquitala's altar stood, fired with the insane zeal of impending destruction, the high priest of the little marae—who had been warned—sorrowfully gathered the three clumsy wide-eyed stone gods into his canoe. He must, of course, before he did this, have prostrated himself before the ancient shades of the gods of his people and begged them to forgive what he was about to do, since he did it only to save the magnificent memory of Parquitala. At all events he steered his canoe to the deepest part of the lagoon and there dropped the gods one by one into the inscrutable cerulean depths. When Laval and his assistants arrived, nothing was left to destroy but the terraces of the altar, which in frustrated fury he ripped apart till scarcely a stone was left where the altar had stood.

As time went on and Catholicism replaced the idols of paganism with painted plaster effigies, the simple natives humbly accepted the substitute and immolated themselves on the altar of Laval's mad ambition. But Parquitala, untouched by the occult splendor of the long glittering arm of the church, walked abroad unmolested by the holy water, spells, or incantations which were thrown upon his name. Perhaps he embodies the spirit of all the ancient gods and is deathless. At any rate when he chose to appear no power could be raised against him. The years passed, and the silent shadow of Parquitala moved as though Catholicism had never existed. . . .

The Polynesians reckon time by the moon, and it is on the eighteenth, nineteenth, and twentieth nights of the moon month that the ghosts walk. The full moon has risen, and its lower rim just touches the horizon at sunset. It is an ideal time for ghosts to walk at will. Of course suggestion plays a great part in our lives, and to a simple South Sea islander the suggestion that on these nights the *tupapau* are abroad is extremely potent.

However, with all my philosophy and understanding of scientific metaphysics, I will say that there is some very powerful force at work, not only on the nights mentioned but on other nights as well, especially on Manga Reva and the near-by islands. The *tupapaus* on The Forgotten Islands seem to possess more freedom than those of Tahiti, which rarely walk save on the three nights of the moon on which they are set at liberty from their ghostly fourth-dimensional state of confinement.

On the island of Maupiti, one of the Leeward group of the Society Islands where I once lived for several months, I retired on the first night of my arrival on the island in a small bedroom which opened doorless from the main living room, where the family of Pihau Tane, my host, slept. Tired and exhausted from my trip I slept soundly. But at about two in the morning I found myself awakened by some force outside myself. Raising myself on one elbow, I looked about. Sitting in the middle of the doorway was a vague figure which slowly took the very tangible form of an old man. He was so old that his eyes had sunk to pinpoints and his long upper and lower teeth protruded beyond his gums. One hand was raised in a gesture of command and he looked straight in front of him, as though looking out the window. When I first saw him he was wavering and mistlike, but before long I saw him with absolute distinctness. Where the light came from I do not know. While I watched, wide awake but powerless to move because of the strange effect on me of this curious phenomenon, I saw shapes slowly rising from the floor. They were black shapes, half seal, half cat, with long black bodies that curled around one side of the ancient figure. They were like seals in their movements, but each animal—if that is what they were—had four very short paws, no tail, and in their catlike heads were set enormous eyes.

This continued for some time. There seemed no end to the stream of little black monsters that rose from the floor, caressed the mummylike figure, and then circled upward and vanished into the ceiling. Although some curious things happened to me before, this was my first real occult experience in the South Seas and a sort of hypnotic terror came over me. I began to repeat a formula for the banishment of demons and the powers of darkness.

I had scarcely started when the seated figure turned its head slowly toward me, and from what I had thought were eyeless sockets shot dark gleams, like fires glowing in a pit.

The head grew large, the shriveled gums and protruding teeth still hideously plain, and the body assumed proportions to match the head. The arm raised in command slowly reached out till the long bony fingers were just within reach of my face.

I had the feeling that I was being hypnotized, first into a daze and then into a deep sleep, and I sank away, dimly remembering that the demon's head had swelled until it touched the ceiling before I lost consciousness. The black stream of animals had ceased the moment I commenced the formula. As I dropped into sleep I seemed to fall into an ancient state of being, something from thousands of years ago, so that I was terrified at first, happy at last that I could do so.

From that day I had no trouble with my life in Polynesia. All forces, material and occult, reached out to help me in every way.

When I told the natives some time after this about my experience, I received nothing but belief, and then I was told the story of Pihau's house.

Pihau built his house, against the approval of every one on the island, on the site of a ruined marae, which happened to be situated on land which he owned. Now while the natives have accepted the Christianity presented to them by the missionaries, they yet have a deep-rooted fear and respect for the ancient altars of their ancestors, and to build a house on the site of one of them is sacrilege indeed.

According to the natives the high priest of the Tieopolo has a kind of vicarious life if he finds a living person through whom he may express himself. Old Nairou, the Marquesan father of Pihau's wife, was such a person. He saw the *tupapau* every night. In the morning he described the form under which the demon had appeared to him the night before. Sometimes he took the form of an animal; again he was a huge half animal, half human being, terrifying to behold; again he appeared as a black and uneasy cat or dog that ended his wanderings by darting from the ground suddenly straight for the sky and disappearing. Sometimes he appeared as a very old man accompanied by black animal-like forms, and again he appeared as a ball of faintly luminous fire.

The natives believed that my seeing him without warning or preparation on that first night of my island visit was a sign that I was accepted by their ancient powers. Their ancient gods were pleased with me for some unknown reason. This of course established an easy atmosphere for my work, for if you have the sympathy of the people with whom you are living you have nothing to fight against. The natives christened me "ghost cousin," an appellation which my neighbors of Manga Reva took over, and which they seem to feel I rightly deserved.

There is no middle ground in sympathy with that half world. One either wanders farther and farther into the intricacies of the fabulous jungles of the old Manga Revan world, or one does not. Nothing rests for a second where it was, up to that fractional margin which divides what we call the past and present understanding of time.

That the gray guardians of the other world had listened to Tom's plaintive desire to know more definitely the phantoms that haunted the island and his brain alike was made evident about a week after the storm and the finding of the skull.

The night before Tom's final acceptance of the unseen had been a peculiar one for me. I slept fitfully, hearing voices and steps of people passing. Mad fancies played hide-and-seek in my mind. The dog slept uneasily, turning and twisting in her sleep, making a new bed for herself in that ancient fashion peculiar to animals, turning around and around before settling down for the night. Finally I got up, unlocked the door, and went out on the porch. The wind had blown ragged clouds across the moon. It was chill, and I felt uneasy in the dimness of the half-shrouded night.

Suddenly beside me, close beside me, flashed a gray cat, apparently fast asleep. It lay curled up, suspended in midair. I jumped. It flew with an abrupt movement beside me, so close that it touched me. I felt it distinctly. Then it dashed around me and circled out into the vagueness of the garden beyond.

All my adjustments, mental and emotional, were so ragged that I had difficulty in finding myself. I reentered the house, locked the door, crept into bed and deliberately slugged myself with my mind into sleep.

Next morning as I was having my coffee Tom wandered over in his leisurely fashion. I told him what I had seen. All his features lighted up.

"Bob, do you think it will happen again? Could I see it?"

"Heavens, I hope not, old man! This restless flitting about of sleeping cats, without obedience to the laws of gravity, is getting on my nerves."

After supper that night Tom and I were smoking the last of a precious package of cigarettes. The sun had long since disappeared, yet enough light remained to shape trees and houses in a half-distinct way. We were standing on the porch, relaxed, talking about a proposed trip to Agakaouitai and the burial place of the old kings. Tom suddenly stiffened and slowly turned his head. I followed his eyes and there in the black velvet depths of the open cookhouse we saw a dimly outlined shape like a man, a half man rather, as the outline stopped at the waist. The figure was a line drawing, such a sight as a child might crudely sketch in white chalk on a blackboard, a child's conception of what a man might be. While we watched—and it seemed an eternity—it came swiftly toward us, faster than a frightened fish in the lagoon. It seemed to be drawn upon the air, the lines not luminous but white, and though I knew that it was coming rapidly toward us I cannot tell just how I knew this. It darted around us and disappeared into the garden, as the cat had done the night before.

Speechless and choking with emotion, Tom pointed to where it had disappeared. I was the first to come to myself.

"Well, Tom, how about that?"

But Tom couldn't articulate his thoughts clearly for several minutes. Finally all his curiosity, fright, and wonder came out in jerky sentences as he asked what it was, why it didn't stay longer, and what it meant.

Ignoring these, I answered calmly (outwardly I was calm, though I confess I was inwardly rather shaken): "Well, are you convinced now?"

"You bet I am!" he answered with explosive conviction. "But, Bob . . . " and on and on he wandered, asking me questions impossible to answer.

From that night on Tom lost his puzzled look, but he liked less than ever wandering about in the night, and I always had to turn the flashlight on to the path which led to the road before he would leave my house.

Charis Crockett

Sejak the Witch Killer

Charis Dennison, a Radcliffe graduate born in 1905, married Frederick Eugene Crockett. He had accompanied Commander Richard Byrd to the South Pole, and the couple spent a honeymoon among the recently reformed cannibals in western New Guinea. Of her book, *The House in the Rain Forest* (1942), about the experiences of these anthropologists who set up housekeeping in the jungle, Professor Ernest Hooton says in his introduction: "It is jammed with good descriptive writing, excellent anthropology, and good humor."

This selection asserts the former belief that death among the tribesmen is almost always assumed to be the result of the actions of an enemy, so that the person charged with the duty of revealing the murderer is an important personage.

DOUBTLESS in the tangled growth of the Rain Forest poisonous plants exist, but the most popular method of disposing of an enemy is by a magical plant known only to graduates of the Newun. *Kwi* is the powdered bark of a tree; all that it requires to be fatal is to be placed on someone's head, preferably while he is sleeping. It has another property which would endear it to the writer of detective stories: it permits the "poisoner" to establish a perfect alibi for the time of his victim's death. All he need do is murmur under his breath the moment when the *kwi* is to take effect and then arrange to be innocently poking in his garden a respectable distance away at that time.

The force of this alibi is naturally rather diminished by the fact that every Madik knows the idiosyncrasies of *kwi*, and also that every Madik is constitutionally averse to the verdict "death from natural causes." When a man dies the chances are ten to one that a human or supernatural being has killed him. The murderer is nevertheless protected to some extent. Although the finger of suspicion may point at him, it probably points at a number of others also—anyone believed to have held any sort of grudge against the dead man. The laying-on of *kwi* cannot be traced to him without subsequent thorough investigation.

Sejak told us about a case at which he had assisted. Nakari, his father's sister's husband's brother, had waked one morning feeling very unwell. Nakari's brother examined him closely and diagnostically. On Nakari's forehead he saw a small black spot.

"Oh, my brother, it is *kwi*," he cried, "and the *kwi* is on your forehead. You must surely die."

Although they had little hope of saving Nakari, his relations rushed out and collected all sorts of medicines, with which they anointed him profusely, while the brother scratched away at his forehead with a loop of rattan in a forlorn effort to draw out the fatal *kwi*. As the day wore on, Nakari turned greener and greener and began to bleed from his mouth and nose in a ghastly symphony of color. By nightfall he was dead.

All the most remote appendages of the family tree were assembled, including Sejak, and the usual verdict was promptly reached of murder by a person or persons unknown.

A list was made of all the people who might feel inimically towards Nakari. There was Yakwo; he had been dunning Nakari for a piece of cloth due him for several generations, and Nakari had been too shiftless to do anything about it. And Dim; Nakari's son had had an affair with Dim's niece, but neither father nor son had ever shown any signs of producing the cloth which would have made an honest woman of her. Then Nakari and Shubul had recently had words—no one knew exactly why. These three men were obviously the favorites, but several less likely candidates were added for the pleasure of prolonging the oratorical discussion, airing private grudges, and the assurance of having left no stone unturned.

The cast was now chosen; it remained to decide on the play. The Madik have ingeniously evolved two forms of murder trial, both of which simultaneously reveal and execute the murderer—a vast improvement over the cumbersome paraphernalia of our criminal law. The choice between the two trials depends on the condition of the *corpus delicti.* Nothing ever happens in a hurry in New Guinea; to decide on a course of action, to notify the proper people, and to gather a suitable group in a suitable place at a suitable time is not the affair of a Papuan moment. It sometimes happens that by the time the stage is set the murdered man has been some time dead, and only his clean white bones remain.

Under these conditions, and with such a reliable representative of the deceased available, the ensuing proceedings take place by the rack whereon his relics repose. While the guests wait uneasily at one side, the family build a fire. Over the coals they place big flat leaves and on them arrange a layer of the murdered man's bones garnished with raw sago and green bananas. Once properly roasted, this macabre goulash is passed around to each of the unenthusiastic suspects. As they start to eat, the ghosts of the vicinity are called upon to see that the bones, having penetrated to the stomach of the murderer, dispatch him on the spot. And so, according to all accounts, they infallibly do. In the meantime the pure in heart, undeterred by the unusual ingredients, are one more meal to the good, sufficient recompense for any trouble to which they may have been put.

There was no dining off bones in the case of Sejak's father's sister's husband's brother. Sejak was about as unprocrastinating as a Madik could be, and he was eager to clear matters up as soon as possible.

"We will have the 'Undashulko'—the trial of the knife in the bamboo," he said. "Blit and I will go to tap the saguer tree and you and you—go gather rattan to make the '*guns.*'"

A *gun* is a strip of rattan which serves as the Papuan calendar, and by which meetings and future events are arranged. A knot is made for every day before the specified date. The recipient cuts off one knot each morning. When there is no knot left to cut, he realizes the set day has dawned. For a large gathering they are sent out in all directions, carefully tallied with the mother *gun,* which the expectant host keeps at home for his own information.

Yakwo, Dim, Shubul, and the other suspects received their rattan invitations for the Undashulko. Such an invitation cannot very well be refused; failure to put in an appearance would be construed as an admission of guilt. The chance of supernaturally invoked punishment would immediately be replaced by a very certain volley of spears hurled by human hands.

Sejak's eyes always began to dance with excitement when he recounted the Undashulko. All the guests had arrived promptly and sat in a circle on the floor of Nakari's brother's house. In the corner stood an enormous bamboo node brimming with the liquid and mildly intoxicating results of Sejak's labors on the saguer tree. Grouped around it were several cane saguer-drinking tubes, incised with crisscross lines and gaily stained with red. Sejak was convinced—or so he said afterwards—that it was Dim who had killed Nakari.

"If someone's son had an affair with my niece and never paid me for it, I think I would kill him," he explained with gentle logic. "Or the son," he added reflectively.

"So," he said, "I filled one of the cane tubes with saguer, and in it I placed a new sharp knife I had bought from a Moi man. Then I called in a very loud voice to the ghost of Nakari. I told him: 'The man who killed you with *kwi* is here somewhere. When he drinks the saguer from this tube, do you, with your ghostly hand, plunge the knife into his insides and kill him.' Then I gave the tube to Dim to drink. Dim's eyes were rolling like this" (it was almost impossible for Sejak's eyes to roll any more in demonstration) "and his hands were shaking like leaves in the wind, but he tipped up the tube and drank the saguer while we all waited and watched. Suddenly," shouted Sejak, throwing his comb on the floor with a clatter, "he dropped the tube like this and doubled up like this and he vomited blood, pools and pools of blood, from where the knife had cut his insides. And then he died." Sejak slapped his thighs and rocked back and forth in retrospective enjoyment. "Nakari's ghost had killed him; he knew his murderer. You can't fool a ghost."

"That must have been very satisfactory," we said, impressed. "What happened then? Was Dim's family annoyed?"

"Oh, no," said Sejak, "How could they be? Dim had killed Nakari and it was justice."

We mulled over this for a while until we heard Sejak give vent to several heavy sighs. We looked at him in surprise.

"Were you, after all, sorry to see Dim die?"

"Oh, no," he said again. "But I was remembering that then we left the house with the big bamboo full of saguer and we drank it all up. It had little red peppers in it. It was the best I ever tasted."

Sejak was a patriotic and important member of his tribe. In the present degenerate days there are few men as well educated as he, for Sejak had not been satisfied with the preliminary general instruction received at the Newun. With a few others he had pursued a postgraduate course under the tutelage of the wise old teacher of the young men's house. This advanced curriculum had one rather peculiar characteristic. The pupils were instructed in the art of curing a number of complicated diseases which could only be contracted by those who had learned these cures. It would really seem that these ambitious students made very little actual forward progress save in the business of indefinitely checkmating themselves. Why learn to cure smallpox, for instance, if you were immune to it until you knew the cure?

There was one compensation for this mass of ambivalent information. It was only a postgraduate who knew how to kill a witch.

Sejak was modest about his accomplishments. It was not from him but from some of his admirers that we were first told the tale of how he slew a witch and saved a human life. When we first commented on the subject to him he blushed becomingly and shrugged his shoulders as though to say, "Of course, anyone can kill a witch." But he would have been deeply hurt had we appeared to agree with this attitude.

Angry ghosts, bad words, broken tabus lead often to disaster and occasionally to death. But not even the battle cry of men with spears so congeals the hearts of the people with fear as the very thought of a witch, the terror that stalks by day and by night through the forest and through the houses of sleeping men.

A great advantage to a Madik witch is that she remains incognito, exhibiting none of the insignia of her profession. More wily than her sisters of the western world, she conducts her nefarious business entirely through the agency of her familiar spirit, thereby obviating any necessity for mumbling spells, harnessing broomsticks, or exposing herself at a coven.

This familiar spirit is always of the male gender, a twin brother of the witch born either in material or ethereal form at the same time and of the same mother witch. If he appears as a human baby his mother hastily disposes of him, for he is an incarnate accusation of witchcraft against both herself and her daughter. But even as she presses the breath from his tiny body, she is consoled by the assurance that his powerful spirit will never wander far from his sister's side.

The reason that this semi-supernatural brood is such a menace to society is not because they are activated by malice or ill will towards their fellows; it is purely a question of dietetics. Ordinary mortals may be tempted to dine off the bodies of their acquaintances, but the sublimated palates of the Tubwi and her brother crave the titillation of a meal of human souls.

It is appropriately the disembodied male twin who sets out on the quest for food, armed with a barbed spear or a sharpened bamboo as invisible to human eyes as he himself. Several men described to us having been attacked by a hungry Tubwi—the sensation of a sharp stab in the chest followed by the agonizing wrench which they knew meant the slicing off of a piece of soul. The huntsman nibbles off this as he heads for home, but he is careful to save a presentable portion for the sister who awaits him.

"I have found a good edible soul," he says to her, "that will last us for some time. As soon as we have finished this, I will go back for more."

For the Tubwis skillfully preserve their food supply in the same manner accredited to some of the South Coast Papuans, who are said to tie their victim to a tree and cut off a steak whenever they are hungry, solicitously tending the wounds to keep him alive and the meat fresh in between meals.

The wounded soul meanwhile is in a torment of apprehension. It knows that it is marked as Tubwi food; that unless it can escape unseen by its vigilant enemy it will be gradually hacked away to nothing. In the hope of eluding its persecutor, its human habitation may make a dash for obscurity. Crawling under creepers, doubling in its tracks, stealing silently along unfrequented paths, it seeks to dodge its lynx-eyed hunter, to find somewhere a far-off shelter unknown to him. Sometimes it is successful and the angry Tubwis, balked of their prey, attack another soul with redoubled energy and viciousness, eager simultaneously to satiate their whetted appetites and revenge themselves against mankind. More often the hunted soul is run to earth, for swift and clever beyond the power of ordinary mortals must he be who can outwit a spirit, who can hide from invisible eyes and guard himself from unseen weapons.

One day Sejak's friend, the walleyed Unsit, was traveling through the forest. Impatient and foolhardy, he had decided not to wait until someone else felt impelled to follow the same route, but to risk the trip by himself. He arrived in Sejut with haunted eyes and a terrible pain in his chest. He had felt the bamboo blade of a Tubwi entering into him and he was a man without hope. His friends called in Sejak, and Sejak said:

"Do not try to run away from the Tubwi yet. First I will see if I can kill it."

That night after Unsit had laid his *kakoya* on the floor and gone to sleep, Sejak sat up watching on the steps to the house, his spear and a big stick lying beside him.

'The Tubwi,' he thought to himself, 'will be following Unsit closely. Probably he will attack again tonight.'

Now, a Tubwi, as I have mentioned, is invisible to most people, and that is why men like Sejak require very special training to sharpen their eyes sufficiently to see into the unseen world. It was very late and Sejak was beginning to despair when suddenly his well-trained ears heard an inaudible rustling. He stiffened and peered into the flickering shadows; then with a great shout he leapt from the steps and the aroused and astonished household saw him engaging in a wild struggle with nothing at all. After a last tremendous whack at the ground he gave a triumphant cry and returned to the house saying:

"The Tubwi is dead. It came in the form of a snake and I have killed it. Unsit will now be well."

His trembling friends peered at the spot where Sejak had demolished the snake, but there was nothing to be seen. The following morning Unsit was miraculously recovered, but it was not until several days later that the actual identity of the Tubwi was revealed. Then it was heard that the same night in which Sejak slew the invisible snake, a woman named Malanu had died for no apparent reason at Swailbe. The human female Tubwi cannot survive her alter ego, nor he her. As they came into the world together, so together they must leave it, and when Malanu's death became known it was obvious that Sejak had truly killed his witch.

Sometimes a dying man is vouchsafed a glimpse of his Tubwi murderer. The woman witch is unmistakably the higher in command—and though she sends her brother out to the preliminary skirmishes, she is apt to take a hand herself towards the end. The last morsel of a soul is supposed to be the most delectable, and frequently she chooses to give the *coup de grâce* and avail herself of it. As she lifts her bamboo dagger to plunge it into her victim's throat, his clouded eyes may clear for one brief and horrible vision. and with a strangled cry he shouts the name of his psychophagous murderer.

One cannot help feeling sorry for the woman who has, by the hallucinations or the spite of a dying man, been branded as a Tubwi. The kin of the man she is supposed to have murdered are prancing for justice against her. If her family stand by her, unconvinced of her guilt, she may be given the dubious opportunity of taking the hot-water test, with a fifty-fifty chance of proving herself innocent. But often her husband and her relations are so appalled at the thought of the dangerous monster they have unwittingly harbored that they hand the woman over without a protest, receiving gratefully in exchange some child recently captured in a raid. For the self-appointed agents of justice the disposal of the Tubwi that they have acquired is no sinecure. They dare not kill her and they dare not keep her alive.

It is here that the San or trading partners come in very usefully again. Her first captor marches the witch as fast as possible to his nearest San and requests, in the name of friendship, that he take her over. This San, anxious to be relieved as quickly as possible of his unwelcome responsibility, sets out immediately with her on the journey to a San of *his*. If anyone is lucky enough to have a San among the wild Mari tribe of the Karon, she is rushed to them, for the Mari have no fear of a Madik Tubwi and murder her without the slightest hesitation. Failing a Mari San, the only hope is that the woman, kept incessantly on the run, will very soon die from sheer exhaustion.

This sounds distressingly brutal, but the Madik, like our own not so remote forebears, believes he is ridding the community of a very present danger, and his method is surely no more inhuman than a well-attended bonfire in which the witch is burnt alive. I am thankful that while we lived in Sainke Doek the Tubwis were quiescent. Just before our arrival, Sassodet had died the sort of death that was apparently suggestive of a Tubwi's greed, but the flash of second sight was denied to his last moments and, with no clue to the identity of the devourer of his soul, the matter was not pursued any further.

There is pathos in the fate of the starved and weary woman, powerless to prove herself an ordinary human being, driven like a pariah through the jungle until she dies. But she is not the only pitiful figure. There must be compassion, too, for those enslaved by the beliefs that cause her fate, for the natives who live afraid, never daring to be alone, haunted by the specter of unseen presences hungering to gobble up their souls. To the Madik the soul is an integral necessity; with its loss his body dies. His fragile soul-substance is as much at the mercy of attack from the invisible world as is his bare brown body vulnerable to the enemy's spear. It is small wonder that he has developed a philosophy of resignation, of casual acceptance of the march of life and death, that he lives only in the present moment with the future so insecure.

Don Blanding

Gods and Old Ghosts

Donald Benson Blanding (1894–1957), sometimes called "the poet laureate of Hawaii," was born in Kingfisher, Oklahoma, but lived for some years at Laston, where his father was deputy sheriff. He graduated from The Chicago Art Institute and first came to Hawaii in 1916. In these early days he wrote advertising copy for a Chinese shop in Honolulu. He was a popular lecturer and the author and illustrator of seventeen books. In 1928 he proposed, along with Grace Tower Warren, that May 1 should be celebrated as "Lei Day" in Hawaii.

Blanding died of a heart attack in Los Angeles but his ashes were scattered at sea. His only marriage was to Dorothy Putnam, former wife of George Palmer Putnam, whose later wife was Amelia Earhart. "Gods and Old Ghosts" is part of a chapter in his prose volume, *Hula Moons* (1930).

ON one of these nights I met the Old Man of the Mountain. He was reputed to be a kahuna. A kahuna is a sort of astrologer, philosopher, doctor, and unwritten history of Hawaii. He is a survival of the powerful clan of priests who ruled the kings and the kingdom in the days of the monarchy. Ignorant haoles call them witch doctors; but the term is incorrect, although they are credited with the ability to put good or bad kahuna (spell) on people, and pray individuals to death if they choose. They are respected and feared by most of the Hawaiians, who are quite superstitious, as are any people who live in close touch with nature.

The Old Man (I never heard him called any other name) looked like an inspired prophet who had survived through the ages from the beginnings of the islands. In repose his features were lost in a tangle of crossing and crisscrossing wrinkles. He had no teeth, and so his face collapsed into folds, resembling a brown lichen. When he spoke, the black gape of his mouth and the dim fires of his eyes identified him as human.

I *never saw him arrive.* In the midst of chatter and laughter he'd suddenly *be* among us, looking like a gnarled root at the base of a hau tree. On the first night that I met him, he made this grown-from-the-ground appearance. All of the Hawaiians fell silent, even the children. He sat for half an hour, his old eyes watching the stars unwinkingly. Pua brought him a cup of okolehao. He drank it with relish but without comment. After the corrosive fire of the liquor percolated and filtered through his aged bones, he broke into speech, half chant half talk, lifting his face into the light. With the muscles of his long throat quivering and the strange quavers of his voice, he looked like an aged wolf baying the moon.

Although I could not understand much Hawaiian, I saw at once that he was speaking in a different manner from the conversational tongue of my friends. A *th* sound which is not in the modern language softened the hard *k*, giving a smoother slur to the unbroken flow of words which continued for half an hour. I don't know when or how he breathed.

He told a dramatic tale full of gestures. His pantomime was so vivid that I could get the larger drawing of the story.

"He talks *old-style* Hawaiian," Aunty Pinau whispered. "These keikis (children) do not understand."

After he had finished his story, Aunty Pinau translated what he had told. It was the legend of the demigod, Maui, whose exploits resembled those of Hercules. It related his colossal feat of lifting the sky, which was crushing the earth, and placing it on top of the mountain so that the trees could grow and the people go about the business of living. He told also of Maui's mother Hina, a famed tapa maker, and her difficulty in getting the bark-cloth dried, owing to the shortness of the days. She appealed to her son for aid. He climbed to the top of Haleakala, lassoed the sun, and broke off some of its rays so that it couldn't roll across the sky so swiftly, thus lengthening the days and allowing his mother to complete her beautiful tapa robes.

In the nights that followed he told many other stories. They were delightful, embroidered with poetic metaphor and classical references too intricate to follow. The Hawaiians are natural orators, after the William Jennings Bryan style of silver-tongued eloquence.

The simple sagas differed only a little from the folk tales of Grimm and Andersen and the Bible. There were the brave princes of remarkable accomplishment, and the villains with low and scoundrelly sculduggery in their hearts, the Cinderellas, the giant killers and Jonahs.

During those long, pleasant hours, the civilized world became very remote. It was difficult to realize that, just across the channel, Honolulu buzzed with activity, with chittering tourists, honking motors, and the confusion of progress. My mind rested in the simple, unroutined current of life that flowed so aimlessly through the uncounted days and nights.

My unfeigned enjoyment and interest in the legends were richly rewarded. I did not realize that I was being studied and weighed, and that I had passed critical inspection, until one day the Old Man appeared in the door of the palm-leaf lean-to which I used for studio. Nalani was with him.

"He want you come along," she said. "He show you something. I go too."

I put aside the sketch that I was making and we started out along the beach. The Old Man took the lead. I had to realize shortly that the ancient gargoyle was a better man than I was. Although he seemed to stumble and waver, his stride was long and steady, as we wove through guava and lantana thickets and tangled jungle growth, over sand and broken lava. I soon saw that we were going in a tortuously devious way and that the Old Man wanted to confuse me. I stopped Nalani.

"Tell Old Man I no look see."

"He taking you sacred place," she explained.

"Tell him go straight. I lost now. I no can find again."

Nalani spoke to our guide. He measured me with his squinting eyes and made decision. We started off across a desolate field of lava, among sharp, broken fragments that chewed my tennis sneakers to ribbons. Nalani and the Old Man wore Hawaiian fiber sandals which seemed to protect their feet. I was soon a mass of scratches and gouges up to my knees. Sweat poured into the abrasions and smarted mightily, but I suspicioned that it was all worth while. The wildness of the setting promised well for adventure.

Finally we came to a large well about thirty feet across, a dark hole in the center of the lava flow. Down twenty feet, among ferns, roots, and mosses, lay a pool of water, so still and clear that every detail, of rock, cloud, and our peering faces was reflected. No breath disturbed the glassy surface.

The Old Man spoke.

"Wai-napa-napa."

"Mirror-water," Nalani translated, deeply impressed.

As I peered into the water-mirror I had a ghostly feeling that many brown faces of long-dead Hawaiians stared over my shoulders; there were warriors and women, maidens and young men. Was this an oracle, a crystal in which one read the future? What had brought them; what had they found in the dark pool?

We scrambled down the steep sides to a ledge near the water, descending from the warm sunlight into a grave-cold shadow. The Old Man stripped off his shirt and trousers and stood in short, spotless drawers (Drawers, in a spot like that!) Nalani kept on her flimsy shift, I improvised a breechclout from the sleeves of my shirt. Having gotten down to essentials, I waited, prepared for anything.

Although the Old Man, with his withered, wrinkled flesh hanging in loose folds on his spare frame, looked like a molting condor, I could see that he had been a grand figure in his youth (some time B. C. if one judged by appearances).

The Old Man took several deep breaths and dived, groping his way down the black wall of the pool. Quite startlingly he started to disappear, first his head, then shoulders and trunk, finally legs. We had a last pale glimmer of the soles of his feet . . . and he was gone; into the face of the rock apparently. He "went out," as frogs "go out" down the gullet of a snake. The sight was not comforting.

"Where Old Man go?" I asked Nalani anxiously.

"Inside," she replied briefly, poising for a dive. "You come."

"Come, my eye! I want to know where we're going."

"Inside." She smiled as though it were the most natural thing in the world to prowl around in dark underwater grottos.

"Wait," I insisted. "I go same time you go."

This was tricky business. I've always had a dislike of being cooped up in trappy places. Diving into unknown "insides" of rocks was not appealing. To back out was to lose all I had gained of the confidence of these people. Auwe!

I filled my lungs to the last crowded inch. We dived. The water was colder and seemed damper than any I had ever entered before. I could follow the flash of Nalani's legs as we turned under a submerged ledge and fumbled into murky darkness. It was creepy. Panicky thoughts invaded my mind. These Hawaiians were regular fishes in the water and could stay under indefinitely. Suppose I couldn't hold out. I couldn't turn back, we'd gone too far. I plowed on. My lungs began to heave and I knew things were getting out of control. I wanted to gasp. My eyes felt as though they would pop out like grape pulps.

I saw Nalani slant up toward a faint glow of light, and nearly strained a ligament following after. I must have shot completely out of the water in my anxiety to breathe again.

We were in a cave about the size of a large room. The roof arched about fifteen feet above our heads. The only light was that which reflected through the hole by which we had entered. I was surprised to see how short the distance was to the pool outside. It had seemed like a city block.

A greenish corpse-light illumined the cave faintly. Our faces showed an unhealthy mauve tint; our bodies, under the water, were the white of eggshells. Dark rocks hung heavily above us, veined with a clotted blood-red and speckled with small spatters of white deposit which seemed to glow with phosphorescence against the black surface. The air was stale with the musty smell of roots and decay. There was a steady drip-drip of seeping water from stubby stalactites (if they're the things that hang down) on the ceiling.

The Old Man pointed to two ledges about as large as bench seats that jutted from the wall on either side. Nalani perched on one of them; I crawled up on the other. Our guide swam back and forth, pointing to the seats and at the red veins in the rocks and the white specks, fixing them in our attention. He said nothing. I think he saved up his words until he had enough and then told a story.

By this time I was dull blue with cold and my flesh felt like stucco; and despite the fact that I was deeply appreciative of the honor of dipping into this sanctified mysterious water, I wanted to get out.

The Old Man led off toward the exit. His rear view, with the legs and arms paddling grotesquely in silhouette against the dim greenish light, looked ridiculously like an enormous, skinny frog. Nalani followed; she was always a mermaid in the water. I had no one to view my exit, so I made it hurriedly and without grace.

In the first seconds after emerging and scuttling up the walls of the well we got a curious illusion. The sudden blinding light, flooding over everything, made the lava and the distant trees and mountains look as though they had been freshly painted with many shades of gold lacquer.

We stretched on the warm rocks and thawed, letting the sunlight seep into our very bones, melting them pleasantly. I felt as a jellyfish must feel when stranded on the sand.

Finally the Old Man broke into his chanting talk, gesturing toward the cave and toward the high slopes of Haleakala. I gathered that something horrible had happened here at some time. Nalani translated the story. The cold black and white of print can catch only the skeleton of the legend. It needs the soft, slurring voice, the gestures, the setting, to give the real flavor of the Legend of the Mirror-Water Cave and the Princess Popoalaia.

A very long time ago (legends begin this way in Hawaii, France, China, or Madagascar) high up on the slopes of Haleakala lived the Princess Popoalaia. She was married to a man far beneath her in station. Although he was strong as the strongest of men, and his skill in games and contests was great, although he was a splendid, fearless warrior and hunter, he was not a kind husband. He was a sullen, suspicious man, jealous of his beautiful wife's every movement. He watched her constantly, and when he had to go down to the sea for fishes and seaweed (which the Hawaiians use for medicine and food) as he often did, his heart was heavy with suspicion. On his return he invariably questioned her closely, and, not content with her avowed innocence, he also questioned the men of the family and the women who were with her.

Often he threatened his wife until she feared for her life. Yet she was as innocent and pure as the flowers that she wove into leis that she bound about her hair.

On returning from one of his frequent trips, Kaaka, the husband, was filled with unreasoning jealousy. He had listened to tales told by malicious neighbors, and so angry was his mood that he lost all sight of her gentle sweetness and beauty. He strode into the house in rage, and, when his wife spoke to him, he answered her harshly.

"Your time is short," he said.

He went out, and to the frightened ears of the princess came the sounds of Kaaka sharpening his stone axe. Often before he had spoken threatening words, but none so terrible as these.

Summoning her little maid, she said, "I must go quickly or my life will not be spared." Together they collected a few of the princess' belongings, some precious keepsakes, among them the kahili, a wand that was tipped with feathers in a certain arrangement, which indicated her rank and family. They cut a hole in the rear wall of the grass house and fled from the place into the forest. Then, by underground passages and lava tubes, they made their way to the sea near Hana.

Kaaka searched the countryside, first in anger, later in despair. There was no sign of the princess. Finally, coming to the village of Hana, he inquired of the people if they had seen her. No one could say yes. They did mention that the beach nearby was haunted by spirits, and that at night figures could be seen dancing in the moonlight. These figures disappeared as soon as human presence was recognized. Kaaka attached no significance to this.

Finally, weary with his long search, he came to the pool of Wainapanapa and rested beside it. Because it looked cool and shadowy, he crept down the rocks to the ledge and stared idly into the bright water. His eyes were almost closing with fatigue when suddenly he saw something moving slowly back and forth, apparently deep in the pool. He thought it was a fish or bit of seaweed. He was startled to discover that it was the reflection of a kahili, the kahili of Princess Popoalaia. He knew then that within the cave the woman he sought was hiding. His anger seethed in his heart.

He called to his men, and, with two of the strongest, slipped into the water, dived under the ledge and, before the women could escape, seized them. The warriors dashed the little maid to death against the rocks, while Kaaka, blind with rage and brutal with savage strength, murdered Popoalaia violently. Her blood stained the black rocks and her brains were scattered over the roof of the cave. The earth shuddered and huge boulders fell from the ceiling. The men fled from the place of horror.

Because the princess was of royal blood, and so related to the gods, and because she was innocent, the spirits that ruled the islands decreed that the rocks of the Mirror-water Cave should bleed forever. It is said that on the nights of Ku, when the moon is in a certain phase, the waters of the cave run red.

André Dupeyrat

The Man Who Turned into a Cassowary

The Catholic Mission in New Guinea, second largest island in the world, was founded by Father Henry Verjus and two lay brothers of the newly born religious order of the Missionaries of the Sacred Heart in 1885 on Yule Island, off the southern coast some seventy miles west of Port Moresby. To this spot Father André Dupeyrat came at the age of twenty-seven and spent two decades ministering to the Melanesian people of the region.

Born in Cherbourg and having served in the French cavalry, Father Dupeyrat was ordained in 1929. He was returned to France in 1951, charged with spreading news of the missionary efforts in the New Guinea area then under Australian administration. He became a member of several learned societies but is best known for several popular volumes in translation, such as *Papuan Conquest* (Melbourne, 1948), *Festive Papua* (London, 1955), *Papua: Beasts and Men* (London, 1963), and *Savage Papua: A Missionary among Cannibals* (New York, 1954; British title *Mitsinari*), from which "The Man Who Turned into a Cassowary" is selected.

I WAS once more making an expedition with the cure. Now, it was true, I had tried my wings and was allowed to go off alone, but we still made fairly frequent trips together, like two old black toucans which, like the ravens, always fly in pairs. Besides, these shared journeys were a necessity. To live perpetually alone among natives proves in the end as wearisome to mind as to body. One is separated by several thousand miles from any center of culture and civilization, severed from the ideas and events that agitate and change the rest of the world. This is not necessarily a bad thing, even quite the contrary. But the lack of any cultural or intellectual interchange, and the easy way one slips into the laziness and lassitude almost inevitably encountered in primitive countries, mean that the mind grows blunt and rusty. All these factors, in addition to the generally harsh conditions of existence, might well reduce the isolated missionary to the mentality and level of his primitive and wretched charges, whom he is nevertheless expected to educate and guide.

We had reached Mondov'Imakoulata—a charming little mission station situated in the territory of the Mondo tribe, and dedicated to the Immaculate Virgin. It consisted of a single-roomed house, built however with proper planks, and a church built of palm trunks with a roof of glinting corrugated iron. It lay only two hours distant from Fané-les-Roses, in the direction of the great central range. Built on a tiny plateau which overlooked the whole upper valley of the Auga, Mondov'Imakoulata served four villages, of which one quite close by was called Mondo.

That evening, the grave and dignified Josepa, who was catechist for the region, together with two village notables and three old men from Mondo, had arrived to keep us company. The conversation soon grew animated in the comfortable intimacy of our little house. Outside, the night was dark, a thick darkness without moon. Whenever there was a momentary silence, one could hear the rumble of mountain torrents, and the wind rustling and rattling through the foliage of the great trees. Meanwhile, as we sat by lantern light, with our guests squatting around us, we talked of a hundred and one items of local gossip. The talk happened to turn to someone who had recently been much in the public eye—a certain Isidoro Ain'u'Ku.

Isidoro was still a young man, a member of the Ilidé tribe who lived near the sources of the Dilava. Extremely intelligent, and full of verve and energy, he had been one of the first to take instruction when Father Norin and Father Bachelier had visited his village for the first time a few years earlier. In a very short time, he had grasped their teachings and had passed his catechumen's examination brilliantly.

Then, after the compulsory period of probation, he had been accepted for baptism.

Before giving him the sacrament, however, the missionary had asked him: "Are you married?" Ain'u'Ku had replied in the negative, and all the villagers had confirmed his assertion.

In actual fact, he had been married, but against his will. For while he was still a child of no more than fifteen months, his parents had chosen an even younger girl child to be his future bride. For a long time, he had thought of her as his sister—a sister whom, besides, he could not bear. Growing older, and realizing the truth, he had refused to accept her as his wife.

Unfortunately, they had already lived together beyond the age of puberty, and he had thus given at least tacit, and in any case, public consent to the union. And even though a pagan one, his marriage was indissoluble. Now that he had become a Christian, he was obliged to take back his legitimate wife, who, for her part, had also been converted.

When he learned of this decision, Ain'u'Ku argued for a time, and ended up by shouting furiously:

"If that is how it is, I shall no longer belong to God—now I shall go and place myself in the devil's hands! . . . "

He kept his word.

For nearly a year, he disappeared from view. In the mysterious depths of the forest, he went through his novitiate as a sorcerer, guided by some hierophant who taught him the magic rites and formulas, the incantations, and the various ways of killing people. He appeared once more in his own village, thin, gaunt, and sunken-eyed, but with the title and already the reputation of sorcerer. And as he was very subtle, clever, and enterprising, his renown, and the fear it inspired, rapidly spread.

"Father, we tell you this is the truth," said one of the old men. "Ain'u'Ku has the power to change himself into a cassowary."

The cassowary is a bird rather like the ostrich. It is strong, stupid, and voracious. One can hear a cassowary coming along the forest tracks from a long way off. As it runs, it beats its side with short wings, producing a sound rather like the *chuff-chuff* of a railway engine that is still getting up steam. Its huge feet, armed with redoubtable claws, strike thudding echoes even from the spongy and elastic floor of the forest.

We could not help laughing when our other guests earnestly seconded the old man's story. We had heard all those ancient legends about men who turned into beasts before—for did not Europe as well as Papua have its tales of werewolves and other lycanthropic monsters? Rather indulgently, we set about delivering them from these backward notions. Suddenly, one of them made a sign, and we all fell silent. From far away, we could just hear the sound of a cassowary running.

Now the interesting thing was this: everyone knows that cassowaries do not travel by night. Nor, for that matter, do the Papuans. There are too many dangers lurking on the rough mountain trails as they wind along the precipices, and even worse, there are the spirits of the forest. The notion that someone might be playing a trick on us was thus ruled out. Besides, the practiced ears of our guests, and even our own hearing, could not have deceived us. It was without doubt a cassowary.

"We were talking about Isidoro," someone murmured in a strangely altered voice. "He must have heard us. He's coming. . . ."

At this point, it should be mentioned that Isidoro's village, Ilidé, was beyond the main range of mountains, on the opposite side to its western slopes on which was perched the little mission station of Mondo. Thus, the journey from Ilidé to Mondo, even for a Papuan, entailed a good five hours of steep climbs and almost vertical descents over a series of razor-backed ridges, plunging ravines, and narrow gorges, the whole way lying through dense virgin forest at altitudes varying from three thousand to nearly eight thousand feet.

We shrugged our shoulders. No one could possibly make such a journey by night, unless he took pains to light his way with resinous torches and advanced with great caution—a process which would stretch the traveling time to at least ten hours, instead of five.

Meanwhile, the sound of the cassowary drew rapidly nearer. Soon, we heard clearly the drumming of its massive feet on the clay floor of our small courtyard. Then, abruptly, it ceased. A few seconds later, our door was pushed open and someone entered. It was Isidoro.

"I heard that you were here," he declared, all smiles. "I have become bad, but you are still my fathers. I have come to see you and to say your name" [i.e., to welcome you]. "Give me a little tobacco to eat"—[that meant, to smoke]—" so that we can talk comfortably together."

He squatted down before us, shredded up with his nails the hard little wedge of tobacco I had given him, rolled it in a scrap of newspaper, then lit his cigarette with my lighter. We began to talk of one thing and another. Our Mondo friends, gray with fear, said nothing.

Isidoro, who appeared quite fresh and at ease, stayed nearly an hour. We did not, at any point, make any mention of the cassowary. Nor did he.

"I am paying a visit to Mondo," he said, finally getting up. "I am going back there to sleep. I'll see you tomorrow."

We shook hands, and he departed.

Scarcely had the door closed behind him, than we heard once more the thudding of the cassowary's feet and wings.

I leaped outside. The night was black as ink. I could see nothing, and my shout received no answer. But beneath the black sky with its sparse spangling of winking stars, under the loud rustling of the wakeful forest, could be heard, unmistakable and baleful, the dying thunder of the cassowary's running feet.

It became imperative to throw some daylight on this mystery. Otherwise, the superstitious beliefs that held our villagers in thrall would only be confirmed and strengthened.

Without waiting further, we set off for the village of Mondo by lantern light: it was no more than five minutes' walk from the mission station. There, we at once visited the communal hut where travelers are received, and then ruthlessly went into each smaller hut, questioning its inhabitants. We knew our Papuans and they knew us. They knew—and openly admitted—that we were not "whites just like the others," to whom one could tell any tall story. I do not need, therefore, to go into details. We were quickly convinced of one thing: not only was Isidoro not at Mondo, but he had not been seen in the village for a long time, nor for that matter in the surrounding district.

We decided therefore to set off at dawn the next day for Ilidé. We arrived there toward noon, panting, perspiring, and exhausted. The first person to greet us, wearing a broad smile, was Isidoro.

We were careful not to show the least trace of astonishment. The villagers themselves were certainly surprised by our unexpected visit, but we found some plausible excuse, and in the most casual way possible, pursued our detailed and rather anxious investigation. Even then, we were forced back to the conclusion: Isidoro had remained in the communal hut of the village on the preceding evening, smoking and gossiping, until "two pipes after the hour of the *ghélélé*" —that is to say, until after seven, for it is at about six-thirty that the mountain cicada salutes with his strident cries the coming of twilight. He had said that he was going back to his own hut to sleep. Others had seen him enter it, but not come out again. Early next morning, he had appeared on the veranda of his hut in the usual way, yawning and stretching. There had, in short, been nothing unusual in his whole behavior.

The bare facts, however, gave rise to much more troubling conclusions. Isidoro had been in his village the previous evening until after seven o'clock. By about nine-thirty that same evening, he had been in our hut at Mondo. Let us recall at this point that it was physically impossible to cover the distance between these two points in less than five hours, above all at night. For the return journey, it is true, the time factor presented less difficulty. Even then, there are limits to human endurance, above all among the Papuans who, for lack of rich and sustaining foods, have little stamina. Even supposing he could have made the journey by night, which in itself was highly improbable, and counting the time he had spent with us, Isidoro would have had to accomplish in about nine hours a return trip which, by day, would normally take at least ten, and by night at least sixteen hours.

It was a complete mystery. However, the next day, while I was alone, Isidoro came to see me. I had grown weary of turning the problem over and over in my mind. Looking him straight in the eyes, I asked him bluntly:

"Where were you, the other evening?"

"With you, at Mondo. You know that. You gave me some tobacco. We talked. We talked about different things. We shook hands."

"Yes, but you deceived me. You said you were going to sleep at Mondo. No one saw you in the village."

"Oh! . . . That was just an *av'ur'elafé* [a manner of speaking]."

"Yet the people here say that you were with them, in this village, until quite late that same evening, and early the next day again."

"Yes—there they speak the word of truth—*av'akaï*."

"In that case, perhaps you flew like the birds to come and see us?"

His face darkened and his eyes grew fierce. His mouth twisted into a grimace of smiling hatred that I had never seen before, as he said jeeringly:

"You, a priest, have powers to do extraordinary things. I wanted to show you that I, too, have such powers."

And abruptly, he departed.

Robert Dean Frisbie

Over the Reef

Born in Cleveland, Ohio, Robert Dean Frisbie (1896–1948) left for the South Seas after World War I. After "going native" for several years near Papeete, he began twelve years of drifting about the islands. "Ropati," as he was called, in 1924 became a resident trader on Puka-Puka or Danger Island in the northern Cook group. He stayed for four years, married twice, and by his first wife Nga had five children. Encouraged by his friend James Norman Hall, he began writing. *The Book of Puka-Puka* (1929) is his best known work.

In "Over the Reef," Frisbie narrates a horrifying personal adventure among the coral-crusted, iron-toothed shoals of a surf-beaten atoll.

A FEW months ago, while surfboarding across the shallows near Windward Village, I was swept into a depression in the reef, where a rapid current washed me through the breakers into the open sea. It was as much as my life was worth and I knew it.

The sun was just setting behind a heavy screen of storm clouds; half a gale chopped the sea to whitecaps; and between me and the shore was a line of gigantic breakers raising their backs twenty feet above the jagged coral, to crash with terrific violence the whole length of the reef. Even a Puka-Pukan would have considered it impossible to regain the shore.

I had clung to my surfboard, a piece of one-by-four planking, four feet long. It buoyed me up somewhat; otherwise I could not have survived three minutes in that frothy sea.

The news was yelled across the island and soon the beach was black with people; some of the stronger men were on the reef vainly trying to throw me pieces of wood. They watched me with morbid excitement, for they expected momentarily to witness my last agonies.

Three desperate chances were open to me. One was to swim round to the lee side of the island, a distance of about five miles. This was impossible; night was setting in and the gale increasing. Furthermore, my strength was rapidly ebbing in the fight for breath against the waves that constantly bashed against my face. Or I might wait for a canoe to cross the lagoon to the lee reef and come round to me. Only the largest of the canoes could have weathered that sea, and at least two hours would be needed to make the passage. I should be dead long before they could reach me.

The third chance was to swim straight for the reef, and this I did, without hope of getting across but with a strangely exhilarating determination not to give up my life without a struggle. I have sometimes had moments of absurd panic while swimming in deep water far out from shore, as when turtle-fishing with Benny; but now I was nerved by a sort of reckless courage and looked forward without fear to the coming fight, as though the combers were human enemies whom I should somehow injure before they crushed and buried me. When one believes that death is inevitable, one is indifferent to everything except a final splendid demonstration of one's ego—at least, so it was with me that murky evening, a chip flung, buried, raised, derided by the relentless sea.

Coming within the grasp of the combers, I looked back again to see an immense wave about to hurl itself upon me. All my courage ebbed in an instant. The struggle was too hopeless; the contrast between that mighty wall of water and my puny self was too clearly apparent.

Then, strangely, my courage returned. I refused to lose this last opportunity for self-assertion. As the comber curled to fall, I dove straight into it as the only means of protecting myself from its impact.

I could feel the concussion as it hurled itself on the reef; the water became milky with foam, and I knew that I was being tossed about perilously close to the jagged coral.

Fighting my way to the surface, my head was buried in two feet of foam. I beat the water frantically, trying to raise myself above that layer of soft choking froth. My lungs were bursting when it had subsided sufficientiy for me to gasp the fresh air.

I scarcely had time to empty and refill my lungs before another comber reared above me with the malice of a cat playing with a mouse.

Subconsciously I was fighting the greatest battle of all, suppressing an almost overpowering fear which prompted me to dive, fill my lungs with water, and put an end to the struggle. But consciously I was still exhilarated: I was ending my life with gusto, with almost sensual gratification.

The comber fell just as I was diving. Half-stunned, I was whirled around like a chip. I had a vague impression that my head had grazed the coral; in fact, as I afterward learned, a deep gash had been laid open half-way across my scalp. It now seemed that the end was at hand, for again there was the deep layer of light foam above my head. I held my breath, expecting to hear the peculiar hissing sound of the next toppling sea.

As the foam subsided, coughing and gasping for breath I exerted my last strength, making a few feeble strokes toward the reef, now but a few yards distant. Dimly I could see naked figures along the reef gesticulating frantically. I knew that they were warning me of the approach of the next breaker, but I didn't turn my head. There was nothing more that I could do. In my own mind I was already dead, for I had been through the terror of dying, and the final annihilating stroke had only been delayed for a few seconds, that was all. On the beach I saw a hazy line that seemed to waver and melt into blackness as I watched it. I knew it was the villagers standing as close as they could to get to me, watching the end.

There was now less than a fathom of water beneath me, and even though I had had the strength, I could not have dived. I heard the roaring of the oncoming comber; lights flashed in the darkness, and in that second I saw, with uncanny vividness, the form of my mother sitting in her armchair, quietly knitting and gazing up at me with her thoughtful, compassionate eyes.

I lived, of course, but it was a near thing. The last comber had buried me, hurled me across the reef, and rolled me like a log to a spot where the natives rushed out to grasp me.

I remember little of what followed, although I have a faint recollection of people carrying me inland, and of the great little Ura waving his arms and crying: "He is a superman *(toa)!* A Puka-Pukan would have been killed by the first wave!" My pride is so strong that I remember his words more vividly than any other circumstance. He was right: a Puka-Pukan would have philosophically allowed the first wave to kill him, not being sufficiently egotistical to make a final grandiose gesture in the face of death.

That night old William and Mama, Little Sea and Desire sat by my mat. Little Sea had my feet in her lap, massaging them. Desire sat huddled in a corner, whimpering. Mama stroked my forehead, while the whole night through William repeated the story of the incident, adding details with each narration, so that, long before dawn, he had placed me in the same class with Great Stomach, who flew over the sea. It was annoying, to say the least, to have the one thing I wished to forget dinned everlastingly into my ears.

I was aware of a cutting pain in my side and that my breath was coming laboriously, but this was nothing to the mental pain; for when I shut my eyes great combers would rise above me to hang there on the verge of breaking for moments at a time; then they would subside, giving place to others. They seemed to have human faculties and to be leering at me in a cruel, implacable manner. They were screaming that they had pounded the reefs of Puka-Puka for thousands of years and that no mere human should interrupt their endless toil even for a moment.

Toward morning I sent for my medicine chest and took five grains of opium. In a few minutes I was asleep.

I awoke in the evening, coughing up quantities of blood. The pain in my side had grown to a steady burning pang, aggravated by the least movement, and, when I coughed, forcing me to use all my strength to keep from screaming. I could still see the combers rising with horrible deliberation over my head, and I realized vaguely that all during my sleep I had been harassed by a dream-fugue of curling, crashing breakers.

About midnight, after a fit of coughing, I sank back on my mat to feel the pain gradually lessening. Dimness veiled my eyes, and it was with a feeling of immense relief that I awaited the approach of death. To this day I am more than half-convinced that I did die. At any rate, the watchers thought me dead, and all but one of them resigned me to the shades of the ancients.

Half an hour later I awoke, or was revivified. I was dimly conscious, and yet my whole body was as lifeless as though the blood had congealed in my veins. Only my mind functioned, refusing to give up life even though the body was stiff and cold. As though coming from an infinite distance, I could hear the death songs being chanted over me, the patter of footsteps as people ran back and forth on the road below, and the barely audible cry: "Ropati is dead! Ropati is dead!"

I believed that I was dead, and I remember the dim thought came to me that, after all, there is a life after death, a belief I had always scoffed at.

Little Sea and Desire were wailing, with their bodies thrown across my legs, and who but evil—or, rather, good old Bones, the village libertine, the most degenerate soul on the island, was leaning over me, absolutely refusing to give me up as he vigorously massaged my body with those powerful, gorillalike hands of his. Without lecherous old Bones I am convinced that I would have died that night; but by some mysterious Polynesian method of massage *(tarome),* a method which I have often seen used to as much as bring a man out of the grave, Bones saved me. God—if there is one—bless his sinful old soul—if he has any.

Still the death chant went on much as it had over the body of Wail-of-Woe, and at last another half-hour passed before I was sufficiently restored to show signs of life. Consciousness had returned by imperceptible degrees. At first I was only dimly aware of something touching my body lightly. Then I associated this with Bones, whom I could vaguely see leaning over me. A tingling sensation suffused my muscles, much like that one feels when one's foot is asleep. It was at about this time that I blinked my eyes, bringing the death wail to an abrupt end and sending Bosun-Woman home, doubtless greatly disappointed at being balked in her expectation of revels over a fine white corpse. I can still see the ghastly smile on her witchlike face as she turned to leave; and now, when I meet her in the village, she looks at me as much as to say: "Wait, Ropati—just wait! You fooled me once, but I'm in no hurry. I'll be laying you out one of these fine days."

What a lovable, incompetent nurse garrulous old Mama was! Little Sea and Desire could have taken much better care of me, but Mama would not hear of it. What! Allow two mere "drinking-nuts" and one of them no more than an undeveloped *koua,* to nurse me? Never! So dear old Mama settled herself comfortably in my house to attend to my wants.

In the height of my fever she fed me roast pork, lobster, taro pudding, and tinned beans; and when convalescent, arrowroot starch, eggs, and milk; but thanks to a reasonably good constitution and Bones's daily massaging, I managed to pull through, and in a month's time I could sit up and take notice of the world of Puka-Puka.

Once Jeffrey, the village witch doctor, came to visit me with his bottles of noxious medicines and a leering, conceited smile on his lips. Possibly Bosun-Woman had sent him, aware of his skill at hastening the departure of the ailing. I sent him away with an outburst of curses that only old William could appreciate. The old heathen had increased respect for me from that time on, and I think I have never, either before or since, shown such profane versatility.

Merlin Moore Taylor

Two Sorcerers of Black Papua

An American journalist, Merlin Moore Taylor, penetrated the mountain regions of New Guinea with an expedition consisting of three white men, a guard of native police, and a hundred and twenty carriers. In villages in the heart of Papua, never before visited by outsiders, Taylor—who was strongly opposed to "faking stuff from the four corners of the earth"—met a number of characters portrayed in this selection from his 1926 volume, *The Heart of Black Papua.*

THE sorcerer still is a power in New Guinea. Mostly he follows the same path that Tata Koa trod, with variations of his own. One sorcerer, after a period of incarceration at Samarai, somehow discovered the big radio station there and grasped the idea that it enabled the white man to talk to other white men far away, out of sight and hearing. In his village today you will find a miniature wireless tower, a fearsome and intricate thing of sticks and vines and what not, and hanging from its top two long vines with huge sea shells at their ends. With these shells clapped to his ears, the sorcerer maintains he is able to hear what is being said by anyone whose fear and respect he wishes to gain.

Another has a glass bottle, salvaged from the sea, to which he ascribes potent powers. In his district the natives hold what they call a bottle—a length of hollowed bamboo fashioned in that shape—in great reverence. A "bottle" may be handed down for generations, gaining "strength" with the years, and he whose bottle is the "strongest" will have the best hunting, the best gardens, the most successful fishing, and other good fortune. Needless to say, the glass bottle of the sorcerer leads them all.

So the superstition and ignorance of the savage makes sorcery a lucrative business. He buys charms for this and that, he believes implicitly the words of the maker of *puri-puri,* he sees his enemy die as the sorcerer he has hired promises, he steps softly lest he incur the magician's wrath, and he pays tremendous prices, according to his ideas, to protect himself against the machinations of the hired sorcerer of his enemies. But he does not take matters into his own hands—that is, not often.

A native constable, ordered to arrest the sorcerer of his village, declined. The sorcerer threatened him with a lingering death if he obeyed. Faced at last, however, with the alternative of being stripped of his uniform and the prestige attached, he bore the maker of magic to the ground and handcuffed him.

As they crossed the Sound to the government post, the sorcerer took from a tiny bag a long string with many small sticks attached. With his manacled hands he began to finger each stick and to each he gave the name of some villager who had died. "These," he explained to the curious constable, "represent the people I have killed by *puri-puri.* This stick is your grandfather, this stick your father, this your uncle," and so on, until he had named seventeen blood relatives of his captor.

"And those?" asked the constable, pointing to six loose sticks in the palm of the sorcerer.

"Those," was the reply, "are you, your wife, and four children. Some day, and soon, they will be tied to the string."

Whereupon the constable, in a frenzy of desperation and fear, upset the canoe and held the old sorcerer under water until life was extinct. Then he gave himself up to the magistrate and went joyfully to jail. Perhaps in the months he spent there he reasoned out things pretty accurately, for when he returned home, no longer a constable, he declared that the sorcerer, being an old man, had compelled the constable to kill him and in return had imparted to him the secret of his *puri-puri.*

So the ex-constable became the new sorcerer, and where before he had been the white man's aid, today he is his handicap. . . .

"*Taubada* [master]," said Dengo, the policeman who was to be my orderly and bodyguard, pointing to the sorcerer, "I savvee this black cow. He try *puri-puri* (magic) on you, I break his bloody head."

It was a promise that Dengo could easily make. He was a native of Mambare, in the mountains hundreds of miles away, and he had no respect for the black arts of this sorcerer of a coast village. Yet when the time came for him to make good, Mira-Oa used the one thing calculated to make my policeman-orderly show the white feather—a snake. For in the Mambare district flourishes that strange cult, the Baigona, with its overlord a huge snake which is believed to dwell on the top of a mountain, and whose slightest wish, as expressed through the mouths of those who pose as his representatives, is to be obeyed under penalty of death. A native of Mambare gives every snake the right of way and turns his eyes in the other direction, lest by chance he seem to be curious as to the destination or movements of his master.

For five days our trail lay through dismal sago swamps, knee-deep in mud and water, or fighting our way through thick saw-edge grass higher than a man's head. The sun beat down fiercely on our heads and, because we were all trail-tender, we suffered intensely. As soon as we should leave the lowlands and get into the foothills we would be out of civilized territory and rapidly getting into country that never had been explored and where the people live in the same primitive style that their ancestors did hundreds of years ago.

Meanwhile we were in no danger. Fear of the white man's police and jails keeps the Mekeo district which we were traversing under control.

Old Mira-Oa seemed to be resigned to his fate, so far as outward appearance went. It no longer was necessary to throw him down and fasten a load to him, and he ate as heartily as any of his fellows. But he didn't mingle with them much, but sat apart, wrapped in the blanket we had furnished each of the carriers. When he chose to walk around the camp at night, the other natives respectfully stepped aside and he stalked through their midst with tightly compressed lips. But his eyes gave him away. When he looked at us there was a venom and hate in them that was unmistakable.

Humiliated before those he dominated through the fear he was able to inspire in them, forced to carry a load and shown no special favors, he was cut to the quick and he brooded over the manner of his revenge.

When we halted for a rest the old man did not sink upon the ground and relax while he smoked and chewed betel nut, as did the others. Instead he poked about in the bushes at the side of the trail or in the long grass where the sun was hottest. He was looking for something, as we noticed rather casually, but he smothered the rebellion within him when we were looking.

We thought he had decided he was licked, and Humphries was about ready to relieve him of his load, lecture him on the folly and uselessness of pitting his will against that of the white man, and sending him back to his home. Then something happened that revealed the deep cunning of the sorcerer.

Api and Kauri, our cooks, were pottering around over the evening meal, just beyond the canvas fly we occupied at night, when old Mira-Oa came stalking by. He stopped for a moment, flashed a keen glance at us where we were changing our sweat-sodden garments for pajamas, then came forward and, speaking in the Motuan tongue, which is the dialect used between white men and those coastal natives with whom they deal, offered to spread the clothes out to dry.

It was astonishing, almost unbelievable, but we tossed them to him and he laid them out on top of the sloping roof of the fly. Then he departed without saying a word. The next morning, when our orderlies brought the garments to us, each of us three white men made a discovery. The big khaki handkerchiefs we wore about our necks and used to mop the sweat from our faces were gone. During the night someone had taken them.

We did not at that time associate Mira-Oa with the theft, nor did we dream that the offer to hang up our clothing and the stealing of the handkerchiefs was an essential part of his plot to gain his revenge. Neither did we have the faintest suspicion that the old sorcerer intended that vengeance should take the shape of the most horrible death his wicked old brain could conceive. That he failed was due entirely to the fact that loyalty and devotion overcame superstition and tradition in the brain of a black man who five years before had been as wild and untamed a cannibal as ever stalked another.

The first attempt was made the night we camped in the village of Oriro Petana. As soon as he had dumped his load the old man hurried to the far end of the village and entered a hut which stood by itself, surrounded by a tiny fence. It is thus that the home of the village sorcerer may be picked out. We saw him go and Humphries chuckled and made some remark about the old man hunting for sympathy. Then we forgot Mira-Oa in the many camp duties.

In some of the villages the government picks out one of the leaders and makes him a village constable. He is given a uniform, a big brass badge which he hangs about his neck, and a pair of handcuffs. Mostly his duties consist of keeping the village clean and the trails between villages open, and, in case of serious offenses, to arrest offenders and take them to the magistrate of the district.

At Oriro Petana the constable was a rather portly old chap called Kiali, who bustled about officiously and ordered his villagers around in an effort to get us settled for the night. As a matter of fact, his ideas of what we wanted done were rather hazy and he was somewhat of an annoyance.

Just outside our fly we heard him gruffly taking a small boy to task and Humphries, overhearing their words, went out. Kiali was holding in his hands three coconuts with the ends lopped off and was trying to find out from the youngster who had sent them to us. For some reason a village constable always takes to himself the task of supplying white men with coconuts so that they may refresh themselves with the milk. It gives the constable a chance to stand stiffly at attention, snap up his right hand in a salute, then with a flourish of his knife whack off the end and tender it to the visitors.

Kiali had been away when we reached the village and had been deprived of this privilege. Naturally he was peeved when the urchin came to the tent with three opened nuts. The boy seemed tonguetied with awe, and Kiali wasn't getting very far with his inquisition when Humphries stepped in.

"Give me a nut," he ordered. "The boy should be praised, not chided for bringing them."

Kiali was standing well within the light of a hurricane lamp fastened to a tent pole and he was holding each nut in turn where the light would reveal the amount of milk within. Probably his idea was to give the magistrate the best nut. But suddenly he grew quite excited and hurled the nuts to the ground.

"Why did you do that?" cried Humphries angrily. It looked like a case of insubordination, in which case Kiali would have been in for severe punishment.

The old man's bare heels came together, he stiffened abruptly, and his fingers touched his forelock.

"Master," he said, "the nuts were poisoned!"

And so it proved when we had picked them up, broken them open, and examined the meat closely. To it was clinging infinitesimal bits of bamboo pounded almost into a powder. That is the favorite method of murder of the Papuan sorcerer. Mixed with food or drink, the slivers pierce the intestines, set up inflammation, cause a high fever, and prove fatal within a few days.

"Mira-Oa!" cried Humphries, hazarding a good guess, and sent the police corporal to seize the old sorcerer and bring him to us. But Mira-Oa had disappeared, and when we resumed the march next day another man carried his load.

As for Kiali, whose keen eyes had seen the slivers floating on top of the coconut milk and probably saved some of us from great agony if not death, he was rewarded with five sticks of tobacco worth about two cents each. Had he received more than that he wouldn't have appreciated it, but in his black mind would have concluded that we were simpletons.

Downing and I were properly horrified by the incident, but Humphries dismissed it with a shrug of the shoulders. A man who has been a magistrate in New Guinea for ten years becomes a great deal of a fatalist and he expects such things.

"When we get back to Yule Island I'll make a report of the affair and send a policeman over to Mira-Oa's village to pick him up," he said. "The old fellow probably will hide out in the jungle for a while, then he'll go back home. I'll give him a good scare and let it go at that. We can't connect him directly with the thing, anyhow, even though we are morally certain he is guilty."

Neither could we connect the old sorcerer directly with another attempt which took place some twelve hours later, but in view of all that had gone before, the theory that he was guilty seems reasonable.

Oriro Petana is built on the east bank of a river and, poring over a rude map that night, we decided to cross it there the next morning.

"The country on the other side will be disagreeable to go through," said Humphries, "but we had better take it. It will put us on a direct line to where we want to go. Dress lightly, because it will be baking hot in the tall grass."

When we all had managed to get across in the one or two canoes which were available, the order of march for the day was laid out. Dengo and Waimura were to be the leading police and were to accompany Humphries and myself, as they were our orderlies. The other policemen were scattered through the line to keep the carriers moving, and Corporal Sonana and two men were to bring up the rear. Downing was to go anywhere he wished with his camera. As long as we were not in hostile territory the arrangement would work very well, and would permit us white men to push on ahead of the heavily laden blacks if we wished.

So, having seen the line in motion, we hurried on. Waimura was swinging along with Humphries, myself, and Dengo following in the order named.

Suddenly Waimura leaped over something in the path between the high grass that rose on every side of us and yelled. I did not know the meaning of the word which he shrieked over and over, but before Humphries could cry out a warning Dengo had seized me by the shoulders, spun me around behind him, and leaped in front of Humphries.

Then it was that I saw coming straight toward us a snake. It was between three and four feet long, and plainly it was very angry. It did not swerve to either side in fright, but seemed bent on attacking us.

"My God, come away!" yelled Humphries, and seizing me by the wrist started to run. It seemed rather childish to me to flee from such a small snake, but his grasp on my wrist forced me along. His eyes and those of the police had seen something that I, a tenderfoot in New Guinea, had overlooked.

As we fled Humphries called back over his shoulder to Dengo to kill the snake.

"*Io, taubada* (yes, master)," replied the policeman, and a moment later the report of his rifle rang out. How much mental anguish it caused Dengo to fire that shot it is easy to guess, for to him it represented the lord of all things. But Humphries was his master and he obeyed that master's command, although I have no doubt that in his mind there were plenty of misgivings as to what penalty would accrue to him.

It speaks volumes for the training which the government of Papua gives its police. Recruited from savage life, with its freedom and absence of heavy work, and turned into a hard-fighting, competent, loyal upholder of law and order in six months, Dengo in one instant had violated a tradition bequeathed to him by generations of ancestors simply because a white man had ordered him to do so.

Dengo was squatted on the ground beside the reptile, crooning something in the dialect of his people. What, I do not know, but as we approached he rose and stood impassively awaiting further orders.

"I thought so," said Humphries, as he turned over the dead snake with the toe of his boot. To me he pointed out a noose of pliant vine tightly fastened back of the snake's head. The free end of the vine was several feet long.

"Mira-Oa," he said, although how he could tell puzzled me. But he refused to satisfy my curiosity and insisted on going on, after Dengo had tenderly borne the snake's carcass off the trail and laid it in the grass.

"Unless I'm mistaken I can show you better than I can tell you," said Humphries. A few yards farther on, around a bend in the trail, we found the other policeman standing beside a bed of hot coals. On the fire was a deep earthenware pot and beside it a piece of wood and a stone, evidently the cover to the pot and the weight which held it down. In the dust about the fire were the prints of naked feet. To one side a peg had been driven deep into the ground, and fastened to it was another length of the same kind of pliant vine which had been tied to the snake.

It was all very mystifying to me.

"Look inside the pot," said Humphries, although he himself had not done so. With the stick I carried I turned the hot vessel over and fished inside it. What I brought to light was a handkerchief, khaki-colored and unmistakably one of ours, which had disappeared two nights before when the old sorcerer had hung up our clothing to dry.

"I'll explain it as we go along," Humphries promised, and after he had given orders that the pot be thrown into the grass, the fire put out and all traces of it removed and the peg pulled up and tossed away, we struck out again.

"If those carriers had been close to us we would have had a nice little mutiny on our hands," the magistrate told me. "That is one of the favorite methods of a sorcerer to get rid of an enemy whom he cannot poison and dares not face. Old Mira-Oa did steal our handkerchiefs, after all. Probably that one you saw in the pot was mine, as he would want to get rid of me most of all.

"It isn't hard to guess what happened after you have come to know natives as I do. Mira-Oa fled from the village last night when his powdered bamboo trick was discovered, and crossed the river to this side. Early this morning he took that handkerchief and put it with the snake in the pot after fastening a noose about the snake and tying the other end of the vine to the peg. Then he put the lid on the pot and weighted it down and built a fire under the pot.

"The snake, tortured by the heat, associated its suffering with the smell that was closest to him, that of the sweaty handkerchief. When we drew near the sorcerer tilted the lid off the pot and let the snake out. Then he cut the vine, knowing that the snake, infuriated by his agony, would make straight for the thing that had the same smell as the handkerchief which he blamed for his pain. In other words, that snake was bent on attacking the person whose scent was on the handkerchief. In this case I believe it was me, but it might have been you, so when I ran I pulled you along too."

It sounded preposterous then. It sounds that way now, even though I have seen in official reports of the government of New Guinea similar cases narrated.

But that marked the last of old Mira-Oa so far as we were concerned. We made inquiries for him when we got back to the coast weeks later, but he hadn't been seen for several days. Probably word of our return reached him when we still were a long way off. Such messages travel rapidly by means of "bush telegraph," and Mira-Oa no doubt decided that a short exile from his village was preferable to facing us.

James Norman Hall

From the Faery Lands

The first collaboration on a book about the South Pacific by the authors who were later celebrated for producing the *Bounty* trilogy was entitled *Faery Lands of the South Seas* (1921).

James Norman Hall (1887–1951), the "woodshed poet" born in Colfax, Iowa, joined Kitchener's Volunteer Army in August, 1914, and after two years serving as a machine gunner switched to the Lafayette Flying Corps of the French Foreign Legion. Later, when flying for the United States Air Service, he was downed in Germany and spent the last six months of World War I as a prisoner.

After the war he jointly edited *The Lafayette Flying Corps* (1920) with Charles Nordhoff (1887–1947). In 1920 both friends sailed for the Pacific regions and later settled near each other in Tahiti, where they took Polynesian wives and made the South Seas their literary province. *Faery Lands* contains sketches by both authors. Here is a selection from Hall's contribution to the book—a yarn dealing with the atoll of Ahu Ahu in French Oceania.

DUSK came on as we sat over our meal. Ruau sat with her hands on her knees, leaning back against a tree, talking to Crichton. I understood nothing of what she was saying, but it was a pleasure merely to listen to the music of her voice. It was a little below the usual register of women's voices, strong and clear, but softer even than those of the Tahitians, and so flexible that I could follow every change in mood. She was telling Crichton of the *tupapaku* of her atoll which she dreaded most, although she knew that it was the spirit of one of her own sons. It appeared in the form of a dog with legs as long and thick as the stem of a full-grown coconut tree, and a body proportionally huge. It could have picked up her house as an ordinary dog would a basket. Once it had stepped lightly over it without offering to harm her in any way. Her last son had been drowned while fishing by moonlight on the reef outside the next island, which lay about two miles distant across the eastern end of the lagoon.

She had seen the dog three times since his death, and always at the same phase of the moon. Twice she had come upon it lying at full length on the lagoon beach, its enormous head resting on its paws. She was so badly frightened, she said, that she fell to the ground, incapable of further movement; sick at heart, too, at the thought that the spirit of the bravest and strongest of all her sons must appear to her in that shape. It was clear that she was recognized, for each time the dog began beating its tail on the ground as soon as it saw her. Then it got up, yawned and stretched, took a long drink of salt water, and started at a lope up the beach. She could see it very plainly in the bright moonlight. Soon it broke into a run, going faster and faster, gathering tremendous speed by the time it reached the other end of the island. From there it made a flying spring, and she last saw it as it passed, high in air, across the face of the moon, its head outstretched, its legs doubled close under its body. She believed that it crossed the two-mile gap of water which separated the islands in one gigantic leap.

That is the whole of the story as Crichton translated it for me, although there must have been other details, for Ruau gave her account of it at great length. Her earnestness of manner was very convincing, and left no doubt in my mind of the realness to her of the apparition.

As for myself, if I could have seen ghosts anywhere it would have been at Tanao. Late that night, walking alone on the lagoon beach, I found that I was keeping an uneasy watch behind me. The distant thunder of the surf sounded at times like a wild galloping on the hard sand, and the gentle slapping of little waves nearby like the lapping tongue of the ghostly dog having its fill of sea water . . . .

It was an hour before sunset when we sighted the land— the merest blue irregularity on the horizon, visible from one's perch in the shrouds each time the schooner rose to the crest of a sea. The mellow shout of landfall brought a score of native passengers to their feet; at such a moment one realizes the passionate devotion of the islander to his land. Men sprang into the rigging to gaze ahead with eager exclamations; mothers held up their babies—born on distant plantations—for a first glimpse of Ahu Ahu; seasick old women, emerging from disordered heaps of matting, tottered to the bulwarks with eyes alight. The island had not been visited for six months, and we carried a cargo of extraordinary variety—hardware, bolts of calico, soap, lumber, jewelry, iron roofing, cement, groceries, phonograph records, an unfortunate horse, and several pigs, those inevitable deck-passengers in the island trade. There were scores of cases of bully beef and ship's biscuit—the staple luxuries of modern Polynesia, and, most important of all, six heavy bags of mail.

As we drew near the land, toward midnight, I gave up the attempt to sleep in my berth and went on deck to spread a mat beside Tari, our supercargo, who lay aft of the mainmast, talking in low tones with his wife. It was calm, here in the lee of the island; the schooner slipped through the water with scarcely a sound, rising and falling on the long gentle swell. Faint puffs of air came off the land, bringing a scent of flowers and wood smoke and moist earth. We had been sighted, for lights were beginning to appear in the village; now and then, on a flaw of the breeze, one heard a sigh, long drawn and half inaudible—the voice of the reef. A party of natives, seated on the forward hatch, began to sing. The words were modern and religious, I believe, but the music—indescribably sad, wild, and stirring—carried one back through the centuries to the days when man expressed the dim yearnings of his spirit in communal song. It was a species of chant, with responses; four girls did most of the singing, their voices mingling in barbaric harmonies, each verse ending in a prolonged melodious wail. Precisely as the last note died away, in time with the cadence of the chant, the deep voices of the men took up the response, *"Karé, aué!"* ("No, alas!"). Tari turned to me.

"They sing well," he said, "these Ahu Ahu people; I like to listen to them. That is a hymn, but a stranger would never suspect it—the music is pure heathen. Look at the torch-lights in the village; smell the land breeze—it would tell you you were in the islands if you were set down here blindfold from a place ten thousand miles away. With that singing in one's ears, it is not difficult to fancy oneself in a long canoe, at the end of an old-time voyage, chanting a song of thanksgiving to the gods who have brought us safely home."

He is by no means the traditional supercargo of a trading schooner, this Tari; I have wasted a good deal of time speculating as to his origin and the reasons for his choosing this mode of life. An Englishman with a hint of Oxford in his voice—quite obviously what we call a gentleman—a reader of reviews, the possessor (at his charming place on Nukutere) of an enviable collection of books on the natural history and ethnology of the South Seas, he seldom speaks of himself or of his people at home. For twenty years he has been known in this part of the world—trading on Penrhyn, Rakahanga, Tupuai, the atolls of the Paumotu. He speaks a dozen of the island dialects, can join in the singing of *utes*, or bring a roar of applause by his skill in the dances of widely separated groups. When the war broke out he enlisted as a private in a New Zealand battalion, and the close of hostilities found him with decorations for gallantry, the rank of captain, and the scars of honorable wounds. As a subject for conversation, the war interests him as little as his own life, but this evening he had emptied a full bottle of rum, and was in the mildly mellow state which is his nearest approach to intoxication. . . .

"My wife's mother lives on Ahu Ahu, where her ancestors have been hereditary rulers since Maui fished the island out of the sea. I've known the family a good many years, and long before I married Apakura the old lady was kind enough to take a motherly interest in me. I always put up with her when we touched at Ahu Ahu. Once, after I had been away for several months, I sat down to have a yarn with her, and was beginning to tell about where I'd been and what I'd done when she stopped me. 'No, let me tell you,' she said, with an odd smile; and, upon my honor, she did—down to the details! I got the secret out of her the same evening. She is very friendly, it seems, with an ancestor of hers—a woman named Rakamoana, who lived twenty-eight generations—seven hundred years—ago, and is buried in the big marae behind the village. When one of the family is off on a trip, and my mother-in-law suspects that he is in trouble or not behaving himself, she puts herself into a kind of trance, calls up old Rakamoana, and gets all the facts. I hope the habit won't come into general use—might prove jolly awkward, eh? Seriously, though, I can't account for the things she told me without accepting her own explanation. Strange if there were a germ of truth in the legends of how the old seagoing canoes were navigated—the priests, in a state of trance, directing the helmsmen which way to steer for land.

"There is another old woman on Ahu Ahu whose yarns are worth hearing. Many years ago a Yankee whaling vessel called at the island, and a Portuguese harpooner, who had had trouble with the captain, deserted and hid himself in the bush. The people had taken a fancy to him and refused to give him up, so finally the captain was obliged to sail away without his man. From all accounts this harpooner must have been a good chap; when he proved that he was no common white waster, the chief gave him a bit of land and a girl of good family for a wife—now the old lady of whom I spoke. I think it was tools he needed, or some sort of gear for a house he was building; at any rate, when another whaler touched he told his wife that he was going on a voyage to earn some money and that he might be gone a year. There was a kind of agreement, current in the Pacific in those days, whereby a whaling captain promised to land a man at the point where he had signed him on.

"Well, the harpooner sailed away, and, as might have been expected, his wife never saw him again; but here comes the odd part of the story. The deserted wife, like so many of the Ahu Ahu women, had an ancestor who kept her in touch with current events. Being particularly fond of her husband, she indulged in a trance from time to time, to keep herself informed as to his welfare. Several months after his departure the tragedy occurred—described in detail by the obliging and sympathetic dweller in the marae. It was a kind of vision, as told to me, singularly vivid for an effort of pure imagination—the open Pacific, heaving gently and ruffled by a light air; two boats from rival vessels pursuing the same whale; the Portuguese harpooner standing in the bows of one, erect and intent upon the chase, his iron the first, by a second of time, to strike. Then came a glimpse of the two boats foaming side by side in the wake of the whale; the beginning of the dispute; the lancing and death flurry of an old bull sperm; the rising anger of the two harpooners, as the boats rocked gently beside the floating carcass; the treacherous thrust; the long red blade of the lance standing out between the shoulders of the Portuguese.

"The woman awoke from her trance with a cry of anguish; her husband was dead—she set up the widow's *tangi.* One might have thought it an excellent tale, concocted to save the face of a deserted wife, if the same vessel had not called at Ahu Ahu within a year, to bring news of the husband's death under the exact circumstances of the vision.

"What is one to believe? If seeing is believing, then count me a believer, for my own eyes have seen an incredible thing. It was on Aitutaki, in the Cook group. An old chief, the descendant of a very ancient family, lay ill in the village. I had turned in early, as I'd promised to go fishing on the reef when the tide served, an hour after midnight. You know how the spirits of the dead were believed to flee westward, to Hawaiki, and how their voices might be heard at night, calling to one another in the sky, as they drove past, high overhead. Early in the evening, as I lay in bed, a boy came into the next room, panting with excitement. He had been to a plantation in the hills, it seemed, and as he returned, just after dusk, had heard the voices of a shouting multitude passing in the air above him. I was tired and paid little attention to his story, but for some reason I found it impossible to sleep. It was a hot night, very still and sultry, with something in the air that made one's nerves twitch every time a coconut frond dropped in the distance. I was still lying awake when my fishing companions came to get me; a little ahead of time, for, like me, they had been unable to sleep. We would wait on the reef, they suggested, where it was sure to be cool, until the tide was right.

"We were sitting on the dry coral, smoking. I had just looked at my watch, I remember; it lacked a few minutes to one o'clock. Our canoes were hauled up on one side of the

Arutunga Passage—the western pass, by the way. There was no moon. Suddenly one of the boys touched me. 'What is that?' he exclaimed, in a startled voice. I looked up; the others were rising to their feet. Two flaring lights were moving across the lagoon toward us—together and very swiftly. Nearer and nearer they came, until they revealed the outlines of a canoe larger than any built in the islands nowadays—a canoe of the old time, with a flaming torch set at prow and stern. While we stood there, staring in silence, it drew abreast of us, moving with the rush of a swift motorboat, and passed on—out to sea. I was too amazed to think clearly until I heard one of the boys whisper to another, '*Kua mate te ariki*—the chief is dead; the great canoe bears him out to the west.' We launched our canoes and crossed the lagoon to the village. Women were wailing; yes, the old man was dead—he had drawn his last breath a little before one o'clock. Remember that I saw this thing myself. . . .Perhaps it was a dream—if so, we all dreamed alike."

Robert James Fletcher

Siva and the Devil

A restless young English schoolmaster, having read too much of Robert Louis Stevenson, worked his way to the legendary South Seas. He landed in what at the time was the worst possible place—an island in the New Hebrides (now the Republic of Vanuatu). There he spent more than seven years as a plantation manager, encountering such adventures as the one here narrated. It is taken from *Isles of Illusion,* a collection of letters written to an Oxford classmate and published in 1923 under the pseudonym of "Asterisk." He also published a semi-autobiographical novel, *Gone Native* (1924).

September 10th, 1912.

A CURIOUS thing happened last night. I had just fallen asleep about ten o'clock, and was awakened by a most fearsome din. Someone or something was uttering the most awful screams that I have ever heard. Every scream was worse than the last, and each one spoke mortal terror. Mixed with the screams were reports of guns and a general shouting and hullabaloo, but the screams dominated everything.

My first thought was an attack on the plantation by bush tribes. I hopped out of bed, put on a pair of top-boots and my revolver belt and, collaring a Winchester, nipped out at the front door. The row was all coming from the back, so I thought "to fetch a compass" about the attackers and at any rate have a bit of a run for my money. However, to my surprise, at the gate of the house I found all the "labor" assembled and clamoring for "master." I could see at once that they were in an awful state of funk, for they were all stark naked. (As soon as these kanakas are either frightened or ill, off come their clothes.) I called for the head man, and he came up shaking with fright and pitched me the rummiest yarn I ever heard. (I will omit the *biche-la-mar* and give you the gist of the story.)

A certain laborer named Siva had seen a devil at sunset when he went to draw water at the well. The devil had said that he would come and take him off to the bush during the night. Siva had told all his pals and they had sat up with lights and singing all the proper songs, but apparently to no purpose. The devil had come and dragged Siva from his hut and was now trying to catch him behind my house. His pals had rushed after him with their guns and were firing at the devil. As long as they fired the devil couldn't catch Siva, but their weekly allowance of four cartridges apiece was giving out. Would I come and fire some dynamite to frighten the devil right away?

I persuaded the head man (who is a dungaree-clad Christian on ordinary occasions) to come round to the back of the house, and there in the moonlight I saw the strangest sight. I could never have believed it, but for the unmistakable evidence of my own eyes. In the clearing behind the house the wretched Siva was running for his life, doubling and dodging backwards and forwards, his eyes starting out of his head, and uttering the awful screams that had awakened me. Three or four pals shouting at the top of their voices were loading and firing as quick as they could. They were firing apparently at Siva, but really just behind him. I made sure he would get a charge of shot in him, so I ran towards him and roared at him in my most mighty tone of command.

Ordinarily he is a most tractable youth, and obeys me like a dog, but he took not the slightest notice of me. When I was about thirty yards from him and was beginning to be afraid of getting shot myself, the firing ceased. Immediately after the last shot he set off hell-for-leather towards the bush and—here is the odd part—his right hand was stretched out to the right front of his body as if clasped by somebody running beside him, and fast as he went he seemed to be leaning back and pulling against a resistless force. I was too blown to follow, and top-boots are bad for running through thick scrub, so I turned back expecting to find all the other niggers where I had left them.

There was not one to be seen. Every mother's son had bolted for his hut, and was safely inside with lights burning, howling songs for all he was worth. I went from hut to hut trying to cajole and threaten them to make up a party to go and catch the poor beast. I could do absolutely nothing. Ordinarily servilely obedient, now they were as stubborn as mules. I offered lanterns, dynamite, cartridges, even "trade" mouth organs, but nothing would give them confidence. I could do nothing by myself, and feeling fever coming on I turned in to see what morning brought.

In the morning I sent for the head man and gave him a long jaw. He seemed partly ashamed and partly sulky at my interference with what didn't concern me. He would only tell me his old story over and over again, so I sent them all to work. About an hour afterwards in walked Mr. Siva, not a penny the worse for his adventure. He wouldn't tell me a word about it, but went and got his tools and went off to work. I noticed that none of the other men would work near him all day, and if he tried to speak to a man, that man immediately put his fingers in his ears. Whether the fact that Siva had returned whole meant that he had made some fearful pact with the devils or not, I can't say. Anyhow the whole thing was odd.

September 11th.

THE wretched Siva is dead. When I called the roll this morning he didn't answer, and no one would tell me anything, so I went straight off to his hut and found him stiff. I am convinced he has been poisoned, but what can I do? I couldn't perform a post-mortem even if I wanted to; and these beggars use vegetable poisons that are instantaneous in action and quite undiscoverable. I don't know what to do. I suppose I must let the matter drop. If I pressed things much further I should have an open revolt, and I can't fight a hundred niggers with guns single-handed. I have the moral support of the man-of-war at Vila, which might arrive six months after I was dead and buried (or eaten), so I shall wait on events.

W. Somerset Maugham

My South Sea Island

One of the most versatile and widely read English authors of this century, W. Somerset Maugham (1874–1965), while serving as a British secret agent during World War I, spent several months in 1916 and 1917 visiting various islands of Polynesia. He stopped first at Hawaii and then went on to Samoa and Tahiti. These islands provided him with material for two of his best books of fiction: *The Moon and Sixpence* (1919), a novel based on the life of Paul Gauguin; and *The Trembling of a Leaf* (1921), a collection of six stories, including "Red," which he regarded as his most successful short story, and "Rain," the one that is best known.

In the brief tale that follows, a true one which has never been collected, Maugham tells of a curious experience he had while living on a small coral island near Tahiti.

I HAVE always thought it must be the most delightful thing in the world to own an island; not Ireland, of course, or Borneo—that would really be too much of a good thing—but an island that you could walk round without hurrying yourself in a couple of hours; and now and then I have been offered one, if not for a song, at least for no more than I shall get for this article. But it was always at least a thousand miles from where I happened to be, and that seemed a considerable distance to go (especially as there was no means of getting there) in order to inspect an island which, after all, might not be exactly the sort of island I wanted. Besides, if I were not living on it, I should always be worried about it; I should awake in the night in London and wonder anxiously whether anyone had run away with it. You have to be so careful with portable property in the South Seas.

But in Tahiti I met a man who owned an island, and when I told him that I envied him he offered to lend it to me. There was something so casual about the suggestion, like a man in a railway carriage who asks you if you would like his *Punch*, that I accepted at once.

The island happened to be no more than a hundred miles away from anywhere else (that in the Pacific is cheek by jowl, no farther than Piccadilly Circus from Trafalgar Square), so that it was a wonderful chance to enjoy the satisfaction of proprietorship.

I found a small cutter with a gasoline engine to take me over; I had a native servant whose extraordinary incompetence was only equaled by his unfailing good nature, and I engaged a Chinese cook—for I thought this was an occasion to do things in style.

I bought a bag of rice, a quantity of tinned goods, a certain amount of whisky, and a great many bottles of soda, for the owner had warned me that there was no water on the island.

I set my foot on the beach. The island was mine for as long as I chose to inhabit it. The beach really had the silver whiteness that you read of in descriptions of the South Sea islands, and when I walked along in the sunshine it was so dazzling that I could hardly bear to look at it. Here and there were the white shells of dead crabs and the skeletons of sea birds.

I walked up through the coconuts and came upon a grove of enormous, old, and leafy trees; they gave coolness and a grateful shade. It was among these that the tiny settlement was built. There was the headman's hut and another for the workman, two more to store the copra, and a somewhat larger one, trim and clean, which the owner of the island used when he visited it and in which I was to dwell.

I unloaded my stores and bedding and proceeded to make myself at home. But I had not reckoned with the mosquitoes. There were swarms of them; I have never seen so many; and they were bold and fierce and pitiless. I rigged up a net in the veranda of my hut and placed a table and a chair beneath it, but the mosquitoes were ingenious to enter, and I had to kill twenty at least before I could sit down in peace.

Here I took my frugal meals, but when a dish was hurriedly passed between the curtains a dozen mosquitoes dashed in and I had to kill them one by one before I could eat.

I set about exploring the island. It had evidently been raised from the sea at a comparatively recent date, and much of the interior was barren and almost swampy, so that

I sank in as I walked. I suppose what was now dry land had not very long ago been brackish lake. Beside the coconuts nothing much seemed to grow but rank grass and a shrub something like a broom.

There were no animals on the island but rats, perhaps, and though throughout the Pacific you find everywhere the mynah bird, noisy and quarrelsome, to this lonely spot he had never found his way; and the wild fowl I saw were great black gulls with long beaks. They had a piercing, almost a human, whistle. I thought that in them abode, restless and menacing, the souls of dead seamen drowned at sea. They gave something sinister to the smiling sunlit island.

But it was not till I had been on the island for several days that I discovered they were not the only sinister things there. I thought I had explored every inch of it, and I was surprised one evening to catch through the coconuts a glimpse of a little grass hut. I saw a moving shape, and I wondered if it was possible that anyone lived there.

I strolled toward the hut and I saw what was certainly a man, but as I approached he vanished. I supposed that I had startled him and he had slunk away among the brushwood. But I wondered why he had chosen this lonely dwelling, who he was, and how he lived.

The Polynesians are a friendly and sociable race, and I was intrigued to find anyone in that tiny island who needed solitude so much that he must live away even from the half-dozen persons who formed the island's entire population. I puzzled my brains. It could not be a watchman, for among the coconuts there was nothing to watch and no danger to guard against.

When I returned to my own house I told the headman what I had seen and asked him who this solitary creature was; but he would not, or could not, understand me. It was not till I was once more in Papeete that I found out. I thanked the owner of the island for the loan of it and then I asked him who was the mysterious man who seemed so to shun the approach of his fellows.

"Oh, that's my leper," he said. "I thought he'd amuse you."

"He tickled me to death," I answered. "But haven't you rather a peculiar sense of humor?"

Sir Arthur Grimble

A Stinking Ghost

With a degree from Cambridge University and further education in France and Germany, Arthur Grimble (1888–1956) joined the British Colonial Service at the age of twenty-six. On his first assignment he was posted to the Gilbert and Ellice Islands Protectorate, a remote possession in the equatorial Pacific. There he served for nineteen years, first as cadet and then, having proved his competence, as resident commissioner, chief administrator of both groups. Later he became governor of the Seychelles Islands, was knighted in 1938, and ended his career in the Colonial Service as governor of the Windward Islands.

His experiences in the Gilberts, now the Republic of Kiribati, resulted in two volumes of recollections: *We Chose the Islands* (1953) (the British title is *A Pattern of Islands*); and *Return to the Islands* (1957). "A Stinking Ghost" is chosen from the latter volume.

THERE were five European houses scattered through the whispering glades of the palm forest on Betio station in 1923. Two of these had been put up by myself in 1916; the other three were much older; and every one of them, according to the people of Betio village next door, was haunted. The basic trouble was not, I gathered, that they had all happened to be built on prehaunted ground; there wasn't a foot of soil anywhere up the creeping length of Tarawa that wasn't the lurking place of one fiend or another, and you had to take these as you found them. It was how you dealt with them when you laid out your ground plan and built your house that really mattered. If you didn't turn on the proper spells—and how could you if you were a white man?—it followed as a matter of course that the ghosts or the elementals got in.

One of the two bungalows that I had built had been occupied without delay by an earth spirit called Na Kun, who showed himself in the form of a noddy. He croaked "Kun-kun-kun" at you in the dark of night, and aimed his droppings at your eye, and blinded you for life if he made a bull's-eye of it. The other house had a dog on its front veranda: not just a *kamea* (that is, a "come-here"), as the white man's dogs were called, but a *kiri*—one of the breed the ancestors had brought with them out of the west when, shortly after the creation of the world by Naareau the Elder, they came to settle on Tarawa. I could never make out why everyone was so frightened of this beast. He never *did* anything, simply *was* in the house. For my own purposes, I came to the conclusion that he was like the "mopoke" in the celebrated Australian story, so deceptive that what I occasionally thought I saw on the front veranda and took to be something else actually was what I took it for, namely, a mongrel of the old *kiri* strain from the village.

There was a cheerful tale among the villagers that, round about 1910, an aged friend of mine, a widely loved sorcerer who dealt in what was called the magic of kindness (meaning any kind of ritual or charm not intended to hurt anybody) had posted one of his familiars, the apparition of a gray heron, on the front veranda of a decrepit bungalow near the hospital. His intent, so the story went, was to get hold of a few medical secrets for the improvement of his repertoire of curative potions, especially those which had to do with the revitalization of flagging manhood. But his constructive plan was most untimely frustrated when the resident medical officer was tranferred to another house, only just built, but nevertheless already haunted by a hag with two heads. This unpleasant creature made a most frightful scene when the wizard tried to take the new premises over for his inquisitive bird. I learned all these facts from a glorious burlesque show put up for me one Saturday night by the lads, young and old, of Betio village. The miming of the demon lady's fury, her inhospitable gestures, the rout of the sorcerer, and the total desolation of the heron left all of us, including the venerable gentleman himself, helpless with laughter. But, in the last analysis, behind all the mirth of that roaring crowd, there wasn't a soul present except myself who didn't accept both the familiar and the demon for cold and often terrifying fact.

The oldest house on our station, the one we called the old residency, was a pleasant, two-floored structure near the lagoonside haunted by a nameless white beachcomber. This ghost was held in peculiar dread by the villagers, because they regarded it as earthbound for ever, its body having been murdered and left unburied on the beach for the Betio dogs to devour. That kind of revenant was always more *iowawa* (malicious) than any other, everyone believed.

The unhappy man, so the story ran, had been killed on the site of the residency with a glass bottle by a fellow beachcomber named Tom, a generation or so before the coming of the British flag in 1892, which is to say, somewhere back in the late 1860's. Nothing else was remembered of him except that he was wearing a sailor's dark shore clothes and thick black boots when he came by his death. Or, at least, that is how his ghost was said to be dressed whenever it allowed itself to be seen about the house.

The villagers talked about him so much and with such conviction that Europeans began to accept the haunt as a fact. It is hard to resist belief in such things when you are lonely and the whole air around you palpitates with horrified credulity. Good Father Guichard of the Sacred Heart Mission, bless him, came down-lagoon fifteen miles when Olivia and I arrived at Tarawa in 1916, especially to warn us against living in the house. But we did live there. We couldn't see why the poor ghost, if it existed, should want to do us any harm. So we had our beds and the baby's cot on the airy gable veranda where he was supposed to walk, clump-clump, in his great thick boots; and all the time we were there, we never saw or heard a thing or had the smallest feeling of his unseen presence.

But when I was transferred to the central Gilberts in 1917, I found a house that gave me quite different sensations. That was the district officer's transit quarters on Tabiteuea, built by George Murdoch, my predecessor in the central islands. It used to stand in a rustling grove of coconut palms by the lagoon beach, a hundred yards or so north of Utiroa village and about the same distance south of the big, white-washed island prison. It was an airily built, two-roomed shelter of local thatch and timber, a heavenly cool refuge from the ferocious glare of sea and sand beyond the grove. I found it a cheerful place, too, all through the daylight hours, with the talkative Utiroa villagers padding back and forth along the road that passed it to landward. It changed, though, when darkness fell and the village slept. An uneasiness came upon it then. Or perhaps it was I who changed—I don't know—only I couldn't pass a night there without being haunted by a thought that something was on the edge of happening: something so imminently near, I always felt, that if nothing but one gossamer-fold of the darkness could be stripped aside, I should see what it was. The idea would come back and back at me as I sat reading or writing. Once or twice, it pulled me up out of sleep, wide-awake on the instant, thinking, "Here it is!" But if it was, it never showed itself.

Had this been all, I should never have had the place pulled down. Not even the horrifying odor that visited me there one night would have sufficed of itself to drive me to that extreme. You don't destroy a house built by your predecessor—especially an old stager like George Murdoch—for the sole reason that it was once, for about thirty seconds in your experience, invaded by a smell you couldn't explain. It was what George himself said to me afterwards, when I told him (among other things) how my dog had behaved, that set me looking for another site.

The dog was my terrier, Smith. He was lying in the draft of the roadside doorway one night, while I sat reading. I wasn't deeply absorbed because I was worried about Anterea, an old friend of mine, who lay ill in the village—so ill I was sure he wouldn't last the night. Perhaps that made me particularly susceptible to whatever it was. Anyhow, I felt myself suddenly gripped, as I sat, by a more than usually disturbing sense of that imminent something. It had never had any particular direction before, but now it seemed to impend from the roadway. I was aware, also, of having to fight a definite dread of it this time, instead of greeting it with a kind of incredulous expectancy. I sprang up, staring nervously out into the dark beyond the door. And then I noticed Smith. Hackles bristling, gums bared, he was backing step by step away from the door, whimpering and trembling as he backed.

"Smith!" I called. He gave me one quick, piteous look, turned tail and bolted, yelping as if I had kicked him, through the seaward door. I heard him begin to howl on the beach, just as that unspeakable odor came sweeping into the room, wave upon wave of the breath of all corruption, from the road.

Plain anger seized me as I stood. That was natural, I think. I had made myself a fine figure of fun, for whoever was outside, leaping to my feet and goggling like a scared rabbit through the doorway, a glorious butt for this nasty trick. It hurt: I forgot Smith and dashed out into the road. But there wasn't a clue for eye, or ear, or nose in the hissing darkness under the wind-blown palms. I found nobody and nothing, until my running feet brought me to the fringe of Utiroa village; and there I heard a sound that stripped me of all my anger. It was the noise of women wailing and men chanting, mixed with the rhythmic thud-thud of heavy staves on the ground. I couldn't mistake it. A Gilbertese *bomaki* ceremony was in full swing: some villager's departing soul was being ritually sped on its difficult road from earth to paradise. I knew then that my old friend Anterea had not lasted the night, and I lost all heart for my silly chase.

There was no taint on the air of the house when I got back. I fell asleep untroubled by anything but my own sadness. But Smith stayed out on the beach, and I couldn't persuade him to remain indoors after dark for the few more days I spent on Tabiteuea.

The rest of the story is George Murdoch's. He had settled down to trading on Kuria Island after his retirement from the administrative service, so I took the next chance I could of running across to tell him of my feelings about the house, and Smith's queer behavior, and the fetid smell someone had put across me.

"So he's been making friends with you, has he?" said George reflectively when I had finished. And, instead of answering when I asked who "he" might be, he went on,

"From about the middle of Utiroa village to a bit north of the prison—that's his beat. Aye, he's a stinking old nuisance. But mind you, there's no real harm in him."

"He," in short, according to George, was an absurd ghost known to the villagers as *Tewaiteaina,* or One Leg, whose habit for several centuries it had been to walk—or, rather, hop—that particular stretch of Tabiteuea, every night of the year without exception, scaring everybody stiff who saw him go by. George spoke of him with a sort of affectionate irritation, as if he really existed. It was too ridiculous.

"But, Mr. Murdoch," I interrupted, "there's a ghost for every yard of the Gilberts, if you swallow all that village stuff!"

He eyed me humorously. "But there's only one ghost who stinks, young fella-me-lad, and that's old One Leg. Not that he plays that trick often, mind you. Just sometimes, for friendship's sake. Now, if you'll stop interrupting, I'll tell you. . . .

"I'd heard nothing about him when I had the prison and the resthouse built where they are," he went on, "otherwise, I might have chosen somewhere else. Or I might not. What's the odds, anyway? The creature's harmless. So there I was one dark, still night, with a prison nicely full of grand, strong lads up the road, and myself sitting all serene in the resthouse, enjoying a page or two of the King's Regulations. I say I was all serene, you'll note. The house had stood three years, and I'd never been troubled by the something's-going-to-happen notion you've made such a point of. Sheer nonsense that, I'm telling you straight!"

"Yes, Mr. Murdoch," I said humbly.

"Well, you'll grow out of it, I suppose," he comforted me. "So there I sat, a grown man, with not one childish fancy to make a fool of me, when in from the roadway crashed that stinking thing and hit me like a wall. Solid. A fearful stench. You were right about that. Corruption and essence of corruption from the heart of all rottenness—that's what I said to myself as I fought my way through it to the door. . . . How did I know it came from the road, you say? What does that matter—I *did* know; so don't interrupt me with your questions.

"I'll admit the uncanny suddenness of it gave me the shudders at first. But I was angry, like you, by the time I reached the road. I thought some son of a gun was taking a rise out of me. So I dashed back into the house, snatched up a hurricane lamp and started running hell for leather towards the prison. The reek was as thick as a fog that way, and I followed my nose.

"I hadn't gone far, though, before I heard a patter and a rush from ahead, and a great ox of a prison guard came charging full tilt out of the darkness and threw himself at me, gibbering like a cockatoo. As I struggled out of his clutches, I caught something about someone called One Leg who'd gone hop-hopping past him into the prison yard. Well . . . there was my clue. 'Is it One Leg that raised this stink?' I shouted. 'Yes,' he screamed back. 'One Leg . . . the ghost!' I only stayed to call him a blanky fool and belted on.

"But I wasn't quick enough to catch up with the trouble. When I got near the prison yard, something else had started. The whole crowd inside the men's lockup had gone mad . . . raving mad . . . yelling their heads off . . . and the noise of them flinging themselves against the door was like thunder. I knew the padlock wouldn't last if that went on; I heard it crack like a pistol as I came up to the yard entrance; and, begum, before you could say knife, I was down under the feet of a maniac mob stampeding out into the bush.

"I picked myself up and made a beeline for the lockup; ran halfway down the gangway between the beds, swinging my lamp around; found not a soul there; charged out again to Anterea's house in the corner of the yard—why, what's the matter now?"

I had sat bolt upright and exclaimed, "Anterea?" When I repeated it, he said, "Yes, the head warder. Retired before your time, but he's still going strong in Utiroa. One of the few who never gave a damn for old One Leg. Would you believe it? He was sleeping like a baby when I got to him. Hadn't heard a sound and said he couldn't smell a thing, though the place was still humming fit to knock you down. But he got going quick enough when I told him the news. He and I hunted the bush for those poor idiots till the crack of dawn. They came in willingly enough at sunup—all but Arikitaua, that's to say—and we had a fine powwow together round Anterea's shack, waiting for him to turn up. That's when I got all the dope about One Leg.

"They'd all seen him hopping up the gangway between the beds, so they claimed. There wasn't a light, but they'd seen him. 'Fiddle!' I said to that, and Anterea backed me. So, just for the hell of it, I turned on him then, and asked him what of the smell I'd smelt and he hadn't; and immediately about half of them butted in to say they hadn't smelt it, either; and, by the same token, the other half had. It was all very puzzling until somebody explained that One Leg only brought his saintly odor along for the particular friends of the deceased, and then, of course, it was as clear as mud. 'Which deceased?' I wanted to know. 'Oh, anyone who dies within the limits of his beat,' says my clever friend. 'He turns it on as soon as the soul has left the body.'

"You could have knocked me down with a feather if there had been a corpse in sight. But there wasn't. So I said a few words and left them to think up another story. I had a mind to go and inquire in the village after our missing number, Arikitaua . . . an Utiroa man. . . . I liked him a lot. But I hadn't gone fifty steps, when a new hullabaloo from the lockup stopped me in my tracks. I thought they were starting another One Leg stunt. But it was only poor Arikitaua this time. Yes . . . there he was—rolled off his bed on the floor up against the far end wall—where my lamp hadn't reached him—quite dead. I reckon it was just heart disease."

We sat silent a long time; then George said reflectively, "What with this and that, I'm surprised you didn't hear of a friend's death in Utiroa after the old stinker put it across you."

I told him then of Anterea.

"Well . . . well . . . think of that now," said George, ". . . and Anterea an unbeliever. Kind of friendly, I call it. There never was any real harm in old One Leg."

He was furious when I had a new resthouse built on the other side of the island—as furious as a man might be who has led you up the garden path to his own confusion. But he never would admit he'd been pulling my leg. And then again, what was it that scared my dog so?

Florence Coombe

Savagery Among the Black Islands

A woman who was brought up on the South Pacific island of Norfolk and became a worker with the Melanesian Mission produced a volume from which vignettes may be drawn of early days in such Melanesian lands as the Banks Group, the Torres Group, Tikopia, San Cristoval in the New Hebrides, and Ulawa and Bugotu in the Solomons.

"Savagery Among the Black Islands" is taken from various chapters in *Islands of Enchantment* (1912). Florence Coombe is also author of *School-Days in Norfolk Island* (1904).

Motalava, Banks Islands

THE wizard must be persuaded with money to prepare a ghost-shooter. With preparatory fasting, and the accompaniment of the inevitable magic song, the bamboo is packed with its fatal ingredients, such as dead man's bone and leaves hot with mana. The weapon is then ready to be delivered to the man who has set his heart upon killing his enemy. It is such a little bamboo that it can be carried in the hand without attracting notice, and the open end is covered with the thumb until the unsuspecting foe is near at hand. Then with malicious triumph the hand is outstretched towards him—not in friendship! The thumb is lifted and the magic influence released in his direction. If the unlucky mortal sees the ghost-shooter he loses all power of resistance and falls to the ground. He might not die at once, but he will crawl home a doomed man whose hours are numbered. Yet nothing external has so much as touched him. Such was the power of the ghost-shooter.

A story comes from Ra of a rich man with a grudge against somebody, unknowing and unknown. All that was known was that the great man had made ready a ghost-shooter and a feast at the same time. So strong is Melanesian curiosity that all the Ra world came to the feast, while perfectly aware that among them must be the individual whose life was forfeit. The feast would be crowned by a "kill," but who would be the victim?

The host, to make his magic stronger, fasted unwashed for so many days beforehand that the feast found him too weak to walk forth to it. The excited guests assembled in the *tinesara* for the dance which, according to custom, must precede the feast, and presently a grisly object appeared, carried between two supporters—a blackened, shrunken skeleton of a man. There they set him down, at the edge of the dancing-ground, and all saw the thin trembling arm straightened ready, holding the ghost-shooter.

The drum began to tap and the dancers to circle round, while two burning eyes from out a wasted face watched each as he passed and waited still for his opportunity. The time went on, the dancers passed and repassed, and the watcher's gaze from intensity gradually gave way to bewilderment. Which was his victim? This? He raised his arm and uncovered the bamboo. Even in the midst of the dance's whirl all saw, all felt what had happened. The wretched man who stood in the line of the magic shot fell stiff and prostrate, and the dancing stopped. The same moment the shooter became aware that he had felled the wrong man, and loudly proclaimed his distress. Friends gathered round the poor fallen one, and urged him to put out his strength to resist the magic, since there was no harm wished to him in the act. And when the fainting man understood, he revived, and presently recovered. Of what afterwards befell the unknown who had so fortunately escaped I can find no record.

Toga, Torres Islands

THE eye is caught at once by a white cross of coral cement, which evidently marks a Christian grave. The wife of a former teacher was buried here. A year or two ago the priest-in-charge saw a crowd clustered round this grave, the center of their interest being a woman who was handling a land-crab of a species whose bite the natives fear. She, however, seemed quite unafraid, allowing the creature to crawl about her at will. Presently she put it down on the ground, and at once it sidled off into a hole under the cross.

The scene was interpreted afterwards in the confidence that evening brings. The woman was one reputed to be in touch with the spirit-world, and able to communicate with ghosts and see beings invisible to ordinary eyes. When she was thus engaged it was said that her face changed and her eyes protruded crabwise. The crab itself was the soul of the teacher's dead wife, whose remains were buried there. The hole was the passage by which it came up from Panoi, always taking the same visible shape.

Remembering the legend, I questioned one of the women who was standing by me, and she corroborated it, adding that the Toga belief is that all dead folks' souls go down into Panoi by crab holes, and reappear on occasion in crab form. "But some there are among us now who do not believe it," she added.

Tikopia

WHILE writing of customs I must mention that which concerns betrothal. An offer of marriage in Tikopia is made by the handing of a nut to a girl by her admirer, and if she accepts him she accepts the nut. Nor will she refuse him lightly, for if that significant nut be rejected, the girl by her action signs her own death-warrant. She is actually compelled by social custom to commit suicide, and it is said that every year several girls drown themselves rather than marry the man who handed the nut.

San Cristoval

OLD Taki, the chief of Waño, evolved a grudge against a certain man, and resolved to punish him for it. He killed a large pig, and sent it as a gift to the offender, accompanied with a huge quantity of yams.

San Cristoval etiquette does not admit of the refusal of a chiefly gift: such would be an open and flagrant insult, bringing speedy chastisement. It is obligatory on the recipient to accept both pig and yams, and to make therewith a banquet. This does not sound like a very dire punishment. But the sting lies in the tail.

By the inexorable law of native custom the poor fellow knew himself compelled to send in return a present equal to, if not exceeding in value, what he had received. Taki was rich; his victim, poor already, was by the chief's lavish generosity reduced to beggary. His small garden was insufficient to supply the yams required, and all his money was exhausted in buying food for the man of abundance!

Taki still lives and flourishes—an interesting character, whose portrait I am able to reproduce. Until about 1890 he was notorious as a leading headhunter and cannibal.

Perhaps thirty years ago some influence induced him to give his son to the white men to be trained in our Norfolk Island Industrial College. But on the lad's return Taki would have none of his newfangled ways. He dragged the lad down again into shameless savagery, and gloried in it. But the youth had hardly attained maturity when he was killed by a bite from a shark, and about the same time Taki lost both wife and brother. We have in our possession the stock which Taki caused to be carved to memorialize his son. It represents a shark's head, with the miniature figure of a man in its jaws. Thenceforth Taki declared war upon all sharks; the whole ocean tribe suffer for the act of the one. But he wanted something more valuable than the life of many sharks in revenge for the loss of his nearest. He wanted *heads!* And they were not so easy to obtain in 1885 as they had been in, say, 1880.

In vain he urged and gibed at the young men of his village for their cowardice; in vain he lamented and bewailed their desertion and his desolation. They were learning the new way, and could not be prevailed upon to organize one of the night-raids so dear to them of old time. Taki bound around him the girdle that signifies married-womanhood in San Cristoval. It was a sign to the world that he was in the position of an old woman, having lost his nearest and dearest, and yet being unable to obtain human heads with which to honor their tombs.

But in 1887 the girdle was put off. His desire was fulfilled. Two laborers returning from the Queensland sugar plantations, afraid to set foot in their native land, the wild island of Mala, pleaded for shelter in Taki's village, hoping for safety, no doubt, where a Mission school was planted. Taki was more than willing to receive them; he was delighted. Forthwith he sent money and instructions to some heathen down the coast, and the heads of the two Mala men were added to Taki's trophies.

The murder accomplished, Taki explained that a vow he had made necessitated his action, but that now all was over he would like to make a fresh start, follow his people in forsaking savagery, and learn the Peace Teaching! . . .

Touching David Bo, it may be mentioned that one of our head boys at Norfolk Island, a native of Heuru, remarked one morning a few months ago that he believed his chief had died. On inquiry he said that he had dreamed of him, and that although the chief seemed perfectly happy and full of life, he himself had wept greatly. A few weeks later the *Southern Cross*, returning from the islands, brought news of David Bo's death on the very night of the lad's dream. . . .

Ulawa, Solomon Islands

AS San Cristoval is the heart of snake-worship, so Ulawa seems to have been in former days of shark worship. Throughout the Solomons these creatures are looked upon with much dread, and regarded as the abode of ghosts. A man on his deathbed will predict his future appearance in the form of a shark, and when one distinguished in any way by its size or color is observed to frequent a certain rock or strip of beach, it is regarded as representing the deceased or his ghost, and his name is bestowed upon it. I believe off Ulawa there still ranges a fierce maneating shark, called after one Sautahimatawa, to whom propitiatory money is offered in the much-prized porpoise teeth.

In the two or three heathen villages yet remaining in Ulawa, the sharks are worshiped by all the people, who not merely expect to inhabit them hereafter, but in a vague, quasi-totemic way consider themselves the descendants of sharks. It is not every one who can communicate with them; only certain men are possessed of the requisite mana. The test is from a canoe, by means of a very heavy red stone or a very large, light fruit. The man who wishes to prove his power throws out either one or the other, and should the fruit sink or the stone miraculously float, it is clear evidence that he has the desired mana.

The sharks seem to have a very proper feeling, for it is said that where they are worshiped they harm no one. They strictly confine themselves to *killing to order;* there is no freelance work. Their worshipers supply them with occupation, dispatching them on killing expeditions as far as San Cristoval and Ugi.

One of the villages boasts a famous school of sacred sharks. A certain man has mana to summon them when wanted, and a second knows how to send them about their business. According to the native account, which is very precise on the subject, they come when called in a regular order—two in front, and ten couples behind, nose level with nose, swimming straight into the small enclosed harbor where they are to receive their instructions.

Every shark is named. The leader is addressed, and to him is confided the name of his victim-designate. If possible, something connected with the man is supplied to the shark to assist the scent, even if it be only a handful of sand scraped by his foe from his footprints on the beach. Having heard their instructions, the sharks turn again and swim orderly off to work.

The shark especially named selects a large skate for its companion, whose duty it is to lash with its tail the doomed man's canoe until it is upset. Then it is the part of the shark to swallow the man headfirst, but without killing him. Off he goes, a pair of legs sticking out of his mouth, to the spot where his worshiper awaits him, and at his feet the prey is disgorged. The man will not be dead: he must not be! No sacred shark will eat a man unless he has been formally strangled to death. But he is extremely weak, "trembling and sobbing," they say. He knows he can hope for no mercy from the ruthless enemy at whose feet he lies. He is strangled and flung back to the shark for a meal.

Cases are told of a shark sent to destroy a man taking instead a capricious fancy to him—holding him under water once or twice for fun, playing with him, and then releasing him.

There was a famous shark-leader named Huaaha, particularly proficient in his profession. One day when the shark clan was summoned, Huaaha was not amongst them. At the same time came the news of the killing of a great shark in another village where they were no longer held in honor. Thither hurried the shark worshippers, to find that the body of the shark had been already consumed, and only the head remained on the shore.

The question was solemnly addressed to it, "Are you Huaaha?" and forthwith it stood up on end! Upon such conclusive evidence the infuriated people went straight up into the village, where the terrified inhabitants made no show of resistance, and ransacked the houses, burning and destroying everywhere. Down they surged to the beach, and broke up every canoe; up to the gardens in the bush, and ravaged them utterly; and then, glutted with vengeance, returned home.

In the same place there is said to be a hybrid sea monster, with the head of a shark and the legs of a man, who harms no one, but swims sadly about, off the village where sharks are worshipped, with which he is friendly.

The bodies of great chiefs only are buried in the heathen parts of Ulawa. All other corpses are the recognized food of the sharks, offered, as it were, in sacrifice to please them. Many were the battles waged in the Mission's early days between Christian and heathen relatives touching the disposal of the bodies of the baptized. Great and real was the terror of the sharks' indignation at being deprived of their accustomed privilege. But now, of course, burial is the rule, and shark propitiation the exception.

Bugotu, Solomon Islands

AMONG the first of the chiefs of Bugotu with whom the Mission came in contact was one Bera, a very savage ruffian, whose worst barbarities were the offspring of his mother's brain, she being a terrible old hag, who might have served as model for the character of "Gagool" herself!

It pleased Bera (and his mother) to appoint as his successor his grandson, Kikolo, a quiet, well-dispositioned young fellow, who had already joined the Mission school as a hearer. But shortly afterwards signs of wasting and decline were visible in the youth, and Bera was almost beside himself with anxiety. Curiously enough, he seems to have attached no blame to the New Teaching with which Kikolo had connected himself; but, making up his mind that his grandson had offended the local *tindalo,* he bore him hither and thither, from islet to islet, in a vain endeavor to escape out of his jurisdiction. Kikolo's weakness increased, and at last in despair he was brought back to Bera's own house, that there he might die and be buried in chiefly fashion. But one last resource remained, and that should be tried. The *tindalo* might perchance yet be appeased by a human sacrifice.

A mother was working in her garden with her little child beside her, three or four years of age. She never noticed the stealthy approach of one of Bera's men, who, from a short distance away, attracted the infant's attention, and lured it towards him. As soon as it could safely be done, the child was seized and carried off in a canoe to where Bera impatiently awaited the fulfilment of his command.

The poor little innocent was borne into the presence of the dying youth, and its throat was cut so that the blood flowed around him, while Bera cried to the *tindalo* to accept the child's life in lieu of his grandson's. But the same day Kikolo died.

On hearing of the death, the teacher hurried to the chief, and offered to make a coffin and bury the body. Something induced Bera to accede to his suggestion, but he reckoned without his mother, who insisted on the old ceremonies being performed.

A large, deep grave was dug according to custom, in which the corpse was placed upright. Then Kikolo's wife and child were dragged thither, strangled on the brink, and cast into the grave. All the dead man's goods followed—his rifle, his money, and so forth. Every one owning allegiance to Bera next advanced bearing an offering of some sort, which was in like manner thrown into the grave. Then the earth was filled in up to the dead man's neck, the head protruding from the ground. Round this fires were lighted, and kept burning until the flesh was cinders and the skull bare. This was then carried to the great canoe house, and there deposited, henceforth to receive worship and sacrifice as a *tindalo.*

The dead man's property—coco palms and banana groves—were all hacked down, a heap of stones was piled over the grave, and the period of howling and wailing set in. An expedition for compensatory heads would be set afoot as soon as possible, for until these are obtained, no one leaves the village or resumes ordinary life.

Jack London

The Amateur M.D.

In the spring of 1907, Jack London (1876–1916) and his wife Charmian sailed their ketch *Snark* to Hawaii to begin two years of cruising the Pacific, including the Marquesas group, the Societies, Samoa, Fiji, the New Hebrides, and the Solomons. No fewer than nine books by London deal with the Pacific region. Before his death he became the best known, highest paid, and most popular writer in the world.

After adventures among "the terrible Solomons," including the grim island of cannibal Malaita and black Guadalcanal, the Londons took a horrifying cruise on a blackbirding vessel and then, against dangerous odds, headed the *Snark* for a visit to Ontong Java or Lord Howe Island. On their return to their base at Guadalcanal, it became alarming clear that their dream voyage must end.

"The Amateur M.D." comprises the final chapter of London's fascinating chronicle, *The Cruise of the Snark* (1913).

WHEN we sailed from San Francisco on the *Snark*, I knew as much about sickness as the Admiral of the Swiss Navy knows about salt water. And here, at the start, let me advise any one who meditates going to out-of-the-way tropic places. Go to a first-class druggist—the sort that have specialists on their salary list who know everything. Talk the matter over with such an one. Note carefully all that he says. Have a list made of all that he recommends. Write out a check for the total cost, and tear it up.

I wish I had done the same. I should have been far wiser, I know now, if I had bought one of those ready-made, self-acting, foolproof medicine chests such as are favored by fourth-rate shipmasters. In such a chest each bottle has a number. On the inside of the lid is placed a simple table of directions: No. 1, toothache; No. 2, smallpox; No. 3, stomach ache; No. 4, cholera; No. 5, rheumatism; and so on, through the list of human ills. And I might have used it as did a certain venerable skipper, who, when No. 3 was empty, mixed a dose from No. 1 and No. 2, or, when No. 7 was all gone, dosed his crew with 4 and 3 till 3 gave out, when he used 5 and 2.

So far, with the exception of corrosive sublimate (which was recommended as an antiseptic in surgical operations, and which I have not yet used for that purpose), my medicine chest has been useless. It has been worse than useless, for it has occupied much space which I could have used to advantage.

With my surgical instruments it is different. While I have not yet had serious use for them, I do not regret the space they occupy. The thought of them makes me feel good. They are so much life insurance, only, fairer than that last grim game, one is not supposed to die in order to win. Of course, I don't know how to use them, and what I don't know about surgery would set up a dozen quacks in prosperous practice. But needs must when the devil drives, and we of the *Snark* have no warning when the devil may take it into his head to drive, ay, even a thousand miles from land and twenty days from the nearest port.

I did not know anything about dentistry, but a friend fitted me out with forceps and similar weapons, and in Honolulu I picked up a book upon teeth. Also, in that subtropical city I managed to get hold of a skull, from which I extracted the teeth swiftly and painlessly. Thus equipped, I was ready, though not exactly eager, to tackle any tooth that got in my way. It was in Nuku Hiva, in the Marquesas, that my first case presented itself in the shape of a little, old Chinese. The first thing I did was to get the buck fever, and I leave it to any fair-minded person if buck fever, with its attendant heart palpitations and arm tremblings, is the right condition for a man to be in who is endeavoring to pose as an old hand at the business. I did not fool the aged Chinaman. He was as frightened as I and a bit more shaky. I almost forgot to be frightened in the fear that he would bolt. I swear, if he had tried to, that I would have tripped him up and sat on him until calmness and reason returned.

I wanted that tooth. Also, Martin wanted a snapshot of me getting it. Likewise Charmian got her camera. Then the procession started. We were stopping at what had been the clubhouse when Stevenson was in the Marquesas on the *Casco.* On the veranda, where he had passed so many pleasant hours, the light was not good—for snapshots, I mean. I led on into the garden, a chair in one hand, the other hand filled with forceps of various sorts, my knees knocking together disgracefully. The poor old Chinaman came second, and he was shaking, too. Charmian and Martin brought up the rear, armed with kodaks. We dived under the avocado trees, threaded our way through the coconut palms, and came on a spot that satisfied Martin's photographic eye.

I looked at the tooth, and then discovered that I could not remember anything about the teeth I had pulled from the skull five months previously. Did it have one prong? two prongs? or three prongs? What was left of the part that showed appeared very crumbly, and I knew that I should have to take hold of the tooth deep down in the gum. It was very necessary that I should know how many prongs that tooth had. Back to the house I went for the book on teeth. The poor old victim looked like photographs I had seen of fellow countrymen of his, criminals, on their knees, waiting the stroke of the beheading sword.

"Don't let him get away," I cautioned to Martin. "I want that tooth."

"I sure won't," he replied with enthusiasm, from behind his camera. "I want that photograph."

For the first time I felt sorry for the Chinaman. Though the book did not tell me anything about pulling teeth, it was all right, for on one page I found drawings of all the teeth, including their prongs and how they were set in the jaw. Then came the pursuit of the forceps. I had seven pairs, but was in doubt as to which pair I should use. I did not want any mistake. As I turned the hardware over with rattle and clang, the poor victim began to lose his grip and to turn a greenish yellow around the gills. He complained about the sun, but that was necessary for the photograph, and he had to stand it. I fitted the forceps around the tooth, and the patient shivered and began to wilt.

"Ready?" I called to Martin.

"All ready," he answered.

I gave a pull. Ye gods! The tooth was loose. Out it came on the instant. I was jubilant as I held it aloft in the forceps.

"Put it back, please, oh, put it back," Martin pleaded. "You were too quick for me."

And the poor old Chinaman sat there while I put the tooth back and pulled over. Martin snapped the camera. The deed was done. Elation? Pride? No hunter was ever prouder of his first pronged buck than I was of that three-pronged tooth. I did it! I did it! With my own hands and a pair of forceps I did it, to say nothing of the forgotten memories of the dead man's skull.

My next case was a Tahitian sailor. He was a small man, in a state of collapse from long days and nights of jumping toothache. I lanced the gums first. I didn't know how to lance them, but I lanced them just the same. It was a long pull and a strong pull. The man was a hero. He groaned and moaned, and I thought he was going to faint. But he kept his mouth open and let me pull. And then it came.

After that I was ready to meet all comers—just the proper state of mind for a Waterloo. And it came. Its name was Tomi. He was a strapping giant of a heathen with a bad reputation. He was addicted to deeds of violence. Among other things he had beaten two of his wives to death with his fists. His father and mother had been naked cannibals. When he sat down and I put the forceps into his mouth, he was nearly as tall as I was standing up. Big men, prone to violence, very often have a streak of fat in their makeup, so I was doubtful of him. Charmian grabbed one arm and Warren grabbed the other. Then the tug of war began. The instant the forceps closed down on the tooth, his jaws closed down on the forceps. Also, both his hands flew up and gripped my pulling hand. I held on, and he held on. Charmian and Warren held on. We wrestled all about the shop.

It was three against one, and my hold on an aching tooth was certainly a foul one; but in spite of the handicap he got away with us. The forceps slipped off, banging and grinding along against his upper teeth with a nerve-scraping sound. Out of his mouth flew the forceps, and he rose up in the air with a bloodcurdling yell. The three of us fell back. We expected to be massacred. But that howling savage of sanguinary reputation sank back in the chair. He held his head in both his hands, and groaned and groaned and groaned. Nor would he listen to reason. I was a quack. My painless tooth-extraction was a delusion and a snare and a low advertising dodge. I was so anxious to get that tooth that I was almost ready to bribe him. But that went against my professional pride and I let him depart with the tooth still intact, the only case on record up to date of failure on my part when once I had got a grip. Since then I have never let a tooth go by me. Only the other day I volunteered to beat up three days to windward to pull a woman missionary's tooth. I expect, before the voyage of the *Snark* is finished, to be doing bridgework and putting on gold crowns.

I don't know whether they are yaws or not—a physician in Fiji told me they were, and a missionary in the Solomons told me they were not; but at any rate I can vouch for the fact that they are most uncomfortable. It was my luck to ship in Tahiti a French sailor, who, when we got to sea, proved to be afflicted with a vile skin disease. The *Snark* was too small and too much of a family party to permit retaining him on board; but perforce, until we could reach land and discharge him, it was up to me to doctor him. I read up the books and proceeded to treat him, taking care afterwards always to use a thorough antiseptic wash. When we reached Tutuila, far from getting rid of him, the port doctor declared a quarantine against him and refused to allow him ashore. But at Apia, Samoa, I managed to ship him off on a steamer to New Zealand. Here at Apia my ankles were badly bitten by mosquitoes, and I confess to having scratched the bites—as I had a thousand times before. By the time I reached the island of Savaii, a small sore had developed on the hollow of my instep. I thought it was due to chafe and to acid fumes from the hot lava over which I tramped. An application of salve would cure it—so I thought. The salve did heal it over, whereupon an astonishing inflammation set in, the new skin came off, and a larger sore was exposed. This was repeated many times. Each time new skin formed, an inflammation followed, and the circumference of the sore increased. I was puzzled and frightened. All my life my skin had been famous for its healing powers, yet here was something that would not heal. Instead, it was daily eating up more skin, while it had eaten down clear through the skin and was eating up the muscle itself.

By this time the *Snark* was at sea on her way to Fiji. I remembered the French sailor, and for the first time became seriously alarmed. Four other similar sores had appeared — or ulcers, rather, and the pain of them kept me awake at night. All my plans were made to lay up the *Snark* in Fiji and get away on the first steamer to Australia and professional M.D.'s. In the meantime, in my amateur M.D. way, I did my best. I read through all the medical works on board. Not a line nor a word could I find descriptive of my affliction. I brought common horse sense to bear on the problem. Here were malignant and excessively active ulcers that were eating me up. There was an organic and corroding poison at work. Two things I concluded must be done. First, some agent must be found to destroy the poison. Secondly, the ulcers could not possibly heal from the outside in; they must heal from the inside out. I decided to fight the poison with corrosive sublimate. The very name of it struck me as vicious. Talk of fighting fire with fire! I was being consumed by a corrosive poison, and it appealed to my fancy to fight it with another corrosive poison. After several days I alternated dressings of corrosive sublimate with dressings of peroxide of hydrogen. And behold, by the time we reached Fiji four of the five ulcers were healed, while the remaining one was no bigger than a pea.

I now felt fully qualified to treat yaws. Likewise I had a wholesome respect for them. Not so the rest of the crew of the *Snark*. In their case, seeing was not believing. One and all, they had seen my dreadful predicament; and all of them, I am convinced, had a subconscious certitude that their own superb constitutions and glorious personalities would never allow lodgment of so vile a poison in their carcasses as my anaemic constitution and mediocre personality had allowed to lodge in mine. At Port Resolution, in the New Hebrides, Martin elected to walk barefooted in the bush and returned on board with many cuts and abrasions, especially on his shins.

"You'd better be careful," I warned him. "I'll mix up some corrosive sublimate for you to wash those cuts with. An ounce of prevention, you know."

But Martin smiled a superior smile. Though he did not say so, I nevertheless was given to understand that he was not as other men (I was the only man he could possibly have had reference to), and that in a couple of days his cuts would be healed. He also read me a dissertation upon the peculiar purity of his blood and his remarkable healing powers. I felt quite humble when he was done with me. Evidently I was different from other men in so far as purity of blood was concerned.

Nakata, the cabin boy, while ironing one day, mistook the calf of his leg for the ironing block and accumulated a burn three inches in length and half an inch wide. He, too, smiled the superior smile when I offered him corrosive sublimate and reminded him of my own cruel experience. I was given to understand, with all due suavity and courtesy, that no matter what was the matter with my blood, his number-one, Japanese, Port-Arthur blood was all right and scornful of the festive microbe.

Wada, the cook, took part in a disastrous landing of the launch, when he had to leap overboard and fend the launch off the beach in a smashing surf. By means of shells and coral he cut his legs and feet up beautifully. I offered him the corrosive sublimate bottle. Once again I suffered the superior smile and was given to understand that his blood was the same blood that had licked Russia and was going to lick the United States someday, and that if his blood wasn't able to cure a few trifling cuts, he'd commit hari-kari in sheer disgrace.

From all of which I concluded that an amateur M.D. is without honor on his own vessel, even if he has cured himself. The rest of the crew had begun to look upon me as a sort of mild monomaniac on the question of sores and sublimate. Just because my blood was impure was no reason that

I should think everybody else's was. I made no more overtures. Time and microbes were with me, and all I had to do was wait.

"I think there's some dirt in those cuts," Martin said tentatively, after several days. "I'll wash them out and then they'll be all right," he added, after I had refused to rise to the bait.

Two more days passed, but the cuts did not pass, and I caught Martin soaking his feet and legs in a pail of hot water.

"Nothing like hot water," he proclaimed enthusiastically. "It beats all the dope the doctors ever put up. These sores will be all right in the morning."

But in the morning he wore a troubled look, and I knew that the hour of my triumph approached.

"I think I *will* try some of that medicine," he announced later on in the day. "Not that I think it'll do much good," he qualified, "but I'll just give it a try anyway."

Next came the proud blood of Japan to beg medicine for its illustrious sores, while I heaped coals of fire on all their houses by explaining in minute and sympathetic detail the treatment that should be given. Nakata followed instructions implicitly, and day by day his sores grew smaller. Wada was apathetic, and cured less readily. But Martin still doubted, and because he did not cure immediately, he developed the theory that while doctor's dope was all right, it did not follow that the same kind of dope was efficacious with everybody. As for himself, corrosive sublimate had no effect. Besides, how did I know that it was the right stuff? I had had no experience. Just because I happened to get well while using it was not proof that it had played any part in the cure. There were such things as coincidences. Without doubt there was a dope that would cure the sores, and when he ran across a real doctor he would find what that dope was and get some of it.

About this time we arrived in the Solomon Islands. No physician would ever recommend the group for invalids or sanitariums. I spent but little time there ere I really and for the first time in my life comprehended how frail and unstable is human tissue. Our first anchorage was Port Mary, on the island of Santa Anna. The one lone white man, a trader,

came alongside. Tom Butler was his name, and he was a beautiful example of what the Solomons can do to a strong man. He lay in his whaleboat with the helplessness of a dying man. No smile and little intelligence illumined his face. He was a sombre death's-head, too far gone to grin. He, too, had yaws, big ones. We were compelled to drag him over the rail of the *Snark*. He said that his health was good, that he had not had the fever for some time, and that with the exception of his arm he was all right and trim. His arm appeared to be paralyzed. Paralysis he rejected with scorn. He had had it before, and recovered. It was a common native disease on Santa Anna, he said, as he was helped down the companion ladder, his dead arm dropping, bump-bump, from step to step. He was certainly the ghastliest guest we ever entertained, and we've had not a few lepers and elephantiasis victims on board.

Martin inquired about yaws, for here was a man who ought to know. He certainly did know, if we could judge by his scarred arms and legs and by the live ulcers that corroded in the midst of the scars. Oh, one got used to yaws, quoth Tom Butler. They were never really serious until they had eaten deep into the flesh. Then they attacked the walls of the arteries, the arteries burst, and there was a funeral. Several of the natives had recently died that way ashore. But what did it matter? If it wasn't yaws, it was something else—in the Solomons.

I noticed that from this moment Martin displayed a swiftly increasing interest in his own yaws. Dosings with corrosive sublimate were more frequent, while, in conversation, he began to revert with growing enthusiasm to the clean climate of Kansas and all other things Kansan. Charmian and I thought that California was a little bit of all right. Henry swore by Rapa, and Tehei staked all on Bora Bora for his own blood's sake; while Wada and Nakata sang the sanitary paean of Japan.

One evening, as the *Snark* worked around the southern end of the island of Ugi, looking for a reputed anchorage, a Church of England missionary, a Mr. Drew, bound in his whaleboat for the coast of San Cristoval, came alongside and stopped for dinner Martin, his legs swathed in Red Cross

bandages till they looked like a mummy's, turned the conversation upon yaws. Yes, said Mr. Drew, they were quite common in the Solomons. All white men caught them.

"And have you had them?" Martin demanded, in the soul of him quite shocked that a Church of England missionary could possess so vulgar an affliction.

Mr. Drew nodded his head and added that not only had he had them, but at that moment he was doctoring several.

"What do you use on them?" Martin asked like a flash.

My heart almost stood still waiting the answer. By that answer my professional medical prestige stood or fell. Martin, I could see, was quite sure it was going to fall. And then the answer—O blessed answer!

"Corrosive sublimate," said Mr. Drew.

Martin gave in handsomely, I'll admit, and I am confident that at that moment, if I had asked permission to pull one of his teeth, he would not have denied me

All white men in the Solomons catch yaws, and every cut or abrasion practically means another yaw. Every man I met had had them, and nine out of ten had active ones. There was but one exception, a young fellow who had been in the islands five months, who had come down with fever ten days after he arrived, and who had since then been down so often with fever that he had had neither time nor opportunity for yaws.

Every one on the *Snark* except Charmian came down with yaws. Hers was the same egotism that Japan and Kansas had displayed. She ascribed her immunity to the pureness of her blood, and as the days went by she ascribed it more often and more loudly to the pureness of her blood. Privately I ascribed her immunity to the fact that, being a woman, she escaped most of the cuts and abrasions to which we hardworking men were subject in the course of working the *Snark* around the world. I did not tell her so. You see, I did not wish to bruise her ego with brutal facts. Being an M.D., if only an amateur one, I knew more about the disease than she, and I knew that time was my ally. But alas, I abused my ally when it dealt a charming little yaw on the shin. So quickly did I apply antiseptic treatment that the yaw was cured before she was convinced that she had one. Again, as an M.D., I was without honor on my own vessel; and, worse than that, I was charged with having tried to mislead her into the belief that she had had a yaw. The pureness of her blood was more rampant than ever, and I poked my nose into my navigation books and kept quiet. And then came the day. We were cruising along the coast of Malaita at the time.

"What's that abaft your ankle-bone?" said I.

"Nothing," said she.

"All right," said I; "but put some corrosive sublimate on it just the same. And some two or three weeks from now, when it is well and you have a scar that you will carry to your grave, just forget about the purity of your blood and your ancestral history and tell me what you think about yaws anyway."

It was as large as a silver dollar, that yaw, and it took all of three weeks to heal. There were times when Charmian could not walk because of the hurt of it; and there were times upon times when she explained that abaft the ankle-bone was the most painful place to have a yaw. I explained, in turn, that, never having experienced a yaw in that locality, I was driven to conclude the hollow of the instep was the most painful place for yaw-culture. We left it to Martin, who disagreed with both of us and proclaimed passionately that the only truly painful place was the shin. No wonder horse racing is so popular.

But yaws lose their novelty after a time. At the present moment of writing I have five yaws on my hands and three more on my shin. Charmian has one on each side of her right instep. Tehei is frantic with his. Martin's latest shin-cultures have eclipsed his earlier ones. And Nakata has several score casually eating away at his tissue. But the history of the *Snark* in the Solomons has been the history of every ship since the early discoverers. From the *Sailing Directions* I quote the following:

"The crews of vessels remaining any considerable time in the Solomons find wounds and sores liable to change into malignant ulcers."

Nor on the question of fever were the *Sailing Directions* any more encouraging, for in them I read:

"New arrivals are almost certain sooner or later to suffer from fever. The natives are also subject to it. The number of deaths among the whites in the year 1897 amounted to 9 among a population of 50."

Some of these deaths, however, were accidental.

Nakata was the first to come down with fever. This occurred at Penduffryn. Wada and Henry followed him. Charmian surrendered next. I managed to escape for a couple of months; but when I was bowled over, Martin sympathetically joined me several days later. Out of the seven of us all told, Tehei is the only one who has escaped; but his sufferings from nostalgia are worse than fever. Nakata, as usual, followed instructions faithfully, so that by the end of his third attack he could take a two hours' sweat, consume thirty or forty grains of quinine, and be weak but all right at the end of twenty-four hours.

Wada and Henry, however, were tougher patients with which to deal. In the first place, Wada got in a bad funk. He was of the firm conviction that his star had set and that the Solomons would receive his bones. He saw that life about him was cheap. At Penduffryn he saw the ravages of dysentery, and, unfortunately for him, he saw one victim carried out on a strip of galvanized sheet-iron and dumped without coffin or funeral into a hole in the ground. Everybody had fever, everybody had dysentery, everybody had everything. Death was common. Here today and gone tomorrow—and Wada forgot all about today and made up his mind that tomorrow had come.

He was careless of his ulcers, neglected to sublimate them, and by uncontrolled scratching spread them all over his body. Nor would he follow instructions with fever, and, as a result, would be down five days at a time, when a day would have been sufficient. Henry, who is a strapping giant of a man, was just as bad. He refused point blank to take quinine, on the ground that years before he had had fever and that the pills the doctor gave him were of different size and color from the quinine tablets I offered him. So Henry joined Wada.

But I fooled the pair of them, and dosed them with their own medicine, which was faith-cure. They had faith in their funk that they were going to die. I slammed a lot of quinine down their throats and took their temperature. It was the first time I had used my medicine-chest thermometer, and I quickly discovered that it was worthless, that it had been produced for profit and not for service. If I had let on to my two patients that the thermometer did not work, there would have been two funerals in short order. Their temperature I swear was 105°. I solemnly made one and then the other smoke the thermometer, allowed an expression of satisfaction to irradiate my countenance, and joyfully told them that their temperature was 94°. Then I slammed more quinine down their throats, told them that any sickness or weakness they might experience would be due to the quinine, and left them to get well. And they did get well, Wada in spite of himself. If a man can die through a misapprehension, is there any immorality in making him live through a misapprehension?

Commend me the white race when it comes to grit and surviving. One of our two Japanese and both our Tahitians funked and had to be slapped on the back and cheered up and dragged along by main strength toward life. Charmian and Martin took their afflictions cheerfully, made the least of them, and moved with calm certitude along the way of life. When Wada and Henry were convinced that they were going to die, the funeral atmosphere was too much for Tehei, who prayed dolorously and cried for hours at a time. Martin, on the other hand, cursed and got well, and Charmian groaned and made plans for what she was going to do when she got well again.

Charmian had been raised a vegetarian and a sanitarian. Her Aunt Netta, who brought her up and who lived in a healthful climate, did not believe in drugs. Neither did Charmian. Besides, drugs disagreed with her. Their effects were worse than the ills they were supposed to alleviate. But she listened to the argument in favor of quinine, accepted it as the lesser evil, and in consequence had shorter, less painful, and less frequent attacks of fever. We encountered a Mr. Caulfeild, a missionary, whose two predecessors had died after less than six months' residence in the Solomons. Like them he had been a firm believer in homeopathy, until after his first fever, whereupon, unlike them, he made a grand slideback to allopathy and quinine, catching fever and carrying on his Gospel work.

But poor Wada! The straw that broke the cook's back was when Charmian and I took him along on a cruise to the cannibal island of Malaita, in a small yacht, on the deck of which the captain had been murdered half a year before. *Kai-kai* means to eat, and Wada was sure he was going to be *kai-kai'd.* We went about heavily armed, our vigilance was unremitting, and when we went for a bath in the mouth of a freshwater stream, black boys, armed with rifles, did sentry duty about us. We encountered English war vessels burning and shelling villages in punishment for murders. Natives with prices on their heads sought shelter on board of us. Murder stalked abroad in the land. In out-of-the-way places we received warnings from friendly savages of impending attacks. Our vessel owed two heads to Malaita, which were liable to be collected any time. Then, to cap it all, we were wrecked on a reef, and with rifles in one hand warned the canoes of wreckers off while with the other hand we toiled to save the ship. All of which was too much for Wada, who went daffy, and who finally quit the *Snark* on the island of Ysabel, going ashore for good in a driving rainstorm, between two attacks of fever, while threatened with pneumonia. If he escapes being *kai-kai'd,* and if he can survive sores and fever which are riotous ashore, he can expect, if he is reasonably lucky, to get away from that place to the adjacent island in anywhere from six to eight weeks. He never did think much of my medicine, despite the fact that I successfully and at the first trial pulled two aching teeth for him.

The *Snark* has been a hospital for months, and I confess that we are getting used to it. At Meringe Lagoon, where we careened and cleaned the *Snark's* copper, there were times when only one man of us was able to go into the water, while the three white men on the plantation ashore were all down with fever. At the moment of writing this we are lost at sea somewhere northeast of Ysabel and trying vainly to find Lord Howe Island, which is an atoll that cannot be sighted unless one is on top of it. The chronometer has gone wrong. The sun does not shine anyway, nor can I get a star observation at night, and we have had nothing but squalls and rain for days and days. The cook is gone. Nakata, who has been trying to be both cook and cabin boy, is down on his back with fever. Martin is just up from fever, and going down again. Charmian, whose fever has become periodical, is looking up in her date book to find when the next attack will be. Henry has begun to eat quinine in an expectant mood. And, since my attacks hit me with the suddenness of bludgeon blows, I do not know from moment to moment when I shall be brought down. By a mistake we gave our last flour away to some white men who did not have any flour. We don't know when we'll make land. Our Solomon sores are worse than ever, and more numerous. The corrosive sublimate was accidentally left ashore at Penduffryn; the peroxide of hydrogen is exhausted; and I am experimenting with boracic acid, lysol, and antiphlogystine. At any rate, if I fail in becoming a reputable M.D., it won't be from lack of practice.

P.S. It is now two weeks since the foregoing was written, and Tehei, the only immune on board, has been down ten days with far severer fever than any of us and is still down His temperature has been repeatedly as high as 104, and his pulse 115.

P.S. At sea, between Tasman atoll and Manning Straits.

Tehei's attack developed into blackwater fever—the severest form of malarial fever, which, the doctor-book assures me, is due to some outside infection as well. Having pulled him through his fever, I am now at my wit's end, for he has lost his wits altogether. I am rather recent in practice to take up the cure of insanity. This makes the second lunacy case on this short voyage.

P.S. Some day I shall write a book (for the profession), and entitle it, "Around the World on the Hospital Ship *Snark*." Even our pets have not escaped. We sailed from Meringe Lagoon with two, an Irish terrier and a white cockatoo. The terrier fell down the cabin companionway and lamed its nigh hind leg, then repeated the maneuver and lamed its off fore leg. At the present moment it has but two legs to walk on. Fortunately, they are on opposite sides and ends, so that she can still dot and carry two. The cockatoo was crushed under the cabin skylight and had to be killed.

This was our first funeral—though for that matter, the several chickens we had, and which would have made welcome broth for the convalescents, flew overboard and were drowned. Only the cockroaches flourish. Neither illness nor accident ever befalls them, and they grow larger and more carnivorous day by day, gnawing our fingernails and toenails while we sleep.

P.S. Charmian is having another bout with fever. Martin, in despair, has taken to horse-doctoring his yaws with bluestone and to blessing the Solomons. As for me, in addition to navigating, doctoring, and writing short stories, I am far from well. With the exception of the insanity cases, I'm the worst off on board. I shall catch the next steamer to Australia and go on the operating table. Among my minor afflictions, I may mention a new and mysterious one. For the past week my hands have been swelling as with dropsy. It is only by a painful effort that I can close them. A pull on a rope is excruciating. The sensations are like those that accompany severe chilblains. Also, the skin is peeling off both hands at an alarming rate, besides which the new skin underneath is growing hard and thick. The doctor-book fails to mention this disease. Nobody knows what it is.

P.S. Well, anyway, I've cured the chronometer. After knocking about the sea for eight squally, rainy days, most of the time hove to, I succeeded in catching a partial observation of the sun at midday. From this I worked up my latitude, then headed by log to the latitude of Lord Howe, and ran both that latitude and the island down together. Here I tested the chronometer by longitude sights and found it something like three minutes out. Since each minute is equivalent to fifteen miles, the total error can be appreciated. By repeated observations at Lord Howe I rated the chronometer, finding it to have a daily losing error of seven-tenths of a second. Now it happens that a year ago, when we sailed from Hawaii, that selfsame chronometer had that selfsame losing error of seven-tenths of a second. Since that error was faithfully added every day, and since that error, as proved by my observations at Lord Howe, has not changed, then what under the sun made that chronometer all of a sudden accelerate and catch up with itself three minutes?

Can such things be? Expert watchmakers say no; but I say that they have never done any expert watchmaking and watch-rating in the Solomons. That it is the climate is my only diagnosis. At any rate, I have successfully doctored the chronometer, even if I have failed with the lunacy cases and with Martin's yaws.

P.S. Martin has just tried burnt alum, and is blessing the Solomons more fervently than ever.

P.S. Between Manning Straits and Pavuvu Islands. Henry has developed rheumatism in his back, ten skins have peeled off my hands and the eleventh is now peeling, while Tehei is more lunatic than ever and day and night prays God not to kill him. Also, Nakata and I are slashing away at fever again. And finally up to date, Nakata last evening had an attack of ptomaine poisoning, and we spent half the night pulling him through.

Genevieve Taggard

The Plague

Genevieve Taggard (1894–1948), born at Waitsburg, Washington, was two years old when her parents went to the Hawaiian Islands to teach there in the public schools. Up to the time she entered Punahou High School in Honolulu, her playmates were almost entirely children of the various groups that predominate in the islands—Hawaiians, Chinese, Japanese, and Portuguese. She taught for a year in a rural school on the island of Oahu and then in 1914 left to study at the University of California. Later she taught at several colleges for women and published half a dozen volumes of verse. The following sketch, drawn from memory of her life in Hawaii, shows an equal mastery of prose.

ONE evening my father came in late to supper just as we had lighted the kerosene lamp and put it in the middle of the cleared dining table. He had been off seeing the superintendent about building the new school.

"Hayashida is sick," said my mother, "and wants to see you before you go to bed."

My father took a little hand lamp and went out into the tropic blackness, down the latticed walk to Hayashida's little whitewashed house, where he lived with Kiko. The screen door banged after him, and he was gone a long time, while I watched the mealy damp baby moths who came under the lamp shade and got cooked on the kerosene surface of the silver lamp. Then the screen door closed lightly, and my father came back holding his lamp up.

"Mama," he said as he blew out the light and stood some distance from us, "Hayashida has a bubo under his arm as big as an egg."

He washed himself with kerosene and called up the doctor on the telephone, sitting down as he waited for a connection. Mother sent us to bed. We didn't know what a bubo was.

The next day the doctors—about four of them and several health officials—came to see Hayashida. They told my father to say that Hayashida had measles and dismiss the school indefinitely. This my father did, because he had to, although he hated to stand up before all his schoolchildren and tell a lie. Hayashida besides being our Japanese boy was the janitor of the school. He had swept it out on Monday afternoon just before he was taken sick.

The neighbors knew what they knew—the measles story wasn't very convincing. The doctors went in and out of the little whitewashed house where Hayashida lived, and Kiko could be seen standing limp against one window—all her lovely oiled hair pressed against the glass. We children loved Hayashida and Kiko. He was a big raw-boned Japanese, gaunt and yellow, and very merry. He had come to us right off a plantation when he couldn't speak any English.

Only Kiko could speak, because she had been a silkworm girl in Tokyo. Under the lattice of the passion vine over our door they stood beside each other and wished to come and work for us. Hayashida took care of our huge garden and the lawn; he clipped the hedges and swept the walks, and all afternoon long, while he ran the sprinklers and changed them, he kept our swings going too, and carried us around on his shoulders. Once a centipede crawled up inside his blue denim pants and he caught hold of the cloth and called to us to look while he squeezed it to death, so that it wouldn't bite him. He also sang very sweet songs to himself in a high silly voice all the time he worked.

Now with a great bang, we were overridden with doctors who tramped into our house and brushed past us children as if we didn't even exist.

"You've got to fumigate," said one. "How solid is this house anyway?" and he poked at the new wallpaper and made a hole. "I thought so—built out of sticks," he said.

I wanted to yell at him for that; to bang him on the head; to tell him to get out of my house. While some of the strange men were talking to my mother, the same one who had broken the paper went over and yanked down the curtains.

"Take down all the hangings," he ordered my father.

Then the death wagon came for Hayashida. They carried him out with masks over their faces and gloves on, and little Kiko walked sorrowfully after him in a kimono which she had ceased to wear since she lived with us. Now she reverted to a kimono, and carried a few belongings in a little handkerchief. She sat at his head in the wagon, and a few children were there to see what was happening. My father tried not to cry; so did we all. Hayashida was going for good. No one ever got well of the plague.

"Good-bye, Hayashida," said my father, "you have been a good boy with us."

Hayashida sat up in the wagon.

"Will you take care of Kiko if I die, Mr. Taggard?"

"Yes, Hayashida."

"If I get well, can I have my old place back?"

"Yes, Hayashida."

So he went away. The doctors hurried him off to the receiving station and he was put in quarantine. Now two health officials fastened on us.

"Take your children and go away for three or four days while we fumigate. Go anywhere. There is no danger. You haven't been exposed. Go visit friends. Don't let anybody know. There mustn't be a scare. This is only the sixth case. We must keep it quiet."

"I won't go to a friend's house," replied my indignant mother. "Where shall we go? There isn't a place in the world."

"You've got to get out for about four days," they said savagely, wishing she wouldn't quibble with them.

I started to take down some dresses.

"Little girl," one of them bawled at me. "Don't touch those things. Get out of the house in the fresh air. You can't take anything with you."

So we went, headachy and driven, forlorn in our old clothes, about four o'clock, knowing that all the neighbors down the long road to the streetcar were looking out from behind the doors and whispering that there was Plague in our family.

The streetcars go very fast in the Islands, because there are such long stretches. They are open—a row of seats and a roof. On these flying platforms you go across rice fields and wait at switches for the other car; you climb a hill with a drone, and then branch off into Palama where the Japanese live.

At four o'clock on a school day it seemed strange to be riding through Palama. Dimly, the reason for this ride—the distinction of having Plague in the family, the awful importance of an event that seizes you the way a cat does a rat, the very great satisfaction of having something happen that is huge and terrible, that may end in darker, grimmer events—all this was in our minds as we went through Palama, looking at the Japanese and Chinese, the children, the withered women in their flat-chested black sateen coats and earringed ears. On all the faces that turned up to our car as it danged its bell through the crowded streets and down across the bridge, I extended the now gently painful knowledge that Hayashida would die, that our house would be fumigated and that my head ached and my feet were cold.

On we went through Honolulu, past the hardware store where the Sherwin Williams paint folders were tucked in little boxes—(we always helped ourselves to the little booklets with their shiny inches of blue and tan); past our little church looking brown and dusty on a weekday with the shutters closed and the bougainvillea vine next it blooming cerise in the heat; past the Palace, the Opera House, the statue of Kamehameha, where the idiot Portuguese boy stood all day, worshiping and rubbing his hands; past the rich people's houses on the way to Waikiki.

Waikiki was our heaven always. It was always reserved for the greatest occasions of joy. A sharp turn—our car was running wildly over the swamp in the stiff breeze from the sea, with Diamond Head lifted up, brown as a niggertoe nut, running parallel with our track. Another curve and wind and a switch, and the smell of salt, and the first turn of a wave, between two hedges as we started up again, running headlong into Diamond Head,—headlong for the place where the water came into the arm of the old brown-purple mountain.

(Oh, the sea, the sea, the sea, the sea, the waves; the high clouds; the bright water, the crazy foam on the surf away out, the blue limpid lovely empty water. Oh, the sea.) So I cried to myself, and got up to stand on the seat.

"Sit down," said my mother wearily. She had a headache, I could tell.

We sat fixed, waiting for the great joy of seeing it suddenly, as we knew we would—the mountain, the surf running in with its arched neck and blowing mane, the dizzy blue water level on the sand. There it was. Oh, sea, sea. My brother and sister wouldn't sit still. My father cheered up, and lifted his head and his dreamy gaze to focus on it; my mother sat dully, because her head ached so. I could tell, by the narrowed slits of her eyes. She didn't look. The sun hit the water and the sunlight hit you as it shot off the surface. Black things danced in the air. It hurt between the eyes to look at it.

We got off at the Waikiki Inn and my mother and father hurried ahead. We ran for the sand.

They came out of the office in a minute, looking very embarrassed and troubled and trying to look untroubled. A Japanese boy led them to a little cottage under some vines and unlocked the door. My mother looked in and then came down to get us.

"You can't go in the water today. I'm sorry. Get out right away. You look like little wild children. You mustn't get wet," she said in a lower tone when we came, holding up our skirts to our waists, all wet-legged from the first tumbled wave. "Mother doesn't dare let you get in the water. One of us may have it."

With that her face looked so terrified and in such dull pain that we came limping in, letting down our dresses, and picking up our shoes and stockings. As we walked away from sand to grass lawn, the sea talked and roared and mumbled and swished at our backs. We didn't dare even turn around.

That night I was sick. The black dots in the air turned to balls of fire; the terrible sunlight on the water, the terrible water we couldn't go in, that became noisy torment, throbbing like the heart in illness; fever that took the bones and broke them and wrenched the stomach. My mother was sick too. We were sick together. The others slept. I lay under the thick mosquito net as if I were as wide as the Pacific Ocean and the fever took one arm off to the east, the other to the west; my legs stretched into dimness, I gazed flat upward, fixed, at some immensity—I immense, and facing immensity. The kerosene lamp purred on the table, a yellow torment. My mother sat retching with a sick headache. Now and then she would come and bow her head on the bed outside the mosquito net and say, "Oh, Genevieve, will this night never be over?" and then she would vomit again.

The sea rose outside in a great wind. A hard tropic tree scratched and clanged on the iron roof of the cottage. It was utterly black except for the torment of the little flame in the lamp. The ocean broke outside so near, the same wave sounds as in daylight, but so interminable at night, and no one to hear it, but us, me and my mother. The waves hit the shore like a blow on a wound; the lamp burned in its chimney stifling the air, never wiggling, just burning. Horror, the black death!

She fanned me and called out that I was her first born, and rubbed the wet hair from my head and chafed my feet. Her hand on my legs made them limited again at the bottom of the bed, not so long that they had no feet as a moment before. "Oh, mother, will this night never end?"

It ended—fear and a sick headache and a little fever—that was all. And I did not die except in some experience of the mind.

Pacific Commercial Advertiser

The Lanai Horror

Although the Hawaiian people have always been kindly and gentle as a group, and even in the heat of battle seldom tortured their foes, they were victims of a cult of sorcery that sometimes caused outbreaks of fiendish fame. Such an episode took place as late as February 12, 1892, on the smaller island of Lanai.

The *kahuna anaana* or sorcerer could be either male or female. His professional calling included murder, in which he was guided by a familiar demon. "He usually does his victims to death by secret administration of poison, or quite as commonly, perhaps, by some occult influence upon them, possibly of a hypnotic sort," an editorial ran in the July issue of *The Friend*, a Protestant missionary journal founded in Honolulu in 1843. "He first establishes himself in business by killing one or more of his nearest relations. This creates for him a reputation of remorseless truculence, which makes him greatly feared, and ensures large emoluments. All these murders he professes to execute by means of his demon, often claiming to have produced deaths in which he really had no hand. Sometimes he overdoes the business, and has to fly before the wrath of the outraged people whom he has held in terror. This is very rare; their fear of his demon masters their anger."

The behavior of Pulolo, the sorceress of Lanai, follows the classic formula. Again to quote the article in *The Friend*, "A significant fact is that Pulolo learned her trade of sorceress during a residence of some years in this city. Under the fostering patronage of royalty for a little more than thirty years, Honolulu has grown to be a headquarters of superstition and a chief seminary of sorcery. This began when Prince Lot's agent Kapu issued printed licenses to about three hundred kahunas or native doctors, with schedules of fees ranging up to fifty dollars. These kahunas rarely knew much of real remedies. Their chief stock in trade was the superstitious fears of the people, who would hire their incantations to propitiate or exorcise the evil demons that made them ill. In order to educate and develop those fears, they immediately formed private classes in idolatry and sorcery throughout the kingdom. Since then this culture of diabolism has gone steadily on. Fresh accessions of force were largely made to it during the late reign."

The story of the Lanai outbreak may best be told by quoting from successive issues of the *Pacific Commercial Advertiser,* a Honolulu newspaper which ran weekly from 1856 to 1888 and resumed publication daily in 1882. A sequel to the event described is to be found in *The Friend* for October, 1892: "The scene of the Pulolo murders and *hoomanamana* frenzy is at the steamer landing at the western end of the island. A curse rests on the place. The houses that stand there have been abandoned, and the place where the killing was done and where the bodies and the house were given to the flames is now but a bit of sand marked off by the stumps of the fence posts."

February 17, 1892.

THE steamer *Mokolii,* which arrived on Tuesday, brings a strange story from Lanai. At the quiet little hamlet of Awalua, the landing at Lanai, there stood near the shore a grass hut, occupied by a family of about ten persons, one of them an old Hawaiian supposed to be crazy *(pupule).* A female kahuna attended the old gentleman. During the evening of the 12th inst., several bowls of awa were consumed by the family, the children included, to appease the *aumakua* deity.

After the awa, it is conjectured that the entire party went to sleep, with the exception of the female kahuna, the spirit not allowing her to rest until the aumakua had brought the desired relief. The story goes that she waited until after midnight, when the aumakua, continuing conspicuous by his absence, she lost patience and determined to hasten the steps of the dilatory god by the application of fire to the house. The flames woke the sleepers, who rushed out of the burning hut. When nothing was left but ashes, it turned out that a young man of twenty was missing.

And now comes the strangest part of the story. When the steamer *Mokolii* reached Lanai, an astonishing sight met their gaze. The once well-beloved occupants of the hut at Awalua were running wild on the rocks, clad in nature's attire. The whole family had been seized with real or apparent insanity. When approached, they appeared to have lost all means of communication, and no intelligible account of their condition could be obtained. When the *Mokolii* left for Honolulu, Hon. F. H. Hayselden of Lanai had sent a boat to Lahaina to fetch Deputy Sheriff Makalua to investigate the matter. According to the chief officer's story, it seems that the unfortunate young man who perished in the flames had a pretty wife, to whom another native in the same house had taken a fancy, and the belief is that the rest of the family, not being in sympathy with the husband set the house on fire, with the intention of murdering him.

This is as much of this strange eventful history as has yet reached Honolulu. A family all going crazy at one fell swoop in an event unparalleled since the days of the Bacchic frenzy.

February 22, 1892.

A horrible outbreak of heathenish superstition has occurred on the island of Lanai, leading to deeds of the most frightful violence, to the murder of a man, a woman, and a child, and the savage torturing of still another unfortunate. The first rumors of these shocking events reached Honolulu on the *Mokolii* last Tuesday. Yesterday the *Kinau* brought confirmation of these rumors, together with twelve prisoners, an entire family all charged with murder, some of them on three indictments. The names of the twelve [*sic*] persons are as follows: Kaaaio; Kala; Keliikuewa; Keola; Puulolo (wahine); Nawai (wahine); Kanae (wahine); Kahikina; Kanoenoe (wahine); and Kalakaa.

The murdered persons are the three following: Kula (liilii) [infant], six years; Puni (wahine), sister; and Kaholokai.

There are three charges of murder: (1) Puulolo (wahine) is charged with the murder of Puni (wahine); (2) all twelve are charged with the murder of Kala [*sic:* Kula], (liilii); and (3) Kahikina, Puulolo, Kakaio ([*sic:* Kaaaio], Kala, Keola, and Kealake [*sic:* Kalakaa] are charged with the murder of Kaholokai.

The police are cautious in their utterances, and it is difficult to ascertain the course of the whole dreadful history. Much of it will not be known until the trial; some of it will never be known. The following brief sketch of the facts is derived from the most trustworthy sources accessible.

On Monday, the 15th inst., news reached Lahaina that murders had occurred at Awalua, on Lanai. The deputy sheriff dispatched Mr. Chillingworth, R. P. Hose, and other constables to the scene. They left Lahaina at 10 a.m. Tuesday, reaching Awalua at 12:30, where they found Puulolo (wahine) and Kealaka [sic] tied with ropes. It appears that sometime before the events described below, Puulolo had cured, or was credited with curing, a child of Kaholokai's which had been very sick. This had gained for her the reputation of a kahuna, and she probably was convinced of the reality of her supernatural powers. The *aumakua,* or spirit, which had power over her was called Kihilikini. Acting under the guidance of this spirit, on the night of Thursday, February 11, she beat and killed her sister Puni, beating her to death with a club. Puni, it is said, had expressed disbelief in her power, which had angered her. The following night was marked by events still more bloodcurdling. The furious woman clubbed to death her nephew Kala [sic], a boy of six years, the rest of the family acquiescing or assisting. After this action was completed, the other members of the family held Paa, a young man of about thirty and a brother of the kahuna, while she burned him over the face, body, and arms with a flaming torch made of cloth dipped in oil or lard. Later in the night her fourth victim, Kaholokai, was seized and held while she beat him with a club until he became unconscious. At this point the rest left him and went away, leaving the murderess alone with the dying man, to whom she was supposed to have dealt the finishing strokes. The family returned and went to sleep, and early in the morning the fire was started which destroyed the hut. Into its flame the body of Kaholokai was thrown, the other corpses being left to die on the ground outside, where the sickening horror had been enacted.

Saturday morning a native by the name of Palau, who lived about a mile away, came down and asked questions about what had occurred, but receiving no answers went to the other side of the island, about eight miles away, to inform the constable. Returning, he with another native, by the name of Kahulu, made some rough wooden coffins in which the three murdered Hawaiians were buried. Some of the family, who by this time may be supposed to have come partially to their senses, dug the graves.

This was on Saturday night. On Tuesday the four police officers arrived from Lahaina, and on Wednesday morning at four o'clock they started back with two boats, in the second of which were the twelve prisoners. They reached Lahaina at 6:30 and were met by an excited crowd, among them women armed with sticks. The face of the burned man, Paa, was covered from sight with a veil, it being feared that his disfigured appearance would incite the people to violence against Puulolo.

The examination of the prisoners was set for the following day but was postponed until Friday owing to the absence of Mr. Chillingworth in Wailuku. All twelve prisoners were sent down to Honolulu and arrived on the *Kinau* on Sunday morning. They were taken first to the station house, and afterwards to the Oahu Jail. It is said that Dr. Davison, of Lahaina, from an examination of the kahuna Puulolo, found no reason to suppose her insane. An officer who had a good deal of conversation with her on the voyage from Lahaina says that she seems perfectly rational. She is a young woman between twenty and thirty years of age, rather slender in figure. An eyewitness in the Oahu Prison speaks of her as cowering in a blanket, with her head bent down and muttering to herself.

The murders of Kaholokai and the child Kala [sic] were perpetrated, it is believed, in the expectation that the kahuna would bring them to life again. Paa, the brother, who was so horribly burned, is said to be improving, with a prospect of recovery.

The natives have all deserted Awalua, and the scene of this sickening outburst of heathenism and superstition is now a desert.

June 8, 1892

The steamer *Claudine* was detained till six o'clock last evening waiting for the court.

Pulolo, the Lanai murderess, and her band of accomplices in that horrible tragedy were marched from the prison to the steamer by policemen, a crowd of natives following them all the way. Pulolo was dressed in a new blue dress but had no shoes on. She wore a native *loulu* hat. Several native women were eager to catch a glimpse of the tragical kahuna, but when they saw her, she being only a small woman, they gnashed their teeth, wishing that she was in glory. The police encountered no small trouble in their efforts to prevent the eager visitors from coming too close to the person of Pulolo.

June 16, 1892

The *Kinau* arrived yesterday and brought news of the conclusion of the famous Lanai murder case, full particulars of which were published at the time. The evidence of the witnesses placed on the stand fully authenticated the accounts previously published and showed that the murders committed were due to what must be regarded as an outbreak of cruelty, animal ferocity, and degraded superstition all combined. A *nol. pros.* was entered as to five of the defendants, and a verdict of murder in the second degree found by the jury in the case of five others, *viz.* Pulolo the kahuna and four of the men implicated with her. Kala, the father of the murdered child, was sentenced to thirty years' imprisonment and Keola Kakaia and Keliikuewa to twenty years' each. In the case of Pulolo, the principal, sentence was reserved, owing to a discrepancy between English and Hawaiian versions, but it will be for life. The cause of the difficulty is the use of the word "term" in English, which led to some doubt in the mind of the court whether a simple sentence for life would be sufficient, or whether a term of years would have to be fixed.

June 20, 1892

Owing to the nature of this extraordinary murder case, it was found impossible to give a full report of it by furnishing the lengthy evidence produced in court, which was the most revolting ever placed on record in this kingdom. The following narrative covers the principal facts brought out in the trial, which, it will be seen, has not been concluded, only one of the several indictments having been tried.

On Thursday afternoon, June 9, after great difficulty in selecting a native jury, occurred the trial of the Lanai murderers before the Circuit Court at Wailuku. A brief abstract of the case, from the testimony presented to the jury, is as follows: On Thursday, February 11, the woman Pulolo, who claimed to be a kahuna and to have at her command a spirit named Kiilikina, had two of her soldiers, Keliikuewa and Kakaio, seize her husband and hold him, while she beat him cruelly and cut his feet with broken bottles till he could not walk. Not satisfied with this, she commenced punishing a little boy, six years old, the son of her eldest brother, Kalu.

Another brother, Hoopii, being sceptical as to her supernatural powers, at her command was seized and held by some of her attendants, while this inhuman wretch burned him most horribly with torches ignited from a large fire in the dwelling nearby. While in the witness box, Hoopii brought tears to the eyes of some of the audience, and caused execrations to come from the lips of others, by exhibiting the fearful scars received during this fiendish torturing. At the time he was so exhausted by the pain and punishment that he could scarcely move, only groan with agony.

Her vampire instincts remaining still unquenched, she took the boy, Kaialiilii, in hand again, and buffeted him about till he bled profusely at the nose and mouth, while his father and others stood by and silently witnessed this new act of cruelty. The poor stripling cried to his parent again and again for help, but the poor superstitious creature did not dare (or perhaps wish) to move hand or foot to succor his tortured offspring.

This brutal sorceress finally put an end to the boy's sufferings by sitting on his head till it bent to his waist, like a broken reed, and life was extinct. The poor little corpse was then taken and laid out on a mat, and the helpless Hoopii was placed beside it with his face to the wall guarded by the so-called soldiers.

Her next victim was her sister, whom she suffocated with the assistance of Kaholokai, by thrusting her head into hot sand. After this, the body of her dead sister was placed on the matting beside the boy's; she then ordered her satellites to seize her late assistant Kaholokai, and they held him fast while she beat him to death.

During the night the house, which at this time much resembled a morgue, caught fire, but was saved from destruction by the men near at hand. Early the next morning, February 12, a council of war was held to decide how best to cover up the dark deeds of the previous night. Her instructions to her tools were to say, when interrogated, that the boy's death resulted from sickness; that the man, Kaholokai, lost his life in the fire which attacked the house on the night before; that the girl, her sister, died in a fit.

The next move in this frightful tragedy after removing the bodies of the boy and woman was to cremate Kaholokai's corpse, by burning the house, with all its furniture and effects; thus hoping to give an appearance of accidental conflagration. The other two bodies were afterwards burned. After the destruction of the dwelling and the bodies, the murderess and her retinue spent the night at a neighbor's house some distance away.

The jury, on Friday, the 10th inst., brought in a unanimous verdict of murder in the second degree against Pulolo (twenty years in prison) and four of the men, for the murder of the boy. The remainder of the ten persons arrested were discharged on this count, but were held (as well as the five already found guilty) to answer two other indictments—for the murders of the woman and man. Owing to the terrible pitch of popular feeling on Maui, there will probably be a change of venue granted before another trial takes place.

As to the motive for these unprecedented crimes, it is difficult to conjecture. The reason given out generally among Hawaiians is this: that Pulolo and her brother-in-law, one of her willing tools, wished to marry, and in order to consummate their purpose, it was necessary to put the husband of one and the wife of the other out of the way. The other horrible acts were perpetrated to conceal their real intention. The intensity of popular feeling among the natives is not directed against kahunaism as a practice, but against this imposter, who has falsely claimed the powers of a Hawaiian magician.

During Thursday, p.m., the 16th and 17th inst., the foreign jury distinguished itself by rapid and thorough work. The jury is probably the best one, taken as a whole, that has been summoned to try cases on Maui for a number of years. Last night Judge Bickerton excused them until Monday morning. Today some native divorce cases are under consideration.

June 23, 1892

News came by the steamer *W. G. Hall* that a native wahine by the name of Kaaiai, of Kailua, Hawaii, tried to imitate the fiendish work of Pulolo, the notorious Lanai murderess. This woman is also a kahuna, and her neighbors are said to have obeyed her commands with superstitious fear. It is said that a few weeks ago, she ordered her sentinels to drag a kanaka about the place, after which a hole was dug to bury him alive. The sentinels were about to carry out her instructions, but were prevented by the timely appearance of others who took him out. The kahuna and her attendants were tried before the district judge of the place and were fined $100 each and costs.

June 27, 1892

Pulolo, the kahuna murderess, was sentenced to fifty years' imprisonment.

Robert Louis Stevenson

Another Molokai

Stevenson (1850–1894), wandering Scottish author of *Treasure Island* and *Kidnapped* who spent his last years in the South Seas, twice visited Hawaii. In May, 1889, he spent twelve days residing in the isolation colony on the island of Molokai, where the devoted Father Damien de Veuster had labored among the lepers until his recent death. On his return to Honolulu, Stevenson remarked: "There are Molokais everywhere." He was to confirm this truth the following year on another cruise of the South Pacific.

"Another Molokai" concluded a series of letters contributed to the New York *Sun* in 1891 and seldom reprinted.

IN 1890, when I was at Penrhyn [in the Cook Islands], Mr. Hird was supercargo on the *Janet Nicoll;* and knowing I had visited the Lazaretto on Molokai, he called me in consultation. "It is strange," said he. "When I was here there was no such thing as leprosy upon the island; and now there seems a great deal. Look at that man, and tell me what you think." The man was leprous as Naaman.

The story goes that a leper escaped from Molokai in an open boat and landed, some say in Penrhyn, some say first in Manihiki. There are many authentic boat voyages difficult to credit; but this of thirty degrees due north and south, and from the one trade to the other across the equatorial doldrums, ranks with the most extraordinary. We may suppose the westerly current to have been entirely intermitted, the easterly strong, and the fugitive well supplied with food. Or we may explain the tale to be a legend, framed to conceal the complaisance of some ill-judging skipper. One thing at least is sure: a Hawaiian leper, in an advanced stage of the disease, and admitting that he had escaped from Molokai, appeared suddenly in these distant islands, and was seen by Mr. H. J. Moors of Apia walking at large in Penrhyn. Mr. Moors is not quite certain of the date, for he visited the atoll in 1883 and again in 1884; but another of my neighbors, Mr. Harper, was trading in Penrhyn all the first year. He saw nothing of the Hawaiian, and this pins us to the later date. I am tediously particular on this point, because the result is amazing. Seven years is supposed to be the period of leprous incubation; and the whole of my tale, from the first introduction of the taint to the outbreak of a panic on the island, passes (at the outside) in a little more than six. At the time when we should have scarce looked for the appearance of the earliest case, the population was already steeped in leprosy.

The Polynesians assuredly derive from Asia; and Asia, since the dawn of history, has been a camping ground for this disease. Of two things, either the Polynesian left, ere the disease began, and is now for the first time exposed to the contagion, or he has been so long sequestered that Asiatic leprosy has had the time to vary, and finds in him a virgin soil. The facts are not clear; we are told, on one hand, that some indigenous form of the disease was known in Samoa within the memory of man; we are assured, on the other, that there is not a name for it in any island language. There is no doubt, at least, about the savage rapidity with which it spreads when introduced. And there is none that, when a leper is first seen, the islanders approach him without disaffection and are never backward to supply him with a wife. I find this singular; for few races are more sensitive to beauty, of which their own affords so high a standard; and I have observed that when the symptoms are described to him in words, the islander displays a high degree of horror and disgust. His stringent ideals of courtesy and hospitality and a certain debile kindliness of disposition must explain his conduct. As for the marriage, the stranger once received, it follows as a thing of course. To refuse the male is still considered in most parts of Polynesia a rather unlovely rigor in the female; and if a man be disfigured, I believe it would be held a sort of charity to console his solitude. A kind island girl might thus go to a leper's bed in something of the same spirit as we visit the sick at home with tracts and pounds of tea.

The waif who landed on Penrhyn was much marred with the disease; his head deformed with growths; a thing for children to flee from screaming. Yet he was received with welcome, entertained in families, and a girl was found to be his wife. It is hard to be just to this Hawaiian. Doubtless he was a man of a wild strain of blood, a lover of liberty and life; doubtless he had harbored in the high woods and the rains, a spectral Robin Hood, armed to defend his wretched freedom; perhaps he was captured fighting; and of one thing we may be sure, that he had escaped early from the Lazaretto, still untamed, still hot with resentment. His boat voyage was a discipline well fitted to inspire grave thoughts; in him it may have only sharpened the desire of pleasure; for to certain shallow natures the imminence of death is but a whet. In his own eyes he was an innocent prisoner escaped, the victim of a nameless and senseless tyranny. What did he ask? To taste the common lot of men, to sit with the house folk, to hear the evensong, to share in the day's gossip, to have a wife like others, and to see children round his knees. He landed in Penrhyn, enjoyed for a while simple pleasures, died, and bequeathed to his entertainers a legacy of doom.

They were early warned. Mr. Moors warned them in 1884, and they made light of his predictions, the long incubation of the malady deceiving them. The leper lived among them; no harm was seen. He died, and still there was no harm. It would be interesting, it is probably impossible, to learn how soon the plague appeared. By the midst of 1890, at least, the island was dotted with lepers, and the *Janet Nicoll* had not long gone before the islanders awoke to an apprehension of their peril. I have mentioned already traits which they share with their Paumotuan kindred; their conduct in this hour of awakening is another. There were certain families—twenty, I was told; we may imply a corrective and guess ten—entirely contaminated; the clean waited on these sick and bade them leave the settlement.

Some six years before they had opened their doors to a stranger; now they must close them on their next of kin.

It chanced that among the tainted families were some of chief importance, some that owned the land of the village. It was their first impulse to resent the measure of expulsion.

"The land is ours," they argued. "If any are to leave, let it be you," and they were thought to have answered well; "let them stay" was the reconsidered verdict; and the clean people began instead to prepare their own secession. The coming of the missionary ship decided otherwise; the lepers were persuaded; a *motu* [islet] of some size, hard by the south entrance, was now named Molokai, after its sad original; and thither, leaving their lands and the familiar village, self-doomed, self-sacrificed, the infected families went forth into perpetual exile.

The palms of their lost village are easily in view from Molokai. The sequestered may behold the smoke rise from their old home; they can see the company of boats skim forth with daylight to the place of diving. And they have yet nearer sights. A pier has been built in the lagoon; a boat comes at intervals, leaves food upon its seaward end, and goes again, the lepers not entering on the pier until it be gone. Those on the beach, those in the boat, old friends and kinfolk thus behold each other for a moment silently. The girl who bid Mr. Hird flee from the settlement opened her heart to him on his last visit. She would never again set eyes, she told him, on her loved ones, and when he reminded her that she might go with the boat and see them from a distance on the beach, "Never!" she cried. If she went, if she saw them, her heart would pluck her from the boat; she must leap on the pier, she must run to the beach, she must speak again with the lost; and with the act the doors of the prison isle would close upon herself. So sternly is the question of leprosy now viewed, under a native rule, in Penrhyn.

Long may it so continue! and I would I could infect with a like severity every isle of the Pacific. But self-indulgence and sentiment menace instead the mere existence of the island race; perhaps threaten our own with a new struggle against an enemy refreshed. Nothing is less proved than this peril to ourselves; yet it is possible. To our own syphilis we are inured, but the syphilis of eastern Asia slays us; and a new variety of leprosy, cultivated in the virgin soil of Polynesian races, might prove more fatal than we dream.

So that ourselves, it may be, are no strangers to the case; it may be it was for us the men of Penrhyn resigned their acres, and when the defaced chimera sailed from Molokai, bringing sorrow and death to isles of singing, we also, and our babes may have been the target of his invisible arrows. But it needs not this. The thought of that hobgoblin boatman alone upon the sea, of the perils he escaped, of the evil he lavished on the world, may well strike terror in the minds even of the distant and the unconcerned. In mine, at the memory of my termagant minstrel, hatred glows.

Eric Kundsen

The One-Eyed Akua

Son of Valdemar Knudsen, Norwegian pioneer in Hawaii who for some time was manager of Grove Farm plantation at Lihue, Kauai, and purchaser of properties on that island that are still retained in the family, Eric A. Knudsen (1872–1957) was born on that island. He early learned the Hawaiian language and listened to many stories told by the local people. He was educated in New Zealand and Europe and later earned a Harvard law degree. He served as cattleman and trailblazer on the Garden Isle and was speaker of the Territorial House of Representatives and president of the Senate, as well as a member of the Kauai Board of Supervisors. He is the author of *Teller of Tales,* a 1944 collection of stories told over the radio, and, in collaboration with Gurre P. Noble, *Kanuka of Kauai,* about the Knudsen and Robinson families of his native island. "The One-Eyed Akua" is a true recollection of an adventure that befell a cowboy on the home ranch.

WE HAD just finished breakfast and all of us children were out on the lawn. Makaawaawa, the cook, and his wife Makae, our nurse, were washing dishes. The sun was shining through the trees; early to bed and early to rise was an old Hawaiian custom and Papa ran the camp on that rule. The days were wonderful but the nights cold and dark and the woods were not good places to be in when night came on. The natives said they were full of evil spirits and akua and we children believed that. Even though Papa used to laugh at the stories, we knew the natives were right. Hadn't they lived in the mountains for thousands of years before the white man came? They ought to know.

Suddenly Papa came out of the camp carrying his Winchester rifle, the good old .44. That was always the sign that something was going to happen.

"Makaawaawa," he called, and the cook came out of the kitchen wiping his hands. "Take my rifle and go kill a wild cow or calf. We have no fresh meat in camp."

Makaawaawa's eyes sparkled. Hunting wild cattle was fun, so he quickly took the rifle, stuck his hunting knife in his belt, called his dog, Liona, and strode up the trail until he was soon lost to sight. That excitement over, we children settled down and went playing in the woods.

Lunchtime came and the hunter was still away. No one worried, for sometimes one had to hunt a long time before one found cattle. Then afternoon began to lengthen out and the sun dipped toward the west. Makae began to look out towards the hills and finally she confided to us children that something terrible had happened to her man; he should have been back long before this. We children ran and told Papa but he only laughed and told us not to listen to such nonsense. But when the sun disappeared behind Puu Hinahina, Papa began to agree with us that something might have gone wrong and when the sun set, he walked to the top of Halemanu ridge and shouted long and loud, hoping to get an answer from the long valleys and ridges that sloped away to the west. No answer came. He returned to camp and sent two big natives up the trail towards the north to shout. In no time at all, they too, came back. It was getting dark and no Hawaiian wanted to be out in the woods.

Poor old Makae sat in the servants' house and wept long and loud. She knew her man was dead and she was not to be consoled. Black night settled over the mountains and you couldn't see your hand before your face. We lit the lamps and gathered round the little stove. Mama made us some tea and toast and finally the camp settled down for the night, with only the chirping of the crickets and the low sobbing of Makae.

Early next morning we were all up and out. Two of the boys were saddling their horses to go and look for the lost man. Mama and Makae were getting breakfast for us when we heard footsteps and we looked up the trail to the north. We saw Makaawaawa coming down the road as fast as he could trot. We all gave a shout and ran to meet him, and in a moment he was standing by the kitchen door and Makae looked at him as if he had come back from the dead.

"Where have you been?", we all asked at once. "What happened?"

Leaning his rifle against the wall he told us this story:

"As you know," he said, "I went off yesterday and as soon as I reached the high ridge I plunged down into the great koa forests of Kopakaka, a favorite place of the wild cattle, but I saw none so on I went. Hour after hour I tramped along the cattle trails, I looked into Tauhau, crossed the Makaha Valley, hunted through the Milolii Valleys. Up and down I went but I saw nothing and had just decided to go home when to my surprise I saw a big black cow standing right in front of me. I took good aim and fired and down she dropped. I walked up to her, and had just laid down my gun and drew my knife when the cow jumped to her feet and dashed off through the brush. My dog and I had no trouble following her tracks, for she was badly wounded and left a trail of blood on the ferns. But she seemed tireless and led me up the ridges and into the valleys, always farther and farther away. I forgot all about time, I was so determined to get that cow, so I trailed her away over into the Nualolo woods and finally I came upon her. She was standing quite still, so I fired again and this time she was dropped, dead. I drew my knife and was going to butcher her when I realized how tired I was. And no wonder, for as I looked, the sun was setting low over the ocean. I must get home. There was no time to get meat. So I ran as fast as I could, but the sun sank into the sea, and as you know how quickly the night falls, I knew I could never get home.

"I was on a wide ridge all covered with lehua and koa trees. The cattle road ran through a nice little open glade and at the upper end was a big koa tree. In the last light, I just had time to gather a pile of dead sticks and build a fire near the tree. Then I leaned my gun against the tree and sat down with my back against the trunk. With my dog by my side, I settled down for the night.

"It was getting dark in the woods. There was still just enough light in the glade to see objects quite distinctly, when my dogs began to growl and the hair on their back stood straight up and they gazed down the glade with terror in their eyes. I looked also and to my horror I saw a huge monster coming out of the woods. He was about seven feet tall with a great tuft of hair on his head; his great arms swung at his sides as he walked towards me and his large hands almost touched the ground. He came slinking up to me and my dogs lay as if dead by my side. Hurriedly I put more wood on the fire and then I saw that he had but one great big eye large as a saucer, right in the middle of his face, and a great big mouth with teeth showing through the lips. I recognized him for one of the cruel akua that live in the woods and kill every human being they can get hold of. My father had told me about them when I was a boy.

"Slowly he came and luckily for me the new wood made the fire burn brightly. They were afraid of fire, and coming no closer the akua sat down opposite me and looked at me with his one big eye. There he sat all night long waiting for me to go to sleep and the fire to go out so he could come around and kill me. I sat and watched him and every time the fire began to die down I put on more wood, praying my small pile of dried logs would last the night. Woe to me if it ran out! So all night long we sat and watched each other and the night seemed endless.

"The night wind was blowing softly through the trees and I saw the akua turn his eye toward the stars. I looked up quickly and to my joy saw they were fading; dawn was coming, the night would end at last. Still he sat and watched me but the light began to come and the stars faded away. The akua had to go, for the sun would soon be up and its deadly rays would kill the akua. He rose to his feet, giving me one last ugly look, and then slunk slowly across the little glade swinging his huge arms, his great hands almost touching the ground, and then he disappeared into the dark jungle.

"I waited a little while, grabbed my rifle and ran up the trail, my dogs at my heels; and here I am, lucky to be alive."

Hugh Hastings Romilly

A Christmas Ghost on Rotuma

The Polynesian island of Rotuma, lying several hundred miles north of the Fiji Group, was the scene of fierce wars among the various rival chiefs. Finally deciding that this "garden of the Pacific" had suffered enough, in 1879 they petitioned the Queen of England to send a ruler for their people. Meanwhile, Sir Arthur Gordon, governor of Fiji, at their request sent a relative, Arthur Gordon, and an interpreter to study the situation. About a month later they were joined by a staff member, H. H. Romilly, who gives the following story of an encounter with the supernatural.

Hugh Hastings Romilly (1856–1892), colonial administrator and explorer, went to Fiji in 1879 and his visit to Rotuma supplied him with the material for his first book, *A True Story of the Western Pacific* (London, 1882), the source of the present selection. Following Britain's decision to annex Rotuma, Romilly went there as deputy commissioner, and began a varied colonial career not only in the Pacific but in Mashonaland, Africa. Other books of interest are *The Western Pacific and New Guinea* (London, 1886) and *From My Verandah in New Guinea* (London, 1889).

FOR five months I stayed in Rotumah without any news from the outer world, including the infected country of Fiji. In two months after my arrival there I went into my new house. It was very large and luxurious. Every evening Alipati used to come and have a talk and smoke with me. It was always open to any of my friends who cared to come. As I provided tobacco for them I seldom passed an evening by myself. The house was situated about two hundred yards from Albert's—Alipati's—own house, and was just outside the limits of his town. A considerable clearing of four or five acres had been made in the bush to build it in. The short distance between the house and the village was of course very dark at night, as the path between them lay through a thick piece of bush. This sort of life went on with the exception of one break the whole time I was there.

Two days before Christmas Day, I was left all alone by my accustomed friends in the house, and spent the evening by myself. Allardyce and I made some remarks about it, but attached no importance to it of any sort. Next day I went to the other end of the island and did not come back till late. I had not seen Albert or any of his people during the day. In the evening I fully expected him up as a matter of course, but again no one made his appearance. I should have gone down myself to his house, as I thought that possibly a dance might be going on, which would account for no one making his appearance, but as it was raining heavily I did not go. I asked my native servants if anything was going on; they said there was no dance, and they did not know why Albert had not come. I saw by their manner that they knew something more, and I saw also that they were afraid to tell me what it was. I determined to see Albert early next day and find out everything from him.

All that night we were annoyed by a harmless mad woman named Herena, who walked round and round the house crying "Kimueli" — "Kimueli." We thought nothing of it, as we were quite accustomed to her. Next day I went down early to Albert's house. He was just going out to his work in the bush. I said, "Albert, why have you not been to see me for two nights?"

"Me 'fraid,' said Albert, "dead man he walks."

"What dead man?"

"Kimueli."

Of course I laughed at him. It was an everyday occurrence for natives who had been out late at night in the bush to come home saying they had seen ghosts. If I wished to send a message after sunset it was always necessary to engage three or four men to take it. Nothing would have induced any man to go by himself. The only man who was free from these fears was my interpreter, Friday. He was a native, but had lived all his life among white people. When Friday came down from his own village to my house that morning, he was evidently a good deal troubled in his mind. He said,

"You remember that man Kimueli, sir, that Tom killed."

I said, "Yes, Albert says he is walking about."

I expected Friday to laugh, but he looked very serious and said,

"Everyone in Motusa has seen him, sir; the women are so frightened that they all sleep together in the big house."

"What does he do?" said I. "Where has he been to? What men have seen him?"

Friday mentioned a number of houses into which Kimueli had gone. It appeared that his head was tied up with banana leaves and his face covered with blood. No one had heard him speak. This was unusual, as the ghosts I had heard the natives talk about on other occasions invariably made remarks on some commonplace subject. The village was very much upset. For two nights this had happened, and several men and women had been terribly frightened.

It was evident that all this was not imagination on the part of one man. I thought it possible that some madman was personating Kimueli, though it seemed almost impossible that anyone could do so without being found out. I announced my determination to sit outside Albert's house that night and watch for him. I also told Albert that I should bring a rifle and have a shot, if I saw the ghost. This I said for the benefit of anyone who might be playing its part.

Poor Albert had to undergo a good deal of chaff for being afraid to walk two hundred yards through the bush to my house. He only said,

"By-and-bye you see him too, then me laugh at you."

The rest of the day was spent in the usual manner. Allardyce and I were to have dinner in Albert's house; after that we were going to sit outside and watch for Kimueli. All the natives had come in very early that day from the bush. They were evidently unwilling to run the risk of being out after dark. Evening was now closing in, and they were all sitting in clusters outside their houses. It was, however, a bright moonlight night, and I could plainly recognize people at a considerable distance. Albert was getting very nervous, and only answered my questions in monosyllables.

For about two hours we sat there smoking, and I was beginning to lose faith in Albert's ghost when all of a sudden he clutched my elbow and pointed with his finger. I looked in the direction pointed out by him, and he whispered "Kimueli."

I certainly saw about a hundred yards off what appeared to be the ordinary figure of a native advancing. He had something tied round his head, as yet I could not see what. He was advancing straight towards us. We sat still and waited. The natives sitting in front of their doors got closer together and pointed at the advancing figure. All this time I was watching it most intently. A recollection of having seen that figure was forcing itself upon my mind more strongly every moment, and suddenly the exact scene, when I had gone with Gordon to visit the murdered man, came back on my mind with great vividness. There was the same man in front of me, his face covered with blood, and a dirty cloth over his head, kept in its place by banana leaves which were secured with fiber and cotton thread. There was the same man, and there was the bandage round his head, leaf for leaf, and tie for tie, identical with the picture already present in my mind.

"By Jove, it *is* Kimueli," I said to Allardyce in a whisper. By this time he had passed us, walking straight in the direction of the clump of bush in which my house was situated. We jumped up and gave chase, but he got to the edge of the bush before we reached him. Though only a few yards ahead of us, and a bright moonlight night, we here lost all trace of him. He had disappeared, and all that was left was a feeling of consternation and annoyance on my mind.

We had to accept what we had seen; no explanation was possible. It was impossible to account for his appearance or disappearance. I went back to Albert's house in a most perplexed frame of mind. The fact of its being Christmas day, the anniversary of Tom's attack on Kimueli, made it still more remarkable.

I had myself only seen Kimueli two or three times in life, but still I remembered him perfectly, and the man or ghost, whichever it was who had just passed, exactly recalled his features. I had remembered too in a general way how

Kimueli's head had been bandaged with rag and banana leaves, but on the appearance of this figure it came back to me exactly, even to the position of the knots. I could not then, and do not now, believe it was in the power of any native to play the part so exactly. A native could and often does work himself up into a state of temporary madness, under the influence of which he might believe himself to be anyone he chose, but the calm, quiet manner in which this figure had passed was, I believe, entirely impossible for a native, acting such a part and before such an audience, to assume. Moreover, Albert and everyone else scouted the idea. They all knew Kimueli intimately, had seen him every day, and could not be mistaken. Allardyce had never seen him before, but can bear witness to what he saw that night.

I went back to my house and tried to dismiss the matter from my mind, but with indifferent success. I could not get over his disappearance. We were so close behind him that, if it had been a man forcing his way through the thick undergrowth, we must have heard and seen him. There was no path where he had disappeared.

I determined to watch again next night. Till two in the morning I sat up with Albert smoking. No Kimueli made his appearance. Albert said he would not be seen again, and during my stay on the island he certainly never was.

A month after this event I went on board a schooner bound for Sydney; my health had suffered severely, and it was imperative for me to go to a cooler climate. I can offer no explanation for this story. Till my arrival in England I never mentioned it to anyone; at the request of my friends, however, I now consent to publish it.

I am not a believer in ghosts. I believe a natural explanation of the story to exist, but the reader, who has patiently followed me thus far, must find it for himself, as I am unable to supply one.

Louis Becke

A Basket of Breadfruit

George Lewis Becke (1855–1913) is generally acclaimed as the best writer of South Sea stories to have lived for many years in the region he evoked in his fact and fiction.

After spending two decades as a trader, beachcomber, blackbirder, and wanderer "from Rapa to Palau," Louis Becke at the age of thirty-eight began to write stories for the famed Sydney *Bulletin,* and in 1896 went to London to embark on a literary career. Before his death he published thirty-five books about the Pacific, six of them in collaboration with Walter James Jeffery. This selection comes from Becke's first book, *By Reef and Palm* (1894).

"A Basket of Breadfruit," the adventures of a trader during the civil war days in Samoa when Colonel Albert Barnes Steinberger, an American filibuster, was intervening in the three-way struggle of the chiefs for supremacy, has the ring of truth. In fewer than two thousand words, the reader is plunged into a life-or-death situation, following the involvement of a South Sea trader hurrying his small schooner inside the perilous reef.

IT WAS in Steinberger's time. A trader had come up to Apia in his boat from the end of Savaii, the largest of the Samoan group, and was on his way home again when the falling tide caused him to stop awhile at Mulinu'u Point, about two miles from Apia. Here he designed to smoke and talk and drink kava at the great camp with some hospitable native acquaintances during the rising of the water. Soon he was taking his ease on a soft mat, watching the bevy of *aua luma* [the local girls] "chawing" kava.

Now the trader lived at Falealupo, at the extreme westerly end of Savaii; but the Samoans, by reason of its isolation and extremity, have for ages called it by another name—an unprintable one—and so some of the people present began to jest with the trader for living in such a place. He fell in with their humor, and said that if those present would find him for a wife a girl unseared by the breath of scandal, he would leave Falealupo for Safune, where he had bought land.

"Malie!" said an old dame, with one eye and white hair, "the *papalagi* [foreigner] is inspired to speak wisdom tonight; for at Safune grow the sweetest nuts and the biggest taro and breadfruit; and, lo! here among the kavachewers is a young maid from Safune—mine own granddaughter Salome. And against her name can no one in Samoa laugh in the hollow of his hand," and the old creature, amid laughter and cries of *Isa! e le ma le lo matua* [the old woman is without shame], crept over to the trader, and, with one skinny hand on his knee, gazed steadily into his face with her one eye.

The trader looked at the girl—at Salome. She had, at her grandmother's speech, turned her head aside, and taking the "chaw" of kava root from her pretty mouth, dissolved into shamefaced tears. The trader was a man of quick perceptions, and he made up his mind to do in earnest what he had said in jest—this because of the tears of Salome. He quickly whispered to the old woman, "Come to the boat before the full of the tide and we will talk."

When the kava was ready for drinking, the others present had forgotten all about the old woman and Salome, who had both crept away unobserved, and an hour or two was passed in merriment, for the trader was a man well liked. Then, when he rose and said *to fa,* they begged him not to attempt to pass down in his boat inside the reef, as he was sure to be fired upon, for how were their people to tell a friend from an enemy in the black night? But he smiled, and said his boat was too heavily laden to face the ocean swell. So they bade him *to fa,* and called out *manuia oe!* [Bless you!] as he lifted the door of thatch and went.

The old woman awaited him, holding the girl by the hand. On the ground lay a basket, strongly tied up. Salome still wept, but the old woman angrily bade her cease and enter the boat, which the crew had now pushed bow-on to the beach. The old woman lifted the basket and carefully put it on board.

"Be sure," she said to the crew, "not to sit on it, for it is but ripe breadfruit I am taking to my people in Manono."

"Give them here to me," said the trader, and he put the basket in the stern out of the way. The old woman came aft, too, and crouched at his feet and smoked a *sului.* The cool land-breeze freshened as the sail was hoisted, and then the crew besought the trader not to run down inside the reef. Bullets, they said, if fired in plenty, always hit something, and the sea was fairly smooth outside the reef. And old Lupetea grasped his hand and muttered in his ear, "For the sake of this my little daughter, go outside. See, now, I am old, and to lie when so near death as I am is foolish. Be warned by me and be wise; sail out into the ocean, and at daylight we will be at Salua in Manono. Then thou canst set my feet on the shore—I and the basket. But the girl shall go with thee. Thou canst marry her, if that be to thy mind, in the fashion of the *papalagi,* or take her *fa'a Samoa.* Thus will I keep faith with thee. If the girl be false, her neck is but little and thy fingers strong."

Now the trader thought in this wise: "This is well for me, for if I get the girl away thus quietly from all her relations I will save much in presents," and his heart rejoiced, for although not mean he was a careful man. So he steered his boat between the seething surf that boiled and hissed on both sides of the boat passage.

As the boat sailed past the misty line of cloud-capped Upolu, the trader lifted the girl up beside him and spoke to her. She was not afraid of him, she said, for many had told her he was a good man, and not a *ula vale* [scamp], but she wept because now, save her old grandmother, all her kinsfolk were dead. Even but a day and a half ago her one brother was killed with her cousin. They were strong men, but the bullets were swift, and so they died. And their heads had been shown at Matautu. For that she had grieved and wept and eaten nothing, and the world was cold to her.

"Poor little devil!" said the trader to himself—"hungry." Then he opened a locker and found a tin of sardines. Not a scrap of biscuit. There was plenty of biscuit, though, in the boat, in fifty-pound tins, but on these mats were spread, whereon his crew were sleeping. He was about to rouse them when he remembered the old dame's basket of ripe breadfruit. He laughed and looked at her. She, too, slept, coiled up at his feet. But first he opened the sardines and placed them beside the girl, and motioned her to steer. Her eyes gleamed like diamonds in the darkness as she answered his glance, and her soft fingers grasped the tiller. Very quickly, then, he felt among the packages aft till he came to the basket.

A quick stroke of his knife cut the sennit that lashed the sides together. He felt inside. "Only two, after all, but big ones, and no mistake. Wrapped in cloth, too! I wonder—Hell and furies, what's this?"—as his fingers came in contact with something that felt like a human eye. Drawing his hand quickly back, he fumbled in his pockets for a match, and struck it.

Breadfruit? No. Two heads with closed eyes, and livid lips blue with the pallor of death, showing their white teeth. And Salome covered her face and slid down in the bottom of the boat again, and wept afresh for her cousin and brother, and the boat came up in the wind, but no one awoke.

The trader was angry. But after he had tied up the basket again, he put the boat on her course once more and called to the girl. She crept close to him and nestled under his overcoat, for the morning air came across the sea from the dew-laden forests and she was chilled. Then she told the story of how her grandma had begged the heads from those of Malietoa's troops who had taken them at Matautu, and then gone to the camp at Mulinu'u in the hope of getting a passage in some boat to Manono, her country, where she would fain bury them. And that night he had come, and old Lupetea had rejoiced and sworn her to secrecy about the heads in the basket. And that also was why Lupetea was afraid for the boat to go down inside the passage, for there were many enemies to be met with, and they would have shot old Lupetea because she was of Manono. That was all. Then she ate the sardines, and, leaning her head against the trader's bosom, fell asleep.

As the first note of the great grey pigeon sounded the dawn, the trader's boat sailed softly up to the Salua beach, and old Lupetea rose, and, bidding the crew goodbye, and calling down blessings on the head of the good and clever white man as she rubbed his and the girl's noses against her own, she grasped her basket of breadfruit and went ashore. Then the trader, with Salome by his side, sailed out again into the ocean.

Samuel L. Clemens [Mark Twain]

The Burning of the Clipper Ship *Hornet*

Samuel L. Clemens (1835–1910), whose arrival in Honolulu on March 18, 1866, was noted on the passenger list under his recently adopted pseudonym of "Mark Twain," spent four months in the "Sandwich Islands" as a newspaper correspondent. Traveling around the group, he described life as he saw it more than a century ago in the future fiftieth state.

While on a horseback tour of the Kona Coast of Hawaii, the reporter came upon a large temple platform "which was built," he wrote, "in a single night, in the midst of storm and thunder and rain, by the ghastly hands of dead men! Tradition says that by the weird glare of the lightning a noiseless multitude of phantoms were seen at their strange labor far up the mountainside at dead of night—flitting hither and thither and bearing great lava blocks clasped in their nerveless fingers—appearing and disappearing as the pallid luster fell upon their forms and faded away again. Even to this day, it is said, the natives hold this dread structure in awe and reverence, and will not pass it in the night."

While he was in Honolulu, some survivors of one of the most amazing episodes in Pacific annals arrived in the hospital in that port. The clipper ship *Hornet* had accidentally been set on fire near the equator, and Captain Josiah Mitchell and fourteen men had made their way in the ship's longboat to Laupahoehoe on the island of Hawaii, a disastrous voyage of four thousand miles.

Clemens spent the night interviewing the seamen and writing the story of their adventures for the Sacramento, California, *Weekly Union*. Next morning the manuscript was tossed aboard a schooner which had already cast off for San Francisco. This "grand scoop" was widely reprinted, and on his return to California "Mark" boldly billed the newspaper for $300, a sum fifteen times his usual rate for an article. This exciting piece of early reporting made its writer for the first time a "literary personage," and, in his own words, "about the best-known honest man on the Pacific Coast."

Honolulu, June 25, 1866.

IN THE postscript to a letter which I wrote two or three days ago and sent by the ship *Live Yankee,* I gave you the substance of a letter received here from Hilo by Walker, Allen & Co. informing them that a boat containing fifteen men, in a helpless and starving condition, had drifted ashore at Laupahoehoe, Island of Hawaii, and that they had belonged to the clipper ship *Hornet,* Mitchell master, and had been afloat on the ocean since the burning of that vessel, about one hundred miles north of the equator, on the 3d of May — forty-three days.

The third mate and ten of the seamen have arrived here and are now in the hospital. Captain Mitchell, one seaman named Antonio Passene, and two passengers (Samuel and Henry Ferguson, of New York City, young gentlemen aged respectively eighteen and twenty-eight) are still at Hilo, but are expected here within the week.

In the captain's modest epitome of this terrible romance, which you have probably published, you detect the fine old hero through it. It reads like Grant.

I have talked with the seamen and with John S. Thomas, third mate, but their accounts are so nearly alike in all substantial points that I will merely give the officer's statement and weave into it such matters as the men mentioned in the way of incidents, experiences, emotions, etc. Thomas is a very intelligent and a very cool and self-possessed young man and seems to have kept a pretty accurate log of his remarkable voyage in his head. He told his story, of three hours' length, in a plain, straight-forward way, and with no attempt at display and no straining after effect. Wherever any incident may be noted in this paper where any individual has betrayed any emotion, or enthusiasm, or has departed from strict, stoical self-possession, or had a solitary thought that was not an utterly unpoetical and essentially practical one, remember that Thomas, the third mate, was not that person. He has been eleven days on shore, and already looks sufficiently sound and healthy to pass almost anywhere without being taken for an invalid. He has the marks of a hard experience about him, though, when one looks closely. He is very much sunburned and weather-beaten, and looks thirty-two years old. He is only twenty-four, however, and has been a sailor fifteen years. He was born in Richmond, Maine, and still considers that place his home. The following is the substance of what Thomas said:

The *Hornet* left New York on the 15th of January last, unusually well manned, fitted, and provisioned—as fast and as handsome a clipper ship as ever sailed out of that port. She had a general cargo—a little of everything: a large quantity of kerosene oil in barrels; several hundred cases of candles; also four hundred tons Pacific Railroad iron, and three engines. The third mate thinks they were dock engines, and one of the seamen thought they were locomotives. Had no gales and no bad weather; nothing but fine sailing weather, and she went along steadily and well—fast, very fast, in fact. Had uncommonly good weather off Cape Horn; he had been around that Cape seven times—each way—and had never seen such fine weather there before. On the 12th of April, in latitude, say, 35° S. and longitude 95° W., signaled a Prussian bark; she set Prussian ensign, and the *Hornet* responded with her name, expressed by means of Merritt's system of signals. She was sailing west—probably bound for Australia. This was the last vessel ever seen by the *Hornet's* people until they floated ashore in Hawaii in the longboat—a space of sixty-four days.

At seven o'clock on the morning of the 3d of May, the chief mate and two men started down into the hold to draw some "bright varnish" from a cask. The captain told him to bring the cask on deck—that it was dangerous to have it where it was, in the hold. The mate, instead of obeying the order, proceeded to draw a canful of the varnish first. He had an open light in his hand, and the liquid took fire; the can was dropped, the officer in his consternation neglected to close the bung, and in a few seconds the fiery torrent had run in every direction, under bales of rope, cases of candles, barrels of kerosene, and all sorts of freight, and tongues of flame were shooting upward through every aperture and crevice toward the deck.

The ship was moving along under easy sail, the watch on duty were idling here and there in such shade as they could find, and the listlessness and repose of morning in the tropics was upon the vessel and her belongings. But as six bells chimed, the cry of "Fire!" rang through the ship and woke every man to life and action. And following the fearful warning, and almost as fleetly, came the fire itself. It sprang through hatchways, seized upon chairs, table, cordage, anything, everything—and almost before the bewildered men could realize what the trouble was and what was to be done the cabin was a hell of angry flames. The mainmast was on fire—its rigging was burned asunder! One man said all this had happened within eighteen or twenty minutes after the first alarm—two others say in ten minutes. All say that one hour after the alarm, the main and mizzenmasts were burned in two and fell overboard.

Captain Mitchell ordered the three boats to be launched instantly, which was done—and so hurriedly that the longboat (the one he left the vessel in himself) had a hole as large as a man's head stove in her bottom. A blanket was stuffed into the opening and fastened to its place. Not a single thing was saved, except such food and other articles as lay about the cabin and could be quickly seized and thrown on deck. Thomas was sent into the longboat to receive its proportion of these things, and, being barefooted at the time, and bareheaded, and having no clothing on save an undershirt and pantaloons, of course he never got a chance afterward to add to his dress. He lost everything he had, including his logbook, which he had faithfully kept from the first. Forty minutes after the fire alarm the provisions and passengers were on board the three boats, and they rowed away from the ship—and to some distance, too, for the heat was very great. Twenty minutes afterward the two masts I have mentioned, with their rigging and their broad sheets of canvas wreathed in flames, crashed into the sea.

All night long the thirty-one unfortunates sat in their frail boats and watched the gallant ship burn; and felt as men feel when they see a tried friend perishing and are powerless to help him. The sea was illuminated for miles around, and the clouds above were tinged with a ruddy hue; the faces of the men glowed in the strong light as they shaded their eyes with their hands and peered out anxiously upon the wild picture, and the gunwales of the boats and the idle oars shone like polished gold.

At five o'clock on the morning after the disaster, in latitude 2° 20′ N., longitude 112° 8′ W., the ship went down, and the crew of the *Hornet* were alone on the great deep, or, as one of the seamen expressed it, "We felt as if somebody or something had gone away—as if we hadn't any home any more."

Captain Mitchell divided his boat's crew into two watches and gave the third mate charge of one and took the other himself. He had saved a studding sail from the ship, and out of this the men fashioned a rude sail with their knives; they hoisted it, and taking the first and second mates' boats in tow, they bore away upon the ship's course (northwest) and kept in the track of vessels bound to or from San Francisco, in the hope of being picked up.

I have said that in the few minutes' time allowed him, Captain Mitchell was only able to seize upon the few articles of food and other necessaries that happened to lie about the cabin. Here is the list: Four hams; seven pieces of salt pork (each piece weighed about four pounds); one box of raisins; one hundred pounds of bread (about one barrel); twelve two-pound cans of oysters, clams, and assorted meats; six buckets of raw potatoes (which rotted so fast they got but little benefit from them); a keg with four pounds of butter in it; twelve gallons of water in a forty-gallon tierce or scuttle butt; four one-gallon demijohns full of water; three bottles of brandy, the property of passengers; some pipes, matches, and a hundred pounds of tobacco; they had no medicines. That was all these poor fellows had to live on for forty-three days—the whole thirty-one of them!

Each boat had a compass, a quadrant, a copy of Bowditch's *Navigator,* and a nautical almanac, and the captain's and chief mate's boats had chronometers.

Of course, all hands were put on short allowance at once. The day they set sail from the ship each man was allowed a small morsel of salt pork—or a little piece of potato, if he preferred it—and half a sea biscuit three times a day. To understand how very light this ration of bread was, it is only necessary to know that it takes seven of these sea biscuits to weigh a pound. The first two days they only allowed one gill of water a day to each man; but for nearly a fortnight after that the weather was lowering and stormy, and frequent rain squalls occurred. The rain was caught in canvas, and whenever there was a shower the forty-gallon cask and every other vessel that would hold water was filled—even all the boots that were watertight were pressed into this service, except such as the matches and tobacco were deposited in to keep dry. So for fourteen days. There were luxurious occasions when there was plenty of water to drink. But after that how they suffered the agonies of thirst for four long weeks!

For seven days the boats sailed on, and the starving men ate their fragment of biscuit and their morsel of raw pork in the morning, and hungrily counted the tedious hours until noon and night should bring their repetitions of it. And in the long intervals they looked mutely into each other's faces, or turned their wistful eyes across the wild sea in search of the succoring sail that was never to come.

"Didn't you talk?" I asked one of the men.

"No; we were too downhearted—that is, the first week or more. We didn't talk—we only looked at each other and over the ocean."

And thought, I suppose, thought of home—of shelter from storms—of food, and drink, and rest.

The hope of being picked up hung to them constantly—was ever present to them, and in their thoughts, like hunger. And in the captain's mind was the hope of making the Clarion Islands, and he clung to it many a day.

The nights were very dark. They had no lantern and could not see the compass, and there were no stars to steer by. Thomas said, of the boat, "She handled easy, and we steered by the feel of the wind in our faces and the heave of the sea." Dark, and dismal, and lonesome work was that! Sometimes they got a glimpse of the sailor's friend, the north star, and then they lighted a match and hastened anxiously to see if their compass was faithful to them—for it had to be placed close to an iron ringbolt in the stern, and they were afraid, during those first nights, that this might cause it to vary. It proved true to them, however.

On the fifth day a notable incident occurred. They caught a dolphin! and while their enthusiasm was still at its highest over this stroke of good fortune, they captured another. They made a trifling fire in a tin plate and warmed the prizes—to cook them was not possible—and divided them equitably among all hands and ate them.

On the sixth day two more dolphins were caught.

Two more were caught on the seventh day, and also a small bonita, and they began to believe they were always going to live in this extravagant way; but it was not to be; these were their last dolphins, and they never could get another bonita, though they saw them and longed for them often afterward.

On the eighth day the rations were reduced about one half. Thus: breakfast, one fourth of a biscuit, an ounce of ham, and a gill of water to each man; dinner, same quantity of bread and water, and four oysters or clams; supper, water and bread the same, and twelve large raisins or fourteen small ones, to a man. Also, during the first twelve or fifteen days, each man had one spoonful of brandy a day; then it gave out.

This day, as one of the men was gazing across the dull waste of waters as usual, he saw a small, dark object rising and falling upon the waves. He called attention to it, and in a moment every eye was bent upon it in intensest interest. When the boat had approached a little nearer, it was discovered that it was a small green turtle, fast asleep. Every noise was hushed as they crept upon the unconscious slumberer. Directions were given and hopes and fears expressed in guarded whispers. At the fateful moment—a moment of tremendous consequence to these famishing men—the expert selected for the high and responsible office stretched forth his hand, while his excited comrades bated their breath and trembled for the success of the enterprise, and seized the turtle by the hind leg and handed him aboard! His delicate flesh was carefully divided among the party and eagerly devoured—after being "warmed" like the dolphins which went before him.

After the eighth day I have ten days unaccounted for—no notes of them save that the men say they had their two or three ounces of food and their gill of water three times a day—and then the same weary watching for a saving sail by day and by night, and the same sad "hope deferred that maketh the heart sick," was their monotonous experience. They talked more, however, and the captain labored without ceasing to keep them cheerful. (They have always a word of praise for the "old man.")

The eighteenth day was a memorable one to the wanderers on the lonely sea. On that day the boats parted company. The captain said that separate from each other there were three chances for the saving of some of the party where there could be but one chance if they kept together.

The magnanimity and utter unselfishness of Captain Mitchell (and through his example, the same conduct in his men) throughout this distressing voyage are among its most amazing features. No disposition was ever shown by the strong to impose upon the weak, and no greediness, no desire on the part of any to get more than his just share of food, was ever evinced. On the contrary, they were thoughtful of each other and always ready to care for and assist each other to the utmost of their ability. When the time came to part company, Captain Mitchell and his crew, although theirs was much the more numerous party (fifteen men to nine and seven respectively in the other boats), took only one-third of the meager amount of provisions still left, and passed over the other two-thirds to be divided up between the other crews; these men could starve, if need be, but they seem not to have known how to be mean.

After the division the Captain had left for his boat's share two-thirds of the ham, one-fourth of a box of raisins, half a bucket of biscuit crumbs, fourteen gallons of water, three cans of soup-and-bully. [That last expression of the third mate's occurred frequently during his narrative, and bothered me so painfully with its mysterious incomprehensibility that at length I begged him to explain to me what this dark and dreadful "soup-and-bully" might be. With the consul's assistance he finally made me understand the French dish known as soup bouillon is put up in cans like preserved meats, and the American sailor is under the impression that its name is a sort of general title which describes any description of edible whatever which is hermetically sealed in a tin vessel, and with that high contempt for trifling conventionalities which distinguishes his class, he has seen fit to modify the pronunciation into soup-and-bully. —MARK.]

The captain told the mates he was still going to try to make the Clarion Isles, and that they could imitate his example if they thought best, but he wished them to freely follow the dictates of their own judgment in the matter. At eleven o'clock in the forenoon the boats were all cast loose from each other, and then, as friends part from friends whom they expect to meet no more in life, all hands hailed with a fervent "God bless you, boys; good-by!" And the two cherished sails drifted away and disappeared from the longing gaze that followed them so sorrowfully.

On the afternoon of this eventful eighteenth day two boobies were caught—a bird about as large as a duck, but all bone and feathers—not as much meat as there is on a pigeon—not nearly so much, the men say. They ate them raw—bones, entrails and everything—no single morsel was wasted; they were carefully apportioned among the fifteen men. No fire could be built for cooking purposes—the wind was so strong and the sea ran so high that it was all a man could do to light his pipe.

At eventide the wanderers missed a cheerful spirit—a plucky, strong-hearted fellow, who never drooped his head or lost his grip—a staunch and true good friend, who was always at his post in storm or calm, in rain or shine—who scorned to say die, and yet was never afraid to die—a little trim and taut old rooster, he was, who starved with the rest, but came on watch in the stern sheets promptly every day at four in the morning and six in the evening for eighteen days and crowed like a maniac! Right well they named him Richard of the Lion Heart! One of the men said with honest feeling: "As true as I'm a man, Mr. Mark Twain, if that rooster was here today and any man dared to abuse the bird, I'd break his neck!" Richard was esteemed by all, and by all his rights were respected. He received his little ration of bread crumbs every time the men were fed, and, like them, he bore up bravely and never grumbled and never gave way to despair. As long as he was strong enough, he stood in the stern sheets or mounted the gunwale as regularly as his watch came round, and crowed his two-hour talk, and when at last he grew feeble in the legs and had to stay below, his heart was still stout and he slapped about in the water on the bottom of the boat and crowed as bravely as ever! He felt that under circumstances like these America expects every rooster to do his duty, and he did it. But is it not to the high honor of that boat's crew of starving men that, tortured day and night by the pangs of hunger as they were, they refused to appease them with the blood of their humble comrade? Richard was transferred to the chief mate's boat and sailed away on the eighteenth day.

The third mate does not remember distinctly, but thinks morning and evening prayers were begun on the nineteenth day. They were conducted by one of the young Fergusons, because the captain could not read the prayer book without his spectacles, and they had been burned with the ship. And ever after this date, at the rising and the setting of the sun, the storm-tossed mariners reverently bowed their heads while prayers went up for "they that are helpless and far at sea."

On the morning of the twenty-first day, while some of the crew were dozing on the thwarts and others were buried in reflection, one of the men suddenly sprang to his feet and cried, "A sail! a sail!" Of course, sluggish blood bounded then and eager eyes were turned to seek the welcome vision. But disappointment was their portion, as usual. It was only the chief mate's boat drifting across their path after three days' absence. In a short time the two parties were abreast each other and in hailing distance. They talked twenty minutes; the mate reported "All well" and then sailed away, and they never saw him afterward.

On the twenty-fourth day Captain Mitchell took an observation and found that he was in latitude 16° N. and longitude 117° W.—about 1,000 miles from where his vessel was burned. The hope he had cherished so long that he would be able to make the Clarion Isles deserted him at last; he could only go before the wind, and he was now obliged to attempt the best thing the southeast trades could do for him—blow him to the "American group" or to the Sandwich Islands—and therefore he reluctantly and with many misgivings turned his prow toward those distant archipelagoes. Not many mouthfuls of food were left, and these must be economized. The third mate said that under this new program of proceedings "we could see that we were living too high; we had got to let up on them raisins, or the soup-and-bullies, one, because it stood to reason that we warn't going to make land soon, and so they wouldn't last." It was a matter which had few humorous features about it to them, and yet a smile is almost pardonable to this idea, so gravely expressed, of "living high" on fourteen raisins at a meal.

The rations remained the same as fixed on the eighth day, except that only two meals a day were allowed, and occasionally the raisins and oysters were left out.

What these men suffered during the next three weeks no mortal man may hope to describe. Their stomachs and intestines felt to the grasp like a couple of small tough balls, and the gnawing hunger pains and the dreadful thirst that was consuming them in those burning latitudes became almost insupportable. And yet, as the men say, the captain said funny things and talked cheerful talk until he got them to conversing freely, and then they used to spend hours together describing delicious dinners they had eaten at home, and earnestly planning interminable and preposterous bills of fare for dinners they were going to eat on shore, if they ever lived through their troubles to do it, poor fellows. The captain said plain bread and butter would be good enough for him all the days of his life, if he could only get it.

But the saddest things were the dreams they had. An unusually intelligent young sailor named Cox said: "In those long days and nights we dreamed all the time—not that we ever slept, I don't mean—no, we only sort of dozed—three-fourths of the faculties awake and the other fourth benumbed into a counterfeit of a slumber; oh, no—some of us never slept for twenty-three days, and no man ever saw the captain asleep for upward of thirty minutes. But we barely dozed that way and dreamed—and always of such feasts! Bread, and fowls, and meat—everything a man could think of, piled upon long tables, and smoking hot! And we sat down and seized upon the first dish in our reach, like ravenous wolves, and carried it to our lips, and—and then we woke up and found the same starving comrades about us, and the vacant sky and the desolate sea!"

These things are terrible even to think of.

Rations Still Further Reduced. It even startles me to come across that significant heading so often in my notebook, notwithstanding I have grown so familiar with its sound by talking so much with these unfortunate men.

On the twenty-eighth day the rations were: one teaspoonful of bread crumbs and about an ounce of ham for the morning meal; a spoonful of bread crumbs alone for the evening meal, and one gill of water three times a day! A kitten would perish eventually under such sustenance.

At this point the third mate's mind reverted painfully to an incident of the early stages of their sufferings. He said there were two between decks, on board the *Hornet,* who had been lying there sick and helpless for he didn't know how long; but when the ship took fire they turned out as lively as anyone under the spur of the excitement. One was a "Portyghee," he said, and always of a hungry disposition; when all the provisions that could be got had been brought aft and deposited near the wheel to be lowered into the boats, "that sick Portyghee watched his chance, and when nobody was looking he harnessed the provisions and ate up nearly a quarter of a bar'l of bread before the old man caught him, and he had more than two notions to put his light out." The third mate dwelt upon this circumstance as upon a wrong he could not fully forgive, and intimated that the Portyghee stole bread enough, if economized in twenty-eighth-day rations, to have run the longboat party three months.

Four little flying fish, the size of the sardines of these latter days, flew into the boat on the night of the twenty-eighth day. They were divided among all hands and devoured raw. On the twenty-ninth day they caught another, and divided it into fifteen pieces, less than a spoonful apiece.

On the thirtieth day they caught a third flying fish and gave it to the revered old captain—a fish of the same poor little proportions as the others—four inches long—a present a king might be proud of under such circumstances—a present whose value, in the eyes of the men who offered it, was not to be found in the Bank of England—yea, whose vaults were not able to contain it! The old captain refused to take it; the men insisted; the captain said no—he would take his fifteenth—they must take the remainder. They said in substance, though not in words, that they would see him in Jericho first! So the captain had to eat the fish.

I believe I have done the third mate some little wrong in the beginning of this letter. I have said he was as self-possessed as a statue—that he never betrayed emotion or enthusiasm. He never did except when he spoke of "the old man." I always thawed through his ice then. The men were the same way; the captain is their hero—their true and faithful friend, whom they delight to honor. I said to one of these infatuated skeletons, "But you wouldn't go quite so far as to die for him?" A snap of the finger—"As quick as that!—I wouldn't be alive now if it hadn't been for him." We pursued the subject no further.

Rations Still Further Reduced. I still claim the public's indulgence and belief. At least Thomas and his men do through me. About the thirty-second day the bread gave entirely out. There was nothing left, now, but mere odds and ends of their stock of provisions. Five days afterward, on the thirty-seventh day—latitude 16° 30′ N., and longitude 170° W.—kept off for the "American group"—"which don't exist and never will, I suppose," said the third mate. Ran directly over the ground said to be occupied by these islands—that is, between latitude 16° and 17° N., and longitude 133° to 136° W. Ran over the imaginary islands and got into 136° W., and then the captain made a dash for Hawaii, resolving that he would go till he fetched land, or at any rate as long as he and his men survived.

On Monday, the thirty-eighth day after the disaster, "we had nothing left," said the third mate, "but a pound and a half of ham—the bone was a good deal the heaviest part of it—and one soup-and-bully tin." These things were divided among the fifteen men, and they ate it all—two ounces of food to each man. I do not count the ham bone, as that was saved for next day. For some time, now, the poor wretches had been cutting their old boots into small pieces and eating them. They would also pound wet rags to a sort of pulp and eat them.

On the thirty-ninth day the ham bone was divided up into rations, and scraped with knives and eaten. I said: "You say the two sick men remained sick all through, and after awhile two or three had to be relieved from standing watch; how did you get along without medicines!"

The reply was: "Oh, we couldn't have kept them if we'd had them; if we'd had boxes of pills, or anything like that, we'd have eaten them. It was just as well—we couldn't have kept them, and we couldn't have given them to the sick men alone—we'd have shared them around all alike, I guess." It was said rather in jest, but it was a pretty true jest, no doubt.

After apportioning the ham bone, the captain cut the canvas cover that had been around the ham into fifteen equal pieces, and each man took his portion. This was the last division of food the captain made. The men broke up the small oaken butter tub and divided the staves among themselves, and gnawed them up. The shell of the little green turtle, heretofore mentioned, was scraped with knives and eaten to the last shaving. The third mate chewed pieces of boots and spit them out, but ate nothing except the soft straps of two pairs of boots—ate three on the thirty-ninth day and saved one for the fortieth.

The men seem to have thought in their own minds of the shipwrecked mariner's last dreadful resort—cannibalism; but they do not appear to have conversed about it. They only thought of the casting lots and killing one of their number as a possibility; but even when they were eating rags, and bones, and boots, and shell, and hard oak wood, they seem to have still had a notion that it was remote. They felt that someone of the company must die soon—which one they well knew; and during the last three or four days of their terrible voyage they were patiently but hungrily waiting for him. I wonder if the subject of these anticipations knew what they were thinking of? He must have known it—he must have felt it. They had even calculated how long he would last; they said to themselves, but not to each other, I think they said, "He will die Saturday—and then!"

There was one exception to the spirit of delicacy I have mentioned—a Frenchman, who kept an eye of strong personal interest upon the sinking man and noted his failing strength with untiring care and some degree of cheerfulness. He frequently said to Thomas: "I think he will go off pretty soon, now, sir. And then we'll eat him!" This is very sad.

Thomas and also several of the men state that the sick Portyghee, during the five days that they were entirely out of provisions, actually ate two silk handkerchiefs and a couple of cotton shirts, besides his share of the boots, and bones, and lumber.

Captain Mitchell was fifty-six years old on the 12th of June—the fortieth day after the burning of the ship and the third day before the boat's crew reached land. He said it looked somewhat as if it might be the last one he was going to enjoy. He had no birthday feast except some bits of ham canvas—no luxury but this, and no substantials save the leather and oaken bucket staves.

Speaking of the leather diet, one of the men told me he was obliged to eat a pair of boots which were so old and rotten that they were full of holes; and then he smiled gently and said he didn't know, though, but what the holes tasted about as good as the balance of the boot. This man was still very feeble, and after saying this he went to bed.

At eleven o'clock on the 15th of June, after suffering all that men may suffer and live for forty-three days, in an open boat, on a scorching tropical sea, one of the men feebly shouted the glad tidings, "Land ho!" The "watch below" were lying in the bottom of the boat. What do you suppose they did? They said they had been cruelly disappointed over and over again, and they dreaded to risk another experience of the kind—they could not bear it—they lay still where they were. They said they would not trust to an appearance that might not be land after all. They would wait.

Shortly it was proved beyond question that they were almost to land. Then there was joy in the party. One man is said to have swooned away. Another said the sight of the green hills was better to him than a day's rations, a strange figure for a man to use who had been fasting for forty days and forty nights.

The land was the island of Hawaii, and they were off Laupahoehoe and could see nothing inshore but breakers. I was there a week or two ago, and it is a very dangerous place. When they got pretty close to shore they saw cabins, but no human beings. They thought they would lower the sail and try to work in with the oars. They cut the ropes and the sail came down, and then they found they were not strong enough to ship the oars. They drifted helplessly toward the breakers, but looked listlessly on and cared not a straw for the violent death which seemed about to overtake them after all their manful struggles, their privations, and their terrible sufferings. They said, "It was good to see the green fields again." It was all they cared for. The "green fields" were a haven of rest for the weary wayfarers; it was sufficient; they were satisfied; it was nothing to them that Death stood in their pathway; they had long been familiar to him; he had no terrors for them.

Two of Captain Spencer's natives saw the boat, knew by the appearance of things that it was in trouble, and dashed through the surf and swam out to it. When they climbed aboard there were only five yards of space between the poor sufferers and a sudden and violent death. Fifteen minutes afterward the boat was beached upon the shore and a crowd of natives (who are the very incarnation of generosity, unselfishness, and hospitality) were around the strangers, dumping bananas, melons, taro, poi—anything and everything they could scrape together that could be eaten—on the ground by the cartload; and if Mr. Jones, of the station, had not hurried down with his steward, they would soon have killed the starving men with kindness. As it was, the sick Portyghee really ate six bananas before Jones could get hold of him and stop him. This is a fact. And so are the stories of his previous exploits. Jones and the kanaka girls and men took the mariners in their arms like so many children and carried them up to the house, where they received kind and judicious attention until Sunday evening, when two whaleboats came from Hilo, Jones furnished a third, and they were taken in these to the town just named, arriving there at two o'clock Monday morning.

Each of the young Fergusons kept a journal from the day the ship sailed from New York until they got on land once more at Hawaii. The captain also kept a log every day he was adrift. These logs, by the captain's direction, were to be kept up faithfully as long as any of the crew were alive, and the last survivor was to put them in a bottle, when he succumbed, and lash the bottle to the inside of the boat. The captain gave a bottle to each officer of the other boats, with orders to follow his example. The old gentleman was always thoughtful.

The hardest berth in that boat, I think, must have been that of provision keeper. This office was performed by the captain and the third mate; of course they were always hungry. They always had access to the food, and yet must not gratify their craving appetites.

The young Fergusons are very highly spoken of by all the boat's crew, as patient, enduring, manly and kindhearted gentlemen. The captain gave them a watch to themselves—it was the duty of each to bail the water out of the boat three hours a day. Their home is in Stamford, Connecticut, but their father's place of business is New York.

In the chief mate's boat was a passenger—a gentlemanly young fellow of twenty years named William Lang, son of a stockbroker in New York.

The chief mate, Samuel Hardy, lived at Chatham, Massachusetts; second mate belonged in Shields, England; the cook, George Washington (Negro), was in the chief mate's boat, and also the steward (Negro); the carpenter was in the second mate's boat.

Captain Mitchell. To this man's good sense, cool judgment, perfect discipline, close attention to the smallest particulars which could conduce to the welfare of his crew or render their ultimate rescue more probable, that boat's crew owe their lives. He has shown brain and ability that make him worthy to command the finest frigate in the United States, and a genuine unassuming heroism that entitles him to a Congressional medal. I suppose some of the citizens of San

Francisco who know how to appreciate this kind of a man will not let him go on hungry forever after he gets there. In the above remarks I am only echoing the expressed opinions of numbers of persons here who have never seen Captain Mitchell, but who judge him by his works—among others the Hon. Anson Burlingame and our Minister to Japan, both of whom have called at the hospital several times and held long conversations with the men. Burlingame speaks in terms of the most unqualified praise of Captain Mitchell's high and distinguished abilities as evinced at every point throughout his wonderful voyage.

Captain Mitchell, one sailor, and the two Fergusons are still at Hilo. The two first mentioned are pretty feeble, from what I can learn. The captain's sense of responsibility kept him strong and awake all through the voyage; but as soon as he landed and that fearful strain upon his faculties was removed, he was prostrated—became the feeblest of the boat's company.

The seamen here are doing remarkably well, considering all things. They already walk about the hospital a little, and very stiff-legged, because of the long inaction their muscles have experienced.

When they came ashore at Hawaii, no man in the party had had any movement of his bowels for eighteen days, several not for twenty-five or thirty, one not for thirty-seven, and one not for forty-four days. As soon as any of these men can travel, they will be sent to San Francisco.

I have written this lengthy letter in a great hurry in order to get it off by the bark *Milton Badger*, if the thing be possible, and I may have made a good many mistakes, but I hardly think so. All the statistical information in it comes from Thomas, and he may have made mistakes, because he tells his story entirely from memory, and although he has naturally a most excellent one, it might well be pardoned for inaccuracies concerning events which transpired during a series of weeks that never saw his mind strongly fixed upon any thought save the weary longing for food and water. But the logbooks of the captain and the two passengers will tell the terrible romance from the first day to the last in faithful detail, and these I shall forward by the next mail if I am permitted to copy them.

James Cowan

The Slave Ships of Callao

James Cowan (1870–1943), journalist and Maori scholar, was born at Pakuranga, Auckland, of an Irish father who had seen service in the Maori Wars in the Waikato region. Even in childhood, young Cowan absorbed Maori lore. When after an apprenticeship in journalism he took a publicity post with the Tourist Department in Wellington, he was able to travel throughout the islands and study their past. His principal work was a history of the New Zealand wars and the pioneering period, but he also wrote books on other Polynesian islands, such as *Suwarrow Gold* (1936), from which "The Slave Ships of Callao" is taken.

This is a brief account of a horrifying period in South Sea history, when ships from South America raided the islands of the South Pacific for native laborers condemned to die in the guano mines of Peru.

PEACEFUL lay the broad lagoon, peaceful the little thatched-hut villages beneath the palms that swished their fronds in the trade wind. On the outer reef beyond the sheltered glimmerglass, the surf beat with a slow percussive rhythm, softened to a kind of lullaby by distance. Most of the brown folk of the atoll were at their siesta; when the blazing sun westered more they would be making ready for their evening's flying-fish catching by torchlight. Now it was blistering on the beaches; the sunshine was thrown back as from a glittering plate of steel from the surface of the water, a dazzle painful to the eye. The expanse of the lagoon stretched away for some five miles in front of the largest village. To right and left it extended in a crescent; the white heads of the rollers breaking on the coral wall appeared and subsided at regular intervals. Palm-grove isles darkened the long reef line; and in the lagoon there were islets, each bearing its tall leaning coconuts, their heads waving gently in the breeze.

A boy wandering out of one of the quiet dwellings gazed out seaward, shading his eyes from the dazzle. He raised a shrill cry, "*He kaipuké, he kaipuké!*" ("A ship, a ship!"). Out poured the suddenly aroused folk—men, women, and children—just as they jumped up from their mats. They came running to the beach.

There she was, her sails shining pearly white against the blue, a brig, painted black, making for the reef entrance opposite the principal village. Sailing swiftly, and taking in her royals as she opened up the channel, she came in with yards trimmed to the good leading wind. Once well into the lagoon she rounded to and anchored.

The strange craft had an unusually large crew for her size, for while a dozen men were aloft stowing sails, she lowered two whaleboats, each with an officer and five men. By this time the lagoon was alive with outrigger canoes all making for the brig. While some of the clamorous crews were climbing on deck, the two boats had reached the beach.

What could she be, this strongly manned black ship? Vociferous questions went unanswered. But one thing was quickly made clear, she was not a British trader. The officers and sailors who had landed spoke a language strange to the Polynesians. They were dark-avised, their quick black eyes darted here and there; some of them wore cutlasses by their sides; others had holstered revolvers at their belts. But they professed friendship; they had a native of some half-caste breed with them who spoke a dialect understandable by the islanders; and they carried some small presents, tobacco, knives, and beads, which they gave to the headman in the big house for distribution among the people.

When night came down, the strangers returned to the brig. They had arranged that parties of the islanders should visit the ship next morning.

There was little sleep for the people of the palm-grove villages that night. Some of them sat on the beach till late, gazing out at the black shadowy form of the strange ship; the few lights she showed cast long wavering lines of brightness on the face of the lagoon. In the great thatched meetinghouse, most of the excited natives gathered for talk and song and dance. There were improvised chants about the new-come ship. The wooden drums were going with a clatter and a throb that carried far across the waters. The men in the brig could have heard that regular quick rattle of the *pahu,* the sounds that carry their onomatopoeic words to the Polynesian—"Tingiri, ringiri, ranga-ra, ranga-ra, tikirangi-ti."

Daylight had scarcely appeared before the canoes were in the water again. Nearly every man and boy was there, paddling for the brig. A side ladder was down, and men stood in the gangway admitting the natives, one canoe crew at a time. The visitors, tremendously happy and excited, were escorted down below by a ladder in the main hatchway. They were told that there was a feast of biscuit and meat awaiting them.

There were nearly a hundred brown men there, most of the adult male population of the atoll. Crew after crew went below, unsuspecting evil of these strangers almost as dark as themselves.

Suddenly the hatchway was closed, shutting up the islanders in darkness. Their amazed and terrified shouts were faintly heard by the few still left in the canoes. The boats were in the water and the armed crews quickly rounded up the astonished canoe paddlers and forced them up the brig's ladder. Then they made for the shore and compelled the women to load the boats with coconuts, fruit, and yams. Some of the prettiest girls were seized by the officers and thrust into the boats, and off the raiders rowed to the brig. Sails were loosed, the capstan was manned; up came the anchor to the sound of a Spanish chant; the canvas was sheeted home, and under topsails and topgallantsails the black brig stood out through the channel, and into the heaving blue of the Pacific, leaving behind her a ravished land. The coral isle of peace and beauty was a land of mourning, bereft of most of its able-bodied men and its most handsome women, stolen away by whom they knew not, bound they knew not where, victims to the wicked greed of men in high places in a far-off land.

That drama of deceit and tragedy was witnessed in many a South Sea island seventy years ago. At a later date there were somewhat similar episodes in the Black Islands of the Western Pacific, but these raids of which I write were all carried out in the Polynesian islands in the eastern sector of the great South Sea, among a harmless, unsuspecting people, the most pleasing and friendly of all the inhabitants of the Pacific. The piratical marauders were Spanish-American slavers; the vessels were under the Peruvian flag; their raids were carried out systematically over a great area of Polynesia for the purpose of getting free labor for the mines and plantations and guano workings of Peru.

At least a dozen of the coral lands which now fly New Zealand's flag were among the objectives of these forced-labor-getting cruises, and many hundreds of hapless island folk were stolen away for slavery. The tragic recollection of these "thief-ships," as the natives called them, lingers to this day all over the South Pacific.

The records of the raiders and their brutal deeds are scattered and fragmentary. I searched the files of the 'sixties in an attempt to piece together a connected story of the ruffianly business, the lineal successor of the old African negro slave traffic to the United States and Spanish America. Notes on the subject, too, I gathered many years ago from old island traders and sailors.

This cheap labor enterprise began, as nearly as it can be fixed, in the year 1860. The Peruvian government and large private interests found it difficult and expensive to obtain labor for their works in a legitimate way. The mines, the guano islands, the plantations, and other scenes of industry must have men who would work for next to nothing, and if for nothing at all, so much the better. Africa was out of the question, since British warships patroled the slave coast so vigilantly. So Peru turned to the so-far untouched South Sea islands as a likely source of labor which would cost little but the expense of fitting up ships to go and steal it.

The raids by a fleet of Peruvian barks, brigs, and schooners were carried out in the period 1861–63. During that time many vessels were chartered for Callao, to "recruit" labor for the mines. It was said that an engagement was entered into by a Callao house to supply some ten thousand natives. In the year 1863 at least two thousand were actually secured and haled off to lifelong slavery—probably endured only a few years. The trickery and violence, and the murders, the crime and sorrow, make as sorry a tale of sin and suffering as anything in the shocking history of the African slave trade.

At least a score of vessels fitted out at Callao appear to have been for slaving cruises. From lonely Easter Island and that southernmost of the tropic lands, lofty Rapa, up to the Line Islands, and thence as far as the Carolines in the northwest, the pirates roved the Pacific, inveigling the trusting Polynesian people on board by promises, and when trickery failed, capturing them by force of arms. The ships were similar to those employed in the slave trade between West Africa and Brazil, and other American countries. Their holds were fitted with long rows and tiers of bunks, or rather shelves, for the accommodation of the 'livestock'. They carried rice to feed the slaves, and were equipped with large boilers—one brig captured by the French in 1863 had three boilers—for cooking the rice and for condensing seawater for the tanks and casks.

The atolls of the Tokelau group (now under New Zealand's jurisdiction) and the Ellice Islands, both groups lying northward of Samoa, were among the first visited, and hundreds of natives were stolen there. Penrhyn Island, Manihiki, Rakahanga, Pukapuka (Danger Island), the Cook Islands, the Paumotu or Tuamotu Archipelago, the Society Islands—at all of these some of the fleet of thief-ships called. Some places proved unfruitful in recruits—the Society Islands, under the French flag, for instance, and most of the Cook Islands, which are now British. Very few of the vigilant Raratongans fell victims, and none of the Samoans, so far as can be learned. There were many white residents there who would put the natives on their guard against the Spanish-American scoundrels. But the Tokelau people and their like, the atoll-dwellers, among whom there were few white people, fell very easily to the Peruvians' wiles.

When islanders could not be enticed on board by promises of goods, armed parties were landed, the able-bodied men were captured, and those who resisted were shot down. Guns were turned on the canoes, and the terrified people swimming away were rounded up by boats' crews. A trick often used when the natives came aboard unsuspectingly to visit and trade immediately a ship anchored in their lagoons, or lay off the reef, was to ask them down below to have a glass of grog and some biscuits and other white man's food. They were taken into the hold or 'tween-decks, and the hatches were shut down on them.

At Easter Island, that isle of mystery, seven vessels made rendezvous early in the slaving cruise. Their captains landed armed crews, gathered in some hundreds of natives, including the high chiefs and learned men, forced them into the boats, and took them on board. They then made a clean sweep of the island, carrying away all the taro, yams, sweet potatoes, and pigs and fowls, and capped their villainy by setting the houses on fire. Many of the poor people who were captured refused to eat or drink, and died of grief before the ships reached Callao.

At Niué, or Savage Island, two ships from Callao stole ninety men. Only one of these slaves, a young chief named Taolé, lived to see his home island again. His narrative I shall give presently.

At the island of Mauké, in the Cook Group, the Auckland schooner *Flying Fish* in 1863 found the natives in great consternation over the deeds of these Peruvian craft. They feared they would be attacked, and desired that a man-of-war should be sent to cruise in search of the slavers. The schooner *Osprey*, which arrived at Auckland in April, 1863, from the Cook Islands, brought news that a brig, supposed to be Spanish, had visited Mangaia Island, the southernmost of the group, and had stolen away the principal chief's son and several other men. Later, two other vessels, whose people said they were Americans, called and tried to engage two hundred men each, but failed.

Perhaps the most atrocious deed of all was the action of the captain of a bark which put many scores of sick natives on shore at Sunday Island, in the Kermadec group, to recover or die as they might. This was reported in 1863 by a vessel which called at Sunday Island on her way to Samoa. The slaving-vessel was a fast-sailing bark; she had a large crew of Spanish-speaking men from Peru and Chile. This was one of the vessels which had kidnapped natives from Niué. They would probably have had a better chance of recovering from the sickness, whatever it was, on shore, than in the crowded, unsavory ship, but they were callously left there marooned on an all-but-desert island, where nearly all of them died. The epidemic spread too to the family of the one white settler on the island, and his Samoan wife and several children died.

For one particularly vile crime there is no parallel even in the African slave trade. This was the sweeping-off of the Nukulaelae people, in the Ellice Islands. Nukulaelae (or the Mitchell Islands) is a coral reef and lagoon with ten beautiful islands. Before the visit of the Peruvian slavers the population of the atoll was four hundred and fifty, all living in peace and plenty, a happy primitive folk; they had been christianized by native missionaries from Samoa. When H.M.S. *Basilisk* visited the group in 1872 the population was seventy. The story of the great piracy was told to Captain Moresby by the only trader there, a German. He went from Nukulaelae on a cruise to Samoa and when he was away, in 1864, the man-stealers came. He returned to find only fifty worn-out people and children; all the rest had been kidnapped by the ruthless Spanish-Americans. The story told to Moresby was that three large barks, flying the Spanish flag, had appeared off the atoll, and an old man landed and told the natives that the vessels were missionary ships. He invited them on board to receive the Holy Sacrament. In simple faith the islanders went off in their canoes, all the able-bodied men. They were made prisoners and put into the hold. Again the old scoundrel landed and told the women and children that the men had sent him for them. They too went off to the black ships and were thrust into the hold of captivity. Then the wicked ships sailed away. None of those left on shore knew where their friends had gone; they vanished over the horizon. Long afterwards it was found that they had been carried off to Peru; but not a word ever reached Nukulaelae from the stolen people. They disappeared from all ken. "It was sickening," Captain Moresby wrote in his account of his voyage, "to hear the tale told on the spot which had seen all this sorrow." Only two men, one of whom the captain saw, escaped from the thief-ships; they jumped overboard and swam six or seven miles back to the island.

Two or three of the raiders received something of their deserts. In 1863 the French naval authorities at Tahiti had three captured slaving-vessels in Papeete harbor. One of these, the *Cora,* was seized by the natives at Rapa Island. One of the captains was sentenced to ten years' imprisonment and another to five years. It would have been a fitting and dramatic retribution had they been hoisted to the yard-arms of their own black craft, "rigged with curses dark," and sent to the bottom with the scuttled pirate-ship. Unfortunately it does not appear that any of these sea ruffians of the 'sixties were hanged for their crimes.

Thomas Dunbabin

Bully Hayes and Ben Pease

Among the many contributors to the facts and legends of the buccaneering career of William Henry Hayes (1829–1877) was Thomas Dunbabin (1883–1964), journalist and author. Born in Tasmania, Dunbabin was selected as a Rhodes Scholar at Oxford in 1906. On his return he worked on Sydney newspapers. During World War II he served as press attaché at the Australian Legation at Ottawa, and later was director of the Australian News and Information Bureau in London and attaché in New York.

His best known book is *Slavers of the South Seas* (1935), from which "Bully Hayes and Ben Pease" is taken.

AS BLACKBIRDERS, William Henry (Bully) Hayes, once of Cleveland, Ohio, and Benjamin Pease, formerly a lieutenant in the United States Navy, were apparently no worse, and perhaps no better, than scores of others in the trade. Yet these two picturesque, plausible, and daring ruffians stand out from the swarm of blackbirders, Australian, English, American, French, Peruvian, Chilean, who harried the Pacific Islands. Hayes in particular had a certain daredevil and dashing touch about his villainies that marked him off from the crowd of adventurers and riffraff that haunted the South Seas in his day. Like Pease and so many others, he was a stealer of men and of women.

He swept off the people of lonely islets to sell them into slavery. He was also a thorough-paced buccaneer, a sea-robber, a man of many disguises and of many moods. He ranged far and wide over the Pacific, turning up in the most unlikely places and doing the most unexpected things.

His career, too, lasted far longer than that of the usual South Seas pirate. From first to last he was active in the Pacific for nearly twenty years. He had something of the grand manner, and it is no wonder that a Bully Hayes legend has grown up around him.

Hayes was a tall, powerful, upstanding fellow, with a pleasant, open face. Like that stout, smiling contemporary villain of fiction, Count Fosco (whom he resembled in his love of canaries), he went bald early. One sinister touch about him was that the top of his right ear had been bitten off. This fact, however, was concealed by the fact that he wore his hair long and covered his ears. Though he was bald on top of the head he had a luxuriant growth of brown hair at the sides. And he wore a full beard.

Hayes was always well-dressed in the sea-going fashion of the day. Unlike most of the blackbirders he did not drink. He used to say that he could not have made the reputation that he had, and have escaped justice for so long, if he had not been strictly temperate. He had a friendly, plausible manner except when he fell into fits of ungovernable rage. These became more frequent in his later years. Towards the end of his career he shot, it is said, several persons in these accesses of temper. He always professed a becoming sorrow after these events.

A writer who saw Hayes when he brought the brig *Rona* into Hokitika, New Zealand, in 1864—quite early in his Pacific career—describes him as a "stout, bald, pleasant-looking man of good manners." He pictures this dreaded blackbirder and buccaneer as walking about the wharf followed by three white poodle dogs. He was fond of pets, especially of small birds. Like his partner, Pease, Hayes was a marrying man. This observer states that in the cabin of the *Rona* sat the two white wives of Hayes, each with a child.

The elder Hayes is said to have been a bargeman on the Mississippi. And it has been asserted that William Henry worked with his father till he was a strapping lad of eighteen. Then, longing for wider waters than the Mississippi, he ran away to sea. With him went $4,000 from his father's strong box. Where he went for several years and what he did is not recorded. In 1858 he appeared at Hawaii, having been put ashore, perhaps with good reason, from the ship

Orestes. Early in 1859 he went to San Francisco. Two months later he came to Kahului, on the island of Maui, in command of a brig bound for New Caledonia. While bargaining for cattle he was taken in charge by Treadway the sheriff for having entered a closed port without a permit.

Hayes put the blame on his mate for not telling him that it was necessary to enter at Lahaina before coming on to Kahului. He invited Treadway to dinner on the brig, and asked if he would pilot the vessel to Lahaina. Once outside the harbour, Hayes coolly told Treadway that he could either come to New Caledonia or go ashore in his boat, which was alongside. The sheriff went ashore. Next mail brought papers to the United States Consul authorizing the arrest of Hayes and the seizure of the brig.

Hayes had landed in Frisco with fifty dollars—borrowed when on the beach in Hawaii. With this as a basis of credit he had bought the brig, shipped a crew, and fitted the vessel for sea. His actual out-of-pocket expenses were thirteen dollars for water. For this he had to pay cash. This brig was later sunk off Wallis Island. Hayes and others made their way to Samoa in the boat.

Hayes seems to have been seldom long without a vessel. The brig *Rona,* in which he visited Hokitika in 1864, belonged to Lyttelton, New Zealand. It is said that Hayes bought her on terms in Wellington. He then persuaded a merchant in Auckland to fit her out with a cargo for the islands. The merchant's son shipped as supercargo. When they were well out to sea Hayes turned his supercargo adrift in a dinghy. One of the tricks he played when he reached the islands was to kidnap two native chiefs and to keep them on board till the natives filled his vessel with copra. At Hokitika Hayes held a sale of South Sea Island goods and curios. He sold for cash and most of the goods were to be delivered next morning. But when the morning came the *Rona* had gone.

During 1868 Hayes, still master of the *Rona,* landed one hundred and fifty natives of Niue or Savage Island at Tahiti to work on plantations. Their removal from the island, and especially the clandestine departure of the women, was carried out against the laws of the island. The missionary on Savage Island, writing on October 20, 1868, mentions that

Hayes was there in the *Rona*. His ostensible purpose was to buy pigs for Tahiti. But pigs were a secondary object, his primary purpose being to secure a cargo of men and women. Hayes had previously stolen a number of women, many of whom were mothers and wives, and children were left behind uncared for.

Hayes seems to have kept the *Rona* for a period quite without parallel in the case of his other vessels. He seems to have been a reckless navigator; it was a case of "easy come, easy go" with his craft. He usually stole the vessel and was given to piling it up on a reef before very long.

In 1869 we find Hayes associated with that other choice scoundrel, Benjamin Pease. It has been claimed for Pease that he was the first man to import island labor into Fiji. Hayes became master of the brig *Pioneer* (also called the *Leonora*), of which Pease was allegedly the owner. The two worked for a time in the North Pacific. Then their ways diverged.

But they met again at Samoa. Hayes was by this time in command of the schooner *Atlantic* and had been blackbirding and trading, in his own peculiar way, amongst the eastern islands. As a result of a specially audacious bit of blackbirding the *Atlantic* was seized by the British consul at Apia, John L. Williams.

In a report dated March 11, 1870, Williams tells us something of the blackbirding methods of Hayes. He had first of all kidnapped a score of natives of Danger Island, intending to sell them in Fiji. These natives were utterly useless as laborers, for when they could not get their accustomed food, consisting mostly of coconuts and fish, they died. Of the twenty whom Hayes had taken on board his schooner, seventeen were dead when he called at Apia and the other three were dying.

Hayes had then gone to Manihiki, where he had kidnapped a number of lads and girls, intending to sell them in Fiji. Apart from kidnapping these people Hayes had, the consul reported, robbed and defrauded them, taking coconuts, mats, and hats with no intention of paying for them. Promising to pay for the cargo at a neighboring island, Hayes had enticed a large number of natives, young and old, on board the *Atlantic*. He had then turned out of the vessel the older and less valuable natives.

A touch of compassion on the part of this hardened kidnapper proved his undoing. The evidence on which the consul acted in arresting Hayes and releasing his blackbirds was supplied by Moete, a Catholic native of Manihiki. Moete was a middle-aged native who with his wife and some of his children had gone on board the *Atlantic* to sell coconuts. When the schooner was about to make sail with the kidnapped lads and girls, Hayes ordered Moete and Toka to be sent ashore with the other older people. They loved their children so much that they could not bear the idea of being parted from them, perhaps for ever. So they begged to be taken into captivity with the children if the latter could not be released. Hayes allowed Moete and his wife to stay on board. Moete also told the consul that a teacher at Tahiti sent on board the schooner two little girls as a present to Hayes. Knowing that Hayes was a desperate and resourceful ruffian, Williams, who possessed no real force, did not quite know what to do with him. Williams desired to hold him until a war vessel arrived on which he could be sent to Sydney. In the meantime he did not venture to put Hayes in the calaboose but had him kept under surveillance. Just then Ben Pease arrived in the brig *Leonora,* or *Pioneer.* Hayes pointed out to the consul that the chronometers of the *Atlantic* required rating and secured permission to take them on board the *Leonora* for that purpose. When the consul woke up next day the *Leonora* had gone and so had Hayes. It was All Fools' Day, April 1, 1870.

After describing how Hayes had escaped from Apia on April 1, 1870, in Pease's brig, Williams says that the *Pioneer* visited Savage Island where Pease, by means of a forged order, obtained cotton and coconut fiber to the value of £300, the property of J. and T. Skinner of Sydney. After this robbery the two rascals called at Savau in Samoa, where they obtained three thousand yams from a British trader and left without paying for them. Hayes was in the habit of landing an armed party on any island where he could find coconut oil and taking it to his vessel, threatening to fire on any one who interfered.

The stolen goods seem to have been sold in Fiji. The *Leonora* turned up at Shanghai with both Hayes and Pease on board. Within ten days Pease was in prison, charged with murder. Hayes fitted the *Leonora* for sea. He paid only one bill, that for the spare mainyard. Then he went down the China coast, levying blackmail on the villages as he went. He put into Saigon, where he was chartered to carry a cargo of rice to Hong Kong, via ports. At one of these ports on the way, the owner of the rice went ashore on business. Hayes made sail, leaving the owner there, and sold the rice at Bangkok on his own account. A steamer with the owner of the rice on board made Bangkok just after Hayes had gone.

In due course Hayes drifted back to Samoa, where he was again arrested. This time the action was taken by Captain Meade of the United States cruiser *Narragansett.* As no evidence against him seemed to be forthcoming, Meade set Hayes free. Then Hayes persuaded Meade to give him a set of sails. A little earlier in his career Hayes commanded a black brig called the *Water Lily,* which may have been the *Pioneer* or *Leonora* under another name. He was blackbirding in the Western Pacific in her. It was suggested that he lent this vessel to headhunting natives, carrying them on their raids. Probably this accusation was unfounded.

Hayes seems to have had an objection to Frenchmen. He bargained with the French owner of the schooner *Giovanni Apiama* for a share in the vessel. Hayes was to pay a sum in cash and to throw in a share in certain trading stations. One day as they sailed past a lonely islet the Frenchman was struck from behind and stunned. He woke up on shore with the schooner standing away under full sail. Hayes then, so it is said, entrusted the stolen schooner to a skipper named Pinkham, and never saw either the vessel or Pinkham again.

Hayes was caught napping after this episode. He was surprised by the Spaniards at Guam while bathing; he was made prisoner and sent to Manila, where he passed himself off as a devout Catholic. He soon escaped from Manila and turned up again at San Francisco, where he stole the schooner *Lotus.*

Captain Moore, of H.M.S. *Barossa,* came across the track of Hayes in the Line Islands in 1872. A Frenchman named Lechat complained that Hayes had cheated him over the purchase of his vessel and over a proposed partnership in trepang stations. Finally he challenged Hayes to come on shore and fight a duel with revolvers, to which Hayes replied:

"Anyhow, I do not wish to see you any longer on my vessel; be off with you or I will throw you overboard."

When Lechat replied that he was going but would meet Hayes again in China, he was knocked down the side ladder and stunned. When he came to himself his blood stained the deck. There was, Lechat said, a "concert of maledictions" against Hayes.

An Englishman with the remarkable name of Asia James Lowther, trading agent on the Mulgrave Islands for Towns and Company of Sydney, stated that Hayes offered him £20 down for his oil. When he said that the hogsheads containing the oil were not his, Hayes flew into a frightful rage and said:

"If Jesus Christ and God Almighty stood at the door I would fight for it." Hayes took the oil and eight pigs and ordered Asia James off the station.

Captain Simpson of H.M.S. *Blanche* reported on June 6, 1872, that Hayes had apparently abandoned kidnapping and had established himself in the Marshall group, where he carried on a so-called legal trade but was constantly com mitting piratical depredations.

At an early stage in his Pacific career Hayes did a little to aid missionary enterprise. He was trading in the Hervey group in a fifty-ton schooner, said to have been stolen from Singapore, and agreed to take a party of missionaries from Apia to the Herveys. When they reached the islands the goods of the missionaries, to the value of between £200 and £300, were missing. Hayes swore that they had never been put on board. It was found later that he had bartered them away for copra in another part of the group.

Apart from this slip, Hayes behaved well on the trip. When the missionaries suggested that they might hold service on the schooner, Hayes asked them not to be afraid of making the service too long as he wanted to get as much of it as he could while he had the chance. He said that he felt that the voyage was going to do him a great deal of good. On the first Sunday Hayes was there for the service but no other member of the crew:

"Just wait a minute," said Hayes, "I won't have any skulking." The leading missionary said that if the crew did not wish to come he would rather not have them at the service. "I don't care a curse," replied Hayes. "They are on a missionary ship now and as long as you are on board I guess they will have to reform."

About this time Hayes had a supercargo who may, or may not, have been Louis Becke. They quarrelled and Hayes battered his supercargo over the head with a bag containing $250. Then Hayes threw the bag, and the dollars, overboard, saying that the dollars were not fit to keep after touching such a skunk. It was on the same trip that Hayes rebuked the mate for swearing as he went up into the rigging.

"Come down, you skunk," roared Hayes. "If there is any swearing to be done on this trip I'll do it."

A favorite practice of Hayes and one that led to much confusion was to disappear for months and to spread reports that he was dead. Then he would turn up in some quite different region and begin all over again.

He is said to have stolen a vessel at Batavia, in addition to his ship-stealing at San Francisco, Singapore, and other ports up and down the Pacific. He was stopped by an English warship but told so plausible a tale that he was allowed to proceed, after borrowing a few articles from the captain.

After this he returned to San Francisco and conspired with a man, who had once been his cook, to steal a cutter. This, evidently, was the third vessel he had stolen from San Francisco. Hayes stole also the wife of the captain of the cutter and they went cruising in the Pacific.

One day in 1876, as they were sailing among the Line Islands, the cook was steering and something annoyed Hayes. He kicked the cook, who naturally resented this. Hayes, in one of his furious rages, went below to secure his revolver. As he came up on deck again the cook, leaving the steering-wheel to itself, struck the bully over the head with the iron handle of the tiller. Hayes was killed instantly. Such was his reputation, however, that even the slayer (whose name is said to have been Janssen, though others call him Peters) could hardly believe that he was really dead at last.

The cook tied the body to a small anchor and threw it over the side, remarking: "For sure he's dead this time." So perished Bully Hayes and that was his only epitaph.

On St. George's Day, April 23, 1869, the brig *Pioneer,* or *Leonora,* sailed into Port Lloyd in the Bonin Islands. Pease played the part of a gentleman with large but vague interests in various parts of the Pacific. He passed as the owner of the brig while Hayes was the master. Pease persuaded Thomas Webb, one of the most substantial settlers on this remote group, that he had in his gift a profitable post as superintendent of sawmills to be set up on the island of Ascension in the Carolines. Webb placed all his stock at the disposal of the plausible Pease and shipped with all his family on the *Pioneer.* Pease married an island girl, Susan Robinson. Like his associate Hayes, Pease had a habit of marrying. He landed Webb and his family on the island of Ascension and sailed away, stating that he had to hasten on his cruise. Webb found there *was* a sawmill on Ascension, but that Pease had no more to do with it than the man in the moon, and that there was no vacancy for a superintendent. As for Pease's new wife, a Bonin Islander who saw her at the end of the honeymoon trip writes: "Susan is well but not contented, for Captain Pease carried two native women besides her on the vessel."

Mrs. Susan Pease had been one of the heroines of a strange story in which blackbirding and murder were mixed up with a Bonins' feud. Her father, George Robinson, had left a whaler at the Bonins and had settled on the South Island, where he had cleared a good deal of land. After eight years of life on this lonely island he went with his family, including Susan, to Guam and Saipan in the Ladrones. Three years later he returned, bringing with him some natives of the Kingsmill Islands, whom he proposed to employ on his farm. He found the land, however, in the possession of James Mutley, an old-timer who had come to the Bonins in 1846. Mutley refused to give it up.

The kanakas whom Robinson had brought with him left him and sided with Mutley. On the other hand, an ex-whaler named Bob who had been taken in by Mutley came over to the Robinson party. One day in 1860 the Kingsmill

Islanders attacked Bob. He fought bravely and defended himself for a time by getting into a cleft amongst the rocks. Finally the kanakas overpowered him, killed him, and savagely mutilated the body. Robinson fled into the bush with three of his six children. The kanakas pursued and caught the fugitives and brought them to Mutley, who arranged for them to be taken away from the island on a passing whaler.

The other three Robinson children escaped with their old nurse, a woman from the Raven Islands called Hypa. These children were Caroline, the eldest girl, who was nineteen, Susan, and a boy Charles. They crossed the island and stayed there for eleven months, hiding in the bush and living on shell-fish and wild berries. They were then picked up and taken to Port Lloyd by the master of a whaling vessel, Captain William Marsh. Thomas Webb, a leading settler, took them in. He later married Caroline, while Susan in due course married Benjamin Pease. She came back to the Bonins and survived Pease by thirty years, dying in 1912. Hypa, the Raven Island nurse, died in 1897 at the reputed age of one hundred and twelve. At her express wish, she was baptized just before her death.

On what terms Robinson secured the Kingsmill Islanders whom he brought to the Bonins is not stated, but a document signed by Ebenezer F. Nye, master of the bark *Helen Snow,* and dated June 1, 1860, tells of the bringing to the Bonins of some natives of the Marquesas group. It looks as if Ebenezer had been doing a little blackbirding, for he protests rather too much. His statement reads:

"This is to certify that I have brought to this port from Wellington Island at their own request three women, one man, and a child and given them their passage free, and they are at perfect liberty to go where they please and to stop with whom they please, and no one, I hope, will take advantage of them or misuse them in any way."

There is no harm in hoping.

Pease paid further visits to the Bonin Islands and settled there for a time, in the intervals of more exciting episodes such as blackbirding, stealing a schooner from a Frenchman, stealing whale oil, and standing his trial at Shanghai for the murder of his cooper—a charge on which he was acquitted. The end came in 1881, when Pease was master of the schooner *Lotus* (perhaps the one that Hayes had stolen from San Francisco), trading in the Marshall Islands. When the *Lotus* was on her way from Jaluit to Ebon Island, the kanaka crew mutinied and threw Pease overboard, no doubt for good reasons. The schooner was making little way and Pease started to swim after her, calling to the kanakas and asking them to pick him up. The kanakas threw Pease's seachest overboard and told him to go back to Jaluit on it.

Thomas Henry Huxley

Mrs. Thompson Among the Cannibals

One of the greatest English biologists, Thomas Henry Huxley (1825–1895), as a young man spent almost five years as assistant surgeon on the exploring vessel H.M.S. *Rattlesnake* in the South Pacific. Huxley Island in the Louisiade Archipelago was given his name. The following brief extract from his journal, edited by his grandson Julian Huxley, shows some of the literary skill that was to make "Darwin's bulldog" the most readable biologist of his time.

The heroine of the event, who had been cast away on Possession Island and who lived for about five years among the cannibal natives of the Prince of Wales Islands near the tip of Cape York, furnished much information about the manners and superstitions of these aboriginal islanders.

October 6, 1849

THE MOST remarkable occurrence that has yet befallen us happened yesterday. A large party of natives came on from the islands and shortly after their arrival Scott (the captain's coxswain) and several seamen wandering about fell in with a party of them—gins—among whom was a white woman disfigured by dirt and the effect of the sun on her almost uncovered body; her face was nevertheless clean enough, and before the men had time to recover from their astonishment she advanced towards them and in hesitating broken language cried "I am a Christian—I am ashamed." The men immediately escorted her down to Heath's party, ashore watering, who of course immediately took her under their protection, and the cutter arriving very shortly to take the party on board, she found herself once more safe among her own people. Three natives accompanied her off in the canoe whom she called her brothers and who appeared much interested in her.

This is her story, told in half Scotch, half native dialect, for she has been so long among these people as nearly to forget her mother tongue.

Her name is Thompson and her maiden name was Crawford. She was born in Aberdeen and her father was a tinsmith who emigrated when she was about eight years old to Australia. From her account he appears to have been at first in very good business in Sydney but latterly became unsteady and consequently descending lower in the scale, was, when she left him, only a journeyman.

When between fifteen and sixteen she left her father's house without his knowledge or consent and making her way up to Moreton Bay with a lover of hers was there married to him. She wrote to her father to tell him that she was happy and doing well but has never since heard anything of him. The husband was a sailor and appears to have been a very handy sort of man; according to her account he could make everything for himself from the shoes on his feet to the hat on his head and furthermore fitted up very well a small cutter rather larger than our *Asp*.

She tells me he was a great favorite with Captain Wickham and might have done very well at Moreton Bay. However, the tempter came, in the shape of an old sailor who had been wrecked in a large ship, well laden, on an island in Torres Straits, and he gave Thompson such brilliant ideas of the profit to be obtained by any one who should take the trouble to visit the wreck and walk off with "jetsam and flotsam" that the latter resolved to go in his cutter and either return to Moreton Bay or go on to Port Essington (at which place he seems to have had some idea of settling). About this time Dr. Leichhardt was starting on his overland expedition and it appears that he wished Thompson to join him, but the latter, the worse for him, preferred his own exploration, only promising on his arrival at Port Essington to inform the people of the coming expedition and induce them to send a party to meet it.

After living, then, about eighteen months at Brisbane, Thompson with his wife and three men started in the cutter on their ill-omened journey. They had nearly reached the desired island when a heavy squall came on, and their little vessel was utterly wrecked upon a reef running out from the island.

Two native canoes which were out turtle fishing were similarly distressed by the squall but the natives easily reached the shore. Not so with the unfortunate tenants of the cutter: the three men were drowned, and Mrs. Thompson was drowning when one of the blackfellows (Aliki who came on board with her) swam out, and seizing her arm brought her safely to land.

They treated her very kindly, fed her and protected her from insult. One of the old chiefs, who had lately lost a daughter, persisted, according to their common belief that white people are the ghosts of black, that she was this very daughter "jump alive again" and she seems to have been regularly adopted among them, so that she talks of her brothers, nephews, etc. Years rolled on, and by degrees she approximated towards her friends, adopting their language so that she speaks it fluently and at present evidently thinks in it, having in talking to you to translate her native thoughts into plain English, sometimes a matter of considerable difficulty, and at the same time adopting their ways so that her manners present a most ludicrous graft of the gin upon the white woman.

For the first twelvemonth she kept some account of time but afterwards lost it, so that she has no idea of dates at present, and indeed, as she says herself, she would have forgotten her own language had she not been accustomed to sing to herself at night all the old fragments of songs and ballads she could remember.

The natives appear to have treated her quite as a pet; she never shared in the labors of the women but stayed in the camp to look after the children while they went out on "hospitable cares intent." Of the kindness and good disposition of the men she speaks in the highest terms, and of the women too she speaks well but says that some of them were not so kind.

Year after year she saw the English ships sail by on their way to China but never had any opportunity of communicating with them, and sometimes she says she was very sorrowful and despairing.

Last year she knew of our being here but the natives would not let her come, and when the canoes were setting out from the islands to visit us for the purpose of getting tobacco, etc., the women were very unwilling to let her come, and it was only partly by promises to return, partly by the influence of "Toma-gogi," one of her brothers, a gentleman about six feet two and doubtless proportionately respected, that she got away.

So far as we can judge she has been five years among these people, and is therefore even now a very young woman; and indeed notwithstanding the hard life she must have led, she looks young, and I have no doubt when she is appropriately dressed, and gets rid of her inflamed eyes, she will be not bad-looking.

Poor creature! we have all great compassion for her and I am sure there is no one who would not do anything to make her comfortable. Captain Stanley gives her his workshop for a cabin, and as soon as she recovers herself sufficiently to understand the use of a needle, she can have as much calico and flannel as she wants, to make mysterious feminine toggery.

She must be content to take a long cruise with us, but it will be at any rate, I should think, preferable to her late circumstances.

W. D. Alexander

Burial of the Last Prince of Kauai

The funeral rites of the son of Kaumualii, last king of the Hawaiian island of Kauai, were, even as late in island history as 1849, supposed to be accompanied by the death of two retainers who would keep him company in the spirit world.

William DeWitt Alexander (1833–1913), born in Honolulu, eldest son of a pioneer missionary family, graduated from Yale University in 1855, and two years later returned to his birthplace as professor of Greek at Punahou School. He became a member of the privy council of the kingdom and a distinguished geographer and historian. His account of the funeral of Prince Kealiiahonui is taken from the *Hawaiian Historical Society Report* for 1907.

THE FUNERAL rites of Kealiiahonui, in 1849, are a striking example of the survival of pagan supersititions long after the introduction of Christianity into these Islands.

This Kealiiahonui was the son of Kaumualii, the last king of Kauai, and of Kapuaamohu, a Kauai princess of the highest rank. He was, therefore, of the bluest blood in the realm. In addition to this he was considered to be the handsomest chief in the Islands, and was proficient in all athletic exercises. He was six feet six inches in height and finely proportioned; a model for a sculptor.

In 1821 he was married to the Queen Regent, Kaahumanu, whose matrimonial chains were said by Stewart "not to have been altogether silken." After her death, in 1832, he married Kekauonohi, a granddaughter of Kamehameha I through his son Kahoanoku-Kinau. Her mother was Wahinepio, a sister of Kalanimoku.

It is only too evident that Kealiiahonui was kept in the background by the jealousy of the Hawaii chiefs. After Governor Kaikioewa's death, however, in 1840, his wife, Kekauonohi, was for some years Governess of Kauai. The late Levi Haalelea was latterly employed as their private secretary and land agent.

Kealiiahonui died at Honolulu, June 23, 1849, in what is known as the Haalelea House. Haalelea soon afterwards married his widow, who died two years later. There was a famous lawsuit over the genuineness of an alleged will of Kealiiahonui (leaving all his lands to his widow), which has twice been renewed since.

From the *Polynesian* newspaper of the time we learn that he was born August 17, 1800, and that his public funeral took place in Honolulu, June 30, 1849. A niece of his, Kapule by name, who was still living at a very advanced age when this was written, faithfully attended him during his last sickness and death. She was cited as a witness in the lawsuit over his will. Her mother was the daughter of King Kaumualii by Naluahi, a woman of low rank, and her father was an American sailor, "Ako," who is supposed to have been lost at sea. She and her husband were *kahus* of Kealiiahonui, and had a recognized right to be consulted in the disposition of his remains.

It seems that by Kekauonohi's orders the coffin containing her late husband's remains was removed to Puuloa, Ewa, with the view of having it afterwards taken out to sea and there sunk. It was temporarily deposited in a cavern in the coral limestone back of Puuloa, which has long been used for a burial place, and has lately been closed up.

Kapule strongly objected to the plan of sinking the coffin in the sea, and delayed its execution for a considerable time. At last certain chiefs from Honolulu paid her a visit and succeeded in overcoming her opposition. During the following night she and her husband, with one or two assistants, removed the outer coffin, which they afterwards buried somewhere near Puuloa.

In order to test the truth of her story, at the instance of her lawyer, about 1892, the spot was found by her direction, and part of the coffin was dug up, with the brass plate on it in good preservation. There is a peculiar superstition among the native Hawaiians in regard to the disposal of the outer coffin in such cases, of which we have had illustrations in recent times. In their opinion, if such a coffin is left unburied it bodes death to some near relative of the deceased. During the same night they took out the sacred bones, the *unihipili* which they hunakele'd, or concealed, according to the ancient custom. I am informed that they were sunk in the sea.

Kapule took an earring and a finger ring from the body, which she preserved for a long time as relics of her master.

A day or two after this the coffin was taken on a canoe out to the deep sea outside of Pearl Harbor, to a spot five miles out, known to fishermen as *kamole ia,* to be sunk, by six brothers from Kauai who were *kahus,* or retainers, of the dead chief. A son of one of them, Simona, a well-known fisherman, who died a few years ago at Puuloa, gave this account to the late James I. Dowsett.

Two men had been selected as victims, *moe puu,* to be put to death on the occasion, that they might accompany their chief into the other world. But when the time came only one of them, Kanepio by name, could be found; the other, Opiopio, having absconded. He was taken out to sea in the canoe, but when the time came for despatching him, one of the brothers, Kauhini, made a strong plea for his life. He said that the order of their chief was that two should die, but not that either should die without the other. "Either both or neither," he said. He pressed this argument so strongly that he carried his point, and the coffin, with the remains of the last prince of Kauai, was committed to the deep without any attendant to bear him company.

My informant relates that the coffin floated at first, on which a superstitious boatman said it was because they had not made the human sacrifice commanded by the chief. Then Kauhini, raising his paddle, smashed the glass case over the face of the corpse, upon which the coffin filled and sank to the bottom of the sea.

The method of burial was closely connected with the belief in *aumakuas,* or ancestral deities. In this case the *aumakuas* of Kealiiahonui's family may have been shark gods or other marine deities, and the object of sinking his body in the sea was probably to introduce him into the society of these powerful spirits, where he might exert his influence to befriend members of the family in times of danger upon the sea.

In the same way the bones of other chiefs have been thrown into the fiery lake of Halemaumau, that they might join the company of Pele and her numerous family of volcanic deities.

Rev. John B. Stair

A Samoan Poltergeist

An English missionary who spent some years in Samoa was puzzled for many years about the possible existence of supernatural events and native sorcery.

John Bettridge Stair labored in the islands for the London Missionary Society from 1838 to 1845. Because of his wife's precarious health, he returned to England in 1849, but later was transferred to Australia as a Church of England vicar in the dioceses of Melbourne and Ballarat.

"A Samoan Poltergeist" is drawn from an article by Stair in the *Journal of the Polynesian Society,* Vol. V. (1896), pp. 50–53. Later reflections on his adventures among the spirits appear in his *Old Samoa* (London: Religious Tract Society, 1897, pp. 261–265).

I HAVE given some carefully recorded statements of natives and facts bearing upon the belief of the old Samoans upon such matters, and I now, for the first time, make known a few facts and experiences bearing upon this most interesting subject as they occurred to me personally more than fifty years ago. During the earlier years of my residence amongst the Samoans, various circumstances occurred which were so strange and unaccountable that I could not understand them, and thinking of them in connection with many statements of the natives I was forced to the conclusion that they were the results of other than ordinary agencies.

Two or three of these may be mentioned which occurred at Falelatai during my residence there, somewhere about the years 1839 and 1840, and the facts alluded to consisted of a constant succession of extraordinary noises and visitations, which I could never understand or fathom as arising from any ordinary causes.

The house we then occupied was a new one, substantial and well built, so as to be free from easy access for the purpose of annoyance; but for many months, night after night, our sleep, as well as the sleep of all in the house, was disturbed by most uncanny noises and doings that were the occasion of much annoyance and astonishment alike to ourselves, our native servants, and occasional visitors.

A long passage ran through the center of the house from end to end, having rooms on either side opening into it, and in a most unaccountable manner this passage became the scene of nightly doings that utterly perplexed and astonished us all, including our native servants and native friends, so much so that they seemed more perplexed than ourselves. Night after night, after we had all retired to rest, this passage appeared to be taken possession of by a party of bowlers, who kept up an incessant rolling of what seemed to be wild oranges or *molis,* backwards and forwards from end to end. Not a sound could be heard other than the interminable mysterious bowling or rolling of these *molis* or balls backwards and forwards; the most cautious inspection failing to reveal any human agency in producing these uncanny noises and disturbances.

After a time we became so used to them that they lost their novelty in a measure, and we slept in spite of them, but we could never dispossess ourselves of a certain uncomfortable feeling that the nearness of such uncanny visitors and roisterous doings produced. Strangers coming and hearing the noises for the first time were amazed and wondered, and the breakfast table the next morning was sure to be the scene of eager questions and expostulations.

"Stair, I wonder you allow your servants to keep such late hours and indulge in such uncanny sports."

"What do you mean?" I would reply, "there were no servants about, they had all retired to rest long before we did last night."

"Why," the reply would come, "I heard them rolling balls up and down the passage for hours last night, so that I could not sleep." And great indeed was the astonishment when we assured the visitor that these strange noises were of nightly occurrence and the outcome of unknown or apparently ghostly visitants!

At other times loud noises and knockings would be heard on the outer door, which would appear to be battered as though about to be smashed in; but not the slightest trace could be found of the delinquents any more than they could be found in what I have described under the head of native testimony.

One instance especially made a deep impression on my mind. It was a lovely moonlit night, and a number of native chiefs and leading men had gathered in my front room, as their delight was to talk over various matters, especially to discuss foreign customs and doings. The room was well filled, and we were in the midst of an animated discussion when suddenly a tremendous crash came at the front door, as though it must be smashed in. Instantly the whole party jumped up and scattered, some to the front, some to the back, and others to the sides, so as to completely surround the house and capture the aggressors, or so for the moment the whole company thought. Hardly a word was spoken, but a rush was made to capture the offender. Not a soul was to be seen outside, however, and in a very short time the whole party were collected, crestfallen at their want of success, and keenly discussing as to who could have caused the noise. The idea of its being the act of a native was scouted by the whole party, who said it was well known that the gathering of the chiefs was there, and no native would have dared commit the outrage. It was generally decided that it must be the doings of the *aitu* or *aitus,* who were such constant aggressors! Yet for all that every place was still further keenly searched, but without avail.

Later on in the evening we were collected together at one end of the house near to a large *ifi* (chestnut) tree, in which a good-sized bell was hung for use on various occasions. Suddenly the bell began to ring violently, without any apparent cause—no hand was pulling it, but it kept on wildly clanging in full view of the whole party, who looked on in amazement.

"Perhaps there is a string attached and someone pulling it, secreted under that fence," suggested one. Immediately one of the number ran to the fence, but no one was there. Another climbed the tree. There was no string attached, but the bell kept on wildly ringing! There was in reality no need to ascend the tree to ascertain the fact of there being no string attached, for every leaf and twig stood out boldly to view in the bright moonlight; but the mystery was not solved, and the old conclusion was come to that it was part of the mischievous doings of the *aitu.*

Still, another mystery! As we were talking eagerly together, we were suddenly pelted with small stones, thrown obliquely, which struck several of the party with no little force; some on the breast, others on other parts of the body, myself on the foot—leaving us all so mystified that we separated, the outsiders to their homes and we to our haunted dwelling, more astounded than ever.

At last, after many months, my wife's health began to be affected, and at length quite to fail under the effects of much nervous prostration brought on by these continued uncanny visitations, aided by the great humidity of the district, so that it was deemed advisable we should remove to a more healthy place, which we did, at much loss and inconvenience. Our house was left, and with the removal we were happily freed from any further ghostly visitations.

Very much astonishment was expressed by the natives as to what they thought was the occasion of these extraordinary visitations. Some thought the house had been unwittingly built upon an old native burying-ground, others that the *ifi* tree was an old *malumalu,* or temple of an *aitu.* If so, the wrath of the various *folaunga-aitu,* or parties of voyaging spirits, must have been aroused at seeing the sanctity of their temple invaded.

In after years I often visited the spot, but the house was dismantled and, if I mistake not, was not occupied after, certainly it was not by any European.

One old chief and orator, Sepetaio, from Mulinu'u, seemed much concerned at our frequent annoyances, and often discussed them with us. One day he came and, to my amusement, he gravely proposed to capture some one of the *aitus* that caused us so much annoyance. If I would let him have one of my servants named Mu, he declared, he could capture the *aitu* and bring him before me. I thanked him very much, but declined his offer to make me personally acquainted with the *aitu.* Among other things, he told me of an adventure that had happened to this same man Mu many years before, in which he had successfully laid his plans to capture an *aitu.*

Tradition records that an *aitu* was accustomed to sit upon the limb of a tree somewhere near the neighborhood of Palauli (black mud), Savaii, from which he so constantly assaulted travellers as to become the bugbear of the place. At length a traveling party from Falelatai, happening to stay there, were duly informed of the trouble of the villagers, on which Mu proposed to capture the *aitu,* provided the villagers would lend him their assistance and support him in his plans, which they gladly consented to do.

He then procured some putrid fish, with which he rubbed himself over as the night advanced, and started alone for the haunt of the *aitu,* having previously arranged with his companions that they should light a big fire in the marae and appear as if they were having a merrymaking, while some of their number were to lie in ambush near the fire with their clubs.

On nearing the spot Mu saw the *aitu* seated upon a branch, and at once accosted him.

After a little time the *aitu* said, "What a nice smell comes from you."

"Yes," said the man, "I have been feasting upon a dead man, and a famous feast I have had. Would you not like to have some of what is left?"

"Indeed, I should," said the *aitu,* "but if I go you must carry me."

"All right," said Mu, "I will carry you part of the way and you shall carry me the rest."

On this Mu started with the *aitu* on his back, taking the road towards the village, which they reached after mutual carryings. The *aitu* made some remark as to the noises and shouts of laughter that came from the village, when Mu said to his companion, who was riding, "Don't hold so tightly, you will choke me; sit loosely upon my back, and hold lightly by my throat, for as we must pass through this village I shall have to walk quickly, as I know they are a bad lot;

so don't stop my breathing." The *aitu,* anxious to get to the promised feast, did as he was told, and Mu trudged onwards, taking care to pass close by the fire, into which he pitched his burden, then the ambush rushed to the spot and beat fire and *aitu* to pieces with their clubs, and were thus enabled to rid themselves of their tormentor.

George Anson, Lord Byron

Lord Byron Views the Rites

This report on observing in 1825 a ceremony of *pule anaana* or "praying to death" is given by the commander of the British Navy vessel that brought back in state to Hawaii the bodies of King Kamehameha II and his wife, who had died in London of a fatal attack of measles.

George Anson, Captain the Right Honorable Lord Byron, R.N. (1789–1858), unlike his famed poet cousin, was always affable and tactful. At a time when the Hawaiian Kingdom was still considered to be under the protection of Great Britain, he quietly encouraged the ruling chiefs to consider making and enforcing modern laws, such as trial by jury.

His account is taken from a compilation of notes made by gentlemen on the voyage under the title of *Voyage of H.M.S. "Blonde" to the Sandwich Islands, 1824–25*, published in London in 1826.

February 28 [*1825*]

RETURNING from a walk this morning, I witnessed, for the first time, a rite of sorcery. My attention was attracted by a group of people near the path I was crossing. On approaching it, though ignorant of the particular ceremony performing, I at once judged it to be idolatrous.

A small mat was spread on the ground, on which was spread several pieces of tapa, a native cloth, and on those again two of the large leaves of the *ape* (one of the largest of the vegetable productions of the islands—I do not know its scientific name). These last seemed to have been prepared with special care; they were both of the same size; were placed the one directly above the other, both of the stems being split entirely up to the point of the leaves. They were carefully held together by a man kneeling at one end, while the priest or sorcerer, kneeling at the other, repeated prayers over them. These, with two or three others who appeared engaged in the ceremonies, were as solemn as the grave; the rest of the company were light and trifling, and some of them turned to me, and laughing at what they seemed to think the folly of their friends, said, *ino, ino*—bad, bad—*pupuka*—foolish—*debelo*—devilish! On inquiring what it meant, they told me a pipe had been stolen from one of the men, and the incantation was making to discover the thief, and to pray him to death. On reproving them for their superstition and wickedness, they became disconcerted, and the man holding the leaves made some unfortunate movement, which the man praying said had destroyed the effect, and immediately ceased to pray.

Perhaps there is no superstition more general and deep-rooted in the minds of this people than the belief that some have the power of destroying the lives of others by their incantations and prayers. There is not a doubt that many yearly become victims to their credence in this device of darkness, which holds thousands in the bondage of cruel fears. A person gains the displeasure of one of these praying men. He is told that the *kanaka anaana* is exercising his power over him, and that he will die. He cannot shake off the dread of that which he believes to be possible; his imagination becomes filled with pictures of death—his spirits become affected—his appetite fails—these, the natural consequence of his fears are believed to be the effect of the sorcery of his enemy. Under this conviction he takes no nourishment, pines, languishes, and dies, the victim of his own ignorance and superstition. This is no fiction, but a reality that is constantly occurring.

The less enlightened of the people think no one dies a natural death. Every instance of mortality is assigned to the effect of poison administered by some foe, or to the more insidious, but, in their opinion, equally fatal influence of the *pule anaana.*

Before a sorcerer can gain power over the life of a chief, he must possess himself of something that has belonged to the person of the chief, as spittle, or *any excrement,* an article of clothing, etc. In this superstition we find the origin of the care taken of the spittle, etc. of a chief, which is always in charge of a confidential attendant. When a chief became unwell, or had any fear that one of the praying-men had obtained an article which had been worn by him, or had touched his person, he had immediate recourse to sacrifices to counteract the prayer against his life.

The last instance of the kind occurred in October, 1824. According to the custom of disposing of the old clothes of the chiefs, the princess had several boxes of garments she had thrown by carried out from Lahaina and secretly buried in the sea. It was reported that one dress had been stolen with a design of praying her to death, from the power it would give the sorcerer over her life. The consequence was that her ignorant attendants prevailed on her to sacrifice to her old gods to escape the evil. For this purpose she went to a village eight miles from Lahaina (which was said to be too much under the influence of Jehovah to secure success in the rite) under pretext of visiting her plantations in that neighborhood, and sacrificed to the gods of her fathers. This is the last, and probably will remain the last, sacrifice ever made in the islands by order of a high chief.

Owen Chase

The Ship That Was Wrecked by a Whale

The first authentic account of the ramming and sinking of a ship by a whale was written by Owen Chase, first mate of the whaler *Essex*. His *Narrative* (1821) gives not only the details of the attack by the furious whale in the equatorial Pacific, but also describes an open-boat voyage twice as long as that made by the celebrated Captain William Bligh of the *Bounty*.

The attack on the *Essex* is memorable not only in itself but in literary history, for Herman Melville used the incident as the basis for the climax of his classic novel *Moby Dick*.

ON THE 20th of November [1819] (cruising in latitude 0° 40′ S., longitude 119° 0′ W.), a shoal of whales was discovered off the lee bow.

The weather at this time was extremely fine and clear, and it was about eight o'clock in the morning that the man at the masthead gave the usual cry of "There she blows." The ship was immediately put away, and we ran down in the direction for them. When we had got within half a mile of the place where they were observed, all our boats were lowered down, manned, and we started in pursuit of them. The ship, in the meantime, was brought to the wind, and the main-topsail hove aback, to wait for us. I had the harpoon in the second boat; the captain preceded me in the first.

When I arrived at the spot where we calculated they were, nothing was at first to be seen. We lay on our oars in anxious expectation of discovering them come up somewhere near us. Presently one rose, and spouted a short distance ahead of my boat; I made all speed toward it, came up with, and struck it; feeling the harpoon in him, he threw himself, in an agony, over toward the boat (which at that time was up alongside of him), and giving a severe blow with his tail, struck the boat near the edge of the water, amidships, and stove a hole in her.

I immediately took up the boat hatchet, and cut the line, to disengage the boat from the whale, which by this time was running off with great velocity. I succeeded in getting clear of him, with the loss of the harpoon and line; and finding the water to pour fast in the boat, I hastily stuffed three or four of our jackets in the hole, ordered one man to keep constantly bailing, and the rest to pull immediately for the ship; we succeeded in keeping the boat free, and shortly gained the ship.

The captain and the second mate, in the other two boats, kept up the pursuit, and soon struck another whale. They being at this time a considerable distance to leeward, I went forward, braced around the mainyard, and put the ship off in a direction for them; the boat which had been stove was immediately hoisted in, and after examining the hole, I found that I could, by nailing a piece of canvas over it, get her ready to join in a fresh pursuit sooner than by lowering down the other remaining boat which belonged to the ship.

I accordingly turned her over upon the quarter and was in the act of nailing on the canvas when I observed a very large spermaceti whale, as well as I could judge, about eighty-five feet in length; he broke water about twenty rods off our weather bow, and was lying quietly, with his head in a direction for the ship. He spouted two or three times and then disappeared. In less than two or three seconds he came up again, about the length of the ship off, and made directly for us, at the rate of about three knots. The ship was then going with about the same velocity.

His appearance and attitude gave us at first no alarm; but while I stood watching his movements, and observing him but a ship's length off, coming down for us with great celerity, I involuntarily ordered the boy at the helm to put it hard up; intending to sheer off and avoid him. The words were scarcely out of my mouth before he came down upon us with full speed and struck the ship with his head, just forward of the forechains; he gave us such an appalling and tremendous jar as nearly threw us all on our faces. The ship brought up as suddenly and violently as if she had struck a rock, and trembled for a few seconds like a leaf.

We looked at each other with perfect amazement, deprived almost of the power of speech. Many minutes elapsed before we were able to realize the dreadful accident; during which time he passed under the ship, grazing her keel as he went along, came up alongside of her to leeward, and lay on the top of the water (apparently stunned with the violence of the blow) for the space of a minute; he then suddenly started off, in a direction to leeward.

After a few moments' reflection, and recovering, in some measure, from the sudden consternation that had seized us, I of course concluded that he had stove a hole in the ship, and that it would be necessary to set the pumps going. Accordingly they were rigged but had not been in operation more than one minute before I perceived the head of the ship to be gradually settling down in the water; I then ordered the signal to be set for the other boats, which scarcely had I dispatched before I again discovered the whale, apparently in convulsions, on the top of the water, about one hundred rods to leeward. He was enveloped in the foam of the sea that his continual and violent thrashing about in the water had created around him, and I could distinctly see him smite his jaws together, as if distracted with rage and fury. He remained a short time in this situation and then started off with great velocity across the bows of the ship to windward.

By this time the ship had settled down a considerable distance in the water, and I gave her up as lost. I however ordered the pumps to be kept constantly going, and endeavored to collect my thoughts for the occasion. I turned to the boats, two of which we then had with the ship, with an intention of clearing them away, and getting all things ready to embark in them, if there should be no other resource left; and while my attention was thus engaged for a moment, I was aroused with the cry of a man at the hatchway, "Here he is—he is making for us again!"

I turned around and saw him about one hundred rods directly ahead of us, coming down apparently with twice his ordinary speed, and to me at that moment, it appeared, with tenfold fury and vengeance in his aspect. The surf flew in all directions about him, and his course toward us was marked by a white foam of a rod in width, which he made with the continual violent thrashing of his tail; his head was about half out of water, and in that way he came upon, and again struck, the ship.

I was in hopes, when I descried him making for us, that by a dexterous movement of putting the ship away immediately I should be able to cross the line of his approach before he could get up to us and thus avoid what I knew, if he should strike us again, would prove our inevitable destruction. I bawled out to the helmsman, "Hard up!" but she had not fallen off more than a point before we took the second shock. I should judge the speed of the ship to have been at this time about three knots, and that of the whale about six. He struck her to windward, directly under the cathead, and completely stove in her bows. He passed under the ship again, went off to leeward, and we saw no more of him.

Our situation at this juncture can be more readily imagined than described. The shock to our feelings was such as I am sure none can have an adequate conception of that were not there: the misfortune befell us at a moment when we least dreamed of any accident, and from the pleasing anticipations we had formed, of realizing the certain profits of our labor, we were dejected by a sudden, most mysterious, and overwhelming calamity.

Not a moment, however, was to be lost in endeavoring to provide for the extremity to which it was now certain we were reduced. We were more than a thousand miles from the nearest land and with nothing but a light open boat as the resource of safety for myself and companions.

I ordered the men to cease pumping, and everyone to provide for himself; seizing a hatchet at the same time, I cut away the lashings of the spare boat, which lay bottom up across two spars directly over the quarter-deck, and cried out to those near me to take her as she came down. They did so accordingly, and bore her on their shoulders as far as the waist of the ship.

The steward had in the meantime gone down into the cabin twice, and saved two quadrants, two practical navigators, and the captain's trunk and mine; all which were hastily thrown into the boat, as she lay on the deck, with the two compasses which I snatched from the binnacle. He attempted to descend again; but the water by this time had rushed in, and he returned without being able to effect his purpose.

By the time we had got the boat to the waist, the ship had filled with water, and was going down on her beam-ends: we shoved our boat as quickly as possible from the plank shear into the water, all hands jumping in her at the same time, and launched off clear of the ship. We were scarcely two boats' lengths distant from her when she fell over to windward and settled down in the water.

Amazement and despair now wholly took possession of us. We contemplated the frightful situation the ship lay in, and thought with horror upon the sudden and dreadful calamity that had overtaken us. We looked upon each other, as if to gather some consolatory sensation from an interchange of sentiments, but every countenance was marked with the paleness of despair. Not a word was spoken for several minutes by any of us; all appeared to be bound in a spell of stupid consternation; and from the time we were first attacked by the whale to the period of the fall of the ship and of our leaving her in the boat more than ten minutes could not certainly have elapsed! God only knows in what way, or by what means, we were enabled to accomplish in that short time what we did; the cutting away and transporting the boat from where she was deposited would of itself, in ordinary circumstances, have consumed as much time as that, if the whole ship's crew had been employed in it.

My companions had not saved a single article but what they had on their backs; but to me it was a source of infinite satisfaction, if any such could be gathered from the horrors of our gloomy situation, that we had been fortunate enough to have preserved our compasses, navigators, and quadrants. After the first shock of my feelings was over, I enthusiastically contemplated them as the probable instruments of our salvation; without them all would have been dark and hopeless.

Gracious God! What a picture of distress and suffering now presented itself to my imagination. The crew of the ship were saved, consisting of twenty human souls. All that remained to conduct these twenty beings through the stormy terrors of the ocean, perhaps many thousand miles, were three open light boats. The prospect of obtaining any provisions or water from the ship, to subsist upon during the time, was at least now doubtful. How many long and watchful nights, thought I, are to be passed? How many tedious days of partial starvation are to be endured, before the least relief or mitigation of our sufferings can be reasonably anticipated?

We lay at this time in our boat, about two ships' lengths off from the wreck, in perfect silence, calmly contemplating her situation, and absorbed in our own melancholy reflections, when the other boats were discovered rowing up to us. They had but shortly before discovered that some accident had befallen us, but of the nature of which they were entirely ignorant. The sudden and mysterious disappearance of the ship was first discovered by the boat steerer in the captain's boat, and with a horror-struck countenance and voice, he suddenly exclaimed, "Oh, my God! where is the ship?" Their operations upon this were instantly suspended, and a general cry of horror and despair burst from the lips of every man as their looks were directed for her, in vain, over every part of the ocean.

They immediately made all haste toward us. The captain's boat was the first that reached us. He stopped about a boat's length off but had no power to utter a single syllable: he was so completely overpowered with the spectacle before him that he sat down in his boat, pale and speechless. I could scarcely recognize his countenance, he appeared to be so much altered, awed, and overcome with the oppression of his feelings and the dreadful reality that lay before him. He was in a short time however enabled to address the inquiry to me, "My God, Mr. Chase, what is the matter?"

I answered, "We have been stove by a whale." I then briefly told him the story.

After a few moments' reflection he observed that we must cut away her masts, and endeavor to get something out of her to eat.

Our thoughts were now all accordingly bent on endeavors to save from the wreck whatever we might possibly want, and for this purpose we rowed up and got on to her. Search was made for every means of gaining access to her hold; and for this purpose the lanyards were cut loose, and with our hatchets we commenced to cut away the masts, that she might right up again, and enable us to scuttle her decks. In doing which we were occupied about three quarters of an hour, owing to our having no axes, nor indeed any other instruments but the small hatchets belonging to the boats. After her masts were gone she came up about two thirds of the way upon an even keel.

While we were employed about the masts the captain took his quadrant, shoved off from the ship, and got an observation. We found ourselves in latitude 0° 40′ S., longitude 119° W.

We now commenced to cut a hole through the planks, directly above two large casks of bread, which most fortunately were between decks, in the waist of the ship, and which being in the upper side when she upset, we had strong hopes was not wet. It turned out according to our wishes, and from these casks we obtained six hundred pounds of hard bread. Other parts of the deck were then scuttled, and we got without difficulty as much fresh water as we dared to take in the boats, so that each was supplied with about sixty-five gallons; we got also from one of the lockers a musket, a small canister of powder, a couple of files, two rasps, about two pounds of boat nails, and a few turtle.

In the afternoon the wind came on to blow a strong breeze; and having obtained everything that occurred to us could then be got out, we began to make arrangements for our safety during the night. A boat's line was made fast to the ship, and to the other end of it one of the boats was moored, at about fifty fathoms to leeward; another boat was then attached to the first one, about eight fathoms astern; and the third boat the like distance astern of her.

Night came on just as we had finished our operations; and such a night as it was to us! So full of feverish and distracting inquietude that we were deprived entirely of rest. The wreck was constantly before my eyes. I could not, by any effort, chase away the horrors of the preceding day from my mind: they haunted me the livelong night. My companions—some of them were like sick women; they had no idea of the extent of their deplorable situation. One or two slept unconcernedly, while others wasted the night in unavailing murmurs.

I now had full leisure to examine, with some degree of coolness, the dreadful circumstances of our disaster. The scenes of yesterday passed in such quick succession in my mind that it was not until after many hours of severe reflection that I was able to discard the idea of the catastrophe as a dream. Alas! it was one from which there was no awaking; it was too certainly true that but yesterday we had existed as it were, and in one short moment had been cut off from all the hopes and prospects of the living! I have no language to paint out the horrors of our situation. To shed tears was indeed altogether unavailing, and withal unmanly; yet I was not able to deny myself the relief they served to afford me.

After several hours of idle sorrow and repining I began to reflect upon the accident and endeavored to realize by what unaccountable destiny or design (which I could not at first determine) this sudden and most deadly attack had been made upon us; by an animal, too, never before suspected of premeditated violence, and proverbial for its insensibility and inoffensiveness. Every fact seemed to warrant me in concluding that it was anything but chance which directed his operations; he made two several attacks upon the ship, at a short interval between them, both of which, according to their direction, were calculated to do us the most injury by being made ahead and thereby combining the speed of the two objects for the shock, to effect which, the exact maneuvers which he made were necessary. His aspect was most horrible, and such as indicated resentment and fury. He came directly from the shoal which we had just before entered, and in which we had struck three of his companions, as if fired with revenge for their sufferings. But to this it may be observed that the mode of fighting which they always adopt is either with repeated strokes of their tails, or snapping of their jaws together; and that a case, precisely similar to this one, has never been heard of among the oldest and most experienced whalers. To this I would answer that the structure and strength of the whale's head is admirably designed for this mode of attack, the most prominent part of which is almost as hard and as tough as iron; indeed,

I can compare it to nothing else but the inside of a horse's hoof, upon which a lance or harpoon would not make the slightest impression. The eyes and ears are removed nearly one third the length of the whole fish from the front part of the head and are not in the least degree endangered in this mode of attack. At all events, the whole circumstances taken together, all happening before my own eyes, and producing, at the time, impressions in my mind of decided, calculating mischief on the part of the whale (many of which impressions I cannot now recall) induce me to be satisfied that I am correct in my opinion. It is certainly, in all its bearings, a hitherto unheard-of circumstance, and constitutes, perhaps, the most extraordinary one in the annals of the fishery.

Johannes C. Andersen

Two Tales of Old Hawaii

One of the most prominent students of Polynesian lore was Johannes Carl Andersen (1873–1962), born in Denmark. He was librarian for many years of the Alexander Turnbull Library in Wellington, New Zealand, and edited the *Journal of the Polynesian Society* from 1925 to 1947. He was honored by the award of the Royal Society Medal for Ethnology in 1944. During his long life Andersen published a number of articles and several books, such as *Polynesian Literature: Maori Poetry* (1946) and *Myths and Legends of the Polynesians* (1928), from which "The Feather Cloak of Hawaii" and "Hiku and Kawelu" are taken. Based upon the Alexander Fornander Collection of Hawaiian legends, both these lucid retellings deal with the eerie belief in "kapuku," or restoration of a corpse to life.

The Feather Cloak

THE Hawaiians have a story of the feather cloak that served as the first known pattern. Eleio was a kukini, or trained runner, in the service of Kakaalaneo, chief of Maui. He was not only a swift and tireless runner, but was also a kahuna, initiated into the observances that enabled him to see spirits, that made him skilled in medicine, and able to return a wandering spirit to its dead body if the work of dissolution had not begun.

Eleio had been sent to Hana to fetch awa root for the chief, and was expected to be back so that the chief might have his prepared drink for supper. Soon after leaving Olowalu, Eleio saw a beautiful young woman ahead of him. He hastened his steps, but, exert himself as he would, she kept the same distance between them. Being the fleetest kukini of his time, it piqued him that a woman should be able to prevent his overtaking her, so he determined to capture her, and devoted all his energies to that object. She led him a long chase over rocks, hills, mountains, deep ravines, precipices, and gloomy streams, till they came to the cape of Hana-manu-loa at Kahiki-nui, beyond Kaupo, where he caught her just at the entrance to a puoa—a kind of tower made of bamboo, with a platform halfway up, where the dead bodies of persons of distinction were exposed to the elements.

When he caught her she turned to him and said, "Let me live! I am not human, but a spirit, and in this enclosure is my dwelling." He answered, "I have thought for some time that you were a spirit; no human being could have so outrun me."

She then said, "Let us be friends. In yonder house live my parents and relatives. Go to them and ask for a hog, rolls of kapa, some fine mats, and a feather cloak. Describe me to them, and tell them that I give all those things to you. The feather cloak is not finished; it is now only a fathom and a half square, and was intended to be two fathoms. There are in the house enough feathers and netting to finish it. Tell them to finish it for you." The spirit then disappeared.

Eleio entered the puoa, climbed onto the platform, and saw the dead body of the girl. She was in every way as beautiful as the spirit, and had apparently been dead but a short time. He left the puoa and hurried to the house pointed out as the home of her parents, and he saw a woman wailing, whom he recognized, from her resemblance, as the mother of the girl.

He saluted her with an aloha. "I am a stranger here," said he, "but I had a traveling companion who guided me to yonder puoa and then disappeared." At these words the woman ceased her wailing and called to her husband, to whom she repeated what the stranger had said.

"Does this house belong to you?" asked Eleio.

"It does," they answered.

"Then," said Eleio, "my message is to you." He repeated to them the message of the young girl, and they willingly agreed to give up all the things which their loved daughter had herself thus given away. But when they spoke of killing the hog and making a feast for him, he said, "Wait a little, and let me ask if all these people round about me are your friends?"

They answered, "They are our relatives—the uncles, aunts, and cousins of the spirit who seems to have chosen you either as husband or as brother."

"Will they do your bidding in everything?" he asked.

The parents answered that they could be relied on. He directed them to build a large arbor, to be entirely covered with ferns, ginger, maile, ieie—sweet and odorous foliage of the islands. An altar was to be erected at one end of the arbor and appropriately decorated. The order was willingly carried out, men, women, and children working with a will, so that in a couple of hours the whole structure was finished. He then directed the hog to be cooked, also red and white fish, red, white, and black cocks, and varieties of banana called lele and maoli to be placed on the altar. He directed all women and children to enter their houses and assist with their prayers, all pigs, chickens, and dogs to be hidden in dark houses to keep them quiet, and that strict silence be kept. The men at work were asked to remember the gods, and to invoke their assistance for Eleio.

He then started for Hana, pulled up a couple of bushes of awa of Kaeleku, famous for its medicinal virtue, and was back again before the hog was cooked. The awa was prepared, and when everything was ready for the feast he offered all to the gods and prayed for their assistance in what he was about to perform.

The spirit of the girl had been lingering near him all the time, seeming to be attracted to him, but of course invisible to everyone else. When he had finished his invocation he turned and caught the spirit, and holding his breath and invoking the gods he hurried to the puoa, followed by the parents, who now began to understand that he was about to attempt the kapuku, or restoration of the dead to life. Arrived at the puoa, he placed the spirit against the insteps of the girl and pressed it firmly in, meanwhile continuing his invocation. The spirit entered its former body kindly enough until it came to the knees, when it refused to go farther, fearing pollution, but Eleio by the strength of his prayers induced it to go farther, and farther, the father, mother, and male relatives assisting with their prayers, and at length the spirit was persuaded to take entire possession of the body, and the girl came to life again.

She was submitted to the usual ceremonies of purification by the priest, after which she was led to the prepared arbor, where there was a happy reunion. They feasted on the food prepared for the gods, whose guests they were, enjoying the material essence of the food after its spiritual essence had been accepted by the gods.

After the feast the feather cloak, the rolls of fine kapa, and the beautiful mats were brought and displayed to Eleio; and the father said to him, "Take as wife the woman you have restored, and remain here with us; you shall be our son, sharing equally in the love we have for her."

But Eleio, thinking of his chief, said, "No, I accept her as a charge; but, for wife, she is worthy to be one for a higher in rank. If you will trust her to my care, I will take her to my master; for her beauty and her charms make her worthy to be his wife and our queen."

"She is yours to do with as you will," said the father. "It is as if you had created her; for without you where would she be now? We ask only this, that you will always remember that you have parents and relatives here, and a home whenever you may wish it."

Eleio then requested that the feather cloak be finished for him before he returned to the chief. All who could work feathers set about it at once, including the girl herself, whose name, Eleio now learned, was Kanikani-aula. When it was finished he set out on his return, accompanied by the girl and taking the feather cloak and the awa that remained after a portion had been used during his incantations. They traveled slowly, according to the strength of Kanikani-aula, who now, in the body, could not equal the speed she had possessed as a spirit.

Arriving at Launi-upoko, Eleio turned to her and said, "You wait here, hidden in the bushes, while I go on alone. If by sundown I do not return, I shall be dead. You know the road by which we came; return then to your people. But if all goes well I shall be back in a little while."

He then went on, and when he reached Makila, on the confines of Lahaina, he saw a number of people heating an imu, or ground oven. On perceiving him they seized and started to bind him, saying it was the order of the chief that he should be roasted alive; but he ordered them away with the request, "Let me die at the feet of my master," and went on.

When at last he stood before Kakaalaneo, the chief said to him, "How is this? Why are you not cooked alive as I ordered? How came you to pass my guards?"

The runner answered, "It was the wish of the slave to die, if die he must, at the feet of his master; but if so, it would be an irreparable loss to you, my master; for I have that with me which will add to your fame, now, and to posterity."

"And what is that?" asked the king.

Eleio unrolled his bundle, and displayed to the astonished chief the glories of the feather cloak, a garment unknown till then. Needless to say, he was pardoned and restored to favor, the awa he had brought from Hana being reserved for the chief's special use in his offerings to the gods that evening.

When the chief heard the whole story of the reason for the absence of Eleio he ordered the girl to be brought, that he might see her, and express gratitude for the wonderful garment. When she arrived he was so charmed with her appearance, with her manner and conversation, that he asked her to become his queen.

Hiku and Kawelu

NOT far from the summit of Hualalai, on the island of Hawaii, in a cave on the southern side of the ridge, lived Hina and her son Hiku, a kupua, or demigod. During the whole of his childhood and youth Hiku had lived alone with his mother on the summit of the mountain, and had never once been permitted to descend to the plains below to see the abodes of men or to learn their ways. From time to time his ear had caught the sound of the distant hula and the voices of the merrymakers, and he had often wished to see those who danced and sang in those far-off coconut groves. But his mother, experienced in the ways of the world, had always refused her consent. Now at length he felt that he was a man; and as the sounds of mirth arose to his ears again, he asked his mother that he might go and mingle with the people on the shore. His mother, seeing that his mind was made up, reluctantly gave her consent, warning him not to linger, but to return in good time. So, taking in his hand his faithful arrow, Pua-ne, which he always carried, off he started.

This arrow was possessed of supernatural powers, being able to answer his call, and by its flight to direct his steps.

He descended over the rough lava and through the groves of koa that cover the southwestern slopes of the mountain, until, nearing its base, he stood on a distant hill; and, consulting his arrow by shooting it far into the air, he watched its flight until it struck on a distant hill above Kailua. To this hill he directed his steps and picked up his arrow in due time, again shooting it into the air. The second flight landed the arrow near the coast of Holualoa, six or eight miles south of Kailua. It struck on a barren waste of lava beside the water hole of Wai-kalai, known also as the Wai-a-Hiku (Water of Hiku), used by the people to this day.

Here he quenched his thirst; and nearing the village of Holualoa he again shot the arrow, which entered the courtyard of the alii (chief) of Kona, and from the women it singled out the chiefess Kawelu, and landed at her feet. Seeing the noble air of Hiku as he approached to claim his arrow, she stealthily hid it, and challenged him to find it. Then Hiku called to the arrow, "Pua-ne! Pua-ne!" and the arrow answered, "Ne," thus revealing its hiding place.

This incident of the arrow, and the grace and manliness of Hiku, won the heart of the young chiefess, and she was soon possessed by a strong passion for him, and determined to make him her husband. With her arts she detained him for several days at her home, and when he at last was determined to set out for the mountains she shut him up in the house and detained him by force. But the words of his mother came to his mind, and he sought means of breaking away from his prison. He climbed to the roof, and, removing a portion of the thatch, made his escape.

When his flight was discovered by Kawelu, she was distracted with grief; she refused to be comforted, refused all food, and before many days had passed, she died. Messengers were dispatched, who brought back the unhappy

Hiku, the cause of all the sorrow. He had loved her though he had fled, and now, when it was too late, he wept over her. The spirit had departed to the netherworld of Milu, but, stung by the reproaches of her kindred and friends, and urged by his real love for Kawelu, Hiku resolved to attempt the perilous descent into the netherworld, and if possible bring back her spirit to the world it had left.

With the assistance of his friends he collected from the mountains great lengths of kowali (convolvulus vine). He also prepared a coconut shell, splitting it into two closely fitting parts. Then, anointing himself with a mixture of rancid coconut oil and kukui (candle-nut) oil, which gave him a strong, corpselike odor, he started with his companions in canoes for the point on the sea where the sky hangs down to meet the water.

Arrived at the spot, he directed his comrades to lower him into the abyss called the Lua-o-Milu (Cave of Milu). Taking with him his coconut shell, and seating himself on the cross-stick of the swing, he was quickly lowered down by the long rope of vines held by his friends in the canoe above.

Soon he entered the great cavern where the spirits of the dead were gathered together. As he came among them, their curiosity was aroused to learn who he was; and he heard many remarks such as, "Whew! what an odor this corpse has!" and "He must have been dead a long time!" Even Milu himself, as he sat on the bank watching the spirits, was deceived, or he would never have permitted the entry of the living man into the regions ruled by him.

Hiku and his swing, which was like the one with one rope only used in Hawaii, attracted considerable attention. One spirit in particular watched him most intently—the spirit of Kawelu. There was mutual recognition, and with the permission of Milu she darted up to him, and swung with him on the kowali. As they were enjoying together this favorite Hawaiian pastime, the friends above were informed of the success of the ruse by means of a preconcerted signal, and rapidly drew them upward. At first Kawelu was too much absorbed in the sport to notice this; but when at length her attention was aroused by seeing the great distance of those beneath her she was about to flit away like a butterfly. Hiku, however, quickly clapped the coconut shells together, imprisoning her within them, and both were soon drawn up to the canoes above.

They returned to the shores of Holualoa, where Hiku landed at once and hastened to the house where the body of Kawelu still lay. Kneeling by its side, he made an incision in the great toe of the left foot, and into this with great difficulty he forced the reluctant spirit, binding up the wound so that it could not escape from the cold and clammy flesh in which it was now imprisoned. Then he began to rub and chafe the foot, working the spirit farther and farther up the limb. Gradually, as the heart was reached, the blood began to flow through the body; the breast began gently to heave, and soon the eyes opened, and the spirit gazed out from them as if just awakened from sleep. Kawelu was restored to consciousness, and seeing the beloved Hiku bending tenderly over her, she said, "How could you be so cruel as to leave me?"

All remembrance of the Lua-o-Milu and what had taken place there had disappeared, and she took up the thread of consciousness just where she had left it a few days before. Great joy filled the hearts of the people of Holualoa as they welcomed back to their midst the loved Kawelu and the hero Hiku, who from that day was not separated from her.

In this myth the entrance to the Lua-o-Milu is placed out to sea; but the more usual accounts place it at the mouth of the great valley of Waipio, in a place called Keoni, where the sands have long since covered up and concealed this passage to the netherworld.

Every year, it is told, the procession of ghosts marches silently down the Mahiki road, and at this point enters the Lua-o-Milu. This company of the dead is said to have been seen in quite recent times. A man, walking in the evening, saw the company appear in the distance; and, knowing that should they encounter him his death was certain, he hid himself behind a tree, and, trembling with fear, gazed at the dread sight. There was Kamehameha the conqueror, with all his chiefs and warriors in battle array, thousands of heroes who had won renown in the olden time. They kept perfect step as they marched along in utter silence, and, passing through the woods down to Waipio, disappeared from his view.

Benjamin Kaoao

Temple of the Red-Eyed Pigs

This tradition of a forgotten heiau or Hawaiian temple on the north shore of the island of Oahu was narrated by Benjamin Kaoao to L. M. Keaunui and printed in Thrum's *Hawaiian Annual* for 1916.

KAUMAKAULAULA was the temple, and Kamehaikaua the one who built and laid the foundation thereof after the great flood, Kai-a-Kahinalii. Kahonu was the priest, and Kekuaokalani the king. Maliko was the location of the king's house, while Kawaiakane and Kawaiakanaloa were the places where the king was reared in the Punaluu division of land, district of Koolauloa, island of Oahu-a-Lua.

In those very ancient days which are past and gone into obscurity, when the Prince Kekuaokalani was born on the island of Hawaii, his bringing-up was taken in charge by Kahonu, the priest spoken of above, and his royal consort, both of whom were close relatives, *iwikuamoo,* of the prince.

On the third *anahulu* (one month) after the prince had first inhaled the cool airs of this earthly life, the council of chiefs sat in session in accordance with the wishes of the royal guardians of the young prince, to segregate their royal charge to some other island of the group. The council of chiefs, the priests, the omen readers, the statesmen and counselors of the royal court consented to approve this request of Kahonu. And in his capacity as priest, with jealous care and with great regard, Kahonu sought to maintain the dignity and sacredness of his royal charge, for he was of the highest kapu rank, *kapu moe,* the prostration kapu, by which the breath of the common people mingled with the dust, days now long past, when a man was sure to be killed if his shadow even fell upon the king's house.

When the council of chiefs allowed the petition, Kahonu and his wife made immediate preparation, together with his people, the order of priesthood, his omen-readers, statesmen and court attendants for their voyage by canoes for the island of Oahu, and Punaluu was the destination in accordance with the orders of Kahonu to his canoe paddlers.

When the fleet arrived off the breakers at Punaluu, it was evident to the people on the shore that Punaluu was the goal, Kahonu being well acquainted with his birthplace, from which he had gone to reside in Hawaii. The canoes entered the harbor of Mamalu, where vessels nowadays are loaded with pineapples from Punaluu. Makaiwa was the landing place of the canoes, where now there is a wharf with warehouses for the convenience of the shipping public.

When the voyagers arrived in Punaluu, Kahonu and his wife took their young charge to the densest part of the forest in the deep solitude of the uplands of the mountains, a place called the Water of Kane and Water of Kanaloa, where the prince was nurtured. The place is still in existence. The priests, courtiers, and traveling companions of the young prince were made by Kahonu to remain at Maliko, to erect a house for his royal charge and to repair some deficiencies in the temple of Kaumakaulaula herein spoken of.

The house of the chief was so very sacred that the shadow of a man must not cross it, and for he who disobeyed and did not observe this law of the sacredness of the chief, death was his sure penalty, and the body of the unfortunate was placed on the altar of the temple, together with prisoners of war.

The fame of the temple of Kaumakaulaula became known through wonderful things of a mysterious nature, known only to this temple, which was this: In early times the people dwelt on the lands under the chiefs and division overseers. They raised animals such as hogs, dogs, and chickens in those days of darkness, yet full of ingenuity; days in which they asserted that the deity lived with the people and would be kindly disposed to their supplications when accompanied by a cup of awa and the snout of a pig — *ihu o ka puaa.*

On the approach of the sacred nights of the temple these omens of wonder and mystery would be observed: the eyes of all the pigs which were near the boundaries of this temple would turn red, and this has been known to happen even down to the present time. That is how the name of Kaumakaulaula became applicable and has continued famous to this day. It is spoken of as hidden, *"he heiau huna ia,"* a most sacred temple. Wonderful and mysterious things pertaining to it lay hidden in the earth. Sounds of the drum, the nose flute, the whistling gourd, and the voices of the priests in prayer could be heard by our own ears to our wonder and astonishment during the nights of Kane and of the Kaloas, every six months, and this has continued from its founding even to the present day.

One would be in doubt of this to witness the present desolate condition of this temple site, because it is now but a level field lying in desolation but recently put under cultivation. The temple had but one body but divided for its services into two sections. There was a separate division where the priests performed their ritual services, this was just seaward of the house-lot adjoining on the north side of the stream of Maipuna, and above the bridge and government road. The altar of sacrifice was also a separate place where the bodies of men and other sacrifices were offered up in solemn service. Its site is a *kahua*—a hollow place—now occupied by a lime kiln, seaward of Ben Kaoao's residence, above the road. My familiarity with the boundaries of this temple site is from long residence here, and its lines having been pointed out by my parents, who were old residents of Punaluu. In length it is about six chains along the government road, commencing at the bridge of the Maipuna stream on the south and running northward. It was two chains in width on the south adjoining the stream, and one chain on the north end. The altar and temple services were at the south end, while the house of the priest was at the narrower north end.

The several divisions of the temple premises, known from the time of our ancestors, were as follows:

1. Heiau.—A place to offer sacrifices and other things prepared for the deity, with prayer.

2. Loko.—A place where captives are confined; where the vanquished die.

3. Upena.—A place where fish (victims?) are caught, or ensnared; a sign of death.

In this connection I recall certain prayers repeated by some old people who have long ago passed to the other side, wherein the word net (*upena*) is used. It is as follows:

"The man-fishing net of Lono,
The braided net of Kamehaikane,
The double net in which the *luhia* is caught,
The *niuhi,* the *lalakea,* the *mano,*
The *moelawa,* the favorite shark dish of the chief."

Mary Pukui and Martha Beckwith

The Marchers of the Night

The Hawaiians have an oral literature that is particularly rich in tales of ghosts and other night spirits. They are reticent, however, about telling these stories to others, who might scoff, so that not many of them have found their way into printed English. The following authentic Hawaiian ghost story was given in 1930 to Martha Beckwith, an authority to Hawaiian folklore, by Mrs. Mary Pukui, who as a child had heard it told by her Hawaiian mother and older relatives in Ka'u and Puna on the island of Hawaii.

EVERY Hawaiian has heard of the "Marchers of the Night," *Ka huaka'i o ka Po.* A few have seen the procession. It is said that such sight is fatal unless one had a relative among the dead to intercede for him. If a man is found stricken by the roadside, a white doctor will pronounce the cause as heart failure, but a Hawaiian will think at once of the fatal night march.

The time for the march is between half after seven when the sun has actually set and about two in the morning before the dawn breaks. It may occur on one of the four nights of the gods, on Ku, Akua, Lono, Kane, or on the nights of Kaloa. Those who took part in the march were the chiefs and warriors who had died, the *aumakua,* and the gods, each of whom had their own march.

That of the chiefs was conducted according to the tastes of the chief for whom the march was made. If he had enjoyed silence in this life his march would be silent save for the creaking of the food calabashes suspended from the carrying-sticks, or of the litter, called *manele,* if he had not been fond of walking. If a chief had been fond of music, the sound of the drum, nose flute and other instruments was heard as they marched. Sometimes there were no lights borne, at other times there were torches but not so bright as for the gods and demigods. A chief whose face had been sacred, called an *alo kapu,* so that no man, beast, or bird could pass before him without being killed, must lead the march; even his own warriors might not precede him. If on the contrary his back had been sacred, *akua kapu,* he must follow in the rear of the procession. A chief who had been well protected in life and who had no rigid tabu upon face or back would march between his warriors.

On the marches of the chief a few *aumakua* would march with them in order to protect their living progeny who might chance to meet them on the road. Sometimes the parade came when a chief lay dying or just dead. It paused before the door for a brief time and then passed on. The family might not notice it, but a neighbor might see it pass and know that the chief had gone with his ancestors who had come for him.

In the march of the *aumakua* of each district there was music and chanting. The marchers carried candlenut torches which burned brightly even on a rainy night. They might be seen even in broad daylight and were followed by whirlwinds such as come one after another in columns. They cried *"Kapu o moe!"* as a warning to stragglers to get out of the way or to prostrate themselves with closed eyes until the marchers passed. Like the chiefs, they too sometimes came to a dying descendant and took him away with them.

The march of the gods was much longer, more brilliantly lighted and more sacred than that of the chiefs or of the demigods. The torches were brighter and shone red. At the head, at three points within the line and at the rear were carried bigger torches, five being the complete number among Hawaiians, the *ku a lima.* The gods with the torches walked six abreast, three males and three females. One of the three at the end of the line was Hi'iaka-i-ka-poli-o-Pele, youngest sister of the volcano goddess. The first torch could be seen burning up at Kahuku when the last of the five torches was at Nonuapo. The only music to be heard on the marches of the gods was the chanting of their names and mighty deeds. The sign that accompanied them was a heavy downpour of rain, with mist, thunder and lightning, or heavy seas. Their route the next day would be strewn with broken boughs or leaves, for the heads of the gods were sacred and nothing should be suspended above them.

If a living person met these marchers it behooved him to get out of the way as quickly as possible, otherwise he might be killed unless he had an ancestor or an *aumakua* in the procession to plead for his life. If he met a procession of chiefs and had no time to get out of the way, he might take off his clothes and lie face upward, breathing as little as possible. He would hear them cry "Shame!" as they passed. One would say, "He is dead!" Another would cry, "No, he is alive, but what a shame for him to lie uncovered!" If he had no time to strip he must sit perfectly still, close his eyes and take his chance. He was likely to be killed by the guard at the front or at the rear of the line unless saved by one of his ancestors or by an *aumakua*. If he met a procession of gods he must take off all his clothes but his loincloth and sit still with his eyes tightly closed, because no man might look on a god although he might listen to their talk. He would hear the command to strike; then, if he was beloved by one of the gods as a favorite child or namesake, he would hear someone say, "No! he is mine!" and he would be spared by the guards.

Many Hawaiians living today have seen or heard the ghostly marchers. Mrs. Wiggin, Mrs. Pukui's mother, never got in their way but she has watched them pass from the door of her own mother's house and has heard the Kau people tell of the precautions that must be taken to escape death if one chances to be in their path.

A young man of Kona, Hawaii, tells the following experience. One night just after nightfall, about seven or eight in the evening, he was on his way when of a sudden he saw a long line of marchers in the distance coming toward him. He climbed over a stone wall and sat very still. As they drew near he saw that they walked four abreast and were about seven feet tall, nor did their feet touch the ground. One of the marchers stepped out of the line and ran back and forth on the other side of the wall behind which he crouched as if to protect him from the others. As each file passed he heard voices call out "Strike!" and his protector answered, "No! no! he is mine!" No other sounds were to be heard except the call to strike and the creak of a *manele*. He was not afraid and watched the marchers closely. There were both men and women in the procession. After a long line of marchers four abreast had passed there came the *manele* bearers, two before and two behind. On the litter sat a very big man whom he guessed at once to be a chief. Following the litter were other marchers walking four abreast. After all had passed his protector joined his fellows.

A month later the same young man went to call on some friends and was returning home late at night. Not far from the spot where he had met the marchers before was a level flat of ground and drawing near to the spot he heard the sound of an *ipu* drum and of chanting. He came close enough to see and recognize many of the men and women whom he had seen on the previous march as he had sat behind the stone wall. He was delighted with the chanting and drumming, with the dancing of the *ala'apapa* by the women and the *mokomoko* wrestling and other games of the past by the men. As he sat watching he heard someone say, "There is the grandson of Kekuanoi!" "Never mind! we do not mind him!" said another. This was the name of a grandfather of his who lived on the beach and he knew that he himself was being discussed. For a couple of hours he sat watching before he went home. His grandfather at home had seen it all; he said, "I know that you have been with our people of the night; I saw you sitting by watching the sports." Then he related to his grandfather what he had seen on the two nights when he met the chiefs and warriors of old.

In old days these marchers were common in Kau district, but folk of today know little about them. They used to march and play games practically on the same ground as in life. Hence each island and each district had its own parade and playground along which the dead would march and at which they would assemble.

Mrs. Emma Akana Olmsted tells me that when she was told as a child about the marchers of the night she was afraid, but now that she is older and can herself actually hear them she is no longer terrified. She hears beautiful loud chanting of voices, the high notes of the flute and drumming so loud that it seems beaten upon the side of the house beside her bed. The voices are so distinct that if she could write music she would be able to set down the notes they sang.

TALES OF THE PACIFIC

JACK LONDON

Stories of Hawaii by Jack London
Thirteen yarns drawn from the famous author's love affair with Hawai'i Nei.
$6.95 ISBN 0-935180-08-7

The Mutiny of the Elsinore by Jack London
Based on a voyage around Cape Horn in a windjammer from New York to Seattle in 1913, this romance between the lone passenger and the captain's daughter reveals London at his most fertile and fluent best. The lovers are forced to outrace a rioting band of seagoing gangsters in the South Pacific.
$5.95 ISBN 0-935180-40-0

South Sea Tales by Jack London
Fiction from the violent days of the early century, set among the atolls of French Oceania and the high islands of Samoa, Fiji, Pitcairn, and "the terrible Solomons."
$5.95 ISBN 0-935180-14-1

HAWAII

Hawaii: Fiftieth Star by A. Grove Day
Told for the junior reader, this brief history of America's fiftieth state should also beguile the concerned adult. "Interesting, enlightening, and timely reading for high school American and World History groups."
$4.95 ISBN 0-935180-44-3

A Hawaiian Reader
Thirty-seven selections from the literature of the past hundred years, including such writers as Mark Twain, Robert Louis Stevenson and James Jones.
$5.95 ISBN 0-935180-07-9

Hawaii and Its People by A. Grove Day
An informal, one-volume narrative of the exotic and fascinating history of the peopling of the archipelago. The periods range from the first arrivals of Polynesian canoe voyagers to attainment of American statehood. A "headline history" brings the story from 1960 to 1990.
$4.95 ISBN 0-935180-50-8

True Tales of Hawaii and the South Seas **Edited by A. Grove Day and Carl Stroven**
Yarns from the real Pacific by 21 master storytellers, including Mark Twain, W. Somerset Maugham, Robert Louis Stevenson, and James A. Michener. This anthology comprises some of the best nonfiction writing about the South Pacific.
$4.95 ISBN 0-935180-22-2

A Hawaiian Reader, Vol. II
A companion volume to *A Hawaiian Reader.* Twenty-four selections from the exotic literary heritage of the Islands.
$6.95 ISBN 1-56647-207-5

Kona **by Marjorie Sinclair**
The best woman novelist of post-war Hawai'i dramatizes the conflict between a daughter of Old Hawai'i and her straitlaced Yankee husband. Nor is the drama resolved in their children.
$4.95 ISBN 0-935180-20-6

Claus Spreckels, The Sugar King in Hawaii **by Jacob Adler**
Sugar was the main economic game in Hawai'i a century ago, and the boldest player was Claus Spreckels, a California tycoon who built a second empire in the Islands by ruthless and often dubious means.
$5.95 ISBN 0-935180-76-1

Russian Flag Over Hawaii: The Mission of Jeffery Tolamy, **a novel by Darwin Teilhet**
A vigorous adventure novel in which a young American struggles to unshackle the grip held by Russian filibusters on the Kingdom of Kauai. Kamehameha the Great and many other historical figures play their roles in a colorful love story.
$5.95 ISBN 0-935180-28-1

Rape in Paradise **by Theon Wright**
The sensational "Massie Case" of the 1930's shattered the tranquil image that mainland U.S.A. had of Hawaii. One woman shouted "Rape!" and the island erupted with such turmoil that for 20 years it was deemed unprepared for statehood. A fascinating case study of race relations and military-civilian relations.
$4.95 ISBN 0-935180-88-5

Mark Twain in Hawaii: Roughing It in the Sandwich Islands
The noted humorist's account of his 1866 trip to Hawai'i at a time when the Islands were more for the native than the tourists. The writings first appeared in their present form in Twain's important book, *Roughing It.* Includes an introductory essay from *Mad About Islands* by A. Grove Day.
$4.95 ISBN 0-935180-93-1

Hawaii and Points South **by A. Grove Day**
Foreword by James A. Michener
A collection of the best of A. Grove Day's many shorter writings over a span of 40 years. The author has appended personal headnotes, revealing his reasons for choosing each particular subject.
$4.95 ISBN 0-935180-01-X

Pearl, **a novel by Stirling Silliphant**
In a world on the brink of war, the Hawaiian island of Oahu was still the perfect paradise. And in this lush and tranquil Pacific haven everyone clung to the illusion that their spectacular island could never be touched by the death and destruction of Hirohito's military machine.
$5.95 ISBN 0-935180-91-5

Horror in Paradise: Grim and Uncanny Tales from Hawaii and the South Seas, **edited by A. Grove Day and Bacil F. Kirtley**
Thirty-four writers narrate "true" episodes of sorcery and the supernatural, as well as gory events on sea and atoll.
$6.95 ISBN 0-935180-23-0

HAWAIIAN SOVEREIGNTY

Kalakaua: Renaissance King **by Helena G. Allen**
The third in a trilogy that also features Queen Liliuokalani and Sanford Ballard Dole, this book brings King Kalakaua, Hawai'i's most controversial king, to the fore as a true renaissance man. The complex facts of Kalakaua's life and personality are presented clearly and accurately along with his contributions to Hawaiian history.
$6.95 ISBN 1-56647-059-5

Nahi'ena'ena: Sacred Daughter of Hawai'i **by Marjorie Sinclair**
A unique biography of Kamehameha's sacred daughter who in legend was descended from the gods. The growing feelings and actions of Hawaiians for their national identity now place this story of Nahi'ena'ena in a wider perspective of the Hawaiian quest for sovereignty.
$4.95 ISBN 1-56647-080-3

Around the World With a King **by William N. Armstrong, Introduction by Glen Grant**
An account of King Kalakaua's circling of the globe. From Singapore to Cairo, Vienna to the Spanish frontier, follow Kalakaua as he becomes the first monarch to travel around the world.
$5.95 ISBN 1-56647-017-X

Hawaii's Story by Hawaii's Queen by Lydia Liliuokalani
The Hawaiian kingdom's last monarch wrote her biography in 1897, the year before the annexation of the Hawaiian Islands by the United States. Her story covers six decades of island history told from the viewpoint of a major historical figure.
$7.95 ISBN 0-935180-85-0

The Betrayal of Liliuokalani: Last Queen of Hawaii 1838-1917 by Helena G. Allen
A woman caught in the turbulent maelstrom of cultures in conflict. Treating Liliuokalani's life with authority, accuracy and details, *Betrayal* also is tremendously informative concerning the entire period of missionary activity and foreign encroachment in the Islands.
$6.95 ISBN 0-935180-89-3

HAWAIIAN LEGENDS

Myths and Legends of Hawaii by Dr. W.D. Westervelt
A broadly inclusive, one-volume collection of folklore by a leading authority. Completely edited and reset format for today's readers of the great prehistoric tales of Maui, Hina, Pele and her fiery family, and a dozen other heroic beings, human or ghostly.
$5.95 ISBN 0-935180-43-5

The Legends and Myths of Hawaii by David Kalakaua
Political and historical traditions and stories of the pre-Cook period capture the romance of old Polynesia. A rich collection of Hawaiian lore originally presented in 1888 by Hawai'i's "merrie monarch."
$6.95 ISBN 0-935180-86-9

Teller of Hawaiian Tales by Eric Knudsen
Son of a pioneer family of Kauai, the author spent most of his life on the Garden Island as a rancher, hunter of wild cattle, lawyer, and legislator. Here are 60 campfire yarns of gods and goddesses, ghosts and heroes, cowboy adventures and legendary feats among the valleys and peaks of the island.
$5.95 ISBN 1-56647-119-2

SOUTH SEAS

Best South Sea Stories
Fifteen writers capture all the romance and exotic adventure of the legendary South Pacific, including James A. Michener, James Norman Hall, W. Somerset Maugham, and Herman Melville.
$4.95 ISBN 0-935180-12-5

The Blue of Capricorn **by Eugene Burdick**
Stories and sketches from Polynesia, Micronesia, and Melanesia by the co-author of *The Ugly American* and *The Ninth Wave.* Burdick's last book explores an ocean world rich in paradox and drama, a modern world of polyglot islanders and primitive savages.
$5.95 ISBN 0-935180-36-2

The Book of Puka Puka **by Robert Dean Frisbie**
Lone trader on a South Sea atoll, "Ropati" tells charmingly of his first years on Puka-Puka, where he was destined to rear five half-Polynesian children. Special foreword by A. Grove Day.
$5.95 ISBN 0-935180-27-3

Manga Reva **by Robert Lee Eskridge**
A wandering American painter voyaged to the distant Gambier Group in the South Pacific and, charmed by the life of the people of "The Forgotten Islands" of French Oceania, collected many stories from their past—including the supernatural. Special introduction by Julius Scammon Rodman.
$5.95 ISBN 0-935180-35-4

The Lure of Tahiti **selected and edited by A. Grove Day**
Fifteen stories and other choice extracts from the rich literature of "the most romantic island in the world." Authors include Jack London, James A. Michener, James Norman Hall, W. Somerset Maugham, Paul Gauguin, Pierre Loti, Herman Melville, William Bligh, and James Cook.
$5.95 ISBN 0-935180-31-1

In Search of Paradise **by Paul L. Briand, Jr.**
A joint biography of Charles Nordhoff and James Norman Hall, the celebrated collaborators of *Mutiny on the "Bounty"* and a dozen other classics of South Pacific literature. This book, going back to the time when both men flew combat missions on the Western Front in World War I, reveals that the lives of Nordhoff and Hall were almost as fascinating as their fiction.
$5.95 ISBN 0-935180-48-6

The Fatal Impact: Captain Cook in the South Pacific by Alan Moorehead
A superb narrative by an outstanding historian of the exploration of the world's greatest ocean—adventure, courage, endurance, and high purpose with unintended but inevitable results for the original inhabitants of the islands.
$4.95 ISBN 0-935180-77-X

The Forgotten One by James Norman Hall
Six "true tales of the South Seas," some of the best stories by the co-author of *Mutiny on the "Bounty."* Most of these selections portray "forgotten ones"—men who sought refuge on out-of-the-world islands of the Pacific.
$5.95 ISBN 0-935180-45-1

Home from the Sea: Robert Louis Stevenson in Samoa, by Richard Bermann
Impressions of the final years of R.L.S. in his mansion, Vailima, in Western Samoa, still writing books, caring for family and friends, and advising Polynesian chieftains in the local civil wars.
$5.95 ISBN 0-935180-75-3

A Dream of Islands: Voyages of Self-Discovery in the South Seas by A. Gavan Daws
The South Seas... the islands of Tahiti, Hawai'i, Samoa, the Marquesas... the most seductive places on earth, where physically beautiful brown-skinned men and women move through a living dream of great erotic power. *A Dream of Islands* tells the stories of five famous Westerners who found their fate in the islands: John Williams, Herman Melville, Walter Murray Gibson, Robert Louis Stevenson, Paul Gauguin.
$4.95 ISBN 0-935180-71-2

His Majesty O'Keefe by Lawrence Klingman and Gerald Green
The extraordinary true story of an Irish-American sailing captain who for 30 years ruled a private empire in the South Seas, a story as fantastic and colorful as any novelist could invent. Vivid in its picture of Pacific customs, it is also filled with the oddity and drama of O'Keefe's career and a host of other major characters whose adventures are part of the history of the South Pacific. Made into a motion picture starring Errol Flynn.
$4.95 ISBN 0-935180-65-6

How to Order

For book rate (4-6 weeks; in Hawaii, 1-2 weeks) send check or money order with an additional $3.00 for the first book and $1.00 for each additional book. For fiirst class (1-2 weeks) add $4.00 for the first book, $3.00 for each additional book.

1215 Center Street, Suite 210
Honolulu, HI 96816
Tel (808) 732-1709 Fax (808) 734-4094
Email: mutual@lava.net

Praise for the Novels of Karen Marie Moning

FAEFEVER

"Ending in what can only be described as a monumental cliffhanger, the newest installment of this supernatural saga will have you panting for the next. Breathtaking!"
—*Romantic Times*

"Erotic shocks await Mac in Dublin's vast Dark Zone, setting up feverish expectations for the next installment."
—*Publishers Weekly*

BLOODFEVER

"Moning's delectable Mac is breathlessly appealing, and the wild perils she must endure are peppered with endless conundrums. The results are addictively dark, erotic, and even shocking." —*Publishers Weekly*

"Mac is madder and 'badder'—as well she should be—in the second Fever tale, and her creator's pacing is running full tilt. Moning brilliantly works the dark sides of man and Fae for all they are worth." —*Booklist*

"I loved this book from the first page. It sucked me in immediately. . . . More. I want more." —LINDA HOWARD

"Spiced with a subtle yet delightfully sharp sense of humor, *Bloodfever* is a delectably dark and scary addition to Karen Marie Moning's Fever series."
—*The Chicago Tribune*

DARKFEVER

"A wonderful dark fantasy . . . Give yourself a treat and read outside the box." —CHARLAINE HARRIS

"A compelling world filled with mystery and vivid characters . . . will stoke readers' fervor for *Bloodfever*, the next installment." —*Publishers Weekly*

"Clear off space on your keeper shelf—this sharp series looks to be amazing." —*Romantic Times*

SPELL OF THE HIGHLANDER

"Moning's characters are truly loveable; her tales are entertaining, touching, and incredibly hard to put down once begun. *Spell of the Highlander* is another sweeping tale of Highlander romance that longtime fans will treasure and will surely capture the imagination of new fans as well . . . an enchanting tale." —*Romance Reviews Today*

THE IMMORTAL HIGHLANDER

"Seductive, mesmerizing, and darkly sensual, Moning's hardcover debut adds depth and intensity to the magical world she has created in her earlier Highlander books, and fans and new readers alike will be drawn to this increasingly intriguing series." —*Library Journal*

"All readers who love humorous fantasy romance filled to the brim with fantasy-worthy Highlanders will find Moning's latest to be a sensuous treat." —*Booklist*

"Nonstop action for fans of paranormal romance."
—*Kirkus Reviews*

THE DARK HIGHLANDER

"Darker, sexier, and more serious than Moning's previous time-travel romances . . . this wild, imaginative romp takes readers on an exhilarating ride through time and space."
—*Publishers Weekly* (starred review)

"Pulsing with sexual tension, Moning delivers a tale of romance fans will be talking about for a long time." —*Oakland Press*

"*The Dark Highlander* is dynamite, dramatic, and utterly riveting. Ms. Moning takes the classic plot of good vs. evil . . . and gives it a new twist." —*Romantic Times*

KISS OF THE HIGHLANDER

"Moning's snappy prose, quick wit and charismatic characters will enchant." —*Publishers Weekly*

"Here is an intelligent, fascinating, well-written foray into the paranormal that will have you glued to the pages. A must read!" —*Romantic Times*

"*Kiss of the Highlander* is wonderful . . . [Moning's] storytelling skills are impressive, her voice and pacing dynamic, and her plot as tight as a cask of good Scotch whisky." —*Contra Costa Times*

THE HIGHLANDER'S TOUCH

"A stunning achievement in time-travel romance. Ms. Moning's imaginative genius in her latest spellbinding tale speaks to the hearts of romance readers and will delight and touch them deeply. Unique and eloquent, filled with thought-provoking and emotional elements, *The Highlander's Touch* is a very special book. Ms. Moning effortlessly secures her place as a top-notch writer." —*Romantic Times*

"Ms. Moning stretches our imagination, sending us flying into the enchanting past." —*Rendezvous*

BEYOND THE HIGHLAND MIST

"A terrific plotline . . . Gypsies and Scottish mysticism, against the backdrop of the stark beauty of the Highlands . . . an intriguing story. Poignant and sensual." —*Publishers Weekly*

"This highly original time-travel combines the wonders of the paranormal and the mischievous world of the fairies to create a splendid, sensual, hard-to-put-down romance. You'll delight in the biting repartee and explosive sexual tension between Adrienne and the Hawk, the conniving Adam, and the magical aura that surrounds the entire story. Karen Marie Moning is destined to make her mark on the genre." —*Romantic Times*

TO TAME A HIGHLAND WARRIOR

"A hauntingly beautiful love story . . . Karen Marie Moning gives us an emotional masterpiece that you will want to take out and read again and again." —*Rendezvous*

DELL BOOKS BY KAREN MARIE MONING

The Highlander Series

Beyond the Highland Mist

To Tame a Highland Warrior

The Highlander's Touch

Kiss of the Highlander

The Dark Highlander

The Immortal Highlander

Spell of the Highlander

The Fever Series

Darkfever

Bloodfever

Faefever

TO TAME A HIGHLAND WARRIOR

KAREN MARIE MONING

A DELL BOOK

2009 Bantam Books Mass Market Edition

Published in the United States by Dell, an imprint of The Random House Publishing Group, a division of Random House, Inc., New York.

DELL is a registered trademark of Random House, Inc., and the colophon is a trademark of Random House, Inc.

Originally published in mass market in the United States by Dell, an imprint of The Random House Publishing Group, a division of Random House, Inc., in 1999.

ISBN 978-0-440-24555-1

Cover art: Franco Accornero

Printed in the United States of America

www.bantamdell.com

2 4 6 8 9 7 5 3 1

This one is for Rick Shomo—Berserker extraordinaire;
and for Lisa Stone—Editor extraordinaire.

Acknowledgments

Chasing a dream is a risky venture, one made considerably richer by the company and counsel of family and friends. My heartfelt thanks to my mother, who endowed me with her formidable will and taught me never to give up on my dreams, and to my father, who demonstrates daily the nobleness, chivalry, and infinite strength of a true hero.

My deep appreciation to Mark Lee, a repository for the universe's trivia, whose bizarre tidbits feed the writer's soul, and to the special ladies of RBL Romantica for their friendship, insight, and of course the "Bonny and Braw Beefcake Farm."

Special thanks to Don and Ken Wilber of the Wilber Law Firm, who created the perfect fit for my dual careers, allowing them to work in synthesis with each other.

Eternal gratitude to my sister, Elizabeth, who keeps my feet on the ground in so many crucial ways, and to my agent, Deidre Knight, whose professional guidance and personal friendship has enriched both my writing and my life.

And finally, to the booksellers and readers who made my first novel a success.

A CELTIC LEGEND

Legend tells that the power of the Berserker—preternatural strength, prowess, virility, and cunning—can be bought for the going rate of a man's soul.

In the heather hills of the Highlands, the Viking god Odin lurks in shadowy places listening for the bitter howl of a man, brutalized beyond mortal endurance, to invoke his aid.

Legend holds that if the mortal is worthy, the primal breath of the gods blows into the man's heart, making him an undefeatable warrior.

Women whisper that the Berserker is an incomparable lover; legend holds there is a single true mate for him. Like the wolf, he loves but once and for all time.

High in the mountains of Scotland, the Circle Elders say that the Berserker, once summoned, can never be dismissed—and if the man does not learn to accept the primitive instincts of the beast within, he will die.

Legend tells of such a man . . .

Prologue

Death itself is better than a life of shame.
Beowulf

Maldebann Castle
The Highlands of Scotland
1499

THE SCREAMING *HAD* TO STOP.

He couldn't endure it another minute, yet he knew he was helpless to save them. His family, his clan, his best friend Arron, with whom he'd ridden the heather fields only yesterday, and his mother—oh, but his mother was another story; her murder had presaged this . . . this . . . barbaric . . .

He turned away, cursing himself for a coward. If he couldn't save them and he couldn't die with them, at least he owed them the honor of scribing the events into his memory. To avenge their deaths.

One at a time, if necessary.

Vengeance doesn't bring back the dead. How many times had his father said that? Once Gavrael had believed him, believed *in* him, but that had been before he'd discovered his mighty, wise, and wonderful da crouched over his mother's body this morning, his shirt bloodstained, a dripping dagger in his fist.

Gavrael McIllioch, only son of the Laird of Maldebann, stood motionless upon Wotan's Cleft, gazing down the sheer cliff at the village of Tuluth, which filled the valley hundreds of feet below. He wondered how this day had turned so bitter. Yesterday had been a fine day, filled with the simple pleasures of a lad who would one day govern these lush Highlands. Then this cruel morning had broken, and with it his heart. After discovering his da crouched above the savaged body of Jolyn McIllioch, Gavrael had fled for the sanctuary of the dense Highland forest, where he'd passed most of the day swinging wildly between rage and grief.

Eventually both had receded, leaving him oddly detached. At dusk, he'd retraced his path to Castle Maldebann to confront his sire with accusations of murder in a final attempt to make sense of what he'd witnessed, if there was sense to be made. But now, standing on the cliff high above Tuluth, the fourteen-year-old son of Ronin McIllioch realized his nightmare had only begun. Castle Maldebann was under siege, the village was engulfed in flames, and people were darting frantically between pillars of flames and piles of the dead. Gavrael watched helplessly as a small boy sped past a hut, directly into the blade of a waiting McKane. He recoiled; they were only children, but children could grow up to seek vengeance, and the fanatic McKane never left seeds of hatred to take root and bear poisonous fruit.

By the light of the fire engulfing the huts, he could see that the McKane severely outnumbered his people. The distinctive green and gray plaids of the hated enemy were a dozen to each McIllioch. *It's almost as though they knew we'd be vulnerable,* Gavrael thought. More than half the McIllioch were away in the north attending a wedding.

Gavrael despised being fourteen. Although he was tall and broad for his age, with shoulders that hinted at exceptional strength to come, he knew he was no match for the burly McKane. They were warriors with powerfully developed, mature bodies, driven by obsessive hatred. They trained ceaselessly, existing solely to pillage and kill. Gavrael would be no more significant than a tenacious pup yapping at a bear. He could plunge into the battle below, but he would die as inconsequentially as the boy had moments before. If he had to die tonight, he swore he would make it mean something.

Berserker, the wind seemed to whisper. Gavrael cocked his head, listening. Not only was his world being destroyed, now he was hearing voices. Were his wits to fail him before this terrible day ended? He knew the legend of the Berserkers was simply that—a legend.

Beseech the gods, the rustling branches of the pines hissed.

"Right," Gavrael muttered. As he'd been doing ever since he'd first heard the fearsome tale at the age of nine? There was no such thing as a Berserker. It was a foolish tale told to frighten mischievous children into good behavior.

Ber . . . serk . . . er. This time the sound was clearer, too loud to be his imagination.

Gavrael spun about and searched the massive rocks behind him. Wotan's Cleft was a tumble of boulders and odd standing stones that cast unnatural shadows beneath the full moon. It was rumored to be a sacred place, where chieftains of yore had met to plan wars and determine fates. It was a place that could almost make a stripling lad believe in the demonic. He listened intently, but the wind carried only the screams of his people.

It was too bad the pagan tales weren't true. Legend claimed Berserkers could move with such speed that they seemed invisible to the human eye until the moment they attacked. They possessed unnatural senses: the olfactory acuity of a wolf, the auditory sensitivity of a bat, the strength of twenty men, the penetrating eyesight of an eagle. The Berserkers had once been the most fearless and feared warriors ever to walk Scotland nearly seven hundred years ago. They had been Odin's elite Viking army. Legend claimed they could assume the shape of a wolf or a bear as easily as the shape of a man. And they were marked by a common feature—unholy blue eyes that glowed like banked coals.

Berserker, the wind sighed.

"There is no such thing as a Berserker," Gavrael grimly informed the night. He was no longer the foolish boy who'd been infatuated with the prospect of unbeatable strength; no longer the youth who'd once been willing to offer his immortal soul for absolute power and control. Besides, his own eyes were deep brown, and always had been. Never had history recorded a brown-eyed Berserker.

Call me.

Gavrael flinched. This last figment of his traumatized mind had been a command, undeniable, irresistible. The hair on the back of his neck stood up on end and his skin prickled. Not once in all his years of playing at summoning a Berserker had he ever felt so peculiar. His blood pounded through his veins and he felt as if he teetered on the brink of an abyss that both lured and repulsed him.

Screams filled the valley. Child after child fell while he stood high above the battle, helpless to alter the course of events. He would do anything to save them: barter, trade, steal, murder—*anything.*

Tears streamed down his face as a tiny lass with blond ringlets wailed her last breath. There would be no mother's arms for her, no bonny suitor, no wedding, no babes—not a breath more precious life. Blood stained the front of her frock, and he stared at it, mesmerized. His universe narrowed to a tunnel of vision in which the blood blossoming on her chest became a vast, crimson whirlpool, sucking him down and down . . .

Something inside him snapped.

He threw his head back and howled, the words ricocheting off the rocks of Wotan's Cleft. *"Hear me, Odin, I summon the Berserker! I, Gavrael Roderick Icarus McIllioch, offer my life—nay, my soul—for vengeance. I command the Berserker!"*

The moderate breeze turned suddenly violent, lashing leaves and dirt into the air. Gavrael flung his arms up to shield his face from the needle-sharp sting of flying debris. Branches, no match for the fierce gale, snapped free and battered his body like clumsy spears hurled from the trees. Black clouds scuttled across the night sky, momentarily obscuring the moon. The unnatural wind keened through the channels of rock on Wotan's Cleft, briefly muffling the screams from the valley below. Suddenly the night exploded in a flash of dazzling blue and Gavrael felt his body . . . change.

He snarled, baring his teeth, as he felt something irrevocable mutate deep within him.

He could smell dozens of scents from the battle below—the rusty, metallic odor of blood and steel and hate.

He could hear whispers from the McKane camp on the far horizon.

He saw for the first time that the warriors appeared to be moving in slow motion. How had he failed to notice it before? It would be absurdly easy to slip in and destroy them all while they were moving as if slogging through wet sand. So easy to destroy. So easy . . .

Gavrael sucked in rapid breaths of air, pumping his chest full before charging into the valley below. As he plunged into the slaughter, the sound of laughter echoed off the stone basin that cupped the valley. He realized it was coming from his own lips only when the McKane began to fall beneath his sword.

* * *

Hours later, Gavrael stumbled through the burning remains of Tuluth. The McKane were gone, either dead or driven off. The surviving villagers were tending the wounded and walking in wide, cautious circles around the young son of the McIllioch.

"Near to threescore ye killed, lad," an old man with bright eyes whispered when Gavrael passed. "Not even yer da in his prime could do such a thing. Ye be far more berserk."

Gavrael glanced at him, startled. Before he could ask what he meant by that comment, the old man melted into the billowing smoke.

"Ye took down three in one swing of yer sword, lad," another man called.

A child flung his arms around Gavrael's knees. "Ye saved me life, ye did!" the lad cried. "Tha' ole McKane woulda had me for his supper. Thank ye! Me ma's thanking ye too."

Gavrael smiled at the boy, then turned to the mother, who crossed herself and didn't look remotely appreciative. His smile faded. "I'm not a monster—"

"I know what ye are, lad." Her gaze never left his. To

Gavrael's ears her words were harsh and condemning. "I know exactly what ye are and doona be thinking otherwise. Get on with ye now! Yer da's in trouble." She pointed a quivering finger past the last row of smoldering huts.

Gavrael narrowed his eyes against the smoke and stumbled forward. He'd never felt so drained in all his life. Moving awkwardly, he rounded one of the few huts still standing and jerked to a halt.

His da was crumpled on the ground, covered with blood, his sword abandoned at his side in the dirt.

Grief and anger vied for supremacy in Gavrael's heart, leaving him strangely hollow. As he stared down at his father, the image of his mother's body surged to the forefront of his mind and the last of his youthful illusions shattered; tonight had birthed both an extraordinary warrior and a flesh-and-blood man with inadequate defenses. "Why, Da? Why?" His voice broke harshly on the words. He would never see his mother smile again, never hear her sing, never attend her burial—for he would be leaving Maldebann once his da replied, lest he turn his residual rage upon his own father. And then what would he be? No better than his da.

Ronin McIllioch groaned. Slowly he opened his eyes in a blood-crusted squint and gazed up at his son. A ribbon of scarlet trickled from his lips as he struggled to speak. "We're . . . born—" He broke off, consumed by a deep, racking cough.

Gavrael grabbed his father by handfuls of his shirt and, heedless of Ronin's pained grimace, shook him roughly. He would have his answer before he left; he would discover what madness had driven his da to kill his mother or he would be tortured all his life by unanswered questions. "What, Da? Say it! Tell me why!"

Ronin's bleary gaze sought Gavrael's. His chest rose and fell as he drew swift, shallow gasps of smoky air. With a strange undertone of sympathy, he said, "Son, we canna help it . . . the McIllioch men . . . always we're born . . . this way."

Gavrael stared at his father in horror. "You would say that to me? You think you can convince me that I'm mad like you? I'm not like you! I'll not believe you. You lie. You *lie*!" He lunged to his feet, backing hastily away.

Ronin McIllioch forced himself up on his elbows and jerked his head at the evidence of Gavrael's savagery, the remains of McKane warriors who had been literally ripped to pieces. "You did that, son."

"I am *not* a ruthless killer!" Gavrael scanned the mutilated bodies, not quite convinced of his own words.

"It's part of . . . being McIllioch. You canna help it, son."

"Doona call me son! I will never be your son again. And I'm not part of your sickness. I'm not like you. I will *never* be like you!"

Ronin sank back to the ground, muttering incoherently. Gavrael deliberately closed his ears to the sound. He would not listen to his da's lies a moment longer. He turned his back on him and surveyed what was left of Tuluth. The surviving villagers huddled in small groups, standing in absolute silence, watching him. Averting his face from what he would always remember as their reproving regard, his glance slid up the dark stone of Maldebann castle. Carved into the side of the mountain, it towered above the village. Once he had wished for nothing more than to grow up and help govern Maldebann at his da's side, eventually taking over as chieftain. He'd wished to always hear the lovely lilt of his mother's laughter filling the spacious halls, to hear his da's answering rumble as they joked and talked. He'd dreamed of wisely settling his people's concerns; of marrying one day and having sons of his own. Aye, once he had believed all those things would come to pass. But in less time than it had taken the moon to bridge the sky above Tuluth, all his dreams, and the very last part of him that had been human, were destroyed.

* * *

It took Gavrael the better part of a day to drag his battered body back up into the sanctuary of the dense Highland forests. He could never go home. His mother was dead, the castle ransacked, and the villagers had regarded him with fear. His da's words haunted him—*we're born this way*—killers, capable of murdering even those they claimed to love. It was a sickness of the mind, Gavrael thought, which his father said he, too, carried in his blood.

Thirstier than he'd ever been, he half crawled to the loch nestled in a small valley beyond Wotan's Cleft. He collapsed for a time on the springy tundra, and when he wasn't quite so dizzy and weak he struggled forward to drink, dragging himself on his elbows. As he cupped his hands and bent over the sparkling, clear pool he froze, mesmerized by his reflection rippling in the water.

Ice-blue eyes stared back at him.

Chapter 1

Dalkeith-Upon-the-Sea
The Highlands of Scotland
1515

Grimm paused at the open doors of the study and gazed into the night. The reflection of stars dappled the restless ocean, like tiny pinpoints of light cresting the waves. Usually he found the sound of the sea crashing against the rocks soothing, but lately it seemed to incite in him a questing restlessness.

As he resumed pacing, he sifted through possible reasons for his unrest and came up empty-handed. It had been by choice that he remained at Dalkeith as captain of the Douglas guard when, two years ago, he and his best friend, Hawk Douglas, left Edinburgh and King James's service. Grimm adored Hawk's wife, Adrienne—when she wasn't trying to marry him off—and he doted upon their young son, Carthian. He had been, if not exactly happy, content. At least until recently. So what ailed him?

"You're wearing holes in my favorite rug with your pacing, Grimm. And the painter will never be able to finish this portrait if you won't sit down," Adrienne teased, jarring him from his melancholy reverie.

Grimm expelled a breath and ran a hand through his thick hair. Absentmindedly he fiddled with a section at his temple, twisting the strands into a plait as he continued to contemplate the sea.

"You aren't looking for a wishing star out there, are you, Grimm?" Hawk Douglas's black eyes danced with mirth.

"Hardly. And anytime your mischievous wife would care to tell me what curse she laid upon me with her careless wishing, I'd be happy to hear it." Some time ago, Adrienne Douglas had wished upon a falling star, and she steadfastly refused to tell either of them what she'd wished until she was absolutely certain it had been heard and granted. The only thing she would admit was that her wish had been made on Grimm's behalf, which unnerved him considerably. Although he didn't consider himself a superstitious man, he'd seen enough odd occurrences in the world to know that merely because something seemed improbable certainly didn't render it impossible.

"As would I, Grimm," Hawk said dryly. "But she won't tell me either."

Adrienne laughed. "Go on with the two of you. Don't tell me two such fearless warriors suffer a moment's concern over a woman's idle wish upon a star."

"I consider nothing you do idle, Adrienne," Hawk replied with a wry grin. "The universe does *not* behave in a normal fashion where you're concerned."

Grimm smiled faintly. It certainly didn't. Adrienne had been tossed back in time from the twentieth century, the victim of a wicked plot to destroy the Hawk, concocted by a vindictive Fairy. Impossible things happened around

Adrienne, which was why he wanted to know what bloody wish she'd made. He'd like to be prepared when all hell broke loose.

"Do sit down, Grimm," Adrienne urged. "I want this portrait finished by Christmas at the latest, and it takes Albert months to paint from his sketches."

"Only because my work is sheer perfection," the painter said, miffed.

Grimm turned his back on the night and reclaimed his seat by Hawk in front of the fire. "I still doona get the point of this," Grimm muttered. "Portraits are for lasses and children."

Adrienne snorted. "I commission a painter to immortalize two of the most magnificent men I've ever laid eyes upon"—she flashed them a dazzling smile, and Grimm rolled his eyes, knowing he would do whatever the lovely Adrienne wished when she smiled like that—"and all they can do is grumble. I'll have you know, one day you'll thank me for doing this."

Grimm and Hawk exchanged amused glances, then resumed the pose she insisted displayed their muscular physiques and dark good looks to their finest advantage.

"Be certain you color Grimm's eyes as brilliantly blue as they are," she instructed Albert.

"As if I don't know how to paint," he muttered. "I *am* the artist here. Unless, of course, you'd like to try your hand at it."

"I thought you liked *my* eyes." Hawk narrowed his black eyes at Adrienne.

"I do. I married you, didn't I?" Adrienne teased, smiling. "Can I help it if the staff at Dalkeith, to the youngest maid of a tender twelve years, swoons over your best friend's eyes? When I hold my sapphires up to the sunlight, they look exactly the same. They shimmer with iridescent blue fire."

"What are mine? Puny black walnuts?"

Adrienne laughed. "Silly man, that's how I described your heart when I first met you. And stop fidgeting, Grimm," she chided. "Or is there some reason you want those braids at your temples in this portrait?"

Grimm froze, then slowly touched his hair in disbelief.

Hawk stared at him. "What's on your mind, Grimm?" he asked, fascinated.

Grimm swallowed. He hadn't even realized he'd plaited the war braids into his hair. A man wore war braids only during the blackest hours of his life—when he was mourning his lost mate or preparing for battle. So far, he'd worn them twice. What had he been thinking? Grimm stared blankly at the floor, confused, unable to vocalize his thoughts. Lately he'd been obsessed with ghosts of the past, memories he'd tossed savagely into a shallow grave years ago and buried beneath a thin sod of denials. But in his dreams the shadow corpses walked again, trailing behind them a residue of unease that clung to him throughout the day.

Grimm was still struggling to answer when a guard burst through the doors to the study.

"Milord. Milady." The guard nodded deferentially to Hawk and Adrienne as he hastily entered the room. He approached Grimm, a somber expression on his face. "This just came for ye, Cap'n." He thrust an official-looking piece of parchment into Grimm's hands. "The messenger insisted 'twas urgent, and to be delivered into your hands only."

Grimm turned the message slowly in his hand. The elegant crest of Gibraltar St. Clair was pressed into the red wax. Suppressed memories broke over him: *Jillian*. She was a promise of beauty and joy he could never possess, a memory he'd consigned to that same uncooperative, shallow grave that now seemed determined to regurgitate its dead.

"Well, open it, Grimm," Adrienne urged.

Slowly, as if he held a wounded animal that might turn on him with sharp teeth, Grimm broke the seal and opened the missive. Stiffly, he read the terse, three-word command. His hand fisted reflexively, crumpling the thick vellum.

Rising, he turned to the guard. "Prepare my horse. I leave in one hour." The guard nodded and left the study.

"Well?" Hawk demanded. "What does it say?"

"Nothing you need to address, Hawk. Doona worry. It doesn't concern you."

"Anything that concerns my best friend concerns me," Hawk said. "So give over, what's wrong?"

"I said nothing. Leave it, man." Grimm's voice held a note of warning that would have restrained a lesser man's hand. But the Hawk had never been, and would never be, a lesser man, and he moved so unexpectedly that Grimm didn't react quickly enough when he whisked the parchment from his hand. Grinning mischievously, Hawk backed away and uncrumpled the parchment. His grin broadened, and he winked at Adrienne.

" 'Come for Jillian,' it says. A woman, is it? The plot thickens. I thought you'd sworn off women, my fickle friend. So who's Jillian?"

"A woman?" Adrienne exclaimed delightedly. "A young, marriageable woman?"

"Stop it, you two. It's not like that."

"Then why were you trying to keep it a secret, Grimm?" Hawk pressed.

"Because there are things you doona know about me, and it would take far too long to explain. Lacking the leisure to tell you the full story, I'll send you a message in a few months," he evaded coolly.

"You're not getting out of this so easily, Grimm Roderick." Hawk rubbed the shadow beard on his stubborn jaw thoughtfully. "Who is Jillian, and how do you know Gibraltar St. Clair? I thought you came to court directly from England. I thought you knew no one in all of Scotland but for those you met at court."

"I didn't exactly tell you the whole story, Hawk, and I doona have time for it now, but I'll tell you as soon as I get settled."

"You'll tell me now, or I'm coming with you," Hawk threatened. "Which means Adrienne and Carthian are coming as well, so you can either tell me or prepare for company, and you never know what might happen if Adrienne comes along."

Grimm scowled. "You really can be a pain, Hawk."

"Relentless. Formidable," Adrienne agreed sweetly. "You may as well give in, Grimm. My husband never takes no for an answer. Believe me, I know this."

"Come on, Grimm, if you can't trust me, who can you trust?" he coaxed. "Where are you going?"

"It's not a question of trust, Hawk." Hawk merely waited with an expectant look on his face, and Grimm knew he had no intention of relenting. Hawk would push and poke and ultimately do exactly as he'd threatened—come along—unless Grimm gave him a sufficient answer. Perhaps it was time he admitted the truth, although the odds were that once he did, he wouldn't be welcomed back at Dalkeith. "I'm going home, sort of," Grimm finally conceded.

"*Caithness* is your home?"

"Tuluth," Grimm muttered.

"What?"

"Tuluth," Grimm said flatly. "I was born in Tuluth."

"You said you were born in Edinburgh!"

"I lied."

"Why? You told me your entire family was dead! Was that a lie too?"

"No! They are. I didn't lie about that. Well . . . mostly I didn't lie," he corrected hastily. "My da is still alive, but I haven't spoken to him in more than fifteen years."

A muscle twitched in Hawk's jaw. "Sit down, Grimm. You're not going anywhere until you tell me all of it, and I suspect it's a tale that's long overdue."

"I doona have time, Hawk. If St. Clair said it was urgent, I was needed at Caithness weeks ago."

"What relevance has Caithness to any of this, or to you? Sit. Talk. *Now.*"

Sensing no possibility of reprieve, Grimm paced as he began his story. He told them how, at the age of fourteen, he'd left Tuluth the night of the massacre and wandered the forests of the Highlands for two years, wearing his war braids and hating mankind, hating his father, hating himself. He skipped the brutal parts—his mother's murder, the starvation he'd endured, the repeated attempts on his life. He told them that when he was sixteen he'd found shelter with Gibraltar St. Clair; that he'd changed his name to Grimm to protect himself and those for whom he cared. He told them how the McKane had found him again at Caithness and attacked his foster family. And finally, in the tone of a dreaded confession, he told them what his real name had been.

"What did you just say?" Hawk asked blankly.

Grimm drew a deep breath into his lungs and expelled it angrily. "I said Gavrael. My real name is Gavrael." There was only one Gavrael in all of Scotland; no other man would willingly own up to that name and that curse. He braced himself for the Hawk's explosion. He didn't have to wait for long.

"McIllioch?" Hawk's eyes narrowed disbelievingly.

"McIllioch," Grimm confirmed.

"And Grimm?"

"Grimm stands for Gavrael Roderick Icarus McIllioch." Grimm's Highland brogue rolled so thickly around the name, it was a nearly unintelligible burr of *r*'s and *l*'s and staccato-sharp *k*'s. "Take the first letter of each name, and there you have it. G-R-I-M."

"Gavrael McIllioch was a Berserker!" Hawk roared.

"I told you you didn't know so much about me," Grimm said darkly.

Crossing the study in three swift strides, Hawk bristled to a stop inches from Grimm's face and studied him, as if he might uncover some telltale trace of a beast that should have betrayed Grimm's secret years ago. "How could I not have known?" Hawk muttered. "For years I'd been wondering about some of your peculiar . . . talents. By the bloody saints, I should have guessed if only from your eyes—"

"Lots of people have blue eyes, Hawk," Grimm said dryly.

"Not like *yours*, Grimm," Adrienne remarked.

"This explains it all," Hawk said slowly. "You're not human."

Grimm flinched.

Adrienne leveled a dark look at her husband and linked her arm through Grimm's. "Of course he's human, Hawk. He's just human . . . plus some."

"A Berserker." Hawk shook his head. "A fardling Berserker. You know, they say William Wallace was a Berserker."

"And what a lovely life he had, eh?" Grimm said bitterly.

* * *

Grimm rode out shortly thereafter, answering no more questions and leaving the Hawk immensely dissatisfied. He left quickly, because the memories were returning of their own accord and with fury. Grimm knew he had to be alone when full recollection finally reclaimed him. He didn't willingly think about Tuluth anymore. Hell, he didn't willingly think anymore, not if he could help it.

Tuluth: in his memory a smoky valley, clouds of black so thick his eyes had stung from the acrid stench of burning homes and burning flesh. Children screaming. *Och, Christ!*

Grimm swallowed hard as he spurred Occam into a gallop across the ridge. He was impervious to the beauty of the Highland night, lost in another time, surrounded only by the color of blood and the blackness of soul-disfiguring desolation—with one shimmering spot of gold.

Jillian.

Is he an animal, Da? May I keep him? Please? He's an ever-so-glorious beastie!

And in his mind he was sixteen years old again, looking down at the wee golden lass. Memory swept over him, dripping shame thicker than clotted honey off a comb. She'd found him in the woods, scavenging like a beast.

He'd be fiercer than my Savanna TeaGarden, Da!

Savanna TeaGarden being her puppy, all one hundred forty pounds of Irish wolfhound puppy.

He'd protect me well, Da, I know he would!

The instant she'd said the words, he'd taken a silent vow to do just that, never dreaming it might one day entail protecting her from himself.

Grimm rubbed his clean-shaven jaw and tossed his head in the wind. For a brief moment he felt the matted hair again, the dirt and sweat and the war braids, the fierce eyes brimming with hatred. And the pure, sweet child had trusted him on sight.

Och, but he'd dissuaded her quickly.

CHAPTER 2

GIBRALTAR AND ELIZABETH ST. CLAIR HAD BEEN RIDING toward their son's home in the Highlands for over a week before Gibraltar finally confessed his plan. He wouldn't have told her at all, but he couldn't stand to see his wife upset.

"Did you hear that?" Elizabeth said accusingly to her husband as she rounded her mare and cantered back to his side. "Did you?"

"Hear what? I couldn't hear a thing. You were too far away," he teased.

"That's it, Gibraltar. I've had it!"

Gibraltar raised an inquiring brow. "What's it, love?" Flushed with outrage, his wife was even more alluring than she was when calm. He wasn't above gently provoking her to enjoy the show.

Elizabeth tossed her head briskly. "I am sick of hearing men talk about our flawless, saintly, unwed—as in nearly a spinster—daughter, Gibraltar."

"You've been eavesdropping again, haven't you, Elizabeth?" he asked mildly.

"Eavesdropping, schmeavesdropping. If my daughter is being discussed, even if only by the guards"—she gestured in their direction irritably—"I have every right to listen. Our fearsome protectors, who I might point out are perfectly healthy full-grown men, have been trading tributes to her virtues. By virtues they don't mean her breasts or any of her lovely curves, but her sweet temper, her patience, her calling to the cloister, for goodness' sake. Did she breathe a word to you about this sudden inclination to devote herself to the nunnery?" Without waiting for an answer, Elizabeth reined in her mount and glared at him. "They go on and on about how flawless she is and not one of them says a word about tupping her."

Gibraltar laughed as he drew his stallion to a halt beside her mare.

"How dare you think this is funny?"

Gibraltar shook his head, his eyes sparkling. Only Elizabeth would take offense that men didn't talk about seducing their only daughter.

"Gibraltar, I must ask you to be serious for a moment. Jillian is twenty-one years old and not one man has seriously tried to court her. I vow she's the most exquisite lass in all of Scotland, and men walk quietly worshipful circles around her. *Do* something, Gibraltar. I'm getting worried."

His smile faded. Elizabeth was right. It was no longer a laughing matter. Gibraltar had reached that conclusion himself. It wasn't fair to let Elizabeth continue worrying when he'd taken action that would soon put both their fears to rest. "I've already taken care of it, Elizabeth."

"What do you mean? What have you done this time?"

Gibraltar studied her intently. At the moment he wasn't

completely certain which would upset Elizabeth more: continued worry over their daughter's unwed state, or the details of what he'd done without consulting her. A uniquely masculine moment of reflection convinced him she would be dazzled by his ingenuity. "I've arranged for three men to attend Caithness in our absence, Elizabeth. By the time we return, either Jillian will have chosen one of them, or one of them will have chosen her. They are not the kind of men to give up in the face of a wee bit of resistance. Nor are they the kind of men to fall for her 'nunnery stories.' "

Elizabeth's horrified expression deflated his smug pose. "One of them will choose her? Are you saying that one of these men you've selected might compromise her if she doesn't choose?"

"Seduce, Elizabeth, not compromise," Gibraltar protested. "They wouldn't ruin her. They're all honorable, respectable lairds." His voice deepened persuasively. "I selected these three based in part on the fact that they're also all very . . . er"—he searched for a word innocuous enough that it wouldn't alarm his wife, because the men he'd chosen could be patently alarming—". . . masculine men." His perfunctory nod was intended to soothe her concerns. It failed. "Exactly what Jillian needs," he assured her.

"Masculine! You mean randy inveterate blackguards! Probably domineering and ruthless, to boot. Don't prevaricate with me, Gibraltar!"

Gibraltar sighed gustily, any hope of subtle persuasion debunked. "Do you have a better idea, Elizabeth? Frankly, I think the problem is that Jillian has never met a man who wasn't intimidated by her. I guarantee you not one of the men I've invited will be even remotely intimidated. Captivated? Yes. Intrigued? Yes. Ruthlessly persistent? Yes. Precisely what a Sacheron woman needs. A man who is man enough to *do* something about it."

Elizabeth St. Clair, née Sacheron, nibbled her lower lip in silence.

"You know how you've been longing to see our new grandson," he reminded her. "Let's just go on with our visit and see what happens. I promise you that none of the men I've chosen will harm a hair on our precious daughter's head. They might muss it up a bit, but that will be well and good for her. Our impeccable Jillian is long overdue for some mussing."

"You expect me to just go off and leave her with three men? *Those* kind of men?"

"Elizabeth, those kind of men are the only kind of men who will not worship her. Besides, I was once one of those kind of men, if you'll recall. It will take an uncommon man for our uncommon daughter, Elizabeth," he added more gently. "I aim to find her that uncommon man."

Elizabeth sighed and blew a tendril of hair from her face. "I suppose you've the right of it," she murmured. "She truly hasn't met a man who didn't worship her. I wonder, how do you think she'll react when she does?"

"I suspect she might not know what to do at first. It may throw her badly off balance. But I'm wagering one of the men I've selected will help her figure it out," Gibraltar said smoothly.

Alarm vanquished Elizabeth's despondence instantly. "That's it. We'll just have to go back. I can't be somewhere else when my daughter is experiencing these woman things for the first time. God only knows what some man will try to teach my daughter or how he'll try to teach it to her, not to mention how shocked she's certain to be. I can't be off visiting while my daughter is being bullied and bamboozled out of her maidenhead—it simply won't do! We'll have to go home." She gazed expectantly at her husband, awaiting his nod of agreement.

"Elizabeth." Gibraltar said her name very quietly.

"Gibraltar?" Her tone was wary.

"We are not turning back. We are going to visit our son to attend our grandson's christening and spend a few months, as planned."

"Does Jillian know what you've done?" Elizabeth asked icily.

Gibraltar shook his head. "She hasn't a suspicion in her pretty head."

"What about the men? Don't you think they will tell her?"

Gibraltar grinned wickedly. "I didn't tell them. I simply commanded their attendance. But Hatchard knows and is prepared to inform them at a suitable time."

Elizabeth was shocked. "You told no one but our chief man-at-arms?"

"Hatchard is a wise man. And she needs this, Elizabeth. She needs to find her own way. Besides," he provoked, "what man would dare bamboozle a lass's maidenhead with her mother hovering at her elbow?"

"Och! My mother, my da, my seven brothers, and my grandparents being in attendance didn't stop you from bamboozling mine. Or abducting me."

Gibraltar chuckled. "Are you sorry I did?"

Elizabeth gave him a steamy look from beneath her lashes that assured him to the contrary.

"So you see, sometimes a man knows best, don't you think, my dear?"

She didn't reply for a moment, but Gibraltar didn't mind. He knew Elizabeth trusted him with her life. She just needed some time to get used to his plan and to accept the fact that their daughter needed a loving push over the edge of the nest.

When Elizabeth finally spoke, resignation buffered her words. "Just which three men did you choose without my discerning insight and consent?"

"Well, there's Quinn de Moncreiffe." Gibraltar's gaze never strayed from her face.

Quinn was blond, handsome and daring. He'd sailed black-flag for the King before he'd inherited his titles and now commanded a fleet of merchant ships, from which he'd trebled his clan's already considerable fortune. Gibraltar had fostered Quinn when he'd been a young lad, and Elizabeth had always favored him.

"Good man." A lift of a perfect golden brow betrayed grudging admiration for her husband's wisdom. "And?"

"Ramsay Logan."

"Oh!" Elizabeth's eyes grew round. "When I saw him at court he was clad in black from head to toe. He looked as dangerously attractive as a man could be. How is it that some woman hasn't snatched him up? Do go on, Gibraltar. This is becoming quite promising. Who's the third?"

"We're lagging too far behind the guards, Elizabeth," Gibraltar evaded glibly. "The Highlands have been peaceful lately, but we can't be too careful. We must catch up." He shifted in his saddle, grasped her reins, and urged her to follow.

Elizabeth scowled as she plucked the reins from his hand. "We'll catch them later. Who's the third?"

Gibraltar frowned and gazed at the guards, who were fading out of sight around a bend. "Elizabeth, we mustn't tarry. You have no idea—"

"The third, Gibraltar," his wife repeated.

"You look especially lovely today, Elizabeth," Gibraltar said huskily. "Have I told you that?" When his words evoked no response but a cool, level stare, he wrinkled his brow.

"Did I say three?"

Elizabeth's expression grew cooler.

Gibraltar expelled a breath of frustration. He mumbled a name and spurred his mount forward.

"What did you just say?" she called after him, urging her mare to keep up.

"Oh hell, Elizabeth! Give over! Let's just ride."

"Repeat yourself, please, Gibraltar."

There was another unintelligible answer.

"I can't understand a word when you mumble," Elizabeth said sweetly.

Sweet as siren song, he thought, *and every bit as lethal.* "I said Gavrael McIllioch. All right? Leave it, will you?" He rounded his stallion sharply and glared, savoring the fact that at least for the time being he'd rendered her as close to speechless as Elizabeth St. Clair ever came.

Elizabeth stared at her husband in disbelief. "Dear God in heaven, he's summoned the Berserker!"

* * *

On the sloping lawn of Caithness, Jillian St. Clair shivered despite the warmth of the brightly shining sun. Not one cloud dotted the sky, and the shady forest that rimmed the south end of the lawn was a dozen yards away—not close enough to have been responsible for her sudden chill.

An inexplicable sense of foreboding crept up the back of her neck. She shook it off briskly, berating her overactive imagination. Her life was as unmarred by clouds as the expansive blue sky; she was being fanciful, nothing more.

"Jillian! Make Jemmie stop pulling my hair!" Mallory

cried, dashing to Jillian's side for protection. The lush green grass of the lawn was sprinkled with the dozen or so children who gathered every afternoon to cajole stories and sweets from Jillian.

Sheltering Mallory in her arms, Jillian regarded the lad reprovingly. "There are better ways to show a lass that you like her than pulling her hair, Jemmie MacBean. And it's been my experience that the girls whose hair you pull now are the ones you'll be courting later."

"I didn't pull her hair because I *like* her!" Jemmie's face turned red and his hands curled into defiant fists. "She's a *girl*."

"Aye, she is. And a lovely one at that." Jillian smoothed Mallory's luxuriant, long auburn hair. The young lass already showed promise of the beautiful woman she would become. "Pray tell, why *do* you pull her hair, Jemmie?" Jillian asked lightly.

Jemmie kicked at the grass with his toes. "Because if I punched her the same way I punch the lads, she'd probably cry," he mumbled.

"Why must you do anything to her at all? Why not simply talk to her?"

"What could a *girl* have to say?" He rolled his eyes and scowled at the other lads, wordlessly demanding support with his fierce glare.

Only Zeke was unaffected by his bullying. "Jillian has interesting things to say, Jemmie," Zeke argued. "You come here every afternoon to listen to her, and *she's* a girl."

"That's different. She's not a girl. She's . . . well, she's almost like a mother to us, 'cept she's a lot prettier."

Jillian brushed a strand of blond hair back from her face with an inward wince. What had "prettier" ever done for her? She longed to have children of her own, but children required a husband, and one of those didn't appear to be on the horizon for her, pretty or not. *Well, you could stop being so picky,* her conscience advised dryly.

"Shall I tell you a story?" She swiftly changed the subject.

"Yes, tell us a story, Jillian!"

"A romantic one!" an older girl called.

"A bloody one," Jemmie demanded.

Mallory scrunched her nose at him. "Give us a fable. I love fables. They teach us good things, and some of us"—she glared at Jemmie—"need to learn good things."

"Fables are dumb—"

"Are not!"

"A fable! A fable!" the children clamored.

"A fable you shall have. I shall tell you of the argument between the Wind and the Sun," Jillian said. "It's my favorite of all the fables." The children jostled for the seat closest to her as they settled down to hear the tale. Zeke, the smallest of them, was shoved to the back of the cluster.

"Don't squint, Zeke," Jillian chided kindly. "Here, come closer." She drew the boy onto her lap and pushed the hair out of his eyes. Zeke was her favorite maid, Kaley Twillow's, son. He'd been born with such weak eyesight that he could scarcely see past his own hand. He was forever squinting, as if it might one day work a miracle and bring the world into focus. Jillian couldn't imagine the sorrow of not being able to clearly see the lovely landscape of Scotia, and her heart wept for Zeke's handicap. It prevented him from playing the games the other children adored. He was far more likely to be hit by the bladder-skin ball than to hit it, so to compensate Jillian had taught him to read. He had to bury his nose in the book, but therein he'd found worlds to explore he could never have seen with his own eyes.

As Zeke nestled into her lap, she began. "One day the Wind and the Sun were having an argument over who was stronger, when suddenly they saw a tinker coming down the road. The Sun said, 'Let us decide our dispute now. Whichever of us can cause the tinker to take off his cloak shall be regarded as the stronger.'

"The Wind agreed to the contest. 'You begin,' the Sun said, and retired behind a cloud so he wouldn't interfere. The Wind began to blow as hard as it could upon the tinker, but the more he blew, the tighter the tinker clutched his cloak about his body. That didn't deter the Wind from giving it all he had; still the tinker refused to yield his cloak. Finally the Wind gave up in despair.

"Then the Sun came out and blazed in all his glory upon the tinker, who soon found it too warm to walk with his cloak on. Removing it, he tossed the garment over his shoulder and continued on his journey, whistling cheerily."

"Yay!" the girls cheered. "The Sun won! We like the Sun better too!"

"It's a stupid girl story." Jemmie scowled.

"I liked it," Zeke protested.

"You would, Zeke. You're too blind to be seeing warriors and dragons and swords. I like stories with adventure."

"This tale had a point, Jemmie. The same point I was making about you pulling Mallory's hair," Jillian said gently.

Jemmie looked bewildered. "It did? What does the Sun have to do with Mal's hair?"

Zeke shook his head, disgusted by Jemmie's denseness. "She was telling us that the Wind tried to make the tinker feel bad, so the tinker needed to defend himself. The Sun made the tinker feel good and warm and safe enough to walk freely."

Mallory beamed adoringly at Zeke, as if he were the cleverest lad in the world. Zeke continued seriously, "So be nice to Mallory and she'll be nice to you."

"Where do you get your halfwit ideas?" Jemmie asked, irritated.

"He listens, Jemmie," Jillian said. "The moral of the fable is that kindness affects more than cruelty. Zeke understands that there's nothing wrong with being nice to the lasses. One day you'll be sorry you weren't nicer." *When Zeke ends up with half the village lasses hopelessly in love with him despite his weak vision,* Jillian thought, amused. Zeke was a handsome young lad and would one day be an attractive man possessing the unique sensitivity those born with a handicap tended to develop.

"She's right, lad." A deep voice joined their conversation as a man spurred his horse from the shelter of the nearby trees. "I'm *still* sorry I wasn't nicer to the lasses."

The blood in Jillian's veins chilled and her cloudless life was suddenly awash with thick, black thunderheads. Surely *that* man would never be fool enough to come back to Caithness! She pressed her cheek into Zeke's hair, hiding her face, wishing she could melt into the ground and disappear, wishing she had put on a more elegant gown this morning—as ever, wishing impossible things where this man was concerned. Although she hadn't heard his voice in years, she knew it was he.

"I recall a lass I was mean to when I was a lad, and now, knowing what I know, I'd give a great deal to take it all back."

Grimm Roderick. Jillian felt as if her muscles had

melted beneath her skin, fused by the heat of his voice. Two full timbres lower than any other voice she'd ever heard, modulated so precisely it conveyed intimidating self-discipline, his was the voice of a man in control.

She raised her head and stared at him, her eyes wide with shock and horror. Her breath caught in her throat. No matter how the years changed him, she would always recognize him. He'd dismounted and was approaching her, moving with the detached arrogance and grace of a conqueror, exuding confidence as liberally as he exhaled. Grimm Roderick had always been a walking weapon, his body developed and honed to instinctual perfection. Were she to scramble to her feet and feint left, Jillian knew he'd be there before her. Were she to back up, he'd be behind her. Were she to scream, he could cover her mouth before she'd even finished drawing her breath in preparation. She'd only once before seen a creature move with such speed and repressed power: one of the mountain cats whose muscles bunched in springy recoil as they padded about on dangerous paws.

She drew a shaky breath. He was even more magnificent than he'd been years ago. His black hair was neatly restrained in a leather thong. The angle of his jaw was even more arrogant than she remembered—if that was possible; jutting slightly forward, it caused his lower lip to curl in a sensual smirk regardless of the occasion.

The air itself felt different when Grimm Roderick was in it; her surroundings receded until nothing existed but him. And she could never mistake those eyes! Mocking blue-ice, his gaze locked with hers over the heads of the forgotten curious children. He was watching her with an unfathomable expression.

She lunged to her feet, tumbling a startled Zeke to the

ground. As Jillian stared wordlessly at Grimm, memories surfaced and she nearly drowned in the bitter bile of humiliation. She recalled too clearly the day she'd vowed never to speak to Grimm Roderick again. She'd sworn never to permit him near Caithness—or near her vulnerable heart again—as long as she lived. And he dared saunter up now? As if nothing had changed? The possibility of reconciliation was instantly squashed beneath the weighty heels of her pride. She would not dignify his presence with words. She would not be nice. She would not grant him one ounce of courtesy.

Grimm worried a hand through his hair and took a deep breath. "You've . . . grown, lass."

Jillian struggled to speak. When she finally found her tongue, her words dripped ice. "How dare you come back here? You are not welcome. Leave my home!"

"I can't do that, Jillian." His soft voice unnerved her.

Her heart racing, she drew a slow, deep breath. "If you don't leave of your own accord, I'll summon the guards to remove you."

"They won't do that, Jillian."

She clapped her hands. "Guards!" she cried.

Grimm didn't move an inch. "It won't help, Jillian."

"And quit saying my name like that!"

"Like what, Jillian?" He sounded genuinely curious.

"Like . . . like . . . a prayer or something."

"As you wish." He paused the length of two heartbeats—during which she was astonished he'd capitulated to her will, because he certainly never had before—then he added with such husky resonance that it slipped inside her heart without her consent, "Jillian."

Perish the man! "Guards. Guards!"

Her guards arrived on a run, then halted abruptly, studying the man standing before their mistress.

"Milady, you summoned?" Hatchard inquired.

"Remove this iniquitous scoundrel from Caithness before he breeds . . . *brings*"—she corrected herself hastily—"his depravity and wicked insolence into my home," she sputtered to a finish.

The guards looked from her to Grimm and didn't move.

"Now. Remove him from the estate at once!"

When the guards still didn't move, her temper rose a notch. "Hatchard, I said make him leave. By the sweet saints, toss him out of my life. Banish him from the country. Och! Just remove him from this *world*, will you, now?"

The flank of guards stared at Jillian with openmouthed astonishment. "Are you feeling well, milady?" Hatchard asked. "Should we fetch Kaley to see if you've a touch of the fever?"

"I don't have a touch of anything. There's a degenerate knave on my estate and I want him off it," Jillian said through gritted teeth.

"Did you just grit?" Hatchard gaped.

"Pardon?"

"Grit. It means to speak from between clenched teeth—"

"I'm going to scream from between clenched teeth if you disobedient wretches don't remove this degenerate, virile"—Jillian cleared her throat—"*vile* rogue from Caithness."

"Scream?" Hatchard repeated faintly. "Jillian St. Clair doesn't scream, she doesn't grit, and she certainly doesn't have fits of temper. What the devil is going on here?"

"He's the devil," Jillian seethed, motioning to Grimm.

"Call him what you will, milady. I still can't remove him," Hatchard said heavily.

Jillian's head jerked as if he'd struck her. "You disobey me?"

"He doesn't disobey you, Jillian," Grimm said quietly. "He obeys your da."

"What?" She turned her ashen face to his. He proffered a crumpled, soiled piece of parchment.

"What is that?" she asked icily, refusing to move even an inch closer.

"Come and see, Jillian," he offered. His eyes glittered strangely.

"Hatchard, get that from him."

Hatchard didn't budge. "I know what it says."

"Well then, what does it say?" she snapped at Hatchard. "And how do you know?"

It was Grimm who answered. "It says 'come for Jillian' . . . Jillian."

He'd done it again, added her name after a pause, a husky veneration that left her oddly breathless and frightened. There was a warning in the way he was saying her name, something she should understand but couldn't quite grasp. Something had changed since they'd last fought so bitterly, something in him, but she couldn't define it. "Come for Jillian?" she repeated blankly. "My da sent you that?"

When he nodded, Jillian choked and nearly burst into tears. Such a public display of emotion would have been a first for her. Instead, she did something as unexpected and heretofore undone as gritting and cursing; Jillian spun on her heel and bolted toward the castle as if all the banshees of Scotland were nipping at her heels, when in truth it was the one and only Grimm Roderick—which was far worse.

Sneaking a glance over her shoulder, she belatedly remembered the children. They were standing in a half-circle, gaping at her with disbelief. She stormed, absolutely mortified, into the castle. Slamming the door was a bit difficult, since it was four times as tall as she was, but in her current temper she managed.

Chapter 3

"Inconceivable!" Jillian seethed as she paced her chambers. She tried to calm down, but reluctantly concluded that until she got rid of *him*, calm was not possible.

So she stormed and paced and considered breaking things, except that she liked everything in her room and didn't really want to break any of her own belongings. But if she could only have gotten her hands on him, oh—then she'd have broken a thing or two!

Vexed, she muttered beneath her breath while she quickly slipped out of her gown. She refused to ponder her urge to replace the plain gown and chemise that had been perfectly suitable only an hour before. Nude, she stalked to her armoire by the window, where she was momentarily distracted by the sight of riders in the courtyard. She peered out the tall opening. Two horsemen were riding through the gate. She studied them curiously, leaning into the window. As one, the men raised their heads, and she gasped. A smile crossed the blond man's face, giving her the impression he'd glimpsed her poised in the window, clad in nothing but temper-flushed skin. Instinctively she ducked behind the armoire and snatched up a gown of brilliant green, assuring herself that just because she could see them clearly didn't mean they could see her. Surely the window reflected the sun and permitted little passage of vision.

Who else was arriving at Caithness? she fumed. *He* was bad enough. How dare he come here, and furthermore, how dare her da summon him? *Come for Jillian.* Just what had her da intended with such a note? A shiver slipped down her spine as she contemplated the possessive sound of the words. Why would Grimm Roderick respond to such a strange missive? He'd tortured her ceaselessly as a child and he'd rejected her as a young woman. He was an overbearing lout—who'd once been the hero of her every fantasy.

Now he was back at Caithness, and that was simply unacceptable. Regardless of her da's reasons for summoning him, he simply had to go. If her guards wouldn't remove him, she would—even if it meant at sword point, and she knew just where to find a sword. A massive claymore hung above the hearth in the Greathall; it would do nicely.

Her resolve firm, her gown fastened, Jillian marched out of her chambers. She was ready to confront him; her body was bristling with indignation. He had no right to be here, and she was just the person to explain that to him. He'd left once before when she'd begged him to stay—he couldn't arbitrarily decide to come back now. Snatching her hair back, she secured it with a velvet ribbon and made for the Greathall, moving briskly down the long corridor.

She drew to a sudden halt at the balustrade outside the solar, alarmed by the rumble of masculine voices below.

"What did your message say, Ramsay?" Jillian heard Grimm ask.

Their voices floated up, carrying clearly in the open Greathall. The tapestries were currently down for a cleaning, so the words reverberated off the stone walls.

"Said the lord and his lady would be leaving Caithness and called upon an old debt I owe him. He said he wished me to oversee his demesne while he was not here to do it himself."

Jillian peeked surreptitiously over the balustrade and saw Grimm sitting with two men near the main hearth. For an eternal moment she simply couldn't take her eyes off him. Angrily she jerked her gaze away and studied the newcomers. One of the men was tossed back in his chair as if he owned the keep and half the surrounding countryside. Upon closer scrutiny, Jillian decided he would likely act as if he owned any place he deigned to be. He was a study in black from head to toe: black hair, tanned skin, clad in a length of black wool that was unbroken by even one thread of color. Definitely hulking Highland blood, she concluded. A thin scar extended from his jaw to just below his eye.

Her eyes drifted over the second man. "Quinn," she whispered. She hadn't seen Quinn de Moncreiffe since he'd fostered with Grimm under her father years ago. Tall, golden and breathtakingly handsome, Quinn de Moncreiffe had comforted her on the many occasions Grimm had chased her away. In the years since she'd last seen him he had matured into a towering man with wide shoulders, a trim waist, and long blond hair pulled back in a queue.

"It would seem just about every man in Scotia and half of England is indebted to Gibraltar St. Clair for one thing or another," Quinn observed.

Ramsay Logan folded his hands behind his head and

leaned back in his chair, nodding. "Aye. He bailed me out of more than a few tight spaces when I was a younger lad and more prone to thinking with the wee head."

"Och, so you think you've changed, Logan?" Quinn provoked.

"Not so much that I couldn't knock you senseless still, de Moncreiffe," Ramsay shot back.

Ramsay Logan, Jillian mused; she'd been right about his bloodline. The Logans were indeed Highlanders. Ramsay certainly looked like one of those savage mountain men whose notoriety was exceeded only by their massive holdings. They were a land-rich clan, owning a large portion of the southern Highlands. Her eyes crept back to Grimm, despite her best intentions. He relaxed in his chair regally, composed as a king and acting as if he had every bit as much right to be there. Her eyes narrowed.

The corners of Grimm's mouth twitched faintly. "It's like old times with the two of you poking at each other, but spare me your dissension. There's a puzzle here. Why did Gibraltar St. Clair summon the three of us to Caithness? I've heard of no trouble here in years. Quinn, what did your message say? That he needed you to serve Caithness in his absence?"

Above them, Jillian frowned. That was a good question—why *would* her parents bring these three men to Caithness while they attended their grandson's christening? Hatchard, Caithness's chief man-at-arms, commanded a powerful force of guards, and there hadn't been trouble in these parts of the Lowlands for years.

"It said that he wished me to watch over Caithness in his absence, and if I couldn't take the time away from my ships to come for him, I should come for Jillian. I found his message rather odd but got the impression he was worried about Jillian, and truth be told, I've missed the lass," Quinn replied.

Jillian jerked. What was her deceitful da up to?

"Jillian—the Goddess-Empress herself." Ramsay flashed a wolfish grin.

Jillian's nostrils flared and her spine stiffened.

"What?" Grimm looked puzzled.

"He's referring to her much-lauded reputation. Didn't you stop at the stables when you rode in?" When Grimm shook his head, Quinn snorted. "You missed an earful. The lads there prattled on and on about her before we even had a chance to dismount, warning us not to defile her 'saintly' mien. The 'Goddess-Empress Jillian,' one of the young lads called her, saying mere 'Queen' was too commonplace."

"Jillian?" Grimm looked dubious.

Jillian glared at the top of his head.

"Bespelled," Ramsay affirmed. "The lot of them. One lad told me she's the second Madonna, and he believes if she bears children, it will surely be the product of divine intervention."

"I must say, any intervention with Jillian would be divine," Quinn said, grinning.

"Aye, right between those divine thighs of hers. Did you ever see a lass more well fashioned for a man's pleasure?" Ramsay kicked his feet up on the hearth and shifted in his chair, dropping his hands in his lap.

Jillian's eyebrows climbed her forehead, and she placed a hand over her mouth.

Grimm glanced sharply at Ramsay and Quinn. "Wait a minute—what do you mean by 'her divine thighs'? You've never met Jillian, have you? You doona even know what she looks like. And Quinn, *you* haven't seen her since she was a wee lass."

Quinn looked away uncomfortably.

"Does she have golden hair?" Ramsay countered. "Masses of it, falling in waves past her hips? Flawless face and about yay-tall?" He held his hand slightly above his seated head to demonstrate. "Is her bedroom on the second floor, facing due east?"

Grimm nodded warily.

"I *do* know what she looks like. Quinn and I saw her in a window as we rode in," Ramsay informed him.

Jillian groaned softly, hoping he wouldn't continue.

Ramsay continued, "If she's the woman who was changing her gown, the one with the breasts a man could—"

Jillian's hands flew protectively to her bodice. *It's a little late for that,* she rued.

"You did *not* see her getting dressed," Grimm growled, glancing at Quinn for reassurance.

"No," Ramsay supplied helpfully, "we saw her undressed. Framed in the window, sun spilling over the most splendid morning gown of rosy skin I've ever seen. Face of an angel, creamy thighs, and everything golden in between."

Mortification steeped Jillian in a furious blush from the crown of her head to her recently viewed breasts. They *had* seen her; all of her.

"Is that true, Quinn?" Grimm demanded.

Quinn nodded, looking sheepish. "Hell, Grimm, what did you expect me to do? Look away? She's stunning. I'd long suspected the wee lass would ripen into a lovely woman, but I'd never imagined such exquisite charms. Although Jillian always seemed like a younger sister to me, after I saw her today . . ." He shook his head and whistled admiringly. "Well, feelings can change."

"I didn't know Gibraltar had such a daughter," Ramsay hastened to add, "or I'd have been sniffing around years ago—"

"She's not the sniffing around kind. She's the marrying kind," Grimm snapped.

"Aye, she is the marrying kind, and the keeping kind, and the bedding kind," Ramsay said coolly. "The dolts at Caithness may be intimidated by her beauty, but I'm not. A woman like that needs a flesh-and-blood man."

Quinn shot Ramsay an irritated look and rose to his feet. "Exactly what are you saying, Logan? If any man is going to be speaking for her, it should be me. I've known Jillian since she was a child. My message specifically mentioned coming for Jillian, and after seeing her, I intend to do *precisely* that."

Ramsay came to his feet slowly, unfolding his massive frame until he stood a good two inches above Quinn's six-foot-plus frame. "Perhaps the only reason *my* message wasn't worded the same way is because St. Clair knew I'd never met her. Regardless, it's past time I take a wife, and I intend to give the lovely lass an option besides hanging her nightrail—if she ever wears one, although I'm certainly not complaining—beside some common Lowland farmer."

"Who's calling who a farmer here? I am a bleeding merchant and worth more than all your paltry skinny-ass, shaggy-haired cows put together."

"Pah! My skinny-ass cows aren't where I get my wealth, you Lowland skivvy—"

"Aye, raiding innocent Lowlanders, more likely!" Quinn cut him off. "And what the hell is a skivvy?"

"Not a word a *flatlander* would know," Ramsay snapped.

"Gentlemen, please." Hatchard entered the Greathall, an expression of concern on his face. Having served as chief man-at-arms for twenty years, he could foresee a battle brewing half a county away, and this one was simmering beneath his nose. "There's no need to get into a brawl over this. Hold your tongues and bide a wee, for I have a message for you from Gibraltar St. Clair. And do sit down." He gestured to the chairs clustered near the hearth. "It's been my experience that men who are facing off rarely listen well."

Ramsay and Quinn continued to glare at each other.

Jillian tensed and nearly poked her head through the spindles of the balustrade. What was her father up to this time? Shrewd, red-haired Hatchard was her father's most trusted advisor and longtime friend. His vulpine features were an accurate reflection of his cleverness; he was canny and quick as a fox. His long, lean fingers tapped the hilt of his sword as he waited impatiently for the men to obey his command. *"Sit,"* Hatchard repeated forcefully.

Ramsay and Quinn reluctantly eased back into their chairs.

"I'm pleased to see you've all arrived promptly," Hatchard said in an easier tone. "But, Grimm, why is your horse wandering the bailey?"

Grimm spoke softly. "He doesn't like to be penned. Is there a problem with that?"

Like man, like horse. Jillian rolled her eyes.

"No, no problem with me. But if he starts eating Jillian's flowers, you may have a bit of a skirmish on your hands." Hatchard lowered himself into a vacant chair, amused.

"Actually, I suspect you're going to have a bit of a skirmish on your hands no matter what you do with your horse, Grimm Roderick." He chuckled. "It's good to see you again. It's been too long. Perhaps you could train with my men while you're here."

Grimm nodded curtly. "So why has Gibraltar summoned us here, Hatchard?"

"I'd planned to allow you all to settle in a bit before I passed on his message, but the lot of you are already onto the right of it. St. Clair did bring you here for his daughter," Hatchard admitted, rubbing his short red beard thoughtfully.

"I knew it," Ramsay said smugly.

Jillian hissed softly. *How dare he?* More suitors, and among them the very man she had vowed to hate until death. Grimm Roderick. How many men would her da throw at her before he finally accepted that she would not wed unless she found the kind of love her parents shared?

Hatchard leaned back in his chair and regarded the men levelly. "He expects she will choose one of you before they return from their visit, which gives the lot of you till late autumn to woo her."

"And if she doesn't?" Grimm asked.

"She will." Ramsay folded his arms across his chest, a portrait of arrogance.

"Does Jillian know about this?" Grimm asked quietly.

"Aye, is she duplicitous or is she an innocent?" Quinn quipped.

"And if she is innocent, to what degree?" Ramsay asked wickedly. "I, for one, intend to find out at the earliest opportunity."

"Over my dead body, Logan," Quinn growled.

"So be it." Ramsay shrugged.

"Well, whatever he intended, I don't think it was for the three of you to be killing each other over her." Hatchard smiled faintly. "He merely intends to see her wed before she passes another birthday, and one of you shall be the man. And no, Grimm, Jillian doesn't know a thing about it. She'd likely flee Caithness immediately if she had the vaguest inkling what her father was up to. Gibraltar has brought dozens of suitors to Jillian over the past year, and she drove them all away with one shenanigan or another. She and her da relished outwitting each another; the more unusual his ploy, the more inventive her reaction. Although, I must say, she always handled things with a certain delicacy and subtlety only a Sacheron woman can effect. Most of the men had no idea they'd been . . . er . . . for lack of a better word . . . duped. Like her father, Jillian can be the very image of propriety while planning a mutinous rebellion behind her composed face. One of you must court and win her, because the three of you are Gibraltar's last hopes."

Impossible, Jillian silently argued her case with shaky conviction. Her da would not do this to her. Would he? Even as she denied it, the long, considering glances her da had been giving her before he'd left surfaced in her mind. Suddenly his somewhat guilty expression, his last-minute hugs before he'd left made sense to Jillian. By the saints, as dispassionately as he matched his broodmares, her da had locked her in the stables with three hot-blooded studs and gone visiting.

Make that two hot-blooded studs and one cold, arrogant, impossible heathen, she amended silently. For surely as the sun rose and set, Grimm Roderick wouldn't deign to touch her even with someone else's hands. Jillian's shoulders slumped.

As if he'd somehow read her mind, Grimm Roderick's words drifted up, inciting more of that witless fury she suffered in his presence.

"Well, you doona have to worry about me, lads, for I wouldn't wed the woman if she was the last woman in all of Scotia. So it's up to the two of you to make Jillian a husband."

Jillian clenched her jaw and fled down the corridor before she could succumb to a mad urge to fling herself over the balustrade, a hissing female catapult of teeth and nails.

Chapter 4

Maldebann Castle
The Highlands, above Tuluth

"Milord, your son is near."

Ronin McIllioch surged to his feet, his blue eyes blazing. "He's coming here? Now?"

"No, milord. Forgive me, I did not mean to alarm you," Gilles corrected hastily. "He is at Caithness."

"Caithness," Ronin repeated. He exchanged glances with his men. Their gazes reflected concern, caution, and unmistakable hope. "Have you any idea why he's there?" Ronin asked.

"No. Shall we find out?"

"Dispatch Elliott, he blends in well. Discreetly, mind you," Ronin said. Softly he added, "My son is closer than he's come in years."

"Yes, milord. Think you he may come home?"

Ronin McIllioch smiled, but it did not reach his eyes. "The time is not yet right for his return. We still have work to do. Send with Elliott the young boy who draws. I want pictures, with great detail."

"Yes, milord."

"And Gilles?"

Gilles paused in the doorway.

"Has anything . . . changed?"

Gilles sighed and shook his head. "He still calls himself Grimm. And as nearly as our men have been able to ascertain, he has never bothered to ask if you're still alive. Nor has he ever once looked west to Maldebann."

Ronin inclined his head. "Thank you. That will be all, Gilles."

* * *

Jillian found Kaley dicing potatoes in the kitchen. Kaley Twillow was a motherly woman in her late thirties; her curvaceous body couched an equally spacious heart. Originally from England, she'd come to Caithness upon the reference of one of Gibraltar's friends when her husband had died. Maid, cook's assistant, confidante in place of a scheming mother—Kaley did it all. Jillian plunked down on the edge of a chair and said without preface, "Kaley, there's a thing I've been wondering."

"And what might that be, dear?" Kaley asked with a tender smile. She laid her knife aside. "As a rule, your questions are quite peculiar, but they are always interesting."

Jillian edged her chair nearer to the cutting block where Kaley stood, so the other servants in the busy kitchen wouldn't overhear. "What does it mean when a man 'comes for a woman'?" she whispered conspiratorially.

Kaley blinked rapidly. "Comes?" she echoed.

"Comes," Jillian affirmed.

Kaley retrieved her knife, clutching it like a small sword. "In just what context did you hear this phrase used?" she asked stiffly. "Was it in reference to you? Was it one of the guards? Who was the man?"

Jillian shrugged. "I overheard a man saying he was told to 'come for Jillian' and he planned to do just that, precisely to the letter. I don't understand. He already did it—he came here."

Kaley thought a moment, then chortled, relaxing visibly. "It wouldn't have been the mighty, golden Quinn, would it, Jillian?"

Jillian's blush was reply enough for Kaley.

She calmly replaced her knife on the cutting board. "It means, dear lass"—Kaley bent her head close to Jillian's—"that he plans to bed you."

"Oh!" Jillian flinched, eyes wide. "Thank you, Kaley." She excused herself crisply.

Kaley's eyes sparkled as Jillian beat a hasty retreat from the kitchen. "A fine man. Lucky lass."

* * *

As she raced for her chambers, Jillian seethed. While she could appreciate her parents' desire to see her wed, it was their fault as much as hers that she wasn't. They hadn't started encouraging her until last year, and shortly thereafter they'd dumped a barrage of candidates upon her with no warning. One by one, Jillian had brilliantly discouraged them by convincing them she was an unattainable paragon, not to be considered in a carnal, worldly sense—a woman better suited for the cloister than the marriage bed. A declaration of such intent had cooled the ardor of several of her suitors.

If cool civility and frigid reserve failed, she hinted at a family disposition toward madness that sent men scurrying. She'd had to resort to that on only two occasions;

apparently her pious act was pretty convincing. And why shouldn't it be? she brooded. She'd never done anything particularly daring or improper in her entire life, hence she'd acquired a reputation as "a truly good person." "Yuck," she informed the wall. "Chisel that on my headstone. 'She was a truly good person, but she's dead now.' "

Although her efforts to dissuade her suitors had been successful, she'd apparently failed to stop her parents from scheming to marry her off; they'd summoned three more suitors to Caithness and abandoned her to her own straits. Dire straits indeed, for Jillian knew these men were not the kind to be put off with a few cool words and an aloof demeanor. Nor would they likely accept her claims of inherited madness. These men were too confident, too bold . . . *oh, hell's bells,* she dusted off another childhood curse, they were far too masculine for any woman's peace of mind. And if she wasn't careful, these three men could cause her to reclaim all the childhood epithets she'd learned while skipping at the heels of Quinn and Grimm. Jillian was accustomed to gentle, modest men, men gelded by their own insecurities, not swaggering, uncut bulls who thought "insecure" meant an unstable fortress or a weak timber in a foundation.

Of the three men currently invading her home, the only one she might hope to persuade to consider her plight sympathetically was Quinn, and that was far from a certainty. The lad she'd known years ago was quite different from the formidable man he'd become. Even at the far reaches of Caithness she'd heard of his reputation throughout Scotland as a relentless conqueror, both of trade and women. To top it off, if Kaley's interpretation could be trusted and Quinn had truly been making an innuendo about bedding her, his youthful protectiveness had matured into manly possessiveness.

Then there was the intrepid Ramsay Logan. Nobody had to convince Jillian the black-clad Ramsay was dangerous. He dripped peril from every pore.

Grimm Roderick was another matter. He would certainly not push for her hand, but his simple presence was bad enough. He was a constant reminder of the most painful and humiliating days of her life.

Three barbarians who had been hand-selected by her own da to seduce and marry her lurked in her home. What was she going to do? Although it appealed to her immensely, fleeing didn't make much sense. They'd only come after her, and she doubted she'd ever make it to one of her brother's homes before Hatchard's men caught up. Besides, she brooded, she would *not* leave her home just to get away from *him*.

How could her parents do this to her? Worse yet, how could she ever go downstairs again? Not only had two of the men seen her without a stitch of clothing on, they were obviously planning to pluck the overripe, or so her parents had concluded without so much as soliciting her opinion, berry of her virginity. Jillian squeezed her knees together protectively, dropped her head in her lap, and decided things couldn't get much worse.

* * *

It wasn't easy for Jillian to hide in her chambers all day. She wasn't the cowering sort. Nor, however, was she the foolish sort, and she knew she must have a plan before she subjected herself to the perils of her parents' nefarious scheme. As afternoon faded into evening and she'd yet to be struck by inspiration, she discovered she was feeling quite irritable. She hated being cooped up in her chambers. She wanted to play the virginal, she wanted to kick the first person she saw, she wanted to visit Zeke, she wanted to eat. She'd thought someone would appear by lunchtime, she'd been certain loyal Kaley would come check on her if she didn't arrive at dinner, but the maids didn't even appear to clean her chambers or light the fire. As the solitary hours passed, Jillian's ire increased. The angrier she became, the less objectively she considered her plight, ultimately concluding she would simply ignore the three men and go about her life as if nothing was amiss.

Food was her priority now. Shivering in the chilly evening air, she donned a light but voluminous cloak and pulled the hood snug around her face. Perhaps if she met up with one of the oversized brutes the combination of darkness and concealing attire would grant her anonymity. It probably wouldn't fool Grimm, but the other two hadn't seen her with clothes *on* yet.

Jillian closed the door quietly and slipped into the hallway. She opted for the servants' staircase and carefully picked her way down the dimly lit, winding steps. Caithness was huge, but Jillian had played in every nook and cranny and knew the castle well; nine doors down and to the left was the kitchen, just past the buttery. She peered down the long corridor. Lit by flickering oil lamps, it was deserted, the castle silent. Where was everyone?

As she moved forward, a voice floated out of the darkness behind her. "Pardon, lass, but could you tell me where I might find the buttery? We've run short of whisky and there's not a maid about."

Jillian froze in mid-step, momentarily robbed of speech. How could all the maids disappear and that man appear the very instant she decided to sneak from her chambers?

"I asked you to leave, Grimm Roderick. What are you still doing here?" she said coolly.

"Is that you, Jillian?" He stepped closer, peering through the shadows.

"Have so many other women at Caithness demanded you depart that you're suffering confusion about my identity?" she asked sweetly, plunging her shaking hands into the folds of her cloak.

"I didn't recognize you beneath your hood until I heard you speak, and as to the women, you know how the women around here felt about me. I assume nothing has changed."

Jillian almost choked. He was as arrogant as he'd always been. She pushed her hood back irritably. The women had fallen all over him when he'd fostered here, lured by his dark, dangerous looks, muscled body, and absolute indifference. Maids had thrown themselves at his feet, visiting ladies had offered him jewels and lodgings. It had been revolting to watch. "Well, you are older," she parried weakly. "And you know as a man gets older his good looks can suffer."

Grimm's mouth turned faintly upward as he stepped forward into the flickering light thrown off by a wall torch. Tiny lines at the corners of his eyes were whiter than his Highland-tanned face. If anything, it made him more beautiful.

"You are older too." He studied her through narrowed eyes.

"It's not nice to chide a woman about her age. I am *not* an old maid."

"I didn't say you were," he said mildly. "The years have made you a lovely woman."

"And?" Jillian demanded.

"And what?"

"Well, go ahead. Don't leave me hanging, waiting for the nasty thing you're going to say. Just say it and get it over with."

"What nasty thing?"

"Grimm Roderick, you have never said a single nice thing to me in all my life. So don't start faking it now."

Grimm's mouth twisted up at one corner, and Jillian realized that he still hated to smile. He fought it, begrudged it, and rarely did one ever break the confines of his eternal self-control. Such a waste, for he was even more handsome when he smiled, if that was possible.

He moved closer.

"Stop right there!"

Grimm ignored her command, continuing his approach.

"I said *stop*."

"Or you'll do what, Jillian?" His voice was smooth and amused. He cocked his head at a lazy angle and folded his arms across his chest.

"Why, I'll . . ." She belatedly acknowledged there wasn't much of anything she could do to prevent him from going anywhere he wished to go, in any manner he wished to go there. He was twice her size, and she'd never be his physical match. The only weapon she'd ever had against him was her sharp tongue, honed to a razor edge by years of defensive practice on this man.

He shrugged his shoulders impatiently. "Tell me, lass, what will you do?"

Jillian made no reply, mesmerized by the intersection of his arms, the golden slopes of muscle flexing at his slightest movement. She had a sudden vision of his hard body stretched full length above hers, his lips curving, not with his customary infuriating condescension but with passion.

He sauntered nearer, until he stood mere inches from

her. She swallowed hard and clasped her hands inside her cloak.

He lowered his head toward hers.

Jillian could not have moved if the stone walls of the corridor had started crumbling around her. If the floor had suddenly ruptured beneath her feet, she would have hung suspended on dreamy clouds of fantasy. Mesmerized, she stared up into his brilliant eyes, fascinated by the silky dark lashes, the smooth tan of his skin, the aquiline, arrogant nose, the sensual curved lips, the cleft in his chin. He leaned closer, his breath fanning her cheek. *Was he going to kiss her? Could it be Grimm Roderick might actually kiss her? Had he truly responded to her da's summons—for her?* Her knees felt weak. He cleared his throat, and she trembled with anticipation. What would he do? Would he ask her permission?

"So where, milady, pray tell, is the buttery?" His lips brushed her ear. "I believe this ridiculous conversation began by my saying we're out of whisky and there's not a maid about. Whisky, lass," he repeated in a voice oddly roughened. "We men need a drink. Ten minutes have passed and I'm no closer to finding it."

Kiss her, indeed. When pine martens curled up on the hearth like sleepy cats. Jillian glared at him. "One thing has not changed, Grimm Roderick, and don't you ever forget it. I still hate you."

Jillian pushed past him, retreating once again to the safety of her chambers.

Chapter 5

The moment Jillian opened her eyes the next morning, she panicked. Had he left because she'd been so hateful?

He's supposed to leave, she reminded herself grimly. She *wanted* him to leave. Didn't she? Her brow furrowed as she pondered the illogical duality of her feelings. As far back as she could recall, she'd always suffered this vacillation where Grimm was concerned: hating him one moment, adoring him the next, but always wanting him near. If he hadn't been so unkind to her she would have consistently adored him, but he'd made it painfully clear that her adoration was the last thing he wanted. And that obviously hadn't changed. From the first moment she'd met Grimm Roderick, she'd been hopelessly drawn to him. But after years of being brushed away, ignored, and finally abandoned, she'd given up her childhood fantasies.

Or had she? Perhaps that was precisely her fear: Now that he was back she would make the same mistakes again and behave like an adolescent fool over the magnificent warrior he had become.

Dressing quickly, she snatched up her slippers and hastened for the Greathall. As she entered the room, she halted abruptly. "Oh, my," she murmured. Somehow she'd managed to forget there were three men in her home, so consumed had she been with thoughts of Grimm. They gathered near the fire, while several maids cleared dozens of platters and dishes from the massive table centered in the Greathall. Yesterday, safe behind the balustrade, Jillian had been struck by how tall and broad the three of them were. Today, standing only a few feet from them, she felt like a dwarf willow in a forest of mighty oaks. Each man stood at least a foot taller than she did. It was downright intimidating to a woman who was not easily intimidated. Her gaze wandered from one man to the next.

Ramsay Logan was an inch short of terrifying. Quinn was no longer the stripling son of a Lowland chieftain, but a powerful laird in his own right. And Grimm was the only man not looking at her; he stood gazing intently into the fire. She took advantage of his distraction and studied his profile with greedy eyes.

"Jillian." Quinn moved forward to greet her.

She forced herself to drag her gaze away from Grimm and concentrate on what Quinn was saying. "Welcome, Quinn." She pasted a cheerful smile on her lips.

"It's so good to see you again, lass." Quinn took her hands in his and smiled down at her. "It's been years and . . . och, but the years have been generous to you—you're breathtaking!"

Jillian blushed and glanced at Grimm, who was paying no heed to the conversation. She stifled the urge to kick him and make him notice that someone thought she was lovely. "You've changed yourself, Quinn," she said brightly. "It's no wonder I've heard your name linked with one beautiful woman after another."

"And just where would you be hearing that, lass?" Quinn asked softly.

"Caithness isn't exactly the end of the earth, Quinn. We do get visitors here on occasion."

"And you've asked them about me?" Quinn probed, interested.

Behind him, Ramsay cleared his throat impatiently.

Jillian sneaked another glance at Grimm. "Of course I have. And Da always likes to hear about the lads he fostered," she added.

"Well, although I wasn't fostered here, your father *did* ask me to come. That must count for something," Ramsay grumbled, trying to jostle Quinn aside. "And if this dolt would recall his manners, perhaps he'd see fit to introduce me to the loveliest woman in all of Scotland."

Jillian thought she heard Grimm make a choking sound. Her gaze flew to him, but he hadn't moved a muscle and still appeared oblivious to the conversation.

Quinn snorted. "Not that I don't agree with his assessment of you, Jillian, but beware this Highlander's tongue. He's got quite a reputation with the lasses himself." Reluctantly he turned to Ramsay. "Jillian, I'd like you to meet—"

"Ramsay Logan," Ramsay interrupted, thrusting himself forward. "Chieftain of the largest keep in the Highlands and—"

"My ass, you are." Quinn snorted. "The Logan scarcely has a pot to"—he broke off and cleared his throat—"cook in."

Ramsay jostled him aside and moved into his place.

"Give it up, de Moncreiffe, she's not interested in a Lowlander."

"*I'm* a Lowlander," Jillian reminded.

"Merely by birth, not by choice, and marriage could correct that." Ramsay stepped as close to Jillian as he could without actually standing on her toes.

"Lowlanders are the civilized lot of the Scots, Logan. And quit crowding her, you're going to back her right out of the hall."

Jillian smiled gratefully at Quinn, then flinched as Grimm finally looked sidewise at her.

"Jillian," he said quietly, nodding in her general direction before turning back to the fire.

How could he affect her so intensely? All the man had to do was say her name, one word, and Jillian was unable to form a coherent sentence. And there were so many questions she wanted to ask him—years and years of "whys." *Why did you leave me? Why did you hate me? Why couldn't you adore me like I adore you?*

"Why?" Jillian demanded before she knew she'd opened her mouth.

Ramsay and Quinn gazed at her, puzzled, but she only had eyes for Grimm.

She stomped over to the fire and poked Grimm in the shoulder. "Why? Would you just tell me that? For once and for all, why?"

"Why what, Jillian?" Grimm didn't turn.

She poked him harder. "You know 'why what.' "

Grimm glanced reluctantly over his shoulder. "Really, Jillian, I haven't the faintest idea what you're blathering about." Ice-blue eyes met hers, and for a moment she thought she glimpsed a blatant dare in them. It shocked her to her senses.

"Don't be ridiculous, Grimm. It's a simple question. Why have the three of you come to Caithness?" Jillian quickly salvaged the remnants of her pride. They didn't know she'd overheard her father's despicable scheme, and she'd soon discover if any of them would be honest with her.

Grimm's eyes flickered strangely; in another man Jillian might have called it disappointment, but not in his. He scanned her from head to toe, noting the slippers clutched in her hands. When he looked at her bare toes she curled them under her gown, feeling oddly vulnerable, as if she were six again.

"Put your slippers on, lass. You'll catch a chill."

Jillian glared at him.

Quinn moved to her side and offered his arm for her to lean on while she donned her slippers. "He's right. The stones are cold, lass. As to the why of it, your da summoned us to look after Caithness in his absence, Jillian."

"Really?" Jillian said sweetly, adding "liar" to the list of nasty names she was calling men in the privacy of her thoughts. She stuffed one foot in a slipper, then the next. She doubted Grimm would care if she died of a chill. *Put your slippers on,* he ordered, as if she were an unruly toddler who couldn't complete the simple task of dressing herself. "Is there trouble expected in these parts of the Lowlands?"

"It's better to be safe than sorry, lass." Ramsay offered the platitude with his most charming smile.

Safe, my arse, she thought mulishly. Safe certainly wasn't this, surrounded by circling warriors who were inflamed by the mere scent of a woman.

"Your da didn't wish to take the chance trouble might befall Caithness in his absence, and now seeing you, lass, I understand his concern," Ramsay added smoothly. "I'd select only the finest to protect you too."

"I'm all the protection she needs, Logan," Quinn said dryly. He took her by the hand and led her to the table. "Bring breakfast for the lady," he instructed a maid.

"Protection from what?" Jillian asked.

"From yourself, most likely." Grimm's voice was low but still carried clearly in the stone hall.

"*What* did you just say?" Jillian whirled around in her seat. Any excuse for an argument with him was a welcome excuse.

"I said protection from yourself, brat." Grimm met her gaze with a heated one of his own. "You're forever walking into danger. Like when you wandered off with the tinkers. We couldn't find you for *two days*."

Quinn laughed. "By Odin's spear, I'd forgotten about that. We were nearly mad with worry. I finally found you north of Dunrieffe—'

"I would have found her if you hadn't insisted I go south, Quinn. I told you they'd gone north," Grimm reminded him.

Quinn glanced sideways at Grimm. "Hell's bells, man, don't brood about it. She was found, and that's all that matters."

"I wasn't lost to begin with," Jillian informed them. "I knew exactly where I was."

The men laughed.

"And I am not always getting into danger. I just wanted to feel the freedom of the tinkers. I was old enough—"

"You were thirteen!" Grimm snapped.

"I was fully in control of myself!"

"You were misbehaving as usual," Quinn teased.

"Jillian never misbehaves," Kaley murmured as she

entered the room and caught the last of the conversation. She placed a steaming platter of sausage and potatoes in front of Jillian.

"A shame, if it's true," Ramsay purred.

"Then there was the time she got stuck in the pigpen. Remember that one, Grimm?" Quinn laughed, and even Grimm couldn't begrudge him a smile. "Remember how she looked, backed into the corner, jabbering away to the enraged mama pig?" Quinn snorted. "I swear Jillian was squealing louder than the sow was."

Jillian leapt to her feet. "That's quite enough. And quit smiling, Kaley."

"I'd forgotten that one myself, Jillian." Kaley chuckled. "You were a handful."

Jillian grimaced. "I'm not a child anymore. I'm twenty-one years old—"

"And why is it that you haven't wed, lass?" Ramsay wondered aloud.

Silence descended as all eyes, including several curious maids', focused on Jillian. She stiffened, mortification staining her cheeks with a flush of pink. By the saints, these men held nothing back. Not one of her past suitors would have dared such a direct frontal attack, but these men, she reminded herself grimly, weren't like any men she'd ever known before. Even Grimm and Quinn were unknown variables; they'd become dangerously unpredictable.

"Well, why haven't you?" Quinn said softly. "You're beautiful, witty, and well landed. Where are all your suitors, lass?"

Where, indeed? Jillian mused.

Grimm turned from the fire slowly. "Yes, Jillian, tell us. Why *haven't* you wed?"

Jillian's eyes flew to his. For a long moment she was unable to free herself from the snare of his gaze and the strange emotions it incited in her. With an immense effort of will, she averted her gaze. "Because I'm joining the cloister. Didn't Da tell you?" she said cheerfully. "That's probably why he brought you all here, to escort me safely to the Sisters of Gethsemane come fall." She studiously ignored Kaley's reproachful look and plunked down in her seat, attacking her breakfast with newly discovered relish. Let them chew on that. If they wouldn't admit the truth, why should she?

"Cloister?" Quinn said after a stunned silence.

"The nunnery," she clarified.

"As in wed to the Christ and none other?" Ramsay groaned.

"As in," Jillian confirmed around a mouthful of sausage.

Grimm didn't say a word as he left the Greathall.

* * *

A few hours later Jillian was wandering the outer bailey, quite aimlessly, certainly not of a mind to wonder where one specific man might have gotten off to, when Kaley ducked out the back entrance of the castle just as she passed.

"The cloister, is it? Really, Jillian," Kaley reprimanded.

"By the saints, Kaley, they were telling stories about me!"

"Charming stories."

"Humiliating stories." Jillian's cheeks colored.

"Endearing stories. True stories, not outrageous fibs like you told."

"Kaley, they're men," Jillian said, as if that should explain everything.

"Mighty fine men, at that, lass. Your da brings the cream

of the crop here for you to choose a husband, and you go and tell them you're destined for a nunnery."

"You knew my da brought them here for that?"

Kaley flushed.

"How did you know?"

Kaley looked embarrassed. "I was eavesdropping from the solar when you were spying over the balustrade. You really must stop doffing your clothes in front of the window, Jillian," she chided.

"I didn't do it on purpose, Kaley." Jillian pursed her lips and scowled. "For a moment I thought Mother and Da had told you, even though they hadn't told me."

"No, lass. They didn't tell anyone. And maybe they were a bit heavy-handed, but you can approach this in one of two ways: You can be angry and spiteful and ruin your chances, or you can thank Providence and your da for fetching you the best of the best, Jillian."

Jillian rolled her eyes. "If those men are the best, then it's the cloister for certain."

"Jillian, come on, lass. Don't fight what's best for you. Choose a man and quit being mulish."

"I don't want a man." Jillian seethed.

Kaley measured her a long moment. "What are you doing wandering around out here, anyway?"

"Enjoying the flowers." Jillian shrugged nonchalantly.

"Don't you usually ride in the morning, then go to the village?"

"I didn't feel like it this morning. Is that a crime?" Jillian said peevishly.

Kaley's lip twitched in a smile. "Speaking of riding, I believe I saw that handsome Highlander Ramsay down by the stables."

"Good. I hope he gets trampled. Although I'm not certain there's a horse tall enough. Perhaps he could lie upon the ground and make it easier."

Kaley searched Jillian's face intently. "Quinn told me he was going to the village to fetch some whisky from MacBean."

"I hope he drowns in it," Jillian said, then looked at Kaley hopefully.

"Well," Kaley drawled, "I guess I'll be heading back to the kitchens. There's a lot of food to cook for these men." The voluptuous maid turned her back on Jillian and started walking away.

"Kaley!"

"What?" Kaley blinked innocently over her shoulder.

Jillian's eyes narrowed. "Innocent doesn't suit you, Kaley."

"Peevish doesn't suit you, Jillian."

Jillian flushed. "I'm sorry. So?" she encouraged.

Kaley shook her head, chuckling softly. "I'm sure you don't care, but Grimm's gone to the loch. Looked to me like he planned to do some washing."

The moment Kaley was gone, Jillian glanced around to make certain no one was watching, then doffed her slippers and raced for the loch.

* * *

Jillian ducked behind the rock and watched him.

Grimm was crouched at the edge of the loch, scrubbing his shirt with two smooth rocks. With a castle full of servants and maids to do the washing, the mending, his every bidding—even rush to his bed if he so much as crooked a seductive finger—Grimm Roderick walked to the loch, selected stones, and washed his own shirt. What pride. What independence. What . . . isolation.

She wanted to wash the worn linen for him. No, she wanted to wash the muscled chest the soft linen caressed. She wanted to trace her hands over the ridges of muscle that laced his abdomen and follow that silky dark trail of hair where it dipped beneath his kilt. She wanted to be welcomed into his solitary confinement and release the man she was convinced had deliberately walled himself behind a façade of chill indifference.

One knee in the grass, his leg bent beneath him, he scrubbed the shirt gently. Jillian watched the muscles in his shoulders flexing. He was more beautiful than any man had the right to be, with his great height and perfectly conditioned body, his black hair restrained by a leather thong, his piercing eyes.

I adore you, Grimm Roderick. How many times had she said those words safely in the private chambers of her head? *Loved you since the day I first saw you. Been waiting for you to notice me ever since.* Jillian dropped to the moss behind the rock, folded her arms on the stone, and rested her chin upon them, watching him hungrily. His back was bathed golden by the sun, and his wide shoulders tapered to a trim waist, where his kilt hugged his hips. His plunged a hand into his thick, dark hair, pushing it out of his face, and Jillian expelled a breath as his muscles rippled.

He turned and looked directly at her. Jillian froze. Damn his acute hearing! He'd always had unnatural senses. How could she have forgotten?

"Go away, peahen." He returned his attention to the shirt he was washing.

Jillian closed her eyes and dropped her head on her hands in defeat. She couldn't even get to the point where she worked up the courage to try to talk to him, to reach him. The moment she started thinking mushy thoughts, the bastard said something remote and biting and it deflated the sails of her resolve before she'd even lifted anchor. She sighed louder, indulging in a generous dose of self-pity.

He turned and looked at her again. "What?" he demanded.

Jillian lifted her head irritably. "What do you mean, 'what'? I didn't say anything to you."

"You're sitting back there sighing as if the world's about to end. You're making so much noise I can't even scrub my shirt in peace, and then you have the gall to get snippy with me when I politely inquire as to what you're mooning about."

"Politely inquire?" she echoed. "You call a barely grunted and entirely put-upon-sounding 'what' a polite inquiry? A 'what' that says 'how dare you invade my space with your pitiful sounds?' A 'what' that says 'could you please go die somewhere else, peahen?' Grimm Roderick, you don't know the first damned thing about polite."

"There's no need to be cursing, peahen," he said mildly.

"I am *not* a peahen."

He tossed a scathing look over his shoulder. "Yes, you are. You're always pecking away at something. Peck-peck, peck-peck."

"Pecking?" Jillian shot to her feet, leapt the stone, and faced Grimm. "I'll show you pecking." Quick as a cat, she plucked the shirt from his hands, twisted her hands in the fabric, and ripped it down the center. She found the sound of the cloth tearing perversely satisfying. "That's what I really feel like doing. How's *that* for invading your space? And why are you washing your own stupid shirt in the first place?" She glared at him, flapping the tails of his shirt to punctuate her words.

Grimm sat back on his heels, eyeing her warily. "Are you feeling all right?"

"No, I am not feeling all right. I haven't been feeling all right all morning. And stop trying to change the subject and turn it around on me, like you always do. Answer my question. Why are you washing your own shirt?"

"Because it was dirty," he replied with calculated condescension.

She ignored it with admirable restraint. "There are maids to wash—"

"I didn't wish to inconvenience—"

"The shirts of the men who—"

"A maid by asking her to wash—"

"And I would have washed the stupid thing for you anyway!"

Grimm's mouth snapped shut.

"I mean, that is . . . well, I would have if . . . if all the maids were dead or taken grievously ill and there was no one else who could"—she shrugged—"and it was the only shirt you owned . . . and bitterly cold . . . and you were sick yourself or something." She snapped her mouth shut, realizing there was no way out of the verbal quagmire into which she'd leapt. Grimm was staring at her with fascination.

He rose to his feet in one swift graceful motion. Mere inches separated them.

Jillian resented having to tilt her head back to look up at him, but her resentment was quickly replaced by a breathless awareness of the man. She was mesmerized by his proximity, riveted by the intense way he was eyeing her. Had he moved even closer? Or had she leaned into him?

"*You* would have washed my shirt?" His eyes searched hers intently.

Jillian gazed at him in silence, not trusting herself to speak. If she opened her mouth, God only knew what might come out. *Kiss me, you big beautiful warrior.*

When he brushed her tense jaw with the back of his knuckles, she nearly swooned. Her skin tingled where his fingers had passed. His lips were a breath away from hers, his eyes were heavy-lidded and unfathomable.

He wanted to kiss her. Jillian felt certain of it.

She tilted her head to receive his kiss. Her lids fluttered shut, and she gave herself fully over to fantasy. His breath fanned her cheek, and she waited, afraid to move a muscle.

"Well, it's too late now."

Her eyes flew open. *No, it's not,* she nearly snapped. *Kiss me.*

"To wash it, I mean." His gaze dropped to the tattered shirt she still held. "Besides," he added, "I doona need some silly peahen fussing over me. At least the maids doona rip my shirts, unless of course they're in a hurry to remove them from my body, but that's an entirely different discussion which is neither here nor there, and one I'm sure you wouldn't be interested in having with me anyway. . . ."

"Grimm?" Jillian said tightly.

He looked out over the loch. "Um?"

"I hate you."

"I know, lass," he said softly. "You told me that last night. It seems all our little 'discussions' end on those words. Try to be a bit more creative, will you?"

He didn't move a muscle when the remains of his wet shirt slapped him in the face and Jillian stomped away.

* * *

Grimm came to dinner wearing a clean tartan. His hair was wet, slicked back from a recent bath, and his shirt was ripped cleanly in two down the center of his back. The loose ends flapped above his tartan, and entirely too much muscled back could be seen for Jillian's comfort.

"What happened to your shirt, Grimm?" Quinn asked curiously.

Grimm gazed across the table at Jillian.

Jillian raised her head, intending to scowl self-righteously, but failed. He was looking at her with that strange expression she couldn't interpret, the one she'd seen when he'd first arrived and had kept saying her name—and she swallowed her angry words along with a bite of bread that had become impossibly dry. The man's face was flawlessly symmetrical. A shadow beard accentuated the hollows beneath his cheekbones, sharply defining his arrogant jaw. His wet hair, secured by a thong, gleamed ebony in the flickering light. His blue eyes were brilliant against the backdrop of his tanned skin, and his white teeth flashed when he spoke. His lips were firm, pink, sensuous, and presently curved in a mocking expression.

"I had a run-in with an ill-tempered feline," Grimm said, holding her gaze.

"Well, why don't you change your shirt?" Ramsay asked.

"I brought only the one," Grimm told Jillian.

"You brought one shirt?" Ramsay snorted disbelievingly. "Odin's spear, Grimm, you can afford a thousand shirts. Becoming a miser, are you?"

" 'Tis not the shirt that makes the man, Logan."

"Damn good thing for you." Ramsay carefully straightened the folds of his snowy linen. "Have you considered that it may be a reflection of him?"

"I'm sure a maid can mend it for you," Quinn said. "Or I can lend you one."

"I doona mind wearing it this way. As for reflections, who's to see?"

"You look like a villein, Roderick." Ramsay sneered.

Jillian made a resigned sound. "I'll mend it," she muttered, dropping her gaze to her plate so she didn't have to see their stunned expressions.

"You can sew, lass?" Ramsay asked doubtfully.

"Of course I can sew. I'm not a complete failure as a woman just because I'm old and unwed," Jillian snapped.

"But don't the maids do that?"

"Sometimes they do and sometimes they don't," Jillian replied cryptically.

"Are you feeling all right, Jillian?" Quinn asked.

"Oh, will you just hush up?"

Chapter 6

It infuriated her. Every time she glimpsed the line of uneven stitches puckering the center of Grimm's shirt, she felt herself turning into an irascible, beady-eyed porcupine. It was as humiliating as if he'd stitched the words "Jillian lost control of herself and I'm never going to let her forget it" across his back. She couldn't believe she'd torn it, but years of suffering his torment as a child had proved her undoing, and she'd simply snapped.

He was back at Caithness, he was hopelessly attractive, and he still treated her exactly the same as he had when she'd been a child. What would it take to make him see that she wasn't a child anymore? *Well, stop acting like one, to start with,* she remonstrated herself. Since the moment she'd tenderly mended his shirt, she'd been longing to waylay him, divest him of the pernicious reminder, and gleefully burn it. Doing so, however, would have reinforced his perception that she had a penchant for witless action, so instead she'd procured three shirts of finer linen, with flawless stitching, and instructed the maids to place them in his room. Did he wear them?

Nary a one.

Each day that dawned, he donned the same shirt with the ridiculous pleat down the back. She'd considered asking him why he wouldn't wear the new ones, but that would be as bad as admitting that his ploy to make her feel stupid and guilty was working. She'd die before she betrayed another ounce of emotion to the emotionless man who was sabotaging her impeccable manners.

Jillian dragged her eyes from the dark, seductive man walking in the bailey, wearing a badly mended shirt, and forced herself to take a deep, calming breath. *Jillian Alanna Roderick*; she rolled the name behind her teeth, a whisper of exhaled breath. The syllables tumbled euphonically. *I only wish* . . .

"So it's the cloister for you, eh, lass?"

Jillian stiffened. The throaty rumble of Ramsay Logan was not what she needed to hear at this moment. "Umhmm," she mumbled in the direction of the window.

"You won't last a fortnight," he said matter-of-factly.

"How dare you?" Jillian whirled about to face him. "You don't know a thing about me!"

Ramsay smiled smugly.

Jillian blanched as she remembered that he'd seen her naked at the window the day he'd arrived. "I'll have you know that I have a calling."

"I'm sure you do, lass," Ramsay purred. "I simply think your ears are plugged and you're hearing the wrong one. A woman like you has a calling to a flesh-and-blood man, not a God who will never make you feel the joy of being a woman."

"There are finer things in life than being a man's broodmare, Logan."

"No woman of mine would ever be a broodmare. Don't misunderstand me: I don't belittle the Kirk and Christ's chosen, I simply don't see you being drawn to such a lure. You're too passionate."

"I am cool and collected," she insisted.

"Not around Grimm," Ramsay said pointedly.

"That's because he irritates me," Jillian snapped.

Ramsay cocked a brow and grinned.

"Just what do you think is so funny, Logan?"

" 'Irritates' is an interesting word for it. Not the one I might have chosen. Rather, let's see . . . 'Excites'? 'Delights'? Your eyes burn like amber in the sunlight when he enters the room."

"Fine." Jillian turned back to the window. "Now that we've debated our choice of appropriate verbs, and you've selected all the wrong ones and obviously don't know a thing about women, you may continue on with your day. Shoo, shoo." She waved her hand at him.

Ramsay's grin widened. "I don't intimidate you a bit, do I, lass?"

"Aside from your overbearing attitude, and the fact that you use your great height and girth to make a woman feel cornered, I suspect you're more bull than bully," she muttered.

"Most women like the bull in me." He moved closer.

Jillian shot a disgusted look over her shoulder. "I'm not most women. And don't be standing on my toes, Logan, there's only room enough for me on them. You can trundle back home to the land of the mighty Logan, where the men are men and the women belong to them. I am not the kind of woman you're used to dealing with."

Ramsay laughed.

Jillian turned slowly, her jaw clenched.

"Would you like some help with Roderick?" He gazed over her shoulder, out the window.

"I thought we'd just established you're not a cold-blooded murderer, which means you'd be of no use to me."

"I think you need help. That man can be dense as sod."

When the door to the Greathall opened a scant instant later, Ramsay moved so quickly that Jillian had no time to protest. His kiss was swiftly delivered and lingeringly prolonged. It raised her to her tiptoes and left her strangely breathless when he released her.

Jillian gazed at him blankly. Truth be told, she'd had so few kisses that she was grossly unprepared for the skillful kiss of a mature man and accomplished lover. She blinked.

The slam of the door caused the timbers to shudder, and Jillian understood. "Was that Grimm?" she breathed.

Ramsay nodded and grinned. When he started to lower his head again, Jillian hastily clamped her hand over her mouth.

"Come on, lass," he urged, catching her hand in his. "Grant me a kiss to thank me for showing Grimm that if he's too stupid to claim you, someone else will."

"Where do you get the idea I care what that man thinks?" She seethed. "And *he* certainly doesn't care if you kiss me."

"You're recovering from my kiss too fast for my liking, lass. As for Grimm, I saw you watching him through this window. If you don't speak your heart—"

"He has no heart to speak to."

"From what I saw at court I'd wager that's true, but you'll never know for certain until you try," Ramsay continued. "I'd just as soon you try, fail, and get it over with so you can start looking at me with such longing."

"Thank you for such brilliant advice, Logan. I can see by your own blissfully wedded state that you must know what you're talking about when it comes to relationships."

"The only reason I'm not blissfully wed is because I'm holding out for a good-hearted woman. They've become a rare commodity."

"It requires a good-hearted man to attract a good-hearted woman, and you've likely been looking in the wrong places. You won't find a woman's heart between her—" Jillian broke off abruptly, mortified by what she'd almost said.

Ramsay roared with laughter. "Tell me I could make you forget Grimm Roderick and I'll show a good-hearted man. I would treat you like a queen. Roderick doesn't deserve you."

Jillian sighed morosely. "He doesn't want me. And if you breathe one word to him about what you think I feel, which I assure you I don't, I shall find a way to make you miserable."

"Just don't be tearing my shirts." Ramsay raised his hands in a gesture of defeat. "I'm off to the village, lass." He ducked quickly out the door.

Jillian scowled at the closed door for a long moment after he'd gone. By the saints, these men were making her feel like she was thirteen again, and thirteen had not been a good year. A horrid year, come to think of it. The year she'd watched Grimm in the stables with a maid, then gone to stand in her room and gaze sadly at her body. Thirteen had been a miserable year of impossible duality, of womanly feelings in a child's body. Now she was exhibiting childish feelings in a woman's body. Would she ever gain her balance around that man?

* * *

Caithness. Once Grimm had considered the name interchangeable with "heaven." When he'd first arrived at Caithness at the age of sixteen, the golden child who "adopted" him had been lacking only filmy wings to complete the illusion that she could offer him angelic absolution. Caithness had been a place of peace and joy, but the joy had been tainted by a bottomless well of desire for things he knew could never be his. Although Gibraltar and Elizabeth had opened their door and their hearts to him, there had been an invisible barrier he'd been unable to surmount. Dining in the Greathall, he'd listened as the St. Clairs, their five sons, and single daughter had joked and laughed. They had taken such obvious delight in each step along the path of life, savoring each phase of their children's development. Grimm had been acutely aware of the fact that Caithness was not his home but another family's, and he was sheltered merely out of their generosity, not by right of birth.

Grimm expelled a breath of frustration. *Why?* he wanted to shout, shaking his fists at the sky. Why did it have to be Ramsay? Ramsay Logan was an incorrigible womanizer, lacking the tenderness and sincerity a woman like Jillian needed. He'd met Ramsay at court, years ago, and had witnessed more than a few broken hearts abandoned in the savage Highlander's charming wake. Why Ramsay? On the heels of that thought came a silent howl: *Why not me?* But he knew it could never be. *We canna help it, son . . . we're born this way.* Senseless killers—and worse, he was a Berserker to boot. Even without summoning the Berserker, his father had killed his own wife. What would the inherited sickness of the mind, coupled with being a Berserker, make him capable of? The only thing he knew with any degree of certainty was that he never wanted to find out.

Grimm buried both hands in his hair and stopped walking. He pulled his fingers through, loosening the thong and reassuring himself his hair was clean, not matted with dirt from living in the forests. He had no war braids plaited into the locks, he was not brown as a Moor from months of sun and infrequent bathing, he no longer looked as barbaric as he had the day Jillian found him in the woods. But somehow he felt as if he could never wash away the stains of those years he'd lived in the Highland forests, pitting his wits against the fiercest predators to scavenge enough food to stay alive. Perhaps it was the memory of shivering in the icy winters, when he had been grateful for the layer of dirt on his skin because it was one more layer between his body and the freezing temperatures. Perhaps it was the blood on his hands and the sure knowledge that if he was ever fool enough to let himself feel for anyone it might be his turn to come to awareness with a knife in his hand and his own son watching.

Never. He would never hurt Jillian.

She was even more beautiful than he remembered. Jillian was a woman full grown now, and he had no defenses against her but his will. It had been his formidable will alone that had brought him this far. He'd trained himself, disciplined himself, learned to control the Berserker . . . for the most part.

When he'd ridden into the courtyard a few days ago and seen the golden, laughing woman surrounded by delighted children, regret for his lost childhood had almost suffocated him. He'd longed to insert himself into the picture on the gently sloping lawn, both as a child and as a man. Willingly he would have curled at her feet and listened, willingly he would have taken her in his arms and given her children of her own.

Frustrated by his inability to do either, he'd provoked her. Then she'd raised her head and Grimm had felt his heart plummet to the soles of his boots. It had been easier for him to recall her with a younger, innocent face. Now the saucily tilted nose and sparkling eyes were part of a sultry, sensual woman's features. And her eyes, although still innocent, held maturity and a touch of quiet sorrow. He wished he knew who had introduced that into her gaze, so he could hunt and kill the bastard.

Suitors? She'd likely had scores. Had she loved one?

He shook his head. He didn't like that idea.

So why had Gibraltar summoned him here? He didn't believe for a minute that it had anything to do with him being a contender for Jillian's hand. More likely Gibraltar had recalled the vow Grimm had made to protect Jillian if she ever needed it. And Gibraltar probably needed a warrior strong enough to prevent any possible trouble between Jillian and her two "real" suitors: Ramsay and Quinn. Aye, that made perfect sense to him. He'd be there to protect Jillian from being compromised in any way and to break up any potential disputes between her suitors.

Jillian: scent of honeysuckle and a mane of silky golden hair, eyes of rich brown with golden flecks, the very color of the amber the Vikings had prized so highly. They appeared golden in the sunlight but darkened to a simmering brown flecked with yellow when she was angry—which around him was all the time. She was his every waking dream, his every nocturnal fantasy. And he was dangerous by his mere nature. A beast.

"Milord, is something wrong?"

Grimm dropped his hands from his face. The lad who'd

been on Jillian's lap when he'd first arrived was tugging on his sleeve and squinting up at him.

"Are you all right?" the boy asked worriedly.

Grimm nodded. "I'm fine, lad. But I'm not a laird. You can call me Grimm."

"You look like a laird to me."

"Well, I'm not."

"Why doesn't Jillian like you?" Zeke asked.

Grimm shook his head, begrudging a rueful twist of his lips. "I suspect, Zeke—it is Zeke, isn't it?"

"You know my name," the lad exclaimed.

"I overheard it when you were with Jillian."

"But you remembered it!"

"Why wouldn't I?"

Zeke stepped back, gazing at Grimm with blatant adoration. "Because you're a powerful warrior, and I'm, well . . . me. I'm just Zeke. Nobody notices me. 'Cept Jillian."

Grimm eyed the lad, taking in Zeke's half-defiant, half-ashamed stance. He placed his hand on the boy's shoulder. "While I'm here at Caithness, how would you like to serve as my squire, lad?"

"Squire?" Zeke gaped. "I canna be a squire! I canna see well."

"Why doona you let me be the judge of that? My needs are fairly simple. I need someone to see to my horse. He doesn't like to be penned, so his food and water must be brought to him wherever he happens to be. He needs to be brushed and groomed, and he needs to be ridden."

With his last words, Zeke's hopeful expression vanished.

"Well, he doesn't need to be ridden for some time yet, he had a good hard ride on the way here," Grimm amended hastily. "And I could probably give you a few lessons."

"But I canna see clearly. I canna possibly ride."

"A horse has a great deal of common sense, lad, and can be trained to do many things for his rider. We'll take it slowly. First, will you care for my stallion?"

"Aye," Zeke breathed. "I will! I vow I will!"

"Then let's go meet him. He can be standoffish to strangers unless I bring them around first." Grimm took the lad's hand in his own; he was amazed by how the tiny hand was swallowed in his grip. So fragile, so precious. A brutal flash of memories burst over him—a child, no older than Zeke, pinioned on a McKane sword. He shook it off savagely and closed his fingers securely around Zeke's.

"Wait a minute." Zeke tugged him to a stop. "You still didn't tell me. Why doesna Jillian like you?"

Grimm rummaged for an answer that might make sense to Zeke. "I guess it's because I teased and tormented her when she was a young lass."

"You picked on her?"

"Mercilessly," Grimm agreed.

"Jillian says the lads only tease the lasses they secretly like. Did you pull her hair too?"

Grimm frowned at him, wondering what that had to do with anything. "I suppose I might have, a time or two," he admitted after some thought.

"Och, good!" Zeke exclaimed, his relief evident. "So you're courting her now. She needs a husband," he said matter-of-factly.

Grimm shook his head, the merest hint of an ironic grin curving his lips. He should have seen that one coming.

Chapter 7

Grimm clamped his hands over his ears, but it didn't help. He tugged a pillow over his head, to no avail. He considered getting up and slamming the shutters, but a quick glance revealed that he was to be deprived of even that small pleasure. They were already closed. One of the many "gifts" that was part and parcel of being a Berserker was absurdly heightened hearing; it had enabled him to survive on occasions when a normal man couldn't have heard the enemy stealthily approaching. Now it was proving a grave disadvantage.

He could hear *her*. Jillian.

All he wanted to do was sleep—for Christ's sake, it wasn't even dawn! Did the lass never rest? The trill of a lone flute drifted up, scaling the stone walls of the castle and creeping through the slats of the shutters on a chill morning breeze. He could feel the melancholy notes prying at the stubborn shutters on his heart. Jillian was everywhere at Caithness: blooming in the flower arrangements on the tables, glowing in the children's smiles, stitched into the brilliantly woven tapestries. She was inescapable. Now she dared invade his sleep with the haunting melody of an ancient Gaelic love song, soaring to a high wail, then plummeting to a low moan with such convincing anguish that he snorted. As if she knew the pain of unrequited love! She was beautiful, perfect, blessed with parents, home, family, a place to belong. She had never wanted for love, and he certainly couldn't imagine any man denying her anything. Where had she learned to play a heartbreaking love song with such plaintive empathy?

He leapt from the bed, stomped to the window, and flung the shutters open so hard they crashed into the walls. "Still play that silly thing, do you?" he called. *God, she was beautiful.* And God forgive him—he still wanted her every bit as badly as he had years ago. Then he'd told himself she was too young. Now that she was a woman fully grown he could no longer avail himself of that excuse.

She was standing below him on a rocky cleft overlooking the loch. The sun was a buttery gold crescent, breaking the horizon of the silvery loch. Her back was to him. She stiffened; the bittersweet song stuttered and died.

"I thought you were in the east wing," Jillian said without turning. Her voice carried as clearly to his ears as had the melody, despite her being twenty feet below him.

"I choose my own domain, peahen. As I always have." He leaned out the window slightly, absorbing every detail of her: blond hair rippling in the breeze, the proud set of her shoulders, the haughty angle at which she cocked her head, while she looked out over the loch as if she could scarcely bear to acknowledge his existence.

"Go home, Grimm," she said coldly.

" 'Tis not for you that I stay, but for your da," he lied.

"You owe him such allegiance, then? You, who gives allegiance to none?" she mocked.

He winced. "Allegiance is not beyond me. 'Tis merely that there are so few deserving it."

"I don't want you here," she flung over her shoulder.

It irritated him that she wouldn't turn about and look at him; it was the least she could do while they said nasty things to each other. "I doona care what you want," he forced himself to say. "Your da summoned me here, and here I will remain until he releases me."

"I have released you!"

Grimm snorted. Would that she could release him, but whatever kept him bound to Jillian was indestructible. He should know; he'd tried for years to destroy the bond, not to care where she was, how she fared, if she was happy. "The wishes of a woman are insignificant when weighed against a man's," he said, certain insulting the feminine gender at large would bring her around to face him so he could savor the passion of her anger, in lieu of the sensual passion he desperately longed to provoke in her. *Berserker*, his mind rebuked. *Leave her alone—you have no right.*

"You are such a bastard!" Jillian unwittingly accommodated his basest wishes, spinning so quickly she took a spill. Her brief stumble presented him with a breathtaking view of the swell of her breasts. Pale, they sloped to a gentle valley that disappeared beneath the bodice of her gown. Her skin was so translucent that he could see a faint tracing of blue veins. He pressed against the window ledge to hide the sudden rise of his kilt.

"Sometimes I vow you aim to provoke me." She scowled up at him, pushing off the ground with her hand as she stood up straight, stealing his glimpse of cleavage.

"Now, why would I bother to do that, brat?" he asked

coolly—so coolly it was counterpoint and insult to her raised voice.

"Could it be that you're afraid if you ever stopped torturing me, you might actually like me?" she snapped.

"Never suffer that delusion, Jillian." He splayed his hand through his hair and winced self-consciously. He could never manage to tell a lie without making that gesture. Fortunately, she didn't know that.

"Seems to me you've developed an overwhelming fondness for your hair, Grimm Roderick. I hadn't noticed your little vanities before. Probably because I couldn't see that much of you beneath all the dirt and filth."

It happened in a flash. With her words he was dirty again—mud-stained, blood-soaked, and filthy beyond redemption. No bath, no scouring could ever cleanse him. Only Jillian's words could make him clean again, and he knew he didn't inspire absolution.

"Some people grow up and mature, brat. I woke up one day, shaved, and discovered I was a bloody handsome man." When her eyes widened, he couldn't resist pushing her a little harder. "Some women have said I'm too handsome to have. Perhaps they feared they couldn't hold me in the face of so much competition."

"Spare me your conceit."

Grimm smiled inwardly. She was so lovely, temper-flushed and disdainful, and so easily provoked. Countless times he'd wondered what kind of passion she'd unleash with a man. With a man like him. His thoughts took a dangerous segue into the forbidden. "I've heard men say you're too beautiful to touch. Is that true? *Are* you untouched?" He bit his tongue the instant the words escaped.

Jillian's mouth dropped in disbelief. "*You* would ask me that?"

Grimm swallowed. There'd been a time when he'd known from firsthand experience precisely how untouched she was, and that was a memory he'd do well to bury. "When a lass permits virtual strangers to kiss her, it makes one wonder what else she permits." Bitterness tightened his lips, clipping his words.

Jillian stepped back as if he'd flung something more substantial than an insult in her direction. She narrowed her eyes and studied him suspiciously. "Curiously, it sounds like you care."

"Not a chance. I simply doona wish to have to force you into marrying Ramsay before your da returns. I suspect Gibraltar might like to be present to give the *maiden* away."

Jillian was watching him intently, too intently for his liking. He wondered desperately what was going on inside her head. She'd always been far too clever, and he was perilously close to acting like a jealous suitor. When she'd been young, he'd needed every ounce of his will to carry on a convincing charade of dislike. Now that she was a woman grown, drastic measures were necessary. He shrugged his shoulders arrogantly. "Look, peahen, all I want is for you to take your bloody flute off somewhere else so I can get a bit of sleep. I didn't like you when you were a wee lass, and I doona like you now, but I owe your da and I will honor his missive. The only thing I remember about Caithness is that the food was good and your da was kind." The lie practically burned his tongue.

"You don't remember anything about me?" she asked carefully.

"A few things, nothing of any significance." Restless fingers twined through his hair, tugging it free from his thong.

She glared at him. "Not even the day you left?"

"You mean the McKane attacking?" he asked blandly.

"No." She frowned up at him. "I meant later that day, when I found you in the stables."

"What are you talking about, lass? I doona recall you finding me in the stables before I left." He caught his traitorous hand in mid-rise to his hair and crammed it into the waistband of his kilt.

"You remember nothing of me?" she repeated tightly.

"I remember one thing: I remember you following me around until you nearly drove me mad with your incessant chattering," he said, looking as bored and long-suffering as possible.

Jillian turned her back on him and didn't utter another word.

He watched her for a few moments, his eyes dark with memories, before pulling the shutters closed. When a few moments later the haunting silvery notes of her flute wept, he held his hands over his ears so tightly that it hurt. How could he possibly hope to remain here yet continue to resist her when every ounce of his being demanded he make her his woman?

I doona recall you finding me in the stables before I left.

He'd never uttered a greater lie. He recalled the night in the stables. It was seared into his memory with the excruciating permanence of a brand. It had been the night twenty-two-year-old Grimm Roderick had stolen an unforgettable taste of heaven.

After the McKane were driven off and the battle was over, he'd desperately scrubbed the blood from his body, then packed, flinging clothing and keepsakes without care for what they were or where they landed. He'd nearly brought destruction upon the house that had sheltered him freely, and he would never again subject them to such danger. Jillian's brother Edmund had been wounded in the battle, and although it seemed certain he would recover, young Edmund would bear scars for life. Leaving was the only honorable thing Grimm could do.

He found Jillian's note when his fingers had closed upon the book of Aesop's fables she had given him his first Christmas at Caithness. She'd slipped the note with her big, looping scrawl between the pages so it protruded above the binding. *I will be on the roof at gloaming. I must speak to you tonight, Grimm!*

Crumpling the note furiously, he stomped off for the stables.

He dared not risk seeing her before he left. Filled with self-loathing for bringing the McKane to this sacred place, he would not commit another transgression. Ever since Jillian had started to mature, he'd been unable to get her out of his mind. He knew it was wrong. He was twenty-two years old and she was scarcely sixteen. While she was certainly old enough to be wed—hell, many lasses were wed by thirteen—he could never offer her marriage. He had no home, no clan, and he was a dangerously unpredictable beast to boot. The facts were simple: No matter how much he might want Jillian St. Clair, he could never have her.

At sixteen he'd lost his heart to the wee golden lass; at twenty-two he was beginning to lose his head over the woman. Grimm had concluded a month ago that he had to leave soon, before he did something stupid like kiss her, like find reasons to justify carrying her off and making her his woman. Jillian deserved the best: a worthy husband, a family of her own, and a place to belong. He could offer her none of that.

Strapping his packs on the horse's back, he sighed and

shoved a hand through his hair. As he began leading his horse from the stable, Jillian burst through the doors.

Her eyes darted warily between him and his horse, not missing a detail. "What are you doing, Grimm?"

"What the hell does it look like I'm doing?" he snarled, beyond exasperated that he'd failed to escape without encountering her. How much temptation was he expected to resist?

Tears misted her eyes, and he cursed himself. Jillian had seen so much horror today; he was the lowest of bastards to add to her pain. She'd sought him out in need of comfort, but unfortunately he was in no condition to console her. The aftereffects of Berserkergang left him unable to make clear choices and sensible decisions. Experience had taught him that he was more vulnerable after a Berserker rage; both his mind and body were more sensitive. He needed desperately to get away and find a safe, dark place to sleep for days. He had to force her to leave this instant, before he did something unforgivably stupid. "Go find your da, Jillian. Leave me alone."

"Why are you doing this? Why are you leaving, Grimm?" she asked plaintively.

"Because I must. I never should have come here to begin with!"

"That's silly, Grimm," she cried. "You fought gloriously today! Da locked me in my room, but I could still see what was going on! If you hadn't been here, we wouldn't have had a chance against the McKane—" Her voice broke, and he could see the horror of the bloody battle fresh in her eyes.

And Christ, she'd just admitted that she'd watched him when he'd been berserk! "If I hadn't been here—" he began bitterly, then caught himself on the verge of admitting *he* was the only reason the McKane had come at all.

"If you hadn't been here, what?" Her eyes were huge.

"Nothing," he muttered, staring at the floor.

Jillian tried again. "I watched you from the win—"

"And you should have been hiding, lass!" Grimm cut her off before she could prattle glowingly about his "bravery" in battle—bravery that sprang from the devil himself. "Have you no idea what you look like? Doona you know what the McKane would have done to you if they'd found you?" His voice cracked on the words. It had been fear of what the McKane might do to his beloved lass that had driven him even deeper into Berserkergang during battle, turning him into a ruthless killing animal.

Jillian nervously tugged her lower lip between her teeth. The simple gesture shot a bolt of pure lust through him, and he despised himself for it. He was strung tighter than a compound bow; residual adrenaline from the battle still flooded his body. The heightened arousal attained in Berserkergang had the unfortunate effect of lingering, riding him like a demon, goading him to mate, to conquer. Grimm shook his head and turned his back on her. He couldn't continue looking at her. He didn't trust himself. "Get away from me. You doona know what you risk, being here with me."

Straw rustled against the hem of her gown as she moved. "I trust you completely, Grimm Roderick."

The sweet innocence in her young voice nearly undid him. He grimaced. "That's your first mistake. Your second mistake is being here with me. *Go away.*"

She stepped closer and placed a hand on his shoulder. "But I do trust you, Grimm," she said.

"You can't trust me. You doona even know me," he growled, his body rigid with tension.

"Yes, I do," she argued. "I've known you for years. You've lived here since I was a wee lass. You're my hero, Grimm—"

"Stop it, lass!" he roared as he spun and knocked her hand away from him so roughly that she stepped back a few paces. His glacial blue eyes narrowed. "So you think you know me, do you?" He advanced on her.

"Yes," she insisted stubbornly.

He sneered. "You doona know a bloody thing. You doona know who I've killed and who I've hated and who I've buried and how. You doona know what happens to me because you doona know what I really am!"

"Grimm, I'm frightened," she whispered. Her eyes were wide pools of gold in the lantern light.

"So run to your bloody da! He'll comfort you!"

"He's with Edmund—"

"As you should be!"

"I need you, Grimm! Just put your arms around me! Hold me! Don't leave me!"

Grimm's limbs locked, freezing him clear to his marrow. *Hold me*. Her words hung in the air. Oh, how he longed to. Christ, how often he'd dreamed of it. Her deep amber eyes shifted with fear and vulnerability, and he reached for her despite his resolve. He caught his hands in mid-reach. His shoulders bowed, he was suddenly exhausted by the weight of the internal debate he waged. He could not offer her comfort. He was the very reason she needed comforting. Had he never come to Caithness, he would never have brought destruction on his heels. He could never forgive himself for what he'd brought upon the people who'd opened their hearts to him when no one else had cared if he'd lived or died.

"You doona know what you're saying, Jillian," he said, suddenly immensely weary.

"Don't leave me!" she cried, flinging herself into his arms.

As she burrowed against his chest, his arms closed instinctively around her. He held her tightly, offering her shuddering body the shelter of his damned near invincible one.

He cradled her in his arms while she sobbed, suffering a terrible sense of kinship with her. Too clearly he recalled the loss of his own innocence. Eight years before he'd stood and watched his own clan fight the McKane. The sight of such brutality had rendered him nearly senseless with grief and rage, and now his young Jillian knew the same terrors. How could he have done this to her?

Would she have nightmares? Relive it as he had—at least a thousand times?

"Hush, sweet lass," he murmured, stroking her cheek. "I promise you the McKane will never come back here. I promise you that somehow I will always look after you, no matter where I am. I will never let anyone hurt you."

She sniffled, her face buried in the hollow between his shoulder and his neck. "You can't protect me if you're not here!"

"I spoke with your da and told him I'm leaving. But I also told him that if you ever need me, he has only to summon me." Although Gibraltar had been angry with him for leaving, he'd seemed mollified that he would know where to find Grimm should the need arise.

Jillian turned her tearstained face up to his, her eyes wide.

He lost his breath, gazing at her. Her cheeks were flushed and her eyes were brilliant with tears. Her lips were swollen from crying and her hair tumbled in a mane of gold fire about her face.

He had absolutely no intention of kissing her. But one moment they were looking into each other's eyes and the next moment he'd bent his head forward to press a pledge against her lips: a light, sweet promise of protection.

The moment their lips met, his body jerked violently.

He drew back and stared at her blankly.

"D-did you f-feel that?" she stammered, confusion darkening her eyes.

Not possible, he assured himself. *The world does not shake on its axis when you kiss a lass.* To convince himself—he kissed her again. The earthquake began just beneath his toes.

His innocent pledge took on a life of its own, became a passionate, soul-searing kiss between a man and his mate. Her maiden lips parted sweetly beneath his and she melted into the heat of his body.

Grimm squeezed his eyes tightly shut, recalling that long-ago kiss as he listened to the trill of Jillian's flute outside his window.

God, how vividly he recalled it. And he'd not touched another woman since.

* * *

Quinn insisted they go for a ride, and although Jillian initially resisted, before long she was glad she went. She'd forgotten how charming Quinn was, how easily he could make her laugh. Quinn had come to Caithness the summer after Grimm had arrived. Her father had fostered the two lads—a chieftain's eldest son and a homeless scavenger—as equals, although in Jillian's eyes no other boy could ever have been Grimm's equal.

Quinn had been well mannered and thoughtful, but it had been Grimm she'd fallen in love with the day she'd met him—the wild boy living in the woods at the perimeter of Caithness. It had been Grimm who'd upset her so much she'd cried hot tears of frustration. It had been Quinn who'd comforted her when he'd left. Funny, she mused as she glanced over at the dashing man riding beside her, some things hadn't changed a bit.

Quinn caught her sidelong glance and grinned easily. "I've missed you, Jillian. Why is it that we haven't seen one another in years?"

"Judging from the tales I heard of you, Quinn, you were too busy conquering the world and the women to spare time for a simple Lowland lass like me," she teased.

"Conquering the world perhaps. But the women? I think not. A woman is not to be conquered, but to be wooed and won. Cherished."

"Tell that to Grimm." She rolled her eyes. "That man cherishes nothing but his own bad temper. Why does he hate me so?"

Quinn measured her a moment, as if debating what to say. Finally he shrugged. "I used to think it was because he secretly liked you and couldn't let himself show it because he felt he was a nobody, not good enough for the daughter of Gibraltar St. Clair. But that doesn't make sense, because Grimm is now a wealthy man, rich enough for any woman, and God knows the women desire him. Frankly, Jillian, I have no idea why he's still cruel to you. I'd thought things would change, especially now that you're old enough to be courted. I can't say that I'm sorry, though, because it's less competition as far as I'm concerned," he finished with a pointed look.

Jillian's eyes widened. "Quinn—" she started, but he waved his hand to silence any protest.

"No, Jillian. Don't answer me now. Don't even make me say the words. Just get to know me again, and then we'll speak of things that may come to be. But come what may, I will always be good to you, Jillian," he added softly.

Jillian tugged her lower lip between her teeth and spurred her mount into a canter, stealing a glance over her shoulder at the handsome Quinn. *Jillian de Moncreiffe*, she thought curiously.

Jillian Alanna Roderick, her heart cried defiantly.

Chapter 8

JILLIAN STOOD IN THE LONG, NARROW WINDOW OF THE drum tower a hundred feet above the courtyard and watched Grimm. She'd climbed the winding stairs to the tower, telling herself she was trying to get away from "that man," but she knew she wasn't being entirely honest with herself.

The drum tower held memories, and that's what she'd gone to revisit. Splendid memories of the first summer Grimm had been in residence, that wondrous season she'd taken to sleeping in her princess tower. Her parents had indulged her; they'd had men seal the cracks in the stones and hung tapestries so she'd be warm. Here were all her favorite books, the few remaining dolls that had escaped Grimm's "burials at sea" in the loch, and other love-worn remnants of what had been the best year of her life.

That first summer she'd found the "beast-boy," they'd spent every moment together. He had taken her on hikes and taught her to catch trout and slippery salamanders. He'd sat her on a pony for the first time; he'd built her a snow cave on the lawn their first winter together. He'd been there to raise her up if she wasn't tall enough to see, and he'd been there to pick her up if she fell. Nightly he'd told her outlandish stories until she'd passed into a child's exhausted slumber, dreaming of the next adventure they'd share.

To this day, Jillian could still recall the magic feeling she'd had whenever they'd been together. It had seemed perfectly possible that he might be a rogue angel sent to guard her. After all, she'd been the one who'd discovered him lurking in the thickets of the forest behind Caithness. She'd been the one who'd coaxed him near with a tempting feast, waiting patiently day after day on a rumpled blanket with her beloved puppy, Savanna TeaGarden.

For months he'd resisted her offering, hiding in his bracken and shadows, watching her as intently as she'd watched him. But one rainy day he'd melted out of the mist and come to kneel upon her blanket. He'd gazed at her with an expression that had made her feel beautiful and protected. Sometimes, in the years to follow, despite his cruel indifference, she'd caught that same look in his eyes when he thought she wasn't watching. It had kept her hope alive when it would have been wiser to let it die. She'd grown to young womanhood desperately in love with the fierce boy-turned-man who had a strange way of appearing whenever she needed him, rescuing her repeatedly.

Granted, he hadn't always been gentle while he did it. One time he'd trussed her up, high in an oak's lofty branches, before tearing off through the woods to rescue Savanna from a pack of wild dogs he'd saved Jillian from moments earlier. Lashed to the tree, terrified for her puppy, she'd howled and struggled but had been unable to loosen her bonds. He'd left her there for hours. But sure as the sun always rose and set, he had come back for her—cradling the wounded, but remarkably alive, wolfhound in his arms.

He'd refused to discuss with her how he'd saved her puppy from the rabid pack, but she hadn't worried overmuch. Although Jillian had found it mildly astonishing that he'd been unhurt himself, over the years she'd come to expect that Grimm would suffer no harm. Grimm was her hero. He could do anything.

One year after she'd met Grimm, Quinn de Moncreiffe had arrived to be fostered at Caithness. He and Grimm became close as brothers, sharing a world of adventures from which she was painfully excluded. That had been the beginning of the end of her dreams.

Jillian sighed as Grimm disappeared into the castle. Her back stiffened when he reappeared a few moments later with Zeke. She narrowed her eyes when Zeke slipped his hand trustingly into Grimm's. She could still recall how easy it had been to slide her child's hand into his strong grip. He was the kind of man that children and women wanted to keep around, although for wholly different reasons.

There was certainly a mystery about him. It was as if a swirling black mist had parted the day Grimm Roderick had stepped into existence, and no amount of questioning, no relentless scrutiny could ever illuminate his dark past. He was a deep man, unusually aware of the tiniest nuances in a conversation or interaction. When she'd been a child, he'd always seemed to know exactly how she was feeling, anticipating her feelings before she had understood them herself.

If she was honest with herself, the only truly cruel thing she could accuse him of was years of indifference. He'd never done anything terribly unkind in and of itself. But the night he'd left, his absolute rejection had caused her to harden her heart against him.

She watched him swing Zeke up in his arms. What on earth was he doing? Putting him on a horse? Zeke couldn't ride, he couldn't see well enough. She opened her mouth to call down, then paused. Whatever else he might be, Grimm was not a man who made mistakes. Jillian resigned herself to watch for a few moments. Zeke was giddy with excitement, and it wasn't often she saw him happy. Several of the children and their parents had gathered around to watch. Jillian held her breath. If Grimm's intentions went awry it would be a painful, public humiliation for Zeke, and one he'd not live down for a long time.

She watched as Grimm bowed his dark head close to the horse; it looked as if he was whispering words in the prancing gray stallion's ear. Jillian suffered a momentary fancy that the horse had actually nodded his head in response. When Grimm slipped Zeke on the horse's back, she held her breath. Zeke sat rigidly at first, then slowly relaxed as Grimm led the stallion in easy wide circles around the courtyard. Well, that was all fine and good, Jillian thought, but now what would Zeke do? He certainly couldn't be led around all the time. What was the point of putting the child on a horse when he could never ride on his own?

She quickly decided she'd had enough. Obviously Grimm didn't understand; he should not be teaching the boy to want impossible things. He should be encouraging Zeke to read books, to indulge in safer pursuits, as Jillian had done. When a child was handicapped, it made no sense to encourage him to test those limits foolishly in a manner that might cause him harm. Far better to teach him to appreciate different things and pursue attainable dreams. No matter that, like any other child, Zeke might wish to run and play and ride—he had to be taught that he couldn't, that it was dangerous for him to do so with his impaired vision.

She would take Grimm to task over his lapse in judgment immediately, before any more damage was done. Quite a crowd had gathered in the courtyard, and she could already see the parents shaking their heads and whispering among themselves. She promised herself she would handle this problem coolly and rationally, giving the onlookers no cause for gossip. She would explain to Grimm the proper way to treat young Zeke and demonstrate that she wasn't always a witless idiot.

She exited the drum tower quickly and made her way to the courtyard.

* * *

Grimm led the horse in one last slow circle, certain that at any moment Jillian would burst from the castle. He knew he shouldn't spend time with her, yet he found himself deliberately arranging to give Zeke his first riding lesson where she'd be certain to see. Only moments before he had glimpsed a flutter of motion and a fall of golden hair in the tower window. His gut tightened with anticipation as he lifted Zeke down from the stallion. "I suspect you feel comfortable with his gait now, Zeke. We've made a good start."

"He's very easy to ride. But I won't be able to guide him myself, so what's the point? I could never ride by myself."

"Never say never, Zeke," Grimm chided gently. "The moment you say 'never' you've chosen not to try. Rather than worrying about what you can't do, set your mind to thinking of ways that you could do it. You might surprise yourself."

Zeke blinked up at him. "But everybody tells me I canna ride."

"Why do *you* think you can't ride?" Grimm asked, lowering the boy to the ground.

" 'Cause I canna see clearly. I may run your horse smack into a rock!" Zeke exclaimed.

"My horse has eyes, lad. Do you think he'd allow you to run him into a rock? Occam wouldn't let you run him into anything. Trust me, and I'll show you that a horse can be trained to compensate for your vision."

"You really think one day I might be able to ride without your help?" Zeke asked in a low voice, so the onlookers gathered around wouldn't hear the hope in his voice and mock him for it.

"Yes, I do. And I'll prove it to you, in time."

"What madness are you telling Zeke?" Jillian demanded, joining them.

Grimm turned to face her, savoring her flushed cheeks and brilliant eyes. "Go on, Zeke." He gave the lad a gentle nudge toward the castle. "We'll work on this again tomorrow."

Zeke grinned at Grimm, stole a quick look at Jillian's face, and left hurriedly.

"I'm teaching Zeke to ride."

"Why? He can't see well, Grimm. He will never be able to ride by himself. He'll only end up getting hurt."

"That's not true. The lad's been told he can't do a lot of things that he can do. There are different methods for training a horse. Although Zeke may have poor eyesight, Occam here"—Grimm gestured to his snorting stallion—"has keen enough senses for them both."

"What did you just say?" Jillian's brow furrowed.

"I said my horse can see well enough—"

"I heard that part. What did you call your horse?" she demanded, unaware her voice had risen sharply, and the dispersing crowd had halted collectively, hanging on her every word.

Grimm swallowed. He hadn't thought she'd remember! "Occam," he said tightly.

"Occam? You named your horse *Occam*?" Every man, woman, and child in the lower bailey gaped at the uneven timbre of their lady's voice.

Jillian stalked forward and poked an accusing finger at his chest. "Occam?" she repeated, waiting.

She was waiting for him to say something intelligent, Grimm realized. Damn the woman, but she should know better than that. Intelligent just didn't happen when he was around Jillian. Then again, demure and temperate didn't seem to happen when Jillian was around him. Give them a few minutes and they'd be brawling in the courtyard of Caithness while the whole blasted castle watched in abject fascination.

Grimm searched her face intently, seeking some flaw of form that betrayed a weakness of character, anything he could seize upon and stoke into a defense against her charms, but he may as well have searched the seas for a legendary selkie. She was simply perfect. Her strong jaw reflected her proud spirit. Her clear golden eyes shone with truth. She pursed her lips, waiting. Overly full lips, the lower one plump and rosy. Lips that would part sweetly when he took her, lips between which he would slide his tongue, lips that might curve around his . . .

And those lips were moving, but he didn't have the damndest idea what she was saying because he'd taken a dangerous segue into a sensual fantasy involving heated, flushed flesh, Jillian's lips, and a man's need. The roar of blood pounding in his ears must have deafened him. He struggled to focus on her words, which faded back in just in time for him to hear her say

"You lied! You said you never thought about me at all."

He gathered his scattered wits defensively. She was looking much too pleased with herself for his peace of mind. "What are you pecking away at now, little peahen?" he said in his most bored voice.

"Occam," she repeated triumphantly.

"That's my horse," he drawled, "and just what *is* your point?"

Jillian hesitated. Only an instant, but he saw the flicker of embarrassment in her eyes as she must have wondered if he really didn't remember the day she'd discovered the principle of "Occam's Razor," then proceeded to enlighten everyone at Caithness. How could he not recall the child's delight? How could he forget the discomfiture of visiting lords well versed in politics and hunting, yet utterly put off by a woman with a mind, even a lass at the tender age of eleven? Oh, he remembered; he'd been so bloody proud of her it had hurt. He'd wanted to smack the smirks off the prissy lords' faces for telling Jillian's parents to burn her books, lest they ruin a perfectly good female and make her unmarriageable. He remembered. And had named his horse in tribute.

Occam's Razor: The simplest theory that fits the facts corresponds most closely to reality. *Fit this, Jillian—why do I treat you so horribly?* He grimaced. The simplest theory that encompassed the full range of asinine behavior he exhibited around Jillian was that he was hopelessly in love with her, and if he wasn't careful she would figure it out. He had to be cold, perhaps cruel, for Jillian was an intelligent woman and unless he maintained a convincing façade she would see right through him. He drew a deep breath and steeled his will.

"You were saying?" He arched a sardonic brow. Powerful men had withered into babbling idiots beneath the sarcasm and mockery of that deadly gaze.

But not his Jillian, and it delighted him as much as it worried him. She held her ground, even leaned closer, ignoring the curious stares and perked ears of the onlookers. Close enough that her breath fanned his neck and made him want to seal his lips over hers and draw her breath into his lungs so deeply that she'd need him to breathe it back into her. She looked deep into his eyes, then a smile of delight curved her mouth. "You *do* remember," she whispered fiercely. "I wonder what else you lie to me about," she murmured, and he had the dreadful suspicion she was about to start applying a scientific analysis to his idiotic behavior. Then she'd know, and he'd be exposed for the lovestruck dolt he was.

He wrapped his hand around her wrist and clamped his fingers tight, until he knew she understood he could snap it with a flick of his hand. He deliberately let his eyes flash the blazing, unholy look people loathed. Even Jillian backstepped slightly, and he knew that somehow she'd caught the tiniest glimpse of the Berserker in his eyes. It would serve her well to fear him. She *must* be afraid of him—Christ knew, he was afraid of himself. Although Jillian had changed and matured, he still had nothing to offer her. No clan, no family, and no home. "When I left Caithness I swore never to return. *That's* what I remember, Jillian." He dropped her wrist. "And I did not come back willingly, but for a vow made long ago. If I named my horse a word you happen to be familiar with, how arrogant you are to think it had anything to do with you."

"Oh! I am not arrogant—"

"Do you know why your da really brought us here, lass?" Grimm interrupted coldly.

Jillian's mouth snapped shut. It figured that he would be the only one who might tell her the truth.

"Do you? I know you used to have a bad habit of spying, and I doubt much about you has changed."

Her jaw jutted, her spine stiffened, and she threw her shoulders back, presenting him with a clear view of her lush figure—one of the things that had definitely changed about her. She bit her lip to prevent a smug smile when his gaze dropped sharply, then jerked back up.

Grimm regarded her stonily. "Your da summoned the three of us here to secure you a husband, brat. Apparently you're so impossible to persuade that he had to gather Scotia's mightiest warriors to topple your defenses." He studied her stalwart stance and aloof expression a moment and snorted. "I was right—you do still eavesdrop. You aren't at all surprised by my revelation. Seeing as how you know the plan, why doona you just be a good lass for a change; go find Quinn and persuade him to marry you so I can leave and get on with my life?" His gut clenched as he forced himself to say the words.

"That's what you wish me to do?" she asked in a small voice.

He studied her a long moment. "Aye," he said finally. "That's what I wish you to do." He pushed his hands through his hair before grabbing Occam by the reins and leading him away.

Jillian watched him retreat, her throat working painfully. She would not cry. She would never again waste her tears on him. With a sigh, she turned for the castle, only to come smack up against Quinn's broad chest. He was regarding her with such compassion that it unraveled her composure. Tears filled her eyes as he put his arms around her. "How long have you been standing here?" she asked shakily.

"Long enough," he replied softly. "It wouldn't take any persuading, Jillian," Quinn assured her. "I cared deeply for you as a lass—you were as a cherished younger sister to me. I could love you as much more than a sister now."

"What is there to love about me? I'm a blithering idiot!"

Quinn smiled bitterly. "Only for Grimm. But then, you always were a fool for him. As to what one might love about you: your irrepressible spirit, your wit, your curiosity about everything, the music you play, your love for the children. You have a pure heart, Jillian, and that's rare."

"Oh, Quinn, why are you always so good to me?" She affectionately brushed his cheek with her knuckles before she slipped past him and dashed, alone, for the castle.

Chapter 9

"What the hell is your problem?" Quinn demanded, bursting into the stables.

Grimm glanced over his shoulder as he slid the halter from Occam. "What are you talking about? I doona have a problem," he replied, waving an eager-to-assist stable boy away. "I'll take care of my own horse, lad. And doona be penning him up in here. I just brought him in to rub him down. *Never* pen him."

Nodding, the stable boy backed away and left quickly.

"Look, McIllioch, I don't care what motivates you to be such a bastard to her," Quinn said, dropping all pretense by using Grimm's real name. "I don't even wish to know. Just stop. I won't have you making her cry. You did it enough when we were young. I didn't interfere then, telling myself that Gavrael McIllioch had had a tough life and maybe he needed some slack, but you don't have a tough life anymore."

"How would you know?"

Quinn glared. "Because I know what you've become. You're one of the most respected men in Scotland. You're no longer Gavrael McIllioch—you're the renowned Grimm Roderick, a legend of discipline and control. You saved the King's life on a dozen different occasions. You've been rewarded so richly that you're worth more than old St. Clair and myself put together. Women fling themselves at your feet. What more could you want?"

Only one thing—the thing I can never have, he brooded. *Jillian*. "You're right, Quinn. As usual. I'm an ass and you're right. So marry her." Grimm turned his back and fiddled with Occam's saddle. He shrugged Quinn's hand off his shoulder a moment later. "Leave me alone, Quinn. You'd make a perfect husband for Jillian, and since I saw Ramsay kissing her the other day, you'd better move fast."

"Ramsay kissed her?" Quinn exclaimed. "Did she kiss him back?"

"Aye," Grimm said bitterly. "And that man has spoiled more than his share of innocent lasses, so do us both a favor and save Jillian from him by offering for her yourself."

"I already have," Quinn said quietly.

Grimm spun sharply. "You did? When? What did she say?"

Quinn shifted from foot to foot. "Well, I didn't exactly out-and-out ask her, but I made my intentions clear."

Grimm waited, one dark brow arched inquiringly.

Quinn tossed himself down on a pile of hay and leaned back, resting his weight on his elbows. He blew a strand of blond hair out of his face irritably. "She thinks she's in love with you, Grimm. She has always thought she was in love with you, ever since she was a child. Why don't you finally come clean with the truth? Tell her who you really are. Let her decide if you're good enough for her. You're heir to a chieftain—if you'd ever go home and claim it. Gibraltar knows exactly who you are, and he summoned you to be one of the contenders for her hand. Obviously he thinks you're good enough for his daughter. Maybe you're the only one who doesn't."

"Maybe he brought me just to make you look good by comparison. You know, invite the beast-boy. Isn't that what Jillian used to call me?" He rolled his eyes. "Then the handsome laird looks even more appealing. She can't be interested in me. As far as Jillian knows, I'm not even titled. I'm a nobody. And I thought you wanted her, Quinn." Grimm turned back to his horse and swept Occam's side with long, even strokes of the brush.

"I do. I'd be proud to make Jillian my wife. Any man would—"

"Do you love her?"

Quinn cocked a brow and eyed him curiously. "Of course I love her."

"No, do you *really* love her? Does she make you crazy inside?" Grimm watched him carefully.

Quinn blinked. "I don't know what you mean, Grimm."

Grimm snorted. "I didn't expect you would," he muttered.

"Oh, hell, this is a snarl of a mess." Quinn exhaled impatiently and dropped onto his back in the fragrant hay. He plucked a stem of clover from the pile and chewed on it thoughtfully. "I want her. She wants you. And you're my closest friend. The only unknown factor in this equation is what you want."

"First of all, I sincerely doubt she wants me, Quinn. If anything, it's the remains of a childish infatuation that, I assure you, I will relieve her of. Secondly, it doesn't matter what I want." Grimm produced an apple from his sporran and offered it to Occam.

"What do you mean, it doesn't matter? Of course it matters." Quinn frowned.

"What *I* want is the most irrelevant part of this affair, Quinn. I'm a Berserker," Grimm said flatly.

"So? Look what it has brought you. Most men would trade their souls to be a Berserker."

"That would be a damned foolish bargain. And there's a lot you doona know that is part and parcel of the curse."

"It's proved quite a boon for you. You're virtually invincible. Why, I remember down at Killarnie—"

"I doona wish to talk about Killarnie—"

"You killed half the damned—"

"Haud yer wheesht!" Grimm's head whipped around. "I doona wish to talk about killing. It seems that's the only thing I'm good for. For all that I'm this ridiculous legend of control, there's still a part of me I can't control, de Moncreiffe. I have no control over the rage. I never have," he admitted roughly. "When it happens, I lose memory. I lose time. I have no idea what I'm doing when I'm doing it, and when it's over, I have to be told what I've done. You know that. You've had to tell me a time or two."

"What are you saying, Grimm?"

"That you must wed her, no matter what I might feel, because I can never be anything to Jillian St. Clair. I knew it then, and I know it now. I will never marry. Nothing has changed. *I* haven't been able to change."

"You *do* feel for her." Quinn sat up on the hay mound, searching Grimm's face intently. "Deeply. And that's why you try to make her hate you."

Grimm turned back to his horse. "I never told you how my mother died, did I, de Moncreiffe?"

Quinn rose and dusted hay from his kilt. "I thought she was killed in the massacre at Tuluth."

Grimm leaned his head against Occam's velvety cheek and breathed deeply of the soothing scent of horse and leather. "No. Jolyn McIllioch died much earlier that morning, before the McKane even arrived." He delivered the words in a cool monotone. "My da murdered her in a fit of rage. Not only did I sink to such foolishness as summoning a Berserker that day, I suffer an inherited madness."

"I don't I believe that, Grimm," Quinn said flatly. "You're one of the most logical, rational men I know."

Grimm made a gesture of impatience. "Da told me so himself the night I left Tuluth. Even if I gave myself latitude, even if I managed to convince myself I didn't suffer an inherited weakness of mind, I'm still a Berserker. Doona you realize, Quinn, that according to ancient law we 'pagan worshipers of Odin' are to be banished? Ostracized, outcast, and murdered, if at all possible. Half the country knows Berserkers exist and seek to employ us; the other half refuses to admit we do while they attempt to destroy us. Gibraltar must have been out of his mind when he summoned me—he couldn't possibly seriously consider me for his daughter's hand! Even if I wanted with all my heart to take Jillian to wife, what could I offer her? A life such as this? That's assuming I'm not addled by birthright, to boot."

"You're not addled. I don't know how you got the ridiculous idea that because your da killed your mother there's something wrong with *you*. And no one knows who you really are except for me, Gibraltar, and Elizabeth," Quinn protested.

"And Hatchard," Grimm reminded. And Hawk and Adrienne, he recalled.

"So four of us know. None of us would ever betray you. As far as the world is concerned you're Grimm Roderick, the King's legendary bodyguard. All that aside, I don't see how it would be a problem for you to admit who you really are. A lot of things have changed since the massacre at Tuluth. And although some people do still fear Berserkers, the majority revere them. You're some of the mightiest warriors Alba has ever produced, and you know how we Scots worship our legends. The Circle Elders say only the purest, most honorable blood in Scotland can actually call the Berserker."

"The McKane still hunt us," Grimm said through his teeth.

"The McKane have always hunted any man they suspected was Berserk. They're jealous. They spend every waking moment training to be warriors and can never match up to a Berserker. So defeat them, and lay it to rest. You're not fourteen anymore. I've seen you in action. Rouse up an army. Hell, I'd fight for you! I know scores of men who would. Go home and claim your birthright—"

"My gift of inherited madness?"

"The chieftainship, you idiot!"

"There might be a small problem with that," Grimm said bitterly. "My crazy, murdering da has the dreadful manners to still be lingering on this earth."

"What?" Quinn was speechless. He shook his head several times and grimaced. "Christ! How can I walk around all these years thinking I know you, only to find out I don't know a blethering thing about you? You told me your da was dead."

It seemed all his close friends were saying the same thing lately, and he wasn't a man given to lying. "I thought he was, for a long time." Grimm ran an impatient hand through his hair. "I will never go home, Quinn, and there are some things about being Berserk that you doona understand. I can't have any degree of intimacy with a woman without her realizing that I'm not normal. So what am I supposed to do? Tell the lucky woman I am one of those savage killing beasts that have gotten such a bad reputation over the centuries? Tell her I can't see blood without losing control of myself? Tell her that if my eyes ever start to seem like they're getting incandescent, to run as far away from me as she can get because Berserkers have been known to turn on friend and foe indiscriminately?"

"You've never once turned on me!" Quinn snapped. "And I've been beside you when it happened many times!"

Grimm shook his head. "Marry her, Quinn. For Christ's sake! Marry her and free me!" He cursed harshly, dropping his head against his stallion.

"Do you really think it will?" Quinn asked angrily. "Will it free any of us, Grimm?"

* * *

Jillian strolled the wall-walk, the dim passage behind the parapet, breathing deeply of the twilight. Gloaming was her favorite hour, the time when dusk blurred into absolute darkness broken only by a silvery moon and cool white stars above Caithness. She paused, resting her arms against the parapet. The scent of roses and honeysuckle carried on the breeze. She inhaled deeply. Another scent teased her senses, and she cocked her head. Dark and spicy; leather and soap and man.

Grimm.

She turned slowly and he was there, standing behind her on the roof, deep in the shadows of the abutting walls watching her, his gaze unfathomable. She hadn't heard a sound as he'd approached, not a whisper of cloth, not one scuffle of his boots on the stones. It was as if he were fashioned of night air and had sailed the wind to her solitary perch.

"Will you marry?" he asked without preface.

Jillian sucked in a breath. Shadows couched his features but for a bar of moonlight illuminating his intense eyes. How long had he been there? Was there a "me," unspoken, at the end of his sentence? "What are you asking?" she said breathlessly.

His smooth voice was bland. "Quinn would make a fine husband for you."

"Quinn?" she echoed.

"Aye. He's golden as you, lass. He's kind, gentle, and wealthy. His family would cherish you."

"And what about yours?" She couldn't believe she dared ask.

"What about mine, what?"

Would your family cherish me? "What is your family like?"

His gaze was icy. "I have no family."

"None?" Jillian frowned. Surely he had some relatives, somewhere.

"You know nothing about me, lass," he reminded her in a low voice.

"Well, since you keep butting your nose into my life, I think I have the right to ask a few questions." Jillian peered intently at him, but it was too dark to see him clearly. How could he seem such a part of the night?

"I'll quit butting my nose. And the only time I butt my nose in is when it looks like you're about to get in trouble."

"I do *not* get into trouble all the time, Grimm."

"So"—he gestured impatiently—"when will you marry him?"

"Who?" She seethed, plucking at the folds of her gown. Clouds passed over the moon, momentarily obscuring him from her view.

His eerily disembodied voice was mildly reproaching. "Try to follow the conversation, lass. Quinn."

"By Odin's shaft—"

"Spear," he corrected with a hint of amusement in his voice.

"I am not marrying Quinn!" she informed the dark corner furiously.

"Certainly not Ramsey?" His voice deepened dangerously. "Or was he such a good kisser that he's already persuaded you?"

Jillian drew a deep breath. She released it and closed her eyes, praying for temperance.

"Lass, you have to wed one of them. Your da demands it," he said quietly.

She opened her eyes. Praise the saints, the clouds had blown by and she could once again discern the outline of his form. There was a flesh-and-blood man in those shadows, not some mythical beast. "You're one of the men my da brought here for me, so I guess that means I could choose you, doesn't it?"

He shook his head, a blur of movement in the gloom. "Never do that, Jillian. I have nothing to offer you but a lifetime of hell."

"Maybe you think that, but maybe you're wrong. Maybe, if you quit feeling sorry for yourself, you'd see things differently."

"I doona feel sorry for myself—"

"Ha! You're drowning in it, Roderick. Only occasionally does a smile manage to steal over your handsome face, and as soon as you catch it you swallow it. You know what your problem is?"

"No. But I have the feeling you're going to tell me, peahen."

"Clever, Roderick. That's supposed to make me feel stupid enough to shut up. Well, it won't work, because I feel stupid around you all the time anyway, so I may as well act stupid too. I suspect your problem is that you're afraid."

Grimm leaned indolently back against the stones of the wall, looking every inch a man who'd never contemplated the word *fear* long enough for it to gain entrance into his vocabulary.

"Do you know what you're afraid of?" she pushed bravely on.

"Considering that I didn't know I was afraid, I'm afraid you've got me at a bit of a disadvantage," he mocked.

"You're afraid you might have a feeling," she announced triumphantly.

"Oh, I'm not afraid of feelings, lass," he said, dark, sensual knowledge dripping from his voice. "It just depends on the kind of feeling—"

Jillian shivered. "Don't try to change the subject—"

"And if the feeling's below my waist—"

"By segueing into a discussion about your debauched—"

"Then I'm perfectly comfortable with it."

"And perverse male needs—"

"Perverse male needs?" he echoed, suppressed laughter lacing his words.

Jillian bit her lip. She always ended up saying too much around him, because he had the bad habit of talking over her, and she lost her head time and again.

"The issue at hand is feelings—as in emotions," she reminded stiffly.

"And you think they're mutually exclusive?" Grimm prodded.

Had she said that? she wondered. By the saints, the man turned her brain into mush. "*What* are you talking about?"

"Feelings and *feelings*, Jillian. Do you think they're mutually exclusive?"

Jillian pondered his question a few moments. "I haven't had a lot of experience in that area, but I would guess they are more often for a man than a woman," she replied at length.

"Not all men, Jillian." He paused, then added smoothly, "Exactly how much experience have you had?"

"What was my point?" she asked irritably, refusing to acknowledge his question.

He laughed. By the saints, he laughed! It was a genuine uninhibited laugh—deeply resonant, rich, and warm. She shuddered, because the flash of white teeth in his shadowed face made him so handsome she wanted to cry at the unfairness of his miserly dispensation of such beauty.

"I was hoping you'd tell me that anytime now, Jillian."

"Roderick, conversations with you never go where I think they're going."

"At least you're never bored. That must count for something."

Jillian blew out a frustrated breath. That was true. She was elated, exhilarated, sensually awakened—but never, never bored.

"So are they mutually exclusive for you?" she dared.

"What?" he asked blandly.

"Feelings and *feelings*."

Grimm tugged restlessly at his dark hair. "I suppose I

haven't met the woman who could make me feel while I was feeling her."

I could, I know I could! she almost shouted. "But you have those other kind of feelings quite frequently, don't you?" she snipped.

"As often as I can."

"There you go with your hair, again. What is it with you and your hair?" When he didn't reply she said childishly, "I hate you, Roderick." She could have kicked herself the moment she said it. She prided herself on being an intelligent woman, yet around Grimm she regressed into a petty child. She was going to have to dredge up something more effective than the same puerile response if she intended to spar with him.

"No you doona, lass." He uttered a harsh curse and stepped forward, doffing the shadows impatiently. "That's the third time you've said that to me, and I'm getting bloody sick of hearing it."

Jillian held her breath as he moved closer, staring down at her with a strained expression. "You wish you could hate me, Jillian St. Clair, and Christ knows you *should* hate me, but you just can't quite bring yourself to hate me all that much, can you? I know, because I've looked in your eyes, Jillian, and where a great big nothing should be if you hated me, there's a fiery thing with curious eyes."

He turned in a swirl of shadows and descended from the roof, moving with lupine grace. At the bottom of the steps, he paused in a puddle of moonlight and tilted his head back. The pale moon cast his bitter expression into stark relief. "Doona ever say those words to me again, Jillian. I mean it—fair warning. Not ever."

Cobblestones crunched beneath his boots as he disappeared into the gardens, comforting her that he was, indeed, of this world.

She pondered his words for a long time after he'd gone, and she was left alone with the bruised sky on the parapet. Three times he'd called her by name—not brat or lass, but Jillian. And although his final words had been delivered in a cool monotone, she had seen—unless the moon was playing tricks with her vision—a hint of anguish in his eyes.

The longer she considered it, the more convinced she became. Logic insisted that love and hate could masquerade behind the same façade. It became an issue of simply peeling back that mask to peer beneath it and determine which emotion truly drove the man in the shadow. A glimmer of understanding pierced the gloom that surrounded her.

Go with your heart, her mother had counseled her hundreds of times. *The heart speaks clearly even when the mind insists otherwise.*

"Mama, I miss you," Jillian whispered as the last stain of purple twilight melted into a raven horizon. But despite the distance, Elizabeth St. Clair's strength was inside her, in her blood. She was a Sacheron *and* a St. Clair—a formidable combination.

Indifferent to her, was he? It was time to see about that.

Chapter 10

"Well, that's it, then—they're off," Hatchard muttered, watching the men depart. He finger-combed his short red beard thoughtfully. He stood with Kaley on the front steps of Caithness, watching three horses fade into swirls of dust down the winding road.

"Why did they have to choose Durrkesh?" Kaley asked irritably. "If they wanted to go catting about, they could very well have gone to the village right here." She waved at the small town clustered protectively near the walls of Caithness that spilled into the valley beyond.

Hatchard shot her a caustic glance. "Although this may come as a grave shock to your . . . shall we say . . . accommodating nature, not everyone thinks about catting all the time, Missus Twillow."

"Don't be 'Missus Twillowing' me, Remmy," she snapped. "I'll not be believing you've lived nearly forty years without doing a bit of catting yourself. But I must say, I find it appalling that they're off catting when they were brought here for Jillian."

"If you'd listen for a change, Kaley, you might hear what I've been telling you. They went to Durrkesh because Ramsay suggested they go—not for catting, but to acquire wares that can only be purchased in the city. You told me we've run short of peppercorns and cinnamon, and you won't be finding those wares here." He gestured to the village and allowed a significant pause to pass before adding, "I also heard one might find saffron at the city fair this year."

"*Saffron!* Bless the saints, we haven't had saffron since last spring."

"You've kept me perennially aware of the fact," Hatchard said wryly.

"One does what one can to aid an old man's memory." Kaley sniffed. "And correct me if I'm wrong, but don't you usually send your men for the wares?"

"Seeing how Quinn was so avid to buy an elegant gift for Jillian, I certainly wasn't about to stop him. Grimm, I believe, went with them simply to avoid getting stuck alone with the lass," Hatchard added dryly.

Kaley's eyes sparkled, and she clapped her hands together. "A gift for Jillian. So it's to be Jillian de Moncreiffe, is it? A fine name for a fine lass, I must say. And that would keep her nearby in the Lowlands."

Hatchard returned his pensive gaze to the ribbon of road wending through the valley. He watched the last rider disappear around a bend and clucked his tongue. "I wouldn't be so certain, Kaley," he murmured.

"Whatever is that cryptic remark supposed to mean?" Kaley frowned.

"Just that in my estimation the lass has never had eyes for anyone but Grimm."

"Grimm Roderick is the worst possible man for her!" Kaley exclaimed.

Hatchard turned a curious gaze on the voluptuous maid. "Now, why would you say that?"

Kaley's hand flew to her throat, and she fanned herself. "There are men women desire and there are men women marry. Roderick is *not* the kind of man a woman marries."

"Why not?" Hatchard asked, bewildered.

"He's dangerous," Kaley breathed. "Positively dangerous to the lass."

"You think he might harm her in some way?" Hatchard tensed, prepared to do battle if such was the case.

"Without even meaning to, Remmy." Kaley sighed.

* * *

"They've gone where? And for how long did you say?" Jillian's brow puckered with indignation.

"To the city of Durrkesh, milady," Hatchard replied. "I should suppose they'll be gone just shy of a sennight."

Jillian smoothed the folds of her gown irritably. "I wore a dress this morning, Kaley—a pretty one," she complained. "I was even going to ride to the village wearing it instead of Da's plaid, and you know how I hate riding in a dress."

"You look lovely, indeed," Kaley assured her.

"I look lovely for whom? All my suitors have abandoned me."

Hatchard cleared his throat gruffly. "There wouldn't have been one in particular you were hoping to impress, would there?"

Jillian turned on him accusingly. "Did my da put you up to spying on me, Hatchard? You're probably sending him weekly reports! Well, boodle, I'll tell you nothing."

Hatchard had the grace to look abashed. "I'm not sending him reports. I was merely concerned for your welfare."

"You can concern yourself with someone else's. I'm old enough and I worry enough for both of us."

"Jillian," Kaley chided, "crabby does not become you. Hatchard is merely expressing his concern."

"I feel like being crabby. Can't I just do that for a change?" Jillian's brow furrowed as she reflected a moment. "Wait a minute," she said pensively. "Durrkesh, is it? They hold a splendid fair this time of year . . . the last time I went with Mama and Da, we stayed at a perfectly lovely little inn—the Black Boot, wasn't it, Kaley?"

Kaley nodded. "When your brother Edmund was alive the two of you went to the city often."

A shadow flitted across Jillian's face.

Kaley winced. "I'm sorry, Jillian. I didn't mean to bring that up."

"I know." Jillian drew a deep breath. "Kaley, start packing. I've a sudden urge to go a'fairing, and what better time than now? Hatchard, have the horses readied. I'm tired of sitting around letting life happen to me. It's time I make my life happen."

"This doesn't bode well, Missus Twillow," Hatchard told Kaley as Jillian strolled briskly off.

"A woman has as much right to cat about as a man. At least she's catting after a husband. Now we just have to put our heads together and make certain she chooses the right one," Kaley informed him loftily before sauntering after Jillian, twitching her plump hips in a manner that put

Hatchard in mind of a long-forgotten, exceedingly bawdy ditty.

He blew out a gusty breath and headed off to the stables.

* * *

The Black Boot sagged alarmingly at the eaves, but fortunately the rooms Grimm had procured were on the third floor, not the top, which meant they should be reasonably safe from the deluge that had begun halfway through their trip.

Pausing outside the open door to the inn, Grimm fisted double handfuls of his shirt and squeezed it. Water gushed from between his hands and splattered loudly on the great stone slab outside the door.

A thick, swirling mist was settling over the town. Within a quarter hour the dense fog would be impossible to navigate through; they'd arrived just in time to avoid the worst of it. Grimm had settled his horse in the small U-shaped courtyard behind the inn, where a ratty lean-to swayed precariously from the drooping roof. Occam would find sufficient shelter, provided the flood didn't carry him off.

Grimm whisked the beaded water droplets off his plaid before entering the inn. Any weaver worth her salt wove the fabric so tightly it was virtually water-repellant, and the weavers at Dalkeith were some of the finest. He unfastened a length of the woolen fabric and draped it across his shoulder. Quinn and Ramsay were already at the fire, toasting their hands and drying their boots.

"Bloody nasty weather out there, ain't it, lads?" The barkeep beckoned cheerfully through the doorway to the adjoining tavern. "Me, I've got a fire in here s'warm as tha' one, and a fine brew to chase yer chill, so dinna tarry. Me name's Mac," he added with a friendly nod. "Come bide a wee."

Grimm glanced at Quinn, who shrugged. His expression plainly said there wasn't much else to do on such a miserably wet evening than pass it drinking. The three men ducked through the low doorway that partitioned the eatery from the tavern proper and claimed several battered wooden stools at a table by the hearth.

"Seein' as 'tis nearly deserted in here, I may as well pull up a seat once I've seen t' yer drinks. No' many venture out in a downpour such as this." The barkeep ambled unevenly to the bar, then lumbered back to their table, producing a bottle of whisky and four mugs with a flourish.

" 'Tis a fardlin' mess out there, ain't it? An' where be ye travelin'?" he asked, sitting heavily. "Dinna mind me leg, I think the wood's goin' soft," he added as he grabbed a second stool, lifted his wooden leg by the ankle, and dropped it on the slats. "Sometimes it pains me when the weather goes damp. An' in this damn country, tha's all the time, ain't it? Gloomy place, she is, but I love 'er. Y'ever been outside of Alba, lads?"

Grimm glanced at Quinn, who was gazing raptly at the barkeep, his expression a mixture of amusement and irritation. Grimm knew they were both wondering if the lonely little barkeep would ever shut up.

It was going to be a long night.

* * *

A few hours later the rain hadn't abated, and Grimm used the excuse of checking on Occam to escape the smoky tavern and Mac's incessant prattle. Besieged by the same restlessness that had ridden him at Dalkeith, he could scarcely sit still for longer than a few hours. He slipped into the back courtyard of the inn, wondering what Jillian was doing at the moment. A slight smile curved his lips as he pictured her stomping about, tossing her glorious mane of hair, outraged that she'd been left behind. Jillian despised being excluded from anything "the lads" did. But this was for the best, and she would realize it when Quinn returned with his gift and made his formal pledge. Grimm could scarcely look at Quinn without being struck by what a perfect couple they would make, giving birth to perfect, golden children with aristocratic features and not a touch of inherited madness. Perhaps by getting the two of them together he could redeem himself in some small measure, he mused, although the thought of Jillian with Quinn caused his stomach to tighten painfully.

"Get out o' me kitchen and dinna be returnin', ye ratty-ass whelp." A door on the far side of the courtyard suddenly burst open. A child tumbled head over heels into the night and landed prone in the mud.

Grimm studied the man whose wide frame nearly filled the doorway. He was a big, beefy man, well over six feet tall, with a frizzled crown of short-cropped brown curls. His face was mottled red in patches, either due to rage or exertion, or more likely both, Grimm decided. He clutched a wide butcher's knife that gleamed dully in the light.

The lad clambered to his knees, slipping on the sodden ground. He scrubbed at a spattering of mud on his cheek with thin, dirty fingers. "But Bannion always gives us the scraps. Please, sir, we need to eat!"

"I'm no' Bannion, ye insolent whelp! Bannion doesna work here anymore, and no wonder, if he be giving away to such as ye. I'm the meat butcher now." The man cuffed the child with such vigor that the boy collapsed onto his backside in the mud, shaking his head dazedly. "Ye think we spare any cuts fer the likes o' ye? Ye can rot in a gutter, Robbie MacAuley says. I dinna expect anyone to feed me.

It's the likes o' ye rats that grow up to be thieves and murderers of honest, hardworkin' men." The meat butcher stepped out into the rain, dragged the child from the mud by his scruffy collar, and shook him. When the lad began howling, the butcher cracked a meaty hand across his face.

"Release him," Grimm said quietly.

"Eh?" The man glanced around, startled. A sneer crossed his red face as his gaze lit on Grimm, who was partially concealed by the shadows. The meat butcher straightened menacingly, suspending the boy by one hand. "What's yer concern wi' me business? Stay out o' it. I dinna ask yer opinion and I dinna want it. I found the l'il whelp stealing me vittles—"

"Nay! I dinna steal! Bannion *gives* us the scraps."

The meat butcher backhanded the lad across the face, and blood sprayed from the child's nose.

In the shadow of the lean-to Grimm stared transfixed at the bleeding child. Memories began to crowd him—the flash of a silver blade, a tumble of blond curls and a blood-stained smock, pillars of smoke—an unnatural wind began to rise, and he felt his body twisting inside, reshaping itself until he was hopelessly lost to the rage within. Far beyond conscious thought, Grimm lunged for the meat butcher, crushing him against the stone wall.

"You son of a bitch." Grimm closed his hands around the man's windpipe. "The child needs food. When I release you, you're going to go in the kitchen and pack him a basket of the finest meat you've got, and then you're going to—"

"Like 'ell I am!" the butcher managed to wheeze. He twisted in Grimm's grip and plunged blindly forward with the knife. As the blade slid home, Grimm's hand relaxed infinitesimally, and the butcher sucked in a whistling breath of air. "There, ye bastard," he cried hoarsely. "Nobody messes wi' Robbie MacAuley. 'At'll be teachin' ye." He shoved Grimm with both hands, twisting the knife as he pushed.

As Grimm swayed back, the butcher started forward, only to fall instinctively backward again, his eyes widening incredulously, for the madman he'd stabbed with a brutality and efficiency that should have caused a mortal wound was smiling.

"Smile. That's it—go on, smile as ye be dyin'," he cried. " 'Cause dyin' ye are, and that's fer sure."

Grimm's smile contained such sinister promise that the meat butcher flattened himself up against the wall of the inn like lichen seeking a deep, shady crevice between the stones. "There's a knife in yer belly, man," the meat butcher hissed, eyeing the protruding hilt of the knife to reassure himself it was, indeed, lodged in his assailant's gut.

Breathing evenly, Grimm grasped the hilt with one hand and removed the blade, calmly placing it beneath the butcher's quivering jowls.

"You're going to get the lad the food he came for. Then you will apologize," Grimm said mildly, his eyes glittering.

"To 'ell with ye," the butcher sputtered. "Any minute now ye'll be falling on yer face."

Grimm leveled the blade below the butcher's ear, flush across his jugular. "Doona count on it."

"Ye should be dead, man. There's a hole in yer belly!"

"Grimm." Quinn's voice cut through the night air.

Pressing gently, with the care of a lover, Grimm pierced the skin on the butcher's neck.

"Grimm," Quinn repeated softly.

"Gawd, man! Get him offa me!" the butcher cried frantically. "He's deranged! His bleedin' eyes are like—"

"Shut up, you imbecile," Quinn said in a modulated, conciliatory tone. He knew from experience that harshly uttered words could escalate the state of Berserkergang. Quinn circled the pair cautiously. Grimm had frozen with the blade locked to the man's throat. The ragged lad huddled at their feet, gazing up with wide eyes.

"He be Berserk," the lad whispered reverently. "By Odin, look at his eyes."

"He be crazed," the butcher whimpered, looking at Quinn. "Do something!"

"I *am* doing something," Quinn said quietly. "Make no loud noises, and for Christ's sake, don't move." Quinn stepped closer to Grimm, making certain his friend could see him.

"The whelp's just a homeless ne'er-do-well. 'Tis not the thing to be killing an honest man for," the butcher whined. "How was I supposed to know he was a fardlin' Berserker?"

"It shouldn't have made any difference whether he was or not. A man shouldn't behave honorably only when there's someone bigger and tougher around to force him," Quinn said, disgusted. "Grimm, do you want to kill this man or feed the boy?" Quinn spoke gently, close to his friend's ear. Grimm's eyes were incandescent in the dim light, and Quinn knew he was deep into the bloodlust that accompanied Berserkergang. "You only want to feed the boy, don't you? All you want to do is to feed the boy and keep him from harm, remember? Grimm—*Gavrael*—listen to me. Look at me!"

* * *

"I hate this, Quinn," Grimm said later as he unbuttoned his shirt with stiff fingers.

Quinn gave him a curious look. "Do you really? What is there to hate about it? The only difference between what you did and what I would have done is that you don't know what you're doing when you're doing it. You're honorable even when you're not fully conscious. You're so damned honorable, you *can't* behave any other way."

"I would have killed him."

"I'm not convinced of that. I've seen you do this before and I've seen you pull out of it. The older you get, the more control you seem to gain. And I don't know if you've realized this, but you weren't completely unaware this time. You heard me when I spoke to you. It used to take a lot longer to reach you."

Grimm's brow furrowed. "That's true," he admitted. "It seems I manage to retain a sliver of awareness. Not much—but it's more than I used to have."

"Let me see that wound." Quinn drew a candle near. "And bear in mind, the meat butcher would have given no thought to beating the lad senseless and leaving him to die in the mud. The homeless children in this city are considered no better than street rats, and the general consensus is the faster they die, the better."

"It's not right, Quinn," Grimm said. "Children are innocent. They haven't had a chance to be corrupted. We'd do better to take the children off somewhere else to raise them properly. With someone like Jillian to teach them fables," he added.

Quinn smiled faintly as he bent over the puckered wound. "She will be a wonderful mother, won't she? Like Elizabeth." Bemused, he drew his fingers over the already-closing cut in Grimm's side. "By Odin's spear, man, how quickly do you heal?"

Grimm grimaced slightly. "Very. It seems to be getting even quicker, the older I get."

Quinn dropped to the bed, shaking his head. "What a blessing it must be. You never have to worry about infection, do you? How *does* one kill a Berserker, anyway?"

"With great difficulty," Grimm replied dryly. "I've tried to drink myself to death, and that didn't work. Then I tried to labor myself to death. Failing that, I just plunged into every battle I could find, and that didn't work either. The only thing left was to try was to fu—" He broke off, embarrassed. "Well, as you can see, that didn't work either."

Quinn grinned. "No harm in trying, though, was there?"

Grimm begrudged a faint curve of his lip.

"Get some sleep, man." Quinn lightly punched him on the shoulder. "Everything looks better in the morning. Well, almost everything," he added with a sheepish grin, "so long as I wasn't too drunk the night before. Then sometimes the wench looks worse. And so do I, for that matter."

Grimm just shook his head and flopped back on the bed. After folding his arms behind his head, he was asleep in seconds.

Chapter II

Everything looks better in the morning. Watching Jillian from his window, Grimm recalled Quinn's words and agreed wholeheartedly. What lapse of judgment had persuaded him that she wouldn't follow them?

She was breathtaking, he acknowledged as he watched her hungrily, safe in the privacy of his room. Clad in a velvet cloak of amber, she was a vision of flushed cheeks and sparkling eyes. Her blond hair tumbled over her shoulders, casting the sun back at the sky. The rain had stopped—probably just for her, he brooded—and she stood in a puddle of sunshine that shafted over the roof from the east, proclaiming the hour to be shortly before noon. He'd slept like the dead, but he always did after succumbing to the Berserker rage, no matter how brief its duration.

Peering out the narrow casement window, he rubbed the glass until it permitted him an unmarred view. While Hatchard gathered her bags, Jillian linked her arm through

Kaley's and chatted animatedly. When Quinn appeared in the street below a few moments later, gallantly offered his arms to both ladies, and escorted them into the inn, Grimm exhaled dismally.

Ever-gallant, ever-golden Quinn.

Grimm muttered a soft curse and went to feed Occam before worrying about his own breakfast.

* * *

Jillian mounted the main staircase to her room, glanced about to ascertain she was alone, then detoured stealthily down the rear steps, smoothing the folds of her cloak. Biting her lip, she exited into the small courtyard behind the inn. He was there, just as she'd suspected, feeding Occam a handful of grain and murmuring quietly. Jillian paused, enjoying the sight of him. He was tall and magnificent, and his dark hair rippled in the breeze. His plaid was slung too low for propriety, riding his lean hips with sensual insolence. She could see a peek of his back where his shirt had obviously been hastily tucked. Her fingers itched to stroke the smooth olive-tinted skin. When he bent to pick up a brush, the muscles in his legs rippled, and despite her vow to make no sound, she exhaled a breath of unadulterated longing.

Of course, he heard her. She instantly assumed a mask of indifference and volleyed into questions to head off a potential verbal sully. "Why don't you ever pen Occam?" she asked brightly.

Grimm allowed a brief glance over his shoulder, then started brushing the horse's sleek flank. "He was caught in a stable fire once."

"He doesn't appear to have suffered for it." Jillian

traversed the courtyard, eyeing the stallion. "Was he injured?" The horse was magnificent, hands taller than most and a glossy, unmarked slate gray.

Grimm stopped brushing. "You never stop with your questions, do you? And what are you doing here, anyway? Couldn't you just be a good lass and wait at Caithness? No, I forgot, Jillian hates being left behind," he said mockingly.

"So who rescued him?" Jillian was determined not to rise to the bait.

Grimm returned his attention to the horse. "I did." There was a pause, filled only with the rasp of bristles against horseflesh. When he spoke again, he released a low rush of words: "Have you ever heard a horse scream, Jillian? It's one of the most bloodcurdling sounds I've ever heard. It cuts through you as cruelly as the sound of an innocent child's cry of pain. I think it has always been the innocence that bothers me most."

Jillian wondered when he'd heard those screams and wanted desperately to ask, but was hesitant to pry at his wounds. She held her tongue, hoping he might continue if she stayed silent.

He didn't. Silently stepping back from the stallion, he made a sharp gesture, accompanied by a clicking noise with his tongue against his teeth. Jillian watched in amazement as the stallion sank to its knees, then dropped heavily to its side with a soft nicker. Grimm knelt by the horse and motioned her closer.

She slipped to her knees beside Grimm. "Oh, poor, sweet Occam," she whispered. The entire underside of the horse was badly scarred. Lightly she ran her fingers over the thick skin, and her brows puckered sympathetically.

"He was burned so badly, they said he wouldn't live," Grimm told her. "They planned to put him down, so I bought him. Not only was he wounded, he was crazed for months afterward. Can you imagine the terror of being trapped in a burning barn, penned in? Occam could run faster than the fleetest horse, could have left the blaze miles behind, but he was imprisoned in a man-made hell. I've never penned him since."

Jillian swallowed and glanced at Grimm. His expression was bitter. "You sound as if you've been trapped in a few man-made hells yourself, Grimm Roderick," she observed softly.

His gaze mocked her. "What would you know about man-made hells?"

"A woman lives most of her life in a man-made world," Jillian replied. "First her father's world, then her husband's, finally her son's, by whose grace she continues on in one of their households should her husband die before her. And in Scotland, the husbands always seem to die before the women in one war or another. Sometimes merely watching the hells men design for each other—that's horror enough for any woman. We feel things differently than you men do." She impulsively laid her hand against his lips to silence him when he started to speak. "No. Don't say anything. I know you think I know little of sorrow or pain, but I've had my share. There are things you don't know about me, Grimm Roderick. And don't forget the battle I watched when I was young." Her eyes widened with disbelief when Grimm lightly kissed the tips of her fingers where they lay across his lips.

"Touché, Jillian," he whispered. He caught her hand in his and placed it gently in her lap. Jillian sat motionless when he curled his own about it protectively.

"If I were a man who believed in wishes on stars, I would wish on all of them that Jillian St. Clair might never suffer the smallest glimpse of any hell. There should only be heaven for Jillian's eyes."

Jillian remained perfectly still, masking her astonishment, exulting in the sensation of his strong, warm hand cupping hers. By the saints, she would have ridden all the way to England through the savagery of a border battle if she'd known *this* was waiting for her at the end of her journey. She fancied her body had taken root where she knelt; to continue being touched by him she would willingly grow old in the small courtyard, suffering wind and rain, hail and snow without the slightest care. Mesmerized by the glimpse of hesitation in his gaze, her head tilted up; his seemed to move forward and down as if nudged by a serendipitous breeze.

His lips were a breath from hers, and she waited, her heart thundering.

"Jillian! Jillian, are you out there?"

Jillian closed her eyes, willing the owner of the intruding voice to hell and farther. She felt the soft brush of Grimm's lips across hers as he quickly, lightly delivered a kiss that was nothing like the one she'd been anticipating. She wanted his lips to bruise hers, she wanted his tongue in her mouth and his breath in her lungs, she wanted everything he had to give.

"It's Ramsay," Grimm said through his teeth. "He's coming out. Get up off your knees, lass. *Now.*"

Jillian stumbled hastily to her feet and stepped back, trying desperately to see Grimm's face, but his dark head had fallen forward to the spot hers had occupied a moment before. "Grimm," she whispered urgently. She wanted him to raise his head; she needed to see his eyes. She had to confirm that she'd truly seen desire in his eyes as he'd gazed at her.

"Lass." He groaned the word, his head still bowed.

"Yes?" she whispered breathlessly.

His hands fisted in the folds of his kilt, and she waited, trembling.

The door clattered open and shut behind them. "Jillian," Ramsay called as he entered the courtyard. "There you are. I'm so pleased you joined us. I thought you might like to accompany me to the fair. What's your horse doing on the ground, Roderick?"

Jillian released her breath in a hiss of frustration and kept her back to Ramsay. "What, Grimm? What?" she entreated in an urgent whisper.

He raised his head. There was a defiant glint in his blue eyes. "Quinn is in love with you, lass. I think you should know that," he said softly.

Chapter 12

Jillian deftly eluded Ramsay by telling him she needed to buy "woman things"—a statement that appeared to set his imagination to flight. Thus she was able to spend the afternoon shopping with Kaley and Hatchard. At the silversmith she bought a new buckle for her da. From the tanner she purchased three snowy lambskin rugs—thick as sin and soft as rabbit fur. At the goldsmith's she bartered shrewdly for tiny, hammered-gold stars to adorn a new gown.

But all the while her mind was back in the courtyard, lingering on the dark, sensual man who'd betrayed the first glimpse of a crack in the massive walls around his heart. It had stunned her, bewildered her, and fortified her resolve. Jillian didn't doubt for a moment what she'd seen. Grimm Roderick cared. Buried beneath a mound of rubble—the debris from a past she was beginning to suspect had been more brutal than she could comprehend—there was a very real, vulnerable man.

She'd seen in his stark gaze that he desired her, but more significantly, that he had feelings so deep he couldn't express them, and subsequently did everything in his power to deny them. That was sufficient hope for her to work with. It didn't occur to Jillian, even for a moment, to wonder if he was worth the effort—she knew he was. He had everything to offer that she'd ever wanted in a man. Jillian understood that people didn't come perfect; sometimes they'd been so badly scarred that it took love to heal them and allow them to realize their potential. Sometimes the badly scarred ones had the greatest depth and the most to offer because they understood the infinite value of tenderness. She would be the sun beating down upon the cloak of indifference he'd donned so many years ago, inviting him to walk without defenses.

Her anticipation was so strong, it made her feel shaky and weak. Desire had shimmered in Grimm's gaze when he looked at her, and whether he realized it or not, she'd seen an intense, sensual promise on his face.

Now all she had to do was figure out how to release it. She shivered, rattled by the intuitive knowledge that when Grimm Roderick unleashed his passion, it would definitely be worth waiting for.

"Are you chilled, lass?" Hatchard asked worriedly.

"Chilled?" Jillian echoed blankly.

"You shivered."

"Oh please, Hatchard!" Kaley snorted. "That was a daydreaming shiver. Can't you tell the difference?"

Jillian glanced at Kaley, startled. Kaley merely smiled smugly. "Well, it was, wasn't it, Jillian?"

"How did *you* know?"

"Quinn looked very handsome this morning," Kaley said pointedly.

"So did Grimm," Hatchard snapped immediately. "Didn't you think so, lass? I know you saw him by the stables."

Jillian gaped at Hatchard with a horrified expression. "Were you spying on me?"

"Of course not," Hatchard said defensively. "I just happened to glance out my window."

"Oh," Jillian said in a small voice, her glance darting between her maid and man-at-arms. "Why are you two looking at me like that?" she demanded.

"Like what?" Kaley fluttered her lashes innocently.

Jillian rolled her eyes, disgusted by their obvious matchmaking efforts. "Shall we return to the inn? I promised I'd return in time to have dinner."

"With Quinn?" Kaley said hopefully.

Hatchard nudged the maid. "With Grimm."

"With Occam," Jillian flung over her shoulder dryly.

Hatchard and Kaley exchanged amused glances as Jillian dashed down the street, her arms overflowing with packages.

"I thought she brought *us* to carry," Hatchard observed with a lift of one fox-red eyebrow and a gesture of his empty hands.

Kaley smiled. "Remmy, I suspect she could cart the world off on her shoulders and not feel an ounce. The lass is in love, for certain. My only question is—with which man?"

* * *

"Which one, Jillian?" Kaley asked without preface as she fastened the tiny buttons at the back of Jillian's gown, a creation of lime silk that tumbled in a sensuous ripple from clever ribbons placed at the bodice.

"Which one, what?" Jillian asked nonchalantly. She ran

her fingers through her hair, pulling a sleek fall of gold over her shoulder. She perched on the tiny settle before a blurry mirror in her room at the inn, itching with impatience to join the men in the dining room.

Kaley's reflection met Jillian's with a wordless rebuke. She tugged Jillian's hair back and swept it up into a knot with more enthusiasm than was necessary.

"Ouch." Jillian scowled. "All right, I know what you meant. I just don't wish to answer it yet. Let me see how things go this evening."

Kaley relaxed her grip and smiled. "So you admit to this much—you do intend to select a husband from one of them? You'll heed your father's wishes?"

"Yes, Kaley, oh absolutely yes!" Jillian's eyes sparkled as she leapt to her feet.

"I suppose you could wear your hair down this evening," Kaley begrudged. "Although you should at least allow me to dress and curl it."

"I like it straight," Jillian replied. "It's wavy enough of its own accord, and I don't have time to fuss."

"Oh, now the lass who took over an hour to choose a dress doesn't have time to fuss?" Kaley teased.

"I'm already late, Kaley," Jillian said with a blush as she swept from the room.

* * *

"She's late," Grimm said, pacing irritably. They'd been waiting for some time in the small anteroom that lay between the section of the inn that held private rooms and the public eatery. "By Odin's spear, why doona we just send a tray up to her room?"

"And forgo the pleasure of her company? Not a chance," Ramsay said.

"Stop pacing, Grimm," Quinn said with a grin. "You really need to relax a bit."

"I am perfectly relaxed," Grimm said, stalking back and forth.

"No, you're not," Quinn argued. "You look almost brittle. If I tapped you with my sword, you'd shatter."

"If you tapped me with your sword, I'd bloody well tap you back with mine, and not with the hilt."

"There's no need to get defensive—"

"I am not being defensive!"

Quinn and Ramsay both leveled patronizing gazes at him.

"That's not fair." Grimm scowled. "That's a trap. If someone says 'doona get defensive,' what possible response can a person make except a defensive one? You're stuck with two choices: Say nothing, or sound defensive."

"Grimm, sometimes you think too much," Ramsay observed.

"I'm going to have a drink." Grimm seethed. "Come get me when she's ready, *if* that remarkable event manages to occur before the sun rises."

Ramsay shot Quinn an inquiring look. "He wasn't quite so foul-tempered at court, de Moncreiffe. What's his problem? It's not me, is it? I know we had a few misunderstandings in the past, but I thought they were over and forgotten."

"If memory serves me, the scar on your face is a memento from one of those 'misunderstandings,' isn't it?" When Ramsay grimaced, Quinn continued. "It's not you, Logan. It's how he's always acted around Jillian. But it seems to have gotten worse since she's grown up."

"If he thinks he's going to win her, he's wrong," Ramsay said quietly.

"He's not trying to win her, Logan. He's trying to hate her. And if you think you're going to win her, *you're* wrong."

Ramsay Logan made no reply, but his challenging gaze spoke volumes as he turned away and entered the crowded dining room.

Quinn cast a quick look at the empty stairs, shrugged, and followed on his heels.

* * *

When Jillian arrived downstairs, there was no one waiting for her.

Fine bunch of suitors, she thought. *First they leave me, then they leave me again.*

She glanced back up the stairs, plucking nervously at the neckline of her gown. Should she return for Kaley? The Black Boot was the finest inn in Durrkesh, boasting the best food to be had in the village, yet the thought of walking into the crowded eating establishment by herself was a bit daunting. She'd never gone into a tavern eatery alone before.

She moved to the door and peeked through the opening.

The room was packed with boisterous clusters of patrons. Laughter swelled and broke in waves, despite the fact that half the patrons were forced to stand while eating. Suddenly, as if ordained by the gods, the people faded back to reveal a dark, sinfully handsome man standing by himself near the carved oak counter that served as a bar. Only Grimm Roderick stood with such insolent grace.

As she watched, Quinn walked up to him, handed him a drink, and said something that nearly made Grimm smile. She smiled herself as he caught the expression midway through and quickly terminated any trace of amusement. When Quinn melted back into the crowd, Jillian slipped into the main room and hastened to Grimm's side. He glanced at her and his eyes flared strangely; he nodded but said nothing. Jillian stood in silence, searching for something to say, something witty and intriguing; she was finally alone with him in an adult setting, able to engage in intimate conversation as she'd fantasized so many times.

But before she could think of anything to say, he seemed to lose interest and turned away.

Jillian kicked herself mentally. *Hell's bells, Jillian,* she chided herself, *can't you dredge up a few words around this man?* Her eyes started an adoring journey at the nape of his neck, caressed his thick black hair, wandered over the muscled back straining against the fabric of his shirt as he raised an arm for another draught of ale. She reveled in the mere sight of him, the way the muscles in his shoulders bunched as he gripped an acquaintance by the hand. Her eyes traveled lower, taking in the way his waist narrowed to tight, muscular hips and powerful legs.

His legs were dusted with hair, she noted, drawing a shaky breath, studying the backs of his legs below his kilt, but where did that silky black hair begin and end?

Jillian released a breath she hadn't even known she was holding. Every ounce of her body responded to his with delicious anticipation. Merely standing next to this darkly seductive man, her legs felt weak and her tummy was filled with a shivery sensation.

When Grimm leaned back, momentarily brushing against her in the crowded room, she briefly laid her cheek against his shoulder so softly that he didn't know she'd thieved the touch. She inhaled the scent of him and reached brazenly forward. Her hands found the blades of his shoulders and she scratched gently with her nails, lightly scoring his skin through his shirt.

A soft groan escaped his lips, and Jillian's eyes widened. She scratched gently, stunned that he said nothing. He didn't pull away from her. He didn't spin on his heel and lash out at her.

Jillian held her breath, then inhaled greedily, reveling in the crisp aroma of spicy soap and man. He began to move slightly beneath her nails, like a cat having its chin scratched. Could it be he was actually enjoying her touch?

Oh, can the gods just grant me one wish tonight—to feel the kiss of this man!

She slid her palms lovingly over his back and pressed closer to his body. Her fingers traced the individual muscles in his broad shoulders, slid down his tapered waist, then swept back up again. His body relaxed beneath her hands.

Heaven, this is heaven, she thought dreamily.

"You're looking mighty contented, Grimm." Quinn's voice interrupted her fantasy. "Amazing what a drink can do for your disposition. Where's Jillian gotten off to? Wasn't she just here with you a moment ago?"

Jillian's hands stilled on Grimm's back, which was so broad that it completely shielded her from Quinn's view. She ducked her head, feeling suddenly guilty. The muscles in Grimm's back went rigid beneath her motionless fingers. "Didn't she step outside for a breath of fresh air?" she was stunned to hear Grimm ask.

"By herself? Hell's bells, man—you shouldn't let her go wandering outside by herself!" Quinn's boots clipped smartly on the stone floor as she strode off in search of her.

Grimm whipped around furiously. "What do you think you're doing, peahen?" He snarled.

"I was touching you," she said simply.

Grimm grabbed both her hands in his, nearly crushing the delicate bones in her fingers. "Well, doona be, lass. There is nothing between you and me—"

"You leaned back," she protested. "You didn't seem to be so unhappy—"

"I thought you were a tavern wench!" Grimm said, running a furious hand through his hair.

"Oh!" Jillian was crestfallen.

Grimm lowered his head till his lips brushed her ear, taking pains to make his next words audible over the din in the noisy eatery. "In case you doona recall, it is Quinn who wants you and Quinn who is clearly the best choice. Go find him and touch him, lass. Leave me to the tavern wenches who understand a man like me."

Jillian's eyes sparkled dangerously as she turned away and pushed through the crowded room.

* * *

He would survive the night. It couldn't be too bad; after all, he'd lived through worse. Grimm had been aware of Jillian since the moment she'd entered the room. He had, in fact, deliberately turned away from her when it appeared she'd been about to speak. Little good that had done—as soon as she'd touched him he'd been unable to force himself to step away from the sensual feel of her hands on his back. He'd let it go too far, but it wasn't too late to salvage the situation.

Now he studiously kept his back to Jillian, methodically pouring whisky into a mug. He drank with a vengeance, wiping his lips with the back of his hand, longing for the ability to dull his perfect Berserker senses. Periodically he heard the breathless lilt of her laughter. Occasionally, as the proprietor moved bottles upon shelves, he caught a glimpse of her golden hair in a polished flagon.

But he didn't give a damn, any fool could see that much. He'd pushed her to do what she was currently doing, so how could he care? He didn't, he assured himself, because he was one sane man among a race seemingly condemned to be dragged about by violent, unpredictable emotions that were nothing more than unrelieved lust. Lust, not love, and neither one had a damned thing to do with Jillian.

Christ! Who did he think he was kidding? Grimm closed his eyes and shook his head at his own lies.

Life was hell and he was Sisyphus, eternally condemned to push a boulder of relentless desire up a hill, only to have it flatten him before he reached the crest. Grimm had never been able to tolerate futility. He was a man who resolved things, and tonight he would see to it that Jillian solidified her betrothal to Quinn and that would be the end of his involvement.

He couldn't covet his best friend's wife, could he? So all he had to do was get her wed to Quinn, and that would be the end of his agony. He simply couldn't live with this battle waging within him much longer. If she was free and unwed, he could still dream. If she were safely married, he would be forced to put his fool dreams to rest. So resolved, Grimm stole a covert glance over his shoulder to see how things were progressing. Only peglegged Mac behind the counter heard the hollow whistle of his indrawn breath and noticed the rigid set of his jaw.

Jillian was standing halfway across the room, her golden head tilted back, doing that bedazzling woman-thing to his best friend, which essentially involved nothing more than being what she was: irresistible. A teasing glance, vivacious eyes flashing; a delectable lower lip caught between her teeth. The two were obviously in their own little world, oblivious to him. The very situation he'd encouraged her to seek. It infuriated him.

As he watched, the world that wasn't Jillian—for what was the world without Jillian?—receded. He could hear the rustle of her hair across the crowded tavern, the sigh of air as her hand rose to Quinn's face. Then suddenly the only sound he could hear was the blood thundering in his ears as he watched her slender fingers trace the curve of Quinn's cheek, lingering upon his jaw. His gut tightened and his heart beat a rough staccato of anger.

Mesmerized, Grimm's hand crept to his own face. Jillian's palm feathered Quinn's skin; her fingers traced the shadow beard on Quinn's jaw. Grimm fervently wished he'd broken that perfect jaw a time or two when they'd played as lads.

Deeply oblivious to Mac's fascinated gaze, Grimm's hand traced the same pattern on his own face; he mimicked her touch, his eyes devouring her with such intensity that she might have fled, had she turned to look at him. But she didn't turn. She was too busy gazing adoringly at his best friend.

Behind him a soft snort and a whistle pierced the smoky air. "Man, ye've got it bloody bad, and that's more truth than ye'll find in another bottle o' rotgut mash." Mac's voice shattered the fantasy that Grimm was certainly *not* having. "It's a spot of 'ell wanting yer best friend's wife, now, isn't it?" Mac nodded enthusiastically, warming to the subject. "Me, meself, I had a bit o' thing for one o' me own friend's girl, oh let's see, musta been ten years—"

"She's *not* his wife." The eyes Grimm turned on Mac were not the eyes of a sane man. They were the eyes his villagers had seen before judiciously turning their backs on him so many years ago—the ice-blue eyes of a Viking Berserker who would stop at nothing to get what he wanted.

"Well, she sure as 'ell is his *something*." Mac shrugged off the unmistakable warning in Grimm's eyes with the aplomb of a man who'd survived too many tavern brawls to get overly concerned about one irritable patron. "And yer wishing she wasn't, that's fer sure." Mac removed the empty bottle and picked up a full one that was on the counter. He looked at it curiously. "Now where did this come from?" he asked with a frown. "Och, me mind's getting addled, I dinna even recall openin' this one, though fer sure ye'll be drinking it," Mac said, pouring him a fresh mug. The loquacious barkeep ambled into the room behind the bar and returned a moment later with a heaped basket of brandy-basted chicken. "The way yer drinkin', ye need to be eatin', man," he advised.

Grimm rolled his eyes. Unfortunately, all the whisky in Scotland couldn't dull a Berserker's senses. While Mac tended to a new arrival, Grimm dumped the fresh mug of whisky over the chicken in frustration. He had just decided to go for a long walk when Ramsay sat down next to him.

"Looks like Quinn's making some headway," Ramsay muttered darkly as he eyed the chicken. "Mmm, that looks juicy. Mind if I help myself?"

"Have at it," Grimm said stiffly. "Here—have a drink too." Grimm slid the bottle down the bar.

"No thanks, man. Got my own." Ramsay raised his mug.

Husky, melodic laughter broke over them as Jillian and Quinn joined them at the bar. Despite his best efforts, Grimm's eyes were dark and furious when he glanced at Quinn.

"What do we have here?" Quinn asked, helping himself to the basket of chicken.

"Excuse me," Grimm muttered, pushing past them, ignoring Jillian completely.

Without a backward glance, he left the tavern and melted into the Durrkesh night.

* * *

It was nearly dawn when Grimm returned to the Black Boot. Climbing the stairs wearily, he topped the last step and froze as an unexpected sound reached his ears. He peered down the hallway, eyeing the doors one by one.

He heard the sound again—a whimper, followed by a deeper, husky groan.

Jillian? With Quinn?

He moved swiftly and silently down the corridor, pausing outside Quinn's room. He listened intently and heard it a third time—a husky sigh and a gasp of indrawn air—and each sound ripped through his gut like a double-edged blade. Rage washed over him and everything black he'd ever tried to suppress quickened within. He felt himself slipping over treacherous terrain into the fury he'd first felt fifteen years ago, standing above Tuluth. Something more powerful than any single man could be had taken shape within his veins, endowing him with unspeakable strength and unthinkable capacity for bloodshed—an ancient Viking monster with cold eyes.

Grimm laid his forehead against the cool wood of Quinn's door and breathed in carefully measured gasps as he struggled to subdue his violent reaction. His breathing regulated slowly—sounding nothing like the uncontrolled noises coming from the other side of the door. Christ—he'd encouraged her to marry Quinn, not to go to bed with him!

A feral growl escaped his lips.

Despite his best intentions, his hand found the knob and he turned it, only to meet the defiance of a lock. For a moment he was immobilized, stunned by the barrier. A barrier between him and Jillian—a lock that told him she had chosen. Maybe he had pushed her, but she might have taken a bit more time choosing! A year or two—perhaps the rest of her life.

Aye, she had clearly made her choice—so what right did he have to even consider shattering the door into tiny slivers of wood and selecting the deadliest shard to drive through his best friend's heart? What right had he to do anything but turn away and make his path back down the dark corridor to his own personal hell where the devil surely awaited him with an entirely new boulder to wrestle to the top of the hill: the obdurate stone of regret.

The internal debate raged a tense moment, ending only when the beast within him reared its head, extended its claws, and shattered Quinn's door.

* * *

Grimm's breath rasped in labored pants. He crouched in the doorway and peered into the dimly lit room, wondering why no one had leapt, startled, from the bed.

"Grimm . . ." The word pierced the gloom weakly.

Bewildered, Grimm slipped into the room and moved quickly to the low bed. Quinn was tangled in sodden sheets, curled into a ball—alone. Vomit stained the scuffed planks of the floor. A water tin had been crushed and abandoned, a ceramic pitcher was broken beside it, and the window stood open to the chill night air.

Suddenly Quinn thrashed violently and heaved up from the bed, doubling over. Grimm rushed to catch him before he plunged to the floor. Holding his friend in his arms, he gaped uncomprehendingly until he saw a thin foam of spittle on Quinn's lips.

"P-p-poi-son." Quinn gasped. "H-help . . . me."

"No!" Grimm breathed. "Son of a bitch!" he cursed, cradling Quinn's head as he bellowed for help.

CHAPTER 13

"WHO WOULD POISON QUINN?" HATCHARD PUZZLED. "NO one dislikes Quinn. Quinn is the quintessential laird and gentleman."

Grimm grimaced.

"Will he be all right?" Kaley asked, wringing her hands.

"What's going on?" A sleepy-eyed Jillian stood in the doorway. "Goodness," she exclaimed, eyeing the jagged splinters of the door. "What happened in here?"

"How do you feel, lass? Are you well? Does your stomach hurt? Do you have a fever?" Kaley's hands were suddenly everywhere, poking at her brow, prodding her belly, smoothing her hair.

Jillian blinked. "Kaley, I'm fine. Would you stop poking at me? I heard the commotion and it frightened me, that's all." When Quinn moaned, Jillian gasped. "What's wrong with Quinn?" Belatedly she noted the disarray of the room and the stench of illness that clung to the linens and drapes.

"Fetch a physician, Hatchard," Grimm said.

"The barber is closer," Hatchard suggested.

"No barber," Grimm snapped. He turned to Jillian. "Are you all right, lass?" When she nodded, he expelled a relieved breath. "Find Ramsay," he instructed Kaley ominously.

Kaley's eyes widened in comprehension, and she flew from the room.

"What happened?" Jillian asked blankly.

Grimm laid a damp cloth on Quinn's head. "I suspect it's poison." He didn't tell her he was certain; the recent contents of Quinn's stomach pervaded the air, and to a Berserker the stench of poison was obvious. "I think he'll be all right. If it's what I think it is, he would be dead by now had the dose been strong enough. It must have been diluted somehow."

"Who would poison Quinn? Everybody likes Quinn." She unwittingly echoed Hatchard's words.

"I know, lass. Everyone keeps telling me that," Grimm said drolly.

"Ramsay is ill!" Kaley's words echoed down the corridor. "Someone come help me! I can't hold him down!"

Grimm looked toward the hall, then back at Quinn, clearly torn. "Go to Kaley, lass. I can't leave him," he said through his teeth. Some might consider him paranoid, but if his suspicions were correct, it was supposed to have been him lying in a pile of his own vomit, dead.

An ashen-faced Jillian complied quickly.

Biting back a curse, Grimm daubed at Quinn's forehead and sat back to wait for the physician.

* * *

The physician arrived, carrying two large satchels and dashing rain from the thinning web of hair that crowned his pate. After questioning nearly everyone in the inn, he conceded to inspect the patients. Moving with surprising grace for such a rotund man, he paced to and fro, scribbling notes in a tiny book. After peering into their eyes, inspecting their tongues, and prodding their distended abdomens, he retreated to the pages of his tiny booklet.

"Give them barley water stewed with figs, honey, and licorice," he instructed after several moments of flipping pages in thoughtful silence. "Nothing else, you understand, for it won't be digested. The stomach is a cauldron in which food is simmered. While their humors are out of balance, nothing can be cooked, and anything with substance will come back up," the physician informed them. "Liquids only."

"Will they be all right?" Jillian asked worriedly. They'd moved the two men into a clean room adjoining Kaley's for easier tending.

The physician frowned, causing lines to fold his double chin as lugubriously as they creased his forehead. "I think they're out of danger. Neither of them appears to have consumed enough to kill him, but I suspect they'll be weak for some time. Lest they try to rise, you'll want to dilute this with water—it's mandrake." He proffered a small pouch. "Soak cloths in it and place them over their faces." The physician struck a lecturing pose, tapping his quill against his booklet. "You must be certain to cover both their nostrils and mouths completely for several minutes. As they inhale, the vapors will penetrate the body and keep them asleep. The spirits recover faster if the humors rest undisturbed. You see, there are four humors and three spirits . . . ah, but forgive me, I'm quite certain you don't wish to hear all of that. Only one who studies with the zeal of a physician might find such facts fascinating." He snapped his booklet closed. "Do as I have instructed and they shall make a full recovery."

"No bleeding?" Hatchard blinked.

The physician snorted. "Fetch a barber if you have an enemy you wish to murder. Fetch a physician if you have an ill patient you wish to revive."

Grimm nodded vehement agreement and rose to escort the physician out.

"Oh, Quinn," Jillian said, and sighed, placing a hand on his clammy forehead. She fussed at his woolens, tucking them snugly around his fevered body.

Standing behind Jillian on one side of Quinn's bed, Kaley beamed at Hatchard, who was perched across the room, applying cool cloths to Ramsay's brow. *She will choose Quinn, didn't I tell you?* she mouthed silently.

Hatchard merely lifted a brow and rolled his eyes.

* * *

When Grimm checked on the men the following morning, their condition had improved; however, they were still sedated, and not in any condition to travel.

Kaley insisted on acquiring the wares the men had originally come for, so Grimm reluctantly agreed to escort Jillian to the fair. Once there, he rushed her through the stalls at a breakneck pace, despite her protests. When a blanket of fog rolled down from the mountains and sheathed Durrkesh in the afternoon, a relieved Grimm informed Jillian it was time to return to the inn.

Fog always made Grimm uneasy, which proved inconvenient, as Scotland was such foggy terrain. This wasn't a normal fog, however; it was a thick, wet cape of dense white clouds that lingered on the ground and swirled around their feet as they walked. By the time they left the market, he could scarcely see Jillian's face a few feet from him.

"I love this!" Jillian exclaimed, slicing her arms through the tendrils of mist, scattering them with her movement. "Fog has always seemed so romantic to me."

"Life has always seemed romantic to you, lass. You used to think Bertie down at the stables spelling your name in horse manure was romantic," he reminded dryly.

"I still do," she said indignantly. "He learned his letters for the express purpose of writing my name. I think that's very romantic." Her brow furrowed as she peered through the soupy mist.

"Obviously you've never had to fight a battle in this crap," he said irritably. Fog reminded him of Tuluth and irrevocable choices. "It's damned hard to kill a man when you can't see where you're slicing with your sword."

Jillian stopped abruptly. "Our lives are vastly different, aren't they?" she asked, suddenly sober. "You've killed many men, haven't you, Grimm Roderick?"

"You should know," he replied tersely. "You watched me do it."

Jillian nibbled her lip and studied him. "The McKane would have killed my family that day, Grimm. You protected us. If a man must kill to protect his clan, there is no sin in that."

Would that he could absolve himself with such generosity, he thought. She still had no idea that the McKane's attack had not been directed at her family. They'd come to Caithness that foggy day long ago only because they'd heard a Berserker might be in residence. She hadn't known that then, and apparently Gibraltar St. Clair had never revealed his secret.

"Why did you leave that night, Grimm?" Jillian asked carefully.

"I left because it was time," he said roughly, shoving a hand through his hair. "I'd learned all your father could teach me, and it was time to move on. There was nothing to hold me at Caithness any longer."

Jillian sighed. "Well, you should know that none of us ever blamed you, despite the fact that we knew you blamed yourself. Even dear Edmund vowed until his last that you were the most noble warrior he'd ever met." Jillian's eyes misted. "We buried him under the apple tree, just as he'd asked," she added, mostly to herself. "I go there when the heather is blooming. He loved white heather."

Grimm stopped, startled. "Buried? Edmund? What?"

"Edmund. He wished to be buried under the apple tree. We used to play there, remember?"

His fingers closed around her wrist. "When did Edmund die? I thought he was with your brother Hugh in the Highlands."

"No. Edmund died shortly after you left. Nearly seven years ago."

"He was scarcely wounded when the McKane attacked," Grimm insisted. "Even your father said he'd easily recover!"

"He took an infection, then caught a lung complication on top of it," she replied, perplexed by his reaction. "The fever never abated. He wasn't in pain long, Grimm. And some of his last words were of you. He swore you defeated the McKane single-handedly and mumbled some nonsense about you being . . . what was it? A warrior of Odin's who could change shapes, or something like that. But then, Edmund was ever fanciful," she added with a faint smile.

Grimm stared at her through the fog.

"Wh-what?" Jillian stammered, confused by the intensity with which he studied her. When he stepped toward her, she backed up slightly, drawing nearer the stone wall that encircled the church behind her.

"What if creatures like that really existed, Jillian?" he asked, his blue eyes glittering. He knew he shouldn't tread on such dangerous territory, but here was a chance to discover her feelings without revealing himself.

"What do you mean?"

"What if it wasn't fantasy?" he pushed. "What if there really were men who could do the things Edmund spoke of? Men who were part mythical beast—endowed with special abilities, skilled in the art of war, almost invincible. What would you think of such a man?"

Jillian studied him intently. "What an odd question. Do *you* believe such warriors exist, Grimm Roderick?"

"Hardly," he said tightly. "I believe in what I can see and touch and hold in my hand. The legend of the Berserkers is nothing more than a foolish tale told to frighten mischievous children into good behavior."

"Then why did you ask me what I would think if they did?" she persisted.

"It was just a hypothetical question. I was merely making conversation, and it was a stupid conversation. By Odin's spear, lass—*nobody* believes in Berserkers!" He resumed walking, gesturing with an impatient scowl for her to follow.

They walked a few yards in silence. Then, without preamble, Grimm said, "Is Ramsay a fine kisser?"

"What?" Jillian nearly fell over her own feet.

"Ramsay, peahen. Does he kiss well?" Grimm repeated irritably.

Jillian battled the urge to beam with delight. "Well," she drawled thoughtfully, "I haven't had much experience, but in all fairness I'd have to say his kiss was the best I've ever had."

Grimm instantly held her trapped her against him, between his hard body and the stone wall. He tilted her head back with a relentless hand beneath her chin. *By the saints, how could the man move so quickly? And how delicious that he did.*

"Let me help you put it in perspective, lass. But doona think for a minute this means anything. I'm just trying to help you understand there are better men out there. Think of this as a lesson, nothing more. I'd hate to see you wed to Logan simply because you thought he was the best kisser, when such a mistaken perception can be so easily remedied."

Jillian raised her hand to his lips, barring him the kiss he threatened. "I don't need a lesson, Grimm. I can make up my own mind. I loathe the thought of you putting yourself out, suffering on my behalf—"

"I'm willing to suffer a bit. Consider it a favor, since we were once childhood friends." He clasped her hand in his and tugged it away from his lips.

"You were never my friend," she reminded him sweetly. "You chased me away constantly—"

"Not the first year—"

"I thought you didn't remember anything about me or your time at Caithness. Isn't that what you told me? And I don't need any favors from you, Grimm Roderick. Besides, what makes you so certain your kiss will be better? Ramsay's positively took my breath away. I could scarcely stand when he was done," she lied shamelessly. "What if you kiss me and it's not as good as Ramsay's kiss? Then what reason would I have for not marrying him?" Having thrown the gauntlet, Jillian felt as smug as a cat as she waited for the breathtaking kiss she knew would follow.

His expression furious, he claimed her mouth with his.

And the earthquake began beneath his toes. Grimm groaned against her lips as the sensation stripped his waning control.

Jillian sighed and parted her lips.

She was being kissed by Grimm Roderick, and it was everything she'd remembered. The kiss they'd shared so long ago in the stables had seemed a mystical experience, and over the years she'd wondered if she glorified it in her mind, only imagining that it had rocked her entire world. But her memory had been accurate. Her body came alive, her lips tingled, her nipples hardened. She wanted every inch of his body, in every way possible. On top of her, beneath her, beside her, behind her. Hard, muscled, demanding—she knew he was man enough to sate the endless hunger she felt for him.

She twined her fingers in his hair and kissed him back, then lost her breath entirely when he deepened the kiss. One hand cupped her jaw; the other slid down the bow of her spine, cupping her hips, molding her body tightly against his. All thought ceased as Jillian gave herself over to what had long been her greatest fantasy: to touch Grimm Roderick as a woman, as his woman. His hands were at her hips, pushing at her gown—and suddenly her hands were at his kilt, tearing at his sporran to get beneath it. She found his thick manhood and brazenly grasped its hardness through the fabric of his plaid. She felt his body stiffen against hers, and the groan of desire that escaped him was the sweetest sound Jillian had ever heard.

Something exploded between them, and there in the

mist and fog of Durrkesh she was so consumed by the need to mate her man that she no longer cared that they stood on a public street. Grimm wanted her, wanted to make love to her—his body told her that clearly. She arched against him, encouraging, entreating. The kiss hadn't merely rendered her breathless, it had depleted the last of her meager supply of sense.

He caught her questing hand and pinned it against the wall above her head. Only when he had secured both her hands did he change the tempo of the kiss, turning it into a teasing, playful flicker of his tongue, probing, then withdrawing, until she was gasping for more. He brushed the length of his body against hers with the same slow, teasing rhythm.

He tore his lips away from hers with excruciating slowness, catching her lower lip between his teeth and tugging gently. Then, with a last luscious lick of his tongue, he drew back.

"So what do you think? Could Ramsay compare to *that*?" he asked hoarsely, eyeing her breasts intently. Only when he ascertained that they didn't rise and fall for a long moment, that he had indeed managed to "kiss her breathless," did he raise his eyes to hers.

Jillian swayed as she struggled to keep her knees from simply buckling beneath her. She stared at him blankly. Words? He thought she could form words after that? He thought she could *think*?

Grimm's gaze searched her face intently, and Jillian saw a look of smug satisfaction banked in his glittering eyes. The faintest hint of a smile curved his lip when she didn't reply but stood gazing, lips swollen, eyes round. "Breathe, peahen. You can breathe now."

Still, she stared at him blankly. Valiantly she sucked in a great, whistling breath of air.

"Hmmph" was all he said as he took her hand and tugged her along. She trotted beside him on rubbery legs, occasionally stealing a peek at the supremely masculine expression of satisfaction on his face.

Grimm didn't speak another word for the duration of their walk back to the inn. That was fine with Jillian; she wasn't certain she could have formed a complete sentence if her life had depended on it. She briefly wondered who, if either of them, had won that skirmish. She concluded weakly that she had. He hadn't been unaffected by their encounter, and she'd gotten the kiss she craved.

When they arrived at the Black Boot, Hatchard informed the strangely taciturn couple that the men, although still quite weak, were impatient to be moved out of the inn. Analyzing all the risks, Hatchard had concurred that it was the wisest course. He had procured a wagon for the purpose, and they would return to Caithness at first light.

Chapter 14

"Tell me a story, Jillian," Zeke demanded, ambling into the solar. "I sore missed you and Mama while you were away." The little boy clambered up onto the settle beside her and nestled in her arms.

Jillian brushed his hair back from his forehead and dropped a kiss on it. "What shall it be, my sweet Zeke? Dragons? Fairies? The selkie?"

"Tell me about the Berserkers," he said decidedly.

"The what?"

"The Berserkers," Zeke said patiently. "You know, the mighty warriors of Odin."

Jillian snorted delicately. "What is it with boys and their battles? My brothers adored that fairy tale."

" 'Tis not a fae-tale, 'tis true," Zeke informed her. "Mama told me they still prowl the Highlands."

"Nonsense," Jillian said. "I shall tell you a fitting tale for a young boy."

"I don't want a fitting tale. I want a story with knights and heroes and quests. And Berserkers."

"Oh my, you are growing up, aren't you?" Jillian said wryly, tousling his hair.

"Course I am," Zeke said indignantly.

"No Berserkers. I shall tell you, instead, of the boy and the nettles."

"Is this another one of your stories with a *point*?" Zeke complained.

Jillian sniffed. "There's nothing wrong with stories that have a point."

"Fine. Tell me about the stupid nettles." He plunked his chin on his fist and glowered.

Jillian laughed at his sullen expression. "I'll tell you what, Zeke. I shall tell you a story with a point, and then you may go find Grimm and ask him to tell you the story of your fearless warriors. I'm certain he knows it. He's the most fearless man I've ever met," Jillian added with a sigh. "Here we go. Pay attention:

"Once upon time there was a wee lad who was walking through the forest and came upon a patch of nettles. Fascinated by the unusual cluster, he tried to pluck it so he might take it home and show his mama. The plant stung him painfully, and he raced home, his fingers stinging. 'I scarcely touched it, Mama!' the lad cried.

" 'That is exactly why it stung you,' his mama replied. 'The next time you touch a nettle, grab it boldly, and it will be soft as silk in your hand and not hurt you in the least.' " Jillian paused meaningfully.

"That's *it*?" Zeke demanded, outraged. "That wasn't a *story*! You *cheated* me!"

Jillian bit her lip to prevent laughter; he looked like an

offended little bear cub. She was tired from the journey and her storytelling abilities were a bit weak at the moment, but there was a useful lesson in it. Besides, the largest part of her mind was preoccupied with thoughts of the incredible kiss she'd received yesterday. It required every shred of her waning self-control to keep from trundling off to find Grimm herself, nestling on his lap and sweetly begging for a bedtime story. Or, more accurately, just a bedtime. "Tell me what it means, Zeke," Jillian coaxed.

Zeke was quiet a moment as he pondered the fable. His forehead was furrowed in concentration, and Jillian waited patiently. Of all the children, Zeke was the cleverest at isolating the moral. "I have it!" he exclaimed. "I shouldna hesitate. I should grab things boldly. If you're undecided, things may sting you."

"Whatever you do, Zeke," Jillian counseled, "do it with all your might."

"Like learning to ride," he concluded.

"Yes. And loving your mama and working with the horses and studying lessons I give you. If you don't do things with all your might, you may end up being harmed by those things you try halfway."

Zeke gave a disgruntled snort. "Well, it's not the Berserker, but I guess it's all right, from a girl."

Jillian made an exasperated sound and hugged Zeke close, heedless of his impatient squirm. "I'm losing you already, aren't I, Zeke?" she asked when the boy raced from the solar in search of Grimm. "How many lads will grow up on me?" she murmured sadly.

* * *

Jillian checked on Quinn and Ramsay before dinner. The two men were sleeping soundly, exhausted by the return trip to Caithness. She hadn't seen Grimm since their return; he'd settled the patients and stalked off. He'd been silent the entire journey and, stung by his withdrawal, she had retreated to the wagon and ridden with the sick men.

Both Quinn and Ramsay still had an unhealthy pallor, and their clammy skin was evidence of the fever's tenacious grip. She pressed a gentle kiss to Quinn's brow and tucked the woolens beneath his chin.

As she left their chambers, her mind slipped back in time to the summer when she'd been nearly sixteen—the summer Grimm left Caithness.

Nothing in her life had prepared Jillian for such a gruesome battle. Neither death nor brutality had visited her sheltered life before, but on that day both came stampeding in on great black chargers wearing the colors of the McKane.

The moment the guards had sounded the alarm her father had barricaded her in her bedroom. Jillian watched the bloody massacre unfolding in the ward below her window with disbelieving eyes. She was besieged by helplessness, frustrated by her inability to fight beside her brothers. But she knew, even had she been free to run the estate, she wasn't strong enough to wield a sword. What harm could she, a mere lass, hope to wreak upon hardened warriors like the McKane?

The sight of so much blood terrified her. When a crafty McKane crept up behind Edmund, taking him unawares, she screamed and pounded her fists against the window, but what meager noise she managed to make could not compete with the raucous din of battle. The burly McKane crushed her brother to the ground with the flat of his battle-ax.

Jillian flattened herself against the glass, clawing

hysterically at the pane with her nails as if she might break through and snatch him from danger. A deep shuddering breath of relief burst from her lungs when Grimm burst into the fray, dispatching the snarling McKane before Edmund suffered another brutal blow. As she watched her wounded brother struggle to crawl to his knees, something deep within her altered so swiftly that she scarce was aware of it: the blood no longer horrified Jillian—nay, she longed to see every last drop of McKane blood spilled upon Caithness's soil. When a raging Grimm proceeded to slay every McKane within fifty yards, it seemed to her a thing of terrible beauty. She'd never seen a man move with such incredible speed and lethal grace—warring to protect all that was nearest to her heart.

After the battle Jillian was lost in the shuffle as her family fretted over Edmund, tended the wounded, and buried the dead. Feeling dreadfully young and vulnerable, she waited on the rooftop for Grimm to respond to her note, only to glimpse him toting his packs toward the stable.

She was stunned. He couldn't leave. Not now! Not when she was so confused and frightened by all that had transpired. She needed him now more than ever.

Jillian raced to the stables as swiftly as her feet could carry her. But Grimm was obdurate; he bid her an icy farewell and turned to leave. His failure to comfort her was the final slight she could endure—she flung herself into his arms, demanding with her body that he shelter her and keep her safe.

The kiss that began as an innocent press of lips swiftly became the confirmation of her most secret dreams: Grimm Roderick was the man she would marry.

As her heart filled with elation, he pulled away from her

and turned abruptly to his horse, as if their kiss had meant nothing to him. Jillian was shamed and bewildered by his rejection, and the frightening intensity of so many new emotions filled her with desperation.

"You can't leave! Not after *that*!" she cried.

"I must leave," he growled. "And *that*"—he wiped his mouth furiously—"should never have happened!"

"But it did! And what if you don't come back, Grimm? What if I never see you again?"

"That's precisely what I mean to do," he said fiercely. "You're not even sixteen. You'll find a husband. You'll have a bright future."

"I've already found my husband!" Jillian wailed. "You *kissed* me!"

"A kiss is not a pledge of marriage!" he snarled. "And it was a mistake. I never should have done it, but you threw yourself at me. What else did you expect me to do?"

"Y-you didn't want to k-kiss me?" Her eyes darkened with pain.

"I'm a man, Jillian. When a woman throws herself at me, I'm as human as the next!"

"You mean you didn't feel it too?" she gasped.

"Feel what?" he snorted. "Lust? Of course. You're a bonny lass."

Jillian shook her head, mortified. Could she have been so mistaken? Could it truly have been only in her mind? "No, I mean—didn't you feel like the world was a perfect place and . . . and we were meant to be . . ." She trailed off, feeling like the grandest fool.

"Forget about me, Jillian St. Clair. Grow up, marry a handsome laird, and forget about me," Grimm said stonily. With one swift move he tossed himself on the horse's back and sped from the stables.

"Don't leave me, Grimm Roderick! Don't leave me like this! I love you!"

But he rode off as if she hadn't spoken. Jillian knew that he'd heard her every word, though she wished he hadn't. She'd not only flung her body at a man who didn't want her, she'd flung her heart after him as he left.

Jillian sighed heavily and closed her eyes. It was a bitter memory, but the sting had eased somewhat since Durrkesh. She no longer believed she had been mistaken about how the kiss had affected them, for in Durrkesh the same thing had happened and she'd seen in his eyes with a woman's sure knowledge that he'd felt it too.

Now all she had to do was get him to admit it.

Chapter 15

After searching for over an hour, Jillian tracked Grimm down in the armory. He was standing near a low wooden table, examining several blades, but she could tell he sensed her presence by the stiffening of his back.

"When I was seventeen, I was near Edinburgh," Jillian informed his rigid back. "I thought I glimpsed you while I was visiting the Hammonds."

"Yes," Grimm replied, intently inspecting a hammered shield.

"It *was* you! I knew it!" Jillian exclaimed. "You were standing near the gatehouse. You were watching me and you looked . . . unhappy."

"Yes," he admitted tightly.

Jillian gazed at Grimm's broad back a moment, uncertain how to vocalize her feelings. It might have helped immensely if she'd understood herself what she wanted to say, but she didn't. It wouldn't have mattered anyway, because he turned and brushed past her with a cool expression that dared her to humble herself by following him.

She didn't.

* * *

She found him later, in the kitchen, scooping a handful of sugar into his pocket.

"For Occam," he said defensively.

"The night I went to the Glannises' ball near Edinburgh," Jillian continued the conversation where, in her mind, it had recently ended, "it was you in the shadows, wasn't it? The fall I turned eighteen."

Grimm sighed heavily. She'd found him yet again. The lass seemed to have a way of knowing where he was, when, and if he was alone. He eyed her with resignation. "Yes," he replied evenly. *That's the fall you became a woman, Jillian. You were wearing ruby velvet. Your hair was uncurled and cascading over your shoulders. Your brothers were so proud of you. I was stunned.*

"When that rogue Alastair—and do you know, I came to find out later he was *married*—took me outside and kissed me, I heard a dreadful racket in the bushes. He said it was likely a ferocious animal."

"And then he told how grateful you should be that you had him to protect you, right?" Grimm mocked. *I almost killed the bastard for touching you.*

"That's not funny. I was truly frightened."

"Were you really, Jillian?" Grimm regarded her levelly. "By which? The man holding you, or the beast in the bush?"

Jillian met his gaze and licked her lips, which were suddenly dry. "Not the beast. Alastair was a blackguard, and had he not been discomfited by the noise, the saints only know what he might have done to me. I was young and, God, I was so innocent!"

"Yes."

"Quinn asked me to marry him today," she announced, watching him carefully.

Grimm was silent.

"I haven't kissed him yet, so I don't know if he's a better kisser. Do you suppose he will be? Better than you, I mean?"

Grimm did not reply.

"Grimm? Will he be a better kisser than you?"

A low rumble filled the air. "Yes, Jillian." Grimm sighed, and went off to find his horse.

* * *

Grimm managed to elude her for almost an entire day. It was late at night before she finally managed to intercept him as he was leaving the ill men's chambers.

"You know, even when I wasn't sure you were really there, I still felt . . . safe. Because you *might* be there."

The hint of an approving smile curved his lips. "*Yes*, Jillian."

Jillian turned away.

"Jillian?"

She froze.

"Have you kissed Quinn yet?"

"No, Grimm."

"Oh. Well, you'd better get on it, lass."

Jillian scowled.

* * *

"I saw you at the Royal Bazaar."

Finally Jillian had succeeded in getting him all to herself

for more than a few forced moments. With Quinn and Ramsay confined to bed, she'd asked Grimm to join her for dinner in the Greathall and had been astonished when he'd readily consented. She sat on one side of the long table, peering at his darkly handsome face through the vines of a candelabrum that held dozens of flickering tapers. They'd been dining in silence, broken only by the clatter of plates and goblets. The maids had retreated to deliver broth to the men upstairs. Three days had passed since they'd returned, during which she'd tried desperately to recapture the tenderness she'd glimpsed in Durrkesh, to no avail. She hadn't been able to get him to stand still long enough to try for another kiss.

Nothing in his face moved. Not a lash flickered. "Yes."

If he answered her with one more annoyingly evasive "yes," she might fly into a rage. She wanted answers. She wanted to know what really went on inside Grimm's head, inside his heart. She wanted to know if the single kiss they'd shared had tilted his world with the same catastrophic force that had leveled hers. "You were spying on me," Jillian accused, peeping through the candles with a scowl. "I wasn't being truthful when I said it made me feel safe. It made me angry," she lied.

Grimm picked up a pewter goblet of wine, drained it, and carefully rolled the cold metal between his palms. Jillian watched his precise, controlled motion and was overwhelmed with hatred for all deliberate actions. Her life had been lived that way, one cautious, precise choice after another, with the exception of when she was around Grimm. She wanted to see him act like she felt: out of control, emotional. Let *him* have an outburst or two. She didn't want kisses offered on the weak excuse of saving her from bad choices. She needed to know she could get beneath his skin the way he penetrated hers. Her hands fisted in her lap, scrunching the fabric of her gown between her fingers.

What would he do if she quit trying to be civil and collected?

She drew a deep breath. "Why did you keep watching me? Why did you leave Caithness, only to follow me all those times?" she demanded with more vehemence than she'd intended, and her words echoed off the stone walls.

Grimm didn't take his eyes from the polished pewter between his palms. "I had to see that all was well with you, Jillian," he said quietly. "Have you kissed Quinn yet?"

"You never breathed a word to me! You'd just come and look at me, and then I'd turn around and you'd be gone."

"I took a vow to keep you from harm, Jillian. It was only natural that I should check on you when you were nearby. Have you kissed Quinn yet?" he demanded.

"Keep me from harm?" Her voice soared with disbelief. "You failed! *You* hurt me worse than anything else ever has in my entire life!"

"Have you kissed Quinn yet?" he roared.

"No! I haven't kissed Quinn yet!" she shouted back. "Is that all you care about? You don't give a damn that *you* hurt *me*."

The goblet clattered to the floor as Grimm lunged to his feet. His hands came down with unbridled fury. Trenchers flew from the table, untouched pottage stew showered the room, chunks of flatbread bounced off the hearth. The candelabrum exploded into the wall and stuck like a cleft foot between the stones. Soapy white candles rained down upon the floor. His rampage didn't stop until the table between them had been swept clean. He paused, panting, his hands splayed wide on the edge of the table, his eyes feverishly bright. Jillian stared at him, stunned.

With a howl of rage, he crashed his hands into the center of six inches of solid oak, and Jillian's hand flew to her throat to smother a cry when the long table split down the middle. His blue eyes blazed incandescently, and she could have sworn he seemed to be growing larger, broader, and more dangerous. She'd certainly gotten the reaction she'd been seeking, and more.

"I know I failed!" he roared. "I know I hurt you! Do you think I haven't had to live with that knowledge?"

Between them, the table creaked and shuddered in an effort to remain whole. The wounded slab tilted precariously. Then, with a groan of defeat, the ends slumped toward the center and it crashed to the floor.

Jillian blinked as she surveyed the wreckage of their meal. No longer seeking to provoke him, she stood dumbfounded by the intensity of his reaction. He knew he'd hurt her? And he cared enough to get this angry at the memory?

"Then why did you come back now?" she whispered. "You could have disobeyed my da."

"I had to see that all is well with you, Jillian," he whispered back across the sea of destruction that separated them.

"I'm well, Grimm," she said carefully. "That means you can go away now," she said, not meaning a breath of it.

Her words evoked no response.

How could a man stand so still that she might think he had been cursed to stone? She couldn't even see his chest rise and fall as she watched him. The breeze blowing in the tall window didn't ruffle him. Nothing touched the man.

God knows she'd never been able to. Hadn't she learned that by now? She'd never been able to reach the real Grimm, the one she'd known that first summer. Why had she believed anything might have changed? Because she was a woman grown? Because she had full breasts and shiny hair and she thought she could entice him near with a man's weakness for a woman? And since he was so damned indifferent to her, why did she even want him?

But Jillian knew the answer to that, even if she didn't understand the how of it. When she'd been a wee lass and tipped her head back to see the wild boy towering above her, her heart had cried welcome. There had been an ancient knowing in her child's breast that had clearly told her no matter what heinous things Grimm stood accused of, she could trust him with her life. She knew he was supposed to belong to her.

"Why don't you just cooperate?" Frustration peeled the words from her lips; she couldn't believe she'd spoken them aloud, but once they were out, she was committed.

"What?"

"Cooperate," she encouraged. "It means to go along. To be obliging."

Grimm stared. "I canna oblige you by leaving. Your da—"

"I am not asking you to leave," she said gently.

Jillian had no idea where she drew her courage from at that moment; she knew only that she was tired of wanting, and tired of being denied. So she stood proudly, moving her body exactly the way it felt whenever Grimm was in the same room: seductive, intense, more alive than at any other time in her life. Her body language must have signified her intent, for he went rigid.

"How would you have me cooperate, Jillian?" he asked in a flat, dead voice.

She approached him, carefully picking her way over broken platters and food. Slowly, as if he were a wild animal, she reached her hand, palm out, toward his chest. He stared at it with a mixture of fascination and mistrust as she placed it upon his chest, over his heart. She felt the heat of him through his linen shirt, felt his body shudder, felt the powerful beating of his heart beneath her palm.

She tilted her head back and gazed up at him. "If you'd truly like to cooperate"—she wet her lips—"kiss me."

It was with a furious gaze that he watched her, but in his eyes Jillian glimpsed the heat he struggled to hide.

"Kiss me," she whispered, never taking her eyes from his. "Kiss me and *then* try to tell me that you don't feel it too."

"Stop it," he ordered hoarsely, backing away.

"Kiss me, Grimm! And not because you think you're doing me a 'favor'! Kiss me because you want to! Once you told me you wouldn't because I was a child. Well, I'm no longer a child, but a woman grown. Other men wish to kiss me. Why not *you*?"

"It isn't like that, Jillian." Both hands moved in frustration to his hair. He buried his fingers deep, then yanked the leather thong off and cast it to the stones.

"Then what is it? Why do Quinn and Ramsay and every other man I've ever known want me, but not you? *Must* I choose one of them? Is it Quinn I should be asking to kiss me? To bed me? To make me a woman?"

He growled, a low warning rumble in his throat. "Stop it, Jillian!"

Jillian tossed her head in a timeless gesture of temptation and defiance. "Kiss me, Grimm, *please*. Just *once*, as if you mean it."

He sprang with such grace and speed that she had no warning. His hands sunk into her hair, pinning her head between his palms and arching her neck back. His lips covered hers and he took the breath from her lungs.

His lips moved over hers with unrestrained hunger, but in the bruising crush of his mouth she sensed a touch of anger—an element she didn't understand. How could he be angry with her when it was so apparent that he'd wanted desperately to kiss her? Of that she was certain. The instant his lips had claimed hers, any doubts she'd previously suffered were permanently laid to rest. She could feel his desire struggling just beneath his skin, waging a mighty battle against his will. *And losing*, she thought smugly as his grip on her hair gentled enough for him to tilt her head, allowing his tongue deeper access to her mouth.

Jillian softened against him, clung to his shoulders, and gave herself over to dizzying waves of sensation. How could a simple kiss resonate in every inch of her body and make it seem the floor was tilting wildly beneath her feet? She kissed him back eagerly and fiercely. After so many years of wanting him, she finally had her answer. Grimm Roderick needed to touch her with the same undeniable need she felt for him.

And she knew that with Grimm Roderick—just once would *never* be enough.

Chapter 16

The kiss spun out and deepened. It was fueled by years of denied emotion, years of disavowed passion that swiftly clawed to the surface of Grimm's resolve. Standing in the Greathall amidst the wreckage of a feast, kissing Jillian, he realized he hadn't just been denying himself peace, he'd been denying himself life. For this was life, this exquisite moment of blending. His Berserker senses were overwhelmed, stupefied by the taste and touch of Jillian. He exulted in the kiss, becoming a bacchanalian worshiper of her lips as he slipped his hands through her hair, following the silken skein down her back.

He kissed Jillian as he'd never kissed any other woman, driven by hunger sprung from the most profane and the most sacred depths of his soul. He wanted her instinctively and would worship her with the primitiveness of his need. The press of her lips thawed the man, the questing probe of her tongue tamed and humbled the icy Viking warrior who had known no warmth until this moment. Desire flattened all his objections and he crushed her body against his, taking her tongue into his mouth as deeply as he knew she would welcome his body into hers.

They slipped and slid on the bits of food scattered across the stones, stopping only at the stability of the wall. Without lifting his mouth from hers, Grimm slid a hand beneath her hips, braced her shoulders against the wall, and drew her legs around his waist. Years of watching her, forbidding himself to touch her, culminated in a display of frenzied passion. Urgency dictated his movements, not patience or skill. His hands slipped from her ankles as her arms entwined his neck and he pushed her gown up and over her calves, revealing her long, lovely legs. He caressed her skin, groaning against her lips when his thumbs found the soft skin of her inner thighs.

The kiss deepened as he took her mouth the same way he'd laid siege to castles: persistently, ruthlessly, and with single-minded focus. There was only Jillian, warm woman in his hands, warm tongue in his mouth, and she matched him, each wordless demand of his body met by hers. She buried her hands in his hair and kissed him back until he was almost breathless himself. Years of need crashed over him as his hands found her breasts and palmed their curves. Her nipples were hard and peaked; he needed more than her lips—he needed to taste every crevice and hollow of her body.

Cradling his face in her hands with a surprisingly strong grip, Jillian forced him to break the kiss. Grimm stared into her eyes, as if to scry the hidden meaning of her gesture. When she tugged his head down to the curve of her breast, he went willingly. He traced a reverent path with his tongue from peak to peak, tugging gently with his teeth before closing his lips on her nipple.

Jillian cried out in abandon and submission, a breathless sound of capitulation to her own desire. She thrust herself so firmly against his hips that the warm hollow between her thighs snugly fitted him with the sensuous finesse of a velvet glove. The barriers between them incensed him, and ripping his kilt from his waist, he eased her gown aside.

Stop! His mind screamed. *She's virgin! Not like this!*

Jillian moaned and rubbed against him.

"Stop," he whispered hoarsely.

Jillian's eyes slitted open. "Not a chance in hell," she said smugly, a smile curving her lower lip.

Her words ripped through him like a heated iron, raising his blood from molten to boiling. He could feel the beast inside him move, yawning with wicked wakefulness.

The Berserker? Now? There was no blood anywhere . . . yet. What would happen when there was?

"Touch me, Grimm. Here." Jillian placed his hand on her breast and drew his head to hers. He groaned and shifted, rubbing in slow, erotic circles against her open thighs. Dimly he realized that the Berserker was rousing into full awareness, but it was somehow different—not violent, but aroused, violently hard, and violently hungry for every taste of Jillian it could have.

He would have laid her back upon the table, but there was no longer a table, so instead he lowered them both into a chair. He shifted so her legs dangled over its arms, and she sat facing him, her hands on his shoulders, her womanhood bared above him. She needed no encouragement to press herself against him, teasing him with the brush of her peaked nipples across his chest. Jillian dropped her head back, baring the slender arch of her neck, and Grimm froze a long moment, drinking in the vision of his lovely Jillian straddling his lap, her narrow waist curving into those lush hips. Although he'd managed to slide her gown from her shoulders, the fabric pooled at her waist, and she was a goddess rising from a sea of silk.

"Christ, you are the most beautiful woman I've ever seen!"

Jillian's head whipped back, and she stared at him. Her look of disbelief quickly became a look of simple pleasure, then an expression of mischievous sensuality. "When I was thirteen," she said, running her fingers down the arrogant curve of his jaw, "I watched you with a maid and I vowed to myself that one day I would do everything to you that she did. Every kiss." She dropped her mouth to his nipple. Her tongue flicked out as she tasted his skin. "Every touch"—she slipped her hand down his abdomen to his hard shaft—"and every taste."

Grimm groaned and grabbed her hand, preventing her fingers from curling around him. If her lovely hand so much as locked around him one time, he would lose control and be inside her in a heartbeat. Calling upon every ounce of his legendary discipline, he held his body away. He refused to hurt her like that. A confession of his own spilled from his lips. "From the day you began to mature, you drove me crazy. I couldn't close my eyes at night without wanting you beneath me. Without wanting to be beside you, *inside* you. Jillian St. Clair, I hope you're as tough as you like to believe you are, because you're going to need every ounce of strength you possess for me tonight." He kissed her, silencing any reply she might have made.

She melted into his kiss until he pulled back. He regarded her tenderly. "And Jillian," he said softly, "I feel it too. I always did."

His words flung open her heart, and the smile she gave him was dazzling. "I *knew* it!" she breathed.

As his hands slid over her heated skin, Jillian abandoned herself to the sensation. When he palmed her between her thighs, she cried out softly and her body bucked against his hand. "More, Grimm. Give me more," she whispered.

His eyes narrowed as he watched her. Pleasure mingled with amazement and desire on her expressive features. He knew he was large, both in width and length, and she needed to be prepared. When she began to move wildly against his hand, he could deny himself no longer. He positioned her above him. "You're in control this way, Jillian. It will hurt you, but you're in control. If it hurts too much, tell me," he said fiercely.

"It's all right, Grimm. I know it will hurt at first, but Kaley told me that if the man is a skilled lover, he will make me feel something more incredible than I've ever felt."

"*Kaley* told you that?"

Jillian nodded. "Please," she breathed. "Show me what she meant."

Grimm expelled a fascinated breath. His Jillian had no fear. He gently slipped the head of his shaft inside her and eased her down, gauging her every flicker of emotion.

Her eyes flared. Her hand flew down to curl around his shaft. "Big," she said worriedly. "Really big. Are you certain this works?"

A grin of pure delight curved his lip. "Very big," he agreed. "But just right to pleasure a woman." He slipped into her carefully. When he met the resistance of the barrier, he paused. Jillian panted softly. "Now, Grimm. Do it."

He closed his eyes briefly and cupped his hands on her bottom, positioning her above him. When he opened his eyes, resolve glimmered in their depths. With one firm thrust he pierced the barrier.

Jillian gasped. "That wasn't so bad," she breathed after a moment. "I thought it would really hurt." When he began to move slowly, her eyes flared. "Oh!"

She cried out, and he silenced her with a kiss. Moving slowly, he rocked her against him until any trace of pain in her wide eyes disappeared and her face was illuminated by the anticipation of what she sensed was dancing just out of her reach. She initiated an erotic, circular movement with her hips, nipping her lower lip between her teeth.

He watched her, entranced by her innate sensuality. She was abandoned, uninhibited, plunging wholly into their intimate play without reservation. Her lips curved deliciously as a long slow thrust of his hips hinted at the passion to come, and he smiled with wicked delight.

He raised her up and switched places with her, placing her on the chair. Kneeling, he pulled her forward, wrapped her legs around his waist, and slid deep within her, pressing with exquisite friction against the mysterious place deep inside her that would cast her over the edge. He teased the nub between her legs until she squirmed against him, begging with her body for what only he could give her.

The Berserker exulted within him, frolicking in a way he had never thought possible.

When she cried out and shuddered against him, Grimm Roderick made a husky, rich sound that was more than laughter; it was the resonant knell of liberation. His triumph quickly became a groan of release. The sensation of her body shuddering around him so tightly was more than he could resist, and he exploded inside her.

Jillian clung to him, gasping as an unfamiliar sound penetrated her reeling mind. Her muscles fused to molten uselessness, her head fell forward, and she peered through her hair at the nude warrior-man kneeling before her.

"Y-you can laugh! Really, truly laugh!" she exclaimed breathlessly.

He traced his thumbs up the inside of her thighs, over the light skein of blood. Blood of her virginity marked her pale thighs. "Jillian, I . . . I . . . oh . . ."

"Don't freeze up on me, Grimm Roderick," Jillian said instantly.

He began shaking violently. "I can't help it," he said tightly, knowing they weren't talking about the same thing at all. "The Greathall," he muttered. "I am such an ass. I am so damned—"

"Stop it!" Jillian grabbed his head with both hands, leveling him with a furious look. "I wanted this," she said intensely. "I waited for this, I needed this. Don't you dare regret it! I don't, and I never will."

Grimm froze, transfixed by the blood that marked her thighs, waiting for the sensation of lost time to begin. It wouldn't be long before the darkness claimed him and the violence ensued.

But moments ticked by, and it didn't happen. Despite the raging energy that flooded his body, the madness never came.

He gazed at her, dumbfounded. The beast within him was fully awakened, yet tame. How could that be? No bloodlust, no need for violence, all the good things the Berserker brought—and none of the danger.

"Jillian," he breathed reverently.

Chapter 17

"How are you feeling?" Grimm asked quietly. Punching the pillows, he maneuvered Quinn to a sitting position. The window fittings were tied loosely back, swags framed the casements, and the crescent moon cast enough light that his heightened vision allowed him to function as if it were broad daylight.

Quinn blinked groggily at Grimm and peered through the gloom. "Please don't." He groaned when Grimm reached for a cloth.

Grimm stopped in mid-reach. "Doona what? I was merely going to wipe your brow."

"Don't smother me with any more of that blasted mandrake," Quinn muttered. "Half the reason I feel so lousy is because Kaley keeps knocking me out."

One bed over, Ramsay rumbled assent. "Don't let her make us sleep anymore, man. My head is splitting from that crap and my tongue feels as if some wee furry beastie crawled in, kicked over on its back, and died there. Three days ago. And now it's rotting—"

"Enough! Do you have to be so descriptive?" Quinn made a face of disgust as his empty stomach heaved.

Grimm raised his hands in a gesture of assent. "No more mandrake. I promise. So how are you two feeling?"

"Like bloody hell," Ramsay groaned. "Light a candle, would you? I can't see a thing. What happened? Who poisoned us?"

A dark expression flitted across Grimm's face. He stepped into the hallway to light a taper, then lit several candles by the bedside and returned to his seat. "I suspect it was meant for me, and my guess is the poison was in the chicken."

"The chicken?" Quinn exclaimed, wincing as he sat up straight. "Didn't the barkeep bring it? Why would the barkeep try to poison you?"

"I doona think it was the barkeep. I think it was the butcher's attempt at revenge. My theory is that if either of you had consumed the entire basket, you would have died. It was intended for me. But the two of you split it."

"That doesn't make any sense if the butcher meant it for you, Grimm," Quinn protested. "He'd seen you in action. Any man knows you can't poison a Ber—"

"Bastard as ornery as myself," Grimm roared, drowning out Quinn's last word before Ramsay heard it.

Ramsay clutched his head. "Och, man, quit bellowing! You're killing me."

Quinn mouthed a silent "sorry" at Grimm, followed by an apologetic whisper: "It's the lingering effects of the mandrake. I'm stupid right now."

"Eh? What?" Ramsay said. "What are you two whispering about?"

"Even between the two of us we didn't even eat all the chicken," Quinn continued, evading Ramsay's query. "And I thought the innkeeper dismissed the butcher after that incident. I asked him to do it myself."

"What incident?" Ramsay asked.

"Apparently not." Grimm ran a hand through his hair and sighed.

"Did you get his name?" Ramsay asked.

"Who? The innkeeper?" Quinn gave him a puzzled look.

"No, the butcher." Ramsay rolled his eyes.

"Why?" Quinn asked blankly.

"Because the bastard poisoned a Logan, you fool. That doesn't happen without recompense."

"No vengeance," Grimm warned. "Just forget it, Logan. I've seen what you do when you focus on vengeance. The two of you came out of this bungled attempt unharmed. That does not justify murdering a man, no matter how much he might deserve it for other things."

"Where's Jillian?" Quinn changed the subject quickly. "I have these foggy memories of a goddess hovering over my bed."

Ramsay snorted. "Just because you think you were making some progress before we were both poisoned doesn't mean you've won her, de Moncreiffe.

Grimm winced inwardly and sat in pensive silence while Quinn and Ramsay argued back and forth about Jillian. The men were still at it some time later and didn't even notice when Grimm left the room.

* * *

Having spent the early hours of dawn with Quinn and Ramsay, Grimm checked in on Jillian, who was still sleeping soundly as he'd left her, curled on her side beneath a mound of blankets. He longed to ease himself into bed beside her, to experience the pleasure of waking up to the sensation of holding her in his arms, but he couldn't risk being seen leaving Jillian's chambers once the castle roused.

So, as morning broke over Caithness, he nodded to Ramsay, who'd managed to stumble down the stairs in search of solid food, whistled to Occam, and swung himself onto the stallion's bare back. He headed for the loch, intending to immerse his overheated body in icy water. The completion he'd experienced with Jillian had only whetted his appetite for her, and he was afraid if she so much as smiled at him today he would fall on her with all the slathering grace of a starved wolf. Years of denied passion were free, and he realized he possessed a hunger for Jillian that could never be sated.

He nudged Occam around a copse of trees and paused, savoring the quiet beauty of the morning. The loch rippled, a vast silvery mirror beneath rosy clouds. Lofty oaks waved black branches against the red sky.

Strains of a painfully off-key song carried faintly on the breeze, and Grimm circumvented the loch carefully, guiding his horse past sinkholes and rocky terrain, following the sound until, rounding a thick cluster of growth, he saw Zeke hunched near the water. The lad's legs were tucked up, his forearms resting on his knees, and he was rubbing his eyes.

Grimm drew Occam to a halt. Zeke was half crying the broken words of an old lullaby. Grimm wondered who had managed to hurt his feelings this early in the morning. He watched the lad, trying to decide what was the best way to approach him without offending the child's dignity. As he hesitated in the shadows, any decision on his part was rendered obsolete as the crackling of brush and bracken alerted him to an intruder. He scanned the surrounding forest, but before he had detected the source, a snarling animal sprang from the woods a few feet behind Zeke. A great, mangy mountain cat burst onto the bank of the loch, thick white spittle foaming on its snout. It snarled, baring lethal white fangs. Zeke turned, and his song warbled to a stop. His eyes widened in horror.

Grimm instantly flung himself from Occam's back, yanked his *sgain dubh* from his thigh, and drew it across his hand, causing blood to well in his palm. In less than a heartbeat, the sight of the crimson beads roused the Viking warrior and set the Berserker free.

Moving with inhuman speed, he snatched Zeke up and tossed him on his stallion and smacked Occam on the rump. Then he did what he so despised . . . he lost time.

* * *

"Somebody help!" Zeke shrieked as he rode into the bailey on Occam's back. "You must help Grimm!"

Hatchard burst from the castle to find Zeke perched on Occam's back, hanging on to his mane with whitened knuckles. "Where?" he shouted.

"The loch! There's a crazed mountain cat and it almost ate me and he threw me on the horse and I rode by myself but it attacked Grimm and he's going to be hurt!"

Hatchard sped off for the loch, unaware of two other people who'd been alerted by the shouting and were hot on his heels.

* * *

Hatchard found Grimm standing motionless, a black shadow against the misty red sky. He was facing the water, standing amidst the scraps of what had once been an animal. His arms and face were covered with blood.

"Gavrael," Hatchard said quietly, using his real name in hopes of reaching the man within the beast.

Grimm did not reply. His chest rose and fell rapidly. His body was pumped up with the massive quantities of oxygen a Berserker inhaled to compensate for the preternatural rage. The veins in his corded forearms pulsed dark blue against his skin, and, Hatchard marveled, he seemed twice as large as he normally was. Hatchard had seen Grimm in the thick of Berserker rage several times when he'd trained the fosterling, but the mature Grimm wore it far more dangerously than the stripling lad had.

"Gavrael Roderick Icarus McIllioch," Hatchard said. He approached him from the side, trying to enter Grimm's line of vision in as innocuous a manner as possible. Behind him, two figures stopped in the shadows of the forest. One of them gasped softly and echoed the name.

"Gavrael, it's me, Hatchard," Hatchard repeated gently.

Grimm turned and looked directly at the chief man-at-arms. The warrior's blue eyes were incandescent, glowing like banked coals, and Hatchard received a disconcerting lesson in what it felt like to have someone look straight through him.

A strangled noise behind him compelled Hatchard's attention. Turning, he realized Zeke had trailed him.

"Ohmigod," Zeke breathed. He trundled closer, peering intently at the ground, then paused mere inches from Grimm. His eyes widened enormously as he scanned the small bits of what had once been a rabid mountain cat, savage enough to shred a grown man and, driven by the blood sickness, mad enough to attempt it. His astonished gaze drifted upward to Grimm's brilliant blue eyes, and he nearly rose on his tiptoes, staring. "He's a Berserker!" Zeke breathed reverently. "Look, his eyes are glowing! They *do* exist!"

"Fetch Quinn, Zeke. Now," Hatchard commanded. "Bring *no one else but Quinn*, no matter what. Do you understand? And not a word of this to anyone!"

Zeke stole one last worshiping look. "Aye," he said, then fled to get Quinn.

CHAPTER 18

"I TRULY DOUBT HE RIPPED THE ANIMAL TO PIECES, Zeke. It isn't healthy to exaggerate," Jillian reprimanded, masking her amusement to protect the boy's sensitive feelings.

"I didn't exaggerate," Zeke said passionately, "I told the truth! I was down by the loch and a rabid mountain cat attacked me and Grimm threw me on his horse and caught the beastie in mid-leap and killed it with one flick o' his wrist! He's a Berserker, he is! I *knew* he was special! Hmmph!" The little boy snorted. "He doesn't need to be a puny laird—he's king o' the warriors! He's a legend!"

Hatchard took Zeke firmly by the arm and tugged him away from Jillian. "Go find your mother, lad, and do it *now*." He fixed Zeke with a glower that dared him to disobey, then snorted as the boy fled the room. He met Jillian's gaze and shrugged. "You know how wee lads are. They must have their fairy tales."

"Is Grimm all right?" Jillian asked breathlessly. Her entire body ached in a most pleasurable way. Every move was a subtle reminder of the things he'd done to her, the things she'd begged him to do before the night had ended.

"Right as rain," Hatchard replied dryly. "The animal was indeed rabid, but don't worry, it didn't manage to bite him."

"Did Grimm kill it?" A rabid mountain cat could decimate an entire herd of sheep in less than a fortnight. They wouldn't usually attack a man, but apparently Zeke had been small enough and the beast had been sick enough to try it.

"Yes," Hatchard replied tersely. "He and Quinn are burying it now," he lied with cool aplomb. There hadn't been enough left to bury, but neither love nor gold could have persuaded Hatchard to tell Jillian that. He winced inwardly. Had the infected mountain cat bitten Zeke even once, the boy would have been contaminated by the ferocious animal's blood sickness and died within days, foaming at the mouth in excruciating agony. Praise the saints Grimm had been there, and praise Odin for his special talents, or Caithness would have been singing funeral dirges and weeping.

"Zeke rode Occam all by himself," Jillian marveled aloud.

Hatchard glanced up and smiled faintly. "That he did, and it saved his life, milady."

Jillian's expression was thoughtful as she headed for the door. "If Grimm hadn't believed in the lad enough to try to teach him, Zeke might never have been able to escape."

"Where are you going?" Hatchard said quickly.

Jillian paused at the entrance. "Why, to find Grimm, of course." To tell him she was wrong to have doubted him. To see his face, to glimpse the newfound intimacy in his eyes.

"Milady, leave him be for a time. He and Quinn are talking and he needs to be alone."

In a flash Jillian felt thirteen again, excluded from the company of the man she loved. "Did he say that? That he needed to be alone?"

"He's washing up in the loch," Hatchard said. "Just give him time, all right?"

Jillian sighed. She would wait for him to come to her.

* * *

"Grimm, I didn't want to say anything before, but I paid that innkeeper a small fortune to get rid of the butcher," Quinn said as he paced the edge of the loch. Grimm rose from the icy water, finally clean again, and scowled at the remains of the animal.

Quinn caught his look and said, "Don't even start. You saved his life, Grimm. I won't hear one word of your self-loathing for being a Berserker. It's a gift, do you hear me? A gift!"

Grimm exhaled dismally and made no response.

Quinn continued where he'd left off. "As I was saying, I paid the man. If he didn't get rid of the butcher, then I'm going to be heading back to Durrkesh to get some answers."

Grimm waved his hand, dismissing Quinn's concern. "Doona bother, Quinn. It wasn't the butcher."

"What? What do you mean, it wasn't the butcher?"

"It wasn't even the chicken. It was the whisky."

Quinn blinked rapidly several times. "Then why did you say it was the chicken?"

"I trust *you*, Quinn. I doona know Ramsay. The poison was root of thmsynne. The root loses its poisonous properties if simmered, broiled, or roasted. It must be crushed and diluted, and its effect is enhanced by alcohol. Besides, I found the remainder of the bottle downstairs the next morning. Whoever it was wasn't very thorough."

"But I didn't drink any whisky with you," Quinn protested.

"You didn't know you drank whisky." Grimm gave him a wry, apologetic twist of his lips. "I dumped my final mug of whisky, poured from the drugged bottle, over the chicken to get rid of it because I was sick of drinking and getting ready to leave. The poison is odorless until digested, and even my senses couldn't pick it up. Once it mixes with the body's fluids, however, it takes on a noxious odor."

"Christ, man!" Quinn gave him a dark look. "Of all the luck. So who do you think did it?"

Grimm studied him intently. "I've given that a lot of thought over the past few days. The only thing I can conclude is that the McKane have ferreted me out again somehow."

"Don't they know poison doesn't work on a Berserker?"

"They've never succeeded in taking one alive to question."

"So they may not know what feats one of you is capable of? Even they don't know how to kill you?"

"Correct."

Quinn mulled this new information over a moment. Then his eyes clouded. "If that's the case, if the McKane have indeed found you again, Grimm, what's to stop them from following you to Caithness?" Quinn asked carefully. "Again."

Grimm raised his head with a stricken look.

* * *

Jillian didn't see Grimm the rest of the day. Quinn informed her that he'd gone riding and would likely not return until nightfall. Night came and the castle retired. Peering out the casement window, she spied Occam wandering the bailey. Grimm had returned.

Draping a plush woolen over her chemise, Jillian slipped from her chambers. The castle was quiet, its occupants sleeping.

"Jillian."

Jillian stopped in mid-step. She turned, suppressing her impatience. She needed to see Grimm, to touch him again, to investigate their newfound intimacy and to revel in her womanhood.

Kaley Twillow was hurrying down the corridor toward her, tugging a wrapper around her shoulders in the chilly air. The older woman's chestnut curls were unpinned and rumpled, and her face was flushed with sleep.

"I heard your door open," Kaley said. "Did you want something from the kitchen? You should have called for me. I'll be happy to get it for you. What did you want? Shall I prepare you a mug of warm milk? Some bread and honey?"

Jillian demurred and patted Kaley's shoulder reassuringly. "Don't worry, Kaley. You go back to bed. I'll get it."

"It's no problem. I was considering a snack myself." Worried eyes flickered over Jillian's impromptu robe of soft woolen.

"Kaley," Jillian tried again, "you needn't worry about me. I'll be fine. Really, I'm just a bit restless and—"

"You're going to see Grimm."

Jillian flushed. "I must. I need to speak with him. I can't sleep. There are things I must say—"

"That can't wait until the morning light?" Kaley eyed

the sheer chemise peeking from beneath the woolen. "You're not even properly dressed," she said reprovingly. "If you find him clad in that, you'll get more than you bargained for."

"You don't understand," Jillian said, sighing.

"Oh, but my dear lass, I do. I saw the remains of the Greathall this morning."

Jillian swallowed and said nothing.

"Shall we cut to the quick of it?" Kaley said tersely. "I'm not so old that I can't recall what it's like. I loved a man like him once. I understand what you're feeling, perhaps even more so than you do, so let me put it into plain words. Quinn is sexual. Ramsay Logan is sexual, and the power they exude promises a rollicking good time." Kaley took Jillian's hands in hers and regarded her soberly. "But Grimm Roderick, ah, he's an entirely different animal, he's not merely sexual. He drips sensual power, and Jillian, sensual power can reshape a woman."

"You *do* know what I mean!"

"I'm flesh and blood too, lass." Kaley laid a gentle hand against her cheek. "Jillian, I've watched you mature with pride, love, and lately a touch of fear. I'm proud because you have a good, fearless heart and a strong will. I'm fearful because your will can make you headstrong beyond compare. Heed my words before you commit yourself to a course that is irrevocable: Sexual men can be forgotten, but a sensual man lingers in a woman's heart forever."

"Oh, Kaley, it's too late," Jillian confessed. "He's in there already."

Kaley drew her into her arms. "I was afraid of that. Jillian, what if he leaves you? How will you handle that? How will you go on? A man like Quinn would never leave. A man like Grimm, well, the men who are larger than life are also the most dangerous to a woman. Grimm is unpredictable."

"Do you regret yours?"

"My what?"

"Your man like Grimm."

Kaley's features softened rapturously, and her expression was answer enough.

"And there you have it," Jillian pointed out gently. "Kaley, if I knew that I could only have a few nights in that man's arms or nothing, I would take those magic nights and use them to keep me warm for the rest of my life."

Kaley swallowed audibly, her eyes filled with empathy. She smiled faintly. "I understand, lass," she said finally.

"Good night, my dear Kaley. Go back to bed, and permit me the same sweet dreams you once dreamt yourself."

"I love you, lass," Kaley said gruffly.

"I love you too, Kaley," Jillian replied with a smile as she slipped down the corridor to find Grimm.

* * *

Jillian entered his chambers quietly. He wasn't there. She sighed, frustrated, and moved restlessly about his room. His chambers were spartan, as clean and disciplined as the man. Nothing was out of order except for a mussed pillow. Smiling, she stepped to the bed and picked it up to plump it. She pressed it to her face for a moment and inhaled his crisp masculine scent. Her smile faltered and became quiet wonder when she spied the tattered book the pillow had been concealing. *Aesop's Fables.* It was the illustrated manuscript she'd given him nearly a dozen years before, that first snowy Christmas they'd spent together. She dropped the pillow and gathered the manuscript, stroking it tenderly with her fingertips. The pages were frayed, the illustrations faded, and little notes and oddities peeked out from the binding. He'd been carrying it all these years, tucking in his mementos, much as she had done with her volume. She cradled it wonderingly. This book told her everything she needed to know. Grimm Roderick was a warrior, a hunter, a guard, an often hard man who carried a tattered copy of *Aesop's Fables* wherever he went, occasionally secreting dried flowers and verses between the pages. She flipped through, stopping at a note that had been crumpled and resmoothed dozens of times. *I will be on the roof at gloaming. I must speak to you tonight, Grimm!*

He'd never forgotten her.

Sensitive yet strong, capable yet vulnerable, earthy and sensual. She was hopelessly in love with him.

"I kept it."

Jillian spun around. Once again she hadn't heard a sound when he'd entered the room. He was framed in the doorway, his eyes dark and unreadable.

"I see that," she replied in a hushed voice.

He crossed the room and dropped himself into a chair before the fire, his back to her. Jillian stood, hugging the precious book to her chest in silence. They were so close to the intimacy she'd always wanted from him that she was afraid to break the spell with words.

"I can't believe you're not bombarding me with questions," he said carefully. "Like why did I keep it?"

"Why did you keep it, Grimm?" she asked, but it really didn't matter why. He had carried it with him to this day, and that was enough.

"Come here, lass."

Jillian gently placed the book on a table and approached him slowly. She hesitated a few paces from his side.

Grimm's hand shot out and fastened on her wrist. "Jillian, please." His voice was so low, it was almost inaudible.

"Please what?" she whispered.

Swiftly he flicked his wrist and she was standing before him, captured between his thighs. His eyes were fixed in the vicinity of her navel, as if he couldn't summon the strength to raise them. "Kiss me, Jillian. Touch me. Show me I'm alive," he whispered back.

Jillian bit her lip as his words slammed into her heart. The most valiant, intense man she'd ever known was afraid he wasn't fully alive. He raised his head and she cried out softly at his expression. It was dark, his eyes swirling with shadows, memories of times she couldn't even begin to comprehend. She cradled his face between her hands and kissed him, lingering on his lower lip, savoring the sensual curve.

"You're the most incredibly alive man I've ever known."

"Am I, Jillian? Am I?" he asked desperately.

How could he wonder about such a thing? His lips were warm and vital, his hands moved across her skin, awakening nerve endings she'd never suspected existed. "Why did you keep the book, Grimm?"

His hands fastened possessively on her waist. "I kept it to remind me that although there is evil, there is sometimes beauty and light. You, Jillian. You were always my light."

Jillian's heart soared. She'd come seeking confirmation of their fragile intimacy, to prove to herself that the tenderness and physical affection Grimm had offered her the night before had not been an isolated instance. She'd never dreamed that he might offer her words of . . . love? For what else were words like that if not words of love?

Her dreams were finally being realized. She'd always known there was a bond between herself and her wild-eyed beast-boy, but coming together as man and woman exceeded all her childhood fantasies.

Rising to his feet, Grimm pulled her against the muscled length of his body, unselfconsciously offering her the powerful evidence of his desire. The mere brush of him between her thighs made her shiver breathlessly.

"I can't get enough of you, Jillian," he breathed, fascinated by the sensual widening of her eyes, by the instinctive way her tongue wet the fullness of her lower lip. He captured it and kissed her slowly with scorching, lingering, mind-stealing kisses as he backed her toward the bed. Halfway there, he seemed to change his mind. He cupped her shoulders in his strong hands and turned her in his arms. Jillian had thought the sensation of him pressed against her thighs was too exciting to bear, but now the hard length of him rose hot against her, and she pushed back into him in a wordless plea. His hands began a languid journey over her body. He caressed the soft curve of her hips, slid his palms up the bow of her back, then slipped his arms around her to catch her breasts, finding the sensitive nipples and tugging them gently through the thin fabric of her chemise.

Gathering her hair in his hand, he tenderly tugged it to the side and kissed the exposed nape of her neck. The brief nip of his teeth caused her to arch her back and surge against him.

He edged her forward, guiding her past the bed and toward the wall. Pressing her close to the smooth stones, he twined his fingers between hers with his palms flush to the backs of her hands. He placed her palms against the wall above her head.

"Doona remove your hands from the wall, Jillian. No matter what I do, hold on to the wall and simply feel . . ."

Jillian held on to the wall as if it were her last hold on sanity. When he slipped her chemise from her body, she shivered as the cool air met her heated skin. His hands brushed the firm underside of her breasts, trailed over her waist, and hesitated on her hips. Then his fingers tightened on her skin and his tongue traced a lingering path down the hollow of her spine. She leaned against the wall, her palms flat, swaying with pleasure. By the time he was done, there was not one inch of her skin he hadn't kissed or caressed with the velvety stroke of his tongue.

Now she understood why he'd told her to hold on to the wall. It had nothing to do with the wall itself and everything to do with preventing her from touching him. Being touched by Grimm Roderick, yet being unable to touch back, overwhelmed her senses and forced her to accept pure pleasure with no distractions.

He dropped to his knees behind her, and he told her—both with his hands and with a low rush of words—how beautiful she was, what she did to him, and how very much he wanted her, *needed* her.

He slid his hands up the insides of her thighs, trailing slow, heated kisses across the round curves of her bottom. A sudden gasp of pleasure escaped her when his hand found the sensitive center between her legs. As his fingers stroked her with an irresistible friction that coaxed a whimper from her throat, he nipped her buttock.

"Grimm!" she gasped.

Laughter laced with something dangerously erotic heightened her arousal even further. "Hands on the wall," he reminded when she started to turn. He eased her thighs apart and maneuvered himself so that he was on the floor, gazing up at her, his face only inches from the part of her that was aching for his touch. She opened her mouth to protest his being so intimately positioned, when the heat of his tongue silenced any admonishment she may have made. Her neck arched and it took every ounce of her will not to scream from the stunning pleasure he ignited within her.

Then her gaze was drawn down to the magnificent warrior kneeling between her thighs. The vision of his face, intense with passion, coupled with the incredible feelings he was coaxing forth, shortened her breath to tiny, helpless pants. She rocked softly against him, making small, breathless cries unlike any sound she'd ever thought to make before.

"I'm going to fall," she gasped.

"I'll catch you, Jillian."

"But I don't think we should—oh!"

"Don't think," he agreed.

"But my legs . . . won't . . . hold!"

He laughed, and with a swift tug yanked her down on top of him. They tumbled onto a woven rug in a press of heated skin and tangled limbs. "And to think you were afraid to fall," he teased.

She savored the incredible closeness of their bodies, and at that moment she fully let go. As she fell against him, she fell even more completely in love with him, into a mindless passion. He *would* always catch her—that she knew without a doubt. They rolled across the rug in a playful skirmish for the superior position, then he flipped her so suddenly that she landed on her hands and knees. In an instant he was behind her, nudging into the cleft between the soft curves of her bottom, and she gasped aloud.

"Now," she cried.

"Now," he agreed, and drove into her.

She felt him deep inside her, filling her, joining them together. Cupping her breasts, he thrust inside her, and she felt so connected to him that it took her breath away. She made a sound of supreme dismay when he slipped out, leaving an ache deep inside her, and she purred with pleasure when he filled her again so deeply that she arched her back and rose up against him, her shoulders pressing against his hard chest

He must have awakened something inside her, Jillian decided, because it took only a few more thrusts for her body to break free and shatter into a thousand quivering pieces. She would *never* get enough of him.

* * *

Hours later, a sated Jillian was lying in a puddle of contentment on his bed. When his hands began their sensual dance upon her body, she sighed. "I couldn't possibly feel that again, Grimm," she protested weakly. "I haven't a muscle left in my body, and I simply couldn't . . ."

Grimm smiled wickedly. "When I was younger I stayed with Gypsies for a time."

Jillian lay back against the pillow, wondering what this had to do with the earth-shattering explosions he'd been lavishing upon her.

"They had a strange ceremony they practiced to induce 'Vision.' It didn't rely upon a mixture of herbs and spices or the smoking of a pipe. It relied upon sexual excess to achieve a state that transcended the everyday frame of mind. They would place one of their seers in a tent with a dozen women, who repeatedly brought him to climax until he was begging for no more pleasure. The Rom claim climax releases something in the body that causes the spirit to soar, ripping it free from its earthly mooring, opening it to the extraordinary."

"I believe that." Jillian was fascinated. "It makes me feel as if I've drunk too much sweet wine—my head gets swimmy and my body feels weak and strong at the same time." When his fingers found the juncture of her thighs, she shivered. With a few deft movements, he had her tingling, hungering all over again, and when he brought her to a swift release with his hands, it was even more exquisite than the last. "Grimm!" Heat erupted inside her, and she shuddered. He didn't remove his hand, but cupped her gently until she calmed. Then he began again, moving his fingers in a light teasing motion over the sensitive nub.

"And again, my sweet Jillian, until you can no longer look at me without knowing what I can do to you, where I can take you, how many times I can take you there."

* * *

For Grimm there was no rest that night. He paced the stone floor, kicking at the lambskin rugs, wondering how he was going to bring himself to do the right thing this time. Never in his life had he allowed himself to get too attached to anything or anyone, because he'd always known that at any moment he might have to leave, fleeing the hunt the McKane perpetuated against any man suspected of being Berserk.

They'd found him in Durrkesh. Quinn was right. What was to prevent them from coming to Caithness? They could have easily followed the lumbering cart upon which they'd transported the sick men. And if they descended upon Caithness again, what harm would this blessed place suffer? What harm might they do to Jillian's home and Jillian herself? Edmund had died as a result of the last McKane attack. Maybe he'd caught a lung fever, but if he hadn't been wounded to begin with, he would never have caught the disease that had claimed his young life.

Grimm couldn't live with the thought of bringing harm—again—to Caithness and Jillian.

He stopped by the bed, gazed down at her, and watched her with his heart in his eyes. *I love you, Jillian,* he willed to her sleeping form. *Always have, and always will. But I'm Berserk, and you—you're the best of life. I have an insane old da and a crumbling pile of rocks to call home. It's no life for a lady.*

He forced his dark thoughts away, scattering them with his formidable will. Sinking into her body was all he wanted to contemplate. These past two days with Jillian had been the best two days of his life. He should be content with that, he told himself.

She rolled over in her sleep, her hand falling palm open, fingers slightly curled. Her golden hair fanned out across the white pillows, her full breasts spilled above the downy linen. Just one more day, he promised himself, and one more blissful, magical, incredible night. Then he'd leave, before it was too late.

CHAPTER 19

QUINN AND RAMSAY SACKED THE KITCHENS OF CAITHNESS at dawn. Not one piece of fruit, not one slab of meat, not a single savory morsel was spared.

"Christ, I feel like I haven't eaten solid food in weeks!"

"We damn near haven't. Broth and bread don't count as real food." Ramsay tore off a chunk of smoked ham with his teeth. "I haven't had an appetite until now. That damn poison made me so sick, I thought I might never want to eat again!"

Quinn palmed an apple and bit into it with relish. Platters were piled haphazardly atop every available surface. The maids would faint when they discovered the men had wiped out all the food that had been prepared for the coming weekend.

"We'll hunt and replenish." Quinn felt mildly guilty as his gaze swept the decimated larder. "You up to a bit of hunting, Ram, my man?"

"So long as it's wearing a skirt," Ramsay said with a gusty sigh, "and answers to the name of Jillian."

"I don't think so," Quinn replied acerbically. "Perhaps you didn't notice, but Jillian obviously has a bit of a *tendre* for me. If I hadn't gotten sick at Durrkesh, I would have proposed marriage and we would be betrothed by now."

Ramsay took a deep slug of whisky and placed the bottle on the counter with a thump. "You really are dense, aren't you, de Moncreiffe?"

"Don't tell me you think it's you." Quinn rolled his eyes.

"Of course not. It's that bastard Roderick. It always has been, ever since we got here." Ramsay's dark expression was murderous. "And after what happened two nights ago . . ."

Quinn stiffened. "What happened two nights ago?"

Ramsay took another swallow, swished it over his tongue, and brooded a silent moment. "Did you notice the long table in the hall is gone, Quinn?"

"Now that you mention it, yes, it is. What happened to it?"

"I saw pieces of it out back behind the bothy. It was shattered down the center."

Quinn said nothing. He knew of only one man who could shatter a table of such massive proportions with his bare hands.

"I came down yesterday to find the maids sweeping food off the floor. One of the candelabra was wedged into the wall. Someone had a helluva fight in there two nights ago. But nobody has breathed a word about it, have they?"

"What are you saying, Logan?" Quinn asked grimly.

"Just that the only two people who were well enough to dine in the hall two nights ago were Grimm and Jillian. They obviously fought, but today Grimm didn't seem bitter. And Jillian, why, the woman has been wreathed in smiles and good humor. Matter of fact, just as a little test, what say we go wake Grimm right now and talk to him about it? That is, if he's not otherwise occupied."

"If you're insinuating that Jillian might be in his chambers, you're a stupid bastard and I'll call you out for it," Quinn snapped. "And maybe there was a fight in the hall between them, but I guarantee you that Grimm is far too honorable to seduce Jillian. Besides, he can't even bring himself to say a civil word to her. He certainly couldn't be nice to her long enough to seduce her."

"You don't find it curious that just when it seemed like you were making progress with her, you and I get poisoned and put out of the running, but he doesn't?" Ramsay asked. "I'd say it was suspiciously convenient. I think it's damned odd that he didn't get sick too."

"He didn't consume any of the poison," Quinn defended.

"Maybe that's because he knew what was poisoned in advance," Ramsay argued.

"That's enough, Logan!" Quinn snapped. "It's one thing to accuse him of wanting Jillian. Hell, we all want her. But it's entirely another to accuse him of trying to kill us. You don't know a damn thing about Grimm Roderick."

"Maybe you're the one who doesn't know him," Ramsay countered. "Maybe Grimm Roderick pretends to be something he's not. I, for one, plan to wake him right now and find out." Ramsay stalked from the room, muttering under his breath.

Quinn shook his head and vaulted after him. "Logan, would you cool your heels—"

"No! You're so convinced of his innocence, I say let's make him prove it!" Ramsay took the stairs to the west wing three at a time, and Quinn had to lope to keep up. As

Logan sped down the long corridor, Quinn overtook him and placed a restraining hand on his shoulder, but Ramsay shook it off.

"If you're so convinced he wouldn't do it, what are you afraid of, de Moncreiffe? Let's just go rouse him."

"You're not thinking clearly about this, Ram—" Quinn broke off abruptly as the door to Grimm's chambers eased opened.

When Jillian slipped out into the hallway, his eyes widened incredulously. There was unequivocally no reason for Jillian to be leaving Grimm's chambers in the wee hours of the morning but for the reason Ramsay had suggested. She was his lover.

Quinn instantly ducked back, pulling Ramsay with him into the shadowed alcove of a doorway.

Her hair was disheveled, and she wore only a woolen draped about her shoulders. Although it trailed nearly to the floor, it left little doubt that there was nothing beneath it.

"Odin's balls," he whispered.

Ramsay favored him with a mocking smile as they lurked in the dark alcove. "Not the honorable Grimm Roderick, right, Quinn?" he whispered.

"That son of a bitch." Quinn's gaze lingered on Jillian's sweet curves as she disappeared down the hallway. The early rays of dawn coming in the tall windows colored his eyes with a strangely crimson glint as he stared at Ramsay.

"Some best friend, eh, de Moncreiffe? He knew you wanted her. He doesn't even offer her marriage. He just takes it for free."

"Over my dead body he will," Quinn vowed.

"Her da brought three men here so she could choose a husband. And what does he do? Both you and I would do the honorable thing, marry her and give her a name, babes, and a life. Roderick tups her and will likely saunter off into the sunset, and you know it. That man has no intention of wedding her. If he possessed one honorable intention, he would have left her to you or me, men who would do right by her. I'm telling you, you don't know him as well as you think."

Quinn scowled, and the minute Jillian disappeared from view, he stalked off muttering beneath his breath.

* * *

The day passed in a haze of happiness for Jillian. The only moment it was marred was when she encountered Quinn at breakfast. He was distant and aloof, not his normal self at all. He eyed her strangely, fidgeted over his breakfast, and finally stalked off in silence.

Once or twice she brushed past Ramsay, who was also behaving oddly. Jillian didn't spare much thought for it; they were probably still suffering the aftereffects of the poison and would be fine in time.

The world was a magnificent place, in her opinion. She was even feeling magnanimous toward her da for having brought her true love back to her. In a burst of generosity she decided he was as wise as she'd once thought. She would wed Grimm Roderick and her life would be perfect.

Chapter 20

"WELL?" RONIN MCILLIOCH DEMANDED.

Elliott shuffled forward, clutching a sheaf of crisp parchments in his hand. "Tobie did well, milord, although we couldn't risk moving in too close to Caithness. Your son possesses the same remarkable senses you have. Still, Tobie managed to capture his likeness on several occasions: riding, saving a small boy, and twice with the woman."

"Let me see." Ronin thrust an impatient hand at Elliott. He rifled through the pages one by one, absorbing every detail. "He's a bonny lad, isn't he, Elliott? Look at those shoulders! Tobie dinna exaggerate, did he?" When Elliott shook his head, Ronin smiled. "Look at that power. My son's every inch a legendary warrior. The lasses must swoon over him."

"Aye, he's a legend, your son is. You should have seen him kill the mountain cat. He cut his own hand to bring on the Berserker rage, to save the child."

Ronin passed the sketches to the man at his side. Two pairs of ice-blue eyes studied every line.

"By Odin's spear!" Ronin exhaled slowly as he reached the last two drawings. "She's the loveliest thing I've ever seen."

"Your son thinks so," Elliott said smugly. "He's every bit as besotted as you were with Jolyn. She's 'the one,' milord, no doubt about it."

"Have they . . . ?" Ronin trailed off meaningfully.

"Judging by the wreck Gavrael made of the Greathall, I'd say yes." Elliott grinned.

Ronin and the man at his side exchanged pleased glances. "The time is at hand. Get with Gilles and start the preparations for him to be comin' home."

"Yes, milord!"

The man sitting next to Ronin raised ice-blue eyes to the McIllioch's. "Do you really think it's goin' to happen as the old woman foretold?" Ronin's brother, Balder, asked softly.

"Cataclysmic changes," Ronin murmured. "She said this generation would suffer more greatly than any McIllioch, but promised that so, too, would this generation advance, and know greater happiness. The old seer swore that my son would see sons of his own, and I believe that. She vowed that when he chose his mate, his mate would be bringin' him home to Maldebann."

"And how will you transcend his hatred for you, Ronin?" his brother asked.

"I doona know." Ronin sighed heavily. "Maybe I'm hoping for a miracle, that he'll listen and forgive me. Now that he's found his mate he may be sympathetic to my plight. He may be capable of understandin' why I did what I did. And why I let him go."

"Doona be so hard on yourself, Ronin. The McKane would have followed you to him if you'd gone after him. They were waiting for you to betray his hidin' place. They know you won't breed more sons. They doona know I even exist. It's Gavrael they're determined to destroy, and the time is quickenin'. If they discover he's found his mate, they'll stop at nothin'."

"I know. He was well hidden at Caithness for years, so I thought it best to leave well enough alone. Gibraltar trained him better than I could have at the time." Ronin met Balder's gaze. "But I always thought that at some point he would come home of his own volition; out of curiosity or confusion about what he was if nothing else, and long before now. When he didn't, when he never once looked west to Maldebann . . . ah, Balder, I fear I grew bitter. I couldna believe he hated me so completely."

"What makes you think he'll be forgivin' you now?"

Ronin raised his hands in a gesture of helplessness. "A fool's fancy? I must believe. Or else I'd have no reason to go on."

Balder clasped his shoulder affectionately. "You have a reason to go on. The McKane must be defeated once and for all and you must ensure the safety of your son's sons. That in itself is reason enough."

"And it will be done," Ronin vowed.

* * *

Grimm spent the day riding, scouring every inch of Caithness for some sign that the McKane had found him. He knew how they operated: They would set up camp on the perimeter of the estate and wait for the right moment, any moment of vulnerability. Grimm rode the entire circumference, searching for anything: the remains of a recent fire, missing livestock commandeered and slaughtered, word of strangers among the crofters.

He found nothing. Not one shred of evidence to support his suspicion that he was being watched.

Still, a prickling of unease lurked at the base of his neck where he always felt it when something was wrong. There was a threat, unidentified and unseen, somewhere at Caithness.

He rode into the bailey at dusk, battling an overwhelming desire to slip from his horse, race into the castle, and rush to Jillian. To sweep her into his embrace, carry her to his chambers, and make love to her until neither of them could move, which for a Berserker was a very long time.

Leave, his conscience pricked. *Leave this moment. Doona even pack a satchel, doona even say goodbye, just get out now.*

He felt like he was being torn in half. In all the years he'd dreamed of Jillian, he'd never imagined he could feel this way; she completed him. The Berserker had risen in him and been humbled by her presence. She could make him clean again. Merely being with her soothed the beast he'd learned to hate, the beast she didn't even know existed.

He grimaced inwardly as hope, the treacherous emotion he'd never permitted himself to feel, jockeyed for position with his premonition of danger. Hope was a luxury he could ill afford. Hope made men do foolish things, such as staying at Caithness when all his heightened senses were clamoring that despite finding no sign of McKane, he was being watched and a confrontation was imminent. He knew how to handle danger. He didn't know how to handle hope.

Sighing, he entered the Greathall and picked at a platter of fruit near the hearth. Selecting a ripe pear, he dropped into a chair before the fire and brooded into the flames, battling his urge to seek her out. He had to make some decisions. He had to find a way to behave honorably, to do the right thing, but he no longer knew what the right thing was. Nothing was black and white anymore; there were no easy answers. He knew it was dangerous to remain at Caithness, but he wanted to remain more than anything he'd ever desired in his life.

He was so lost in thought, he didn't hear Ramsay approach until the Highlander's deep, rumbling voice jarred him. That alone should have warned him that he'd allowed his guard to slip dangerously.

"Where've you been, Roderick?"

"Riding."

"All day? Damn it, man, there's a beautiful woman in the castle and you go out riding all day?"

"I had some thinking to do. Riding clears my head."

"I'd say you have some thinking to do," Ramsay muttered beneath his breath.

With his heightened hearing, Grimm heard each syllable. He turned and faced Ramsay levelly. "Just what is it you think I should be thinking about?"

Ramsay looked startled. "I'm standing a dozen paces from you! There's no way you could have heard that. It was scarcely audible."

"Obviously I did," Grimm said coolly. "So what is it you presume to tell me I should be thinking about?"

Ramsay's dark eyes flickered, and Grimm could see he was trying to suppress his volatile temper. "Let's try honor, Roderick," Ramsay said stiffly. "Honoring our host. And his daughter."

Grimm's smile was dangerous. "I'll make you a deal, Logan. If you doona bring up my honor, I won't drag yours out of the pigsty where it's been bedding down for years."

"My honor—" Ramsay began hotly, but Grimm cut him off impatiently. He had more important things to occupy his mind than arguing with Ramsay.

"Let's just get to the point, Logan. How much gold do you owe the Campbell? Half of what Jillian's worth? Or is it more? From what I hear, you're into him so deeply you may as well have put yourself six feet under. If you bag the St. Clair heiress, you'll be able to clear your debts and live in extravagance for a few years. Isn't that right?"

"Not all men are as wealthy as you, Roderick. For some of us, whose people are vast in number, it's a struggle to take care of our clan. And I care for Jillian," Ramsay growled.

"I'm sure you do. The same way you care for seeing your belly filled with the finest food and the best whisky. The same way you care for riding a pure-blooded stallion, the same way you like to show off your wolfhounds. Maybe all those expenses are why you've been having a hard time maintaining your people. How many years did you fritter away at court, spending gold as liberally as your clan procreates?"

Ramsay turned stiffly and was silent a long moment. Grimm watched him, every muscle in his body tensed to spring. Logan had a violent temper—Grimm had experienced it before. He berated himself for antagonizing the man, but Ramsay Logan's tendency to put his own needs above those of his starving clan infuriated him.

Ramsay drew a deep breath and turned around, astonishing Grimm with a pleasant smile. "You're wrong about me, Roderick. I confess, my past isn't so exemplary, but I'm not the same man I used to be."

Grimm watched him, skepticism evident in every line on his face.

"See? I'm not losing my temper." Ramsay raised his hands in a conciliatory gesture. "I can see how you might believe such things of me. I was a wild, self-centered reprobate once. But I'm not any longer. I can't prove it to you. Only time will prove my sincerity. Grant me that much, will you?"

Grimm snorted. "Sure, Logan. I'll grant you that much. You may be different." *Worse*, Grimm added in the privacy of his thoughts. He turned his gaze back to the flames.

As Grimm heard Ramsay turn to leave the room, he was unable to prevent himself from asking, "Where's Jillian?"

Logan stopped in mid-step and shot a cool glance over his shoulder. "Playing chess with Quinn in the study. He intends to propose marriage to her tonight, so I suggest you give them privacy. Jillian deserves a proper husband, and if she won't have him, I intend to offer in his stead."

Grimm nodded stiffly. After a few moments of attempting to block all thoughts of Jillian from his mind—Jillian ensconced in the cozy study with Quinn, who was proposing marriage—and failing, he stalked back out into the night, more disturbed by Ramsay's words than he wished to admit.

* * *

Grimm wandered the gardens for nearly half an hour before he was struck by the realization that he'd seen no sign of his stallion. He'd left him in the inner ward less than an hour ago. Occam rarely wandered far from the castle.

Puzzled, Grimm searched the inner and outer wards, whistling repeatedly, but he heard nary a nicker, no thunder of hooves. He turned his thoughtful gaze to the stables that graced the edge of the outer bailey. Instinct quickened inside him, warning him, and he set off at a run for the outbuilding.

He burst into the stables and drew to an abrupt halt. It was abnormally silent, and an odd odor pervaded the air. Sharp, acrid, like the stench of rotten eggs. Peering into the gloom, he catalogued every detail of the room before stepping in. Hay tumbled in piles across the floor—normal. Oil lamps suspended from the rafters—also normal. All the gates shut—still normal.

Scent of a thing sulfuric—definitely not normal. But not much to go on either.

He stepped gingerly into the stables, whistled, and was rewarded with a muffled neigh from the stall at the farthest end of the stables. Grimm forced himself not to lurch forward.

It was a trap.

While he couldn't fathom the exact nature of the threat, danger fairly dripped from the rafters of the low outbuilding. His senses bristled. What was amiss? Sulfur?

He narrowed his eyes thoughtfully, paced forward and gently scuffed at the hay beneath his boot, then stooped to push aside a thick sheaf of clover.

He expelled a low whistle of amazement.

He pushed at more hay, moved forward five paces, did the same, moved left five paces, and repeated the motion. Sweeping his hand across the dusty stone floor beneath the hay, he came up with a fistful of finely corned black powder.

Christ! The entire floor of the stable had been evenly sprinkled with a layer of black powder. Someone had liberally doused the stones, then spread loose hay atop it. Black powder was made from a combination of saltpeter, charcoal, and sulfur. Many clans cultivated their own saltpeter in or near the stables to fashion the weapon, but the stuff spread on the floor was fully processed black powder, painstakingly corned to uniform granules, possessing lethal explosive properties, and planted deliberately. It was a far cry from the raw version of fermenting manure from which saltpeter was derived. Coupled with the flammability of the hay and the natural abundance of fresh manure, the stables were an inferno waiting to blow. One spark would send the entire stable up with the force of a massive bomb. If one of the oil lanterns fell or so much as coughed up an oily spark, the building—and half the outer ward—would be rocked by the explosion.

Occam nickered, a sound of frustrated fear. He was muzzled, Grimm realized. Someone had muzzled his horse and penned him in a deadly trap.

He would never permit his horse to be burned again, and whoever had designed this trap knew him well enough to know his weakness for the stallion. Grimm stood, absolutely motionless, ten paces inside the door—not too far to flee for safety if the hay started to smolder. But Occam was in a locked stall, fifty yards from safety, and therein lay the problem.

A coldhearted man would turn his back and leave. What was a horse, after all? A beast, used for man's purposes. Grimm snorted. Occam was a regal, beautiful creature, possessing intelligence and the same capacity to suffer pain and fear as any human being.

No, he could never leave his horse behind.

He had barely completed that thought when something hurtled through the window to his left and the straw caught fire in an instant.

Grimm lunged into the flames.

* * *

In the coziness of the study, Jillian laughed as she moved her bishop into a position of checkmate. She stole a surreptitious peek toward the window, as she had a dozen times in the past hour, seeking some sign that Grimm had returned. Ever since she'd glimpsed him riding out this morning, she'd been watching for him. The moment Occam's great gray shape lumbered past the study, Jillian feared she would surge to her feet, giddy as a lass, and be off at a run. Memories of the night she'd spent entangled with Grimm's hard, inexhaustible body brought a flush to her skin, heating her in a way a fire never could.

"Not fair! How can I concentrate? Playing you when you were a wee lass was far easier," Quinn complained. "I can't think when I play you now."

"Ah, the advantages of being a woman," Jillian drawled mischievously. She was certain she must be radiating her newfound sensual knowledge. "Is it my fault your attention wanders?"

Quinn's gaze lingered on her shoulders, bared by the gown she wore. "Absolutely," he assured her. "Look at you, Jillian. You're beautiful!" His voice dropped to a confidential tone. "Jillian, lass, there's something I wish to discuss with you—"

"Quinn, hush." She placed a finger against his lips and shook her head.

Quinn brushed her hand away. "No, Jillian, I've kept my silence long enough. I know what you feel, Jillian." He paused deliberately to lend emphasis to his next words. "And I know what's going on with Grimm." He held her gaze levelly.

Jillian was immediately wary. "What do you mean?" she evaded.

Quinn smiled in an effort to soften his words. "Jillian, he's not the marrying kind."

Jillian bit her lip and averted her gaze. "You don't know that for certain. That's like saying Ramsay's not the marrying kind because, from the tales I've heard, he's been a consummate womanizer. But only this morning he convinced me of his troth. Merely because a man has shown no past inclination to wed doesn't mean he won't. People change." Grimm had certainly changed, revealing the tender, loving man she'd always believed he really was.

"Logan asked you to marry him?" Quinn scowled.

Jillian nodded. "This morning. After breakfast he approached me while I was walking in the gardens."

"He offered for you? He knew I planned to do so myself!" Quinn cursed, then mumbled a hasty apology. "Forgive me, Jillian, but it makes me angry that he'd go behind my back like that."

"I didn't accept, Quinn, so it hardly matters."

"How did he take it?"

Jillian sighed. The Highlander hadn't taken it well at all; she had the feeling she'd barely escaped a dangerous display of temper. "I don't think Ramsay Logan is accustomed to being rebuffed. He seemed furious."

Quinn studied her a moment, then said, "Jillian, lass, I wasn't going to tell you this, but I think you should be informed so you can make a wise decision. The Logan are land rich but gold poor. Ramsay Logan needs to marry, and marry well. You would be a godsend to his impoverished clan."

Jillian gave him an astonished look. "Quinn! I can't believe that you would try to discredit my suitors. Heavens! Ramsay spent a quarter hour this morning trying to discredit you and Grimm. What's with you men?"

Quinn stiffened. "I am not trying to discredit your suitors. I'm telling you the truth. Logan needs gold. His clan is starving, and has been for many years. They've scarcely managed to hold on to their own lands lately. In the past, the Logan hired out as mercenaries to get coin, but there've been so few wars in recent years that there is no mercenary work to be found. Land takes coin, and coin is something the Logan have never had. You are the answer to their every prayer. Excuse my crass way of wording it, but if Logan could bag the rich St. Clair bride, his clan would herald him as their savior."

Jillian nibbled her lip thoughtfully. "And you, Quinn de Moncreiffe, why do you wish to wed me?"

"Because I care deeply for you, lass," Quinn said simply.

"Perhaps I should ask Grimm about *you*."

Quinn closed his eyes and sighed.

"Just what's wrong with Grimm as a candidate?" she pressed, determined to have it all out.

Quinn's gaze was compassionate. "I don't mean to be cruel, but he will never marry you, Jillian. Everyone knows that Grimm Roderick has vowed never to wed."

Jillian refused to let Quinn see how his words affected her. She bit her lip to prevent any rash words from escaping. She had nearly worked up the courage to ask him why, and if Grimm had actually said such a thing recently, when a tremendous explosion rocked the castle.

The windows rattled in their frames, the very castle shuddered, and both Jillian and Quinn leapt to their feet.

"What was that?" she gasped.

Quinn flew to the window and peered out. "Christ!" he shouted. "The stables are on fire!"

Chapter 21

Jillian raced into the courtyard after Quinn, crying Grimm's name over and over, heedless of the curious eyes of the staff and the shocked gazes of Kaley and Hatchard. The explosion had roused the castle. Hatchard was standing in the courtyard shouting orders, organizing an attack against the hostile flames that were devouring the stables and moving east to ravage the castle.

The autumn weather had been dry enough that the fire would quickly rage out of control, gobbling buildings and crops. The teeming village of daub-and-wattle huts would ignite like dry grass if the flames encroached that far. A few stray sparks carried on the breeze could destroy the whole valley. Jillian frantically pushed that concern to the perimeter of her thoughts; she had to find Grimm.

"Where's Grimm? Has anyone seen Grimm?" Jillian pushed through the throng of people, peering into faces, desperate to catch a glimpse of his proud stance, his intense blue eyes. Her eyes were peeled for the shape of a great, gray stallion. "Don't be a hero, don't be a hero," she muttered under her breath. "For once, just be a man, Grimm Roderick. Be *safe*."

She didn't realize she'd said the words aloud until Quinn, who'd surfaced in the throng beside her, looked at her sharply and shook his head. "Och, lass, you love him, don't you?"

Jillian nodded as tears filled her eyes. "Find him, Quinn! Make him be safe!"

Quinn sighed and nodded. "Stay here, lass. I'll find him for you. I promise."

The eerie scream of a trapped horse split the air, and Jillian pivoted toward the stables, chilled by a sudden, terrible knowledge. "He couldn't be in there, could he, Quinn?"

Quinn's expression plainly echoed her fear. But of course he could, and would. Grimm could not stand by and watch a horse be burned. She knew that; he'd said as much that day at Durrkesh. In his mind, the innocent cry of an animal was as intolerable as the cry of wounded child or a frightened woman.

"No man could survive that." Jillian eyed the inferno. Flames shot up, tall as the castle, brilliant orange against the black sky. The wall of fire was so intense that it was nearly impossible to look at. Jillian narrowed her eyes in a desperate bid to make out the low rectangular shape of the stable, to no avail. She could see nothing but fire.

"You're right, Jillian," Quinn said slowly. "No *man* could."

As if in a dream, she saw a shape coalesce within the flames. Like some nightmare vision the white-orange flames shimmered, a blurred form of darkness rippled behind them, and a rider burst forth, wreathed in flames, streaking straight for the loch, where both horse and rider plunged into the cool waters, hissing as they submerged. She held her breath until horse and rider surfaced.

Quinn spared her a quick nod of reassurance before racing off to join the fight against the inferno that threatened Caithness.

Jillian darted for the loch, tripping over her feet in her haste to reach his side. As Grimm rose from the water and led Occam up the rocky bank, she flung herself at him, burrowed into his arms, and buried her face against his sodden chest. He held her for a long moment until she stopped shuddering, then drew back, wiping gently at her tears. "Jillian," he said sadly.

"Grimm, I thought I'd lost you!" She pressed frantic kisses to his face while she searched his body with her hands to assure herself he was unharmed. "Why, you're not even burned," she said, puzzled. Although his clothing hung in charred tatters and his skin was a bit pinkened, there wasn't so much as a blister marring his smooth skin. She peered past him at Occam, who also seemed to have been spared. "How can this be?" she wondered.

"His coat has been singed, but overall he's fine. We rode fast," Grimm said quickly.

"I thought I'd lost you," Jillian repeated. Gazing into his eyes, she was struck by the sudden and terrible understanding that although he'd burst from the flames, miraculously whole, her words had never been truer. She *had* lost him. She had no idea how or why, but his glittering gaze was teeming with distance and sorrow. With goodbye.

"No," she shouted. "No. I won't let you go. You are *not* leaving me!"

Grimm dropped his gaze to the ground.

"No," she insisted. "Look at me."

His gaze was dark. “I have to go, lass. I will not bring destruction to this place again.”

“What makes you think this fire is about you?” she demanded, battling her every instinct that told her the fire had indeed been about him. She didn’t know why, but she knew it was true. “Oh! You are so arrogant,” she pressed on bravely, determined to convince him that the truth was not the truth. She would use every weapon, fair or unfair, to keep him.

“Jillian.” He blew out a breath of frustration and reached for her.

She beat at him with her fists. “No! Don’t touch me, don’t hold me, not if it means you’re going to say goodbye!”

“I must, lass. I’ve tried to tell you—Christ, I tried to tell myself! I have nothing to offer you. You doona understand; it can never be. No matter how much I might wish to, I can’t offer you the kind of life you deserve. Things like this fire happen to me all the time, Jillian. It’s not safe for anyone to be around me. They hunt me!”

“Who hunts you?” she wailed as her world crumbled around her.

He made an angry gesture. “I can’t explain, lass. You’ll simply have to take my word on this. I’m not a normal man. Could a normal man have survived that?” He flung his arm toward the blaze.

“Then what are you?” she shouted. “Why don’t you just tell me?”

He shook his head and closed his eyes. After a long pause, he opened them. His eyes were burning, incandescent, and Jillian gasped as a fleeting memory surfaced. It was the memory of a fifteen-year-old who’d watched this man battle the McKane. Watching as he’d seemed to grow larger, broader, stronger with every drop of blood that was shed. Watching his eyes burn like banked coals, listening to his chilling laughter, wondering how any man could slay so many yet remain unharmed.

"What *are* you?" she repeated in a whisper, begging him for comfort. Begging him to be nothing more than a man.

"The warrior who has always—" He closed his eyes. *Loved you.* But he couldn't offer her those words, because he couldn't follow up on what they promised. "Adored you, Jillian St. Clair. A man who isn't quite a man, who knows he can never have you." He drew a shuddering breath. "You must marry Quinn. Marry him and free me. Doona marry Ramsay—he's not good enough for you. But you must let me go, because I cannot suffer your death on my hands, and that's all that could ever come of you and me being together." He met her gaze, wordlessly beseeching her not to make his leaving any harder than it already was.

Jillian stiffened. If the man was going to leave her, she was going to make certain it hurt like hell. She narrowed her eyes, shooting him a wordless challenge to be brave, to fight for their love. He averted his face.

"Thank you for these days and nights, lass. Thank you for giving me the best memories of my life. But say goodbye, Jillian. Let me go. Take the splendor and wonder that we've shared and let me go."

Her tears started then. He had already made up his mind, had already begun putting distance between them. "Just tell me, Grimm," she begged. "It can't be so bad. Whatever it is, we can deal with it together."

"I'm an animal, Jillian. You doona know me!"

"I know you're the most honorable man I've ever met! I

don't care what our life would be like. I would live *any* kind of life, so long as I lived it with you," she hissed.

As Grimm backed away slowly, she watched the life disappear from his eyes, leaving his gaze wintry and hollow. She felt the moment she lost him; something inside her emptied completely, leaving a void she suspected she might die from. "No!"

He backed away. Occam followed, nickering gently.

"You said you adored me! If you truly cared for me, you would fight to stay by my side!"

He winced. "I care about you too much to hurt you."

"That's weak! You don't know what caring is," she shouted furiously. "Caring is love. And love fights! Love doesn't look for the path of least resistance. Hell's bells, Roderick, if love was that easy everyone would have it. You're a coward!"

He flinched, and a muscle jumped furiously in his jaw. "I am doing the honorable thing."

"To *hell* with the honorable thing," she shouted. "Love has no pride. Love looks for ways to endure."

"Jillian, stop. You want more from me than I'm capable of."

Her gaze turned icy. "Obviously. I thought you were heroic in every way. But you're not. You're just a man after all." She cast her gaze away and held her breath, wondering if she'd goaded him far enough.

"Goodbye, Jillian."

He leapt on his horse, and they seemed to melt into one beast—a creature of shadows disappearing into the night.

She gaped in disbelief at the hole he'd left in her world. He'd left her. He'd really left her. A sob welled up within her, so painful that she doubled over. "You coward," she whispered.

CHAPTER 22

RONIN INSERTED THE KEY INTO THE LOCK, HESITATED, then squared his shoulders firmly. He eyed the towering oak door that was banded with steel. It soared over his head, set in a lofty arch of stone. *Deo non fortuna* was chiseled in flowing script above the arch—"By God, not by chance." For years Ronin had denied those words, refused to come to this place, believing God had forsaken him. *Deo non fortuna* was the motto his clan had lived by, believing their special gifts were God-given and had purpose. Then his "gift" had resulted in Jolyn's death.

Ronin expelled an anxious breath, forcing himself to turn the key and push open the door. Rusty hinges shrieked the protest of long disuse. Cobwebs danced in the doorway and the musty scent of forgotten legends greeted him. *Welcome to the Hall of Lords,* the legends clamored. *Did you really think you could forget us?*

One thousand years of McIllioch graced the hall. Carved deep into the belly of the mountain, the chamber soared to a towering fifty feet. The curved walls met in a royal arch and the ceilings were painted with graphic depictions of the epic heroes of their clan.

His own da had brought him here when he'd turned sixteen. He'd explained their noble history and guided Ronin through the change—guidance Ronin had been unable to provide his own son.

But who would have thought Gavrael would change so much sooner than any of them had? It had been totally unexpected. The battle with the McKane following so quickly on the heels of Jolyn's savage murder had left Ronin too exhausted, too numbed by grief to reach out to his son. Although Berserkers were difficult to kill, if one was wounded badly enough it took time to heal. It had taken Ronin months to recover. The day the McKane had murdered Jolyn they'd left a shell of a man who hadn't wanted to heal.

Immersed in his grief, he'd failed his son. He'd been unable to introduce Gavrael to the life of a Berserker, to train him in the secret ways of controlling the bloodlust. He hadn't been there to explain. He'd failed, and his son had run off to find a new family and a new life.

As the passing years had weathered Ronin's body he'd greeted each weary bone, each aching joint, and each newly discovered silver hair with gratitude, because it carried him one day closer to his beloved Jolyn.

But he couldn't go to Jolyn yet. There were things yet undone. His son was coming home, and he would not fail him this time.

With effort, Ronin forced his attention away from his deep guilt and back to the Hall of Lords. He hadn't even managed to cross the threshold. He squared his shoulders.

Clutching a brightly burning torch, Ronin pushed his way through the cobwebs and into the hall. His footsteps echoed like small explosions in the vast stone chamber. He skirted a few pieces of moldy, forgotten furniture and followed the wall to the first portrait that had been etched in stone over one thousand years ago. The oldest likenesses were stone, painted with faded mixtures of herbs and clays. The more recent portraits were charcoal sketches and paintings.

The women in the portraits shared one striking characteristic. They were all breathtakingly radiant, positively brimming with happiness. The men shared a single distinction as well. All nine hundred and fifty-eight males in this hall had eyes of blue ice.

Ronin moved to the portrait of his wife and raised the torch. He smiled. Had some pagan deity offered him a bargain and said, "I will take away all the tragedy you have suffered in your life, I will take you back in time and give you dozens of sons and perfect peace, but you can never have Jolyn," Ronin McIllioch would have scoffed. He would willingly embrace every bit of tragedy he'd endured to have loved Jolyn, even for the painfully brief time they'd been allotted.

"I won't fail him this time, Jolyn. I swear to you, I will see Castle Maldebann secured and filled with promise again. Then we'll be together to smile down upon this place." After a long pause, he whispered fiercely, "I miss you, woman."

Outside the Hall of Lords, an astonished Gilles entered the connecting hallway and paused, eyeing the open door in disbelief. Rushing down the corridor, he burst into the long-sealed hall, barely suppressing a whoop of delight at the sight of Ronin, no longer stooped but standing proudly erect beneath a portrait of his wife and son. Ronin didn't turn, but Gilles hadn't expected him to; Ronin always knew who was in his immediate circumference.

"Have the maids set to cleaning, Gilles," Ronin commanded without taking his eyes off the portrait of his smiling wife. "Open this place up and air it out. I want the entire castle scrubbed as it hasna been since my Jolyn was alive. I want this place sparklin'." Ronin opened his arms expansively. "Light the torchères and henceforth keep them burnin' in here as they did years ago, day and night. My son is coming home," he finished proudly.

"*Yes*, milord!" Gilles exclaimed as he hastened off to obey a command he'd been waiting a lifetime to hear.

* * *

Where to now, Grimm Roderick? he wondered wearily. Back to Dalkeith to see if he might lure destruction to those blessed shores?

His hands fisted and he longed for a bottomless bottle of whisky, although he knew it wouldn't grant him the oblivion he sought. If a Berserker drank quickly enough, he might feel drunk for the sum total of about three seconds. That wouldn't work at all.

The McKane always found him eventually. He knew now that they must have had a spy in Durrkesh. Likely someone had seen the rage come over him in the courtyard of the tavern, then tried to poison him. The McKane had learned over the years to attack stealthily. Cunning traps or sheer numbers were the only possible ways to take a Berserker, and neither of them was foolproof. Now that he had escaped the McKane twice, he knew the next time they struck they would descend in force.

First they'd tried poison, then the fire at the stables.

Grimm knew if he had remained at Caithness they might have destroyed the entire castle, taking out all the St. Clair in their blind quest to kill him. He'd become acquainted with their unique fanaticism at an early age, and it was a lesson he'd never forgotten.

They'd blessedly lost track of him during the years he'd been in Edinburgh. The McKane were fighters, not royal arse-kissers, and they devoted little attention to the events at court. He'd hidden in plain sight. Then, when he'd moved from court to Dalkeith, he'd encountered few new people, and those he had met were abjectly loyal to Hawk. He'd started to relax his guard and begun to feel almost . . . normal.

What an intriguing, tantalizing word: normal. "Take it away, Odin. I was wrong," Grimm whispered. "I doona wish to be Berserk any longer."

But Odin didn't seem to care.

Grimm had to face the facts. Now that the McKane had found him again, they would tear the country apart looking for him. It wasn't safe for him to be near other people. It was time for a new name, perhaps a new country. His thoughts turned to England, but every ounce of Scot in him rebelled.

How could he live without ever touching Jillian again? Having experienced such joy, how could he resume his barren existence? Christ, it would have been better if he'd never known what his life might have been like! On that fateful night above Tuluth, at the foolish age of fourteen, he'd called a Berserker, begging for the gift of vengeance, never realizing how complete that vengeance would be. Vengeance didn't bring back the dead, it deadened the avenger.

But there was really little point in regret, he mocked

himself, for he owned the beast and the beast owned him, and it was that simple. Resignation blanketed him, and only one issue remained. *Where to now, Grimm Roderick?*

He nudged Occam to the only place left to go: in the forbidding Highlands he could disappear into the wilderness. He knew every empty hut and cave, every source of shelter from the bitter winter that would soon ice white caps around the mountains.

He would be so cold again.

Guiding Occam with his knees, he plaited war braids into his hair and wondered if an invincible Berserker could die from something so innocuous as a broken heart.

* * *

Jillian gazed sadly at the blackened lawn of Caithness. Everything was a reminder. It was November, and the hated lawn would be black until the first snowfall came to smother it. She couldn't step outside the castle without being forced to remember that night, the fire, Grimm leaving. The lawn sloped and rolled in a vast, never-ending carpet of black ash. All her flowers were gone. Grimm was gone.

He'd abandoned her because he was a coward.

She'd tried to make excuses for him, but there were none to be made. The most courageous man she'd ever known was afraid to love. *Well, to hell with him!* she thought defiantly.

She felt pain; she wouldn't deny it. The mere thought of living without him for the rest of her life was unbearable, but she refused to dwell on it. That would be the sure path to emotional collapse. So she stoked her anger against him, clutching it like a shield to her wounded heart.

"He's not coming back, lass," Ramsay said gently.

Jillian clenched her jaw and spun to face him. "I think I've figured that out, Ramsay," she said evenly.

Ramsay studied her in stalwart stance. When she moved to leave, his hand shot out and wrapped around her wrist. She tried to snatch it away, but he was too strong. "Marry me, Jillian. I swear to you, I'll treat you like a queen. I will never abandon you."

Not so long as there's coin in keeping me, she thought. "Let go of me," she hissed.

He didn't budge. "Jillian, consider your situation. Your parents will be back any day now and expect you to wed. They'll likely force you to choose when they return. I would be good to you," he promised.

"I will never wed," she said with absolute conviction.

His demeanor altered instantly. When his sneering gaze slid over her abdomen, she was shocked; when he spoke, she was rendered momentarily speechless.

"If a bastard quickens in your belly you may think differently, lass," he said with a smirk. "Then your parents will force you to wed, and you'll be counting your blessings if any decent man will have you. There's a name for women like you. You're not so pure," he spat.

"How dare you!" she cried. The instinct to slap the smirk from his face was overwhelming, and she acted upon it reflexively.

Ramsay's face whitened with rage, and the red welt from her blow stood out in stark relief. He caught her other wrist and pulled her close, bristling with anger. "You'll regret that one day, lass." He shoved her away so savagely, she stumbled. For an instant she saw something so brutal in his eyes that she feared he might force her to the ground and beat her, or worse. She scrambled to her feet and dashed for the castle on trembling legs.

* * *

"He's not coming back, Jillian," Kaley said gently.

"I know that! For God's sake, could everyone please just quit saying that to me? Do I look dense? Is that it?"

Kaley eyes filled with tears, and Jillian was instantly remorseful. "Oh, Kaley, I didn't mean to yell at you. I haven't been myself lately. It's just that I'm worried about . . . things . . ."

"Things like babies?" Kaley said carefully.

Jillian stiffened.

"Is it possible . . ." Kaley trailed off.

Jillian averted her gaze guiltily.

"Oh, lass." Kaley wrapped her in her ample embrace. "Oh, lass," she echoed helplessly.

* * *

Two weeks later, Gibraltar and Elizabeth St. Clair returned.

Jillian was torn by mixed emotions. She was elated to have them home, yet she dreaded seeing them, so she hid in her chambers and waited for them to come to her. And they did, but not until the next morning. In retrospect, she realized she'd been a fool to give her clever da any time to ferret out information before confronting her.

When the summons finally came, she shivered, and the last vestige of excitement at seeing her parents turned to pure dread. She dragged her feet all the way to the study.

* * *

"Mama! Da!" Jillian exclaimed. She vaulted into their arms, greedily snatching hugs before they could launch the interrogation she knew was coming.

"Jillian." Gibraltar terminated the hug so quickly, Jillian knew she was in dire straits indeed.

"How's Hugh? And my new nephew?" she asked brightly.

Gibraltar and Elizabeth exchanged glances, then Elizabeth sank into a chair near the fire, abandoning Jillian to deal with Gibraltar by herself.

"Have you chosen a husband yet, Jillian?" Gibraltar skirted all niceties.

Jillian drew a deep breath. "That's what I wished to speak with you about, Da. I've had a lot of time to think." She swallowed nervously as Gibraltar eyed her dispassionately. Dispassionate never boded well for her—it meant her da was furious. She cleared her throat anxiously. "I have decided, after much consideration, I mean, I've really thought this through . . . that I . . . um—" Jillian broke off. She had to stop warbling like an idiot—her da would never be swayed by tepid protests. "Da . . . I really don't plan to wed. *Ever.*" There, it was out. "I mean, I appreciate everything you and Mama have done for me, never think I don't, but marriage is just not for me." She punctuated her words with a confident nod.

Gibraltar regarded her with an unnerving mixture of amusement and condescension. "Nice try, Jillian. But I'm not playing games anymore. I brought three men here for you. Only two are left, and you will marry one of them. I've had it with your shenanigans. You're going to be twenty-two in a month, and either de Moncreiffe or Logan will make a perfectly good husband. There will be no more moping about and no crafty little ploys. *Which one will you wed?*" he demanded, a bit more forcefully than he'd intended.

"Gibraltar!" Elizabeth protested. She rose from her chair, ruffled by his high-handed tone.

"Stay out of this, Elizabeth. She's played me for a fool for the last time. Jillian will summon up one reason after another why she can't wed until we're both too old to do anything about it."

"Gibraltar, we will *not* force her to wed someone she doesn't want." Elizabeth stamped a dainty foot to punctuate her decree.

"She's going to have to accept the fact that she can't have the man she wants, Elizabeth. He was here and he left. And that's the end of the matter." Gibraltar sighed, eyeing his daughter's rigid back as she stood plucking at the folds of her gown. "Elizabeth, I tried. Don't you think I tried? I knew how Jillian felt about Grimm. But I won't force the man to wed her, and even if I did, what good would that do? Jillian doesn't want a forced husband."

"You knew I loved him?" Jillian exclaimed. She almost ran to him, but caught herself and stiffened further.

Gibraltar almost laughed; a broom handle couldn't have been more rigid than his daughter's spine. Stubborn just like her mother. "Of course, lass. I've seen it in your eyes for years. So I brought him here for you. And now Kaley tells me that he left a sennight ago and told you to marry Quinn. Jillian, he's gone. He's made his feelings clear." Gibraltar drew himself up. "I am not going to fling my daughter at some inconsiderate bastard who's too much a fool to see what kind of treasure he'd be getting. I will not gift my Jillian to a man who can't appreciate how rare a woman she is. What kind of father would I be to chase a man down and throw my daughter after him?"

Elizabeth sniffed, blinking back a tear. "You brought him because you knew she loved him," she cooed. "Oh,

Gibraltar! Even though I didn't think he was right for her, you saw through it all. You knew what Jillian wanted."

Gibraltar's pleasure at his wife's adoration quickly evaporated when Jillian's shoulders slumped in defeat.

"I never knew you knew how I felt, Da," Jillian said in a small voice.

"Of course I did. Just as I know how you feel now. But you have to face the facts. He left, Jillian—"

"I know he left! *Must* you all keep reminding me?"

"Yes, if you persist in trying to fritter your life away. I gave him the chance, and he was too much a fool to take it. You must move on with your life, lass."

"He didn't think he was good enough for me," Jillian murmured.

"Is that what he said?" Elizabeth asked quickly.

Jillian blew a tendril of hair from her face. "Sort of. He said that I couldn't possibly understand what would happen if he married me. And he's right. Whatever terrible thing he thinks it is, I can't even begin to guess. He acts like there's some dreadful secret about him, and Mama, I can't convince him otherwise. I can't even begin to imagine what horrible thing he thinks is wrong with him. Grimm Roderick is the best man I've ever known, except for you, Da." Jillian smiled weakly at her father before crossing to the window to stare out at the blackened lawn.

Gibraltar's eyes narrowed and he gazed thoughtfully at Elizabeth, who had raised her eyebrows in surprise.

She still doesn't know. Tell her, Elizabeth mouthed, shooting a glance at her daughter's stiff back.

That he's a Berserker? Gibraltar mouthed back, disbelieving. *He must tell her himself.*

He can't. He's not here!

He refuses. And I won't fix it for him. If he can't bring

himself to trust her, she shouldn't marry him. He's obviously not man enough for my Jillian.

Our *Jillian*.

He shrugged. Crossing the study, he cupped Jillian's shoulders with comforting hands. "I'm sorry, Jillian. I truly am. I thought maybe he'd changed over the years. But he hasn't. Still, it doesn't alter that fact that you must wed. I'd like it to be Quinn."

She stiffened and hissed softly. "I am not marrying anyone."

"Yes, you are," Gibraltar enunciated sternly. "I am posting the banns tomorrow, and in three weeks' time you are going to marry *someone*."

Jillian whirled around to face him, her eyes flashing. "You should know I became his lover."

Elizabeth fanned herself furiously.

Gibraltar shrugged.

Elizabeth gaped, first at Jillian, then at her unresponsive husband.

"That's all? A shrug?" Jillian blinked at her father disbelievingly. "Well, while you may not care, I hardly think my husband-to-be would cheerily accept it, do you, Da?"

"I wouldn't mind," Quinn said quietly, startling them all with his unannounced presence. "I'd marry you on any terms, Jillian."

All eyes flew to Quinn de Moncreiffe, whose broad golden frame filled the doorway.

"Good man," Gibraltar said firmly.

"Oh, Quinn!" Jillian said sadly. "You deserve better . . ."

"I've told you as much before, lass. I'll take you on any terms. Grimm's a fool, but I'm not. I'll marry you happily. No regrets. I've never understood why a woman's supposed to be untouched when a man's expected to be as touched as possible."

"Then it's settled," Gibraltar concluded quickly.

"No, it's not!"

"Yes, it is, Jillian," Gibraltar said sternly. "You will marry in three weeks. Period. End of conversation." He turned away.

"You can't do this to me!"

"Wait." Ramsay Logan stepped into the doorway behind Quinn. "I'd like to offer for her too."

Gibraltar assessed the two men in the doorway and slowly turned his regard to his daughter, who stood, mouth ajar.

"You have twelve hours to choose, Jillian. I post the banns at dawn."

"Mama, you can't let him do this!" Jillian wailed.

Elizabeth St. Clair drew herself erect and sniffed before following Gibraltar from the study.

* * *

"What on earth do you think you're doing now, Gibraltar?" Elizabeth demanded.

Gibraltar leaned back, resting on the sill of the window in their bedroom, the hair on his chest glinting gold between the folds of his silk robe in the soft glow of the firelight.

Elizabeth reclined on the bed nude and, Gibraltar marveled, breathtaking. "By Odin's spear, woman, you know I can refuse you nothing when I see you like that."

"Then don't make Jillian wed, love," Elizabeth said simply. There were no games between her and her husband, and there never had been. Elizabeth firmly believed most problems in a relationship could be cleared up or avoided entirely by clear, concise communication. Games invited unnecessary discord.

"I don't plan to," Gibraltar replied with a faint smile. "It will never go that far."

"Whatever do you mean?" Elizabeth removed the pins from her hair, allowing it to cascade in golden waves over her bare breasts. "Is this another one of your infamous plans, Gibraltar?" she asked with lazy amusement.

"Yes." He sank to the edge of the bed beside her. He ran his hand down the smooth shape of her side, contouring the lovely indentation of her waist, soaring over the lush curve of her hip. "If she hadn't admitted that she'd become his lover, I might not have felt so confident. But he's a Berserker, Elizabeth. There is only one true mate for each Berserker, and they know it. He cannot allow the wedding to take place. A Berserker would die first."

Elizabeth's eyes brightened, and understanding penetrated her sensual languor. "You're posting the banns to antagonize him. Because it's the most effective way to force him to declare himself."

"As always, we understand each other perfectly, don't we, my dear? What better way to bring him back at a run?"

"How clever. I hadn't thought of that. There's no way a Berserker would allow his mate to wed another."

"Let's just hope all the legends about those warriors are true, Elizabeth. Gavrael's da told me years ago that once a Berserker makes love with his own true mate, he can no longer mate another woman. Gavrael is even more Berserk than his da. He'll come for her, and when he does, he'll have no choice but to tell her the truth. We'll get our wedding in three weeks, no doubt about it, and it will be to the man she wants—Grimm."

"What about Quinn's feelings?"

"Quinn doesn't really believe she'll marry him. He is also of the opinion that Grimm will come. I spoke with Quinn before I made Jillian choose, and he agreed to do this. Although I must admit, Ramsay certainly surprised me with his offer."

"You mean you had this all planned out before you confronted her?" Elizabeth was amazed once again by the twists and turns of her husband's brilliant scheming mind.

"It was one of several possible plans," Gibraltar corrected. "A man must anticipate every possibility when the women he loves are concerned."

"My hero." Elizabeth fluttered her eyelashes.

Gibraltar covered her body with his. "I'll show you a hero," he growled.

* * *

Gibraltar hadn't thought that even his cosseted Jillian could pout, sulk, and be nasty for three solid weeks.

She could.

Ever since the morning she'd slipped a note bearing one word, "Quinn," under her parents' bedroom door, she'd refused to speak to him in anything but single-word replies. Everyone else in the castle she harangued with the same questions: how many banns had been posted, when, and where.

"Were they posted in Durrkesh, Kaley?" Jillian fretted.

"Yes, Jillian."

"What about Scurrington and Edinburgh?"

"Yes, Jillian." Hatchard sighed, knowing it was futile to remind her he'd answered the same question the day before.

"And the smaller villages in the Highlands? When were they posted there?"

"Days ago, Jillian." Gibraltar interrupted her interrogation.

Jillian sniffed and turned her back on her da.

"Why do you care where the banns have been posted?" Gibraltar provoked.

"Just curious," Jillian said lightly as she strode regally from the room.

* * *

"He'll come, Mama. I know he will."

Elizabeth smiled and smoothed Jillian's hair, but weeks passed and Grimm didn't come.

Even Quinn started to get a little nervous.

* * *

"What will we do if he doesn't show?" Quinn asked. He paced the study, moving his long legs silently. The wedding was tomorrow and no one had heard a word from Grimm Roderick.

Gibraltar poured them both a drink. "He has to come."

Quinn picked up the goblet and sipped thoughtfully. "He must know the wedding is tomorrow. The only way he could possibly not know is if he is no longer in Scotland. We posted those blasted banns in every village of over fivescore inhabitants."

Gibraltar and Quinn stared at the fire and drank for a time in silence.

"If he doesn't come, I'll go through with it."

"Now, why would you be doing that, lad?" Gibraltar asked gently.

Quinn shrugged. "I love her. I always have."

Gibraltar shook his head. "There's love and then there's

love, Quinn. And if you're not ready to kill Grimm simply for touching Jillian, then it's not the marrying kind of love you're feeling. She's not for you."

When Quinn made no reply, Gibraltar laughed aloud and slapped him on the thigh. "Oh, she's *definitely* not for you. You didn't even argue with me."

"Grimm said something very similar. He asked me if I *really* loved her—if she made me crazy inside."

Gibraltar smiled knowingly. "That's because she *does* make him crazy inside."

"I want her to be happy, Gibraltar," Quinn said fervently. "Jillian is special. She's generous and beautiful and so . . . och, so damned in love with *Grimm*!"

Gibraltar raised his goblet to Quinn's and smiled. "That she is. If push comes to shove, I'll stop the ceremony and give her a choice. But I won't let her marry you without giving her that choice." As he drank, he regarded Quinn thoughtfully. "Actually, I'm not sure I'd let her marry you even then."

"You wound me," Quinn protested.

"She's my baby girl, Quinn. I want love for her. Real love. The kind that makes a man crazy inside."

* * *

Jillian curled into a ball on the window ledge of the drum tower and stared, unseeing, into the night. Thousands of stars dimpled the sky, but she saw none of them. Staring into the night was like staring into a great vacuum—her future without Grimm.

How could she wed Quinn?

How could she refuse? Grimm obviously wasn't coming.

The banns had been posted throughout the country. There was absolutely no way he could *not* know that tomorrow Jillian St. Clair was going to wed Quinn de Moncreiffe. The whole blasted country knew it.

Three weeks ago she might have run away.

But not tonight, not three weeks late for her monthly flow, not with no word from Grimm. Not after believing in him and being proven a lovesick fool.

Jillian rested her palm on her stomach. It was possible she was pregnant, but she wasn't absolutely certain. Her monthly flow had often been irregular and she had been later than this in the past. Mama had told her that many things besides pregnancy could affect a woman's courses: emotional turmoil . . . or a woman's own devout wish that she was pregnant.

Was that it? Did she so long to be pregnant with Grimm Roderick's child that she'd fooled herself? Or was there truly a baby growing inside her? How she wished she knew for certain. She drew a deep breath and expelled it slowly. Only time would tell.

She'd considered striking out on her own, tracking him down, and fighting for their love, but a defiant shred of pride coupled with good common sense made her refuse. Grimm was in the thick of a battle with himself, and it was a battle *he* had to win or lose. She'd offered her love, told him she would accept any kind of life as long as they lived it together. A woman shouldn't have to fight the man she loved for his love. He had to choose to give it freely, to learn that love was the one thing in this world that *wasn't* frightening.

He was an intelligent man and a brave one. He would come.

Jillian sighed. God forgive her, but she still believed.

He *would* come.

Chapter 23

He didn't come.

The day of her wedding dawned cloudy and cold. Sleet started falling at dawn, coating the charred lawn with a layer of crunchy black ice.

Jillian stayed in bed, listening to the sounds of the castle preparing for the wedding feast. Her stomach rumbled a welcome to the scents of roasting ham and pheasant. It was a feast to wake the dead, and it worked; she stumbled from the bed and groped her way through the dimly lit room to the mirror. She stared at her reflection. Dark shadows marred the delicate skin where her cheekbones met her tilted amber eyes.

She would marry Quinn de Moncreiffe in less than six hours.

The rumble of voices carried clearly into her chambers; half the county was in residence, and had been since yesterday. Four hundred guests had been invited and five hundred had arrived, crowding the massive castle and spilling over into less accommodating lodgings in the nearby village.

Five hundred people, more than she would ever have at her funeral, tramping around the frozen black lawn.

Jillian squeezed her eyes tightly shut and refused to cry, certain she'd weep blood if she allowed even one more tear to fall.

* * *

At eleven o'clock Elizabeth St. Clair dabbed prettily at her tears with a dainty hanky. "You look lovely, Jillian," she said with a heartfelt sigh. "Even more so than I did."

"You don't think the bags under my eyes detract, Mama?" Jillian asked acerbically. "How about the grim set of my mouth? My shoulders droop and my nose is beet red from crying. You don't think anyone will find my appearance a bit suspect?"

Elizabeth sniffed, plunked a headpiece on Jillian's hair, and tugged a thin fall of sheer blue gossamer over her daughter's face. "Your da thinks of everything," she said with a shrug.

"A veil? Really, Mama. No one wears a veil in these modern times."

"Just think of it, you'll start a new fashion. By the end of the year, everyone will be wearing them again," Elizabeth chirped.

"How can he do this to me, Mama? Knowing the kind of love you and he share, how can he justify condemning me to a loveless marriage?"

"Quinn does love you, so it won't be loveless."

"It will be on my part."

Elizabeth perched on the edge of the bed. She studied the floor a moment, then raised her eyes to Jillian's.

"You do care," Jillian said, somewhat mollified by the sympathy in Elizabeth's gaze.

"Of course I care, Jillian. I'm your mother." Elizabeth regarded her a pensive moment. "Darling, don't fret, your da has a plan. I hadn't intended to tell you this, but he doesn't plan to make you go through with it. He thinks Grimm will come."

Jillian snorted. "So did I, Mama. But it's ten minutes to the hour and there's no sign of the man. What's Da going to do? Halt the wedding in the middle if he doesn't show up? In front of five hundred guests?"

"You know your da has never been afraid of making a spectacle of himself—or of anyone else, for that matter. The man abducted me from my wedding. I do believe he's hoping the same will happen to you."

Jillian smiled faintly. The story of her mama's "courtship" by her da had enthralled her since she'd been a child. Her da was a man who could give Grimm lessons. Grimm Roderick shouldn't be battling himself about her, he should be battling the world *for* her. Jillian drew a deep breath, hoping against hope, imagining such a scene for herself.

* * *

"We are gathered here today in the company of family, friends, and well-wishers to unite this man and woman in the holy, unbreakable bonds. . . ."

Jillian blew furiously at her veil. Although it puffed a bit, it didn't clear her view. The preacher was slightly blue, Quinn was slightly blue. Irritably she plucked at the veil. No rose-colored hues for her on her wedding day, and why should there be? Outside the tall windows, sleet fell in vaguely blue sheets.

She stole a glance at Quinn, who stood at her side. She was eye level with his chest. Despite her despair, she conceded he was a magnificent man. Regally clad in ceremonial tartan, he'd pulled his long hair back from his chiseled face. Most women would be thrilled to be standing beside him, saying the vows of a lifetime, accompanying him to be mistress of his estate, to give him bonny blond bairns and live in splendor for the rest of their days.

But he was the wrong man. *He'll come for me, he'll come for me, I know he will,* Jillian repeated silently as if it were a magic spell she could weave from the fibers of sheer redundancy.

* * *

Grimm plucked another bann from the wall of a church as he sped by. He crumpled it and crammed it in a satchel that was overflowing with balled-up parchment. He'd been in the tiny highland village of Tummas when he'd seen the first bann, nailed to the side of a ramshackle bothy. Twenty paces beyond it he'd found the second, then the third and the fourth.

Jillian St. Clair was marrying Quinn de Moncreiffe. He'd cursed furiously. How long had she waited? Two days? He hadn't slept that night, consumed by a rage so violent that it had threatened to release the Berserker without any bloodshed to bring it on.

The rage had only intensified, goading him to Occam's back, sending him in circles around the Highlands. He'd ridden to the edge of Caithness, turned around, and come back, ripping down banns all the way, ranging like a maddened beast from Lowland to Highland. Then he turned around again, compelled to Caithness by a force beyond his understanding, a force that reached into the very marrow of his bones. Grimm tossed his braids out of his face and growled. In the forest nearby, a wolf responded with a mournful howl.

He'd had the dream again last night. The one in which Jillian watched him turn Berserk. The one in which she laid her palm against his chest and looked into his eyes and they connected—Jillian and the beast. In his dream, Grimm had realized the beast loved Jillian as deeply as the man, and was just as incapable of ever harming her. In the light of day, he no longer feared that he might hurt Jillian, not even with the threat of his da's madness. He knew himself well enough to know that not even in the wildest throes of Berserkergang could he harm her.

But in his dream, as Jillian had searched his blazing, unholy eyes, fear and revulsion had marked her lovely features. She'd extended a hand palm out to stay him, begging him to go far away as quickly as Occam could carry him.

The Berserker had made a pathetic sound while the man's heart slowly iced over, cooler than the ice-blue eyes that had witnessed so much loss. In his dream, he'd fled for the cover of darkness to hide from her horrified gaze.

Once Quinn had asked him what could kill a Berserker, and now he knew.

A thing so slight as the look on Jillian's face.

He'd woken from the dream filled with despair. Today was Jillian's wedding, and if dreams were portents, she would never forgive him for what he was about to do should she ever uncover his true nature.

But need she ever know?

He would hide the Berserker inside him forever if necessary. He would never again save anyone, never fight, never view blood; he would never reveal himself. He would live as a mere man. They would stop at Dalkeith, where the

Hawk stored a considerable fortune for Grimm, and, with enough gold to buy her a castle in any country, they would flee far from the treacherous McKane and those who knew his secret.

If she would still have him.

He knew what he was about to do was not the honorable thing, but truth be told, he no longer cared. God forgive him—he was a Berserker who likely suffered his da's madness somewhere in his veins, but he could not stand by and permit Jillian St. Clair to wed another man while he still lived and breathed.

Now he understood what she'd known instinctively, years ago, the day he'd stepped out of the woods and stood looking down at her.

Jillian St. Clair was his.

* * *

The hour was approaching noon and he was no more than three miles from Caithness when he was ambushed.

Chapter 24

Ye gods! Jillian drifted back from her wandering thoughts, alarmed. The pudgy priest was almost to the "I do" part. Jillian craned her neck, searching frantically for her father, with no success. The Greathall was crammed to overflowing; guests angled up the staircase, hung over the balustrade, and were stuffed into every nook and cranny.

Fear gripped her. What if her mother had made up the story of her father's plan merely as a ruse to get her to stand up in front of the crowd? What if her mama had deliberately lied, wagering that once they got to the vows, Jillian wouldn't have the nerve to dishonor her parents and Quinn, not to mention herself, by refusing to wed him?

"If there are any here today who know some reason why these two should remain separate, speak now or forever haud yer wheesht."

The hall was silent.

The pause stretched over the length of several heartbeats.

As it lengthened intolerably into minutes, people began to yawn, shuffle their feet, and stretch impatiently.

Silence.

Jillian puffed at her veil and peeked at Quinn. He stood ramrod straight beside her, his hands clasped. She whispered his name, but either he didn't hear or he refused to acknowledge it. She peered at the priest, who seemed to have fallen into a trance, gazing at the bound volume in his hands.

What on earth was going on? She tapped her foot and waited for her da to say something to bring this debacle to a screeching halt.

"I said, if there are any here who see some reason . . ." the priest intoned dramatically.

More silence.

Jillian's nerves stretched to breaking. What was she doing? If her da wouldn't rescue her, to hell with him. She refused to be cowed by fear of scandal. She was her father's daughter, by God, and he'd never genuflected to the false idol of propriety. She puffed at her veil, flipped it back impatiently, and scowled at the priest. "Oh, for goodness' sake—"

"Don't get snippy with me, missy," the priest snapped. "I'm just doing my job."

Jillian's courage was momentarily quaffed by his unexpected rebuke.

Quinn caught her hand in his. "Is something wrong, Jillian? Are you feeling unwell? Your face is flushed." His gaze was full of concern and . . . sympathy?

"I—*can't marry you*" is what she started to say when the doors to the Greathall burst open, crushing several unsuspecting people against the wall. Her words were swallowed in the din of indignant squeals and yelps.

All eyes flew to the entrance.

A great gray stallion reared up in the doorway, its breath frosting the air with puffs of steam. It was a scene from every fairy-tale romance she'd ever read: the handsome prince bursting into the castle astride a magnificent stallion, ablaze with desire and honor as he'd declared his undying love before all and sundry. Her heart swelled with joy.

Then her brow puckered as she scrutinized her "prince." Well, it was almost like a fairy tale. Except this prince was dressed in nothing but a drenched and muddy tartan with blood on his face and hands and war braids plaited at his temples. Although determination glittered in his gaze, a declaration of undying love didn't appear to be his first priority.

"Jillian!" he roared.

Her knees buckled. His voice brought her violently to life. Everything in the room receded and there was only Grimm, blue eyes blazing, his massive frame filling the doorway. He was majestic, towering, and ruthless. *Here* was her fierce warrior ready to battle the world to gain her love.

He urged Occam into the crowd, making his way toward the altar.

"Grimm," she whispered.

He drew up beside her. Sliding from Occam's back, he dropped to the floor next to the bride and groom. He looked at Quinn. The two men gazed at each other a tense moment, then Quinn inclined his head the merest fraction and stepped back a pace. The Greathall hushed as five hundred guests stood riveted by the unfolding spectacle.

Grimm was at a sudden loss for words. Jillian was so beautiful, a goddess clad in shimmering satin. He was covered with blood, mud-stained and filthy, while behind them stood the incomparable Quinn, impeccably attired, titled and noble—Quinn, who had all he lacked.

The blood on his hands was a relentless reminder that despite his fervent vows to conceal the Berserker, the McKane would always be there. They'd been lying in wait for him today. What if they attacked when he was traveling with Jillian? Four had escaped him. The others were dead. But those four were trouble enough—they would round up more men and continue hunting Grimm until either the last McKane was dead, or he was. Along with anyone traveling with him.

What could he hope to accomplish by taking her now? What fool's dream had possessed him to come here today? What desperate hope had convinced him he might be able to hide his true nature from her? And how would he survive the look on her face when she saw him for what he really was? "I'm a bloody fool," he muttered.

A smile curved Jillian's lip. "Yes, that you've been on more than one occasion, Grimm Roderick. You were most foolish when you left me, but I do believe I might forgive you now that you've come back."

Grimm sucked in a harsh breath. Berserker be damned, he had to have her.

"Will you come with me, Jillian?" *Say yes, woman,* he prayed.

A simple nod was her immediate response.

His chest swelled with unexpected emotion. "I'm sorry, Quinn," Grimm said. He wanted to say more, but Quinn shook his head, leaned close, and whispered something in Grimm's ear. Grimm's jaw tensed, and they stared at each other in silence. Finally Grimm nodded.

"Then you go with my blessing," Quinn said clearly.

Grimm extended his arms to Jillian, who slipped into his embrace. Before he could succumb to the urge to kiss her senseless, he tossed her on Occam's back and mounted behind her.

Jillian scanned the worried faces around her. Ramsay was gazing at Grimm with a shocking amount of hatred in his eyes, and she was momentarily flustered by the intensity of it. Quinn's expression was a blend of concern and reluctant understanding. She finally spotted her da where he stood with her mother a dozen feet away. Elizabeth's face was grim. Gibraltar held her gaze a moment, then nodded encouragingly.

Jillian leaned back into Grimm's broad chest and gave a small sigh of pleasure. "I would live any kind of life I had to live, so long as I lived it with you, Grimm Roderick."

It was all he needed to hear. His arms tightened around her waist, he kneed Occam forward and together they fled Caithness.

* * *

"Now that's my idea of how a man takes a woman to wife," Gibraltar observed with satisfaction.

AN ILLYOCH PROPHECY

Legend tells that the Clan Illyoch will prosper for one thousand years, birthing warriors who will accomplish great good for Alba.

In the fertile vale of Tuluth a castle shall rise around the Hall of Gods and many shall covet what belongs to Scotia's blessed race.

The seers warn that an envious clan shall pursue the Illyoch until they are but three. The three will be scattered like seeds uprooted by the wind of betrayal, cast far and wide, and all will appear to be lost. Much grief and despair will descend upon the holy vale.

But harken to hope, sons of Odin, for the three shall be gathered by his far-reaching grasp. When the young Illyoch finds his true mate, she shall bring him home, the enemy shall be vanquished, and the Illyoch shall thrive for a thousand years more.

Chapter 25

They rode hard until early evening, when Grimm drew Occam to a stop in a copse of trees. Upon leaving Caithness, he'd tugged a plaid from his pack and secured it tightly around Jillian's body, forming a nearly waterproof barrier between her and the elements.

He hadn't uttered a word since then. His face had been so grim that she'd kept her silence, allowing him time and privacy to muddle through his thoughts. She'd nestled back against him, contentedly savoring the press of his hard body against hers. Grimm Roderick had come for her. While such an inauspicious beginning might not be the perfect way to start a life together, it would do. For Grimm Roderick to steal a woman from her wedding, he must intend to care for her the rest of her life, and that's all she'd ever desired—a life with him.

By the time he drew Occam to a halt, the freezing rain had abated but the temperature had plummeted. Winter was encroaching, and she suspected they were headed directly for the Highlands, where the chill winds gusted with twice the vigor as in the Lowlands. She clutched the plaid snugly around her, sealing out the cold air.

Grimm dismounted, lowered her from the saddle, and held her for a moment. "God, I missed you, Jillian." The words exploded from him.

She tossed her head, delighted. "What took you so long, Grimm?"

His expression was impossible to interpret. He glanced self-consciously at his hands, which were badly in need of a washing. He busied himself with a flagon of water and a scrap of clean plaid for a moment, removing the worst of the stains. "I had a wee bit of a skirmish on the way and . . ." he mumbled inaudibly.

She studied his disheveled clothing but decided not to ask him about it then. The mud and blood appeared to be from a recent fight, but what had happened in the last few days wasn't her first concern. "That's not what I meant. It took you over a month. Was it so difficult for you to decide if you wanted me?" She forced a teasing smile to camouflage the wounded part of her that was utterly serious.

"Never think that, Jillian. I wake up wanting you. I fall asleep wanting you. I watch a magnificent sunrise and can think only of sharing it with you. I glimpse a piece of amber and see your eyes. Jillian, I've caught a disease, and the fever abates only when I'm near you."

She flashed him a radiant smile. "You're nearly forgiven. So tell me—what took you so long? Is it that you think you're not good enough for me, Grimm Roderick? Because you're not titled, I mean." When he didn't respond, she hastened to reassure him. "I don't care, you know. A title doesn't make the man, and you're certainly the finest man that I've ever known. What on earth do you think is wrong with you?"

His stubborn silence didn't serve as the deterrent he intended; she scurried down an alternate route of inquiry. "Quinn told me that you think your father is mad and you're afraid you've inherited the madness. He said it was nonsense and I must tell you I agree, because you're the most intelligent man I've ever met—except for the times when you don't trust me, which evidences a glaring lapse in your customary good judgment."

Grimm stared at her, disconcerted. "What else did Quinn tell you?"

"That you love me," she said simply.

He swept her into his embrace in one swift move. He buried his hands in her hair and kissed her urgently. She savored the rock-hard press of his body against hers, his teasing tongue, his strong hands cupping her face. Jillian melted against him, wordlessly demanding more. The past month without him, followed by hours pressed against his muscled body as they'd ridden, had begun a slow burn of desire within her. For the past hour, her skin had tingled at every point of contact with his body, and a trembling heat had gathered in her midsection, seeping lower, awakening shockingly intense feelings of desire. She'd been oblivious to the terrain, her mind fully occupied with imagining, in blush-inducing detail, the many different ways she wanted to make love with him.

Now she practically vibrated with need, and she responded wildly to his kiss. Her body was already prepared for him, and she pressed encouragingly against his hips.

He stopped kissing her as suddenly as he'd begun. "We must continue riding," he said tightly. "We have a long way to go, lass. I doona wish to keep you out here in the cold any longer than I must."

He pulled away so abruptly that Jillian gaped at him and nearly screamed with frustration. She was so heated from his kiss that the chill air was inconsequential, and she certainly had no intention of waiting even a moment longer to make love with him again.

She let her eyes flutter slowly closed and swayed a bit. Grimm eyed her intently. "Are you feeling all right, lass?"

"No," Jillian replied, casting him a sidelong glance beneath her lowered lashes. "Frankly, I feel decidedly odd, Grimm, and I don't know what to make of it."

He moved back to her side instantly, and she prepared to spring her trap.

"Where do you feel odd, Jillian? Have I—"

"Here." She swiftly took his hand and placed it on her breast. "And here." She guided his other hand to her hips.

Grimm took several deep breaths and blew them out, willing his thundering heart to slow, to quit pumping so much blood to his loins and perhaps let his brain in on the bargain so he might entertain a coherent thought. "Jillian," he said, exhaling a frustrated breath.

"Well, my," she said mischievously, moving her hands over his body. "You seem to be suffering the same ailment." Her hand closed over him through his plaid, and he made a low, growling sound deep in his throat.

They both spoke at once.

"It's freezing out here, lass. I won't subject you—"

"I'm not—"

"—to the cold for my own selfish needs—"

"—fragile, Grimm. And what about *my* selfish needs?"

"—and I can't make love to you properly outside!"

"Oh, and is *properly* the only way you've ever wanted me?" she mocked.

His gaze locked with hers, and his eyes darkened with desire. He seemed immobilized, obtusely assessing the cold, considering all of her needs—except for the one that really mattered.

In a low voice she said, "Do it. Take me. *Now.*"

His eyes narrowed and he sucked in a harsh breath. *"Jillian."* A storm gathered in his ice-blue eyes, and she wondered for a moment what she'd called forth. A beast—*her* beast. And she wanted him exactly the way he was.

The force of his passion hit her like a sea gale, hot and salty and primitive in its power, holding nothing back. They exploded against each other, driving their bodies as close together as they could. He backed her against a tree, thrust her gown up, and pushed his plaid aside, all the while kissing her eyelids, her nose, her lips, plunging his tongue so deeply into her mouth that she felt herself drowning in the man's sensuality.

"I need you, Jillian St. Clair. Ever since I tossed you up on my horse I've been wanting nothing more than to drag you back off it and bury myself in you, without a word of explanation or apology—because I need you."

"Yes," she whispered fervently. "*That's* what I want!"

With a swift stroke he plunged deeply into her, but the storm was in her body and it raged with the devastating fury of a hurricane.

She tossed her head back and freed her voice, crying out to him, only the creatures of the wilderness to hear. She moved against him urgently, her hips rising to meet every thrust. Her hands clawed at his shoulders and she raised her legs, wrapping them tightly around his waist, locking her ankles over his muscled hips. With each thrust he pressed her back against the tree trunk and she used it to rock herself back into him, taking him as deeply into her body as she could. Only the sounds of passion escaped their lips; words simply weren't needed. Bonding and pledging through contact, their bodies spoke in a tongue ancient and unmistakable.

"Jillian!" he roared as he exploded inside her. An unfettered laugh of delight escaped her as the rush of his liquid warmth inside her pushed her over the edge of pleasure, and she bucked against him.

They held on to each other for a reverent moment. Leaning against her in a soft crush, he seemed reluctant to move, as if he wanted to stay joined to her forever. And when he began to stiffen inside her, she knew she'd convinced him that a little cold air was good for the soul.

* * *

Grimm whistled for Occam. Summoning his horse from the woods, he tightened the tethers on the packs. It was full dark, and they needed to be on their way. There was no shelter to be secured tonight, but by the following day they would be far enough into the Highlands that he could provide shelter for them each night to come. He glanced over his shoulder at Jillian. It was imperative to him that he keep her happy, warm, and safe. "Are you hungry, Jillian? Are you dry enough? Warm enough?"

"No, yes, and yes. Where are we going, Grimm?" she asked, still feeling dreamy from their intense lovemaking.

"There's an abandoned cottage a day's ride from here."

"I didn't mean now, I meant where are you taking me after that?"

Grimm pondered his answer. He'd originally planned to ride directly to Dalkeith, then leave as soon as they'd gathered his fortune and loaded the horses. But he'd begun to think running might not be necessary. He'd spent much of their time on the ride from Caithness mulling over something Quinn had said. *Hell, man, rouse an army and fight the McKane once and for all. I know scores of men who would fight for you. I would.* As would the Hawk's army, as well as many of the men he'd known at court, men who fought for hire.

Grimm loathed the idea of taking Jillian away from Scotland, from her family. He knew what it was like to be without a clan. If he triumphed over the McKane, he could purchase an estate near her family and have only one demon to battle. He could devote his energy to concealing his nature and making Jillian a fine husband.

Promise me you'll tell her the truth, Quinn had demanded in a low, urgent whisper against his ear.

Grimm had nodded.

But he hadn't said when, he prevaricated lamely as he studied her innocent features. Maybe next year, or a lifetime from now. In the meantime, he had other battles to wage.

"Dalkeith. My good friend and his wife are laird and lady there. You'll be safe with them."

Jillian snapped to attention, dreamy reverie squashed by the thought of an impending separation. "What do you mean, I will be safe there? Don't you mean *we* will be safe there?"

Grimm fidgeted with Occam's saddle.

"Grimm—*we,* right?"

He muttered, deliberately incoherent.

Jillian eyed him a moment and snorted delicately.

"Grimm, you don't plan to take me to Dalkeith and leave me there by myself, do you?" Her eyes narrowed, forecasting a tempest if such was his intention.

Without raising his head from an intent inspection of Occam's tethers, he replied, "Only for a time, Jillian. There's something I must do, and I need to know you'll be safe while I'm doing it."

Jillian watched him fidget and considered her options. "His good friend and his wife," he'd said, people who would know something about her man of mystery. That was promising, if not her preference. She wished he would confide in her, tell her what kept him solitary, but she would work with what she could get. Maybe what had happened in his past was too painful for him to discuss. "Where is Dalkeith?"

"In the Highlands."

"Near where you were born?"

"Past there. We have to circle around Tuluth to get to Dalkeith."

"Why circle around it? Why not ride through it?" Jillian fished.

"Because I've never gone back to Tuluth and I doona plan to now. Besides, the village was destroyed."

"Well, if it was destroyed, that makes it even odder to ride around it. Why avoid nothing?"

Grimm raised a brow. "Must you always be so logical?"

"Must you always be so evasive?" she countered, arching a brow of her own.

"I just doona wish to ride through it, all right?"

"Are you certain it's in ruins?"

When Grimm buried a hand in his hair, Jillian finally understood. The only time Grimm Roderick started messing with his hair was when she asked him a question he didn't want to answer. She almost laughed; if she continued questioning him he might rip it out by the handfuls. But she needed answers, and occasionally her digging resulted in a few treasures. What could possibly make him avoid Tuluth like the darkest plague? "Oh, my goodness," she breathed as intuition pointed an unerring finger toward the truth. "Your family is still alive, aren't they, Grimm?"

Ice-blue eyes flew to hers, and she watched him struggle to avoid her question. He toyed with his war braids and she bit her lip, waiting.

"My da is still alive," he conceded.

Although she'd already arrived at such a conclusion herself, his admission threw her off balance. "What else didn't you tell me, Grimm?"

"That Quinn told you the truth. He's an insane old man," Grimm said bitterly.

"Truly insane, or do you mean you just disagree about things, like most people do with their parents?"

"I doona wish to talk about it."

"How old is your da? Have you other family I don't know about?"

Grimm walked away and started pacing. "No."

"Well, what is your home like? In Tuluth."

"It's not in Tuluth," he said through set teeth. "My home was in a bleak, dreary castle carved into the mountain above Tuluth."

Jillian wondered what other astonishing things might be revealed if he kept answering her questions. "If your home was in the castle, then you must be either a servant—" She eyed him from head to toe and shook her head as comprehension crashed over her. "Oh! Here I am prattling on about titles and you don't even say anything! You're a chieftain's son, aren't you? You wouldn't, by chance, be his oldest son, would you?" she asked, mostly in jest. When he quickly averted his gaze, she exclaimed, "You mean you'll be the laird one day? There's a clan awaiting your return?"

"Never. I will never return to Tuluth, and that's the end of this discussion. My da is a batty old bastard and the castle is in ruins. Along with the village, half my clan was destroyed years ago, and I'm certain the remaining half scattered to escape the old man and rebuild elsewhere. I doubt there's anyone left in Tuluth at all—it's likely nothing but ruins." He stole a surreptitious glance at Jillian to see how she was taking his confession.

Jillian's mind was whirling. Something didn't make sense, and she knew she was lacking vital information. Grimm's childhood home lay between here and their destination, and answers lay in the moldering old ruin. A "batty old da" and insight that would show her the way to Grimm's deepest heart.

"Why did you leave?" she asked gently.

He faced her, his blue eyes glittering in the fading light. "Jillian, please. Not so many questions at once. Give me time. These things . . . I haven't spoken of them since they happened." His eyes wordlessly pleaded with her for patience and understanding.

"Time, I can give. I'll be patient, but I won't give up."

"Promise me that." He was suddenly grave. "Promise me you'll never give up, no matter what."

"On you? I wouldn't. Goodness, as mean as you were to me when I was a wee lass, I still didn't give up on you," she said lightly, hoping to brighten his somber expression.

"On *us*, Jillian. Promise me you'll never give up on us." He tugged her back into his arms and gazed down at her so intensely, it nearly took her breath away.

"I promise," she breathed. "And I take my honor as seriously as any warrior."

He relaxed infinitesimally, hoping he'd never need to remind her of her words.

"Are you certain you're not hungry yet?" He changed the subject swiftly.

"I can wait until we stop for the night," she assured him absently, too occupied with her thoughts to consider physical demands. She no longer wondered why he had appeared so late, bloody and mud-stained. He had come, and that was enough for now.

There were other, bigger questions she needed answered.

As they remounted, he drew her against him and she relaxed, relishing the feel of his hard body.

A few hours later, she reached a decision. *A lass has to do what a lass has to do*, she told herself firmly. By morning she planned to acquire a sudden case of inexplicable illness that would demand they secure permanent shelter long before they reached Dalkeith. She had no idea that, by morning, serendipity would take charge of events for her with a twisted sense of humor.

Chapter 26

JILLIAN ROLLED OVER, STRETCHED, AND PEERED through the dim light at Grimm. Furs hung over the windows of the cottage. They barred entrance to the bitter wind, but also permitted little light. The fire had burned down to embers hours ago, and in the amber glow that remained he looked like a bronzed warrior, a heroic, mighty Viking stretched out on the pallet of furs with one arm bent behind his head, the other curled about her waist.

By the saints, but the man was beautiful! In repose, his face had the kind of perfection that made one think of an archangel, created by a joyous God. His brows winged in black arches above eyes that were fringed with thick lashes. Although tiny lines splayed out from the corners of his eyes, he had few laugh lines around his mouth, a lack she intended to remedy. His nose was straight and proud, his lips . . . she could spend a day just gazing at those firm pink lips that curved sensually even in his sleep. She dropped a whisper-light kiss upon the stubborn cleft in his chin.

When they'd arrived the night before, Grimm had built a roaring fire and melted buckets of snow for a bath. They'd shared a tub, shivering in the frigid air until the heat of passion had warmed them to the bone. On a lush pile of furs, they'd wordlessly renewed their pledge to each other. The man was patently inexhaustible, she thought contentedly. Her body ached pleasantly from the marathon lovemaking. He'd shown her things that made her cheeks flame and her heart race in anticipation of more.

Steamy thoughts decamped abruptly when her stomach chose that moment to lurch alarmingly. Rendered momentarily breathless from the sudden nausea, she curled on her side and waited for the feeling to recede. As they'd had little to eat last night and been very active, she concluded she was probably hungry. An aching tummy would certainly make her plan to convince Grimm she was too sick to ride to Dalkeith easier to enact. What illness could she claim? An upset stomach might not be convincing enough to make him consider stopping in a village he'd sworn never to see again.

Conveniently, another wave of nausea gripped her. She scowled as the possibility occurred to her that she'd actually made herself ill merely by planning to pretend she was. She lay motionless, waiting for the discomfort to subside, and conjured visions of her favorite food, hoping that imagination would quaff the hunger pains.

Thoughts of Kaley's pork roast nearly doubled her over. Baked fish in wine sauce had her gagging in an instant. Bread? That didn't sound so bad. The crustier the better. She tried to inch away from Grimm to snatch the satchel where she'd seen a loaf of brown bread the night before, but in his sleep he tightened his arm around her waist. Stealthily she worked at his fingers, but they were like iron vises. As a fresh wave of nausea assaulted her, she moaned and curled into a ball, clutching her stomach. The sound woke Grimm instantly.

"Are you all right, lass? Did I hurt you?"

Afraid he was referring to their excessive lovemaking, she hastened to reassure him. She didn't wish to give him any reason to think twice before bestowing such pleasure on her again. "I'm only a bit sore," she said, then groaned as her stomach heaved again.

"What is it?" Grimm shot up in bed, and despite her misery she marveled at his beauty. His black hair fell about his face, and although the thought of food made her feel impossibly queasy, his lips still looked inviting.

"Did I harm you in my sleep?" he asked hoarsely. "What is it? Talk to me, lass!"

"I just don't feel well. I don't know what's wrong. My stomach hurts."

"Would food help?" He scuffled through the packs rapidly. Uncovering a large piece of greasy, salted beef, he thrust it beneath her nose.

"Oh, *no*!" she wailed, lunging to her knees. She scuttled away from him as quickly as possible, but made it only a few feet before retching. He was at her side in a heartbeat, smoothing the hair back from her face. "Don't," she cried. "Don't even look at me." Jillian hadn't been sick much in her life, but when she had she loathed anyone seeing her weakened by forces beyond her control. It made her feel helpless.

She was probably being punished for planning to be deceitful. That was hardly fair, she thought crossly. She'd never been deceitful in her life—surely she was entitled to one time, especially since it was for a such good cause. They had to stop at Tuluth. She needed answers that she suspected could be found only by returning to Grimm's roots.

"Hush, lass, it's all right. What can I do? What do you need?" It couldn't be poison, Grimm thought frantically. He'd prepared the food they'd eaten last night himself, of venison he'd tracked and cured while up in the Highlands. Then what was it? he wondered, deluged by a flood of emotions: helplessness, fear, realization that this woman in his arms meant everything to him and that he would take whatever sickness she had and bear it himself, if he could.

She convulsed again in his arms, and he held her trembling body.

It was some time before she stopped heaving. When she finally calmed, he wrapped her in a warm blanket and heated some water over the fire. She lay absolutely still while he washed her face. He was transfixed by her beauty; despite her illness Jillian certainly did seem radiant, her skin a translucent ivory, her lips deep pink, her cheeks flushed with rose.

"Are you feeling better, lass?"

She took a deep breath and nodded. "I think so. But I'm not certain I can ride very far today. Is there a place we might stop between here and Dalkeith?" she asked plaintively.

"Perhaps we shouldn't go at all," he hedged, but they had to move on, and he knew it. Lingering here another day was the most dangerous thing he could do. If the McKane were following, one more day might well cost them their lives. He closed his eyes and pondered the dilemma. What if they started off again and she became sicker? Where could he take her? Where they could they hide away until she was well enough to travel?

Of course, he thought sardonically.

Tuluth.

Chapter 27

As they neared the village of his birth, Grimm lapsed into a protracted silence.

They'd ridden at an easy gait through the day, and Jillian had rapidly recovered her customary vigor. Despite her improved health, she forced herself to continue the charade. They were too close to Tuluth for her to waffle in indecision.

They had to go to Tuluth. It was necessary, whether she condoned her methods or not. She suffered no delusions that Grimm would return voluntarily. If he had his way he'd forget the village ever existed. While she accepted the fact that Grimm couldn't bring himself to talk about his past, she had a suspicion that returning to Tuluth might be more necessary for him than it was for her. It was possible he needed to confront his memories in order to lay them to rest.

For her part, she needed to examine the evidence with her own eyes and hands, speak with his "batty" da, and fish for information. In the rubble and debris of the destroyed castle she might find clues to help her understand the man she loved.

Jillian glanced down at his hand, so big it nearly cupped both of hers, while he guided Occam with the other one. What could he possibly think was wrong with him? He was noble and honest, with the exception of speaking about his past. He was strong, fearless, and one of the best warriors she'd ever seen. The man was virtually invincible. Why, he put the legends of those mythical beasts, the Berserkers, to shame.

Jillian smiled, thinking men like Grimm were where such legends were born. Why, he even had the legendary fierce blue eyes. If such beings truly existed, he might have been one of those mighty warriors, she thought dreamily. She hadn't been surprised to learn he was the son of a chieftain; nobility was evident in every line of his magnificent face. She released a sigh of pleasure and leaned back into his chest.

"We're nearly there, lass," he said comfortingly, misinterpreting the sigh.

"Will we be going to the castle?" she asked weakly.

"No. There are some caves where we can take shelter on a cliff called Wotan's Cleft. I played there when I was a boy. I know them well."

"Wouldn't the castle be warmer? I'm so cold, Grimm." She shivered in what she hoped was a convincing manner.

"If my memory serves me, Maldebann is a shambles." He tucked the plaid more securely about her shoulders and cradled her in the heat from his body. "I'm not certain any of the walls are standing. Besides, if my da is still around anywhere he probably haunts those crumbling halls."

"Well, how about the village? Surely some of your people remained?" She refused to succeed in her bid to reach Tuluth but be denied contact with people who might know something about her Highland warrior.

"Jillian, the entire valley was wiped out. I suspect it will be completely deserted. We'll be lucky if the caves are still passable. A lot of the passageways shifted, even collapsed into rubble during the years I played there."

"More reason to go to the castle," she said quickly. "It sounds as if the caves are dangerous."

Grimm expelled a breath. "You're persistent, aren't you, lass?"

"I'm just so cold," she whimpered, pushing away the guilt she felt about being deceitful. It was for a good cause.

His arms tightened around her. "I'll take care of you, Jillian, I promise."

* * *

"Where are they, Gilles?" Ronin asked.

"Nearly three miles east, milord."

Ronin plucked nervously at his tartan and turned to his brother. "Do I look all right?"

Balder grinned. " 'Do I look all right?' " he mocked in falsetto, preening for an imaginary audience.

Ronin punched him in the arm. "Stop it, Balder. This is important. I'm meetin' my son's wife today."

"You're seein' your *son* today," Balder corrected.

Ronin cast his gaze to the stones. "Aye, that I am," he said finally. His head whipped back and he glanced at Balder anxiously. "What if he still hates me, Balder? What if he rides up, spits in my face, and leaves?"

The grin faded from Balder's lips. "Then I'll beat the lad senseless, tie him up, and we'll both be talkin' to him. Persuasively and at our leisure."

Ronin's face brightened considerably. "Now, there's a plan," he said optimistically. "Maybe we could do that straightaway, what say you?"

"Ronin."

Ronin shrugged. "It just seems the most direct course," he said defensively.

Balder assessed his brother, his nervous, callused fingers smoothing the ceremonial tartan. His sleekly combed black hair, liberally sprinkled with silver. His jeweled *sgain dubh* and velvet sporran. His wide shoulders and not-so-trim waist. He stood taller and with more pride than Balder had seen him stand in years. His blue eyes reflected joy, hope, and . . . fear. "You look like every inch a fine laird, brother," Balder said gently. "Any son would be proud to call you da."

Ronin took a deep breath and nodded tightly. "Let's hope you're right. Are the banners hung, Gilles?"

Gilles grinned and nodded. "You do look regal, milord," he added proudly. "And I must say Tuluth has made a fine showing for us. The valley fairly sparkles. Any lad would be pleased to see this as his future demesne."

"And the Hall of Lords, has it been cleaned and opened? Are the torches lit?"

"Yes, milord, and I've hung the portrait in the dining hall."

Ronin gulped a breath of air and began pacing. "The villagers have been informed? All of them?"

"They're waitin' in the streets, Ronin, and the banners have been hung throughout Tuluth as well. It's a fine homecoming you've planned," Balder said.

"Let's just hope he thinks so," Ronin muttered, pacing.

* * *

Grimm's fingers tightened on Jillian's waist as Occam carefully picked his way up the back pass to Wotan's Cleft.

He had no intention of taking Jillian to the cold damp caves where a fire could smoke them out if the wind suddenly changed course down one of the tunnels, but from the Cleft he could assess the village and the castle. If any part of it was still standing, he could scan for smoke from a hearth if anyone inhabited the ghost village. Besides, he preferred Jillian to see immediately what a desolate place it was so she might wish to hurry on to Dalkeith as soon as she was able. She seemed to be making a rapid recovery, although she was still weak and complained of intermittent queasiness.

The sun topped the peak of the Cleft. It wouldn't set for several more hours, allowing him ample time to assess the potential dangers and secure shelter somewhere in the ruined village. If Jillian was well tomorrow morning they could race for the shores of Dalkeith. To avoid leading the McKane to the Douglas estate, he planned to stop in a nearby village and send a messenger for Hawk. They would meet discreetly to discuss the possibility of raising an army and plan Jillian's and his future.

As the tall standing stones of Wotan's Cleft came into view, Grimm's chest tightened painfully. He forced himself to take deep, even breaths as they navigated the rocky path. He hadn't anticipated the force with which his bitter memories would resurface. He'd last climbed this path fifteen years ago and it had forever changed his life. *Hear me, Odin! I summon the Berserker* . . . He'd ascended a boy and descended a monster.

His hands fisted. How could he have considered coming back here? But Jillian snuggled against him, seeking warmth, and he knew he would enter Tuluth willingly even if it were occupied by hordes of demons, to keep her safe and warm.

"Are you all right, Grimm?"

How typically Jillian, he marveled. Despite her own sickness, her concern was for him. "I'm fine. We'll be warm soon, lass. Just rest."

He sounded so worried that Jillian had to bite her tongue to prevent an instant confession from escaping.

"In just a moment you'll be able to see where the village used to be," he said, sorrow roughening his voice.

"I can't imagine what it would be like to see Caithness destroyed. I didn't mean to bring you back to a place that is so painful . . ."

"It happened many years ago. It's almost as if it happened in another lifetime."

Jillian sat up straight as they topped the crest and searched the landscape with curious eyes.

"There." Grimm directed her attention to the cliff. "From the promontory the whole valley comes into view." He smiled faintly. "I used to come up here and look out over the land, thinking that a lad had never been born luckier than I."

Jillian winced. Occam moved forward, his gait steady. Jillian held her breath as they approached the edge.

"The caves lie behind us, beyond that tumble of stones where the slope of the mountain is steepest. My best friend Arron and I once vowed we would map out every tunnel, every chamber in that mountain, but the passages seemed to go on forever. We'd nearly mapped out a quarter of it before . . . before . . ."

Remorse for dragging him back to face his demons flooded her. "Was your friend killed in the battle?"

"Aye."

"Was your da hurt in the battle?" she asked gently.

"He should have died," Grimm said tightly. "The McKane buried a battle-ax in his chest clear to the hilt. It's amazing he survived. For several years after, I assumed he had died."

"And your mother?" she said in a whisper.

There was a silence, broken only by the sound of shale crushing beneath Occam's hooves. "We'll be able to see it any moment, lass."

Jillian's gaze fixed on the cliff's edge where the rock terminated abruptly and became the horizon. Hundreds of feet down she would find the ashes of Tuluth. She drew herself up straighter, nearly tumbling from the horse in her anxiety, and braced herself for the grim scene.

"Hold, lass," Grimm soothed as they took the last few steps to the cliff and gazed out over the lifeless valley.

For nearly five minutes he didn't speak. Jillian wasn't certain he breathed. On the other hand, she wasn't certain she did either.

Below them, nestled around a crystalline river and several sparkling lochs, a vibrant city teemed with life, white huts washed to soft amber by the afternoon sun. Hundreds of homes dotted the valley in even rows along meticulously maintained roads. Smoke from cozy fires spiraled lazily from flues, and although she couldn't hear the voices, she could see children running and playing. People walked up and down the roads where an occasional lamb or cow wandered. Two wolfhounds played in a small garden. Along the main roadway that ran down the center of the city, brilliantly colored banners waved and flapped in the breeze.

Astonished, she scanned the valley, following the river to the face of the mountain. It bubbled from an underground source at the mountain's base, the castle towering in stone above it. Her hand flew to her lips to smother a cry of shock. This was not what she'd expected to see.

A bleak and dreary castle, he'd called it.

Nothing could have been further from the truth. Castle Maldebann was the most beautiful castle she'd ever laid eyes on. With its exquisitely carved towers and regal face, it looked as if it had been liberated from the mountain by the hammer and chisel of a visionary sculptor. Constructed of pale gray stone, it rose in mighty arches to a breathtaking height. The mountain effectively sealed the valley at that end and the castle sprawled along the entire width of the closure, wings stretching east and west from the castle proper.

Its mighty towers made Caithness look like a summer cottage—nay, like a child's tree loft. No wonder Castle Maldebann had been the focus of an attack; it was an incredible, enviable stronghold. The guard walk at the top was dotted with dozens of uniformed figures. The entrance was visible beyond the portcullis and postern and soared nearly fifty feet. Brightly clad women dotted the lower walkways, scurrying to and fro with baskets and children.

"Grimm?" Jillian croaked his name. Ruins? Her brow furrowed in consternation as she wondered how this could possibly be. Was it possible Grimm had misunderstood who lost that fateful battle years ago?

A huge banner with bold lettering rippled above the entrance to the castle. Jillian narrowed her eyes and squinted, much as she chided Zeke for doing, but she couldn't make out the words. "What does it say, Grimm?" she managed in a hushed whisper, awed by the unexpected vista of peace and prosperity stretching before her eyes.

For a long moment he didn't answer. She heard him

swallow convulsively behind her, his body as rigid as the rocks Occam shifted his hooves upon.

"Do you think maybe some other clan took over this valley and rebuilt?" she offered faintly, latching on to any reason she could find to make sense of things.

He released a whistling breath, then punctuated it with a groan. "I doubt it, Jillian."

"It's possible, isn't it?" she insisted. If not, Grimm might genuinely suffer his da's madness, for only a madman could call this magnificent city a ruin.

"No."

"Why? I mean, how can you be certain from here? I can't even make out their plaids."

"Because that banner says 'Welcome home, son,' " he whispered with horror.

Chapter 28

"How am I supposed to make sense of this, Grimm?" Jillian asked as the tense silence between them grew. He was staring blankly down at the valley. She felt suddenly and overwhelmingly confused.

"How are *you* supposed to make sense of it?" He slid from Occam's back and lowered her to the ground beside him. "You?" he echoed incredulously. He couldn't find one bit of sense in it either. Not only wasn't his home a ruin of ashes scattered across the valley floor as it was supposed to be, there were bloody welcome banners flapping from the turrets.

"Yes," she encouraged. "Me. You told me this place had been destroyed."

Grimm couldn't tear his eyes away from the vision in the valley. He was stupefied, any hope of logic derailed by shock. Tuluth was five times the size it had once been, the land tilled in neatly patterned sections, the homes twice as large. Weren't things supposed to seem smaller when one got bigger? His mind objected, with a growing sense of disorientation. He scanned the rocks behind him, seeking the hidden mouth of the cave to reassure himself that he was standing upon Wotan's Cleft and that it was indeed Tuluth below him. The river flowing through the valley was twice as wide, bluer than lapis—hell, even the mountain seemed to have grown.

Castle Maldebann was another matter. Had it changed colors? He recalled it as a towering monolith carved from blackest obsidian, all wicked forbidding angles, dripping moss and gargoyles. His gaze roved disbelievingly over the flowing lines of the pale gray, inviting structure. Fully occupied, cheerily functional, decorated—by God—with banners.

Banners that read "Welcome home."

Grimm sank to his knees, opened his eyes as wide as he could, closed and rubbed them, then opened them again. Jillian watched him curiously.

"It's still there, isn't it?" she said matter-of-factly. "I tried it too," she sympathized.

Grimm snatched a quick glance at her and was stunned to see a half-smile curving her lip. "Is there something amusing about this, lass?" he asked, unaccountably offended.

Instant compassion flooded her features. She laid a gentle hand on his arm. "Oh, no, Grimm. Don't think I'm laughing at you. I'm laughing at how stunned we both are, and partly with relief. I was expecting a dreadful scene. This is the last thing we expected to see. I know the shock must be doubly hard for you to absorb, but I was thinking it's funny because you look like I felt when you first came back to Caithness."

"How is that, lass?"

"Well, when I was little you seemed so big. I mean huge, monstrous, the biggest man in the world. And when you came back, since I was bigger, I expected you to finally look smaller. Not smaller than me, but at least smaller than you did the last time I'd seen you up close."

"And?" he encouraged.

She shook her head, bewildered. "You didn't. You looked bigger."

"And your point is?" He tore his gaze from the valley and peered at her.

"Well, you were expecting smaller, weren't you? I suspect it's probably much bigger. Shocking, isn't it?"

"I'm still waiting for your point, lass," he said dryly.

"I can see someone should have told you more fables when you were young," she teased. "My point is, memory can be a deceptive thing," she clarified. "Perhaps the village never was completely destroyed. Perhaps it just seemed that way when you left. Did you leave at night? Was it too dark to see clearly?"

Grimm took her hands in his as they knelt together on the cliff's edge. It *had* been night when he'd left Tuluth, and the air had been thick with smoke. It had been a horrifying scene to the fourteen-year-old lad. He'd left believing his village and home destroyed and himself a dangerous beast. He'd left filled with hatred and despair, expecting little of life.

Now, fifteen years later, he crouched upon the same ridge, holding the hands of the woman he loved beyond life itself, gazing upon impossible sights. If Jillian hadn't been with him he might have tucked tail and run, never permitting himself to wonder what strange magic had been worked in this vale. He raised her hand to his lips and kissed it. "My memory of you was never deceptive. I always remembered you as the best that life had to offer."

Jillian's eyes widened. She tried to speak but ended up making a small choked sound instead. Grimm stiffened, interpreting her sound for a cry of discomfort. "Here I am, keeping you out in the cold when you're ill."

"That's not what . . . no," she stammered. "Truly, I feel much better now." When he eyed her suspiciously, she added, "Oooh, but I do need to get somewhere warm soon, Grimm. And that castle certainly looks warm." She eyed it hopefully.

Grimm's gaze darted back to the valley. The castle did look warm. And well fortified. Damn near the safest place he could take her, and why not? There were "welcome home" banners draped in dozens of locations. If the McKane were following him, what better place to stand and fight? How strange it was to return to Tuluth after all these years, with the McKane on his heels once again. Would the pattern finally come full circle and end? Perhaps they wouldn't need to go to Dalkeith to raise an army to fight the McKane after all.

But he'd have to face his da. He blew out a frustrated breath and weighed their options. How could he descend into this valley that cradled all his deepest fears? But how could he explain to Jillian if he turned and rode away? What if her illness returned? What if the McKane caught them? He was confounded by the onslaught of questions with no clear answers. Discovering Tuluth was this . . . this glorious place . . . it was too shocking for his mind to absorb.

Jillian winced and rubbed her stomach. His hands

tightened on hers and he invoked his legendary willpower, aware that before this day was through he would need every ounce of it.

He had no choice. They swiftly remounted and began the descent.

* * *

"They're comin'!"

Ronin looked ready to bolt.

"Relax, man," Balder chided. "It's goin' to be fine, you'll see."

The McIllioch grimaced. "Easy for you to say. He's not your son. I tell you, he's goin' to spit in my face."

Balder shook his head and tried not to laugh. "If that's your worst concern, old man, you have nothin' to worry about."

* * *

Grimm and Jillian descended the back of Wotan's Cleft, circled around the base of it, and picked up the wending road into the mouth of the valley. Five huge mountains formed a natural fortress around the valley, rising like the gentle fingers of an unfurled hand. The city filled its protected palm, verdant, teeming with life. Jillian quickly concluded that when the McKane had attacked Tuluth years ago, they must have been either thoroughly arrogant or impossibly vast in numbers.

As if he'd read her mind, Grimm said, "We weren't always this great in numbers, Jillian. In the past fifteen years, Tuluth seems to have not only regained the men lost in the battle with the McKane, but increased by"—his dumbfounded gaze swept the valley—"nearly five times." He whistled, and shook his head. "Someone has been rebuilding."

"Are you certain your da is insane?"

Grimm grimaced. "Yes." *As certain as I am of anything at the moment,* he appended silently.

"Well, for an insane man, he certainly seems to have done wonders here."

"I doona believe he has. Something else must be going on."

"And the 'Welcome back, son' banner? I thought you said you have no brothers."

"I doona," he replied stiffly. He realized they would soon be in clear sight of the first of those banners and he hadn't told Jillian the truth: that there was absolutely no mistaking who was expected because he hadn't been entirely truthful before—the dozens of banners hung throughout the city really read "Welcome back, Gavrael."

Jillian squirmed, trying to get a better view. Despite his concerns, her lush hips wriggling against his loins sent a bolt of lust through his veins. Memories of last night teased the periphery of his mind, but he could afford no distractions. "Be still," he growled.

"I just want to see."

"You're going to be seeing the sky from your back if you keep wiggling like that, lass." He tugged her against him so she could feel what her squirming had accomplished. He'd love nothing more than to lose himself in the passion of Jillian and, when she was sleepily sated, spirit her miles in the other direction.

They had come within reading distance of the banners when Jillian leaned forward again. Grimm swallowed and braced himself for the questions he knew would follow.

"Why, it's not about you at all, Grimm," she said wonderingly. "This banner doesn't say 'Welcome home, son.' It says 'Welcome home, Gavrael.' " She paused, nibbling her lip. "Who's Gavrael? And how could you manage to read it from so far away yet mistake the word 'son' for 'Gavrael'? The words don't look anything alike."

"Must you be so logical?" he said with a sigh. He reconsidered turning Occam about and tearing off in the other direction without offering an explanation, but he knew it would be only a temporary reprieve. Ultimately, Jillian would bring him back, one way or another.

It was time to face his demons—apparently, all of them at the same time. For winding down the road toward him was a parade of people, replete with a band of pipes and drums, and—if his memory could be trusted on anything at all—the one in front bore a marked resemblance to his da. And so did the man who rode beside him. Grimm's gaze darted back and forth between them, searching for some clue that might tell him which one was his father.

Suddenly a worse realization struck him, one which, stunned to temporary senselessness by the condition of his home, he'd managed to overlook entirely. The moment he'd glimpsed the thriving Tuluth, the shock of it all had caused his deepest fear to recede deceptively to the back of his mind. Now it returned with the force of a tidal wave, flooding him with quiet desperation.

If his memory could be trusted—and that did seem to be the question of the day—familiar faces were approaching, which meant some of the people riding toward them knew he was a Berserker.

In an instant, they could betray his terrible secret to Jillian, and he would lose her forever.

Chapter 29

Grimm drew Occam to such an abrupt halt that the stallion spooked and reared. Mustering the most soothing sounds he could manage in his agitated condition, Grimm calmed the startled gray and slipped from its back.

"What are you doing?" Jillian was bewildered by his rapid dismount.

Grimm studied the ground intently. "I need you to remain here, lass. Come forward when I beckon, but no sooner. Promise me you'll wait until I summon you."

Jillian studied his bent head. After a brief internal debate, she reached out and caressed his dark hair. He turned his face into her hand and kissed her palm.

"I haven't seen these people in fifteen years, Jillian."

"I'll stay, I promise."

He gave her a wordless thank-you with his eyes. He was torn by conflicting emotions, yet he knew he had to approach alone. Only when he had wrung an oath from the villagers to protect his secret would he lead Jillian into the city and address her comfort. Had she been dangerously ill, he would have risked losing her love to save her life, but she was hardly incapacitated, and although he regretted any discomfort she might suffer he was not willing to face the fear and revulsion he'd glimpsed in his dreams. He couldn't afford to take any chances.

Satisfied that she would wait at this distance until he summoned her, Grimm turned and sprinted down the dirt road toward the approaching melee. His heart seemed to have lodged in the vicinity of his throat, and he felt as if he were being wrenched in two. Behind him was the woman he loved; in front of him was the past he'd vowed never to confront by light of day.

At the forefront of the cluster rode two men of equal height and girth, both with thick shocks of black hair, liberally threaded with silver. Both had strong, craggy faces and clefts in their proud chins, both had a similar expression of joy on their features. What was going on here? Grimm wondered.

It was as if everything he'd ever believed had been a lie. Tuluth had been destroyed, but Tuluth was a thriving city. His da had been insane, but someone with a stable mind and a strong back had rebuilt this land. His da seemed extraordinarily happy to see him, and though Grimm had not intended to return, his father apparently had been expecting him. How? Why? Thousands of questions flashed through his mind in the short time it took him to span the distance between them.

The parade of people began roaring as he drew near, their faces wreathed in smiles. How was a man expected to walk into such an exuberant crowd with hatred in his heart?

And why were they so damned happy to see him?

He stopped his sprint a dozen feet from the front line. Unable to hold still, he resorted to jogging in place, breathing harshly, not from the run but from the dreaded encounter to come.

The two men who looked so similar broke away from the crowd. One of them raised a hand to the entourage and the crowd fell silent, maintaining a respectful distance as they rode forward. Grimm sneaked a glance over his shoulder to make certain Jillian hadn't followed him. With relief he saw she had obeyed his command, although if she leaned any farther over Occam's head toward the crowd he'd have to peel her from the road.

"Gavrael."

The deep voice so like his own whipped his head around. He stared up at the two men, uncertain which one had spoken.

"Grimm," he corrected instantly.

The man on the right erupted into an immediate bluster. "What the bletherin' hell kind of name is Grim? Why not be namin' yourself Depressed, or Melancholy? Nay, I have it—Woebegone." He cast a disgusted glance at Grimm and snorted.

"It's better than McIllioch," Grimm said stiffly. "And it's not Grim with one *m*. It's Grimm with two."

"Well, why would you be changin' your name at all, lad?" The man on the left did little to disguise his wounded expression.

Grimm searched their faces, trying desperately to decide which one was his father. He didn't have the faintest clue what he might do when he figured it out, but he'd really like to know which one to treat to the venom he'd been storing for years uncounted. No, not uncounted, he corrected himself—fifteen years of angry words he wanted to fling at the man, words that had festered for half his lifetime.

"Who are you?" he demanded of the man who'd most recently spoken.

The man turned to his companion with a mournful look. "Who am I, he's asking me, Balder. Can you be believin' that? Who am I?"

"At least he dinna spit," Balder said mildly.

"You're Ronin," Grimm accused. If the one was named Balder, the other had to be his da, Ronin McIllioch.

"I'm not Ronin to you," the man exclaimed indignantly. "I'm your da."

"You're no father to me," Grimm remarked in a voice so chill it vied with the bitterest Highland wind.

Ronin gazed accusingly at Balder. "I told you so."

Balder shook his head, arching a bushy brow. "He still dinna spit."

"What the hell does spitting have to do with anything?"

"Well, lad," Balder drawled, "that's the excuse I'm lookin' for to tie your spiteful arse up and drag you back to the castle, where I can be poundin' some good common sense and respect for your elders into you."

"You think you could?" Grimm challenged coolly. His dangerous mix of emotions clamored lustily for a fight.

Balder laughed, the sound a joyous shout rumbling from his thick chest. "I love a good fight, lad, but a man like me could eat a pup like you in one snap of his jaws."

Grimm leveled a dark look at Ronin. "Does he know what I am?" Arrogance underscored the question.

"Do you know what *I* am?" Balder countered softly.

Grimm's eyes swept back to his face. "What do you mean?" he asked so quickly it came out sounding like one word. He studied Balder intently. Mocking ice-blue eyes met his levelly. *Impossible!* In all his years, he'd never encountered another Berserker!

Balder shook his head and sighed. He exchanged glances with Ronin. "The lad is dense, Ronin. I'm tellin' you, he's thick through and through."

Ronin puffed himself up indignantly. "He is not. He's my son."

"The lad doesn't know the first thing about himself, even after all these—"

"Well, how could he, bein' that—"

"And any dolt should have figured—"

"That doesn't mean he's dense—"

"Haud yer wheesht!" Grimm roared.

"There's no need to be roarin' my head off, boy," Balder rebuked. "It's not as if you're the only one with a Berserker's temper here."

"I am not a boy. I am not a lad. I am not a dolt," Grimm said evenly, determined to take control of the erratic conversation. There would be time later to discover how Balder had become a Berserker. "And when the woman who is behind me approaches, you will kindly make it clear to the servants, the villagers, and the entire clan that I am *not* a Berserker, do you understand me?"

"Not a Berserker?" Balder's eyebrows rose.

"Not a Berserker?" Ronin's brow furrowed.

"Not a Berserker."

"But you *are*," Ronin argued obtusely.

Grimm glared at Ronin. "But she doesn't know that. And if she discovers it, she'll leave me. And if she leaves me, I'll have no choice but to kill you both," Grimm said matter-of-factly.

"Well," Balder huffed, deeply offended. "There's no need to be gettin' nasty about things, lad. I'm sure we'll find a way to sort things out."

"I doubt it, Balder. And if you call me lad one more time, you're going to have a problem. I'll spit, and give you the reason you've been looking for, and we'll just see if an aging Berserker can take one in his prime."

"Two agin' Berserkers," Ronin corrected proudly.

Grimm's head snapped around, and he stared at Ronin. Identical ice-blue eyes. The day kept dishing out one bewildering revelation after another. He found sanctuary in sarcasm: "What the hell is this, the valley of the Berserkers?"

"Somethin' like that, Gavrael," Balder muttered, dodging a nudge from Ronin.

"My name is *Grimm*."

"How do you plan to be explainin' the name on the banners to your wife?" Ronin asked.

"She's not my wife," Grimm evaded. He hadn't figured that out yet.

"What?" Outraged, Ronin nearly rose to his feet in the stirrups. "You've brought a woman here in dishonor? No son of mine cavorts with his mate without offerin' her the proper union."

Grimm buried his hands in his hair. His world had gone mad. This was the most absurd conversation he could recall holding. "I haven't had the *time* to marry her yet! I only recently abducted her—"

"Abducted her?" Ronin's nostrils flared.

"With her consent!" Grimm said defensively.

"I thought there was a wedding at Caithness," Ronin argued.

"There nearly was, but not to me. And there will be one

as soon as I can. Lack of time is the only reason she's not my wife. And you"—he pointed furiously at Ronin—"you haven't been a father to me for fifteen years, so doona think you can start acting like one now."

"I haven't been a father to you because you wouldn't come home!"

"You know why I wouldn't come home." Grimm spoke furiously, his eyes blazing.

Ronin flinched. He drew a deep breath, and when he spoke again he seemed deflated by Grimm's anger. "I know I failed you," he said, his eyes brimful of regret.

"Failed me is putting it lightly," Grimm muttered. He was badly thrown off balance by his da's response. He'd expected the old man to rage right back, maybe attack him like the batty bastard he was. But there was genuine regret in his gaze. How was he supposed to deal with that? If Ronin had raged back, he could have released his pent-up anger by fighting with him. But Ronin didn't. He simply sat his horse and gazed sadly down at him, and it made Grimm feel even worse.

"Jillian is ill," Grimm said gruffly. "She needs a warm place to stay."

"She's ill?" Balder trumpeted. "By Odin's spear, lad, did you have to wait until now to say the most important thing?"

"Lad?" The way Grimm uttered the single word made his threat clear.

But Balder was unruffled. His mouth twisted with a sneer. "Listen up, son of the McIllioch, you doona frighten me. I'm far too old to be put off by a young pup's growl. You won't let me call you by your God-given name, and I refuse to call you that ridiculous appellation you've chosen, so it's either goin' to be 'lad' or it's goin' to be 'arsehole.' Which do you prefer?" The older man's grin was menacing.

Grimm caught himself on the verge of a faint smile. If he hadn't been so hell-bent on hating this place, he would have liked blustering old Balder. The man commanded respect and clearly took guff from no one.

"You can call me lad on one condition," he relented. "Take care of my woman and keep my secret. And make sure the villagers do the same."

Ronin and Balder exchanged glances and sighed. "Done."

"Welcome home, lad," Balder added.

Grimm rolled his eyes.

"Aye, welcome—" Ronin began, but Grimm raised a warning finger.

"And you, old man," he said to Ronin. "If I were you, I'd be giving me a lot of breathing room," he warned.

Ronin opened his mouth, then closed it, his blue eyes dark with pain.

Chapter 30

Jillian couldn't stop smiling. It was nearly impossible not to in the midst of such excitement. How Grimm managed to continue looking so somber was beyond her comprehension.

She spared a glance at him, which she nearly begrudged because everywhere else she looked she found something enchanting and Grimm looked so miserable it depressed her. She knew she should feel more compassion for his plight, but it was difficult to feel empathy when his family was so overjoyed to welcome him back into the fold. And what a magnificent fold it was.

Gavrael, she corrected herself silently. Rather than motioning her to join them after he'd greeted his da, he'd sprinted back to get her so they could ride in together. Surrounded by the cheering crowd, he'd explained to her that when he'd left Tuluth years ago he'd assumed a new name. His real name, although he insisted she continue calling him Grimm, was Gavrael Roderick Icarus McIllioch.

She sighed dreamily. Jillian Alanna McIllioch; said aloud it was a tumble of *l*'s that rolled euphonically. She had no doubt that Grimm would marry her once they'd settled in.

Grimm tightened his grip on her hand and whispered her name to get her attention. "Jillian, come back from wherever you are. Balder's going to show us to our chambers, and we'll get you warm and fed."

"Oh, I feel much better, Grimm," she said absently, marveling over a beautiful sculpture that adorned the hall. She trundled after Balder and an assortment of maids happily holding Grimm's hand. "This castle is enormous, breathtaking. How could you have ever thought it was dark and dreary?"

He gave her a glum look. "I haven't a blethering clue," he muttered.

"Here's your room, Gavrael—" Balder began.

"Grimm."

"Lad." Balder stared him down levelly. "And Merry here will see Jillian to hers," he said pointedly.

"What?" Grimm was momentarily dumbfounded. Now that she was his, how could he sleep without Jillian in his arms?

"Room." Balder gestured impatiently. "Yours." He turned abruptly to a dainty maid. "And Merry here will show Jillian to *hers*." His blue eyes reflected a cool challenge.

"I will see Jillian to hers myself," Grimm begrudged after a tense pause.

"As long as you see yourself right back out of it, lad, go on ahead. But you're not married, so doona be thinkin' you can act like you are."

Jillian flushed.

"No reflection on you, lass," Balder hastened to assure

her. "I can see you're a fine lady, but this boy is randy as a goat around you and it's plain to see. If he seeks the joys of wedded bliss, he can wed you. Without a weddin' he'll be havin' no bliss."

Grimm flushed. "Enough, Balder."

Balder arched a brow and frowned. "And try to be a bit nicer to your da, lad. The man did give you life, after all." With that he turned and blustered down the hall, his proud chin jutting like the prow of a ship breaking waves.

Grimm waited until he had disappeared from sight, then sought directions from the maid. "I'll escort Jillian to her chambers," he informed the elfin-looking Merry. To the cluster of maids he said, "See to it that we have a steaming tub and"—he glanced at Jillian worriedly—"what kind of food might your stomach tolerate, lass?"

Anything and everything, Jillian thought. She was famished. "Lots," she said succinctly.

Grimm smiled faintly, finished giving the maids instructions, and escorted Jillian to her rooms.

As they entered the rooms, Jillian exhaled a sigh of pleasure. Her chambers were every bit as luxuriously appointed as the rest of Maldebann. Four tall windows graced the west wall of the bedroom, and from there she could watch the sun set over the mountains. Snowy lambskin rugs covered the floors. The bed was carved of burnished cherry that had been polished to a vibrant luster and canopied with sheer white linen. A cheery fire burned in an enormous fireplace.

"How are you feeling, Jillian?" Grimm shut the door and drew her into his arms.

"I'm much better now," she assured him.

"I know this must all be quite shocking—"

Jillian kissed him, silencing further words. He seemed

startled by the gesture, then kissed her back so urgently it caused her toes to curl with anticipation. She clung to the kiss, spinning it out as long as she could, trying to imbue him with courage and love, for she suspected he'd be needing it. Then she forgot her noble intentions as desire sizzled between them.

A sharp rap on the door dampened it quickly.

Grimm pulled back and stalked to the door, unsurprised to find Balder standing there. "I forgot to tell you, lad, we have supper at eight," Balder said, peering beyond him at Jillian. "Has he been kissin' you, lass? You just tell me and I'll take care of it."

Grimm closed the door without replying, and locked it. Balder sighed so loudly outside the door that Jillian nearly laughed.

As Grimm walked back to her side, she studied him. The strain of the day was evident; even his usual proud posture seemed bowed. When she considered all the man had been through in the past few hours, she felt terrible. He was busy tending to her when he could probably use nothing more greatly than some time alone to sort through all the shocks the day had delivered. She brushed his cheek with her hand. "Grimm, if you don't mind, do you think I could rest a bit before I meet any more people? Perhaps I could take dinner in my room tonight and face the castle tomorrow?"

She hadn't been wrong. His expression was a mixture of concern and relief.

"Are you certain you doona mind being on your own? Are you certain you're well enough?"

"Grimm, I feel wonderful. Whatever was wrong with me this morning has passed. Now I'd just like to relax, soak in a long bath, and sleep. I suspect you probably have people and places you'd like to reacquaint yourself with."

"You're remarkable, do you know that, lass?" He smoothed her hair and tucked a stray tendril behind her ear.

"I love you, Grimm Roderick," she said intensely. "Go meet your people and see your home. Take your time. I will always be here for you."

"What did I do to deserve you?" The words exploded from him.

She brushed her lips against his lightly. "I ask myself the same question all the time."

"I want to see you tonight, Jillian. I need to see you."

"I'll leave my door unlocked." She flashed him a dazzling smile that promised the moon and the stars when he came.

He gave her one last tender look and left.

* * *

"Go to him. I can't," Ronin said urgently.

The two men peered out the window at Grimm, sprawled on the wall in front of the castle, gazing out over the village. Night had fallen, and tiny lights in the village twinkled like a reflection of the stars that dotted the sky. The castle had been constructed to provide an unimpeded view of the village. A wide stone terrace lined the perimeter, east and west. It sloped in tiers down to the fortifying walls, the terrace itself surrounded by a low wall at such a height that from atop it one could look straight out over the valley. Grimm had been sitting alone on the wall for hours, alternating his gaze between the castle behind him and the valley before him.

"What would you like me to be sayin'?" Balder grunted.

"He's your son, Ronin. You're goin' to have to speak with him at some point."

"He hates me."

"So speak with him and try to help him get past it."

"It's not that easy!" Ronin snapped, but in his blue eyes Balder saw fear. Fear that if Ronin spoke with his son, he might lose him all over again.

Balder eyed his brother for a moment and then sighed. "I'll try, Ronin."

* * *

Grimm watched the valley batten down for the night. The villagers had begun to light candles and pull shutters, and from his perch on the low wall he could hear the faint strains of parents calling their children into cozy cottages and farmers rounding up animals before venturing to bed themselves. It was a scene of peace and harmony. He stole an occasional glance over his shoulder at the castle, but not one gargoyle lurked. It was possible, he conceded, that at fourteen he'd been fanciful. It was possible that years of running and hiding had colored his perceptions until all seemed desolate and barren, even a past that had once been bright. His life had changed so abruptly on that fateful day, it might well have skewed his memories.

He could accept that he'd forgotten what Tuluth was really like. He could accept that the castle had never been truly menacing. But what was he to make of his da? He'd seen him with his own eyes, crouched over his mother's body. Had he, in his shock and grief, misconstrued that event too? Once the possibility presented itself, he studied it from every angle, his confusion deepening.

He'd found his da in the south gardens in the early

morning, the time Jolyn strolled the grounds and greeted the day. He'd been on his way to meet Arron to go fishing. The scene was painstakingly etched on his mind: Jolyn beaten and battered, her face a mass of bruises, Ronin crouched above her, snarling, blood everywhere, and that damned incriminating knife in his hand.

"Beautiful, isn't it?" Balder interrupted his internal debate.

"Aye," Grimm replied, mildly surprised Balder had joined him. "I doona remember it like this, Balder."

Balder placed a comforting hand on his shoulder. "That's because it wasn't always like this. Tuluth has grown tremendously over the years, thanks to your da's efforts."

"Come to think of it, I doona remember you either," Grimm said thoughtfully. "Did I know you when I was a lad?"

"No. I've spent most of my life wanderin'. I visited Maldebann twice when you were young, but only briefly. Six months ago the ship I was sailin' broke up in a storm, washin' me ashore old Alba. I figured that meant it was time to check on what remained of my clan. I'm your da's older brother, but I had a fancy to see the world, so I bullied Ronin into bein' laird, and a fine one he's made."

Grimm scowled. "That's debatable."

"Doona be so hard on Ronin, lad. He's wanted nothin' more than for you to come home. Maybe your memories of him are as discolored as your memories of Tuluth."

"Maybe," Grimm allowed tightly. "But maybe not."

"Give him a chance, that's all I'm askin'. Get to know him again and make a fresh judgment. There were things he dinna have time to explain to you before. Let him tell you now."

Grimm shrugged his hand off his shoulder. "Enough, Balder. Leave me alone."

"Promise me you'll give him a chance to talk to you, lad," Balder persisted, undaunted by Grimm's dismissal.

"I haven't left yet, have I?"

Balder inclined his head and retreated.

* * *

"Well, that dinna last long," Ronin complained.

"I said my piece. Now do your part," Balder grumbled.

"Tomorrow." Ronin procrastinated.

Balder glared.

"You know it's foolish to try talkin' about things when people are tired, and the lad must be exhausted, Balder."

"Berserkers only get tired when they've been in a rage," Balder said dryly.

"Quit actin' like my older brother," Ronin snapped.

"Well, quit actin' like my younger brother." Two pairs of ice-blue eyes battled, and Balder finally shrugged. "If you won't face that problem, then turn your mind to this one. Merry overheard Jillian tellin' the lad she'd leave her door unlocked. If we doona come up with somethin', that lad o' yours will be samplin' the pleasures without payin' the price."

"But he already has sampled them. We know that."

"That doesn't make it right. And bein' denied may encourage him to wed her all the sooner," Balder pointed out.

"What do you suggest? Lock her in the tower? The boy's a Berserker, he'll get past anythin'."

Balder thought a moment, then grinned. "He won't be gettin' past righteous indignation, will he, now?"

* * *

The hour was past midnight when Grimm hastened down the corridor to Jillian's chambers. Merry had assured him that Jillian passed a restful evening with no further bouts of illness. She'd eaten like a woman famished, the elfin maid had said.

He let his lips curve in the full smile he felt whenever he thought of Jillian. He needed to touch her, to tell her that he wanted to marry her if she would still have him. He longed to confide in her. She had a logical mind; perhaps she could help him see things he couldn't make sense of by dint of being too near the subjects involved. He stood firm on his position that she must never know what he really was, but he could talk with her about much of what had happened—or *seemed* to have happened—fifteen years ago, without betraying his secret. His gait quickened as he turned down the hall leading to her chambers, and he nearly sprinted around the corner.

He halted abruptly when he spotted Balder, energetically plastering a crack in the stone with a mixture of clay and crushed stone.

"What are you doing here?" Grimm scowled indignantly. "It's the middle of the night."

Balder shrugged innocently. "Tendin' this castle is a full-time job. Fortunately, I doona require much sleep anymore. But come to think of it, what are you doin' here? Your rooms are that way"—he leveled a half-full trowel in the other direction—"in case you've forgotten. You wouldn't be lookin' to spoil an innocent young lass, now, would you?"

A muscle twitched in Grimm's jaw. "Right. I must have gotten turned around."

"Well, turn back around, lad. I expect I'll be workin' on this wall all night," Balder said evenly. "The *whole* night."

* * *

Twenty minutes later, Jillian poked her head out the door. "Balder!" She tugged her wrapper about her shoulders, peering at him peevishly.

Balder grinned. She was lovely, flushed with sleep and obviously intent upon sneaking to Grimm's room.

"Do you need somethin', lass?"

"What on earth are you doing?"

He gave her the same lame excuse he'd given Grimm and plastered heartily away.

"Oh," Jillian said in a small voice.

"Do you wish me to escort you to the kitchens, lass? Can I give you a wee tour? I'm usually up all night, and the only thing I plan to do is plaster here. Wee cracks between the stones can become great cracks in the blink of an eye if left untended."

"No, no." Jillian waved him away. "I just heard a noise and wondered what it was." She bid him good night and retreated.

After she'd closed the door, Balder rubbed his eyes. By the saints, it was going to be a bloody long night.

* * *

High above Tuluth, men gathered. Two of them broke away from the main group and moved toward the bluff, talking quietly.

"The ambush didn't work, Connor. Why the hell did you send a mere score of men after a Berserker?"

"Because you said he was probably on his way back to Tuluth," Connor shot back. "We dinna wish to waste too many that we might be needing later. Besides, how many kegs of our black powder did you waste, only to be failing, yourself?"

Ramsay Logan scowled. "I hadn't thought it through as well as I should have. He won't escape the next time."

"Logan, if you kill Gavrael McIllioch there will be gold enough to last you the rest of your days. We've been trying for years. He's the last one left that can breed. That we know of," he added.

"Are all their children born Berserkers?" Ramsay watched the lights flicker and fade in the valley.

Connor's lip curled in disgust. "Only the sons of direct descent from the laird. The curse confines itself to the primary, paternal line. Over the centuries our clan has gathered as much information about the McIllioch as we could. We know they have only one true mate, and once their mate dies they remain celibate for the duration of their years. So the old man is no longer a threat. To the best of our knowledge, Gavrael is his only son. When he dies, that's the end. However, during various times over the centuries they've managed to hide a few from us. That's why it's imperative that you get inside Castle Maldebann. I want the last McIllioch destroyed."

"Do you suspect the castle is crawling with concealed blue-eyed boys? Is it possible Ronin had other sons besides Gavrael?"

"We don't know," Connor admitted. "Over the years we've heard there is a hall, a place of pagan worship to Odin. It's supposed to be right in the heart of the mountain." His face grew taut with fury. "Damned heathens, it's a Christian land now! We've heard they practice pagan ceremonies there. And one of the maids we captured—before she died—said that they record each and every one of their unholy spawn in that hall. You must find it and verify Gavrael is the last."

"You expect me to slip into the lair of such creatures and spy? How much gold did you say was in this for me?" Ramsay bargained shrewdly.

Connor regarded him with the fanaticism of a purist. "If you prove he's the last and succeed in killing him, you can name your price."

"I'll get into the castle and take the last Berserker down," Ramsay said with relish.

"How? You've failed three times now."

"Don't worry. I'll not only get to the hall, I will take his mate, Jillian. It's possible she's pregnant—"

"By Christ's blessed tears!" Connor shuddered with disgust. "After you use her, kill her," he ordered.

Ramsay raised a hand. "No. We will wait to see if she's pregnant."

"But she's been tainted—"

"I want her. She's part of my price," Ramsay insisted. "If she's carrying his child, I'll keep her under close guard until she gives birth."

"If it's a son you kill it, and I'll be there to watch. You say you hate the Berserkers, but if you thought you could breed them into your clan, you might feel differently."

"Gavrael McIllioch killed my brothers," Ramsay said tightly. "Religion or not, I'll suffer no qualms about killing his son. Or daughter."

"Good." Connor McKane looked down into the valley at the sleeping village of Tuluth. "The city is much larger now, Logan. What's your plan?"

"You mentioned there are caves in the mountain. Once I've captured the woman I'll give you a piece of the clothing she's wearing. You'll take it and confront the old man and Gavrael. They won't fight as long as they know I have Jillian. You'll send him to the caves, and I'll take care of it from there."

"How?"

"I said I will take care of it from there," Ramsay growled.

"I want to see his dead body with my own eyes."

"You will." Ramsay joined Connor behind the shelter of a bluff. The two of them stared down at Castle Maldebann.

"Such a waste of beauty and strength on heathens. When they are defeated the McKane will take Maldebann," Connor breathed.

"When I have done as I promised, the *Logan* take Maldebann," Ramsay said with an icy gaze that dared Connor to disagree.

Chapter 31

When Jillian awoke the next morning, she immediately became aware of two things: She missed Grimm terribly, and she had what women called "breeding woes." As she curled on her side and cradled her stomach, she couldn't believe she had failed to recognize her malady the previous morning. Although she'd suspected she was pregnant, she must have been so distracted by worries of how she would maneuver Grimm to Maldebann that she hadn't pieced the facts together and realized she had the morning nausea the maids at Caithness had often complained of. The thought of suffering it every morning depressed her, but the confirmation that she was carrying Grimm's child replaced her discomfort with elation. She couldn't wait to share the wonderful news with him.

A sudden alarming ache in her stomach nearly made her reevaluate her joy. She indulged herself in a loud, self-pitying groan. Curling into a ball helped, as did the consolation that from what she'd heard, such illness was usually of brief duration.

And it was. After about thirty minutes it passed as suddenly as it had assaulted her. She was surprised to discover she felt hearty and hale, as if she'd not suffered a moment of queasiness. She brushed her long hair, tied it back in a ribbon, then sat gazing sadly at the ruins of her wedding gown. They'd left Caithness with nothing but the dress on her body. The only items of clothing in her chambers were that and the Douglas plaid that Grimm had bundled around her. Well, she wasn't going to be denied breakfast by a lack of clothing, she decided swiftly. Not when her tummy was so temperamental.

A few moments and a few strategic knots later, she was wrapped Scots-style in a plaid and ready to make her way to the Greathall.

* * *

Ronin, Balder, and Grimm were already at breakfast, eating in strained silence. Jillian chirped a cheery good morning; the morose group clearly needed a stiff dose of gaiety.

The three men leapt to their feet, jostling for the honor of seating her. She bestowed it upon Grimm with a bright smile. "Good morning," she purred, her eyes wandering over him hungrily. She wondered if her newfound knowledge of their child growing within her glittered in her eyes. She simply *had* to get him alone soon!

He froze, her chair half pulled out. "Morning," he whispered huskily, stupidly, dazzled by her radiance. "Och, Jillian, you have no other clothes, do you?" He eyed her clad in his plaid and smiled tenderly. "I recall you dressing like this when you were wee. You were determined to be just like your da." He seated her, his hands lingering on her shoulders. "Balder, can you set the maids to finding something Jillian might wear?"

It was Ronin who replied. "I'm certain some of Jolyn's gowns could be altered. I had them sealed away . . ." His eyes clouded with sorrow.

Jillian was astonished when Grimm's jaw tensed. He dropped into his seat and fisted his hand around his mug so tightly, his knuckles whitened. Although Grimm had told her a few things about his family, he'd not told her how Jolyn had died. Nor had he told her what Ronin had done to carve such a chasm between the two of them. From what she'd seen of his da, there was nothing remotely strange or mad about him. He seemed a gentle man, filled with regrets and longing for a better future with his son. She realized Balder was watching Grimm as intently as she was.

"Did you ever hear the fable of the wolf in sheep's clothing, lad?" Balder asked, eyeing Grimm with displeasure.

"Aye," he growled. "I became well acquainted with that moral at an early age." Again he flashed a look of fury at Ronin.

"Then you should be understandin' sometimes it works in reverse—there's such a thing as a sheep in wolf's clothing too. Sometimes appearances can be misleadin'. Sometimes you have to reexamine the facts with mature eyes."

Jillian eyed them curiously. There was a message being conveyed that she didn't understand.

"Jillian loves fables," Grimm muttered, urging the subject in a new direction.

"Well, tell us one, lass," Ronin encouraged.

Jillian blushed. "No, really, I couldn't. It's the children who love fables so much."

"Bah, children, she says, Balder!" Ronin exclaimed. "My Jolyn loved fables and told us them often. Come on, lass, give us a story."

"Well . . ." she demurred.

"Tell us one. Go on," the brothers urged.

Beside her Grimm took a deep swallow from his mug and slammed it down on the table.

Jillian flinched inwardly but refused to react. He'd been stomping and glowering ever since they'd arrived, and she couldn't fathom why. Seeking a way to lessen the palpable tension, she rummaged through her stock of fables and, struck by an impish impulse, selected a tale.

"Once there was a mighty lion, heroic and invincible. He was king of the beasts, and he knew it well. A bit arrogant, one might say, but a good king just the same." She paused to smile warmly at Grimm.

He scowled.

"This mighty lion was walking in the forest of the lowlands one evening when he spied a lovely woman—"

"With waves of golden hair and amber eyes," Balder interjected.

"Why, yes! How did you know? You've heard this one, haven't you, Balder?"

Grimm rolled his eyes.

Jillian stifled an urge to laugh and continued. "The mighty lion was mesmerized by her beauty, by her gentle ways, and by the lovely song she was singing. He padded forward quietly so he wouldn't startle her. But the maiden wasn't frightened—she saw the lion for what he was: a powerful, courageous, and honorable creature with an often-fearsome roar who possessed a pure, fearless heart. His arrogance she could overlook, because she knew from watching her own father that arrogance was often part and parcel of extraordinary strength." Jillian sneaked a quick glance at Ronin; he was grinning broadly.

Drawing succor from Ronin's amusement, she looked directly at Grimm and continued. "The lion was besotted. The next day he sought out the woman's father and pledged his heart, seeking her hand in marriage. The woman's father was concerned about the lion's beastly nature, despite the fact that his daughter was perfectly comfortable with it. Unknown to the daughter, her father agreed to accept the lion's courtship, provided the lion king allowed him to pluck his claws and pull his teeth, rendering him tame and civilized. The lion was hopelessly in love. He agreed, and so it was done."

"Another Samson and Delilah," Grimm muttered.

Jillian ignored him. "When the lion then pressed his case, the father drove him from his home with sticks and stones, because the beast was no longer a threat, no longer a fearsome creature."

Jillian paused significantly, and Balder and Ronin clapped their hands. "Wonderfully told!" Ronin exclaimed. "That was a favorite of my wife's as well."

Grimm scowled. "That's the end? Just what the hell was the point of that story?" he asked, offended. "That loving makes a man weaker? That he loses the woman he loves when she sees him unmanned?"

Ronin gave him a disparaging glance. "No, lad. The point of that fable is that even the mighty can be humbled by love."

"Wait—there's more. The daughter," Jillian said quietly, "moved by his willingness to trust so completely, fled her da's house and wed her lion king." She understood Grimm's fear now. Whatever secret he was hiding, he was afraid that once she discovered it, she would leave him.

"I still think it's a terrible story!" Grimm thundered, waving his hand angrily. It caught his mug and sent it flying across the table, spraying Ronin with cider wine. Grimm stared at the bright red stain spreading on his da's white linen for a long, strained moment. "Excuse me," he said roughly, pushing his chair back and without another glance loping from the room.

"Ah, lass, he can be a handful sometimes, I fear," Ronin said with an apologetic look, mopping at his shirt with a cloth.

Jillian poked at her breakfast. "I wish I understood what was going on." She shot a hopeful glance at the brothers.

"You haven't asked him, have you?" Balder remarked.

"I want to ask him, but . . ."

"But you understand he may not be able to give you answers because he doesn't seem to have them himself, does he?"

"I just wish he'd talk to me about it! If not to me, then at least to *you*," she said to Ronin. "There's so much pent up inside him, and I have no idea what to do but give him time."

"He loves you, lass," Ronin assured her. "It's in his eyes, in the way he touches you, in the way he moves when you're around. You're the center of his heart."

"I know," she said simply. "I don't doubt that he loves me. But trust is part and parcel of love."

Balder turned a piercing gaze on his brother. "Ronin is going to speak with him today, aren't you, brother?" He rose from the table. "I'll get you a fresh shirt," he added, and left the Greathall.

Ronin removed his cider-soaked shirt, draped it over a chair, and mopped his body with a linen cloth. The cider had doused him thoroughly.

Jillian watched him curiously. His torso was well defined and powerful. His chest was broad, darkened by years of Highland sun and dusted with hair like Grimm's. And like Grimm's, it was free of scars or birthmarks, a vast unblemished expanse of olive-tinted skin. She couldn't help herself; she stared, perplexed by the fact that there was not a single scar on the torso of a man who'd allegedly fought dozens of battles while wearing no more protection than his plaid, if he fought in the usual Scots manner. Even her father had a scar or two on his chest. She stared uncomprehendingly until she realized Ronin wasn't moving, but was watching her watch him.

"The last time a pretty lass looked at my chest was over fifteen years ago," he teased.

Jillian's gaze flew to his face. He was regarding her tenderly. "Was that how long ago your wife died?"

Ronin nodded. "Jolyn was the loveliest woman I've ever seen. And a truer heart I've never known."

"How did you lose her?" she asked gently.

Ronin regarded her impassively.

"Was it in the battle?" she persisted.

Ronin studied his shirt. "I fear this shirt's ruined."

She tried another route, one he might be willing to discuss. "But surely in fifteen years you've met other women, haven't you?"

"There's only one for us, lass. And after she's gone there can never be another."

"You mean you've never been with . . . in fifteen years you've—" She broke off, embarrassed by the direction the conversation was taking, but she couldn't suppress her curiosity. She knew men often remarried after their wives died. If they didn't, it was considered natural that they took mistresses. Was this man saying he'd been utterly alone for fifteen years?

"There's only one in here." Ronin thumped a fist against his chest. "We only love once, and we're no good to a woman without love," he said with quiet dignity. "My son knows that, at least."

Jillian's eyes fixed on his chest again, and she remarked upon the cause of her consternation. "Grimm said the McKane split your chest open with a battle-ax."

Ronin's eyes darted away. "I heal well. And it's been fifteen years, lass." He shrugged, as if that should explain all.

Jillian stepped closer and stretched out a wondering hand.

Ronin moved away. "The sun darkenin' my skin covers a lot of scars. And there's the hair as well," he said quickly.

Too quickly, for Jillian's peace of mind. "But I don't even see the *hint* of a scar," she protested. According to Grimm, the ax had been buried to the thick wedge of the hilt. Not only couldn't most men survive that, such an injury would have left a thick ridge of hard white tissue. "Grimm said you'd been in many battles. One would think you'd have at least one or two scars to show. Come to think of it," she wondered aloud, "Grimm doesn't have any scars either. Anywhere. As a matter of fact, I don't think I have ever even seen a small cut on that man. Does he never hurt himself? Slip while shaving that stubborn jaw? Stub his toe? Tear a hangnail?" She knew her voice was rising but couldn't help it.

"We McIllioch enjoy excellent health." Ronin fidgeted with his tartan, unrolled a fold, and draped it across his chest.

"Apparently," Jillian responded, her mind far away. She forced herself back with an effort. "Milord—"

"Ronin."

"Ronin, is there something you'd like to tell me about your son?"

Ronin sighed and regarded her somberly. "Och, and is there," he admitted. "But I canna, lass. He must tell you himself."

"Why doesn't he trust me?"

"It's not you he doesn't trust, lass," Balder said, entering the Greathall with a fresh shirt. Like Grimm, he moved silently. "It's that he doesn't trust himself."

Jillian eyed Grimm's uncle. Her gaze darted between him and Ronin. There was something indefinable nagging at the back of her mind, but she simply couldn't put her finger on it. They were both watching her intently, almost hopefully. But what were they hoping for? Baffled, Jillian finished her cider and placed the goblet on a nearby table. "I suppose I should go find Grimm."

"Just doona go looking down the central hall, Jillian," Balder said quickly, regarding her intently. "He rarely goes there, but if he does, it's because he's wishin' for some privacy."

"The central hall?" Jillian's brow furrowed. "I thought this was the central hall." She waved her arm at the Greathall, where they'd dined.

"No, this is the front hall. I mean the one that runs off the back of the castle. Actually, it tunnels right into the heart of the mountain itself. It's where he used to run to when he was a boy."

"Oh." She inclined her head. "Thank you," she added, but had no idea what she was thanking him for. His cryptic comment seemed to have been issued as a deterrent, but it sounded suspiciously like an invitation to snoop. She shook her head briskly and excused herself, consumed by curiosity.

After she left, Ronin grinned at Balder. "He never went there when he was a boy. He hasn't even seen the Hall of Lords yet! You're a sneaky bastard, you are," he exclaimed admiringly.

"I always told you I got the lion's share o' brains in the family." Balder preened and poured them both another glass of cider. "Are the torches lit, Ronin? You left it unlocked, didn't you?"

" 'Course I did! You dinna get *all* the brains. But Balder, what if she can't figure it out? Or worse, can't accept it?"

"That woman has a head on her shoulders, brother. She's fairly burstin' with questions, but she keeps her tongue. Not because she's meek, but out of love for your boy. She's dyin' to know what happened here fifteen years ago, and she's waitin' patiently for Gavrael to tell her. So we'll be givin' her the answers another way to be certain she's prepared when he finally speaks." Balder paused and regarded his brother sternly. "You dinna used to be such a coward, Ronin. Stop waitin' for him to come to you. Go to him as you wish you had years ago. Do it, Ronin."

* * *

Jillian made a beeline for the central hall, or as much of a beeline as she was capable of given that wandering around inside Castle Maldebann was akin to roaming an uncharted city. She navigated confusing corridors, proceeding in the direction she hoped led back toward the mountain, determined to find the central hall. It was obvious Balder and Ronin wished her to see it. Would it give her answers about Grimm?

After thirty minutes of frustrated searching, she looped through a series of twisting hallways and around a corner that opened into a second Greathall, even larger than the one she'd breakfasted in. She stepped forward hesitantly; the hall was definitely old—perhaps as ancient as the standing stones erected by the mystical Druids.

Someone had conveniently lit torches—the interfering brothers, she concluded gratefully—for there was not one window in this part of the structure, and how could there be? This Greathall was actually inside the belly of the mountain. She shivered, rattled by the idea. She crossed the huge room slowly, drawn by the mysterious double doors set into the wall at the other end. They towered above her, wrapped in bands of steel, and above the arched opening bold letters had been chiseled.

"Deo non fortuna," she whispered, driven by the same impulse to speak in hushed tones that she'd suffered in Caithness's chapel.

She pressed against the massive doors and held her breath as they swung inward, revealing the central hall Balder had spoken of. Wide-eyed, she moved forward with the dreamy gait of a sleepwalker, riveted by what lay before her. The flowing lines of the hall commanded the eyes upward, and she pivoted slowly, arching her head back and marveling at the ceiling. Pictures and murals covered the vast expanse, some of them so vibrant and realistic that her hands begged to touch them. A chill coursed through her as she tried to comprehend what she was seeing. Was she gazing up at centuries of the history of the McIllioch? She dragged her gaze downward, only to discover new wonders. The walls of the hall held portraits. Hundreds of them!

Jillian glided along the wall. It took only a few moments for her to realize she was walking down a historical genealogy, a time line done in portraits. The first pictures were chiseled in stone, some directly into the wall, with names carved beneath them—odd names she couldn't begin to pronounce. As she worked her way down the wall, the methods of depiction became more modern, as did the clothing. It was apparent that much care had been given to repainting and restoring the portraits to maintain their accuracy over the centuries.

As she progressed down the time line toward the present, the portraits became more graphically detailed, which deepened her growing sense of confusion. Colors were brighter, more painstakingly applied. Her eyes darting between portraits, she moved forward and back again, comparing portraits of children to their subsequent adult portraits.

She must be mistaken.

Incredulous, Jillian closed her eyes a minute, then opened them slowly and stepped back a few paces to study an entire section. It couldn't be. Grabbing a torch, she moved nearer, peering intently at a cluster of boys at their mothers' skirts. They were beautiful boys, dark-haired, brown-eyed boys who would certainly grow into dangerously handsome men.

She moved to the next portraits and there they were again: dark-haired, blue-eyed, dangerously handsome men.

Eyes didn't change color.

Jillian retraced her steps and studied the woman in the last portrait. She was a stunning auburn-haired woman with five brown-eyed boys at her skirts. Jillian then moved to her right; it was either the same woman or her identical twin. Five men clustered around her in various poses, all looking directly at the artist, leaving no doubt as to the color of their eyes. Ice blue. The names beneath the portraits were the same. She moved farther down the hall, bewildered.

Until she found the sixteenth century.

Unfortunately, the portraits raised more questions than they answered, and she sank to her knees in the hall for a long time, thinking.

Hours passed before she managed to sort through it all to her satisfaction. When she had, no question remained in her mind—she was an intelligent woman, able to exercise her powers of deductive reasoning with the best of them. And those powers told her that, though it defied her every rational thought, there was simply no other explanation. She was sitting on her knees, clad in a disheveled plaid, clutching a nearly burned-out torch in a hall filled with Berserkers.

CHAPTER 32

GRIMM PACED THE TERRACE, FEELING LIKE A FOOL. HE'D sat across the table and shared food with his da, managing to make civil conversation until Jillian had arrived. Then Ronin had mentioned Jolyn, and he'd felt fury rise up so quickly he'd nearly lunged across the table and grabbed the old man by the throat.

But Grimm was intelligent enough to realize that much of the anger he felt was at himself. He needed information and was afraid to ask. He needed to talk to Jillian, but what could he tell her? He had no answers himself. *Confront your da,* his conscience demanded. *Find out what really happened.*

The idea terrified him. If he discovered he was wrong, his entire world would look radically different.

Besides, he had other things to worry about. He had to make certain Jillian didn't discover what he was, and he needed to warn Balder that the McKane were on his heels. He needed to get Jillian somewhere safe before they attacked, and he needed to figure out why he, his uncle, and his da were all Berserkers. It just seemed too coincidental, and Balder kept alluding to information he didn't possess. Information he couldn't ask for.

"Son."

Grimm spun around. "Doona call me that," he snapped, but the protest didn't carry its usual venom.

Ronin expelled a gust of air. "We need to talk."

"It's too late. You said all you had to say years ago."

Ronin crossed the terrace and joined Grimm at the wall. "Tuluth is beautiful, isn't she?" he asked softly.

Grimm didn't reply.

"Lad, I . . ."

"Ronin, did you . . ."

The two men looked at each other searchingly. Neither noticed as Balder stepped out onto the terrace.

"Why did you leave and never come back?" The words burst from Ronin's lips with the pent-up anguish of fifteen years of waiting to say them.

"Why did I leave?" Grimm echoed incredulously.

"Was it because you were afraid of what you'd become?"

"What *I* became? I never became what you are!"

Ronin gaped at him. "How can you be sayin' that when you have the blue eyes? You have the bloodlust."

"I know I'm a Berserker," Grimm replied evenly. "But I'm *not* insane."

Ronin blinked. "I never said you were."

"You did too. That night at the battle, you told me I was just like you," he reminded bitterly.

"And you are."

"I am not!"

"Yes, you are—"

"You killed my mother!" Grimm roared, with all the anguish built up from fifteen years of waiting.

Balder moved forward instantly, and Grimm found himself the uncomfortable focus of two pairs of intense blue eyes.

Ronin and Balder exchanged a glance of astonishment. "*That's* why you never came home?" Ronin said carefully.

Grimm breathed deeply. Questions exploded from him, and now that he'd begun asking he thought he might never stop. "How did I get brown eyes to begin with? How come you're both Berserkers too?"

"Oh, you really are dense, aren't you?" Balder snorted. "Come on, canna you put two and two together yet, lad?"

Every muscle in Grimm's body spasmed. Thousands of questions collided with hundreds of suspicions and dozens of suppressed memories, and it all coalesced into the unthinkable. "Is someone else my father?" he demanded.

Ronin and Balder watched him, shaking their heads.

"Well, then why did you kill my mother?" he roared. "And doona be telling me we're born this way. You may have been born crazy enough to kill your wife, but I'm not."

Ronin's face stiffened with fury. "I canna believe you think I killed Jolyn."

"I found you over her body," Grimm persisted. *"You were holding the knife."*

"I removed it from her heart." Ronin gritted. "Why would I kill the only woman I ever loved? How could you, of all people, possibly think I could kill my true mate? Could you kill Jillian? Even in the midst of Berserkergang, could you kill her?"

"Never!" Grimm thundered the word.

"Then you realize you misunderstood."

"You lunged for me. I would have been next!"

"You are my son," Ronin breathed. "I *needed* you. I needed to touch you; to know you were alive; to reassure myself that the McKane hadn't gotten you too."

Grimm stared at him blankly. "The McKane? Are you telling me the McKane killed mother? The McKane didn't even attack until sundown. Mother died in the morning."

Ronin regarded him with a mixture of amazement and anger. "The McKane had been waiting in the hills all day. They had a spy among us and had discovered Jolyn was pregnant again."

A look of horror crossed Grimm's face. "Mother was pregnant?"

Ronin rubbed his eyes. "Aye. We'd thought she wouldn't bear more children—it was unexpected. She hadn't gotten pregnant since you, and that had been nearly fifteen years. It would have been a late child, but we were so lookin' forward to havin' another—" Ronin broke off abruptly. He swallowed several times. "I lost everythin' in one day," he said, his eyes glittering brightly. "And all these years I thought you wouldn't come home because you dinna understand what you were. I despised myself for havin' failed you. I thought you hated me for makin' you what you are and for not bein' there to teach you how to deal with it. I spent years fightin' my urge to come after you and claim you as my son, to prevent the McKane from trackin' you. You'd managed to pretty effectively disappear. And now . . . now I discover that all these years I've been watchin' you, waitin' for you to come home, you were hatin' me. You were out there thinkin' I killed Jolyn!" Ronin turned away bitterly.

"The McKane killed my mother?" Grimm whispered. "Why would they care if she was pregnant?"

Ronin shook his head and looked at Balder. "How did I raise a son who was so thickheaded?"

Balder shrugged and rolled his eyes.

"You still doona get it, do you, Gavrael? What I was tryin' to tell you all those years ago: We—the McIllioch men—we're *born* Berserk. Any son born of the Laird's direct line is a Berserker. The McKane have hunted us for a thousand years. They know our legends nearly as well as we do. The prophecy was that we would be virtually destroyed, whittled down to three." He waved his arms in a gesture that encompassed the three of them. "But one lad would return home, brought by his true mate, and destroy the McKane. The McIllioch would become mightier than ever before. *You* are that lad."

"B-b-born Berserk?" Grimm stuttered.

"Yes," both men responded in a single breath.

"But I turned into one," Grimm floundered. "Up on Wotan's Cleft. I called on Odin."

Ronin shook his head. "It just seemed that way. It was first blood in battle that brought the Berserker out. Normally our sons doona turn until sixteen. First battle accelerated your change."

Grimm sank to a seat on the wall and buried his face in his hands. "Why did you never tell me what I was before I changed?"

"Son, it's not like we hid it from you. We started tellin' you the legends at a young age. You were entranced, remember?" Ronin broke off and laughed. "I recall you runnin' around, tryin' to 'become a Berserker' for years. We were pleased you welcomed your heritage with such open arms. Go, go look in the blasted Hall of Lords, Gavrael—"

"Grimm," Grimm corrected stubbornly, holding on to some part of his identity—any part.

Ronin continued as if he hadn't been interrupted. "There are ceremonies we hold, when we pass on the secrets and teach our sons to deal with the Berserker rage. Your time was approachin', but suddenly the McKane attacked. I lost Jolyn and you left, never once lookin' west to Maldebann, to me. And now I know you were hatin' me, accusin' me of the most vile thing a man could do."

"We train our sons, Gavrael," Balder said. "Intense discipline: mental, emotional, and physical trainin'. We instruct them to command the Berserker, not be commanded by it. You missed that trainin', yet I must say that even on your own you did well. Without any training, without any understandin' of your nature, you remained honorable and have grown into a fine Berserker. Donna be thrashin' yourself for seein' things at fourteen with the half-opened eyes of a fourteen-year-old."

"So I'm supposed to repopulate Maldebann with Berserkers?" Grimm suddenly fixated on Ronin's words about the prophecy.

"It's been foretold in the Hall of Lords."

"But Jillian doesn't know what I am," Grimm said despairingly. "And any son she has will be just like me. We can never—" He was unable to finish the thought aloud.

"She's stronger than you think she is, lad," Ronin replied. "Trust in her. Together you can learn about our heritage. It is an honor to be a Berserker, not a curse. Most of Alba's greatest heroes have been our kind."

Grimm was silent a long time, trying to recolor fifteen years of thinking. "The McKane are coming," he said finally, latching on to one solid fact in an internal landscape deluged by intangibles.

Both men's eyes flew to the surrounding mountains. "Did you see something move on the mountains?"

"No. They've been following me. They've tried three times now to take me. They've been on our heels since we left Caithness."

"Wonderful!" Balder rubbed his hands together in gleeful anticipation.

Ronin looked delighted. "How far behind you were they?"

"I suspect scarcely a day."

"So they'll be here anytime. Lad, you must go find Jillian. Take her to the heart of the castle and explain. Trust her. Give her the chance to work through things. If you had known the truth years ago, would fifteen years have been wasted?"

"She'll hate me when she discovers what I am," Grimm said bitterly.

"Are you as certain of that as you were that I killed Jolyn?" Ronin asked pointedly.

Grimm's eyes flew to his. "I'm no longer certain of anything," he said bleakly.

"You're certain you love her, lad," Ronin said. "And I'm certain she's your mate. Never has one of our true mates rejected our heritage. Never."

Grimm nodded and turned for the castle.

"Be certain she stays in the castle, Gavrael," Ronin called to his back. "We canna risk her in battle."

After Grimm had disappeared into Maldebann, Balder smiled. "He dinna try to correct you when you called him Gavrael."

Ronin's smile was joyous. "I noticed," he said. "Prepare the villagers, Balder, and I'll rouse the guards. We put an end to the feuding today. All of it."

Chapter 33

It was early afternoon when Jillian finally rose to her feet in the Hall of Lords. A sense of peace enveloped her as she laid the last of her questions to rest. Suddenly so many things she'd overheard her brothers and Quinn saying when Grimm had been in residence made sense, and upon reflection she suspected a part of her had always known.

Her love was a legendary warrior who had grown to despise himself, cut off from his roots. But now that he was home and given the time to explore those roots, he might be able to make peace with himself at long last.

She strolled the hall a final time, not missing the radiant expressions of the McIllioch brides. She stood for a long moment beneath the portrait of Grimm and his parents. Jolyn had been a chestnut-haired beauty; love radiated from her patient smile. Ronin was gazing adoringly at her. In the portrait, Grimm was kneeling before his seated parents, looking like the happiest brown-eyed boy in the world.

Her hands moved to her belly in a timeless feminine

celebration as she wondered what it would be like to bring another boy like Grimm into the world. How proud she would be, and together with Grimm, Balder, and Ronin, they would teach him what he could be, and how special he was—one of Alba's own private warriors.

"Och, lass, tell me you're not breeding!" a voice filled with loathing spat.

Jillian's scream ricocheted off the cold stone walls as Ramsay Logan's hand closed on her shoulder in a painful, viselike grip.

* * *

"I can't find her," Grimm said tightly.

Ronin and Balder turned as one when he stormed into the Greathall. The guards were ready, the villagers had been roused, and to the last man Tuluth was prepared to fight the McKane.

"Did you check in the Hall of Lords?"

"Aye, a brief glance, enough to assure myself she wasn't there." If he'd looked longer he might never have dragged himself back out, so fascinated was he by his previously unknown heritage.

"Did you search the whole castle?"

"Aye." He buried his hands in his hair, voicing his worst fear. "Is it possible the McKane got in here and took her somehow?"

Ronin expelled a gust of air. "Anythin's possible, lad. There were deliveries from the village this afternoon. Hell, anyone could have sneaked in with 'em. We've grown a bit lax in fifteen years of peace."

A sudden cry from the guardhouse compelled their instant attention.

"The McKane are comin'!"

* * *

Connor McKane rode into the vale waving a flag of Douglas plaid, which, while it confused most of the McIllioch, filled Grimm with rage and fear. The only piece of Douglas plaid a McKane could have obtained was the one from Jillian's body. She'd worn the blue and gray fabric at breakfast only this morning.

The villagers were bristling to fight, eager to demand satisfaction for the loss of their loved ones fifteen years past. As Ronin prepared to order them forward, Grimm laid a restraining hand on his arm.

"They have Jillian," he said in a voice that sounded like death.

"How can you be sure?" Ronin's gaze flew to his.

"That's my plaid they're waving. Jillian was wearing it at breakfast."

Ronin closed his eyes. "Not again," he whispered. "Not again." When he opened his eyes, they burned with the inner fire of determination. "We won't lose her, lad. Bring the McKane laird forward," he commanded the guard.

The McIllioch troops emanated hostility but drew back to permit his approach. When Connor McKane drew up in front of Ronin he scowled. "I knew you'd heal from the battle-ax, you devil, but I didn't think you'd recover so well from me killing your pretty whore of a wife." Connor bared his teeth in a smile. "*And* your unborn child."

Although Ronin's hand fisted around his claymore, he didn't free the sword. "Let the lass go, McKane. She has nothin' to do with us."

"The lass may be breeding."

Grimm went rigid on Occam's back. "She's not," he countered coolly. *Surely she would have told him!*

Connor McKane searched his face intently. "That's what she says. But I don't trust either of you."

"Where is she?" Grimm demanded.

"Safe."

"Take me, Connor, take me in her stead," Ronin offered, stunning Grimm.

"You, old man?" Connor spat. "You're not a threat anymore—we saw to that years ago. You won't be having any more sons. Now, him"—he pointed to Grimm—"he's a problem. Our spies tell us he is the last living Berserker, and the woman who may or may not be pregnant is his mate."

"What do you want from me?" Grimm said quietly.

"Your life," the McKane said simply. "To see the last of the McIllioch die is all I've ever wanted."

"We're not the monsters you think we are." Ronin glowered at the McKane chieftain.

"You're pagans. Heathens, blasphemers to the one true religion—"

"You're hardly one to judge!" Ronin exclaimed.

"Dinna think to debate the Lord's word with me, McIllioch. The voice of Satan will not tempt me from God's course."

Ronin's lip drew back in a snarl. "When man thinks he knows God's course better than God himself is when hundreds die—"

"Free Jillian and you may have my life," Grimm interrupted. "But she goes free. You will entrust her to"—Grimm glanced at Ronin—"my da." He tried to meet Ronin's gaze when he named him his sire, but couldn't.

"I dinna recover you to lose you again, lad," Ronin muttered harshly.

"What a touching reunion," Connor remarked dryly.

"But lose him you will. And if you want her, Gavrael McIllioch—last of the Berserkers—free her yourself. She's up there." He pointed to Wotan's Cleft. "In the caves."

Horrified, Grimm scanned the jagged face of the cliff. "Where in the caves?" Dread filled him at the thought of Jillian wandering in the darkness, skirting dangers she couldn't even know were there: collapsed tunnels, rock slides, dangerous pits.

"Find her yourself."

"How do I know this isn't a trap?" Grimm's eyes glittered dangerously.

"You don't," the McKane said flatly. "But if she is in there, it's very dark and there are a lot of dangerous chasms. Besides, what would I gain by sending you off into the caves?"

"They could be set to explode," Grimm said tightly.

"Then I guess you better get her out fast, McIllioch," the McKane provoked.

Ronin shook his head. "We need proof that she's in there. And alive."

Connor dispatched a guard with a low rush of words.

Some time later, that proof was offered. Jillian's piercing scream ripped through the tense air of the valley.

* * *

Ronin watched in silence as Grimm climbed the rocky pass to Wotan's Cleft.

Balder was far back in the ranks, his features concealed by a heavy cloak to prevent the McKane from realizing there was yet another unmated Berserker still alive. Ronin had insisted they not reveal his existence unless it was necessary to save lives.

From different vantages, the brothers admired the young

man mounting the cleft. He'd left Occam behind and was scaling the sheer face of the cliff with a skill and ease that revealed the preternatural prowess of the Berserker. After years of hiding what he was, he now flaunted his superiority to the enemy. He was a warrior, at one with the beast, born to survive and endure. When he topped the cliff and disappeared over the edge the two clans sat their horses in battle lines, staring across the space that separated them with hatred so palpable it hung in the air as thick and oppressive as the smoke that had filled the vale fifteen years past.

Until Jillian and Grimm—or, God forbid, a McKane—topped the edge of the cliff, neither side would move. The McKane hadn't come to Tuluth to lose any more of their clan; they'd come to take Gavrael and eliminate the last of the Berserkers.

The McIllioch didn't move out of fear for Jillian.

The time stretched painfully.

* * *

Grimm entered the tunnel silently. His every instinct demanded he bellow for Jillian, but that would only alert whoever was holding her to his presence. The memory of her terrible scream both chilled his blood and made it boil for vengeance.

He eased into the tunnel, gliding with the silent stealth of a mountain cat, sniffing the air like a wolf. All his animal instincts roused with chill, predatory perfection. Somewhere torches were burning; the scent was unmistakable. He followed the odor down twisting corridors, his hands outstretched in the darkness. Although the interior of the tunnels was pitch black, his heightened vision enabled him to discern the slope of the floor. Skirting deep pits and ducking beneath crumbling ceilings, he navigated the musty tunnels, following the scent.

He rounded a bend where the tunnel opened into a long straight corridor, and there she was, her golden hair gleaming in the torchlight.

"Stop right there," Ramsay Logan warned. "Or she dies."

It was a vision from one of his worst nightmares. Ramsay had Jillian at the end of the tunnel. He'd gagged and bound her. She was wearing the McKane tartan, and the sight of it on her body filled him with fury. The question of who had stripped and reclothed her tortured him. He assessed her quickly, assuring himself that whatever had made her scream had not drawn blood or left visible sign of injury. The blade Logan was holding to her throat had not pierced her delicate skin. Yet.

"Ramsay Logan." Grimm gave him a chilling smile.

"Not surprised to see me, eh, Roderick? Or should I say McIllioch?" He spat the name as if he'd found a foul thing lying on his tongue.

"No, I can't say I'm surprised." Grimm moved stealthily nearer. "I always knew what kind of man you are."

"I said stop, you bastard. I won't hesitate to kill her."

"And then what would you do?" Grimm countered, but drew to a halt. "You'll never make it past me, so what would killing Jillian accomplish?"

"I'd get the pleasure of ridding the world of McIllioch monsters yet to be. And if I don't come out, the McKane will destroy you when you do."

"Let her go. Release her and you can have me," Grimm offered. Jillian thrashed in Ramsay's tight grip, making it clear that she wanted no such thing.

"I'm afraid I can't do that, McIllioch."

Grimm said nothing, his eyes murderous. A score of yards lay between them, and Grimm wondered if the Berserker rage could get him across it and free Jillian before Ramsay could slice with the knife.

It was too risky to chance, and Ramsay was counting on that to stay him. But something didn't make sense. What did Logan hope to gain? If he killed Jillian, Ramsay knew Grimm would go Berserk and rip him to shreds. What was Logan's plan? He began to ask questions, trying to buy precious minutes. "Why are you doing this, Logan? I know we've had our disagreements in the past, but they were minor."

"It has nothing to do with our disagreements and everything to do with what you are." Ramsay sneered. "You're not human, McIllioch."

Grimm closed his eyes, unwilling to see the look of horror he was certain would be on Jillian's face. "When did you figure it out?" Keeping Ramsay talking might give him insight into what the bastard wanted. If it was his life and his alone, and he could assure Jillian's safety by giving it, he would gladly die. But if Ramsay planned to kill them both, Grimm would die fighting for her.

"I figured it out the day you killed the mountain cat. I was standing in the trees and saw you after you transformed. Hatchard called you by your real name." Ramsay shook his head in disgust. "All those years at court I never knew. Oh, I knew who Gavrael McIllioch was—hell, I think everyone does but your lovely bitch here." He laughed when Grimm stiffened. "Careful, or I cut."

"So you aren't the one who tried to poison me?" Grimm inched forward so gracefully he didn't appear to be moving.

Ramsay roared with laughter. "That was a fine fix. Hell

yes, I tried to poison you. Even that backfired; you switched it somehow. But I didn't know you were a Berserker then, or I wouldn't have wasted my time."

Grimm winced. It was out. But Jillian's face was turned to the side, away from the knife, and he couldn't make out her expression.

"No," Ramsay continued. "I had no idea. I just wanted you out of the running for Jillian. You see, I need the lass."

"I was right. You need her dowry."

"But you don't know the half of it. I'm in to Campbell so deeply, he's holding the titles to my land. In years past the Logans hired out as mercenaries, but there haven't been any good wars lately. Do you know when we hired out as mercenaries last? Stop moving!" he bellowed.

Grimm stood impassively. "When?"

"Fifteen years ago. To the McKane, you bastard. And fifteen years ago, Gavrael McIllioch killed my da and three of my brothers."

Grimm hadn't known. The battle was a blur in his mind, his first Berserker rage. "In fair battle. And if your clan hired out they weren't even fighting for a cause, but murdering for coin. If they were in Tuluth, they were attacking my home and slaughtering my people—"

"You're not people. You're not *human*."

"Jillian's not part of this. Let her go. It's me you want."

"She's part of it if she's breeding, McIllioch. She swears she's not, but I think I'll keep her just to make sure. The McKane told me a lot about you monsters. I know the boys are born Berserkers but don't change until they get older. A boy slips out of her womb, he's dead. If it's a girl, who knows. I may let it live. She could be a pretty toy."

Grimm finally managed to get a glimpse of Jillian's

face. It was drawn in a mask of horror. So it was out. She knew, and it was over. The fear and revulsion he'd glimpsed in his nightmares had indeed been a portent. The fight nearly fled him when he saw it, and would have had she not been in danger. He could die now. He may as well, because inside he already had. But not Jillian; she must live.

"She's not pregnant, Ramsay."

Wasn't she? Memories of her sudden nausea at the cottage surfaced in his mind. Of course Ramsay couldn't know, but the mere possibility of Jillian carrying his child sent a primitive thrill of exultation through Grimm's body. His need to protect her, already all-consuming, became the singular focus of his mind. Ramsay might have the upper hand, but Grimm refused to let him win.

"As if you would tell me the truth." Logan scoffed. "There's only one way to find out. Besides, whether she is or isn't, she'll still be wedding me. I want the gold she brings as her dowry. Between her and what the McKane pay me, I'll never have to worry about wealth again. Don't worry, I'll keep her alive. So long as she breathes, Gibraltar will do anything to keep her happy, which means an endless supply of coin."

"You son of a bitch. Just let her go!"

"You want her? Come and get her." Ramsay taunted.

Grimm stepped forward, eyeing the distance. In the instant he hesitated, Ramsay moved the blade, pricking Jillian's skin, and drops of crimson blood fell.

The Berserker, simmering with rage, erupted.

Even as he wondered why Ramsay would dare goad the Berserker into appearing, instinct plunged him forward. He had been considering cutting himself to bring on the rage, when Ramsay had done it for him. One leap brought him ten paces forward. He tried to stop, sensing an unknown trap, but the floor of the cave disappeared beneath his feet and he plunged into a chasm that hadn't existed when he'd played these tunnels as a boy. A chasm deep enough to kill even a Berserker.

"Good riddance, you bastard," Ramsay said with a smile. He held the torch above the previously concealed pit and peered as deep as the flames would permit. He waited a full five minutes but heard no sound. When he'd selected his trap, he'd tossed stones into the chasm to test the depth. None of the stones had yielded a sound, so deep was the aperture yawning into the core of the earth. If Grimm hadn't been ripped to shreds on rocky slag, the fall itself would crush every bone in his body. Skirting the pit, he dragged Jillian from the caves.

* * *

"It's done!" Ramsay Logan cried. "The McKane!" he roared. He stood on the edge of Wotan's Cleft, raised his arm, and bellowed a cry of victory that was instantly echoed by all the McKane. The valley resounded with triumphant thunder. Exuberant, Ramsay released Jillian's hands and removed her gag. His took her mouth in a triumphant, brutal kiss. She stiffened, revolted, and struggled against him. Angered by her resistance, he shoved her away, and Jillian crumpled to her knees.

"Get up, you stupid bitch," Ramsay shouted, nudging at her with his foot. "I said get up!" he roared again when she responded to his kick by curling into a ball. "I don't need you right now anyway," he muttered, gazing down at the valley that would be his home. Adulation lay in the valley, a reflection of his mighty conquest. He waved his arm again, elated by the kill.

Ramsay Logan had taken a Berserker single-handed. His name would live in legends. The chasm was so deep that not even one of Odin's monsters could survive the fall. He'd carefully covered it with thin sheaves of wood, then scattered stone dust atop it. It had been brilliant, if he had to say so himself.

"Brilliant," Ramsay informed the night.

Behind Ramsay, Grimm blinked, trying to clear the red haze of bloodlust. A part of his mind that seemed lost down an endless corridor reminded him that he wanted to attack the man standing near the balled-up woman, not the woman herself. The woman was his world. When he sprang he must be careful, very careful, for to even touch her with the strength of Berserkergang could kill her. A slight brush of his hand could shatter her jaw, the merest caress of her breast could crush her ribs.

To those sitting the horses in the valley below, listening to Ramsay Logan's victory cry, the creature seemed to explode out of the night with such speed it was impossible to identify. A blur of motion surged through the air, grabbed Ramsay Logan by the hair, and neatly severed his head before anyone could so much as shout a warning.

Because she was on the ground, the clans gathered below couldn't see Jillian roll over, startled by the slight hissing sound the blade made as it whisked through the air for Ramsay's throat. But the creature on the cliffs saw her move, and he waited for her judgment, resigned to condemnation.

It was the worst Jillian might ever see of him, the beast realized. In the full throes of Berserkergang, he towered over her, his blue eyes blazing incandescently. He was bruised and bloody from a fall that had halted abruptly on a jagged outcropping, and he held Ramsay Logan's severed head in one hand. He stared at her, pumping great gasps of air into his chest, waiting. Would she scream? Spit at him, hiss and renounce him? Jillian St. Clair was all he'd ever wanted in his entire life, and as he waited for her to shriek in horror of him, he felt something inside him trying to die.

But the Berserker wouldn't go down so easily. The wildness in him rose to its full height and stared down at her through vulnerable ice-blue eyes, wordlessly beseeching her love.

Jillian raised her head slowly and gazed at him a long, silent moment. She drew herself upright into a sitting position and tilted her head back, her eyes wide.

Berserker.

The truth he'd struggled so hard to hide hung between them, fully exposed.

Although Jillian had known what Grimm was before that moment, she was briefly immobilized by the sight of him. It was one thing to know that the man she loved was a Berserker—it was another thing entirely to behold it. He regarded her with such an inhuman expression that if she hadn't peered deep into his eyes, she might have seen nothing of Grimm at all. But there, deep in the flickering blue flames, she glimpsed such love that it rocked her soul. She smiled up at him through her tears.

A wounded sound of disbelief escaped him.

Jillian gave him the most dazzling smile she could muster and placed her fist to her heart. "And the daughter wed the lion king," she said clearly.

An expression of incredulity crossed the warrior's face. His blue eyes widened and he stared at her in stunned silence.

"I love you, Gavrael McIllioch."

When he smiled, his face blazed with love. He tossed his head back and shouted his joy to the sky.

* * *

The last of the McKane died in the vale of Tuluth, December 14, 1515.

CHAPTER 34

"THEY'RE COMING, HAWK!" ADRIENNE SPED INTO THE Greathall where Hawk, Lydia, and Tavis were busy decorating for the wedding. As the ceremony was being held on Christmas Day, they'd combined the customary decorations with the gaily colored greens and reds of the season. Exquisite wreaths fashioned of pinecones and dried berries had been decorated with brilliant velvet bows and shimmering ribbons. The finest tapestries adorned the walls, including one Adrienne had helped to weave over the past year that featured a Nativity scene with a radiant Madonna cradling the infant Jesus while proud Joseph and the magi looked on.

Today the hall was clear of rushes, the stones scoured to a spotless gray. Later, only moments before the wedding, they would strew dried rose petals across the stones to release a springy floral aroma into the air. Sprigs of mistletoe dangled from every beam and Adrienne eyed the foliage, peering up at Hawk, who stood on a ladder, fastening a wreath to the wall.

"What are those lovely sprigs you've hung, Hawk?" Adrienne asked, the picture of innocence.

Hawk glanced down at her. "Mistletoe. It's a Christmas tradition."

"How is it associated with Christmas?"

"The legends say the Scandinavian god of peace, Balder, was slain by an arrow fashioned of mistletoe. The other gods and goddesses loved Balder so greatly, they begged his life be restored and mistletoe be endowed with special meaning."

"What kind of special meaning?" Adrienne blinked expectantly up at him.

Hawk slid swiftly down the ladder, happy to demonstrate. He kissed her so passionately that the embers of desire, always at a steady burn around her husband, roared into flame. "One who passes beneath the mistletoe must be kissed thoroughly."

"Mmm. I like this tradition. But what happened to poor Balder?"

Hawk grinned and planted another kiss on her lips. "Balder was returned to life and the care of mistletoe was bequeathed to the goddess of love. Each time a kiss is given beneath mistletoe, love and peace gain a stronger foothold in the world of mortals."

"How lovely," Adrienne exclaimed. Her eyes sparkled mischievously. "So essentially, the more I kiss you under this branch"—she pointed up—"the more good I'm doing the world. One might say I'm helping all of humankind, doing my duty—"

"Your duty?" Hawk arched a brow.

Lydia laughed and tugged Tavis beneath the branch as well. "It sounds like a good idea to me, Adrienne. Maybe if we kiss them enough we'll lay all the silly feuding in this land to rest."

The next few minutes belonged to lovers, until the door burst open and a guard announced the arrival of their guests.

Adrienne's gaze darted about the Greathall as she fretted over anything that might be yet undone. She wanted everything to be perfect for Grimm's bride. "How do I say it again?" she asked Lydia frantically. She'd been trying to perfect her Gaelic so she could greet them with a proper "Merry Christmas."

"Nollaig Chridheil," Lydia repeated slowly.

Adrienne repeated it several times, then linked her arm through Hawk's and smiled beatifically. "My wish came true, Hawk," she said smugly.

"What was that blasted wish, anyway?" Hawk said, disgruntled.

"That Grimm Roderick find the woman who would heal his heart as you healed mine, my love." Adrienne would never call a man "radiant"; it seemed a feminine word. But when her husband gazed down at her with his eyes glowing so lovingly, she whispered a fervent "thank you" in the direction of the Nativity scene. Then she added a silent benediction for any and all other beings responsible for the events that had carried her across five hundred years to find him. Scotland was a magical place, rich in legends, and Adrienne embraced them because the underlying themes were universal: Love endured, and it could heal all.

* * *

It was a traditional wedding, if such could be between a woman and a man of legend—a Berserker no less, with two more of the epic warriors in attendance. The women fussed and the men shared toasts. At the last minute, Gibraltar and Elizabeth St. Clair arrived. They had ridden like the devil the moment they'd received the message that Jillian was to be wed at Dalkeith-Upon-the-Sea.

Jillian was elated to see her parents. Elizabeth and Adrienne helped her dress while they resolved that both "das" should escort the bride to the groom's side. Ronin had already been solicited for the honor, but Elizabeth maintained that Gibraltar would never recover if he wasn't allowed to escort her too. Yes, she knew that Jillian hadn't expected them to be able to make it in time, but they had and that was the end of it.

The bride and groom didn't see one another until the moment Gibraltar and Ronin escorted Jillian down the elaborate staircase into the Greathall, after a long pause at the top that permitted all and sundry to exclaim over the radiant bride.

Jillian's heart was thundering as her two "das" lifted her hands from their forearms and tucked her arm through the elbow of the man who was to be her husband. Grimm looked magnificent, clad in ceremonial tartan, his black hair neatly queued. Jillian didn't miss it when Ronin's gaze flickered over the plaid. He looked momentarily astonished, then elated, for Grimm had donned the full dress of the McIllioch for his wedding day.

She hadn't thought the day could be any more perfect until the priest began the ceremony. After what seemed like years of traditional benedictions and prayers, he moved onto the vows:

"Do you, Grimm Roderick, promise—"

Grimm's deep voice interrupted him. Pride underscored each word. "My name is Gavrael." He took a deep breath, then continued, enunciating his name clearly. "Gavrael Roderick Icarus McIllioch."

Chills swept up her spine. Tears misted Ronin's eyes and the hall fell silent for a moment. Hawk grinned at Adrienne, and far in the back of the hall where few had as yet seen him, Quinn de Moncreiffe nodded, satisfied. At long last, Grimm Roderick was at peace with who and what he was.

"Do you, Gavrael Roderick—"

"I do."

Jillian nudged him.

He arched a brow and frowned. "Well, I *do*. Must we go through all this? I do. I swear a man has never 'I do'd' more fervently than I. I just want to be *married* to you, lass."

Ronin and Balder exchanged amused glances. Keeping them apart had certainly heightened Gavrael's enthusiasm for the matrimonial bonds.

Guests tittered, and Jillian smiled. "Let the priest have his turn, because I would like to hear you say it all. Especially the 'loving and cherishing me' part."

"Oh, I'll love and ravish you, lass," Gavrael said close to her ear.

"Cherish! And behave." She teasingly swatted at him and nodded encouragingly to the priest. "Do continue."

And so they were wed.

* * *

Kaley Twillow jostled for room, rising to her toes and peering over heads anxiously. Her precious Jillian was getting married and she couldn't see a dratted thing. It just wouldn't do.

"Watch where yer pokin'," an irate guest barked as she strategically jabbed her elbow in a few tender spots to squeeze past.

"Wait your turn to greet the bride!" another one complained when she stepped on his toes.

"I practically raised the wee bride, and I'll be damned if I'm sitting in back unable to see, so *move* your arse!" She glowered.

A small path appeared as they reluctantly permitted her passage.

Wedging her ample bosom and hips between a cluster of guards created a small furor as dozens of men eyed the shapely woman with interest. Finally she pushed through, crested the last wave of guests, and surfaced beside a man whose handsome height and girth took her breath away. His thick black hair was streaked with silver, revealing his mature years, which, in her experience, meant mature passion.

She peered coquettishly at the black-haired man from the corner of her eye, then turned her head to savor him fully. "My, my, and just who might you be?" She fluttered her long lashes admiringly.

Balder's ice-blue eyes crinkled with pleasure as he beheld the voluptuous woman who was obviously delighted to see him. "The man who's been waiting for you all his life, lass," he said huskily.

* * *

The wedding celebration began the moment the vows had been exchanged. Jillian longed to slip off with her husband the instant the ceremony ended. With Balder and

Ronin strictly monitoring her time with Gavrael for the past two weeks, they'd been able to spend no time alone at all. But she didn't wish to hurt Adrienne's feelings when she had obviously taken great care to ensure Jillian's wedding day was the stuff of dreams, so she dutifully lingered and greeted and smiled. The moment she and Gavrael had sealed their union with a kiss, she'd been snatched from his lips, tugged in one direction by the joyous crowd and able to do nothing but watch helplessly as her husband was dragged in the other.

They were married, the older and wiser had counseled, and they would have plenty of time to spend with each other. Jillian had rolled her eyes and pasted a smile on her face, accepting congratulations.

Finally, the flatbread was broken and the feasting commenced, drawing attention away from the newlyweds. Adrienne helped Jillian slip out of the hall, but instead of showing her to their chambers as she'd expected, the stunning, unusual woman had led her to Dalkeith's study. The light from oil globes and dozens of candles coupled with a cheery fire made the room a welcoming and warm haven despite the banks of fluffy white snow drifting outside the windows.

"It looks like we may get a real doozy." Adrienne eyed the drifts as she bustled about, poking up the fire.

Jillian blinked. "A what?"

"Doozy. Oh . . ." Adrienne paused, then laughed. "A big storm. You know, we might get snowed in for a time."

"You're not from this part of the country, are you?" Jillian frowned, trying to place her strange accent.

Again her hostess laughed. "Not quite." She beckoned Jillian to join her before the fire. "Just tell me, are those two of the hunkiest men you've ever laid eyes on?" Adrienne eyed a picture above the hewn-oak mantel and sighed dreamily.

Jillian followed her hostess's gaze upward to a beautifully rendered portrait of Gavrael and the Hawk. "Oh my. I don't know what 'hunkiest' means, but they certainly are the most handsome men I've ever seen."

"That's it," Adrienne agreed. "Do you know they complained the entire time this was being painted? Men." She rolled her eyes and gestured at the painting. "How could they blame a woman for wanting to immortalize such raw masculine splendor?"

The women spoke quietly for a time, unaware Hawk and Gavrael had entered the study behind them. Gavrael's eyes lingered on his wife and he started to move forward, determined to claim her before someone else dragged him off.

"Relax." Hawk placed a restraining hand on his sleeve. Enough distance separated the men from their wives that the women hadn't heard them yet, but Adrienne's voice carried clearly:

"It was all that fairy's fault. He dragged me back through time—not that I'm complaining a bit, mind you. I love it here and I adore my husband, but I'm originally from the twentieth century."

Both men grinned when Jillian did a double take. "Five hundred years from now?" she exclaimed.

Adrienne nodded, her eyes dancing. Jillian studied her intently, then leaned closer. "My husband's a Berserker," she confided.

"I know. He told us right before he left for Caithness, but I didn't get a chance to ask him any questions. Can he change shapes?" Adrienne looked as if she were about to reach for paper and ink and start scribbling notes. "In the twentieth century there's a great deal of dispute over just what they were and what they were capable of." Adrienne paused as she became aware of the two men standing in the doorway. Her eyes twinkled mischievously, and she winked at her husband. "However, there *was* a general consensus on one thing, Jillian." She smiled impishly. "It was commonly held that Berserkers were known for their legendary stamina—both in battle and in the b—"

"We get the point, Adrienne." Hawk cut her off, his black eyes sparkling with amusement. "Now, perhaps we should let Gavrael show her the rest himself."

* * *

Gavrael and Jillian's chambers were on the third floor of Dalkeith. Adrienne and Hawk escorted them, dropping not-so-subtle hints that the newlyweds could make as much noise as they wished; with the intervening floors, the revelers below would be none the wiser.

When the door closed behind them and they were finally alone, Gavrael and Jillian gazed at each other across the downy expanse of a wide mahogany bed. A fire leapt and crackled in the hearth while fluffy snowflakes fell beyond the window.

Grimm regarded her tenderly and his eyes slipped down, as they'd frequently done lately, to the scarcely noticeable swell of her abdomen. Jillian caught the possessive glance and gave him a dazzling smile. Ever since the night of the attack, when she'd told him they were going to have a baby, she'd caught him smiling at odd times with little or no provocation. It delighted her, his intense delight about the baby growing inside her. When she'd told him, after they'd returned from the caves to Maldebann, he'd sat blinking and shaking his head, as if he couldn't believe it was true. When she'd cradled his face in her hands and drawn his head close to kiss him, she'd been stunned by the glimpse of moisture in his eyes. Her husband was the best of men: strong yet sensitive, capable yet vulnerable—and how she loved him!

As she watched him now, his eyes darkened with desire, and anticipation shivered through her.

"Adrienne said we might get snowed in for a while," Jillian said breathlessly, feeling suddenly awkward. Being chaperoned these past weeks had nearly driven her crazy; to compensate, she'd tried to push her unruly steamy thoughts into a secluded corner of her mind. Now they resisted their confines, broke free, and demanded attention. She wanted her husband *now*.

"Good. I hope it snows a dozen feet." Gavrael moved around the bed. All he wanted to do was bury himself inside her, reassure himself that she was indeed his. This day had been the culmination of all his dreams—he was married to Jillian St. Clair. Gazing down at her, he marveled at how much she had changed his life: He had a home, a clan, and a father, the wife he'd always dreamed of, a precious child on the way, and a bright future. He, who had always felt like an outcast, now belonged. And he owed it all to Jillian. He came to a stop inches from her and flashed her a lazy, sensual smile. "I doona suppose you have any noises you'd like to be making while we're snowbound? I'd hate to disappoint our hosts."

Jillian's awkwardness melted away in a flash. Skirting all niceties, she slipped her hand up his muscular thigh and tugged his plaid away from his body. Her fingers flew over the buttons of his shirt, and within moments he stood before her as nature had fashioned him—a mighty warrior with hard angles and muscled planes.

Her gaze dropped lower and fixed upon what must have

surely been nature's most generous boon. She wet her lip, a wordless gesture of desire, unaware of the effect it had on him.

Gavrael groaned and reached for her. Jillian slipped into his arms, wrapped her hand around his thick shaft, and nearly purred with delight.

His eyes flared, then narrowed as he moved with the grace and power of a mountain cat, dragging her down onto the bed. A rough sigh escaped him. "Ah, I missed you, lass. I thought I was going to go crazy from wanting you. Balder wouldn't even let me kiss you!" Gavrael worked swiftly at the tiny buttons on her wedding gown. When she tightened her fingers around him, he quickly secured her hands, trapping them with one of his. "I can't think when you do that, lass."

"I didn't ask you to think, my big brawny warrior," she teased. "I have other uses for you."

He tossed her an arrogant look that clearly warned her he was in charge for the moment. With her distracting hands temporarily restrained, he lingered over her buttons, tracing kisses over each inch of skin as it was revealed. When his lips returned to hers, he kissed her with a savage intensity. Their tongues met, retreated, then met again. He tasted of brandy and cinnamon; Jillian followed his tongue, caught it with her own, and drew it into her mouth. When he stretched full length on top of her, muscled body to silken skin, her softness accommodating his hardness in perfect symmetry, she sighed her pleasure.

"Please," she begged, shifting her body enticingly beneath him.

"Please what, Jillian? What would you like me to do? Tell me exactly, lass." His heavy-lidded eyes glittered with interest.

"I want you to . . ." She gestured.

He nibbled her lower lip, drew back, and blinked innocently. "I'm afraid I doona understand. What was that?"

"Here." She gestured again.

"Say it, Jillian," he whispered huskily. "Tell me. I am yours to command, but I follow only very explicit instructions." The wicked grin he flashed loosened the last of her restraints, leaving her free to indulge in a bit of wickedness of her own.

So she told him, the man who was her own private legend, and he fulfilled her every secret desire, tasting and touching and pleasing her. He worshipped her body with his passion, celebrated their child in her womb with gentle kisses, kisses that lost their gentleness and became hot and hungry against her hips and blazed into flowing heat between her thighs.

Plunging her hands into his thick dark hair, she rose up against him, crying his name over and over.

Gavrael.

And after she'd run out of demands—or simply had been sated beyond coherent thought—he knelt on the bed, pulled her astride him, and wrapped her long legs around his waist. Her nails scored his back as he lowered her onto his hard shaft one exquisite inch at a time.

"You can't harm the baby, Gavrael," she assured him, panting softly as he held her away, giving her but a tiny taste of what she so desperately wanted.

"I'm not worried about that," he assured her.

"Then why . . . are . . . you . . . going so *slow*?"

"To watch your face," he said with a lazy smile. "I love to watch your eyes when we make love. I see every bit of pleasure, every ounce of desire reflected in them."

"They'll look even better if you'll just—" She pushed

against him with her hips and, laughing, he held her away with his strong hands on her waist.

Jillian nearly wailed. "Please!"

But he took his sweet time—and how sweet it was—until she thought she could no longer bear it. Then, abruptly, he buried himself deep within her. "I love you, Jillian McIllioch." His accompanying smile was uninhibited, his white teeth flashing against his dark face.

She laid a finger to his lips. "I know," she assured him.

"But I wanted to say the words." He caught her finger between his lips and kissed it.

"I see," she teased. "You get to say all the love words while I have to say all the bawdy ones."

He made a rumble low in his throat. "I *love* it when you tell me what you want me to do to you."

"Then do this . . ." Her low rush of words dissolved into a satisfied cry as he fulfilled her demand.

Hours later, her last conscious thought was that she should not forget to mention to Adrienne that the "general consensus" about Berserkers could not even begin to touch the reality.

Epilogue

"I DOONA UNDERSTAND IT," RONIN SAID, WATCHING THE lads. He shook his head. "It's never happened before."

"I doona either, Da. But something is different about me from any of the McIllioch males before. Either that, or there's something different about Jillian. Perhaps it's both of us."

"How do you keep up with them?"

Gavrael laughed, a rich sound. "Between Jillian and me, we manage."

"But with them being, you know, the way they are so young, aren't they constantly getting into mischief?"

"Not to mention impossibly high places. They're forever pulling off incredible feats, and if you ask me, they're just a little too damned smart for anyone's good. It's almost more than any one Berserker could be expected to keep up with. That's why I think it would be useful to have their grandda around too," Gavrael said pointedly.

The flush of pleasure on Ronin's cheeks was unmistakable. "You mean you want me to stay here with you and Jillian?"

"Maldebann is home, Da. I know you felt Jillian and I needed the privacy of newlyweds, but we wish you would come home for good. Both you and Balder; the lads need their great-uncle too. Remember, we McIllioch are the stuff of legends, and how will they come to understand the legends without the finest of our Berserkers to teach them? Quit visiting all those people you've been dropping in on and *come home*." Gavrael studied him out of the corner of his eyes and knew Ronin would not leave Maldebann again. The thought gave him great satisfaction. His sons should know their grandda. Not merely as an intermittent visitor, but as a steady influence.

In a contented silence that bordered on awe, Gavrael and Ronin watched the three young boys playing on the lawn. When Jillian stepped out into the sunshine, her sons looked up as one, as if they could sense her presence. They stopped playing and ranged in around their mother, vying for attention.

"Now, there's a beautiful sight," Ronin said reverently.

"Aye," Gavrael agreed.

Jillian laughed as she tousled the heads of her three young sons and smiled into three pairs of ice-blue eyes.

A NORSE LEGEND
(THE TWILIGHT OF THE GODS)

Legend tells that *Ragnarok*—the final battle of the gods—will herald the end of the world.

Destruction will rage in the kingdom of the gods. In the last battle, Odin will be devoured by a wolf. The earth will be destroyed by fire, and the universe will sink into the sea.

Legend holds that this final destruction will be followed by rebirth. The earth will reemerge from the water, lush and teeming with new life. It is prophesied the sons of the dead Aesir will return to Asgard, the home of the gods, and reign again.

In the mountains of Scotland, the Circle Elders say Odin doesn't believe in taking any chances, that he schemes to defy fate by breeding his warrior race of Berserkers into the Scottish bloodlines, deeply hidden. There they await the twilight of the gods, at which time he will summon them to fight for him once more.

Legend tells that there are Berserkers walking among us, even still. . . .

KAREN MARIE MONING is the *New York Times* bestselling author of the Fever series featuring MacKayla Lane, as well as the Highlander series. She has a bachelor's degree in society and law from Purdue University and currently lives in Kentucky and Georgia. She can be reached at www.karenmoning.com.

Don't miss
the other Highlander adventures . . .

KAREN MARIE MONING'S

BEYOND THE HIGHLAND MIST

THE HIGHLANDER'S TOUCH

KISS OF THE HIGHLANDER

THE DARK HIGHLANDER

THE IMMORTAL HIGHLANDER

and

SPELL OF THE HIGHLANDER

Catch the next book in Karen Marie

Moning's sizzling Fever series...

faefever

Now available from Dell Books

"And I will show you something different from either
Your shadow at morning striding behind you
Or your shadow at evening rising to meet you;
I will show you fear in a handful of dust."

—T. S. ELIOT, *The Wasteland*

"Do not go gently into that good night.
Rage, rage against the dying of the light."

—DYLAN THOMAS

"I keep expecting to wake up and find it was
all a bad dream.
Alina will be alive,
I won't be afraid of the dark,
Monsters won't be walking the streets of Dublin,
And I won't have this terrible fear that, tomorrow dawn
just won't come."

—Mac's journal

PART ONE: BEFORE DAWN

PROLOGUE

I'd die for him.

No, wait a minute... that's not where this is supposed to begin.

I know that. But left to my own devices, I'd prefer to skim over the events of the next few weeks, and whisk you through those days with glossed-over details that cast me in a more flattering light.

Nobody looks good in their darkest hour. But it's those hours that make us what we are. We stand strong, or we cower. We emerge victorious, tempered by our trials, or fractured by a permanent, damning fault line.

I never used to think about things like darkest hours and trials and fault lines.

I used to fill my days with sunning and shopping, bartending at the Brickyard (always more of a party than a job, and that was how I liked my life) and devising ways to con Mom and Dad into helping me buy a new car. At twenty-two, I was still living at home, safe in my sheltered world, lulled by the sleepy, slow-paddling fans of the Deep South into believing myself the center of it.

Then my sister, Alina, was brutally murdered while studying abroad in Dublin, and my world changed overnight. It was bad enough that I had to identify her mutilated body, and watch my once-happy family shatter, but my world didn't stop falling apart there. It didn't stop until I'd learned that pretty much everything I'd been raised to believe about myself wasn't true.

I discovered that my folks weren't my real parents, my sister and I were adopted, and despite my lazy, occasionally overblown drawl, we weren't southern at all but descended from an ancient Celtic bloodline of *sidhe*-seers, people who can see the Fae—a terrifying race of otherworldly beings that have lived secretly among us for thousands of years, cloaked in illusions and lies.

Those were the easy lessons.

The hard lessons were yet to come, waiting for me in the *craic*-filled streets of the Temple Bar District of Dublin, where I would watch people die, and learn how to kill; where I would meet

Jericho Barrons, V'lane, and the Lord Master; where I would step up to plate as a major player in a deadly game with fate-of-the-world stakes.

For those of you just joining me, my name is MacKayla Lane, Mac for short. My real last name might be O'Connor, but I don't know that for sure. I'm a *sidhe*-seer, one of the most powerful that's ever lived. Not only can I see the Fae, I can hurt them and, armed with one of their most sacred Hallows—the Spear of Luin or Destiny—I can even kill the immortal beings.

Don't settle into your chair and relax. It's not just my world that's in trouble; it's your world, too. It's happening right now, while you're sitting there, munching a snack, getting ready to immerse yourself in a fictional escape. Guess what? It's not fiction, and there's no escape. The walls between the human world and Faery are coming down—and I hate to break it to you, but these fairies are *so* not Tinkerbell.

If the walls crash completely... well... you'd just better hope they don't. If I were you, I'd turn on all my lights right now. Get out a few flashlights. Check your supply of batteries.

I came to Dublin for two things: to find out who killed my sister and to get revenge. See how easily I can say that now? I want revenge. Revenge with a capital *R*. Revenge with crushed bones and a lot of blood. I want her murderer dead, preferably by my own hand. A few months here and I've shed *years* of polished southern civilities.

Shortly after I stepped off the plane from Ashford, Georgia, and planted my well-pedicured heels on Ireland's shores, I probably would have died, if I hadn't stumbled into a bookstore owned by Jericho Barrons. Who or what he is, I have no idea. But he has knowledge that I need, and I have something he wants, and that makes us reluctant allies.

When I had no place to turn, Barrons took me in, taught me who and what I am, opened my eyes, and helped me survive. He didn't do it nicely, but I no longer care how I survive, as long as I do.

Because it was safer than my cheap room at the inn, I moved into his bookstore. It's protected against most of my enemies with wards and assorted spells, and stands as a bastion at the edge of what I call a Dark Zone: a neighborhood that has been taken over by Shades, amorphous Unseelie that thrive in darkness and suck the life from humans.

We've battled monsters together. He's saved my life twice. We've shared a taste of dangerous lust. He's after the *Sinsar Dubh*—a million-year-old book of the blackest magic imaginable, scribed by the Unseelie King himself—which holds the key to power over both the worlds of Fae and Man. I want it because it was Alina's dying request that I find it, and I suspect it holds the key to saving our world.

He wants it because he says he collects books. Right.

V'lane is another story. He's a Seelie prince and a death-by-sex Fae, which you'll be learning more about soon enough. The Fae consist of two adversarial courts with their own Royal Houses and unique castes: the Light or Seelie Court, and the Dark or Unseelie Court. Don't let the light and dark stuff fool you. Both are deadly. However, the Seelie considered the Unseelie *so* deadly that they imprisoned them roughly seven hundred thousand years ago. When one Fae fears another, be afraid.

Each court has their Hallows, or sacred objects of immense power. The Seelie Hallows are the spear (which I have), the Sword, the Stone, and the Cauldron. The Unseelie Hallows are the amulet (which I had and the Lord Master took), the Box, the Sifting Silvers, and the highly sought after Book. They all have different purposes. Some I know, others I'm not so clear on.

Everybody wants me. So I stay alive in a world where death darkens my doorstep daily.

I've seen things that would make your skin crawl. I've done things that make my skin crawl.

But that's not important now. What's important is starting at the right place. . . . Let's see . . . where was that?

I peel the pages of my memory backward, one at a time, squinting so I don't have to see them too clearly. I turn back, past that whiteout where all memories vanish for a time, past that hellish Halloween, and the things Barrons did. Past the woman I killed. Past a part of V'lane piercing the meat of my tongue. Past what I did to Jayne.

There.

I zoom down into a dark, damp, shiny street.

It's me. Pretty in pink and gold.

I'm in Dublin. It's nighttime. I'm walking the cobbled pavement of Temple Bar. I'm alive, vibrantly so. There's nothing like a recent brush with death to make you feel larger than life.

There's sunshine in my eyes and a spring in my step. I'm wearing a killer pink dress, my favorite heels, and I'm accessorized to the hilt, in gold and rose amethyst. I've taken extra care with my hair and makeup. I'm on my way to meet Christian MacKeltar, a sexy, mysterious young Scotsman who knew my sister. I feel *good* for a change.

Well, at least for a short time I do.

Fast-forward a few moments.

Now I'm clutching my head and stumbling from the sidewalk into the gutter. Falling to all fours. I've just gotten closer to the *Sinsar Dubh* than I've ever been before, and it's having its usual effect on me. Pain. Debilitating.

I no longer look so pretty. In fact, I look positively wretched.

On my hands and knees in a puddle that smells of beer and urine, I'm iced to the bone. My hair is in a tangle, my amethyst hair clip bobs against my nose, and I'm crying. I push the hair from my face with a filthy hand, and watch the tableau playing out in front of me with wide, horrified eyes.

I remember that moment. Who I was. What I wasn't. I capture it in freeze-frame. There are so many things I would say to her.

Head up, Mac. Brace yourself. A storm is coming. Don't you hear the thunderclap of sharp hooves on the wind? Can't you feel the soul-numbing frost? Don't you smell spice and blood on the breeze?

Run, I would tell her. Hide.

But I wouldn't listen to me.

Like Barrons, V'lane is after the *Sinsar Dubh*. He's hunting it for the Seelie queen, Aoibheal, who needs it to reinforce the walls between the realms of Fae and Man, and keep them from coming down. Like Barrons, he has saved my life. (He's also given me some of the most intense orgasms of it.)

The Lord Master is my sister's murderer; the one who seduced, used, and destroyed her. Not quite Fae, not quite human, he's been opening portals between realms, bringing Unseelie—the worst of the Fae—through to our world, turning them loose, and teaching them to infiltrate our society. He *wants* the walls down so he can free all of the Unseelie from their icy prison. He's also after the *Sinsar Dubh,* although I'm not certain why. I think he may be seeking it to destroy it, so no one can ever rebuild the walls again.

That's where I come in.

These three powerful, dangerous men *need* me.

Not only can I see the Fae, I can sense Fae relics and Hallows. I can feel the *Sinsar Dubh* out there, a dark, pulsing heart of pure evil.

I can hunt it.

I can find it.

My dad would say that makes me this season's MVP.

On my knees, watching that . . . *thing* . . . do what it's doing, I'm in the stranglehold of a killing undertow.

Reluctantly, I merge with the memory, slip into her skin . . .

ONE

The pain, God, the *pain*! It was going to splinter my skull!

I clutch my head with wet, stinking hands, determined to hold it together until the inevitable occurs—I pass out.

Nothing compares to the agony the *Sinsar Dubh* causes me. Each time I get close to it, the same thing happens. I'm immobilized by pain that escalates until I lose consciousness.

Barrons says it's because the Dark Book and I are point and counterpoint. That it's so evil, and I'm so good, that it repels me violently. His theory is to "dilute" me somehow, make me a little evil so I can get close to it. I don't see how making me evil so I can get close enough to pick up an evil book is a good thing. I think I'd probably do evil things with it.

"No," I whimper, sloshing on my knees in the puddle. "Please . . . no!" Not here, not now! In the past, each time I'd gotten close to the Book, Barrons had been with me, and I'd had the comfort of knowing he wouldn't let anything too awful happen to my unconscious body. He might tote me around like a divining rod, but I could live with that. Tonight, however, I was alone. The thought of being vulnerable to anyone and anything in Dublin's streets for even a few moments terrified me. What if I passed out for an hour? What if I fell facedown into the vile puddle I was in, and drowned in mere inches of . . . ugh.

I *had* to get out of the puddle. I would not die so pathetically.

A wintry wind howled down the street, whipping between buildings, chilling me to the bone. Old newspapers cartwheeled like dirty, sodden tumbleweeds over broken bottles and discarded wrappers and glasses. I flailed in the sewage, scraped at the pavement with my fingernails, left the tips of them broken in gaps between the cobbled stones.

It was there—straight ahead of me: the Dark Book. I could feel it, fifty yards from where I scrabbled for purchase. Maybe less. And it wasn't just a book. Oh, no. It was nothing that simple. It pulsated darkly, charring the edges of my mind.

Why wasn't I passing out?

Why wouldn't this pain *end*?

I felt like I was dying. Saliva flooded my mouth, frothing into foam at my lips. I wanted desperately to throw up but I couldn't. Even my stomach was locked down by pain.

Moaning, I tried to raise my head. I had to see it. I'd been close to it before, but I'd never *seen* it. I'd always passed out first. If I wasn't going to lose consciousness, I had questions I wanted answered. I didn't even know what it looked like. Who had it? What were they doing with it? Why did I keep having near brushes with it?

Shuddering, I pushed back onto my knees, shoved a hank of sour-smelling hair from my face, and looked.

The street that only moments ago had bustled with tourists making their merry way from one open pub door to the next was now scourged clean by the dark, arctic wind. Doors had been slammed, music silenced.

Leaving only me.

And *them*.

The vision before me was not at all what I'd expected.

A gunman had a huddle of people backed against the wall of a building, a family of tourist with deep Texan accents, cameras swinging around their necks. The barrel of a semiautomatic weapon gleamed in the moonlight. The father was yelling, the mother was screaming, trying to gather three small children into her arms.

"No!" I shouted. At least I think I did. I'm not sure I actually made a sound. My lungs were compressed with pain.

The gunman let loose a spray of bullets, silencing their cries. He killed the youngest last—a delicate blond girl of four or five, with wide, pleading eyes that would haunt me till the day I died. A girl I couldn't save because I couldn't fecking *move*. Paralyzed by pain-deadened limbs, I could only kneel there, screaming inside my head.

Why was this happening? Where was the *Sinsar Dubh*? Why couldn't I see it?

The man turned, and I inhaled sharply.

A book was tucked beneath his arm.

A perfectly innocuous hardcover, about 350 pages thick, no dust jacket, pale gray backing, red binding. The kind of well-read hardcover you might find in any used bookstore, in any city.

I gaped. Was I supposed to believe *that* was the million-year-old book of the blackest magic imaginable, scribed by the Unseelie King? Was this supposed to be funny? How anticlimactic. How absurd.

The gunman glanced at his weapon with a bemused expression. Then his head swiveled back toward the fallen bodies, the blood and bits of flesh and bone spattered across the brick wall.

The book dropped from beneath his arm. It seemed to fall in slow motion, changing, transforming as it tumbled end over end, to the damp, shiny brick. By the time it hit the cobbled pavement with a heavy *whump,* it was no longer a simple hardcover but a massive black tome, nearly a foot thick, engraved with runes, bound by bands of steel and intricate locks. Exactly the kind of book I'd expected: ancient and evil looking.

I sucked in another breath.

Now the thick dark volume was changing again, becoming something new. It swirled and spun, drawing substance from wind and darkness.

In its place rose a . . . *thing* . . . of such . . . terrible essence and pitch. A darkly animate . . . again, I can only say *thing* . . . that existed beyond shape or name: a malformed creature sprung from some no-man's land of shattered sanity and broken gibberings.

And it *lived.*

I have no words to describe it, because nothing exists in our world to compare it to. I'm glad nothing exists in our world to compare it to because if something did exist in our world to compare it to, I'm not sure our world would exist.

I can only call it The Beast, and leave it there.

My soul shivered, as if perceiving on some visceral level that my body was not nearly enough protection for it. Not from this.

The gunman looked at It, and It looked at the gunman, who turned his weapon on himself. I jerked at the sound of more shots. The shooter crumpled to the pavement and his weapon clattered away.

Another icy wind gusted down the street, and there was movement in my periphery.

A woman appeared from around the corner as if answering a summons, gazed blankly at the scene for several moments, then walked as if drugged straight to the fallen book *(crouching beast with impossible limbs and bloodied muzzle!)* that abruptly sported neither ancient locks nor bestial form, but was once again masquerading as an innocent hardcover.

"Don't touch it!" I cried, goose bumps needling my flesh at the thought.

She stooped, picked it up, tucked it beneath her arm and turned away.

I'd like to say she walked off without a backward glance, but she didn't. She glanced over her shoulder, *straight at me*, and her expression choked off what little breath inflated my lungs.

Pure evil stared out of her eyes, a cunning, bottomless malevolence that *knew* me, that understood things about me I didn't, and never wanted to know. Evil that celebrated its existence every chance it got through chaos, demolition, and psychotic rage.

She smiled an awful smile, baring hundreds of small pointy teeth.

And I had one of those sudden epiphanies.

I remembered the last time I'd gotten close to the *Sinsar Dubh* and passed out, and reading the next day about the man who'd killed his entire family, then driven himself into an embankment, mere blocks from where I'd lost consciousness. Everyone interviewed had said the same thing—the man couldn't have done it, it wasn't him, he'd been behaving like someone possessed for the past few days. I recalled the rash of gruesome news articles lately that echoed the same sentiment: whatever the brutal crime—*it wasn't him/her; he/she would never do it*. I stared at the woman who was no longer who or what she'd been when she'd turned the corner and entered this street. A woman possessed. And I understood.

It *wasn't* those people committing the terrible crimes.

The Beast was inside her now, in control. And it would retain control of her until it was done using her, when it would dispose of her and move on to its next victim.

We'd been so wrong, Barrons and I!

We'd believed the *Sinsar Dubh* was in the possession of someone with a cogent plan who was transporting it from place to place with a purpose; someone who was either using it to accomplish certain goals, or guarding it, trying to keep it from falling into the wrong hands.

But it wasn't in the possession of anyone with a plan, cogent or otherwise, and it wasn't being moved.

It was *moving*.

Passing from one set of hands to the next, transforming each of its victims into a weapon of violence and destruction. Barrons had told me that Fae relics had a tendency to take on a life and purpose of their own in time. The Dark Book was a million years old. That was a lot of time. It had certainly taken on some kind of life.

The woman disappeared around the corner and I dropped to the pavement like a stone. Eyes closed, I gasped for shallow breaths. As she/It moved farther away, vanishing into the night where God only knew what she/It would do next, my pain began to ease.

It was the most dangerous Hallow ever created—and it was loose in our world.

Creepy thing was, until tonight, it hadn't been aware of me.

It was now.

It had looked at me, seen me. I couldn't explain it, but I felt it had somehow *marked* me, tagged me like a pigeon. I'd gazed into the abyss and the abyss had gazed back, just like Daddy always said it would: *You want to know about life, Mac? It's simple. Keep watching rainbows, baby. Keep looking at the sky. You find what you look for. If you go hunting good in the world, you'll find it. If you go hunting evil . . . well, don't.*

What idiot, I brooded as I dragged myself up onto the sidewalk, had decided to give *me* special powers? What fool thought I could do something about problems of such enormity? How could I *not* hunt evil when I was one of the few people who could see it?

Tourists were flooding back into the street. Pub doors opened. Darkness peeled back. Music began playing, and the world started up again. Laughter bounced off brick. I wondered what world *they* were living in. It sure wasn't mine.

Oblivious to them all, I threw up until I dry-heaved. Then I dry-heaved until not even bile remained.

I pushed to my feet, dragged the back of my hand across my mouth, and stared at my reflection in a pub window. I was stained, soaked, and I smelled. My hair was a soppy mess of beer and... *oh!* I couldn't bear to think about what else. You never know what you'll find in a gutter in Dublin's party district. I plucked the clip from my hair, scraped it back, and secured it at my nape where it couldn't touch much of my face.

My dress was torn, I was missing two buttons down the front of it, I'd broken the heel off my right shoe, and my knees were scraped and bleeding.

"There's a lass that gives a whole new meaning to falling-down drunk, eh?" a man sniggered as he passed by. His buddies laughed. There were a dozen of them, wearing red cummerbunds and bow ties over jeans and sweaters. A bachelor party, off to celebrate the joy of testosterone. They gave me a wide berth.

They were so clueless.

Was it really only twenty minutes ago I'd been smiling at passersby? Walking through Temple Bar, feeling alive and attractive, and ready for whatever the world might decide to throw at me next? Twenty minutes ago, they'd have circled around me, flirted me up.

I took a few lopsided steps, trying to walk as if I weren't missing three and a half inches of spike beneath my right heel. It wasn't easy. I ached everywhere. Although the pain of the Book's proximity continued to recede, I felt bruised, head to toe, from being held in the crushing vise of it. If tonight turned out anything like the last time I'd encountered it, my head would pound for hours, and ache dully for days. My visit to Christian MacKeltar, the young Scot who'd known my sister, was going to have to wait. I looked around for my missing heel. It was nowhere to be seen. I'd *loved* those shoes, darn it! I'd saved for months to buy them.

I sighed inwardly and told myself to get over it. At the moment, I had bigger problems on my mind.

"You're a good man, Mark."

"Don't be so sure of that."

"Why?" Brooke wanted to know. "Are you a hit man?"

"No."

"A bigamist?"

"No."

"Cruel to small children and medium-sized animals?"

"No."

"Okay, that qualifies you as a good man."

"You don't know anything about me."

"Then tell me," she urged. "It won't change my opinion of you, but it'll satisfy my curiosity."

"Your curiosity," Mark echoed. He was accustomed to thinking of himself as someone who blended into the background. It seemed odd to him to have someone actually wonder about him. "You're curious about me."

She looked into his eyes for a long moment. "Immensely."

Dear Reader,

Well, the lazy days of summer are winding to an end, so what better way to celebrate those last long beach afternoons than with a good book? We here at Silhouette Special Edition are always happy to oblige! We begin with *Diamonds and Deceptions* by Marie Ferrarella, the next in our continuity series, THE PARKS EMPIRE. When a mesmerizing man walks into her father's bookstore, sheltered Brooke Moss believes he's her dream come true. But he's about to challenge everything she thought she knew about her own family.

Victoria Pade continues her NORTHBRIDGE NUPTIALS with *Wedding Willies,* in which a runaway bride with an aversion to both small towns and matrimony finds herself falling for both, along with Northbridge's most eligible bachelor! In Patricia Kay's *Man of the Hour,* a woman finds her gratitude to the detective who found her missing child turning quickly to…love. In *Charlie's Angels* by Cheryl St. John, a single father is stymied when his little girl is convinced that finding a new mommy is as simple as having an angel sprinkle him with her "miracle dust"—until he meets the beautiful blonde who drives a rig called "Silver Angel." In *It Takes Three* by Teresa Southwick, a pregnant caterer sets her sights on the handsome single dad who swears his fatherhood days are behind him. Sure they are! And the MEN OF THE CHEROKEE ROSE series by Janis Reams Hudson concludes with *The Cowboy on Her Trail,* in which one night of passion with the man she's always wanted results in a baby on the way. Can marriage be far behind?

Enjoy all six of these wonderful novels, and please do come back next month for six more new selections, only from Silhouette Special Edition.

Gail Chasan
Senior Editor

MARIE FERRARELLA

DIAMONDS AND DECEPTIONS

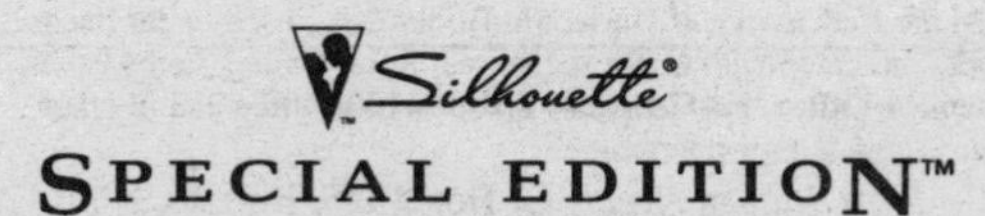

Published by Silhouette Books
America's Publisher of Contemporary Romance

Special thanks and acknowledgment are given to Marie Ferrarella for her contribution to THE PARKS EMPIRE series.

To Charlie with love, forever and always

SILHOUETTE BOOKS

ISBN 0-373-24627-7

DIAMONDS AND DECEPTIONS

This edition published by arrangement with Harlequin Books S.A.

Visit Silhouette Books at www.eHarlequin.com

Printed in U.S.A.

Books by Marie Ferrarella in Miniseries

ChildFinders, Inc.
A Hero for All Seasons IM #932
A Forever Kind of Hero IM #943
Hero in the Nick of Time IM #956
Hero for Hire IM #1042
An Uncommon Hero Silhouette Books
A Hero in Her Eyes IM #1059
Heart of a Hero IM #1105

Baby's Choice
Caution: Baby Ahead SR #1007
Mother on the Wing SR #1026
Baby Times Two SR #1037

The Baby of the Month Club
Baby's First Christmas SE #997
Happy New Year—Baby! IM #686
The 7lb., 2oz. Valentine Yours Truly
Husband: Optional SD #988
Do You Take This Child? SR #1145
Detective Dad World's Most
Eligible Bachelors
The Once and Future Father IM #1017
In the Family Way Silhouette Books
Baby Talk Silhouette Books
An Abundance of Babies SE #1422

Like Mother, Like Daughter
One Plus One Makes Marriage SR #1328
Never Too Late for Love SR #1351

The Bachelors of Blair Memorial
In Graywolf's Hands IM #1155
M.D. Most Wanted IM #1167
Mac's Bedside Manner SE #1492
Undercover M.D. IM #1191

Two Halves of a Whole
The Baby Came C.O.D. SR #1264
Desperately Seeking Twin Yours Truly

***The Reeds**
Callaghan's Way IM #601
Serena McKee's Back in Town IM #808

Those Sinclairs
Holding Out for a Hero IM #496
Heroes Great and Small IM #501
Christmas Every Day IM #538
Caitlin's Guardian Angel IM #661

The Cutlers of the Shady Lady Ranch
(Yours Truly titles)
Fiona and the Sexy Stranger
Cowboys Are for Loving
Will and the Headstrong Female
The Law and Ginny Marlow
A Match for Morgan
A Triple Threat to Bachelorhood SR #1564

***McClellans & Marinos**
Man Trouble SR #815
The Taming of the Teen SR #839
Babies on His Mind SR #920
The Baby Beneath the Mistletoe SR #1408

***The Alaskans**
Wife in the Mail SE #1217
Stand-In Mom SE #1294
Found: His Perfect Wife SE #1310
The M.D. Meets His Match SE #1401
Lily and the Lawman SE #1467
The Bride Wore Blue Jeans SE #1565

***The Pendletons**
Baby in the Middle SE #892
Husband: Some Assembly Required SE #931

The Mom Squad
A Billionaire and a Baby SE #1528
A Bachelor and a Baby SD #1503
The Baby Mission IM #1220
Beauty and the Baby SR #1668

Cavanaugh Justice
Racing Against Time IM #1249
Crime and Passion IM #1256
Internal Affair Silhouette Books
Dangerous Games IM #1274
The Strong Silent Type SE #1613
Cavanaugh's Woman SE #1617
In Broad Daylight IM #1315

*Unflashed series

MARIE FERRARELLA

This RITA® Award-winning author has written over one hundred and twenty books for Silhouette, some under the name Marie Nicole. Her romances are beloved by fans worldwide.

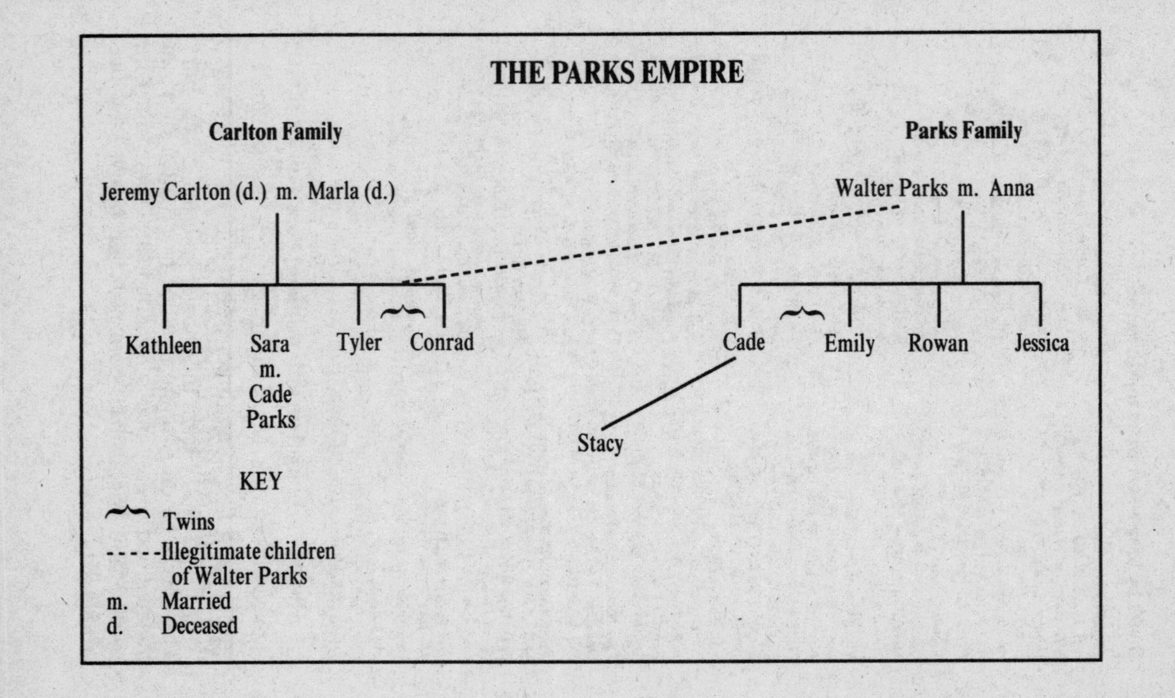

THE PARKS EMPIRE
Carlton Family
Parks Family
Jeremy Carlton (d.) m. Marla (d.)
Walter Parks m. Anna
Kathleen
Sara m. Cade Parks
Tyler
Conrad
Cade
Emily
Rowan
Jessica
Stacy
KEY
Twins
Illegitimate children of Walter Parks
m. Married
d. Deceased

Chapter One

"Ow."

The exclamation of pain, entirely involuntary, was followed by a darker curse. The edge of his razor, on its final pass over the sensitive area of his throat, had nicked him. A small, red blotch appeared.

He had to be more careful, he admonished himself.

Swallowing another curse, he splashed water over the nick, then waited for the wound to dry.

His hands braced on either side of the small, utilitarian bathroom sink, Mark Banning stared into the small, oval mirror that hung directly above it. The glass was still slightly hazy from the shower he'd just taken, but not hazy enough to obliterate the scar that his eyes instantly gravitated toward. The scar that was his anchor to his own reality.

It vaguely occurred to Mark that he'd had the scar for five years now. Five years as of last month. Oh, there were plenty of plastic surgeons around who could readily relieve him of that, who could smooth and tug and resurface the area just below his right eye until their pockets were full and the scar was all but a jagged memory. Nick had even gone so far as to give him several brochures that he'd gathered from a few of the various plastic surgeons who made San Francisco their home.

Mark wasn't even sure if he'd thanked his younger brother for his concern. Probably not. A great deal that went between them went unspoken.

In any case, it was a futile exercise on Nick's part. He didn't want to get rid of the scar. The ugly welt set him apart. It kept the world at arm's length and from growing too friendly. From trying to draw him into a realm where he knew he had no business being. A realm that, if he even ventured into, held only disappointment for him at the end.

Besides, the scar was a symbol of more than just the knife fight he'd been involved in back in New York. It stood for all the scars that he'd sustained within. The scars that no amount of surgery could ever remove or cover up.

The last blow had been the final one. When he'd come home to find that Dana, in a fit of overwhelming depression, had taken her own life, he knew that he was not one of those people destined for happiness. Holding his wife's nude, lifeless body in his arms, willing her back into an existence that Dana had found fruitless and pointless despite all the love he'd tried to show her, he'd felt his own tenuous grasp on happiness irretrievably slipping from his fingers.

Shutting off the water, Mark continued to stare at the scar, at the face of the man who had become little more than an empty shell.

He'd had a hell of a life up to the day it had finally dawned on him that he wasn't meant to be happy, to *ever* be happy. One of the other guys on the force had kidded him the day he'd made detective, saying that seeing his own parents gunned down in front of him at a downtown restaurant when he was little more than ten years old gave him something in common with Batman. Or at least his alter ego Bruce Wayne. And maybe it did.

It'd stolen his childhood away from him, made him old and somber before his time. Filled him with a sense of responsibility that should have, by all rights, come to him years later. But he was the older one, never mind that it was just by a year. His brother, Nick, needed someone to have faith in, even as they were separated, time and again, and sent to different foster homes.

So he had to be strong even when there was no strength left inside.

And throughout it all, he'd always managed to keep track of Nick, never losing sight of his brother no matter what. There were times that Nick had been his sole focus in life, the only reason he kept on going. The reason he made something of himself. Because Nick needed him. In a way, Nick had been his salvation, just as he had been Nick's.

And then things had changed. For the better, he'd thought. And for a precious time, it had been.

While he was still in college, he'd met Dana Dean. Beautiful, adventurous, ambitious, wonderful Dana, who actually made him believe that there really was such a thing as happiness in the world and that maybe, just maybe, he was as entitled to it as the next person.

So he'd married her.

That's what you did when you thought you'd found your soul mate, your main reason for living. Married her and moved, with Nick in tow, to New York because Dana had dreams, huge, boundless dreams of seeing her name up in lights. Of someday—and soon—being the biggest star on Broadway.

That was when the doubts began to appear. They hovered about like giant enemy fighterjets, searching for a place to land. Doubts that everything would work itself out after all.

Dana irrationally insisted that the process from aspiring actress to world-famous icon was going to be a short one, at least for her. She believed in overnight successes. When she was handed rejections instead of accolades, she began to withdraw into herself. Time and again she would come home and alternately rant and sob over her lack of achievement, her lack of progress. The light that had drawn him to her was very quickly extinguished no matter how hard he tried to keep it going, no matter how much support he gave her.

When she quit the part-time job she was holding down, he took on more shifts, determined that money worries were not to be added to Dana's burdens. He wanted her free to pursue her goals.

She became angrier and more depressed. He thought it was all part of the process. Actors were supposed to be a moody lot, there were all those untapped emotions running through them. In his heart, he'd felt sure that once things began going her way, she'd snap out of it and become the Dana he'd fallen in love with. The Dana he still loved with all his heart.

Some detective he was.

He never saw it coming.

Never had a clue that Dana had become so enormously despondent that she could actually end her own life, end it while he was part of her life. He dealt with the rawer side of life every day, but it had never dawned on him that Dana could be sucked down to those kinds of dark depths.

He'd learned. Learned that having him there, loving her, wasn't enough for Dana. That *he* wasn't enough. It was something he wasn't about to get over.

Ever.

Because when he came home after working a longer shift than usual and found her in the tub, her wrists slashed, the water a cold, red, transparent shroud around her body, he blamed himself. Blamed himself for working an extra shift and not finding her in time. If he had seen the signs, he could have saved her. If he had come home at his usual time, he could have saved her.

If.

If.

If.

After a while, there were no more ifs, there was only blame. It began to feel as if Death followed him wherever he went. At least, the death of those he loved. So he decided not to love anymore. There was only Nick left in his world to remind him that he had once been something other than the walking wounded.

He'd wanted to kill himself then. Nick had seen him through the first night and several of the ones that followed, acting as his anchor. Keeping him in this world instead of letting him follow Dana and his parents into the next.

So, unable to take his own life, he'd tried the next best thing. He tried to lose himself in his work.

The mouth on the face in the mirror curved ever so slightly. No, that wasn't strictly true. He didn't try to lose himself in his work, he'd tried to find a way to have his work conduct the execution he couldn't, in all good conscience, carry out himself. If he couldn't hold the gun barrel to his head and pull the trigger himself, then he'd volunteer for the roughest assignments, forge recklessly ahead when common sense had others hanging back. And he did.

He felt he had nothing to lose.

But he was wrong.

He still had Nick to lose. And in the end, he supposed, in an offbeat way, Nick once again wound up being his salvation, saving him from self-extermination or death in the line of duty.

But not before the knife fight in the alley almost became the answer to his unspoken prayers. Foiling a robbery, he'd run after the so-called suspect, only to have the latter ambush him in the alley with a hunting knife. He'd had only his wits, his hands and a discarded trash lid to fight back with. When the suspect had drawn blood, his innate will to live had mysteriously kicked in, making him fight back.

It was a fight he nearly lost. It left him with the jagged scar and had almost ended his life. Twice he'd closed his eyes in that hospital bed and hoped that he'd die.

It was Nick, showing up at the hospital E.R., Nick, who looked at him with such sadness in his eyes, who had managed to catch his soul before it spiraled down, to be sucked into an endless black hole. Nick, who begged him to get well.

So he got better, at least physically. And when he was well enough, he quit the force, took Nick and himself and moved as far away from New York, from the constant reminder of who and what he had lost, as he could. He'd picked San Francisco because the city was anonymous enough for him to get lost in.

It was on the impersonal streets of San Francisco that Mark finally began to pick up the strands of his life, moving forward because he had no other choice. Death was no longer an option.

But neither was living, not really. He made his way as a private investigator, observing others, watching others have lives while he had an existence, nothing more. But then, he figured he wasn't entitled to anything more.

Eventually, over the course of the last five years, he built a reputation. Now, at thirty, he was sought after, able to pick and choose his assignments. He needed little money, just enough to pay the rent, nothing more. Personal indulgences didn't factor into anything, and Nick was independent, pursuing his own career on the San Francisco police force.

Mark was on a case now, one he'd taken on as a personal favor to Nick, actually. Nick's best friend on the force, Tyler Carlton, needed help locating a man by the name of Derek Ross. It seemed that the forty-seven-year-old man was Tyler's long-lost uncle.

The trail was twenty-five years cold, but if Derek was still alive, Mark had no doubt that he would be able to pick it up, be able to find Derek and bring him safely back to the man who had hired him. Tyler was rather vague about certain details, but from what he could piece together, Derek Ross held the key to the secrets Tyler needed to be made privy to.

Secrets that could well bring down Parks Mining and Exploration, currently one of the largest, most powerful gem empires in the country.

He'd been on Derek's trail for the past two weeks and there wasn't the slightest doubt in Mark's mind that he could find the man, because there was nothing else he had to do, nothing else in his life to draw his attention away. Nick was a grown man, leading his own life, and he—he was just marking time.

The ironic term almost made him smile.

Almost.

With a sigh he straightened up and took a towel from the rack to dry his face. There was no telltale smear. The blood had dried.

Mark walked out of the tiny bathroom. It was almost six in the morning. He had a fresh lead to follow. And a man to find.

The shivers were still zipping along up and down her spine, even though the reading was now half an hour in the past.

She loved good poetry, she always had. Loved the sound of it, the endless meanings behind it, the layers that begged to be peeled away, a little at a time, like a big, silver-foil-wrapped Christmas present that promised something wonderful once the wrapping paper was finally dispensed with.

Poetry nurtured the spirit, enriched the soul.

At twenty-three, Brooke Moss was still young enough to dream, to believe in white knights and happily-ever-after endings that metamorphosed into new beginnings filled with promise and wonder.

She hugged the books she'd picked up so far to her soft breast, knowing that her friends sometimes called her naive behind her back. And maybe she was, but she enjoyed being naive if that meant believing in all the things that life had to offer and believing that life was, in the end, good.

Her philosophy hadn't evolved because she was a

child of privilege. Quite the opposite was true. She worked in her father's bookstore, a quaint little San Francisco shop that went by the name of Buy the Book and specialized in not just current books, but rare first editions, as well. Over the past few months she had found herself taking on more and more of the burdens of running the business. During that time she watched with a saddened heart as her father slowly faded before her eyes.

Derek Moss had never been what she would have called a vital man, but ever since he'd returned from the funeral, that funeral he'd attended for a woman she had no recollection of ever having met or even hearing about, it seemed to Brooke that her father was losing his hold on life.

He should have been here, to preside over the reading. Instead he was home. She stifled a sigh.

Setting the first stack of books down, she went back to pick up more. They'd been left on the seats of the forty or so folding chairs she and her father had put out earlier. She was going to have to clear those away, too, she thought. Otherwise the customers who came in tomorrow would find themselves sashaying in between rows of metal chairs as they tried to find books.

Maybe she should talk to her father about hiring part-time help. There'd be no need if he took an active interest in the shop again, but that didn't look as if it was in the cards. At least, not anytime soon.

She had to find a way to make him come around

again, she told herself as she deposited a second pile next to the first on the side of the table.

They'd had a poetry reading at the bookstore tonight. It was a biweekly tradition her father had instituted years ago. Sometimes more frequently if a famous writer was passing through and they managed to prevail upon him or her for a reading. Then advertising would go into high gear and she'd cover the local stores around their shop, as well as all the ones where they lived in Mill Valley with flyers announcing the event. They always had a healthy turnout.

Readings brought in the diehard fans of whoever they chose for the reading, not to mention the curious and those who were seeking something novel to do. Brooke smiled to herself. No pun intended.

Books had always been her life—books and daydreams. And her father, she silently added on. Her father had been her first hero, her first knight in shining armor. It killed her to see him like this.

The moment she'd become aware of his waning interest, she'd tried to get him involved in the store again, in making the decisions. But even the simplest of questions, such as who they should have for their next reading, had gotten nothing but the vaguest of responses from him, coupled with an empty stare, as if he was looking right through her.

He'd shrugged his thin shoulders when she'd asked and said, "Whoever you want, honey," before turning back to the window.

Since he'd returned from the funeral, he'd spent endless hours just staring through the window, completely lost in thought. Certainly lost to her.

Who was that woman? she wondered. What had she meant to him?

He hadn't wanted her to go to the funeral with him, almost hadn't allowed her to know that he was going himself. But she'd wheedled the information out of him, saying she needed to know where to reach him in case there was something about the shop she needed to ask. He'd told her that she was capable of running the store completely without him.

His willingness to relinquish all claim had been her first sign that something was wrong. The shop had always been as much his child as she was.

Just thinking about it now aroused the fear she'd been struggling to bank down. Because her mother had died of leukemia shortly after she was born, Derek Moss was the only parent she had, the only one she'd ever known. And maybe it was childish and selfish of her, but she wasn't ready to let him go. She needed him and loved him and wanted him to be happy.

Happiness was everyone's birthright. Brooke sincerely believed that and she meant to make a believer out of her father.

God knew he'd had little to be happy about over these years. The man had done nothing but work and devote himself to her over the past twenty-three years, and now he was drawing away from even that.

Brooke thought back to the funeral. The changes had gone into high gear then. Had the woman been someone he'd once known, before her mother? Someone he'd once loved? Was that why he seemed so deeply affected, like a man who saw the best that life had to offer behind him instead of in front of him?

She'd be the first to admit that her father had no social life. To her recollection, he had never dated, never even seen women in any other capacity than as a bookstore owner.

What he needed, she decided firmly, was a life. And somehow, it was up to her to give him one.

Somehow.

Maybe that nice Mrs. Sammet, she thought suddenly. The woman came to most of the readings, and she knew that her father was just as much an attraction for the widow as anyone they invited into the store to give a reading.

Maybe she should extend an invitation to Mrs. Sammet to come to dinner....

Brooke set the last pile of books down on the desk, her eyes suddenly drawn to the corner of an envelope that was hiding beneath the blotter. Pulling it out, she saw that it was addressed to her father. There were several forwarding addresses stamped on it.

It was also opened. Had he put it here intentionally, or had it just slipped his mind? Lately he'd allowed things to slip away from him. He'd forgotten to pay the rent on the shop, and there was that shipment of books whose billing had somehow gotten mixed up in the recycled newspapers....

She frowned, taking the letter out of the envelope.

She'd made the transition into her father's keeper without knowing it.

Temporary, she promised herself, it was only temporary.

As Brooke read, her frown deepened. The letter was from a Tyler Carlton. She gathered by reading it that the man didn't know her father, but was asking him to come forward about something. Some sort of secret that would bring Walter Parks to his knees.

She was familiar with the name. Walter Parks was a gem czar. It was his diamonds that graced the hands of half the engaged women in the country. Who was this Tyler and what did he want with her father, anyway? Was this the reason her father had become so reticent, so removed?

She flipped the envelope, looking at the address again. That was when she realized that the letter had come here by mistake. It was addressed to a Derek Ross, not Moss. This Tyler Carlton had to have confused her father with someone else whose name was almost the same.

Still, maybe reading this letter had upset her father for some reason, triggered something in his mind.

She had no answers, but she knew that if she left this lying around, her father would see it again and maybe it would send him deeper into his depression. She folded it and slipped it into her pocket. Maybe hiding it wouldn't accomplish anything, but there was that old saying—out of sight, out of mind, and right now she was desperate to try anything to jar her father out of his mental malaise. At least it was worth a try.

Brooke stopped, listening. Was there someone still in the store?

There it was again, a noise at the far end of the store, she was sure of it. She heard it above the wheezing air-conditioning system they had. It needed to be fixed. Something else to look into, she told herself, tacking the task onto the endless list in her head.

Brooke raised her voice. "I'm sorry, the store's closing. It's closed, really," she amended.

The reading had ended at nine and the hangers-on had lingered for another half hour, asking Jericho Hazley questions about his motivation, his vision and, very possibly, his exercise regimen, the one that left his frame filled out with delicious muscles that were not the usual part and parcel of a dramatic poet. But even the hangers-on had all cleared out ten minutes ago.

Or so she thought.

Maybe this was some kind of groupie, hoping to get Jericho's personal address or his phone number. They were going to be sorely disappointed if that was the case. She firmly believed that *private* meant *private.*

Brooke made her way to the rear of the shop. Maybe her father had decided to come down after all. Maybe he'd changed his mind about going to bed, she thought, hurrying around a row of folding chairs. Usually her father never went to bed before eleven, but lately that had changed, too, another sign that things were very, very wrong.

"Dad, is that you?"

Circumventing another row of chairs, she came

around the corner of the last row of books, the ones reserved for romances, both the tried-and-true and the new, and came to an abrupt halt.

Her gasp hung in the air as she all but walked into a tall, dark-haired stranger standing by the window. Her heart pounded with surprise as her eyes locked on the angry scar that was just below his right eye. A second gasp followed the first.

For one terrifying moment, although he was handsome, the man looked like someone out of Dickens's *Great Expectations*.

She was acutely aware that they were the only two people in the whole store.

It was times like this she wished for a dog. Or, at the very least, an attack cat.

Chapter Two

Damn it, he'd scared her.

Terrified her, if that expression on her face was any indication of what she was feeling. And small wonder, Mark silently upbraided himself. He probably looked like something only several degrees short of Dr. Frankenstein's experiment to her.

He turned slightly, so that the scar was hidden from her.

People always saw the scar first, the man second, and although Mark told himself that it didn't bother him and that the starkness of the scar helped reinforce the separation he wanted to maintain between himself and the world, he didn't particularly relish the idea of frightening small children or fragile women.

His eyes swept over her. And the young woman did

look fragile, despite the fact that he judged she was close to five-ten in those three-inch heels she was wearing.

Mark shifted slightly, moving out from behind the cover of the last row of books and into the main area of the bookstore, careful to keep her on his left side.

He'd spent the better part of the day sitting in his car across the street, scouting this bookstore and its occupants, watching the comings and goings of the various customers from a distance with the aid of his telephoto lens. The woman before him was the owner's daughter. His only child.

Yesterday had been spent checking out their neighborhood in Mill Valley, as well as going through some county records.

He was fairly certain he was on the right trail. She looked like the photograph of Marla Carlton he had tucked away in his car. Tyler had given him the photograph of his late mother as a young girl. It was taken of her and a young man. She'd told Tyler that was his uncle. Tyler had handed it over to him, along with everything else the man had thought might be remotely useful in tracking down his quarry.

Quickly, efficiently, Mark took advantage of his close proximity and studied the young woman's face. The family resemblance was there, in the structure of her heart-shaped face, her high cheekbones, her black hair, her green eyes.

She was a Ross, all right.

Derek Ross's love of rare, old books had brought

him to this quaint, thriving bookstore in the first place. As Mark had pursued his line of work, he'd discovered that while people might change their names, move to a different location, dye their hair a different color, they didn't take as meticulous care about changing who they were inside. Hobbies, interests, preferences, those were far less likely to be abandoned or changed than hair color or names.

So he'd followed a paper trail, so to speak, and discovered that a man fitting Derek Ross's age and general description often made the rounds of estate auctions and old curio shops, always on the lookout for rare old books. The man called himself Derek Moss, not much of a stretch, really, Mark had mused, and for the past twenty-four years he'd owned a bookstore, Buy the Book, in the heart of the more touristy region of San Francisco.

Looking back, Mark judged that this was probably going to be one of his easier assignments. He'd only been at it for a little more than two weeks. It hadn't really been that difficult finding the man. Initially Mark had expected to have to widen his net, stretching it at the very least just outside the state. Instead he'd discovered that, for whatever reason, Moss had decided to remain fairly close to his place of origin. In a city the size of San Francisco, it was relatively easy to get lost among the faces.

Hide in plain sight, the best device of all.

Sight.

The word brought him jarringly back to the expression on Brooke's face.

He must have been a real sight, a real shock for the girl just now, although she appeared to be doing her best to gather herself together, to look as if he hadn't just managed to scare about ten years off her life and probably give her nightmares for the next five.

"Sorry," he apologized with a vague shrug of his shoulders. "I guess I should have called out or said something." A smattering of contrition entered his voice. "I didn't mean to frighten you."

The poor man.

Instantly Brooke's heart went out to him, creating all kinds of romantic scenarios revolving around a long-suffering, misunderstood, hauntingly handsome hero. The man before her transformed from a Dickensian character into Emily Brontë's Heathcliff, the hero who had brooded across the pages of *Wuthering Heights.*

"You didn't frighten me. I mean, you did, but you didn't." She was tripping over her own tongue. Backing up, Brooke started again. For all the time she spent reading books, communication was not always her best subject. "I mean, there's not supposed to be anyone here." She pressed her lips together, offering him an apologetic smile. "I thought you were a rat."

Faced with such innocent honesty, Mark could feel his mouth curving. He was probably more surprised than she was at the smile that was trying to get a toehold. "I'm a little tall for that."

Brooke's eyes widened as, just for a second, she thought of a vermin vaguely approaching the man's proportions. That would have made the rat about six feet tall.

"I'll say." Realizing that he might think it strange that she mistook the noise he made for the movements of a rodent, she made a stab at explaining. "We had a vermin problem several months ago. It was nothing major," she added quickly in case the man, a potential customer after all, was turned off by the idea of thumbing through pages of a book while some rodent hovered about, looking over his shoulder. "Just one wayward rodent." She held up an index finger to underscore the number. "A mouse, really. Not even a large one."

His smile widened just a fraction of an inch. "And you exterminated it."

"Not really." She'd never had the heart to kill anything, outside of mosquitoes, but that was a battle of nature that fell into a "them *vs.* me" arrangement. "I caught it in one of those safe traps, then took it out to where I live and let it go. There's a field not too far from the house."

She was talking too much, Brooke thought. She did that when she was nervous. She debated telling him that, then abandoned the idea as being a tad too honest. He might misunderstand and to protest might just make things worse. But it wasn't the man's scar that made her nervous, it was stumbling across him in a shop she'd thought with a fair amount of certainty was empty.

"I don't like killing things," Brooke finally explained.

He looked into her eyes for a moment. Green, like the first shoots of spring. And soft. "You have a kind heart."

The observation made her smile. She took his words as a compliment, and because it was a compliment, she was compelled to frame a denial.

"Maybe I'm just squeamish."

Despite the fact that she still looked fragile, she didn't strike him as the squeamish type. "If you were squeamish, you would have had the exterminator come in and kill it, not carried it off in a little wire cage to an open field."

His voice was deep, low. Romantic, she thought, although she'd been willing to bet he probably didn't think so. And now that she looked, aside from being soft and brown, his eyes were sad. Incredibly sad. He was a man who'd been through a great deal. Maybe even a tragedy. He had been a star-crossed lover, she guessed, her mind leaping to the topic that was never far from her thoughts. Romance was what made the world go around and someday, she was going to have one of her own.

Someday.

Abruptly Brooke stopped herself before her mind slipped into high gear. She still had a lot to do before she went home herself.

"Um, we are closed, Mr.—" Pausing, she looked at him expectantly.

He thought of giving her an alias. It was a simple enough thing to do. He certainly had enough identification on him to back him up if he gave her another name. But then he decided there was no need for the extra deception. He sincerely doubted that she had any idea who he was or what he did for a living.

From what he'd managed to gather about her,

Brooke Moss had led a very sheltered life. Young, sheltered women had no need to concern themselves with people who made their living as private investigators.

And keeping the lies down to a minimum made them easier to keep track of.

"Banning," he finally told her. "Mark Banning."

"Banning," she repeated, wrapping her tongue around the name. She liked it. It was strong, uncomplicated. Uncompromising. Like him. "Were you here for the poetry reading?"

She didn't remember seeing him, but then, there'd been a lot of people here tonight, she might have not noticed him—although a man like Mr. Banning was hard to miss.

He shook his head. "I just missed it. I slipped in afterward." On purpose. He wanted to mill around the store when it was filled to capacity so that he wouldn't attract too much attention. "During the autographing period."

"Are you interested in collecting autographs?" Even as she asked, Brooke knew the answer had to be no. The man she was talking to didn't look like someone who cared about collecting other people's names scribbled on pieces of paper.

"No, but I am interested in San Francisco." It was the cover story he'd prepared for himself. Ross owned a bookstore that specialized in the unique, the books that didn't turn up on the shelves at local chains, as well as a sampling of the usual current fare. Going out of his way to seek out Moss's establishment because of the kind of books it carried seemed to be a good excuse for him to be there.

"Well, we are in San Francisco." She laughed as she stated the obvious, then sobered just a little. "I don't mean to be rude, Mr. Banning—"

He realized he was staring at her smile and forced himself to focus.

"Mark," he corrected.

He'd also found that people tended to talk more easily to people they were on a first-name basis with, although now that he had met her, he had a feeling that talking was the one thing Brooke Moss or Ross had absolutely no trouble with.

"Mark," she echoed, punctuating his name with a smile before taking another stab at evicting him. She'd let people linger after hours before, but she was tired tonight, and besides, she wanted to go home to her father to make sure he was all right. "I don't mean to be rude, Mark, but we are closed."

He nodded. There was nothing to be gained by pushing. And he did want to verify that he was right about Moss. Besides, his job wasn't over once he was sure the man was who he'd been sent to find. There was more to the assignment than that. "What time do you open in the morning?"

Brooke looked up at him. Apart from the scar, he had nice features. Strong features. He was a very nice-looking man, actually. Handsome in a dark, brooding sort of way. She felt contrite over her initial reaction. The man probably thought she was some kind of empty-headed idiot.

"Officially we open at ten, but the door's usually unlocked by nine, if not before." Her father always liked to come in early to spend time with his books. If a customer wandered in and joined him, that was fine, too. The tomes that lined the shelves of the store were so much more than just books to him. They were his friends, his link with the past as well as his portal to the future. He'd tried to instill the same sort of feelings within her and to a great extent, he'd succeeded. "This is kind of my home away from home."

He pretended to look confused. "Then you don't work here?"

She hadn't meant to mislead him. "I do. I mean—never mind." The more she talked, the more tangled her tongue seemed to become. Maybe she should quit while she wasn't too far behind. "It's late and I'm afraid I'm beginning to sound as if I'm babbling."

That wasn't exactly the word he would have applied to it. "Actually, I find your voice very pleasant to listen to."

Having done what he'd set out to do, which was just to lay a tiny bit of groundwork for future visits, Mark slowly began to make his way to the door.

"I'll be here at ten tomorrow," he promised.

She really wanted him to come back. Maybe tomorrow she could make up for being such a dolt tonight. Walking with him toward the door, she stopped by the front desk. "Nine if you like. It's my turn to open the store and I'll be here at nine."

Were there other clerks here he hadn't taken into account? "You take turns?"

"With my father."

But that wasn't strictly true, at least, not anymore. For the past two weeks, she had been the one to open every day. Even so, that didn't mean she had to give up hope that her father would come around and pick up his routine again. The one that had always given his life such structure, such purpose. With all her heart she longed to see the man who had been her very first hero restored to his former self. She wished he'd confide in her, tell her what was wrong.

"This is his store," she explained, not bothering to hide the pride that came into her voice.

Glancing at the chair beside her, she sighed inwardly. She'd forgotten about those. They still had to be put back in the storeroom and they weren't about to walk themselves in there.

Holding the back of the chair with one hand, she lifted the seat, folding it into place. "He's had it ever since I could remember."

There were at least forty chairs in the small bookstore, five rows of tightly lined-up chairs all but rubbing against one another. Stacking them was going to take her a while.

Mark always believed that opportunities were there to be made use of. This would give him more time to talk to her, to draw more information out of her while putting her at her ease.

Abandoning the door, he picked up the chair closest to him and folded it. He leaned it against the one she'd just put against the wall.

She looked at him in surprise. "Oh, you don't have to do that," she protested.

But even as the words left her mouth, Brooke was pleased by the gesture. She *knew* that he was a kind-hearted man.

He was already folding his third chair. "It'll go quicker if you have help."

She could feel her heart warming toward him. As far as heroic deeds went, this wasn't exactly slaying a dragon for her, but it was a good start.

"Well," Brooke allowed cheerfully, "there's no arguing with that, but I was just chasing you out of the store."

He passed very close to her as he leaned another chair against the vertical stack. The tiniest sliver of guilt went through him as he saw what appeared to be a slightly dreamy look enter her eyes before it faded again. He was just doing his job, nothing more, he reminded himself.

"You can chase me out once we're finished."

She smiled at him as, again, she amended her image of him. Still Heathcliff, but a softer version now.

Heathcliff on a good day, she decided.

She shook her head, starting on the next row of chairs. "It wouldn't seem right, then."

He slapped together another chair. Metal clanged against metal. "All right, you can walk me out of the store when we're finished."

She tilted her head, as if that would help her absorb the nuances of his speech better. There'd been something in his pattern that had caught her attention right after her initial shock had vanished.

Alarms went off in his head. Was something wrong? Had she recognized him from somewhere? "What?"

She smiled, embarrassed that she'd been so obvious. "You're not from around here, are you?"

Relief descended over him. He folded another chair and forced a smile to his lips. "Why, do I have an accent?"

She grinned. "New York, right?"

Her grin was dazzling, he realized. Like sunshine caught in a prism, shooting out shafts of rainbows everywhere. He forced himself back into his role and to focus on what she'd just said.

Mark frowned ever so slightly. It had been five years since he and Nick had moved out here, leaving New York and all the dark memories behind. He thought he'd shed everything about that life.

Apparently not.

He'd never thought of himself as having an accent to begin with, but if he had, five years should have been enough time to at least mute it if not disintegrate it altogether.

She was still looking at him, waiting to see if she was correct.

"Right," he told her, picking up another chair. "Does it show?"

Brooke picked up on the trace of annoyance in his voice. Maybe she shouldn't have said anything. Was he ashamed of where he came from? Or was he trying to live something down?

"It's not as pronounced as some I've heard," she told him quickly, then, because honesty demanded it, softly added, "but no one would mistake you for a native Californian."

He didn't want the focus on him, on anything about him. He wanted it on her. And so he turned the conversation 180 degrees.

"Are you? A native?" he added when she didn't respond immediately.

He knew the answer to that, just as he knew the answer to a lot of other questions about her. She would have been surprised, he thought, at the amount of things he did know about her. And that he was going to know more. But that was his job, to find things out. To pull the pieces of puzzles together until some grand whole emerged.

Besides, he'd learned long ago that the more information you had at your disposal, the less likely you were going to be caught off-guard.

"Born and bred," she told him with a laugh.

He saw her struggling with the chair she'd picked up. It groaned slightly, resisting being folded. He crossed to her and took the chair out of her hands. With a little effort, he folded it.

He liked her laugh. It sounded like a light spring rain, falling on thirsty flowers. She was, he thought, everything he once thought life could be, if only the right things happened. Happy, optimistic, hopeful.

All the things he was not and hadn't been for a very long time. Almost forever, except for that short period of time with Dana, he thought.

But that was so far in the past now, it was as if it had happened to someone else. All but for the very last part.

Brooke picked up another chair and started to fold it when she looked at him. The expression on his face had her stopping. "Where are you?"

Her softly voiced question broke through the haze forming around his brain.

"Hmm?" Quickly he stacked the chair and picked up another. "Here, in your shop."

She wasn't talking about his body. "No, I meant just now. In your head. You looked as if you were a million miles away."

He fell back on his cover story. "Just thinking about the book I'm working on."

Brooke's eyes suddenly became as huge as proverbial saucers and he found himself fascinated despite efforts not to be.

"You're working on a book?" Of all the things he could have said to her, this was the one thing that was guaranteed to rivet her interest. She adored writers and thought of them as being several degrees above mortal men and women. "What kind of a book?"

He started on the last row. "A history of San Francisco."

She cocked her head, contemplating his answer. "Odd subject for a New Yorker."

"I've always been interested in the city." The lie, practiced, came easily to his lips. "First time I heard the term *earthquake,* it was about the 1906 one they had here."

She stopped working. "And that's what attracted you? Our earthquakes?"

He didn't want her thinking he was some kind of a ghoul. God knew the scar underscored that aspect of him enough.

"No, the many layers within the city, the rich history." He forced enthusiasm into his voice. "San Francisco is a great deal like New York, you know, in many ways. You've got a melting pot here, too. There're different pockets of culture and—" Choosing the right place, Mark deliberately stopped abruptly. "I'm talking too much."

"No, you're not," she encouraged. "Keep talking. I'll keep listening."

Just then she heard the front door opening behind her. Hadn't she locked it?

Reproaching herself for being careless, Brooke turned around just in time to see her father walking in. There was a troubled expression on his face.

"So, you *are* here."

Bingo, Mark congratulated himself as he looked at the man crossing the threshold. If this wasn't his quarry, then the man had a doppelgänger running around somewhere in the city.

Chapter Three

The man standing in the doorway had the wiry body of a runner, another hobby Mark knew Derek Ross had once pursued. In his youth Derek had been into track and field. He still maintained a strong interest in running, although his routine had been cut back somewhat over the years.

An easier way to strike up an acquaintance would have been to observe him jogging along a customary route and then fall into place and run with him. Joggers welcomed others experiencing the same punishing regimen they were enduring.

But for one reason or another, Derek Ross wasn't jogging these days. Mark knew, because he'd sat outside his house, both early in the morning and early evening, and waited for the man to emerge for a run. He'd waited in vain.

Still, it couldn't have been that long since he'd given up the hobby. His body was still lean, still very trim. His thin state made him look taller than the five feet, eleven inches Mark had been given as a description. The eyes were the right color, green, and his hair was black, like his daughter's, with only flecks of gray beginning at the temples.

He bore a strong resemblance to his daughter, Mark thought. And to the young man in the photograph of Marla Carlton and her brother that he'd been given.

Any lingering doubts he had that he was on the wrong trail all but vanished entirely. Granted, there was still a small margin for possible error, but by and large, Mark was as sure that this was the man he'd been asked to find as he had ever been of anything.

However, he was nothing if not thorough. The job had taught him to check and then double-check and then check one more time before allowing a sense of accomplishment to enter into the picture. Not that there was ever any triumph attached to it. He'd stopped feeling positive things like triumph a long time ago. That side of him, that part that could feel anything except anger, had faded out of existence that evening in the small bathroom of his barely post-World-War-II Queens apartment.

A sliver of remorse jabbed at Brooke and she flashed her father an apologetic look.

"I didn't mean to make you worry, Dad." He looked so wan, so pale these days she thought, like a ghost of his former self. But at least this was a good sign, that he'd come to look in on her. It meant that he wasn't completely detached and oblivious to things and that gave her a smattering of hope. "The reading ran over and then Mr. Hazley stayed to sign autographs and talk to some of his fans...."

Brooke saw the way her father was looking at the other man. There was just a hint of suspicion in his eyes. It was the same glimmer of wariness that seemed to arise every time someone new would walk into the store. It never remained for long, but it was always there, as if her father didn't really trust anyone beyond her in this world.

She was tired and she was letting her imagination run away with her again. What was in her father's eyes was the natural kind of suspicion that every father exhibited about his only daughter's life. He probably thought she was meeting someone after hours.

As if her life wasn't an open book to him.

An open, rather boring book, she thought with just a touch of despair. But that could change. That *would* change, she promised herself. Just as soon as she got a chance to do something about it. Just as soon as she was sure her father was all right and she got a few things squared away.

Just as soon as. The very words silently mocked her.

Derek Moss turned his attention to the man in his bookstore, a small hint of a frown forming as he studied him. The man he'd found talking to his daughter certainly didn't look like the usual sort of patron who came through Buy the Book's doors. If asked, Derek would have ventured a guess that the only thing the man read was the newspaper. And only the headlines at that.

There was an edgy air about him. He looked as if he might be more at home on Fisherman's Wharf than a shop known for its rare books. If this had been a hundred years ago or so, he would have placed the man at the helm of a pirate ship, or a blockade runner at the very least.

But then, Derek mused, you really couldn't tell a book by its cover, could you? Look at *him,* after all.

Closing the door behind himself, Derek crossed to his daughter and the man. "I don't believe I've had the pleasure. I'm Derek Moss. This is my shop. Mine and Brooke's," he amended.

He'd almost said Derek Ross. He'd hidden beneath the name Moss for almost as many years as he'd once used his own surname. By now, the names should have all been one and the same to him, yet ever since the funeral, there'd been this yearning within him. A yearning to go back, to reclaim his name. To return to his roots, his youth.

To maybe somehow do it all again, just differently this time.

But then, if things had been different, if they had arranged themselves according to a different plan, he might have missed out on being Brooke's father. And Brooke represented the greatest triumph of his life. She was his most precious treasure.

If he hadn't gone into hiding, he would never have met Brooke's mother, and although he'd never loved her the way he had Anna, Jenna had brought a peacefulness to his life that had long been missing.

Brooke quickly took the lead. "This is Mr. Banning, Dad. Mark."

Derek noted that his daughter said the name as if she already liked it. As if she already liked the man even though he was fairly certain that Banning was a stranger to her. But then, Brooke liked everyone. She was such an innocent that way. He supposed that was his fault. He'd gone out of his way to shelter her, to allow her to continue believing that the world was a place where the just and the good triumphed over the bad and the corrupt. Instead of the other way around.

She would learn that all too soon, and it was a lesson destined to remain with her all of her natural life.

Reclaiming the role of the friendly proprietor, Derek put his hand out to the younger man. Banning appeared to hesitate for just a beat before he took it. The man had a firm grip. You could tell a lot about a man by his grip. Derek smiled. "Happy to make your acquaintance, Mr. Banning."

"Mark," Mark prompted. "And I'm the one who's happy." As he said the words, he forced a smile to his lips, slipping into the role he'd cast for himself. It occurred to Mark that ever since Dana had died, he'd been playing one part after another, deliberately losing sight of himself. It was as if one way or another, acting had to remain in the family.

"Oh?" Derek raised an inquisitive eyebrow, glancing toward his daughter for an explanation. When none was volunteered, he looked back at Mark. "And why would that be?"

Mark's natural inclination was to hang back, to observe, to lose himself in the background of life. But that wouldn't give him the answers he needed, wouldn't ultimately allow him to find a way to prevail upon the bookstore owner to come forward.

So he pushed ahead. "I was hoping that you could help me."

"Help you do what?" Derek asked.

"He's writing a book, Dad," Brooke informed him with no small measure of enthusiasm and excitement.

It made Derek smile. Brooke was far more impressed with writers than he was. To Brooke every person who put pen to paper or, these days, glided their fingers across a computer keyboard, creating something out of nothing, was godlike.

Although he loved books—good books—experience had taught him otherwise. Most people spent far more time talking about writing than they actually spent writing, and even those who did apply themselves...well, few were worth the trouble of reading. But those who proved to be worth the effort, they were a world apart.

He couldn't help wondering which category this young man with the dark scar fell into.

Derek studied him with real interest now. "Are you, now?"

Mark nodded. This was not a man who was easily hoodwinked, but he already knew that after preparing himself by reading extensively about his background. "Yes."

Derek leaned his hip against his desk, half perching on it. "Would you mind if I asked what it was about?"

"Not at all. It's a—"

"History of San Francisco," Brooke finished for Mark when the exchange felt as if it was moving too slowly.

Derek continued looking at the other man. "Why would a New Yorker want to do that? I would think that you would have more than enough to write about in New York about New York."

"San Francisco's history is richer." Mark figured that would be what a native would want to hear. One glance at the smile on Brooke's face told him he was right. And then he paused, shaking his head, making this more personal. "Your daughter already commented on my accent. I guess I'm going to have to work hard on getting rid of it."

Brooke's eyes widened. There was an eager, hopeful look there that was hard to miss. "Why would you want to do that? Are you planning on making San Francisco your home?"

He was tempted to say yes because that was what she appeared to want to hear and it would keep things simple. But he had always found it best to keep things without confining parameters. "At least while I'm working on my book."

Brooke looked from Mark to her father. Wheels began to move in her head. This was the most amount of interest she had seen him display in anything since he'd come home from that funeral. Slipping her hand into her pocket, her fingers came in contact with the letter she'd shoved in there. The letter that might or might not have been meant for her father. The letter whose contents she knew had to have upset him, at least a little. He needed to be distracted, and this tall, dark, mysterious stranger with his lofty goal seemed to fit the bill perfectly. He'd come into their lives just in time and appeared to be nothing short of a godsend.

"Do you know anyone here, Mark?"

He'd never quite heard his name said that melodiously before. It almost sounded as if she was singing his name instead of saying it. The question wasn't one that he'd expected, not so soon, but nonetheless he was prepared for it.

"I know the two of you." It wasn't what he would have normally said, not by any stretch of the imagination. But then he wasn't being himself now, he was being whoever he had to be in order to bring his case to a successful close.

"And no one else?" She could feel her father looking at her in confusion, probably trying to guess where she was going with this. She wasn't usually this brazen. *This is for you, Dad, not for me.*

These days Mark made sure that his mind was always several steps ahead of any square he found himself in. He'd learned the hard way. Had his mind worked like that five years ago, maybe he would have realized that Dana wasn't just being moody, but that she had slipped into a full-fledged, raging depression that only got worse and worse with each rejection she sustained.

No time to dwell on what might or might not have been now, he admonished himself. There was nothing he could do about the past. He had the present to worry about, and to be successful there meant that he had to be sure there were no slipups in this charade he was being paid to play.

"Well—" he hedged a moment "—technically there is one other person."

"Technically?" Her mind given to romance, Brooke immediately assumed that Mark was referring to an ex-girlfriend or worse, perhaps an ex-wife. Was that why his eyes looked so sad? Had the woman broken his heart and moved away and now he was here, trying to work up his courage to see her?

She struggled to control her thoughts before they completely ran away with her.

"A friend of mine has an apartment here," Mark explained, "but he's out of the country right now. On location," he added, seeing that there was a question hovering on Brooke's full lips and guessing at what she'd want to ask. "He's letting me stay there while I get my bearings."

It was a plausible enough story based on a kernel of truth from the past. When he and Nick had originally moved out here, it was Nick who had looked up someone he'd known back in New York, a struggling actor who had since moved on to a more stable way of making a living. He and Nick had stayed with Stan until they could find a place of their own. And from there Nick had eventually moved on to his own place.

He'd set up the excuse in case, for some unforeseeable reason, he needed to give her an address where she could reach him. From what he had gathered about her, Brooke Moss seemed like the kind who could spring that kind of question on him without warning. All bases had to be covered for this to work.

"How fortunate for you," Derek commented.

Mark looked at him sharply, expecting to see either doubt or a sarcastic expression on the man's thin face. But there was nothing. Apparently, despite his background, the father seemed to be almost as trusting as the daughter. Good, that would make things easier for him. He needed to gain their confidence so that asking the right questions wouldn't be a problem.

"Sometimes I get lucky," Mark allowed.

But most of the time, a small, bitter voice echoed inside of him, *you don't.*

"Would you like to come to dinner tomorrow night?"

The question that had been forming, waiting to escape, popped out of her mouth the second there was a moment without conversation in it.

Both men turned to look at her, surprise written on both their faces.

Mark wondered if he was dreaming. He'd hoped that getting close to these two people, to Derek, wouldn't take too much time or prove to be too difficult, but this was going along at a speed he would never have predicted. His eyes shifted toward Derek, who looked as surprised as he felt.

He decided to downplay the invitation, in case the

older man became defensive over this sudden invasion of his privacy.

"That's very kind of you, Ms. Moss, but I don't want to impose—"

He expected Brooke to be the one to shoot down his protest. Instead, it was Derek. The man smiled warmly at him.

"You wouldn't be imposing, Mark, trust me. It's been a while since we had anyone to dinner, and I think that maybe Brooke is getting a little tired of the stilted conversation."

"There isn't any stilted conversation," Brooke protested, more out of a sense of protectiveness than anything else. The truth was she'd spent a lot of time trying to get her father to talk to her about anything these days.

"No, you're right," her father agreed. "There's hardly any conversation at all. There's been a death in the—"

Derek abruptly stopped. He'd almost said "family" but had caught himself just in time. He couldn't very well just drop this bombshell on Brooke, not like this. She deserved to hear this the right way. As far as his daughter knew, there were no other family members, just her and him. She hadn't a clue that there was actually an extended family she knew nothing about. That there were cousins and that she was related, by marriage, to the affluent Walter Parks, perhaps one of the most manipulative, odious men to have walked the earth.

Someday, Derek thought, he'd sit her down and tell her who her father really was and where he had come from. As it stood right now, she knew very little about him. And wouldn't it surprise Brooke to discover that she was related to Kathleen Carlton, the mystery author she held in such high regard? He could almost see her face.

But not tonight. He didn't feel up to telling her the long story that led up to his being here in this small bookstore with her tonight. Maybe he wouldn't feel up to telling her about it for a long time.

"A death in my circle of acquaintances," Derek concluded.

Sorry, Marla, he silently apologized to his late sister, *sorry to have to shove you aside like this one last time, but this is for Brooke, you understand.*

Twenty-five years had gone by since he'd actually spoken to his older sister. Twenty-five years, and in all that time he'd always believed that someday he would attempt to bridge that gap with her, attempt to regain the ground they'd once shared as siblings when life had been so much less complicated. He would come to her and they'd patch things up and things could, for a little while, be the way they had once been.

But now there was no time. Death had seen to that, and the gap that had been created so long ago by that horrid man who had ruined so many of their lives yawned before him, deep and dark and bottomless.

If it wasn't that he had accidentally stumbled across her obituary, which he'd discovered that her son had printed in all the major newspapers in the country per her request, he wouldn't have even known she was dead. Because of his own reticence, there would be no reunions, no forgiveness, no restitutions. There would be, and was, only guilt—guilt and a deep, all-pervading sadness for the time that had somehow managed to slip by without contact.

Sorry, Marla, he apologized again.

It was what he had been doing ever since he'd learned of his sister's untimely death, apologizing to her spirit since he could no longer apologize to her person, apologize for dropping out of sight, for allowing his fear to get the better of him. For allowing his fear to make him abandon her to the life she had wound up living.

It was all Walter Parks's fault. Walter Parks had killed her as surely as if he'd put a gun to her head and pulled the trigger.

But then, one way or another, the diamond czar was no stranger when it came to killing people, Derek thought. He'd witnessed it firsthand.

Derek became vaguely aware that Brooke was tugging on his arm. "Dad?"

Banning was looking at him curiously. Embarrassed, Derek forced himself to focus on the present before he totally slipped away into the quagmire that had become his thoughts.

He cleared his throat. "As I was saying, Mark, I've been rather poor company for my daughter lately and you would be doing me a great favor if you would agree to join us for dinner tomorrow night. It won't be anything fancy, but it will be home-cooked, something I suspect you don't get very much of."

Mark wondered if the man was just making idle conversation, or if Ross sensed that the man who was attempting to entrench himself into the perimeter of his life took most of his meals in the form of frozen dinners and take-outs.

Probably just idle conversation, Mark decided. He was getting too paranoid.

"You're right," he agreed. "A home-cooked meal would be a really nice change from what I'm used to." He looked from Brooke to her father. "If you're sure I wouldn't be barging in."

"We're sure," Brooke assured him with feeling.

She liked this man fate had brought into their bookstore, she decided. He was thoughtful and polite, two traits that weren't all that common these days. Romantic traits, she mused.

Brooke wondered if he wrote poetry. Probably wouldn't admit it even if he did, but thinking that he might gave her thought wings again. She didn't want Mark leaving just yet.

"Dad, why don't you take him over to the domestic history section while I finish putting the chairs away in the storeroom?"

"She fancies herself a little dictator," Derek explained fondly as he looked at his daughter. "I tell you what, *you* show Mark to the domestic history section and *I'll* put the chairs away."

"I—"

And then she stopped. While she and her father were busy debating who would put the chairs away, the man she hoped would bring some kind of spark back into her father's life was quietly doing it.

Mark had picked up four of the folding chairs, two in each hand, and was carrying them toward the door that was opened in the rear of the store. Quickly she grabbed two chairs and followed his lead.

"So, you're a doer," she said to him as she caught up, "not a talker."

It amused Mark that for all intents and purposes, the naive young woman had hit the nail on the head. He preferred doing to talking. It seemed rather ironic to him that he was now in a position where he had to use verbal skills to get by.

"Pretty much," he agreed.

Chapter Four

Walter Parks slowly paced around his spacious office, his small, brown eyes cold and drawn into slits as he chewed on the information he'd just gotten wind of. A rumor, really, but rumors had a nasty way of turning out to be true when they could cause the most trouble.

And that's what this now meant. Trouble.

The expression on the diamond czar's face was one that would have sent an enormous chill through the souls of those who worked for him. When the head of Parks Mining and Exploration was displeased, hardened men had been known to break out in a cold sweat and run for cover.

The sixty-year-old owner of the largest diamond import-export firm in the country was several levels above displeased and quickly approaching enraged.

An expensive bust of Hannibal caught his eye and he cleared it off its pedestal with one sweep of his arm. The sculpture by a then up-and-coming, now renowned, artist that he had picked up during his last visit to Florence broke into more than a dozen pieces at his feet. He kicked the largest one aside.

God damn it all to hell, why now?

As each decade of his life went by, bringing with it more and more financial success achieved in an above-board manner, Parks increasingly became more of a force to be reckoned with, and he knew it, prided himself on it. Based all of his fragile self-esteem on it. He'd gone from being a shrewd, calculating man who knew how to make the best of every opportunity that came his way, to a man who created his own opportunities, then on to someone who didn't care what he had to do in order to maintain his position at the top of the mountain. And he meant to keep it at all costs.

Along the way he had shed what little conscience he'd possessed to begin with.

There were skeletons in his closet as well as bodies, specifically *one* that had marked the beginning of his meteoric rise in the diamond field. He had married Anna to gain possession of her father's firm, but it had been the demise of his chief rival, Jeremy Carlton, that had cleared the playing field for him and placed him on the track to exclusive power.

Thoughts of the late Jeremy Carlton, once his naive, so-called friend, had put that haunted look in his eyes.

The look that, when flashed, sent lightning bolts of terror slashing through to his underlings.

And they were all underlings.

As far as he was concerned, everyone in his acquaintance was an underling. And he meant to keep it that way.

Walter fisted his hands, wanting to punch something, knowing that destroying something else wouldn't remove the problem.

Frustration ate at him.

He refused to be toppled because of some sniveling, gutless man who had run like a frightened jackrabbit more than twenty-five years ago.

That was the rumor. That Derek Ross was still alive, that he had surfaced after all this time, and that somehow the younger brother of Jeremy's wife, Marla, the woman he'd had an affair with a quarter of a century ago, posed a threat to him.

Damn Marla.

He'd thought that with her death he'd finally be free of the specter of fear that had whispered along the outer fringes of his mind all these years. Instead her funeral must have brought her brother out of the woodwork. It was then that the rumor had taken hold.

Flowering.

Growing.

The rumor that Derek Ross knew something, had seen something. That was the reason the man he'd just finished speaking to had told him that Tyler Carlton had hired a private investigator to find the man.

But what could Ross have seen? There'd been no one

on board the yacht when he'd topped off Jeremy's cognac with something that had more of a kick to it. A fatal kick. He'd set out straight to sea the moment the man had dropped dead and dumped his body into the dark waters. There hadn't even been a full moon out.

What the hell could Ross have seen?

Parks cursed loudly. He didn't know what Ross knew, and it could very well be nothing, but it was far too late in the game to take any chances. He was sixty years old, still in his prime with years ahead of him. And he meant to enjoy those years to the fullest. Without the threat of exposure.

His mind racing, he rubbed a hand over his face, over skin that had grown leathery before its time, a testimony to his love of sailing and the sun. There was nothing confining about the ocean. A man could be free there, free to be alone with his thoughts, not a prisoner of the endless details which always required him to be alert, to be forever on his guard.

Because if he let down his guard, even for a little while, it could prove to be the end of him.

Well, he wasn't about to think about that, because it wouldn't happen. He was Walter-God-Damn-Parks and he was damn well going to stay that way. He intended to remain a force to be reckoned with. A power. And if that meant having to snuff out yet another useless life, well, so be it.

Jeremy Carlton had been worth two of Derek Ross, maybe even three, and he'd had no trouble killing him. Killed him because Jeremy was the competition, because Jeremy had proof that he was involved in gem smuggling and because Jeremy was the better man. Eventually, if they persisted enough, good men triumphed.

But only if they were alive.

So he'd taken matters into his own hands and become the sole czar of the diamond world.

And he was going to remain that way.

Parks found himself back at his desk. He knew what he had to do.

Sitting down, he drew his telephone closer to him. It was safe to use—for the time being. Because industrial espionage was something he had had to live with on a daily basis, he had his rooms, both here and at home, as well as the telephone lines all checked for bugs first thing every morning. They'd been pronounced clear so he was free to make the call without worrying that someone was listening in. For now.

His mouth curved as he contemplated his solution. There were men who would do anything for a price. Men who lived in the shadows of life and did what they did not only for the money, but for the sheer love of it. For the thrill. For the challenge of the kill. He knew several such men and chose the best to do what needed to be done. Eliminate the source of his concern.

With an annoyed sigh, Parks upbraided himself for not having thought of doing this years earlier. Ross had always been a concern, no matter how minor. He was a loose end that hadn't been tied or destroyed.

It was time to see to that. To destroy it. Maybe then,

when Ross was dead, he would finally be able to get a decent night's sleep.

Parks didn't bother looking the number up in the electronic file that resided in his personal Palm Pilot. He knew the number by heart.

This wasn't the first time he'd used the man's services.

And it probably wouldn't be the last.

"So, how are you doing?"

As Nick Banning walked into his brother's small, austere apartment, he instantly made himself at home. And why not? They'd once shared this place together. He'd moved on to get one of his own, a bigger place, thinking that eventually Mark would do the same.

But his brother remained where he had first planted his roots, despite the fact that he knew Mark was doing very well in his P.I. business these days. Mark Banning's name was well known among the police officers he worked with and mentioned with the kind of respect that wasn't often given to private eyes. It was a tribute to Mark's integrity and his ability, and Nick was more than a little proud of his older brother.

And more than a little concerned. Which was what had brought him here rather than going home after putting in a full day patrolling the streets with some of San Francisco's finest.

Nick stopped by the refrigerator and took out a beer, then walked into the living room. Mark wasn't there. Nick kept walking, reaching the main bedroom. It was the larger of two by about six inches.

Mark was in the closet, shifting hangers around, obviously looking for something.

At least he looked fairly all right, Nick thought, taking a drag from the amber bottle he held. Maybe things were getting better.

Last month had marked five years since it had happened. Five years since his brother had found his wife's lifeless body in their small apartment. He'd come as soon as Mark had called him. When Mark had opened the door, he'd never seen anyone looking so shattered.

Even now Nick doubted if all the pieces had been glued together.

"It's going," Mark finally replied noncommittally. "I'm fine," he added, knowing that was probably what his brother wanted to hear. He wasn't fine, but that was beside the point.

Shoving another hanger aside, he frowned. All his shirts looked as if they could stand to be ironed. But he didn't have time for that now. He was going to be running late if he spent any more time in his closet, and he still needed to get some wine to take to dinner.

With a half shrug, he made his selection. A long-sleeved light-blue shirt that looked less wrinkled than the others. Pulling it off the hanger, he shoved his arms through it as he came out of the closet.

Curious, watching Mark put on the new shirt, Nick sat down on the corner of the double bed.

"I tried calling you a couple of times today, but you weren't answering."

Mark finished buttoning his shirt, then tucked it into his pants. "I wasn't home."

"I tried your cell, too."

"I shut it off." He felt a wave of impatience. He'd only been here about five minutes before Nick had knocked on his door. He looked down at his shirt. Maybe he should start sending his shirts out. God knew he wasn't any good at ironing them. Rather than get wrinkles out, he tended to get scorch marks in. "I was in a bookstore, seemed like the thing to do," he explained about the cell.

His fingers about the bottle's neck, Nick rolled the bottle back and forth as he looked at his brother thoughtfully. "The whole day?"

"Most of it."

Looking into the mirror that hung over his bureau, Mark spread his hands over the front of the shirt, trying to press the wrinkles out of existence. After a few passes, it looked marginally better.

"Research?" Nick asked.

Mark thought of the lie he'd fed Ross and his daughter. "In a manner of speaking."

Nick laughed, shaking his head. Nothing had changed. It was like trying to get information out of an echo chamber.

"You know, conversations with you were never marked with an overabundance of words flowing around." Nick paused to take a drag of the bottle of beer he'd purloined from the refrigerator. "You on a case?"

"Yeah." That was it, a case, a simple by-the-numbers

case. Except that something in his gut told him that it wasn't by the numbers at all. Something had told him that the moment he'd met Brooke Ross/Moss up close and personal.

Nick frowned, trying to pull the pieces together. "In a bookstore."

"In a bookstore." He yanked open the top drawer, looking for a tie. He vaguely remembered shoving in a few when he first came here. Which drawer was it? He let out an impatient breath. "It's the one Tyler wanted me to take." That was safe enough to say, considering it was Nick who had brought Tyler to him. "You know I can't say anything more about it than that."

"Not asking you to," Nick reminded him. "Asking you how you are."

He shoved one drawer closed and pulled open another. He knew he had ties somewhere, the question was where. "I already said fine."

Nick moved a little closer to the edge of the bed. "Yeah, and that's a preprogrammed response. People say 'fine' automatically, even if they've just been shot five times."

Mark gave him an annoyed look over his shoulder. "I promise, if I'm ever shot five times, I won't say fine if you ask me how I am."

Nick knew what Mark was doing, he was throwing up a smoke screen, the way he always did. Mark never talked about how he'd felt about that day, not once. "You know what I mean."

"Yeah, I know what you mean." And he did. He

knew Nick was worried about him and that he was thinking of the recent anniversary of Dana's suicide, of the anniversary of his neglect.

He and Nick had always had a way of communicating that transcended words, a way of honing in on each other's thoughts. Whether it was something that could be termed inherently genetic or something that had developed perforce because of all the separations they'd had to endure as children, he didn't know. What he did know was that he and Nick had a very special, very real bond, and he'd been able to feel what Nick was feeling more than once. He figured the same was true in reverse.

Nick studied him as his brother moved from one drawer to the next, searching for something. He tried again, feeding his brother a line to build on. "It's been five years."

Mark's tone was guarded. He didn't want to talk about this and he was doing his very best to try to hold on to his temper. "Bound to happen. One month piles on top of another, eventually, five years has to come. Six should be next."

Nick lost his temper first. "Damn it, Mark, you need to talk about it."

Finally finding the nest of ties he'd tossed years ago into the bottom drawer, Mark pulled out the first one on the heap. Holding it aloft, its end moved in the air like a newly freed snake as he swung around to face Nick. Why couldn't he take a hint?

"Talk about what? That I was blind? That I didn't see it coming? That I was so into being the best damn cop

I could be, so into going after that gold shield that I didn't realize my own wife was going down for the third time?" Each sentence was punctuated with an abrupt movement as he went through the motions he only vaguely remembered of tying a tie, or a noose, around his neck.

Glaring at Nick, he turned back to the mirror and saw that he'd gotten it wrong. With a huff, he began the process again.

Nick talked to the back of his head. "She had problems, Mark, problems that had nothing to do with you," he insisted.

His eyes met Nick's in the mirror. "I was her husband, damn it, they had everything to do with me. Look, talking about it isn't going to change a damn thing, so why don't you just drop it? I don't get to see you enough to waste time like this."

Nick blew out a breath. "Okay." He paused and then his eyes widened as the image he was looking at in the mirror sank in. "Is that a tie?"

Finished, Mark dowerly examined his handiwork. This time he'd gotten it right. He glanced toward Nick. "You the sharpest they got on the force? Because if so, I'd say the city was in big trouble."

"Very funny, I know it's a tie, what I mean is what's it doing on you?"

Mark looked into the small mirror hanging over his equally small bureau one last time to make sure the ends of the odious appendage were where they were supposed to be. "Hanging."

More teeth pulling, Nick thought with a shake of his head. "You hate ties."

Yes, he did. Ties were the most useless articles of clothing in the world as far as he was concerned. Even worse than vests. "Part of the uniform."

And then it hit him. Nick was off the bed and beside Mark as if someone had just set the comforter on fire. "You got a date?"

His brother looked so happy, so hopeful, as he blurted out the question that Mark was sorely tempted to say yes, he did. But that would have been a lie, and he had never lied to Nick, not when it mattered. The white lies of their childhood didn't count.

He knew that Nick worried about him, that his brother wanted to see him socializing again, but dating had never been a really big priority for him, not even in high school. Maybe that was why, when Dana came along, he'd fallen for her like a ton of bricks. And that was why, since her death, he hadn't gone out, not once. He'd staunchly resisted all the attempts of the other men on the NYPD force to set him up with someone. Resisted, too, all of Nick's efforts to the same end.

He didn't need to date. He was fine just the way he was. Unattached. A loner. At least he'd finally managed to find a kind of purpose for his life again. Which was a great deal better than looking for an end with every breath he took, the way he had when he'd come to the end of his police detective career back in New York City.

Nick was still looking at him hopefully, the half-empty bottle all but dangling from his fingertips.

No, Mark thought, *no lies.* "No, this is work related."

Nick looked at him doubtfully. "They asked you to wear a tie?"

Mark tightened the knot. "Seemed like the occasion called for it." He glanced at his watch. Now he was late. Time to hustle. "Look, I gotta go pick up a bottle of wine." He grabbed a sports jacket. Outside the humidity was doing terrible things to the city at large, but he didn't think he could very well turn up in shirtsleeves. "You're welcome to stay here as long as you like."

Nick followed him to the door, surprise building on surprise. He knew about the case Mark was on. Tyler had filled him in as much as possible. But this didn't sound like any case Mark had ever worked before. Mark was hiding something.

"Wine? You getting clients drunk these days?"

Mark checked his pockets for his keys. "Loosening their tongues," Mark corrected. With that, he walked out, feeling his brother's eyes boring into the back of his head.

There was a liquor store on the next block that seemed a little classier than the norm. Maybe he could find something there, he thought as he hurried away.

Half an hour later he was standing before a quaint, Tudor-styled two-story house in the center of Mill Valley, a bottle of some fancy-named red wine tucked under his arm. It occurred to him, as he reached for the doorbell, that he hadn't asked if she was serving meat or fish. Somehow, he had a feeling she wasn't the type to be strict about things like that.

The door flew open before his fingers had a chance to make contact with the bell.

The next instant Brooke was standing in the doorway, her eyes warmly greeting him even before her lips did. Her hair, dark as midnight, was brushed away from her face and held in place by two tiny clips with white daisies on them. She looked younger than springtime and as sensual as a temptress all at the same time.

He'd spent the entire day in her company, or at least with her being somewhere in the immediate vicinity. There was a table and chairs in the back of the bookstore for people who wanted to browse through the books they were deciding whether or not to purchase. It was there that she had planted him—him and the more than a dozen books she thought he might find helpful.

When he'd made a comment that she was going to have him buying up half the store, she'd looked stunned. Brooke had been quick to tell him that he was welcome to glean everything he needed from the books and then return them to the shelves.

He'd almost laughed at her expression. She'd appeared so clearly distressed that he would take offense. "Then, how are you and your father ever going to make any money?"

"Oh, it's not about making money," she'd told him with no small amount of sincerity. "It's about making friends. Money's only a distant second."

He'd thought that she really was very, very innocent and idealistic. "Try telling that to the electric company when it calls about an overdue bill."

It was then that he had seen compassion enter her eyes. She'd sat down beside him, lowering her voice to a level he found unnervingly sensual even though he knew she meant nothing by it.

"Mark," she began hesitantly, taking his hand, "if you need a loan—"

His mouth had dropped open then, astounded by the generosity she was displaying to someone who was a virtual stranger to her. Someone who, if he was right about her father, might very well be responsible for ultimately turning her world on its ear.

Someone who, at the very least, was lying to her.

Her offer, her generosity of spirit, made him feel guilty, and he didn't like it.

"No," he'd assured her very firmly. "I was just talking figuratively. Thinking about you and your father," he emphasized.

It was then that she'd surprised the hell out of him. She'd leaned over and brushed a quick butterfly kiss against his cheek. The entire episode was so fleeting that it might have not happened at all.

Except that it had.

And the imprint was still there now, softly throbbing against his skin, as he stood on the doorstep, looking at her.

If her smile was any wider, it would take over her entire face. "You came."

She looked so happy to see him that someone might have thought he was a long-lost lover. It seemed ridiculous, and yet he knew she was being genuine. She didn't belong in this century, he thought. She belonged back with knights and poets, in an era where a man's word was his bond.

"I said I would."

"Yes." Ignoring the bottle he was holding, she hooked her arm through his and drew him into the house, subtly closing the door behind him. "You did."

Chapter Five

Seated at the small dining-room table, Mark was listening to Derek Ross talk about his store. It had taken a little coaxing, mostly on the part of the man's daughter, but Derek now seemed to be warming to his subject and even more so, Mark noted, to his guest.

Anyone privy to the scene would have thought that he was an old family friend instead of someone they'd only met yesterday.

These people were much too open, Mark thought. That made his job a lot easier, yet he couldn't help feeling somewhat protective and a little annoyed that they were so incredibly trusting. He would have thought that at his age, Ross would have known better. Trusting people were eaten up alive.

Glancing toward the doorway that led between the

kitchen and the dining room, Mark saw Brooke walking in, holding a large platter before her. Mark quickly rose to his feet. Rounding the table, he went to take the platter from her.

Or attempted to, but she stopped him with a smile. "I'm stronger than I look."

He scanned her slender frame. Her height only added to her look of frailty.

"You'd have to be," Mark heard himself saying, though not quite loud enough that he thought anyone else would hear him.

But she did.

Rather than take offense at some imagined slight, she just smiled more warmly. Brooke placed the platter down in the center of the table. The pot roast was surrounded by tiny, perfect potatoes she'd painstakingly peeled. "Why, do I look like I'll break?"

He sat down again, aware that her father was studying him. More aware of the look in Brooke's eyes. He doubted he'd ever met anyone quite so guileless and yet quiet so captivating.

Mark nodded at the platter she'd just set down. "You don't look as if you weigh much more than that serving of meat you're carrying."

At the mention of dinner, Brooke's attention was drawn back to the meal she'd been working on so diligently. For the first time in weeks she'd left her father to close up the shop and come home to start cooking.

Still, she didn't want Mark to know just how much

effort she'd put into it, in case the meal wasn't to his liking. "It's only pot roast."

Listening to her inflection, Mark detected a note of apology in her voice. She needn't have. It had been more years than he could count since he'd eaten anything from the supermarket that didn't have microwave instructions slapped across the side of the container. Focusing on the career that never came her way, his late wife hadn't been much of a homebody. When Dana cooked at all, her preferred setting was usually "broil" which inevitably escalated to "burn" because she'd always become distracted and forget to take whatever she was preparing out in time. As a result, they'd lived predominantly on take-out of the pizza and Chinese food variety.

The last meal of any import he remembered had been served to him by his mother. An odd twist of fate had made that pot roast, too.

"I'm partial to pot roast," he told her, negating her undeclared apology.

"Well then, I guess you are in luck, Mark," Derek told him as he helped himself to the bowl of peas and carrots that Brooke had put out earlier, "because nobody I know makes a better pot roast than Brooke."

"Dad." She tried not to look as pleased as she felt. Or as embarrassed. She passed a small basket of rolls to Mark. "You don't have to brag."

"Sure I do." Derek chuckled, feeling better than he had in a long while. Life was beginning to regain some of its shape. He realized just how much he needed to live in the present, not the past or the future, just in the moment. He was glad Brooke had extended the invitation to this man. "It's one of the few pleasures I have left in life."

Taking a roll, Mark noticed that it was still warm from the oven. Strange how such small pleasures could seem so important. "Odd thing to say for a man who couldn't be more than, what, forty-seven?"

Standing up to carve several slices of the pot roast for the others, Derek looked mildly surprised at the accuracy of the guess. He made an observation of his own. "That seems like an odd number to pick." He offered the first slices to Mark. "Most people would have said forty-five or fifty."

Mark moved his plate forward as he looked up at the man. "Well, you don't look fifty, but you don't sound forty-five. I thought I'd split the difference, in a manner of speaking, then shave it closer to the younger than the older."

Satisfied at the reasoning, Derek smiled. "You're being kind." Finished serving his guest, he took his seat again, then gave himself several slices after first coaxing his daughter to take a few.

"I'd rather think it was insightful." For form's sake, Mark took the smallest sip he could of the wine he'd brought, his eyes on his quarry.

"Well, you are," Brooke told him with a laugh that sounded like one of the tiny silver bells that had once hung on his family Christmas tree.

The memory startled him, and he looked at her, for one solitary moment completely captivated.

"Because he is," Brooke continued, utterly unaware of the effect she'd just had on her guest. She was looking at her father. "Forty-seven. A very young forty-seven," she insisted when she saw the protest rising on her father's lips.

Enjoying the game, Derek nodded. "All right, since you seemed to be so insightful," he allowed, "how old is Brooke?"

"Dad."

Brooke pressed her lips together. Whether out of embarrassment or because that seemed like the proper response, Mark couldn't tell. He only knew that the sight of her looking like that did something to him that he hadn't expected and didn't welcome.

There was a tolerant, reproving expression on her father's face. These were two people who really loved each other, Mark thought. His own family life was so far in the past that it seemed to have happened to someone else.

And yet, being here, amid these people who were supposed to be strangers to him, he could feel faint rumblings of a connection he hadn't felt in years.

"You're much too young to take offense at age, Brooke," Derek was saying.

She loved her father dearly, but he had a habit of treating her as if she were a child. "You make me sound as if I'm twelve."

"Twice that, minus one," Mark corrected, feeling mildly guilty over the so-called game.

The week he'd spent scouting out the store and its owner, he had also used every means at his disposal to learn everything he could about them. That way he could casually claim to have the same likes and dislikes, the same interests they did. In his experience, people had a tendency to be more open with those whom they felt had something in common with them.

During that time he'd kept himself separated from his subjects, the way he always did. As always, it had been easy for him.

It wasn't quite so easy now.

Watching Brooke's eyes widen with surprise was almost hypnotic. "That's amazing. Have you always been this intuitive?"

"More observant that intuitive," he corrected. He didn't want her getting the wrong idea. If he strayed too far from the truth, he might not find his way back. "For instance, looking at you someone might say that you were older, but you're very exuberant—"

Derek leaned forward, intrigued. "And in your experience, Mark, have you found that older people are less exuberant?"

Mark suddenly realized that the man he'd been sent to find reminded him of his father in a way. They had the same earnest way of talking, of creating a small haven within a world of turmoil.

He shook himself free of the feeling. "Older people tend to realize that life weighs more heavily than they'd first believed it might."

"So, you're a philosopher as well as a historian," Derek concluded genially. He paused to take a sip of his wine, his eyes never leaving his guest.

"Neither, really. Like I said, just an observer." Mark looked down at his plate. He wasn't here to focus attention on himself. He was trying to get as much information about Ross as subtly as he could. "You were right, Mr. Moss. This is very good."

The laugh was surprisingly hearty for a man as wirily built as Derek. "Derek, please, and yes," he looked toward his daughter, "I know."

When Mark looked at her, as well, Brooke could feel a blush rising to her cheeks. Damn, now he was going to think she was a child instead of a fully-grown woman. It was very important to her that he not think of her as a child. That he see the woman she was.

She felt herself wanting to lower her gaze, but she managed not to. "I'm glad you like it. I wasn't sure what to make for someone like you."

He wasn't sure how to take that. Did she somehow suspect…? "Someone like me?"

"A New Yorker." Seeing that he had finished what was on his plate, she rose to cut several more slices of the quickly shrinking pot roast. Not waiting to offer it to him, she placed the three slices on his plate instead, then placed the remaining two on her father's. "You're probably used to fine restaurants—"

Mark made no effort to hide the small smile that came to his lips. In her own way she really was a little dictator, just like her father had claimed. "The finest restaurant food can't compare with a home-cooked meal."

"You don't get very many of those?" she heard herself prodding. Was there a woman in his life, someone back in New York who he would be returning to before long? Who he might, even now, miss?

As she waited for some kind of answer to her silent question, Brooke held her breath.

"None, really," he freely admitted. "I never really learned how to cook very well myself. Somehow it always seemed like too much trouble to go through for just one person."

Rays of hope began to dance through Brooke as she looked at the dark, handsome, mysterious stranger fate had brought to her doorstep. There was no point in trying not to smile.

"Well, while you're here," she heard her father saying, "feel free to drop by after the store's closed. Nothing Brooke likes better than to cook for someone with a healthy appetite."

Looking down at his plate, he realized that he'd finished not only the first serving, but the second, as well. The meat had all but melted like butter in his mouth, and he hadn't paid attention to how quickly he was eating. Which was unusual for him because he always paid attention to all the details, small and large. "I guess I am digging in a little too much."

"No, no," Derek protested quickly and with feeling, "that wasn't meant as a criticism, that was meant to encourage you." He glanced toward his daughter. Very little of what she thought eluded him. "She's been worried about me because I've been picking at my food. Picking at life, too, I suppose," he admitted. He saw the surprised look on Brooke's face. "Didn't think I noticed you noticing? I did and I'm sorry, Brooke. I have a great deal to be grateful for. I just forgot about it for a while."

Because the moment seemed to call for it and because he'd kept so much bottled up inside of him all these years, Derek went on to say in terms as veiled as he could manage, "I recently attended a funeral for someone I used to know a long time ago." An ironic smile twisted his lips, much the way the same feeling had twisted his gut. "I always thought there would be time to get back in touch."

He sighed, defeated for a moment and struggling not to be, "But obviously, time comes in limited supplies. I think I allowed that to get in the way of my making the most of the present." He looked at his daughter, trying to convey his heartfelt apologies for putting her through all this. She shouldn't have to spend her days worried about him. "Like enjoying good food. And good company." Looking from Brooke to Mark, he raised his glass in a toast. "To good company."

"To good company," Brook echoed, turning her eyes toward Mark.

From the shadows, a full measure of guilt skewered into him, entirely unannounced. Mark had no choice but to lift his glass to join them.

"To good company."

He watched Brooke sip from her glass and found himself staring. It took him a moment before he brought the rim of his own to his lips. Somewhere deep inside of him something stirred insistently. It was so foreign to him that at first he wasn't even aware of it happening, and then, once he was, he wasn't certain just what it was that *was* happening.

But this wasn't a time for any self-exploration. He was here to do a job, to lay groundwork. To continue laying groundwork until he was certain he was right, that this was Derek Ross. And then, if this was Derek Ross, to get the man to meet with Tyler Carlton. His nephew.

What was more, not only was Tyler the late Marla Carlton's son, but he and his twin brother, Tyler had told him in the strictest of confidence, were actually the illegitimate sons of Walter Parks. They'd been conceived that summer when Marla's husband, Jeremy, once a friend of Walter's and then his major competitor, mysteriously vanished from the face of the earth.

Mark's eyes remained on the young woman. That would make Brooke, by marriage, the niece of one of the most rich and powerful men in the country.

It didn't seem possible. With her flashing green eyes and quick, ready smile, she was such an innocent. And Parks, from everything that he had heard, was the epitome of corruption and evil.

But even evil could be overcome, destroyed. In this case it would just take a few courageous men to bring him down.

Men like Derek Ross.

If he was Derek Ross.

And if he could be convinced.

"You really don't have to do this." Brooke raised her voice above the sound of running water. It was her third protest, born of guilt. You didn't make your guests help clean up. But it seemed to come naturally to him. She'd known the man for a little more than twenty-four hours and already he'd helped her twice, last night at the shop and now again here. Her father had conveniently faded away into the living room, sharing the company of a glass of the wine Mark had brought and one of his favorite books while he waited for them to return.

The dish washing was going slowly, and she was secretly happy that it was.

Mark turned away from the counter and the dishes he'd just brought in from the dining room.

"And you didn't have to invite me over," he pointed out, hoping that was the end the argument. It was all part of the image he was trying to spin, part of getting close to her father. She seemed the most direct route, and if his conscience was grumbling, well, he'd just have to turn a deaf ear to it. A greater good than just his fee was at stake here. "It really was a delicious meal."

She started to protest, then bit down on her tongue. She had to learn how to accept compliments without trying to bury them beneath a pile of disclaimers. So instead, she smiled at him and murmured, "Thank you."

Her whole being seemed to be smiling, he observed. Sparkling. It took effort not to let himself be drawn in. "I'm very partial to pot roast," he heard himself saying, and realized that he'd already told her that. He tacked on, "My mother used to make it a lot."

Brooke slipped the three dinner plates and utensils

into the sink first. An army of suds moved to close over the temporary space. She glanced over her shoulder at Mark.

"She doesn't anymore?" The moment she said it, she upbraided herself. The trace of a smile that had been on his lips vanished.

"My mother died when I was ten." Even after all this time, the words still had a sharp, prickly taste to them as they came out of his mouth.

She wanted to hug him, to tell him she knew how it felt to lose a parent.

"How awful for you. And for your father," she added, thinking of how lonely her own had been all these years without her mother.

"Yes and no," he confessed before he could give any thought to it. He was usually guarded when it came to what he said. But for some reason, in the presence of her compassionate eyes, the words seemed to be coming a little faster and far more freely than he had intended. "My father died along with her."

Then he was an orphan, she thought. "Car accident?" It was the first thing that occurred to her.

"No, a shooting."

He had every intention of cutting it off right here. Nowhere was it written that he needed to bare any of his soul in the pursuit of his quarry. Yet he couldn't find it in himself to just shut down. Not when Brooke was looking at him that way. As if she was right there, sharing it all.

"We'd just finished eating at a restaurant for my mother's birthday." A small bittersweet smile played on his lips as he remembered. "My dad didn't think she should have to cook on her birthday, so he took us all out to this new, fancy French restaurant that she'd been wanting to go to." His face sobered as the events rose up before him. The noises, the smells, the screams—he remembered them all. And always would. "The police were chasing this robber, and he swung around to fire at them. Ran right past us as we were coming out. My parents were in the way, trying to protect my brother and me and—" He couldn't continue the narrative. It was far too painful for him.

"They died," he concluded roughly. Though it had happened so long ago, his throat still felt scratchy as he talked about it. Still felt as if it was going to close off, taking away all his air with it.

Her hands flew up to her mouth and her heart pounded hard as she relived the moments with him. "Oh my God, I'm so sorry."

Deeply moved, Brooke dropped her hands from her face, her eyes riveted on his face, on the extreme pain she saw there. This was a man who'd loved his parents, a man who still grieved for them after all this time. She understood, because there were times she still ached for the mother she'd never known, the one who existed in the stories her father had told her over the years.

The one who existed in his eyes whenever he mentioned her name.

Without thinking, she took a step closer to him, inclined her head, brushing her lips against his cheek.

She'd meant the contact to be only one kindred spirit—because she did feel so close to him right now—offering comfort to another. There was nothing sexual intended, nothing more.

But the moment her lips touched his cheek, something more came into existence.

She blinked and drew her head back, looking at him. The next moment, she moved forward again and submerged herself once again in the kiss, but this time on his lips.

He caught hold of her shoulders, meaning to push her away. Gently but firmly.

But the intention somehow never came to fruition.

Instead, he found himself holding her to him. Holding his breath as well. And trying very hard to keep his head, his senses, from spinning out of control.

She tasted of innocence, of sweetness and of everything he'd felt he lost all those years ago, standing before that restaurant, holding on to Nick who was crying, doing his very best to be brave while everything inside of him was screaming *No!*

Any noble inclination Mark might have had of drawing away from this woman was aborted in the face of the sustenance she, wittingly or unwittingly, offered him. Like someone hovering above the scene he was watching, Mark cupped her face with his hands and kissed her as if the very act could somehow unaccountably save his soul.

He knew it wasn't possible. His soul had been lost a long time ago.

He couldn't stop kissing her anyway.

Chapter Six

The next moment, as he felt Brooke lean into him, Mark felt his restraints breaking apart one by one like so many brittle slats of a sun-bleached fence. Desire came out of nowhere, assaulting his senses, taking them completely by surprise. He hadn't felt anything remotely like this since he'd first held Dana in his arms.

It was like coming out of a coma to discover that he hadn't died, that he was still alive. That he could feel things that normal men felt.

And then he caught sight of his reflection in the window above the sink. Caught sight of the scar, livid and disfiguring, that zigzagged just beneath his eye.

He was a monster.

What the hell was he thinking, allowing this to happen? Was he trying to create his own version of *Beauty and the Beast?* If nothing else, this was unprofessional. Worse than that, it was morally wrong. Brooke was a young woman who had all of life before her, he was a jaded thirty-year-old man who, for all intents and purposes when it came to love, to home, hearth, family, had left all of that far behind him.

He had nothing to give her and she had every right to everything that life had to offer.

The sweetness of her mouth had seduced him for a moment, but only for a moment. His common sense had returned to keep him from compounding what was a grave mistake.

This time, when Mark took hold of Brooke's shoulders, he gently pushed her away. Her eyes looked dazed at the sudden feel of air against her face. The soft lines of her lips were blurred from the imprint of his. Mark felt something tighten within his gut, but he held his ground. He had to.

"I'm sorry, I shouldn't have done that."

She blinked, as if to clear her head. A smile slowly curved her lips. He found it incredibly sensual. "You didn't. At least, not to begin with. *I* did." And then a look that was a little akin to embarrassment touched her features. "Didn't I do it right?"

"What?"

How could she possibly ask that question? The kiss had been so perfect, it had left him dazzled. If she had been older, or he younger, and not who he was… But he was who he was and too much of life had left its mark on him. There was no excuse for his allowing this to have happened.

Her tongue darted along her lips, moistening them. Making something inside of him ache.

"I mean," she began again, "I realize that you must be accustomed to women who are sophisticated and experienced—"

Mark stared at her. Was she apologizing? For perfection? How insane was that?

"That has nothing to do with it. And I'm not." There were no women, sophisticated or otherwise, in his life and there hadn't been, not since Dana. He made an effort to begin again. "There's nothing wrong with the way you kiss."

Confusion creased the brow beneath her jet-black bangs. "Then why did you stop? Why did you push me away?"

"Because—" The words wouldn't come, wouldn't arrange themselves into neat, precise sentences that explained everything. He fell back on the visual. That should have been enough, anyway. "Look at me, Brooke."

She turned her face up to his, her gaze unwavering. "I am looking at you."

Unable to take it, he turned the offending part of his face from her. "Doesn't my scar frighten you?"

"Not particularly." She thought of their first meeting, but this time the color didn't rise to her cheeks. This wasn't about her reaction to him; this was, she had a feeling, about his reaction to himself. Brooke did her best to downplay the whole incident. "I admit that you did make me jump last night in the shop, but that was only because I didn't think there was anyone else there." Her eyes twinkled as she made an admission. "Sometimes when it's late and I'm alone in the shop, I hear things."

He didn't follow her. "Things?"

She nodded. "Things that aren't there. That go 'bump in the night,'" she elaborated. She quickly finished washing the rest of the utensils, leaving them on the rack to dry. "I'm afraid that I have a very vivid imagination. I always have." Turning toward him again, she took a towel and wiped her hands. "When I first saw you, I thought you were one of those people come to life."

He tried not to notice how the light was playing across her face. How the soft wisps of her hair framed her face. How much he wanted to kiss her again and break all of his own rules.

"Those people?"

"You know the ones." She leaned her hip against the side of the sink, her expression becoming a shade dreamy. "The romantic heroes in the classics. Like Heathcliff in *Wuthering Heights.*"

"I know who Heathcliff is," he told her. It had been required reading in some high school English class he'd taken more than a decade ago. He couldn't remember the teacher's name, but he remembered relating to Heathcliff because the protagonist had been an introverted orphan, like him. "He didn't have a scar."

"Not on his face," she allowed. "But his soul was scarred. That's what made him do the things he did." She looked up into his eyes. "I've always believed that it's what's inside, not outside, that counts." She drew her courage to her, resisting the temptation to place her hand on his chest. She was a toucher by nature, but she sensed that he was just the opposite. That touching made him back away. "Is your soul scarred, Mark?"

If the words had come from anyone else, he would have said they were empty platitudes said for form's sake. But he felt Brooke genuinely believed what she was saying to him. She was still young enough to believe in things like hope and goodness. She had yet to learn that they were myths, like Santa Claus and elves.

Mark looked at her for a long moment, weighing his answer.

Then finally he said "No," because to say yes, to say that any human being over the age of fifteen had some kind of scarring of his soul unless he—or she—was very, very sheltered, would have led her to launch another volley of questions at him, none of which he wanted to answer. He'd already shared far too much of himself tonight.

"Brooke, are you interrogating our guest?" Mark turned to see that Derek was standing in the doorway. Had he been there long?

"No, Dad." She lifted her head, a soft laugh escaping her lips. "Just making polite conversation."

The nod Derek sent his way told Mark the man knew better. And then he laughed as well.

"I apologize if she's been asking things she shouldn't. Brooke has an insatiable thirst to know everything." There was no missing the affection that came into the man's eyes as he looked toward his daughter. "I always told her that she would make a great private investigator, delving completely without shame into places she had no right to be."

"She was just making conversation," Mark echoed her response.

It earned him a wink and a smile from Brooke, both of which astonished him as they homed in on and hit him right where he lived.

It was time to leave.

He didn't want to overstay his welcome. And more than that, he needed time to pull himself together and do a little damage control. He'd committed a breach tonight, a serious breach of protocol during which he'd allowed the lines between his professional and personal life to blur. That was so wrong, he didn't know where to begin. Because he hadn't kissed her as the temporarily transplanted New York City would-be writer, but as himself. As Mark Banning, lost soul, veteran of the tragedies that life sometimes carelessly throws in your path, not once but as many times as it felt like it.

He was going to have to get that under control before he ventured on with this investigation. If he didn't, there would only be trouble ahead.

Mark pretended to look at his watch. "Well, it's getting late and I'd better get going."

Brooke bit her lower lip. She'd frightened him off. Damn, she hadn't meant to do that. She was going to have to work on not letting her impulses get the better of her. Still, she didn't want to see him leave. She looked toward her father to say something, but it was obvious that to him, part of being a good host meant allowing your guest to leave when he wanted to.

So it was up to her. "But it's not even ten o'clock yet."

There was just a hint of a pout to her protest. Mark had a sudden urge to kiss the pout out of existence. He was leaving just in time.

"I want to get an early start in the morning." He addressed his words to both Derek and Brooke. "I came across several sections in a couple of the books I bought that I want to digest a little more fully." He took Derek's hand, shaking it. "Mr. Moss, Brooke, thank you for your generous hospitality."

"It's I who should be thanking you," Derek told him, returning his handshake. "It was a wonderful evening. You made me remember why I love this city so much."

Brooke hooked her arm through Mark's and began to walk him to the living room and the front door beyond. "Will you be stopping by the shop anymore?"

She was saying exactly what he wanted her to say. He felt no triumph. It was a little like the sensation he imagined fisherman felt about shooting fish in a barrel. The quota was guaranteed to be met but the feeling was far from satisfying.

"You've already been more than generous with your time."

Was that a no, she wondered. Oh God, she hoped not. Brooke mentally scrambled for a way to make him return to the store.

"If you feel that way, you can dedicate the book to me," she told him suddenly. "To me and to my father."

The moment she uttered the words, she liked that idea even better. Her father deserved to have a book dedicated to him. He deserved to have a library's worth of books dedicated to him. Over the years he'd done more than his share to help one struggling poet or short-story writer after another and had yet to gain any recognition for it. And he did love books so much.

Brooke opened the front door, then stopped and looked up at the somber man before her. She had a feeling that Mark Banning was not about to forget a promise he might make.

"A dedication," he repeated. "I hadn't thought about that. Sure, why not?" Another lie to add to the others, he thought.

Overjoyed, she had to restrain herself to keep from kissing him again.

"I really hope you decide to come back. To the bookstore," she qualified, although if he came there, she meant to have him come to the house again, too. "I can't begin to tell you how wonderful this has been for my father."

The declaration surprised him. He hadn't expected her to say that. "Your father?"

He watched as her brow furrowed ever so slightly beneath the silky black bangs. "Yes, he's been so withdrawn lately. This evening has been wonderful for him. He's so much more like his old self." Taking Mark's hands in hers, she literally beamed at him. He could all but feel the rays seeping into his being. "I can't thank you enough."

Gratitude always made him feel uncomfortable. And misplaced gratitude did the job that much more so. "There's no need."

"Oh, but there is," she insisted.

She couldn't remember when she'd last met a man as humble as this one. The flesh-and-blood heroes of her world were the poets and writers who came to give readings at the store, and, to a man, they were all full of themselves. This man was an incredible breath of fresh air.

"I believe that everyone should know when they've done something exceptional." Afraid of being overheard, she slipped outside with Mark and pulled the door closed behind her. "Until you came along, my father had transformed from a sweet, brilliant, outgoing man to someone who spent hours just staring out the window. It was as if his soul had been stolen from him. As if he was waiting for something to return to him."

That would be in keeping with the profile he'd mentally sketched out of his quarry. "Like what?"

"I don't know. Every time I tried to talk to him about it, to get him to tell me what was wrong, he would just put me off or say that I was imagining things again. But I wasn't," she insisted. "I know what I saw, and I didn't see my father, just an empty shell he'd left behind." And then she smiled again, her serious moment passing. He found the transformation almost hypnotic. "But you brought him back. You got him talking about what he loves. Thanks to you, he looks alive again."

"It would have happened anyway," he told her. And then he paused, his eyes on hers, another salvo of guilt threatening to hit him. This was his job, he reminded himself. There were a great many questions left that needed to be answered. He'd played roles before, taking on the guise of a friend, a confessor. This was no different, he insisted silently. "Any idea what might have made him change like that?"

She shrugged helplessly. "I know it has something to do with the funeral he went to."

How much did she know, he wondered. She seemed too open to keep anything back if he asked. "Do you know whose?"

Brooke shook her head. Again that helpless, frustrated look came into her eyes. "He wouldn't tell me. Said he would someday, when he could talk about it, but that I should give him a little time." It seemed as if she was silently appealing to him for help. He grew more uncomfortable. "My father's never talked like that before, either. I was always the first one he turned to, the first one to know whatever he knew. He shared everything with me."

Brooke paused. She saw the hint of a grin on Mark's lips. It had a way of blotting out all traces of the scar he was so self-conscious about. Had she said something funny? "What?"

Maybe it was the language of families, Mark thought. "You sound like someone I met recently."

He'd almost said client. It had been a runaway case. A sixteen-year-old boy had asserted his independence, as well as his shortsightedness, and run away from home. It had taken Mark over three weeks of nonstop tracking to finally corner the boy in Dearborn, Michigan, more than a thousand miles from home. Broke, hungry and lost, the boy was ready to admit that independence on its own wasn't all it was cracked up to be.

"She was saying the exact same things," he told Brooke, "except that she was saying them about her teenage son."

She supposed it did sound a little like that. Brooke lifted a shoulder, letting it drop carelessly.

"Maybe this is my father's second childhood," she allowed, then thought better of it, "but I really don't think so. Something has him upset, very upset. He's even letting the business slide, and he's never done that before."

"Maybe he thinks you're old enough to handle it for him now."

Maybe, but that wasn't the point. "But tonight, dinner here with you was like old times." She made an appeal to him, not like a dreamy-eyed woman smitten with a handsome, mysterious stranger, but a daughter who loved her father and wanted him back again. "I don't want to lose that, Mark."

She was holding his hand, as if trying to seal him to a bargain. There was no way he could have refused her, even if the plan hadn't been to turn up at the bookstore tomorrow to leech more information out of them, out of Derek, as he pretended to have more questions about this city of the seven hills that Brooke and her father were so passionate about.

That was another connection between Derek Ross and Derek Moss, Mark mused. Ross had been born here. He'd had family here. Granted there had been a twenty-five-year mysterious rift, but it would stand to reason that he would want to remain close by, in case there was ever an opportunity to mend that rift.

Mark eased into his own opportunity. He was beginning to think he should reduce the fee he was charging Tyler. Brooke was making it almost too easy for him. "Then you won't mind if I come by the bookstore tomorrow and continue to browse around some more?"

"Mind?" she laughed. "I'll even bring the coffee and cake." It was a tradition her father had begun at Buy the Book long before the book chains had decided to incorporate small, trendy coffee shops beneath the roofs of their stores.

"I don't need coffee and cake," he told her. "Just make sure the books are there." And then, because the look in her eyes required it, he added, "And you," hating himself for doing it.

Because while it was true, while he did look forward to seeing her, he shouldn't. He was leading her on. Once this case was solidly locked up, once he was certain that Derek Moss was Derek Ross and delivered him to Tyler, most likely he would never see Brooke again.

And she would be a little less innocent for it, discovering that men could lie for their own ends. Even to a face as pure, as compellingly beautiful and fresh as hers.

"I'll be there," she promised.

She slid the tip of her tongue along her lips, an unabashedly hopeful look in her eyes. He knew what she wanted. What he wanted, as well. But because he wanted it, he kept a tight rein on himself. So he leaned forward and brushed a fleeting kiss to her lips, then forced himself to walk away before anything more could come of the moment.

There was a very special seat in the hottest corner of hell reserved for him, Mark decided as he quickly walked away from the warm, inviting glow of Brooke and her house and toward his car. If there hadn't been already, there was one now.

Telling himself that he was only working a case, that he was trying to further the cause of a very good man—a man who was being denied his birthright due to circumstances beyond his control—hardly did anything to assuage his conscience.

There was no way to sugarcoat the fact that he was deliberately using Brooke. Not ruthlessly, but still, for his own ends, not hers.

The fact that he meant her no harm didn't alter the fact that he was kissing her under false pretenses. She thought he was some romantic knight in rusty armor while he was actually behaving like someone far less noble. He knew exactly how someone as impressionable, as innocent as Brooke Ross would see it. Once she discovered his true identity and his real purpose in being here, she would be crushed by the deception.

That settled it, he promised himself as he got into his vehicle. His lips were not going to touch hers again. Never mind that she tasted of sweet, ripened strawberries with the first kiss of the summer sun on their skin. He had no need of strawberries. A man who had nothing to offer had no right sampling strawberries.

From now on he was going to conduct this investigation by the book, the way he always had before. And no one was going to be hurt.

That meant keeping her at a proper distance.

Easier said than done, he thought the following morning as he walked into Buy the Book.

He had purposely waited until after the store was officially open for business before coming in. He wanted Brooke to be busy so that he could seek out her father and see if he could learn anything more, perhaps see if the man was willing to admit to ever "meeting" Walter Parks. All it took was properly manipulating the conversation in the right directions. He figured he could accomplish that better without Brooke around as a distraction.

But the moment he walked into the store, he saw her. It was as if he had his own built-in radar and it was tuned to her.

Brooke's long, shiny black hair was loose about her shoulders, and for all her innocence and young age, she looked like a temptress. He found himself wanting her the moment her eyes turned in his direction. The moment her lips peeled back into a smile that could rival the sun that was shining so brightly just outside the store's front door.

Murmuring something to the customer she was with, Brooke apparently excused herself and made her way over to him. The wattage from her smile increased. He could almost feel the rays.

Or was that just a precursor to the fires of hell he'd thought about last night?

"Hi," she said brightly. "So, what'll it be today?"

He realized he was staring at her and forced himself to focus. "Excuse me?"

"What'll it be?" she repeated. "Are you interested in exploring San Francisco's past history or its current one? Because we just received a book this morning that my father got in an estate sale. It was a diary of someone written in the first half of the twentieth century. It might be just the thing you need to look over if you're really interested in San Francisco's history."

He'd already done a little boning up on the subject before he'd ever approached Brooke and her father in his present guise as a writer. And yesterday had contained a great deal of reading material he'd had to go through the motions of perusing. As far as he was concerned, he was full up on history, but he knew that the person he was pretending to be would have been fairly enthusiastic about the find she was describing.

"I'd like to see it, if your father wouldn't mind."

She liked that he was so mindful of her father's feelings. Liked a lot about him, she thought.

"We haven't had a chance to unwrap it yet." She nodded toward the rear of the shop. "It's in the storeroom." With that, she turned on her heel and started to walk back.

He tried not to notice the way her hips swayed as she led the way.

Chapter Seven

Music softly playing in the background was the only sound that Tyler Carlton heard within the small San Francisco apartment he now called home. That and the occasional shuffling of papers as he turned a page. He wasn't even sure what kind of music it was. It didn't matter. He'd flipped on the radio as a block against an all-pervading silence as he did what he did every night after he came home from work. He waded through a mountain of old papers. Searching.

Tyler's frown made him appear far older than his twenty-four years. He felt far older, at least, he had these past few weeks.

It wasn't that he'd exactly had a life of hardship up to this point, but dealing with the emotional issues that had swept over him recently without warning like a mile-high tidal wave had definitely taken their toll on him. In a way he was still reeling, even as he desperately tried to tread water.

He and his twin brother, Conrad, were the younger two in a family of four siblings. From the day he was born, he'd grown up fatherless, but with a mother he adored. Marla Carlton had been the best mother he could have asked for. But he'd always felt that she was harboring some sort of secret. A secret that made her eyes look so sad in unguarded moments, even when she was laughing and playing with her children.

Up until the week before her death, he'd always felt that the sadness had been due to his father's untimely death. Marla Carlton had been widowed early in her life. Her husband, Jeremy, the man Tyler had always believed to be his father, a solid, hardworking man in the up-and-coming diamond import company he had founded, had just begun to see the true measure of success when he had suddenly died under extremely mysterious circumstances. His father had left her widowed and pregnant with twins at the age of thirty.

Rallying, his mother had moved her tiny family to Colorado and made a life for them all as best she could. Granted, while he was growing up, they hadn't been what could be termed well off, but they'd been happy and had never lacked for love.

It wasn't until his mother was on her deathbed nearly eight months ago that she'd told them all something that completely rocked his world and tore out the carefully laid foundations from beneath him.

Looking pale and worn, her beautiful green eyes silently asking for forgiveness for the lie she had allowed them to believe all these years, she'd told his brother and him that the sisters they'd grown up playing with were only their half sisters. That she'd had a brief affair with Walter Parks and that Tyler and his twin were the result of that affair.

It had been a bitter pill to swallow, and at first he'd thought that maybe it was the illness playing with her mind, making her believe things that weren't true. But it wasn't. His mother had been very lucid that afternoon. And very determined to tell them everything before there was no more time left.

He'd held her hand in his and let her talk. And let her shatter his world.

He'd grown up loving a father whom he'd thought had been taken from him. Now, sitting here at his kitchen table, old correspondences and papers spread out in all directions, he was looking for proof that his father wasn't dead, and if not noble or kind the way he'd always believed, at least alive.

He had mixed feelings about that. Mixed feelings about giving up his hold on Jeremy Carlton and admitting to the world that he was actually the product of an illicit affair between his impressionable mother and a man who was feared by many and well thought of by none.

Tyler didn't like the idea of being Walter Parks's son.

If it were up to him, he would have let the matter

slide, the way Conrad had after their mother's funeral. But his conscience wouldn't let him. His mother had begged him to find proof that would allow his brother and him to claim their heritage from a man who had destroyed their lives. She made it clear to them that in her heart she felt that Walter Parks, the man who had pretended to love her, to be mesmerized by her, had done it all with an ulterior plan.

He'd done it to gain her help in preventing Jeremy from exposing him as a thief and a smuggler. He'd done it to get hold of Jeremy's thriving business. She was convinced that the man she'd taken to her bed was responsible for her husband's death. And, she had whispered, there was proof.

She'd begged him on her death bed, and he had given her his word to do everything possible to bring all the hidden facts to light.

No matter how much he ached to continue believing that the kind, upstanding, honest man whose picture was on the mantel was really his father, he knew he had to follow his mother's wishes. And, in so doing, to claim what would have been his mother's due.

With any luck, once that was accomplished, he could also bring the man who had given Conrad and him life to justice.

The frown on his lips softened into an ironic smile. A smile that held no humor behind it. Life was very strange and twisted sometimes.

Tired, Tyler leaned back and took a moment to sip from the can of beer he'd taken from the refrigerator.

Dinner. According to his mother, he had an uncle he knew nothing about. An uncle who could help him prove what she had told him and his brother and sisters. Uncle Derek Ross, her younger brother.

It was hard picturing his mother as an older sister, he thought. She'd probably been more like Sara than Kathleen, he mused. Bossy, with a heart of gold.

His mother had long since lost track of Uncle Derek and had only a photograph taken of the two of them some twenty-five years ago to offer him.

When he'd looked at it for the first time, he'd experienced a strange feeling undulating through him. The man looked like his mother.

She'd died less than a week after extracting her promise from him. The pain hadn't lessened any. Pulling strings, he'd seen to it that his mother's obituary had been printed in all the major newspapers in the country, citing where and when the funeral would be held. He'd done it hoping to flush out Parks and perhaps this mysterious uncle.

Parks had been a no-show. No real surprise there, Tyler thought. But there had been someone at the funeral who'd looked a great deal like the computer-aged photo he'd generated of Derek Ross. He'd only noticed the man at the back of the crowd at the cemetery right after the service was over.

But just as he'd started to approach him, the man he thought was his uncle had abruptly walked away. By the time he'd caught up to where he'd been, the man had pulled away in a taxicab.

Not about to give up this slim lead, Tyler had managed to track down the cab driver who had brought the mysterious mourner to the funeral and then driven him away. The cabby had told him he had no idea who his fare was, only that he had taken the man straight to the airport after the funeral and that he'd said something about catching a plane for San Francisco. The cabby said the man made it sound as if he lived there.

Since San Francisco was also where his alleged father lived, it seemed like the place to go. Tyler had called a family meeting, proposing that they pool their resources and move to San Francisco. But Kathleen and Conrad hadn't wanted to pursue this, hadn't wanted to possibly drag their mother's name through the mud. They preferred leaving things just as they were. With their mother gone, who would be the wiser?

But all he could do was remember that he'd held his mother's hand in his and given her his word. So he and Sara were left to continue this crusade on their own. Together they'd moved to San Francisco, to do what needed to be done.

But somewhere along the line, Sara had dropped out, too. In an attempt to get close to the family, she'd wound up falling for Parks's son, Cade. That left only Tyler to bring Parks to justice and avenge the wrong done to his mother.

He didn't intend to get sidetracked.

He joined the police force shortly after arriving in San Francisco. That was where he met and struck up a friendship with Nick Banning, who told him about his brother, Mark, a former NYPD detective who now earned his living as a private investigator. Tyler knew that he couldn't do this all on his own, that he needed help. One meeting with Mark Banning told him he had the right man for the job.

So he had hired Mark to find Derek, telling him as much as he could about the case, hoping that between the two of them he could fulfill his mother's dying wish, if not resolve matters to his own satisfaction.

And if they did find Derek—even if the man couldn't be convinced to tell all he knew about Parks in a court of law—when this was over he would have at least gained an uncle.

Gaining a notorious, much-disliked father was another matter.

He sighed as he continued going through the box of correspondence he'd discovered in a strongbox amid his mother's things. It was a hunt he took no pleasure in, but then, revenge was a dish best served cold.

And, he reminded himself for the umpteenth time, he was doing this for his mother, not himself.

He took another sip of beer and then settled in to get back to work.

Hearing her laugh, Mark glanced up from the book he'd been leafing through for the past hour.

Brooke was at the far end of the store, talking to a customer, charming them without even knowing it. He doubted she was aware of the kind of effect that she had on people. That's what made her even more charming.

Five days had passed.

Five days in which he had steadily gotten himself more and more entrenched in the lives of these two unsuspecting people who were ultimately going to be deeply—and, no doubt, harshly—affected by his discovery.

There was almost no doubt in his mind that Derek Moss was the man he'd been sent to find. Even so, he felt he needed a little more evidence to back up what his gut already knew to be fact.

Gut instincts were not admissible in court.

And circumstantial evidence was the first to fall prey to an able attorney.

He wanted more. According to the story that Tyler Carlton had told him, twenty-five years had gone by, so a few more days wouldn't hurt. After all, it wasn't as if they were involved in some kind of race against time. Walter Parks wasn't going anywhere.

Mark gave himself a myriad of reasons for his need for more evidence, not once admitting that perhaps the true reason he was taking such painstaking time with this case was because he was enjoying Brooke's company. Enjoying the company of a woman when he had ceased to believe that pleasures like that were possible for him.

He didn't want it to end.

And once he told Derek that he knew who he really was, once he made the attempt to convince Marla Carlton's brother not only to allow his nephew to get in contact with him, but to talk to the D.A. about what he knew, the charade would be over. And Brooke would be out of his life.

Permanently.

It was like asking a prisoner who had recently been released from a cave to willingly give up the sunshine he'd discovered and return to darkness. Mark knew he had to, that it was inevitable, but he wanted just a little more time in the light. So that when the prison of darkness was a reality again, he could look back and remember what it was like to sit in the sun, to feel its warmth along his skin. To pretend that he was able to enjoy life's innocent pleasures just like everyone else.

He didn't think it was too much to ask.

Sending the customer on his way, Brooke turned on her heel and began to walk toward him. She nodded at another customer who said goodbye and then left the store. She seemed to be sweeping the place clear.

Mark closed the book he hadn't been reading and moved it aside on the table. As he stood up, she picked the book up. "Not to your liking?"

"Some of the others are more in keeping with what I'm looking for," he lied.

She nodded, accepting his excuse and went to put the book back on the shelf. He followed in her wake. It occurred to him that there were only a couple of customers left in the shop and that they were now in the checkout line.

"Are you closing up early?" he asked.

She knew Mark was referring to the reading they were holding tonight. It was scheduled for six-thirty.

A great many of their regulars were expected, people whose fancies were still stimulated by the power of the spoken word. People who needed no visual aides to help their imaginations take flight. She'd always looked forward to readings, but now she was looking forward to the one tonight for a different reason.

Always before, the authors who came to read here would captivate her so that by evening's end, she would be more than half in love with them. But tonight all she wanted to do was share the experience of a dramatic reading with Mark.

She wanted to watch his face, to hopefully see something stirring within him the way it did within her every time she attended a reading. She supposed that what she wanted so desperately was proof to substantiate her belief—her hope—that they were kindred spirits.

"Just a little earlier." She picked up another book that had been left behind and placed it in the right order on a shelf. Looking around, she satisfied herself that the store was neat. Behind her, the front door opened and closed as another customer left. "I need to set up the chairs."

He placed his hand on her shoulder, stopped her before she could run off. "Why don't you take care of whatever else needs doing? I'll set up the chairs."

"That's very nice of you," she murmured, pleased. She didn't particularly like having to drag out all the chairs. "If you wouldn't mind doing it—"

"Consider it done," he told her.

She watched him walk back to the storeroom, a smile spreading on her lips.

So this was what it felt like, she thought. This was what it felt like to have someone you cared about doing things for you. And she cared about Mark, maybe had even fallen for him. Not in the same fanciful way she always found herself falling for whatever struggling poet or writer her father would invite for a reading, but for a flesh-and-blood real man.

She realized now that the authors who came here looked upon her as an empty vessel they could infuse with their rhetoric, allowing them to bask in their own self-perceived glory.

Mark hadn't allowed her to read a single word of what he was writing. He'd told her that it wasn't ready for anyone's eyes, but that she would be the first one he'd show it to once it was.

The first.

She liked the sound of that. Liked the promise of that.

"That last sigh sounded big enough for you to float away on."

Brooke turned around to find that her father was standing right beside her, an indulgent smile on his lips. She flushed slightly. "Sorry, I wasn't even aware that I was sighing."

"You were." He nodded toward where Mark had begun setting up chairs. "Does it have anything to do with our young writer friend over there?"

She'd never managed to hide things from her father and, frankly, she never really attempted to. He wasn't just her father, but because of all the things they had in common, all the interests they shared, he was her best friend. "Maybe."

"Brooke, I like him, but I don't want you getting carried away." He knew she had a tendency to let her heart rule her head and to fall in love far too quickly, only to be disappointed.

"No carrying," she promised with a wink before she went off to join Mark.

There was a fond smile on Derek's lips as he shook his head. Brooke seemed so young, so impressionable to him. But then, he recalled, he had been even younger than Brooke when he had lost his heart for the first time.

Lost it to another man's wife.

His memory traversed the years, melting them into mists. Anna Parks had been so beautiful that day he'd first met her on the yacht and so happy to be allowed out among Parks's friends. Normally, Parks saw to it that the mother of his four children remained home while he entertained. But the man must have been feeling magnanimous that day, and Derek had been the richer for it. Because up until that moment he hadn't believed that angels could walk the earth.

He'd quickly witnessed that Parks treated his wife as if she were a pet monkey who existed solely for his entertainment. Derek's sister, Marla, who had invited him along for the outing, had told him that Parks confided to her that he had married Anna for her father's considerable fortune and for the ownership of the man's gem company.

Even back then Walter Parks had been the personification of pure ambition, looking only to further his own end. And even then he used people, especially women, to get what he wanted. Anna for her money and Marla as a way of undermining Jeremy. Derek doubted that there was an ounce of real love within the man.

Poor Jeremy.

Derek hadn't thought of his late brother-in-law in years. He suppressed a sigh as he watched his daughter with Mark. He'd been the last one to see Jeremy Carlton on this earth, he thought. He and Parks. But then, if it hadn't been for Parks, Jeremy might still be alive today.

Damn it, where had all these dark thoughts come crowding in from?

He was too young to feel this old, Derek thought. But he did, he realized the next moment. He did feel old. Worse, he felt as if all of life had somehow just managed to go on, leaving him standing behind.

Leaving him with a lovely daughter who depended on him, Derek reminded himself. He had to stop thinking as if he already had two feet in the grave. He was only forty-seven, for God sakes. Medicine being what it was these days, he could have another forty-seven years left ahead of him.

But Marla had had only fifty-five. And for Jeremy there had only been thirty-five.

The thought was sobering. He had to make the most of what there was, he told himself, which meant being there for his daughter. Like a father, not like some specter about to cross over to the other side.

He'd watched his sister being buried. That didn't mean he had to bury himself, as well.

Derek heard the door being opened behind him and he turned to see who was coming in. Several people entered the shop, all clustered around James Holden, this evening's guest reader. The author was obviously basking in all the attention he was receiving.

"Looks like our author is here," Derek called out to his daughter.

He saw her look up, smile and then go back to what she was doing. She seemed completely unaffected by the man's arrival. The last time the writer was here, he'd spent some time after the reading talking to her. Turning her head. She'd floated around for several days, until she had seen a photograph of Holden with a supermodel he was taking to some Hollywood party.

Holden was closer to his daughter's age than Mark was, but in Derek's opinion, the author was far less suitable. The serious man who had entered their lives such a short time ago seemed a far more decent sort. A man who had lived hard and still managed to come out of the fray standing up, ready to take whatever else life had to throw at him.

Mark Banning was the kind of man who could keep his daughter safe, just in case he wasn't around for the next forty-seven years. It never hurt, Derek thought, to have a plan, to be prepared.

If he'd had a plan all those years ago, things might have turned out differently. For everyone.

There was no use thinking about what might have been, he thought. There was only the present and the future to work with.

And tonight's reading, he thought as he walked over to greet Holden.

He'd watched her. All through the reading, he'd studied her, watched her react to the words the man at the podium was reciting with such passion. Brooke seemed to be transported to another place.

If he tried, he could almost visualize her as someone from the last century. She had a timelessness about her, an innocence that was sorely lacking in girls even half her age.

Damn it, now he was the one waxing poetic, Mark noticed. But it was hard not to, given the circumstances. In an effort to create an atmosphere, Derek had lowered the lights, so that all they could focus on was the author's hypnotic, deep voice as it took them on a journey into another world.

It had seemed endless, but finally the author had stopped reading. He'd thought that was the end of it, but it wasn't. There was a question-and-answer period, conducted solely, in his opinion, to further inflate the author's already overinflated ego.

He'd noticed that James Holden had attempted to make eye contact with Brooke several times during the question-and-answer period. But the dreamy expression on her face had vanished and she seemed to be Brooke again.

And her attention, he'd noted with no small satisfaction, even though he knew it shouldn't have mattered to him, had been directed toward him.

Chapter Eight

Derek paused as he came away from the front door. For a moment he watched as Mark went methodically down the rows, collapsing chairs and stacking them against the far wall.

He smiled to himself.

"You know," Derek commented, crossing to the young man and his daughter, "you help out any more around here and I might have to give serious thought to putting you on the payroll."

He had just ushered the last of the people who had attended the reading out the door. At nine-thirty the bookstore was finally closed for the night.

It had been a profitable evening for everyone. The people who had come to listen to James Holden had been given an extra bonus. The author had been in rare form tonight, offering his audience not only words from his previously published tome, but a taste of the next book, as well. The latter wasn't slated to appear on the stands for almost another three months.

It had whetted everyone's appetite. Not only had there been healthy sales of the book Holden had been scheduled to read from, but many of the people who'd attended the reading had preordered the next book, as well. Holden had been properly grateful, with just enough studied humbleness to set the hearts of his female listeners fluttering.

The only time the dark, good-looking writer hadn't been the last word in gracious smugness was when he had failed to draw Brooke's attention away from Mark. Derek noted it had put the author off, though he tried to hide it. The last time James Holden had conducted a reading here, Brooke had hung on his every word and they had gone out afterward for coffee.

His daughter had been completely taken with the man, a condition Derek knew lasted for weeks. She'd spent her days and nights waiting for the telephone to ring. It never did. His heart ached for Brooke.

That the man, who was always a promising draw at Buy the Book, had failed in his attempt to reel Brooke in tonight gave Derek a great deal of pleasure.

He knew it was due in no small part to this new writer who had happened on their horizon. So far Mark seemed like a fine, upstanding, if somewhat quiet, young man. He sincerely hoped Mark wouldn't wind up breaking Brooke's heart.

Setting the chair he was holding down against the

others he'd previously stacked, Mark glanced over his shoulder at Derek. "If I don't find any publishers for this book when I'm finished working on it, I'll keep that in mind."

"Why not now?" Brooke suggested suddenly. Both men turned to look at her. "I mean, you have to eat. Unless you've got an independent source of income," she added as the thought struck her.

"Brooke." There were times when he thought his daughter was a bit too honest, a bit too uncomplicated. "You can't ask Mark something like that." A man's business was his own. He above all people knew that. God knew he couldn't risk having someone pry into his life.

Brooke didn't see that she'd said anything really wrong. She believed in being open. Her own life was an open book and she didn't see why everyone else's couldn't be. Especially, she thought, her father's.

She secretly hoped that if she conducted herself this way, that if she got Mark to open up, as well, it might coax her father to be more open with her. She wanted him to tell her who that woman whose funeral he'd attended really was. And, more important, what that woman had meant to him and why he'd been so unlike himself since he'd received the news of her death.

Brooke flashed a smile bright enough to spread itself across both men, drawing them in, and informed her father, "I just did."

Mark shook his head. There it was again, that innocence. That innocence and honesty that made him feel so damn guilty about doing his job.

"I don't think your father's really serious," he confided to her in what was meant to be taken as a stage whisper.

Brooke raised a single slim eyebrow and looked at her father expectantly. "Dad?"

Because it meant something to her, Derek gave the comment he'd uttered in jest some serious thought now. "Well, I suppose that we could use an occasional hand with the Monday shipments."

It was their heaviest day. Monday was the day when boxes of mass-market books would arrive and he'd always have to stop Brooke from taking it upon herself to see that they were all placed on the shelves as quickly as possible.

She worked harder than any three people, putting him to shame. What was more, she seemed to thrive on constant activity.

"All right." He nodded, looking at Mark. "Maybe something could be arranged on a part-time basis—if it didn't interfere with your research."

Mark wished they'd both stop being so kind to him. He thought about the line about stealing candy from a baby. "Sounds like an offer I'm not supposed to refuse. I'll keep that in mind," he repeated evasively.

It gave him another excuse to hang around in case the one he had grew too thin. Sooner or later they were going to catch on to the fact that he wasn't a writer. Or even a lover of San Francisco the way he claimed. Something was bound to trip him up.

The next moment Mark upbraided himself. He was

thinking as if this was going to take a long time. He knew that it wasn't. He'd already satisfied himself sufficiently that this was the man Tyler had asked him to locate. What he needed now was the right moment, the right opening, to let Derek know that he knew and that someone needed him to go public.

Which meant, in turn, hurting Brooke because she would think he'd used her, the way he'd already gleaned that Holden and a few of the other authors who'd been here giving readings had used her.

They had done it to enhance their own egos. He'd done it to help him get close to her father. He sincerely doubted that she would find his reason any better than theirs. No matter how you looked at it, a wounded heart was still a wounded heart.

"But right now," Mark continued as he picked up another chair, collapsing it, "let's just keep this arrangement informal."

Brooke stepped forward, placing her hand on the same chair that he reached for. "Then you don't have to do this." She tried to take the chair away from him.

He deftly pulled the chair back, out of her reach. "You don't understand, after spending all day thinking and reading, I *need* to do something physical. It's a healthy counterbalance."

Brooke raised both hands up in surrender. "Wouldn't want to stand in the way of your counterbalance," she murmured. And then she glanced toward her father. He was definitely looking better these last few days, but right now she judged that bed would be the best place for him. "Why don't you go on home, Dad? I'll do the register and then lock up."

Derek made no attempt to hide his smile. She always could read him like a book. "I guess I am a little tired." He looked toward Mark. "Thank you again."

A chair beneath each arm, Mark merely nodded as he headed toward the back and the storeroom.

The door closed, ushering in a wave of silence and a far more intimate atmosphere than had existed just a few moments ago. As she stood there alone for a moment, it reminded her a little of the first night she'd stumbled across Mark.

Picking up a chair, Brooke followed him to the storeroom.

The area was small and, except for one small window that looked out onto a dark alley, it appeared as if it was almost completely sealed off from the world. The bulb that hung overhead should have been a higher wattage, she thought, not for the first time.

But right now she was glad that it wasn't. It made her think of the cellar of a castle. And Mark was her reluctant knight.

Setting down the chair beside the others, she caught her lower lip between her teeth. "I guess I can be a little outspoken. I'm sorry."

He glanced at her over his shoulder. She was standing too close. He looked away again, trying to sound casual and not like a man who wanted to kiss her.

"About what?"

He was just being polite now. Something else to like

about him, she thought. "I shouldn't go prying into your personal affairs."

Fighting off urges that had no business being there, it took him a second to figure out what she was talking about.

"Oh, you mean my monetary situation?" He shrugged the incident aside carelessly as he went to bring in more chairs. She followed in his wake like a sensual shadow he couldn't shake. "You meant no harm." He was beginning to doubt if she could mean anyone harm if her own life depended on it. She was the kind of woman you wanted to protect and keep safe. "And the image of the starving artist is part of society's folklore. You were just being thoughtful."

More than polite, she thought. Picking up another chair to his two, she went back into the storeroom again. "How is it that you can turn all my faults into virtues with a phrase?"

He put the chairs aside, then turned. Again, she was a hair's breadth away from him. The urge to take her into his arms grew stronger.

Mark focused on the chairs and nothing else. "Maybe because, from where I'm standing, you don't have any faults."

"Everyone has faults."

He laughed softly to himself. If she only knew.

"Believe me, anything you might consider a fault pales in comparison to what I've seen." Depositing the chairs, he went back out into the store again.

She cocked her head as she looked up at his face.

Somehow she managed to lengthen her stride and get ahead of him.

"What have you seen, Mark? Tell me about yourself. Give me details," she coaxed softly. "I don't know very much, except that you're from New York and that you like San Francisco. And to be helpful." Tactfully she omitted the fact that she also knew he was an orphan.

He'd already told her more than he ought to have. "Maybe we should leave it at that."

Ordinarily, she would have backed away. But there was something about this man, something that had been hurt and that made her want to help him heal, that wouldn't allow her to back away.

"What are you afraid of, Mark?" Her eyes were wide, innocent, as she asked to be allowed to look into his dark soul.

Feelings moved through him. She was too young and innocent for him. And his soul was decades too old for her. His life had seen to that.

"That if you knew more, you'd like me less."

She moved her head slowly from side to side, her eyes never leaving his as her silky hair softly moved against her cheeks. "Not possible."

"Why? Because you like me so little, you couldn't like me less?"

She began to protest vehemently, then realized he was teasing her. "You're playing with words."

Turning his back on her, he went out to gather more chairs. "It's what I do."

Brooke doggedly followed him. "You're a good man, Mark."

He thought of the life he'd led, the times he had come face-to-face with despair and it had almost conquered him. There'd been a time, right after Dana had terminated her life, that he had contemplated taking his own. Unable to, he'd attempted the next best thing, to be killed by some lowlife while executing the duties of his job. But he'd been disappointed even then.

Those were not the actions of the hero she was looking for. "Don't be so sure of that."

"Why?" she wanted to know, refusing to retreat. "Are you a hit man?"

"No."

Popping up like toast in front of him, she had another one for him. "A bigamist?"

The suggestion was so far from the truth, it almost made him laugh. "No."

When he turned to bring the last grouping of chairs in, she got in front of him for a third time. "Cruel to small children and medium-size animals?"

This time he did laugh. Depositing the last bunch of chairs against the wall, he looked at Brooke. "No."

Her point was made. "Okay, that qualifies you as a good man."

She was so far from right. A good man would have somehow been able to see the signs and kept Dana from taking her own life. A good man wouldn't be pretending to be something he wasn't in order to get close to a trusting man and his daughter.

His face was very, very somber as he reiterated, "You don't know anything about me."

"Then tell me," she urged again, adding quickly, "It won't change my opinion of you, but it'll satisfy my curiosity."

"Your curiosity," Mark echoed. He was accustomed to thinking of himself as a nonentity, as something that blended into the background. It seemed odd to him to have someone actually wonder about him. It gave his life depth and dimension, and he wasn't altogether sure how to feel about that. "You're curious about me."

She looked into his eyes for a long moment. "Immensely."

He supposed there was an argument for telling her things about himself. For letting her into his life, not all the way, but just enough to make her feel as if she did know him.

In a way it was manipulative of him, but she *was* asking and if he put her off, it might raise her suspicions. He didn't want that.

And if he told her lies, if he fabricated things about himself, there was a chance one of them might trip him up.

He had already told her enough lies to try to keep straight.

So he made his decision. "You want to go somewhere and get some coffee after we finish up in here?"

Happiness went through her like a rubber ball set off inside of a rubber room.

"We can get coffee here after I finish with the register," she told him, already walking to the front counter. "I can brew a fresh pot." She'd turned the coffeemaker off for the night and had cleaned it out, but it would take nothing to start it again. "We don't have to go anywhere else if you don't feel like it."

"No sense in wasting a whole pot," he told her. He closed the door to the storeroom, locking it with the key she'd given him earlier. He crossed to her and handed the key back to her. "We'll go out."

She was hardly aware of putting the key back in the drawer. Their first date, she thought. Unofficial and last minute, but it was still a date. She'd always loved spontaneity.

On automatic pilot, Brooke went about the business of shutting down the register. Her mind was elsewhere.

There was something very romantic about being swept away by the moment. Just as she had been when she'd kissed him, she thought. It would have been nice to have had him make the first move, but she didn't regret what she did for one second.

It felt as if she'd been born in that small instance. As if everything else she'd experienced had just been marking time until that moment.

Looking back, it had been a little like Sleeping Beauty or Snow White, she mused, writing down the total sales for the day, waiting for true love's first kiss. She was too old to believe in fairy tales, but not too old, she thought, slanting a glance toward Mark, to believe in the existence of Prince Charming.

That described Mark Banning to a T. A little scarred, a little world weary, but Prince Charming nonetheless.

And for the moment he was hers.

The small coffee shop he took her to was doing brisk business, despite the hour and the fact that it was a weekday and the next morning stood waiting in the wings with all that that entailed. It took a while before they finally got their order.

Brooke didn't mind standing in line with Mark, didn't mind waiting on the side until the order was filled. She wouldn't have minded standing anywhere, as long as it was with him.

The day had been hot. Evening brought with it a slight lessening in the sticky humidity, but the air still moved as if it had been soaked in warm molasses.

She thrilled to the feel of his hand against the small of her back as he guided her to a table for two just outside the coffee shop's front doors.

"I'd have thought there wouldn't be so many people drinking coffee this time of night." She could feel her heart all but jumping at his touch and tried very hard to keep her voice steady. "I guess it's never too late for trendy coffee."

He nodded his head in response, and she wondered if perhaps he was regretting agreeing to come out like this. She should have gone with her first instincts and just made coffee at the shop.

Sitting down, she looked at him, waiting until he

took his seat. She didn't want to lose the moment, didn't care what he talked about, as long as he talked.

"So," she began, leaning forward, "what did you think of Holden?"

The hazy air had shifted, moving in his direction. He could just detect a whiff of her perfume. Didn't things like that have a time limit? Weren't they supposed to fade after a few hours? He could swear that he'd been breathing in the light scent all day, and at this point, he was dangerously on overload.

Dangerously at the point where reason was slipping into the shadows, deserting him.

He picked up his cup with both hands and concentrated on her questions, not on what he wanted to do. "It was entertaining."

She laughed and he looked at her. "You hated him, didn't you?"

For an innocent she could be very intuitive. "*Hate* is a little strong."

She cocked her head, her hair sweeping along her shoulder. He held on to his cup a little tighter. "Disliked a lot?"

He shrugged and took a sip. Bypassing the trendy coffee, he'd ordered espresso. As if sitting beside her wasn't enough of an adrenaline kick. "He wasn't worth the effort for emotion."

She liked the sound of that. Liked what it said. In a way he'd succeeded in neatly putting the author in his place.

"I guess you're right. Although I'm sure he thinks so."

He had a hunch that she knew that for a firsthand

fact, but said nothing on the subject. Instead he took another sip of his coffee, then said, "And he seems to have a lot of the audience buying into it, as well."

Almost all of the audience had been comprised of women, a good many over the age of forty. She supposed that was one of the reasons Holden had played up to her in the beginning. She was always the youngest in the room. That made her a clean slate, as he liked to say, for him to write on.

But not anymore, Brooke thought with the kind of triumph one felt at finally getting rid of a bad habit.

"But not you." It wasn't a guess. Brooke was sure of it.

She was waiting for an answer. He tried to think of one that was suitable for the man he was pretending to be. Reading had not been a priority for him for a very long time, but he tried to recall the kind of thing that had once held his interest.

"I like my prose grittier. More real and less introspective."

"Why?" The question surprised him. And the look in her eyes as she leaned her chin against her hand held him captive. "What are you afraid you'll see if you look inside?"

"Everything I've lived through so far." He could see the eager look that came into her eyes. She was a romantic, through and through. He didn't want her romanticizing him. It just made things worse. "It's not poetic or particularly tragic." He had a feeling that was the way her mind worked. "It's just my life."

Like someone diving into icy water, she held her breath and plunged in.

"And you were going to open a tiny window into it tonight." Pressing her lips together, she started him off. "You already told me that you were an orphan by the time you were ten. Was it terrible, living in foster homes all that time?"

Yes, it was terrible, he thought. He'd spent the next eight years living out of a suitcase, ready to leave at a moment's notice if there was the slightest change in the situation. He learned early on that his own behavior didn't affect things greatly. Trying hard didn't help, so he'd stopped trying.

But he didn't want to get into that. Still, she was waiting for something, so he gave her a small piece. "I never got over the feeling that I didn't belong."

She drew her own conclusions. "So no one adopted you."

There'd been one couple, a couple he'd liked, and they had been close to putting through the paperwork. They'd been childless for ten years and had all but given up. He'd thought he'd found a home, but then the woman had gotten pregnant and he was once again sent to another foster home, to begin the process of going from stranger to stranger all over again.

He shook his head and said simply, "No." That covered it, he thought.

"And what did you do after you turned eighteen?"

What had he done, he thought, turning her question over in his mind. He'd gone to work, started attending

CCNY and kept his eye out on his brother, waiting for Nick to turn eighteen so that his brother could come and live with him.

"I started my life," he told her.

Chapter Nine

He'd started his life.

She knew Mark's pronouncement was meant to cut her off, to put an end to that line of conversation. But she was nothing if not persistent.

The noise around them, as customers entered and left the café, grew in volume. Brooke found she either had to raise her voice or lean in, in order to be heard. She leaned in.

"By doing what?" she prodded. "Did you start writing right away? Or was that something you started slowly, after you tried other things?"

He stuck with the truth. "It's a relatively new calling."

She judged him to be in his late twenties, maybe even thirty. That left a lot of time unaccounted for. "What did you do before then?"

"I was a cop."

She'd all but had to read his lips. The information, delivered quietly and without ceremony, caught her totally by surprise. But only for an instant. The moment she thought about it, being a policeman was the kind of thing she could easily visualize him doing. It went with her image of him: a protector. After all, a knight had been the policeman of his day.

The noise from the street and the shop directly behind them increased. Brooke moved her chair in closer to him. Their knees were now touching. The contact sent a small, delicious shiver through her.

"Is that how you got your scar?"

She saw him stiffen slightly. "Yes." It was dark enough that she couldn't read his eyes. "You're just full of questions, aren't you?"

Rather than take offense, she smiled at him brightly. "That's how you learn things."

In response, she saw him drain his coffee and set the cup down. It was a signal to leave. But she wasn't ready to go just yet.

Stubbornly Brooke dug in. "You know," she told him softly, "it's really not as bad as you think it is."

To prove her point, her eyes on his, she lightly glided her fingertips just beneath the scar.

He jerked his head back as if she'd touched him with a hot poker. The look in his eyes warned her off, but she refused to listen. He was a soul in pain and she wanted to help him.

"Actually," she went on, "it transforms you into a rather romantic figure."

He didn't know if she was just being incredibly naive or incredibly kind. In either case, if she'd chosen him to have romantic fantasies about, she'd chosen poorly.

When she reached for him again, he closed his hand around hers, pushing it back down to the table. Mark's voice was dark, low.

"I appreciate what you're trying to do, Brooke, but this is the real world. You have no idea what you're getting yourself into." His eyes told her to back off. "You don't know who I am."

And he wasn't about to tell her, she thought. All right, so be it. That wasn't the point anymore. He needed to be reached more than she needed details. "I know you're a good man."

Mark laughed shortly. She just didn't give up, did she? "And how do you know that?"

Her expression was completely guileless. So guileless he found himself struggling against the temptation of leaning across the tiny table and kissing her. "Instincts."

"Instincts." What kind of instincts could a sheltered twenty-three-year-old have? It took effort to keep the mocking tone from his voice. "And these instincts, they've been infallible up to now?"

She knew what he was saying to her. That she really hadn't lived yet, not the way he had. That she had no experiences to draw on. But you didn't have to take up residence in hell to know you didn't want to be there. And now, looking back at the other men who had captured her fancy, she realized that they had all been shallow. Not like Mark.

What she felt about him, for him, was different. *He* was different. "They're getting better all the time."

He needed to get her to back away before his own resolve crumbled. Before he gave in and allowed himself to get lost in the look in her eyes. Without preamble, he said, "I was married."

She'd thought of him as a free spirit. Free spirits remained unattached. Brooke picked up on the key word. "Was?"

Mark studied his hands, trying to divorce himself from what he was saying. "She died."

Brooke felt a lump growing in her throat. The romantic way she perceived him only became more enhanced. "Oh, Mark, I'm so sorry."

He saw the sympathy in her eyes. And something more. He realized he'd only succeeded in bringing her closer to him, not further away.

She needed to hear the full story.

Mark braced himself. Dana's death wasn't something he talked about, wasn't even something he allowed himself to think about. But maybe if Brooke heard, she'd stop thinking of him as some kind of romantic hero and see him for what he was: a man she should want no part of.

"I met Dana in college. She was everything I wasn't. Bright, outgoing, stunningly beautiful." As he said the words, he could almost see Dana, the way she had once been. He found it difficult to continue. "And she wanted to be an actress. After graduation, we got married.

"I joined the police force and she set about making her dream come true. Except that it didn't." He set his mouth grimly. "When she'd started out, Dana had been so incredibly full of hope. She was so sure she was going to make it. At first, she got a couple of jobs, but then nothing." He sighed. Looking back, the signs had all been there. But he'd been blind to them. Blind to everything except the vision of life the way he'd hoped it would someday be. "With each rejection, she withdrew a little more."

His voice became bitter. "I was so busy trying to make a difference out on the street, trying to make detective, putting in overtime so that she could have those new clothes for those auditions that didn't pan out, I never saw it."

Something cold and sharp slithered across her heart. Her eyes never left his face. "It?"

Mark barely nodded in response. "The way Dana was deteriorating. The way it became harder and harder to reach her, to communicate. There were crying jags. When she wouldn't talk, I left her alone and didn't think anything of it. Nobody likes being rejected, I thought she was just being moody." His expression grew dark, unreadable. "And then one night, I came home to find her. She was in the bathtub."

He realized that Brooke had taken his hand, her fingers curling around his. The slight pressure was meant to somehow give him the strength to get through his narrative. Something nudged at his heart, but he refused to acknowledge it. Not while he was talking about Dana's suicide.

"The water was red." If he closed his eyes, he could

still see it, that horrible off-color red permeating everything within the tub. Leaving a thin layer on Dana. "She'd slashed her wrists." Mark paused, trying to work his way through the pain he felt. He looked up at her. "There was nothing I could do. I couldn't bring her around. She was already dead."

Words seemed so inadequate. Brooke tried, anyway. "Oh, Mark, I am so, so sorry."

An ironic smile twisted his lips. "That's what she said." He saw the confused look on Brooke's face. "In the note she left. Just that—'Mark, I'm sorry.'" The sigh caught in his raw throat. He shook his head. "I was the one who had to be sorry. I never saw it coming. I should have paid more attention."

She realized what he was saying. He blamed himself. That was so like the man she was coming to know. "It's not your fault." She said the words so firmly, he looked at her. "You can't blame yourself."

Who else could he blame? The producers who hadn't wanted her? The directors who always wanted someone else? No, he knew where the blame could squarely be placed. On the doorstep of the man who should have been looking out for her. Who should have taken care of her. "I was her husband."

"Right, her husband, not her keeper," Brooke insisted. He couldn't do this to himself, she thought. If he didn't let go of the guilt, it would eventually destroy him. Suddenly her mission in life gained a new focus, to save him. "Every person is responsible for themselves." As he looked at her in silence, she crawled out further on the shaky limb. "I'm sorry, maybe this sounds cruel, but she let herself get that way. She was the one who gave up. You had nothing to do with it. You didn't beat her, didn't imprison her, didn't demand that she remain at your side, barefoot and pregnant—"

She was making a hell of a lot of assumptions. "How do you know that?"

For a second he'd taken some of the wind out of her sails. She rallied, looking at him unabashedly.

"Because I just do. You're not that kind of person." She saw him start to protest. She had no idea how she knew what she knew, but she did. She was that sure of him. "You're not the kind of person who would force his will on someone else."

Mark didn't think he'd ever been as innocent as Brooke, not even when he was a young boy and had thought himself invincible. "You're romanticizing again. You've known me for less than a month—"

She knew what was coming and cut him off. "For some people, an entire lifetime isn't enough, for others it only takes a few days, hours, maybe even moments."

He laughed and shook his head. There was almost something endearing about how she saw the world. If only it were that way.

"Now you really are romanticizing."

Crossing her arms before her, she looked at him, completely convinced of her stand. "You haven't told me anything to make me change my mind."

He had a feeling that she could probably argue until Gabriel sounded his horn, signaling the end of the world. He didn't have that much time. "You finished?" He nodded at her cup.

It was empty. She hadn't even realized that she'd drained the last drop. All of her attention had been focused on him. And she had a feeling that he wasn't asking strictly about the coffee. But for now she relented. "I guess I am."

He rose, then leaned over the small table and helped her with her chair. "Then I'll take you home."

Standing beside him just before they made their way out to the street proper, she turned her face up to his. "Take me to *your* home."

The softly spoken entreaty moved along his skin like early-morning mist. If only things were that simple, he thought again.

He took her arm and guided her around the scattered tables, beyond the two-foot wrought-iron fencing, out onto the sidewalk. When she turned to look at him, his smile was small, tolerant and genuine. "You don't know what you're asking for."

"Yes, I do. I want to see how you live." She knew what he was thinking. "We're adults, Mark."

The car was parked more than a block away. Finding a spot that close to the coffee shop had been nothing short of a miracle. He began to escort her toward it. "Some of us have been there longer than others."

She laughed. "Residency doesn't count." She felt comfortable with him. Safe. Yet very excited. "I know you're not going to jump me the minute we walk into the apartment."

"Maybe not," he allowed. Then the barest hint of a twinkle entered his eyes as he looked down at her face. "But you might jump me."

"Only if you play your cards right," Brooke teased. And then she added a tad more seriously, "Please? After that coffee, I feel completely wired, and I don't want to go home yet."

The last place he wanted to take her was his apartment. Out here he couldn't act on what he was feeling. If they were alone together...well, he just didn't want to put himself in that kind of a situation. "Then, we'll go for a drive."

They were approaching his car. She had a feeling a drive would quickly turn into a drive to her house. Holding on to his arm, she turned her face up to his. "I'd rather go for a walk."

He felt himself weakening. "I had no idea you were this contrary."

"Surprise."

He paused beside his car, debating. He supposed it wouldn't do any harm to indulge her a little. And there was no denying that he liked being with her. These were the best of circumstances.

"All right, a walk then. But a short one." He saw her opening her mouth to protest. He cut her off. "Take it or leave it."

She knew when she was outmaneuvered. With a surrendering shrug, she said, "I'll take it."

Her arm tucked through his, they walked along one of the city's busier streets. As a concession, she searched for a neutral topic and talked about the new rare first edition of Mark Twain's *A Connecticut Yankee in King Arthur's Court* her father had uncovered several months ago at an estate sale in Maryland.

"You just never know where the next treasure might turn up," she told him.

No, he thought, looking at her, *you just never did.*

He found that he was having difficulty drawing in a lungful of air. Rather than cooling off, the night seemed to be getting balmier. He felt he could almost touch the air around them.

They'd gone about three blocks when a sudden shower came from nowhere, falling hard, the drops sizzling against the hot pavement. Brooke squealed. When he looked at her, he expected her to be annoyed. Dana had hated it when her hair was mussed, but Brooke was laughing.

Looking around for shelter, he almost hurried her into the first store front he saw, but then he spotted something better three doors down. It was a bakery. The store itself was closed, but whoever had locked up had forgotten to retract the green-and-white awning. It provided the perfect shelter.

Mark grabbed her hand and made a run for it.

Once beneath the awning, Brooke all but collapsed, laughing. She huddled against him, drenched even though the shower had only begun minutes ago.

"Nothing like a little hot rain to perk you up," she told him.

Her hair was plastered against her face, even her

eyelashes were wet. Mark tried to remember when he'd seen something so beautiful and couldn't. Feeling clumsy, unable to help himself, he pushed her hair away from her cheeks.

"See, I told you I should have taken you home."

But she shook her head. She didn't regret begging to stay. "This is more fun."

He raised an eyebrow. She certainly was different from his late wife. "Getting drenched?"

"No, running through the summer rain." The street lamp illuminated the laughter in her eyes as she looked up at him. "It's all in how you look at things."

He supposed it was.

And right now he was looking at her the way he knew he shouldn't. The way he hadn't looked at another woman since Dana.

He'd never thought that he would ever feel anything again, except rage. Even things like hunger, exhaustion were reactions that he was only vaguely aware of, like a distant itch felt along skin whose nerve endings had been severed. There was only the mildest of sensations.

But being with this woman, who was everything he was not, everything he had never been, made him aware that he was still breathing, still alive.

Still a man.

Without thinking, Mark stopped brushing back her hair with his fingertips and framed her face instead. His heart pounding in his chest, his common sense struggling to regain its lost control over him, he brought his mouth down to hers and kissed her.

The moment he did, everything else faded away.

There was only her, only Brooke.

Only the life-affirming reality of her. If she was surprised by the kiss, she gave him no indication. Instead she leaned her body into his, igniting flames through all of him.

He kissed her because he had no choice in the matter. He kissed her because to not do so meant the last tiny spark within him was going to be forever extinguished, taking all that he was along with it.

Her soft curves yielded against him, hardening him. Making him want her the way he knew he couldn't have her. It was a line in the deception he just couldn't afford to cross.

No matter how much his body begged him to.

Brooke knew he wanted her. Knew it! He wanted her. But no more than she wanted him.

This felt so right, so wonderful.

The hot wind drove the rain beneath the awning, wetting them further. She didn't notice. Pushing herself up on her toes, Brooke pressed her mouth harder against his. Fell deeper into the kiss. She dug her fingers into his hair, glorying in the way it felt.

This was the man.

The thought throbbed in her brain. This was the man she wanted to spend forever with. Never mind that she was young and inexperienced. Never mind that some people spent a lifetime looking for their soul mate, never to find them. She had found hers.

She knew her heart, knew that this was no mistake.

Everything else that had come before had been just a dry run, a rehearsal, for this. To prepare her for this. Because she knew that it wasn't going to be easy. Mark Banning wasn't a romantic extension of her daydreams, he was a real man and real men never made life easy. She didn't care. She was ready.

From this moment forward, she belonged to him. The hard part was going to be in getting him to want to belong to her.

Mark felt urges plunging through him, demanding attention. With the inner strength that arose from diligent self-discipline and denial, he pulled himself away from the situation. As gently as he could, he pushed her away from him.

The air he tried to draw into his lungs felt heavy. It did nothing to help him gain his bearings. Neither did holding her, so he stopped.

It wasn't easy.

It didn't help.

Neither did looking down into her smile. He struggled against the urge to seal its imprint into his soul.

She blew out a breath, waiting for her pulse to settle down. "I think we just dried our clothes."

"I'm surprised we didn't set the bakery on fire." He glanced back at the store as if to make sure they hadn't. Even with Dana, he'd never felt this kind of mind-numbing reaction.

That was because Brooke represented forbidden fruit, he told himself. If this moment wasn't wrapped up in lies, then perhaps he would have reacted differently to her.

The excuse he gave himself was just another lie that joined the others.

Just as abruptly as the shower had begun, it stopped. Mark put his hand out, but no drops fell to meet his upturned palm. He took hold of her arm. The sooner he got her beneath her father's roof, the better.

"We'd better take advantage of the break and get back to the car. I need to take you home."

She nodded her head solemnly, knowing that there was no room for wordplay this time. He was taking her to her home. She would have been lying if she hadn't admitted, at least to herself, that what had just happened had shaken her up a bit. But it had also made her aware that the next time—and there was going to be a next time—it would end differently. They were going to be together.

"Progress," she murmured as she linked her arm through his.

Venturing out from beneath the awning, he spared her a glance. He wasn't sure if he had heard her correctly. "What?"

"Progress," she repeated. When the confusion didn't leave his features, she explained, "This time you didn't apologize."

There was a reason for that. "You would only talk me out of it."

Her eyes crinkled into her smile. "See, you're getting to know me, too."

This couldn't be allowed to continue. Not when there was a very real and present danger of his forgetting every single professional ethic he had ever taught himself. He had no right to do that to her. Abruptly, he stopped walking and took hold of her shoulders, his expression deadly serious.

"Brooke, listen to me. There are things about me I can't tell you." At least, he added silently, not yet. "I'm not some romantic figure in a two-hundred-year-old book. I'm not one of those authors your father has at the shop."

Her eyes were wide as she looked up at him, innocent and yet somehow oddly knowing. "I know."

He sighed, shaking his head. "Nothing can happen between us."

Her smile was unnervingly serene. "But it already has."

He had no way of arguing that. Because, in his heart, whether he willingly admitted it to himself or not, he knew she was right.

Chapter Ten

He felt like a family friend.

He felt like a traitor.

He'd been a private investigator for five years now and in all that time, Mark could not remember ever being this ambivalent about a case before.

Of course, always before he'd either dealt with out-and-out criminals, like the time he'd gone undercover within a client's company to discover which of the man's employees was embezzling funds from him, or he was just tracking down missing persons. In the latter scenario, he'd never had to get under a so-called missing person's skin before. Never tried to gain that person's complete confidence. In every instance, once the party was located, that was that. He would hand over the information and leave it to his client to approach the person in whatever manner they felt was right.

But this was different. This meant at least pretending to get involved. And somewhere along the line the pretense had become real. He'd gotten involved. Too involved.

Mark stood in front of the mirror over the bureau, wearing the jacket he put on when the situation required something more formal than just the workshirts and jeans he favored.

He didn't see the navy sports jacket, or the light-blue shirt, or the crisply pressed—thanks to the dry-cleaning shop down the block—light-gray pair of pants. He saw the scar. For a while as he grew used to it, the angry red welt had begun to fade. Over time it had almost seemed to become smaller to him until he barely noticed it at all.

But now he felt as if the scar was taking over his entire face.

Like the portrait hidden in Dorian Gray's attic, he thought, that wound up taking on the outward signs of the evil that its namesake was committing over the years.

To the casual observer, it didn't appear as if he was doing anything "evil," he told himself. He was getting paid to help Tyler Carlton claim his birthright and avenge his mother's honor in the bargain. He opened a drawer and took out his tie, the same tie he'd worn to dinner that first night.

He knew where Tyler was coming from. God knew

if there'd been a way he could have avenged his own parents' death, especially his mother's, he would have gladly done it.

But when he'd taken on this case, he hadn't thought about the fact that there might be trusts that would have to be forged and then broken. That was what he was faced with now; that was what was chafing so badly at his conscience. Within a relatively short amount of time, Derek Ross had taken to him as if he were some long-lost son.

And Brooke—well, Brooke looked at him as if he were her knight in shining armor, come to rescue her from the tower so that they could live happily ever after.

Mark stopped trying to knot his tie and stared into the mirror.

If only.

But he knew there was no happily ever after in the offing. There was no happily now, either. Except for the few moments when he forgot who and what he was, what he was about, and focused only on the way she laughed. On the way the light in every room she entered seemed to gather around her and make love to her. The way it lightly slid along her skin, the way it got caught up in her hair, adding highlights to the rich blue-black color.

Mark stopped abruptly. He wasn't helping his case any.

Or this stupid tie.

With an impatient tug, he pulled off the tie he was vainly attempting to knot, then just said the hell with it. Balling it up, he shoved it back into the drawer and slammed it shut.

He blew out a long breath and reined his emotions in. He couldn't afford to go off like this. The second she saw him, Brooke would know there was something wrong and then he'd be subjected to endless questions. The woman would have made one hell of an interrogator, he thought.

What would she have said if she knew that when he'd slipped out of the shop today at one, he hadn't been going to some mysterious appointment, but to her house? To let himself stealthily in through the back door and methodically go through Derek's things, looking for that one last bit of proof that would seal things as to his identity?

He'd found it, too. After going through the man's things, he'd found the photograph hidden in one of the man's beloved old first editions. The same photograph that Tyler had given him. It was of Derek and his sister taken a quarter of a century ago.

He'd put it back, but seeing it was enough. Now there was no room for doubt. He hadn't told Tyler about it, but he would have to. Soon.

The guilt didn't go, but at least he felt a little calmer. Squaring his shoulders, he walked out of his apartment. He was supposed to be picking up Derek and Brooke within the hour. There was a gallery opening he'd promised to attend with them.

But when he arrived, only one of the two was ready. Derek greeted him at the door, wearing a comfortable-looking old sweater whose hem had come unraveled on one side and slacks that looked more appropriate to puttering around in his garden, coaxing flowers to blossom than for a gallery opening.

"Am I too early?" Mark asked. He could have sworn the man said to come at seven-thirty. He'd pulled up in front of the house at seven-twenty-five, then waited five minutes.

"No, you're right on time," Derek assured him. "But I'm afraid I won't be going with you."

Mark's next question faded into oblivion because Brooke came down the stairs just then. She was wearing a black cocktail dress that trailed after her in the back, but was cut high in the front, displaying legs that would have made a dancer envious. Her hair was artfully piled up on her head, making her look hopelessly sexy and far older than her years.

He was a dead man, Mark thought.

The next moment he forced his attention back to Derek. The last thing he wanted to do was be alone with Brooke, especially when she looked like every man's fantasy come true. "Are you sure you can't go?"

"You look lovely, Brooke." Derek turned from his daughter and shook his head as he looked at him. "I'm afraid that I'm really not feeling very well."

Just a hint of concern entered Brooke's eyes, doing battle with indecision. "Maybe I should stay home, too, then, Dad. Take care of you." She started to shed the shawl she'd thrown about her shoulders.

Derek was quick to move the shawl back into place.

"No, no, I'll be fine, really. This passes," he assured her. "I'd feel worse if I knew I was responsible for the two of you missing out on Waller's show. Go, have a good time. For all three of us." A hand firmly on each of their elbows, Derek ushered the younger people across the threshold.

Brooke pressed her lips together. Mark had the vague impression that she was trying to stifle a laugh.

"If you're sure..." she was saying.

"I'm positive," Derek told her. "Now go."

With that, the door was suddenly closed, leaving them standing on the doorstep.

Not trusting himself to touch her, Mark shoved his hands into his pockets and led the way to the car he'd parked in the driveway.

"I'm sorry about that," Brooke apologized as she fell into step beside him.

Mark nodded his head. "Yeah, it's a shame your father can't come with us."

He was surprised to hear a laugh escape her lips. "I mean about the setup."

He opened the passenger door for her, but was careful not to take her hand. "Setup?"

"Yes, my father thinks he's playing Cupid. He's not sick." Wrapping the shawl a little more tightly around her shoulders, she got into the car. "He just wants us to go out together, and I'm afraid he's being very, very obvious."

"Not that obvious," Mark admitted, closing her door for her. "I bought it."

To which Brooke could only shake her head. Men could be so dense sometimes. "Like I said the other day, you're very sweet."

He really didn't know about that.

Champagne was not his drink of choice, but he'd been nursing the contents of the flute for the past hour or so. Mark looked around the small, packed gallery with its illusion of space and intellect.

It seemed longer.

He touched the rim to his lips, pretending to take a sip. There was no doubt about it. He felt out of his element here, the way he had whenever Dana had made him attend one of those gatherings of "creative people" as she liked to refer to them, where everyone else was talking about technique and motivation and things that he couldn't begin to fathom.

It was a little like being in a completely foreign country.

They'd come to a new showing of someone named Waller Kerr, an artist of some renown if he was to believe the flyers put out by the gallery owner. It could have been an exhibition put on by a plumber for all he knew. But for Brooke's sake he made the appropriate noises and, for the most part, faded into the background. It was what he was good at. Observing.

Brooke, on the other hand, was very good at being, if not center stage, then stage left or stage right. She seemed to know half the people at the gallery. At least, it appeared that half the people there extended greetings her way.

Or maybe they just wanted to know her, he thought, allowing himself to once again take in the way she looked in her dress.

When she turned her head in his direction, he pretended to be studying the painting directly in front of him.

He had no idea what he was looking at.

Excusing herself from the man who was talking to her, Brooke crossed the small distance to Mark. She stood beside him for a moment, watching him take in the painting, then inclined her head toward him, her voice low so that only he could hear.

"You don't like this very much, do you?"

It was a large, rectangular canvas that seemed angry at the metallic dots that were spread over it like a horde of incoming warrior ants. "I might if I could understand what it was supposed to be."

"What do you think it is?"

He said the first thing that had come to mind when he'd seen it. "Someone drying off their paint brush by flicking it across the canvas."

She hid her mouth behind her hands, but he could tell she was laughing. Holding on to his shoulder, she rose on her toes and whispered, "Me, too," in his ear. Then, withdrawing her hand slowly, she said, "I've had enough, how about you?"

"Don't have to ask me twice." And then he stopped. Everything he'd learned about her told him she loved these kind of things. "You're doing this because you think I'm bored, aren't you?"

"No, I'm doing this because I *know* you're bored. But that's all right," she assured him, "it's not like this is my very first gallery opening." She took his hand and began to thread her way to the front entrance. It wasn't easy. "I've been to dozens. Dad likes to make sure I have a steady exposure to culture, and between the gallery shows and the readings at the store, I say I'm probably set through the next decade."

He was reluctant to take her away. "So you don't mind leaving?"

"I'd mind staying, knowing you were counting the moments to your escape."

For a moment she stopped and looked around for the gallery owner. It would be polite to bid the woman good-night, but at the moment she was unavailable. The owner of the trendy gallery appeared to be deeply embroiled in a conversation with one of the more affluent patrons. Diamonds were winking on both hands as gestures were being exchanged.

"Wanda's probably trying to haggle up the price," Brooke mused. Making up her mind, she forged ahead. "Let's go."

Leaving the shelter of the air-conditioned gallery was a shock to the system, but their successfully executed getaway was a relief to the soul as far as he was concerned.

For San Francisco, the streets appeared to be fairly empty. He placed his hand against the small of her back, guiding Brooke into the parking structure where he'd left his car.

"Your father might be disappointed if I take you home this early."

Her heels clicked rapidly along the concrete as she hurried beside him to the vehicle. "There's a solution for that." Stopping beside his car, she waited for him to unlock it. "Don't take me home. Not yet," she tagged on.

Mark said nothing in response.

Buckling up, Brooke waited until he had rounded the hood and gotten in on his side before making another stab at conversation. She changed topics. "So, how's the book coming along?"

This topic made him no more comfortable than the last one did. "It still has a long way to go," he told her evasively.

It was exciting to her to be there at what seemed like the beginning of the process. "Have you found a focus for it yet?"

Mark slowly began to inch his way out of the bowels of the structure.

"I thought I did, but..."

He let his voice trail off as he shook his head. He figured the less he talked about his excuse for being at the shop, the less there was to trip him up. This would all be over with soon. He had his proof, what he was still looking for was his opening.

She settled back in her seat, hoping she didn't appear as nervous to him as she was. She was still hoping that he would take her to his apartment.

"I'm sure it'll come to you," she told him with confidence. "And, if you need a fresh pair of eyes, I've got two at your disposal."

"I'll keep that in mind." He eased the car out of the half-filled parking structure and up onto the street level. He'd come out on the side that gave him the option of going left or right. Back to Mill Valley. Or his place.

The latter shouldn't have even been a consideration, he told himself. And yet he couldn't quite get himself to bank down the desire. "So, where do you want to go?"

She looked at him, the answer in her eyes if not on her lips. "I'll let you choose."

If he had half a brain in his head, he'd take her to another coffee shop, or for a long stroll. Anything but to where he was thinking. "When do these things normally end?"

She glanced at her watch. "We've got at least two hours before we would be labeled one of the early departees. Three, four hours if we want to seem decadently carefree." This time the smile she gave him was slow as it filtered its way to her lips and into his soul.

For a second, as his breath caught in his throat, it felt as if the world stood still. It wasn't until he heard someone beep a horn behind him that he realized he'd allowed his mind to wander. In fields he had no business trespassing.

Making a quick decision, he turned right. "And why," he asked, playing along for the moment, "would we want to be decadent?"

She shrugged, her shawl slipping from her shoulder.

She left it there. "I don't know. You're a writer, we just came from a gallery opening, it seemed like the word to use."

She was letting her imagination run away with her, he thought. "I'm a nonfiction writer," he reminded her. Decadence didn't enter into that world.

Brooke seemed to weigh his protest. "Maybe that's the problem. Maybe you need a little fiction in your life."

She'd lost him. "Come again?"

She dug into her subject with enthusiasm. "Maybe you need to pretend that you're this gay—"

His mouth dropped opened. "What?"

"Sorry, I'm old-fashioned, I meant happy. You need to pretend you're this happy-go-lucky guy without a care in the world. Someone who lives just for the day. The moment," she amended. She twisted in her seat, hampered somewhat by the seat belt that insisted on executing a death grip on her. "If you could be that guy, what would you do? Right at this moment, what would you do? Where would you go?"

All right, what was the harm? He supposed he could indulge her and pretend. As long as it was only for the moment. "I'd take the most beautiful girl at the opening to my apartment."

Her mouth suddenly felt dry. Beautiful. He'd called her beautiful. "Fine. Except there's one thing wrong with that."

Well, at least one of them had sense, he thought, relieved. "What?"

"You said girl. You meant woman. The most beautiful woman at the opening."

The smile he gave her was indulgent. She could feel herself balking. She wanted him to think of her as a woman, not a child.

"You're twenty-three."

"And at the turn of the last century," she said, "I would have been thought of as some lamentably poor spinster. At twenty-three I wouldn't be a woman, I'd be an old woman, over the hill, someone the other women would talk about behind their fans and pity." She smiled at him brightly as they came to a stop at a light. "Which means that for this century, I'm just right."

He laughed softly as he shook his head. By now he should have learned. "Anyone ever win an argument with you?"

"Not that I recall." She looked at him for a long moment, her heart suddenly climbing up into her throat. "Play your cards right and you might be the first," she whispered.

Again he found himself a prisoner of her eyes, of the moment. And again someone leaned on their horn behind him, breaking the spell.

Coming to, he drove through the intersection just as the yellow light turned red again. He could almost hear the man in the car behind him cursing.

"You know, this keeps up, I'm going to wind up with a ticket tonight because of you."

He glanced at her as he heard her laugh. "I'm not

sure, but I think that's one of the nicest compliments I've ever gotten."

Against what he would have, until recently, termed his better judgment, he took Brooke to his apartment. After he parked the car in the street, he led her into the venerable old brick structure and then pointed out the stairs to his second-floor apartment. The building had no elevator. Until just now, he hadn't given that much thought.

Following her up, watching the way her hips swayed with each step, he began to rethink the wisdom of bringing her here.

He told himself he did it so that he couldn't arouse her suspicions by repeatedly putting her off. A part of him had even been prepared for this. He'd gone through his apartment and hidden everything that might have given away his true purpose for being at her father's bookstore.

"It's not much," he warned her, unlocking the door.

Brooke walked in ahead of him. She moved about the small living room slowly, like a detective absorbing the scene of the crime, he thought, watching her.

And then, as if she'd made her decision about the apartment, she turned toward him. "Your friend, you said he's an actor?"

"Yes. He's been cast in a television pilot shooting in Canada." He'd read a story in the Sunday entertainment section about a new series that was about to begin filming in Canada because of the reduced production costs. It sounded plausible enough.

"He's very self-contained for an actor."

He felt as if he was treading on shaky ground, trying to avoid quicksand. "What do you mean?"

Glancing around the corner, she saw a small kitchenette. "Well, outside of the appliances, there doesn't seem to be anything that shows he lives here." She indicated the near-empty shelves and the nude walls. "No books on the theater. No photographs of productions he's been in."

That was a mistake, but since there really was no friend, there was nothing he could have done about it—other than have given this phantom a different occupation to begin with. "He's a minimalist."

She seemed perfectly willing to accept the excuse. "Oh. Like you." She crossed back to him. "Is that why the two of you hit it off?"

"I don't know about 'hit it off.'" He didn't want to have to go into any elaborate fabrications about a friendship. This was already beginning to trip him up. "I met him in New York. He knew my wife."

Something tightened within her when she heard him refer to the woman. Jealousy? She wasn't sure. If it was, it wasn't the kind of green-eyed monster she'd heard about, merely envy that someone had won his heart and now he kept it on ice. Out of reach.

"I see." She turned around. "And you ran into him out here?"

"Yes. No." He should have had a story more securely in place. Another oversight. But as he tried to think, nothing came to mind. Why was he blanking out like this? Why did the room seem smaller, more intimate, now than it did when he was in it by himself? "Look, I really don't want to talk about him or the past."

"Fine."

She turned so that she was before him, her body a whisper away. Her dress brushed against his arm. He could feel his body heating as he just stood there, looking at her, letting his mind entertain thoughts it shouldn't have.

When had he turned down this road? When had desires suddenly risen up and seized him by the throat, demanding release?

Her eyes rose to meet his. Her breath felt like seduction along her skin. "What do you want to do?" she asked softly.

Chapter Eleven

Mark didn't remember taking her into his arms.

One moment he was envisioning holding Brooke, the next, she was there. Giving, supple, breaking down his walls of defense faster than if it had been created completely out of ice and she was a tropical heat wave sweeping over him.

The walls buckled, melting in her path until they evaporated, leaving only puddles behind to give testimony to ever having existed at all.

She felt fragile in his arms, and yet she held his entire life in the palm of her hand.

He felt as if he would disintegrate, fade completely out of view, if he couldn't have her. If he couldn't keep on kissing her, holding her, feeling her body mold against his.

He was stealthily slipping into her life under false

pretenses, deliberately burrowing into it so that someone would pay him money for a job well done.

That was the bottom line.

He was using her for money.

Guilt chewed chunks out of him, leaving the rest to be ravaged by desire.

How had it gotten this complicated? He wasn't supposed to have turned down this road. He wasn't supposed to allow his attraction to take the governing seat and rule him like this.

But he couldn't push her away. She was making it too difficult.

She was too warm, too giving, too eager. Even as he tried to draw his head back, to somehow find the strength to break away before this got completely out of hand, Brooke didn't allow him to gain the space he needed. He moved, she moved and he couldn't find it in his heart to push her away.

Not when he wanted her this much.

She was purity and light and everything he had once believed he could attain if he just tried hard enough.

Before he knew better.

Dana's suicide had robbed him of his dreams, his beliefs, his future, but Brooke, with her bright eyes and quick smile, made him think that, just for one night, all that and more could be within his grasp.

He could hold his dreams in his hand for just a few timeless moments.

She was on fire.

Everywhere he touched her went up like a torch until

she felt as if she was standing in the middle of an inferno and only he could put it out.

And yet he was the source of it all.

It made her head spin.

Brooke didn't want to think, didn't want to untangle anything except this dress that was holding her back from him.

Her mouth still sealed to his, she reached behind to get at the zipper. His fingers were there a heartbeat before hers. She shivered in anticipation as she felt the long line of soft nylon teeth part, exposing her flesh to the air.

To his touch.

Her breath caught in her throat as she felt him slip the straps from her shoulders, as she felt the material sigh away from her body, momentarily pausing at the swell of her breasts before slipping down further.

Bypassing her hips, the dress sank in a pool around her feet.

She moaned as he kissed her.

The very sound echoed in his brain, driving him crazy, fueling the hunger that was growing almost too large to contain.

He had to look at her. Just for a second he needed to see her, here in his home.

With him.

The knot in his belly tightened, threatening to cut off his air supply.

She wasn't wearing a bra, just tiny black lace underwear that revealed more than it hid.

Very slowly he slid the tips of his fingers along her torso, pausing at the rim of her panties. He heard her sharp, inviting intake of breath.

He felt as if his gut was going to snap in two.

What the hell was he doing? Struggling with the fragments of a conscience already frayed, Mark told himself to back off, issuing ultimatums that burned away in the heat of his desire.

Pulling her to him, he sealed his fate. And hers.

Mark couldn't stop caressing her, couldn't stop touching her as his lips slanted over and over again against her mouth, her throat, her tender part along her neck.

And with each sigh he heard, with each sharp intake of breath that escaped her lips, his own excitement grew to proportions he hadn't known were humanly possible.

He felt like a man possessed.

And throughout it all, he knew he was doomed. A man whose soul had been plunged in darkness and would be again, once this was over.

Anticipation sank iron teeth into him, jetting up a hundred more notches as he felt Brooke stripping away his jacket, tugging out his shirttails. Urgently working away his belt.

She was undressing him, and he didn't know which excited him more, unwrapping her or having her do away with his clothes.

Every moment brought with it something more, something new. Something he wasn't prepared for. It was like finally being resigned to a fate of dying of thirst, only to be thrown headfirst into a life-affirming pool of water.

She was his pool of water, his salvation.

And he had done nothing but lie to her from the very beginning.

But that was logic and sense, and right now all he knew was that he wanted her, here, now, before sanity and reason rushed back at any moment on winged feet, to take hold of him again.

There'd been less than a handful of women in the last five years. Faceless women just passing through his life. Women he'd slept with to fill a void that couldn't be filled, to blot out a pain that refused to be made any smaller. He couldn't remember their names, their faces, or anything else about them.

Brooke's face was burned into his brain and always would be, no matter what happened.

And no matter what happened he was grateful to her. Would always be grateful to her for making him feel again, however briefly.

He knew that she would look back at this night and curse him, but he was determined that in the quiet moments of the night, when her anger had burned away, Brooke would look back on this and secretly smile.

It was about her pleasure, not his temporary salvation.

He made love with her, not as if this was their first time but their last.

Brooke felt arrows of heat and sunshine shoot

through her, ushering in the brightest lights she'd ever seen.

This was beyond anything she had ever imagined. Her wildest fantasy couldn't begin to hold a candle to what she was feeling right at this moment.

Anticipation came from nowhere, with no basis from which to draw, yet it scrambled her senses and whisked them up to heights Brooke had never conceived were possible.

Her body was vibrating like a struck tuning fork, its beat rushing along with her pulse and heartbeat. It seemed as if her entire body was singing a melody she'd never heard before as it rushed off to somewhere she had never been before.

She had no idea what was waiting for her at the end, only that if she didn't reach it, she was going to die right here, right now, despite the wondrous journey he had already taken her on.

She felt as if all of her body was singing madly. She didn't know the words, only that she had been waiting to hear them, to feel them all of her life.

Each time he moved from her, she cleaved to him, unwilling to let him pull away. Unwilling to bear the burden of separation.

Her body pulsed and craved something it had never had before.

Fulfillment.

He was laying her down on the sofa, anointing her body with hot kisses that sizzled along her skin a beat before they even arrived. She twisted and turned, arching into him, trying to absorb the sensation, wishing she knew what to do to make him feel just a little of what she was feeling.

She reached for him, but even as she did, she was surprised by the firmness that met her touch. For a moment she was almost frightened, but the next moment she left the child she'd been behind and raced across this new threshold that shimmered before her.

It was time. And he was her choice.

Her fingers wrapped themselves around him as she stroked him. The sound he made against her ear filled her with power. With excitement.

With hunger.

She raised her hips against his invitingly, her breath rushing away from her as she felt his mouth taking possession of her breast. She could feel his tongue teasing, suckling her nipple, and she moaned in ecstasy as waves of wild sensations danced through her. Her breathing became more and more labored as she grasped at ecstasy with both hands.

And then he was above her, parting her legs with his knee.

Her heart was hammering so hard she was afraid it was going to burst out of her chest.

An urgency seized her.

Raising her hips higher, Brooke gave herself up to him willingly. The first wave of pain came as a surprise and made her wince, just for a moment.

Brooke felt him hesitating, saw the surprised look in his eyes.

He was going to stop, she knew it. Panicked, not wanting it to end, not now, not so abruptly, Brooke pushed herself up against him.

Whether Mark drove himself into her or she pulled him in by pushing her hips against his wasn't clear to her. But as the rhythm began, the questions, the order, none of it mattered. All that mattered was that this race that she was suddenly so wrapped up in be taken all the way across the finish line.

That it be won.

She moved with him, her own urgency almost outstripping his. An explosion racked her loins, filtering out to all parts of her. And then a wild burst of colors and heat danced through her that she couldn't begin to describe.

He'd erased every word from her head, and all she could do was gasp for air and hold on him.

If she could have picked her moment to die, this would have been it. Die in his arms, with a smile on her face. And her body singing.

He'd suspected.

Known.

In his soul he'd known, somehow known that Brooke was a virgin despite her age. There was something virginal about the look in her eyes. About her. And yet he'd completely disregarded that in pursuit of his own needs. How reprehensible was that?

But she'd given him no choice.

He'd always had a choice, he argued.

He had a will, damn it, a will that had been forged out of steel and coated with iron over these years. Why had he abandoned it, allowing himself to crumple just because the very sight of her, the very feel of her brought him to his knees, literally and figuratively?

What was he going to say? How could he make this up to her? Ever?

Drawing back, Mark slid off her warm, heaving body. He would have gotten up from the sofa entirely, except that there was this look in her eyes that forbid him to leave her.

So, clumsily now, he tucked his arm around her and held her to him.

If his guilt had weighed any more heavily on his chest, it would have suffocated him completely. "Why didn't you tell me?"

A cold chill descended over her body.

The words felt as if they had been sealed with some kind of paste to the roof of her mouth and she had to peel them off one by one.

"Tell you what?"

Mark raised himself up on his elbow, furious with himself. He'd gone too far, and there was no way to make this right. You couldn't unring a bell. "That you were a virgin."

Her heart froze within her breast. She felt naked, exposed, and struggled not to allow the tears she felt forming to fall. He looked so angry. Had she been that much of a disappointment to him? Did he feel that cheated, wasting time with her?

She told him the truth. "Because I didn't want you to stop." Her eyes, bright with unshed tears, met his. "Because I didn't want to be a virgin anymore."

He dragged his hand through his hair, hating what he'd just done. Hating himself because he still wanted her. Again.

"Then why didn't you pick someone else?" For lack of a name, he chose the first that came to him. "Why didn't you go with that Holden character?"

"Because I didn't want 'that Holden character,'" She knew that now, knew that any daydreams she might have had were just that, daydreams. They didn't involve a real person. Not like Mark. He wasn't all about pretenses and ego, he was real. "I wanted you. I wanted you to be the first." Unable to stare at the anger on his face any longer, she looked away. "I'm sorry if I disappointed you, but—"

"Disappointed me?" he echoed the words as if he was repeating something in a foreign language, something that made no sense to him. "Is that what you think this is about?"

"Isn't it?" She licked lips that were suddenly incredibly dry. "I mean, a man has a right to expect a good time if he—"

"No." He cut her short, not wanting to hear any more. Not wanting to have her berate herself. "No, this isn't about disappointment, at least, not mine," he looked at her pointedly, "and this isn't about a man's expectations. If it was, then you more than surpassed anything I could have thought up."

A half smile played across her lips. She wanted to take his face between her hands and kiss it. He was being incredibly sweet. "You're a nonfiction writer, you don't think up things."

He would have been arrested for what he was thinking now, Mark told himself. "I'm a man and men have fantasies."

Her breath hitched in her throat. Her eyes never left his face. "And?"

Unable to help himself, he slid the back of his hand along her cheek. She was so sweet, so innocent. And he had changed all that, damn it. But at the same time, he couldn't help being touched by the import of her gift to him. No one had ever offered themselves to him, body and soul, this way.

It made him infinitely humble.

And infinitely guilty. He doubted if that weight was ever going to be lifted from his shoulders.

"And," he went on to tell her, "I've never had a fantasy to match this." His smile faded as he became serious. "But you have a right to have the first time be with someone who matters—"

She put her finger to his lips to silence him. "It was."

His heart swelled. If he lived to be a tortured hundred, he was never going to forget the way she'd felt in his arms or the way she was right now. "Brooke, you don't know me."

He was beginning to feel as if he sounded like a broken record, but it was true. She didn't know him. The real him. If she had, they would never have been here like this.

Brooke held her ground. "I know all I need to know." She saw he needed more convincing. "Look, there've been others who tried. But I didn't want them. You," she laughed softly, "you didn't even try. But I knew I wanted you. To be the first," she tagged on, afraid that he would see through her, that he would suddenly realize that what she meant was that she wanted it to be him forever. Nothing made a man run faster than knowing his future had been settled without his consent.

She wanted him forever, but she was bright enough to settle for just a night.

But Mark remained unconvinced. It was just the moment talking. She was feeling euphoric. He was being sensible. And hating it.

"You don't know what you're saying."

"Yes, I do," she insisted. Her voice became sterner than he would have thought. She took his attention hostage. "Don't treat me as if I were some addle-brained teenager, Mark. I might not be experienced, but I already told you, that was by choice. I had other...opportunities—" a smile played on her lips "—if you will, but I didn't want them. I've even thought I was in love, but it still didn't seem right. No one ever made me feel safe before. Not the way you do."

Brooke took a deep breath, trying to fortify herself. "Now, if you're disappointed, I am very sorry, but I'm not sorry this happened." The tears she'd been fighting insisted on breaking through. She blinked them back as furiously as she could. It didn't help. She began to rise off the sofa. "If you'll excuse me, I have clothes to get into."

But before she could move, he caught her by the wrist, stopping her. She looked at him quizzically, but he didn't release his hold.

The deed had been done, there was nothing he could do to change that, to undo it. But he could change the way she felt right at this moment.

Slowly he began to brush his thumb along the inside of her wrist. He could feel her pulse begin to jump.

A shaft of guilt went through him, but he knew he had to do this. This wasn't about his own needs, which seemed to be multiplying again at a phenomenal rate. This was about her.

It had always been about her.

He pressed a kiss to her bare shoulder and felt her shiver in response. "How long did you say it would be before your father starts to worry that you're not home?"

Brooke felt her pulse quickening, beating erratically. Could feel her inner core moistening again. Monitoring her heart was out of the question. It was doing things she hadn't thought possible.

Her body was beginning to turn fluid again. She relaxed...and tensed with anticipation at the same time. She was no longer sure what was up, what was down—and didn't care.

"Not for another few hours or so."

Damn it, just looking at her made him feel happy. He knew it wasn't right, and yet he couldn't help himself. Very slowly he ran his fingertips along her lips. Lips that had already sealed his fate once. "How would you like to kill that time?"

"How do you think?"

The words were scarcely out of her mouth before her breathing became labored. Mark was pressing his lips to the hollow of her throat, short-circuiting all her nerve endings within her.

Knowing what to anticipate, she felt as if her body burst into flame almost instantly.

But this time, she promised herself, she was going to show him. This time, he wasn't going to feel as if he was making love with a dewy-eyed novice.

She wrapped her legs around his torso, locking them together and then rocked so that their positions suddenly became reversed before he knew what was happening.

The unconscious anticipation of pleasure had him smiling as he looked at her in surprise.

"Brooke?"

She grinned from ear to ear just before she brought her mouth down to his. "I'm not a virgin anymore," she whispered against his lips.

The next moment, her body splayed across his, she began to make love with him as if they had always done this, as if they had always been two halves of a whole.

His pulse began to throb, alert, ready.

A very special corner of hell, Mark thought again, that was the place reserved for him. He was going to burn for all eternity for this.

But if that was so, he was going to need memories to last him for all eternity.

He started gathering them.

Chapter Twelve

The phone had been ringing off the hook all morning. Which was good for her business but bad for the headache that was beginning to grow right behind Emily Parks's eyes. What's more, she felt as if her face had frozen in place. She'd been perky, smiling and sharp since she'd sailed into work at eight.

Because of the preponderance of couples who had decided that they just *had* to make August their wedding month, there hadn't even been time for lunch today. Six straight hours was an awfully long time to be perky.

The wedding planner, Emily decided, *is taking a break.*

And with that goal in mind, she closed the door of her office, shut off the phone and poured herself a much-deserved cup of coffee.

Maybe the extrastrong shot of caffeine would do something to make her headache go into hiding. It was worth a try.

Pretending for a moment that she wasn't addicted to the fast-paced life she was living and that she would actually want to have it any other way than it was, Emily sat down at her desk and spread open today's copy of the as-yet-unread *San Francisco Tribune*.

Miscalculating, she hit her coffee cup with the California section. Within less than a horrified heartbeat, a black river was suddenly running down her desk.

Not bothering to swallow the curse that rose swiftly to her lips, Emily grabbed the tissue box off her desk and proceeded to stem the tide, dabbing madly at the desk and the newspaper. She offered up a silent thanks that none of her disks had been haphazardly left there to meet the flowing liquid.

Emily Parks's green eyes widened as the words beneath the soaked tissue in her hand came into focus. The article, no more than two inches in height, was buried on the last page of the California section.

Appropriately enough, it was an engagement announcement. One of Rowan's old girlfriends was getting married. Not to him.

She smiled to herself. Probably knew that if she waited for Rowan to pop the question, she was fated to wait forever. Rowan wasn't the marrying kind.

Rowan also wasn't the orthodox kind. Rules, proper behavior, thoughtfulness, all that was completely foreign to her motorcycle-loving sibling. The last time she'd seen him, he was riding that bike off to parts unknown. Right after he'd told them at the family gathering their father had called together that he wanted no part of being Walter Parks's son. Moreover, that he was ashamed of her, Cade and Jessica if they were going to continue to knuckle under to the old man.

Her younger brother by only a year, Rowan had always been the black sheep of the family. Or maybe the white sheep, she amended, thinking of the reputation their father had earned over the years.

But she hadn't heard from him since then. Not that he made a habit of clocking in. Still, she'd called a couple of times and not gotten a call back.

She glanced at the paper. This was as good an excuse as any to call him again. Pulling the telephone over to her, she hit the familiar number on the keypad. This time, as she listened to the answering machine, she struggled to hold on to her patience.

"Rowan, it's Emily, I—" A shrill sound met her ear. It meant his machine was too full for another message. Which meant he hadn't listened to any of his messages so far.

Which meant he hadn't been home in days.

The tips of her fingers suddenly felt icy. Something was wrong.

Ordinarily levelheaded and driven, able to multitask in her sleep, twenty-eight-year-old Emily suddenly felt a chill passing over her spine as she struggled with a premonition. Something had happened to Rowan, she just knew it.

The first thing she needed to do was to call her twin brother, Cade, and see if maybe he'd heard from Rowan. But even as she dialed, she knew what the answer would be. Cade would have mentioned something, if only to voice his displeasure with Rowan's actions.

She couldn't shake the feeling that Rowan was missing. And that he was in trouble.

"You know, you still haven't shown me any of your work."

Every word out of Brooke's mouth sounded like a siren's song.

Sitting on the edge of the bed, his back to her, Mark looked at Brooke over his shoulder. She made him think of that picture he'd once seen. *Venus Rising out of the Sea.* Except she wasn't rising, she was lying on her stomach on his bed. Looking like every young red-blooded male's biggest fantasy come true.

Looking like the reality he wished with all his heart was actually his instead of just borrowed under false pretenses.

Mark struggled to get his mind back on the subject and not on what he wanted to spend the rest of eternity doing with her.

She'd been subtly asking about his book in progress for several days now and he'd been evasive. The inquiry had finally become blunt.

"That's because there's nothing to show yet," he told her. "Just notes."

Knowing he should be getting dressed, he paused

anyway, drinking in the sight of her as if he hadn't already done it countless times.

They'd just made love. Again. The way they had every day for the past week. He could still feel the imprint of her body against his. Feel the heat, the fire. Unable to do without it, he allowed himself to absorb it.

He'd tried to stay clear of her. Heaven knew, he'd tried to keep her at arm's length that very first day after he'd taken her virginity from her. But she'd looked so surprised, so hurt when he'd cut her off the second time and retreated, all he could think of was Dana and how her deplorably low self-esteem had made her take her own life.

He was to blame for that. Somehow, some way, he was to blame for that.

He couldn't allow anything to happen to Brooke because of him. Couldn't let her think that he was one of those men who was consumed with only the conquest and lost interest once that was achieved. That had never been his way and never less than right now.

He wanted Brooke more than ever after their first time.

So he stopped trying to hold her at bay for her own good and allowed her to move in closer. That having her there pleased him was something he knew he was going to have to pay for later. But he was far more interested in now.

So he gave himself excuses and allowed her to come to his apartment. More than once she'd commented on how his "friend" seemed to leave no traces of himself.

If she had been anyone else, he would have been certain that her suspicions had been aroused and that they were trying to draw him out. Trip him up.

But not Brooke. She was an innocent in more ways than one.

His heart ached because he knew she actually didn't believe someone would lie to her. She believed in things like honesty and integrity, and it ate him up alive that he was going to be the one responsible for stealing that from her, too.

First her virginity, then her faith. He could easily grow to hate himself.

But trying to do the noble thing and keep away from her was impossible. He had to go to the bookstore, and she was there every day, appearing at his side with books, with suggestions. Or just to tug on his arm and drag him off to view a piece of history, restored or otherwise, somewhere in the city. And through it all, she'd be leaning into him, wearing that scent that drove him crazy, that expression that reduced his resolve to the consistency of ice cream left out on the counter.

They played tourists.

They played lovers.

Whatever good intentions he had, they amounted to just so much rumble in the face of her sensual enthusiasm. A part of him hoped that if he gave in to his desire enough, his appetite for her would fade. Nothing could be further from the truth. The more he had Brooke, the more he wanted her, until he was completely consumed with the thought, the feel, the reality of her.

Lying on her stomach, her ankles crossed, nude as the moment she was born, Brooke seemed completely oblivious to the effect the sight of her was having on him. You'd think that after making love with her for the past hour, he would be completely spent, and yet there was still more left in the account. And the interest was accruing with each moment that passed.

He'd left the shop early today, telling Brooke he had something to do. He had an appointment to meet with Tyler and give him a progress report. But there were no readings scheduled at the shop for this evening, no special events of any kind and much to her joy, her father was regaining his former interest in running the store. That meant, she'd told him, that she was free to "tag along." He knew he couldn't tell her not to without either hurting her feelings or arousing her suspicions. He wanted to do neither.

So he'd stopped at his apartment on the pretext of picking something up and made a quick call to Tyler, rescheduling. When he'd come out of his bedroom, she was waiting for him. Looking so damn delectable that he lost track of his own thoughts.

Rather than coming up with an excuse, he resorted to distracting her. And himself. He began separating her from her clothing and reunited her with him.

And all the while, as he made love with her, he felt like the kid he'd never been.

"You have to have something," she insisted. "A paragraph, snatches of brilliant thoughts."

A smile playing on her lips, Brooke raised her eyes

to his face as if she didn't have a clue what she was doing to him. He reached for his jeans, telling himself he'd stand a better chance resisting her if he were dressed.

It was a lie.

"Nothing intelligible," he muttered.

Behind him she scrambled to her knees, placing her hand on his shoulder. Holding the sheet to her only as an afterthought.

If it was meant to cool his ardor, it wasn't very effective. He found the sight of her like that impossibly arousing.

"Let me be the judge of that. Please," she coaxed. "I want to read something you wrote."

This part of the plan had fallen by the wayside. He didn't have anything to show her. "It's not ready to have anyone read it."

She put her own interpretation on his reluctance. She'd been around enough writers to know that they always had something they'd written down, bursts of inspiration that came to them out of the blue and which they felt were brilliant.

"You think I'll be disappointed."

Grateful for the lifeline, he grabbed at the excuse. "Something like that."

Brooke sat back on her heels, her eyes intent on his face. And they were laughing. "Oh, Mark, don't you know that there's nothing you could do that would disappoint me."

Wrong. Guess again, he thought.

But she was already drawing closer to him again, nuzzling against him. He could feel her breasts moving against him beneath the thin cotton. He wondered if she had any idea what her body was doing to him? If she had a clue just how much he wanted her?

And then he saw the smile on her lips, the look in her eyes.

She knew.

He gave up the pretense of getting dressed. Letting his jeans drop to the floor, Mark cupped her chin in his hand.

"Have you always been such a temptress?"

"I've never been anything until you came along," she whispered to him.

And it was true. She felt as if she'd been asleep all this time, waiting for him to come into her life. Waiting for him to wake her up with a kiss. He *was* her Prince Charming, even if he did appear to be more on the brooding side. She liked that about him, too. Liked everything about him.

There it was again, guilt, standing in the middle of his soul like some kind of steel edifice being constructed, girder by girder. Cutting off his air. Crushing him.

He had to tell her.

Somehow, some way, he needed to tell her who he really was, that he'd been hired by Tyler Carlton and, indirectly, by the D.A., Robert Jackson, to find her father. That falling for her hadn't been part of the plan.

She wasn't going to believe him. Why should she? He'd lied to her about everything else.

She was by far the best thing that had ever happened to him. And he was going to lose her the moment she found out, because she valued truth above all else and he had done nothing but lie to her from the first moment they had met.

Brooke's cool fingers smoothed out the furrow forming on his brow. Pulling himself back from the quagmire of his thoughts, he raised his eyes to hers.

"You're thinking too much again," she told him softly. "And every time you do, you start having doubts."

It had become her personal mission, her goal, to show him that he couldn't live without her. To that end, she intended to use everything she had at her disposal. That included making love with him as often and as much as she could.

He had to stay.

Because life without him had become unthinkable. Without meaning to, he had stolen her heart and she had to go where it went.

Rising on her knees again, Brooke laced her arms around his neck, her sheet falling seductively away from her body. Murmuring his name, she lightly pressed her lips against his. When he began to deepen the kiss, she abruptly pulled back.

He looked at her, confused.

There was a teasing expression on her face. A laugh echoed in her throat.

He laughed as he shook his head. "You are *such* a temptress," he said again.

Her eyes slowly slid down his torso, and a satisfied smile took hold of her features. Triumph pumped through her veins. She was affecting him again.

The next moment the laughter was gone. Only the desire remained.

"I'll be anything you want me to be," she told him a moment before she brought her mouth back to his.

His arms tightened around Brooke, holding her hard against him. Wanting her so much that it scared the hell out of him.

He hardly knew himself.

Even after being with her, he still wasn't accustomed to the level of desire that repeatedly took hold of his body. Until he'd met her, his had been a life devoid of emotion. Yes, he was close to Nick, but even there, things went unsaid, undemonstrated. He'd been as open with Dana as he thought was possible for him. But it was nothing compared to how he felt around Brooke.

He wanted to be with her all the time, make love with her all the time. She had become his obsession as well as his salvation. Being with her kept him back from the brink of despair.

It was as if he became someone else in her presence. Someone for whom there were still possibilities left in life instead of only a barren desert. When he was with her, there was hope and light.

And most of all, there was her.

For the short duration that this would last, he felt blessed.

Locked in an embrace and each other, they fell onto the bed again. Time, schedules, responsibilities, everything was forgotten.

The only thing that existed was the bed they were on and each other.

He was strumming her like a guitar, Brooke thought. Making every part of her vibrate, creating music out of thin air. He used his hands, he used his mouth, caressing, branding, making her moist. Creating small tidal waves throughout her being.

The tempo increased, snatching away the very air out of her lungs.

Mark showed her the way to paradise, to places that she hadn't even suspected existed. She lost control over her own body. It became entirely his, an instrument of pleasure for him to play however he chose.

When she felt the heat of his mouth at her inner core, she couldn't keep the sounds from escaping her lips. Guttural sounds born of ecstasy, surrounding her and fading into the very walls.

His ardor branded her.

Forever and always.

In her heart, she knew this. Even if Mark left her, she would always, always be his. No matter what happened after today.

Exhausted, panting, she looked up at him as he slid himself over her. She felt every nuance of his body against hers.

"Just when I thought I knew everything, you surprise me," she whispered.

Mark looked down into her eyes, a sadness all but overwhelming him.

If you only knew.

She blinked and looked at him. There was something in his eyes, something she couldn't fathom but that frightened her all the same. Everything within her went on the alert.

"Mark, what is it?"

Mark placed his finger to her lips. "Shh," he cautioned.

He would tell her. By and by he'd tell her. He had to. But not now. Not tonight.

He wanted just one more night with her. Just one more time to make love with her until they were both completely senseless. If that made him a terrible human being, well, he was already slated to burn in hell, what difference did one more offense make?

And it meant so much to him.

The look in his eyes was really scaring her. She tried desperately to interpret it.

Was he growing tired of her? Was he searching for some way to tell her that he was going to be leaving soon? Maybe back to New York or somewhere else?

Didn't he know that she'd go anywhere with him? All he had to do was ask.

But maybe he didn't want to ask.

No, she wasn't going to think about that. That was for tomorrow, not now. She wanted now. More than that, she wanted forever, but she had to have now. Because, if she was very, very lucky, forever would be created out of the building blocks of now.

With renewed energy and purpose, Brooke raised her head, bringing her mouth to his, kissing him over and over again with ardor. Surprising him.

She felt Mark giving way under her assault, and she made her move, shifting their positions until she was the one on top.

With a wicked laugh she straddled him, then slipped him inside of her.

The surprised look on his face empowered her. Fused against his body, she began to move, at first slowly, then faster and faster until she had gotten completely caught up and entangled in her own trap. In the end, it was difficult to say whose breath was whose. Two streams mingled, becoming one.

Just the way they had.

An exhilaration filled him. He felt as if he was free-falling through space. Mark held on to her hips, moving her against him, trying to control the uncontrollable. And then he gave up.

Surrendering himself to the feeling.

To her.

She was like some kind of wild force of nature, and she was the most magnificent thing he had ever beheld.

And just for the moment she was his.

He couldn't lie to himself, even in the throes of the climax that was seizing him. She wouldn't be his much longer. But, for this one moment, this one eternity, she was his, and that was all any of them ever really had.

Only now.

When it was over, when the climax had come and

gone, slowly taking euphoria along with it in its wake, he held Brooke in his arms a long time. And pretended that he really was nothing more than a hopeful would-be nonfiction writer.

And the luckiest man on the face of the earth. Because he had found her, and with her, a corner of heaven.

Chapter Thirteen

Walter Parks was not a patient man. He never had been. He had always wanted things to be done yesterday. As far as he was concerned—and he firmly believed that his was the only opinion that mattered—this hunt for Marla's brother, Derek, that spineless weasel, was taking far too long.

He frowned as he absently swirled his snifter of cognac, sending the dark liquid to and fro in the glass like a drunken tidal wave. He shouldn't have to worry. A man in his position should have been able to coast for the rest of his life instead of still looking over his shoulder, still wondering if the empire he had put all of his energy into creating was in jeopardy.

It wasn't fair.

This was his legacy, and the vultures were after it, damn them.

The small, annoying pain began again. The one just beneath his breastbone.

Rubbing his chest in small, concentric circles, he watched the rain as it slid down in sheets against the pane of his study window.

It was late but he felt wide awake. Wired, even though he was tired. Sleep, as always, was not his friend. Ever since he could remember, it had eluded him, playing an elaborate game of hide-and-seek with a mind that knew no peace, that always felt as if it had to be alert, waiting for some kind of subversive attack.

Even when things were going well he couldn't sleep, and things were not going well.

The telephone beside him rang, disturbing the silence. Putting down his glass, Parks snatched up the receiver before the sound faded. "Yes?"

The voice against his ear was deep, low. "I've located him, Mr. Parks."

Parks jolted to attention. There was no need for the voice to say who "him" was. The fewer details revealed over the telephone, the better. Some bugs defied the electronics expert's sweep.

His hand tightened on the receiver. "You're sure?"

"I'm sure."

"About time," he snapped. Maybe now it could finally be ended. "You know what to do."

"Yes, sir."

"Call me when it's over."

With that, Parks let the receiver fall back into its cradle. He smiled to himself for the first time in days. Even the pain in his chest abated.

Hands on either side of the easy chair, he pushed himself up to his feet.

Maybe now he could finally get some sleep.

Today. He would tell her today, Mark silently promised the reflection in his bathroom mirror.

He washed the last of the shaving lather from his face, trying to lay out a plan. Trying to pretend that he didn't feel as if his life, the life he'd so recently attained, hung in the balance.

Leaving the bathroom, he went to his closet to get dressed. Outside, the wind howled and pelted the window with rain. He hardly heard it. His mind was elsewhere. On a street seven miles away, in front of a bookstore.

He'd go to Buy the Book and tell Brooke who he really was. And then he would approach her father and ask him to come forth and talk to Tyler and the D.A. It was the right thing to do.

As he quickly got dressed, his mouth curved in a mirthless smile. He shook his head.

The right thing.

Like he was the one who should be telling people what the right thing to do was. That he hadn't meant for any of this to happen this way was no excuse. It had, and a wonderful woman was probably going to be irreversibly scarred because of it.

Buttoning his shirt, he tucked it in. He wondered if she would ever find it in her heart to forgive him. No, he suspected not. In her place, he didn't know if he would have been able to handle a deception of this magnitude. He would have felt used. Just as she undoubtedly would, once she knew.

If Brooke let him, he knew he would be willing to spend the rest of his life trying to make it up to her. But in his heart, he had a feeling that really wasn't a possibility.

The rain that was lashing against his windows added to the pall that he felt closing around him.

If he could, he would gladly have held all this at bay just a little longer, resisting the inevitable. But it wasn't up to him. He'd called Tyler Carlton late last night, after he'd taken Brooke home. He'd told him about the matching photograph. The man had been eager for details and happy that his long-lost uncle had finally been found.

Tyler wanted to approach Derek himself, but Mark felt that there was protocol to follow. These things had to be done a certain way. He needed to prepare Derek for the fact that his cover had been blown. By a man he'd taken into his home. A man who had made love to his daughter.

Mark blew out a breath as he finished getting ready. Right now it felt as if his conscience weighed about a thousand pounds. And it was getting heavier with every passing minute.

* * *

She'd woken up smiling. Smiling despite the less than spectacular weather outside. The rain had begun just before Mark had brought her home. She'd felt like dancing between the raindrops. And had. He'd laughed at her.

God, but she loved the sound of his laugh. Loved everything about him, even the way his mouth turned down when he was deep in thought.

She'd hurried through her shower and gotten dressed in record time, sailing down the stairs and beating her father to the kitchen by a good twenty minutes.

Breakfast was waiting for him by the time he came down.

Brooke had watched her father eat, too keyed up, too happy to eat. She toyed with the cup of coffee she'd poured for herself. When her father sneezed and then coughed, she expressed the proper amount of sympathy, offering to go and open up the store in his place. After all, until just recently, she'd been doing it for him for the past couple of months.

"You stay home, Dad," she urged when he demurred. "Take it easy for a while."

But he shook his head. "Don't baby me, Brooke. As it is, I've been taking it easy for too long, letting you carry more than your load." She began to protest, but he cut her off. "I'm not a sack of sugar, I won't disappear if a little rain hits me."

He ended his statement with a sneeze. She pushed the box of tissues closer to him.

"It's more than a little rain. If it was raining any

harder, there'd be a man with a long beard out there, collecting two of everything and loading them onto an ark."

She was given to exaggeration, and it amused him. "Then you shouldn't go out, either."

Brooke tossed her head, sending a curtain of black hair flying over her shoulder. "But I'm young, invincible—"

He homed in on the real reason she wanted to get to the bookstore. "And in love."

There was no point in denying it, even if she was given to being secretive, which she wasn't.

"Yeah, that, too." She leaned her chin on her upturned hand and looked at her father, grinning. "Does it show?"

He laughed. "Only in a lighthouse-beacon kind of way. Does he know?"

She spread a healthy dose of marmalade over the English muffin she'd toasted for him, then pushed the serving in front of him.

"Probably. Oh, Dad, I've never felt this way before. There's this glow, this happiness just shining all over the place inside of me." She looked at him hopefully. "Does it last?"

Does it last? Derek thought of Anna rather than his wife. Anna Parks, the first woman he'd given his heart to on what was to be the most fateful day of his life, the one that changed it forever. He'd heard that Parks had sent her off somewhere, but he'd never managed to discover just where.

He felt that old familiar ache in his heart.

After all these years, he still thought of Anna, even before he thought of the woman who had given him his precious daughter. He knew he always would. What was it that his mother had once said? *You never forget your first one.* And he never had.

He felt Brooke watching him. "If it's the right one, yes, it lasts."

"Like you and Mom?"

In all the years that followed her mother's death, her father had never once had anything that even remotely came close to a female companion. He'd centered his world on her and the store, nothing else. She supposed that she was looking for that kind of love, the kind that hit you squarely between the eyes and burrowed its way into your heart forever. And she thought she'd found it with Mark.

"Is that why you never dated after she died?" she pressed.

A sliver of guilt went through him. Brooke's mother had been a fine, good woman, but she'd never made him forget about Anna, even when he tried. But that was something he wasn't about to get into right now.

"Something like that." When Brooke looked at him, a puzzled expression slipping over her features, he added, "It's complicated, honey. Someday I'll explain it all to you, but not right now." Finished with his breakfast, he began to rise. "I've got a store to open."

Having poured another cup of coffee, Brooke moved that in front of him, then pressed her hand on his shoulder, making him take his seat again.

"*I've* got a store to open," she corrected. "You come in later. I don't want you getting sick on me. It's supposed to stop raining by eleven." Brooke took her empty cup to the sink and quickly rinsed it out. She wanted to get going. "I'll open up."

He didn't bother hiding the knowing smile that came to his lips. "Mark coming in early?"

"Maybe," she said with a mysterious smile on her lips as she wiped her hands on a kitchen towel.

Brooke started for the front door, pausing to pick up her purse and the black, slouch hat she favored whenever it rained. She hated wrestling with an umbrella.

He had a clear view of her as she crossed to the door. "Don't forget your raincoat."

Brooke paused by the coat rack. "It's at the cleaners."

"Then take mine."

She looked at what amounted to a black rain slicker. It looked like a minor pup tent. "It's too big."

"Not that much," he protested. For a man, he was built thin and wiry. "Besides, you're trying to stay dry, not make a fashion statement."

She caught her lower lip between her teeth, thinking. If she took the raincoat, then he wouldn't have one. He'd be forced to wait out the storm.

"Okay, if it keeps you home." Slipping the slicker on, she laughed as she pushed the sleeves back enough to have her hands emerge. Doubling back, she pressed a kiss to his cheek, too happy for words. "I'll see you later."

Brooke left the house singing, her mood in direct contrast to the weather outside.

* * *

The man pulled up the collar of his jacket.

Miserable weather.

He'd been standing in this alley for forty minutes, waiting, getting wet. More opportune times might present themselves later, but Parks had been firm. And you didn't get anywhere in life getting on the wrong side of Walter Parks.

Parks had said he wanted the man eliminated now. Now meant now. It didn't get any clearer than that.

He sneezed. His mood, already foul, darkened. He was going to come down with goddamn pneumonia if his target didn't show up soon.

And then he saw his target approaching. Every nerve ending on heightened alert, he slipped his hand over the hilt of his gun.

His index finger tightened on the trigger.

Brooke felt water splashing on the back of her ankles. The puddle had been deeper than she'd anticipated.

Wouldn't you just know that on a day like today, the street in front of her store would be lined with cars? She'd had to park in the lot across the street.

The rain seemed to get worse with every step she took. Every step of the short distance between the lot and the store had been marked with a struggle with the oversize umbrella her father, at the last minute, had insisted she take with her. Fighting the wind for possession got her wetter than if she'd just made a dash for it.

But she didn't care if she got wet. She felt too happy.

She was going to see Mark today and all was right with the world.

Mark brought his car to a screeching halt in the tight spot, leaving it between a BMW SUV and a sports car, vintage unknown. He made his way out of the parking structure, his eyes on the front of Derek's store.

Brooke's store.

He'd planned to be earlier. But traffic had been really bad. It always was whenever it rained. Maniacs wove in and out of lanes like deranged hummingbirds while the cautious types slowed down to a crawl, completely impeding his progress, making him stop at every light between his apartment and the bookstore.

As he waited for the light to change, allowing him to cross, Mark saw a figure in a black raincoat standing before the door of the bookstore, fumbling with a set of keys.

He recognized the coat. He'd seen it hanging on the rack the last time he'd been over for dinner. Was Derek alone this morning? Where was Brooke?

Disappointed, he decided that maybe this was for the better after all. Maybe if he told Derek first who he was, the rest of it would somehow work itself out. Maybe Derek would even be willing to act as a buffer between him and Brooke.

Right, and maybe Santa would come down his chimney this Christmas.

Mark squared his shoulders resolutely. One way or

another, this had to be done. He might as well get it over with. The light turned green. He began to cross the street.

Everything happened so fast that at first, Mark thought he was imagining it. And then, when the events began to penetrate his brain, they seemed like something he might have seen on a newsreel or in a movie. In less than a heartbeat, he was kicked back to his days on the force in New York.

A man jumped out of the shadows behind Derek. Despite the rain, Mark saw the gun.

Instantly he pulled his own weapon out. The irony of the fact that this was the first time he'd worn it since he began perpetrating the charade didn't occur to him until later. He'd taken it because he meant to use it as a backup for his story.

Instead, he found himself employing it in defense of the man he'd been sent to find.

"Derek, duck!" he cried out.

And then it happened. He saw the person he'd taken to be Derek turn and look straight at him.

Brooke!

It was Brooke in the raincoat, not her father.

The same moment the realization hit him, he heard the shot.

And then he saw Brooke go down.

He felt as if the bullet had penetrated his gut. Air stopped flowing in his lungs even as he raced across the street. A car making a turn careened sharply to avoid hitting him. The driver leaned on his horn, the sound adding to the cacophony of noise throbbing in his head.

Mark never hesitated. His weapon was in his hand and he used it. Shooting at the man who'd shot at Brooke. The other man crumpled, screaming.

And then there was silence, deafening silence, except for the sound of sobs that wouldn't come.

Mark wasn't sure just how he got through it. How everything fell into place. The events moved through his head like broken shards of colored glass forming macabre pictures. He felt like a man trapped in a nightmare as he rushed to Brooke's side.

She looked up at him with wide, dazed eyes.

"Oh, thank God," he cried. "You're alive. Hang on, baby, hang on," he pleaded.

He wanted to cradle her, to shield her from the rain and hold her against him, but he was afraid to move her, afraid that if he did, life would seep away from her just as the blood was doing now.

There was blood, so much blood.

He'd never, ever been so afraid in his life.

White with rage, with fear, he wanted to empty his magazine into the slime who had done this. Instead he kept his weapon trained on the unconscious man on the sidewalk.

Struggling to keep from falling apart, Mark pulled out his cell phone with his other hand and called 911, demanding police backup and paramedics. For a split second he blanked out on the address. And then it came to him.

His heart tightened in his chest as he looked at Brooke. The color had left her face.

He saw her lips move, forming a word. Forming no sound. He leaned closer, his ear to her lips. "What, baby, what?"

"Mark?" Brooke felt as though everything was spinning, and she had a horrible, fiery pain in her shoulder. The pain was spreading, burning into her. Breathing hurt, made it worse. "What...what's happening?" she finally managed to gasp.

"Shhh, don't try to talk, baby." He smoothed away the hair from her face. "Some lowlife tried to mug you, but he can't hurt you anymore." He wasn't sure if the vermin was dead or alive and he didn't care. All he cared about was her. "Hang on, the paramedics are on their way. Just hang on, all right?"

She tried to say "All right," but there was no strength with which to move her lips.

His voice was getting further and further away, melting into the rain and the darkness. Her eyelids felt as if they each weighed fifty pounds, and she gave up trying to hold them up.

She slipped into the darkness.

When the police first arrived, they thought he was the perpetrator. In their defense, Mark supposed he was acting like a deranged man. But he was completely overcome with grief and guilt and terrified that Brooke was going to die. After identifying himself, he managed to regain a little of his control. As quickly, as succinctly as possible, he gave the two patrolmen the details, also giving them Nick's name.

Once they knew he was Nick Banning's brother, the tone of the inquiry changed. His brother was called, arriving almost immediately. Nick dashed out of the car, concern etched on his handsome face.

"You all right?"

"He shot her." Mark looked at his brother, his eyes hollow, reflecting the condition of his soul. "The son of a bitch shot her."

Nick looked at the paramedic. "How is she?"

"The bullet's still inside. One inch closer..." The man didn't have to finish the sentence. Moving swiftly, the paramedics had temporarily stopped the bleeding, but Brooke hadn't regained consciousness. "We need to take her to the hospital," he told Mark.

"Not without me." He started to climb into the ambulance behind the gurney.

When the two patrolmen moved forward to detain Mark, Nick waved them back. "You need to come down to the station to give a statement."

The younger of the two paramedics was closing the rear doors. "Count on it," Mark told his brother.

No one would tell him how she was doing.

He'd accompanied her into the hospital, running alongside the gurney until one of the nurses gently but firmly held him back. He was cut off from her as Brooke was whisked away into a trauma room and then into emergency surgery.

Mark felt as if his legs had been cut off at the knees. In an attempt to keep his mind occupied, he called Derek, telling the man in as precise details as possible that there had been a mugging.

"Oh my God, is Brooke all right?"

Mark dragged his hand through his hair. He wished to God he knew. It took supreme effort to keep his voice calm as he said, "They have her in surgery right now." And then, for the man's benefit, he added, "The doctor says there's every chance she'll be fine."

It was a lie. No doctor had said anything to him. They hadn't taken the time because every second had been precious. But Mark felt he owed the man at least a tiny bit of hope.

"I'll be right there." The line went dead, leaving Mark to pace and to pray to a deity he hadn't spoken a word to or acknowledged in five years.

Derek arrived less than twenty minutes later, looking like a man who had come face-to-face with mortality. He seemed to have aged ten years from the day before.

Mark did what he could to comfort him, but the effort was futile. At the core of Derek's pain was guilt. He blamed himself for what had happened to his daughter.

"I shouldn't have let her go. I shouldn't have let her go," he repeated numbly. His eyes were wild as he looked at Mark. "That should be me lying on that operating room table, not her."

Mark knew all the right words to say, even if he couldn't convince himself of them. Because at bottom he felt that this was all because of the search he'd initiated. Somehow, without knowing how, he'd led this vermin to Brooke's door.

"You can't blame yourself. These things happen. San Francisco is a big city. People get mugged. It's not your fault."

"Actually, technically, it is."

Both men turned to see Nick coming toward them. He'd ridden to the hospital in the second ambulance, the one that had brought the supposed mugger to the hospital. It had been an informative trip.

It was time for the charade to be over, Mark thought. He took the first step to ending it. "Derek, this is my brother. Detective Nick Banning."

Derek looked a little uncertain as he nodded at the other man. "What do you mean, 'technically'?"

Nick told him what he knew. "The guy who shot your daughter was out of his head in the ambulance. He kept saying he didn't know it was a girl, that he thought he was getting Ross, not a girl. Derek Ross," Nick repeated as he looked at Derek. "Is that you?"

The question was a formality. Derek could tell by the way the police detective looked at him as he asked it. Maybe, just maybe, it was time to come out of hiding. There was no point in hiding anymore, not if they could find him. Not if they could threaten the only thing in his life that meant anything to him.

Derek took a deep breath. A measure of relief came with his decision. He looked at Mark's brother. "Yes, it's me."

Chapter Fourteen

Mark saw his chance.

It was obvious to him that Derek thought his past had caught up to him. The man had no idea about his involvement in any of this. Glancing at Nick, Mark knew that his brother wouldn't implicate him, not without his saying something to that effect first.

It would be so easy.

It was so tempting.

He could let everything slide, pretend to be just an innocent bystander in this drama that was unfolding, and neither Derek nor Brooke—especially not Brooke—needed to know that he'd actually been recruited by Nick and hired by Tyler to locate him.

That was the coward's way out, though, and for a moment, Mark seriously entertained the thought of going that route. But because he was afraid of risking Brooke's anger, her loathing and, most of all, her absence from his life, he knew that he couldn't continue with the lie.

Because somehow, some way, the truth would surface, and he couldn't live the kind of life that Derek had endured for the past twenty-five years. He couldn't live with looking over his shoulder, wondering when the truth would accidentally come out and what the consequences of that, of keeping a lie going, would be.

Frustrated, edgy, Mark shoved his hands deep into his pockets.

The longer the lie lived, the larger it became. The harder it would be to make amends. If she even let him make amends. If her father let him.

Making up his mind, he interrupted Derek before the man could get started telling his story to Nick.

"I was sent to find you."

Wrapped up in the jumble of events that had just transpired, worried about Brooke, anxious to make his confession, Derek looked at the man he considered his daughter's savior with complete confusion.

"What?"

"Tyler Carlton hired me to find you," Mark said slowly. He was aware that his brother was looking at him, but he didn't bother to see if the expression was surprise or something else. He needed to get this out. "To find his mother's brother."

At a loss as to what to think about this newest piece

of information, Derek could only stare at him, dumbfounded. "Why?"

Mark glanced at Nick before explaining. His brother looked a little surprised that he'd chosen this setting to make the facts evident, but he didn't want to wait any longer. "Because before she died, his mother told him that you had been a witness to what happened back then. That you'd seen his father—his *real* father—kill her husband, Jeremy. That you could help finally bring Walter Parks to justice and allow Jeremy to finally have the justice he deserved."

Derek felt as if he was reeling. "Marla had a child by that monster?"

"Two," Nick put in. "Tyler and Conrad. Twins."

"I never knew, never suspected," Derek whispered. So much time had been lost. He should have made the attempt to find her, to be there for her. And now it was too late. His heart ached.

"No one did," Mark told him. "She only told her children when she was on her deathbed. I guess she was tired of living a lie. And so am I."

Derek looked at him for a long moment, his expression unreadable. "Then you're not a writer from New York."

Feeling guilty, Mark offered the man a half smile. "I'm from New York all right, but I'm a private investigator. I'm sorry, it was the only way I could think of to get close to you."

Derek shook his head. The attack on Brooke, his own identity outed, the true parentage of his nephews, this was all so much to absorb. His ordered life had been sent reeling on its ear. For the second time in his life, he realized that nothing would be as it was before.

But he'd run from doing what was right all these years. It was time to stop running.

"Don't be sorry," he told Mark. "If you hadn't been there, Brooke would have died. And saving her life means everything to me." And then his eyes darkened. "Walter Parks was behind this, wasn't he?"

It was Nick who answered his question. "The man we've got in custody didn't say as much when he was ranting, but we've got a pretty good idea that Parks is the responsible party."

Derek's mouth hardened as he remembered that day over a quarter of a century ago. The day that had been both the happiest and the worst day of his life. The day he had both found and lost Anna.

"He's an evil, evil man," Derek pronounced. He straightened his shoulders, and it looked to Mark as if Derek had suddenly shed a very heavy weight from them. "I'll tell you anything you want to know."

"Good, I'll set up a meeting for you with Tyler and the D.A. as soon as possible," Nick promised him.

He looked back over his shoulder to where the would-be hit man had been left. The man had been handcuffed to his hospital bed with a guard watching over him, but Nick didn't want to take any chances.

"Now if you'll excuse me, I've got a prisoner to see to." He looked at Mark. "You going to be okay?"

"Yeah, fine." He didn't want his brother fussing over him. "Go do what you have to do."

"I'll call you later," Nick told him.

He left the two men standing in the hall, keeping vigil, sharing unspoken, fearful thoughts.

Derek was the first to finally break the silence. "Tell me the truth, Mark," he said suddenly, then stopped. "It is Mark, isn't it?"

He didn't blame the man for having doubts. "Yes, it's Mark."

Derek nodded, accepting the assurance. He struggled to keep the fear at bay. "How bad was she when they took her in?"

For a moment they were just two men sharing the same fear, loving the same person. "Brooke was unconscious. But I heard the doctor say that the bullet had missed her heart." He'd had to restrain himself from shaking the physician, trying to get answers, to get assurances when he knew there were none.

"Thank God." Struggling against caving in emotionally, Derek searched for something to distract him. He looked at the man with him. "You really do care about her, don't you? That wasn't an act."

He couldn't explain why, when other people's opinions never meant anything to him, that he was relieved that Derek understood. But he was.

"No, that wasn't an act. I care about your daughter more than I can possibly say." A rueful smile came to his lips. "I'm not very good with words. I guess I should have said I was something other than an writer."

There was a sadness in Derek's eyes as he said, "Brooke always had a soft spot in her heart for writers."

Which made what he'd done even that much more manipulative, Mark thought. "Yes, I know."

Derek sighed wearily as he shook his head again. "She's going to be devastated when she finds out about all this. About you. About me."

Mark looked at Brooke's father in surprise. He hadn't even thought about that part of it. He'd been so wrapped up in his own dilemma, in how to make a clean breast of it to Brooke, that he hadn't even considered what this other revelation might do to her. It hadn't crossed his mind that she was ignorant of the facts.

"Then she doesn't know."

"Nothing." Derek looked at the stricken man beside him, taking pity on him. "I can break it to her if you like." When Mark raised an eyebrow in a silent question, he added, "All of it."

Another easy way out. But how reprehensible would she find it to have her father as the messenger and not him? No, there was no easy way out, Mark told himself. No way around it. Not if he ever hoped to win her.

And even if he didn't, he owed this to her, owed it to her to tell her the truth himself, not by proxy. "No, I need to tell her myself."

Derek solemnly nodded his head. "I understand."

Mark only hoped that Brooke would.

Easing the door open, Mark tiptoed into the room. The nurse had told him Brooke was awake and asking for him, but he still thought she might be asleep when he entered.

Her eyes were closed.

Holding his breath, Mark moved in a little closer. He stood by the bed for a moment just looking at her, his heart aching. She was alive, but she looked so frail, so delicate, as pale as the sheet she was lying on.

The doctor had told Derek and him that the surgery had gone exceptionally well and he had every confidence that she would recover. They'd gotten the bullet, and Brooke had lost very little blood, considering the circumstances.

But he needed to see for himself. Needed to assure himself that she was still alive, still breathing.

He stood by her bed for a long time.

Her eyes fluttered open just as he began to back away. She looked right at him, spearing his soul. Holding him fast.

"Don't go."

Her voice was small, barely penetrating the air around her. Barely audible.

He moved back to her side immediately, taking her hand in both of his. Acutely aware that this might be the last time he could be with her like this. The last time he might be with her at all.

She tried to smile. Only one corner of her mouth rose. "My hero," she whispered.

The word pierced his heart, bringing with it a fresh assault of guilt. "Don't."

"You've...got to...get...over this...modesty..."

Mark," she said with effort. "You were my…hero. You saved…me. Always there…watching…over…me."

Her eyes fluttered shut. The even breathing told him that she'd fallen asleep again.

He didn't let go of her hand.

They took turns, Derek and he, sitting by her bed, keeping vigil, waiting for her to wake up again.

Waiting to tell her what he didn't want to tell her, Mark felt as if his very life was on hold. He knew how prisoners on death row felt, waiting for that fateful call from the governor.

The call that might not come. The forgiveness that might not be there.

Brooke woke up again six hours later, during his portion of the vigil.

Stirring, she murmured in her sleep, calling his name. When he answered, she opened her eyes. And then smiled. It came slowly, unfurling like a sleeping flower in the morning sun.

"I was dreaming about you, and here you are. My hero."

He couldn't have her calling him that, believing that, not until she knew everything.

For a moment, because of her condition, he thought of waiting. But that was the fear talking. He had waited too long already.

Maybe, he realized, if he'd told her last night, the way he was going to before changing his mind at the last minute, she might not be lying here like this.

There were a thousand different ways to play the scenario through his head. It didn't matter. It had happened, and thank God she had survived it.

He had to do what needed to be done.

Though her head felt as if it was in danger of spinning again, she tried to focus on Mark's face. He looked so solemn, so bereft. Was that because of her? She was sorry she'd put him through this.

"Is the mugger dead?"

"No."

Nick had told him that the man had regained consciousness and shown every sign of pulling through. He had also made a partial confession, admitting he was paid to kill Derek Ross, but refusing to give them the name of the man who'd hired him. Nick said the hardened man said something about not living out the night if he gave the man up.

"He wasn't a mugger," Mark told her. Brooke looked at him with eyes that didn't understand. "He was a hit man."

"A hit man?" she echoed incredulously. How was that possible? They didn't move in those kinds of circles. "Did he get lost? Why would a hit man want to kill me?"

"He didn't." Mark measured out his words slowly, giving each one weight. Waiting for each to sink in. "He wanted to kill your father. He thought you were Derek. You were wearing his raincoat, opening up the shop..."

His voice trailed off for a moment along with his courage.

It still didn't make any sense to her. "I don't understand. Why would someone want to kill my father? He's just a bookstore owner."

"No, he's not." Standing over her, Mark looked down into her eyes. Hoping he could find forgiveness there as he began to approach the truth of his part in all this. "He's Derek Ross."

In her mind's eye, she suddenly saw the letter. The letter she'd found in his desk drawer and had thought was misaddressed. The letter written by a Tyler Carlton, urging her father to come forward.

It had to be a mistake. Stubbornly she said, "Moss, our name is Moss."

"No," he told her quietly, taking her hand in his, "it's Ross. Your father is Derek Ross, Marla Carlton's younger brother."

"Marla Carlton?" She wrinkled her brow. "Who's Marla—the woman whose funeral Dad went to?"

Mark nodded.

"And someone wants to kill him because he's her brother?" Why? Who was this Marla Carlton? For that matter, who was her father?

He knew this was hard for her, hard to comprehend, but there was no turning back now. "No, because he witnessed Walter Parks kill her husband, Jeremy Carlton."

Her head was aching and spinning at the same time. Was she really hearing all this, or was this just part of a bad dream, induced by the anesthesia?

"How do you know all this?" she asked him. "Did my father tell you?" Why would her father confide in

Mark and not her? Why had he kept all this from her all these years?

Mark braced himself. This was it. "No, I was sent to find him."

This was getting more and more confusing. "They sent a writer?"

"No." He took a deep breath. "They sent a private investigator."

She stared at him. What was he saying to her? That her father was someone else? That *he* was someone else?

"You?" she finally asked, her voice shaking. She felt as if the very walls of her life were being systematically shattered.

"Me."

She stared at him as she tried desperately to align the information she'd just received with what she'd thought, until two minutes ago, was true. None of the jagged edges fit together. Everything felt all jumbled. The only thing she knew was that she knew nothing. Everything she'd believed to be true was a lie.

Her eyes narrowed as she focused on the man she loved. The man who didn't exist. "You lied to me."

The words rang like a condemnation. "About some things."

Hairs, he was splitting hairs. She knew better. "About everything."

"No." He couldn't have her believing that. But when he started to take her hand, she pulled it away, nearly yanking the needle out of her vein.

The expression on her face cut him dead.

"How do I know that?" she demanded hotly. "You could be lying now."

There was no way he could prove that he wasn't. He could only give her his word. "I'm not."

She shook her head. "I don't believe you." How could she have been so stupid, so blind? She'd literally thrown herself at him. And he'd been there to catch her. Humiliated, she hated him. "Boy, what an assignment you got. Find a missing person and, oh, yes, make love to his stupid twit of a daughter while you're at it. And you got paid for this?"

It sounded disgusting. He couldn't blame her for being angry. But it hadn't been like that, and he had to make her believe that it wasn't.

"You're not a stupid twit, and it wasn't supposed to happen that way."

"Right, regrets." She nodded, remembering the look on his face when he'd discovered that she was a virgin. "Sorry I wasn't more experienced for you."

"Stop it." There was a dangerous edge to the warning. For a second, she was silent, looking at him. Daring him to prove her wrong. He felt as helpless as he had when he'd seen the hit man aiming his gun at her. More, because he had no weapon of his own to use. "That wasn't part of it."

And then Brooke laughed shortly, anger entering her eyes. "Well, you can't exactly call it a bonus now, can you?"

How did he make her understand that he hadn't used her, not that way.

Hadn't he? a small voice echoed in his brain. Hadn't he used her to bring him back among the living? He could have kept her at arm's length; it wouldn't have cost him the investigation. But it had been easier for him not to. And in the final analysis, that was using her.

He came as close to pleading as he ever had in his life. "Brooke, you have to believe me when I say that what happened between you and me was beside the point."

But her eyes were flat, unapproachable. "Was anything you told me true? Are you even from New York, or was that an act, too?" Sarcasm twisted her mouth. "You know, you really should be in the movies, you're very convincing."

"I am from New York." His voice was tight as he fought to rein in his emotions. Losing his temper wasn't going to further his case. Nothing, he knew, was going to further his case. "And I told you as much of the truth as I could. My brother's best friend hired me to find your father—"

"Your brother?" she echoed. "You have a brother?" She knew nothing about him. The thought hit her right between the eyes. She'd given herself to a stranger, a lie, a fabrication. For all she knew he was married with three children.

He nodded. "His name is Nick and he's with the police department—"

But she was shaking her head, her one good hand to her ear. The IV bottle tottered dangerously, then settled again. "I don't want to hear it," she cried. "You'll just tell me more lies."

He stood his ground, feeling as if he was fighting for his life. "Brooke, I—"

"Get out," she cried. Tears sprang to her eyes. Tears of anger, of hurt and humiliation.

It couldn't end like this. She hated him; he could see it in her eyes. And he couldn't stand to see her crying like this.

"Brooke, please—"

"Get out," she repeated, struggling not to scream. Her emotions were all over the map. "I want you to get out of here."

He wanted to stay and fight for her, to make her understand that he'd done what he had to do but that making love with her hadn't been part of it. That was in a separate place all its own. And above all, he wanted her to believe that she was the most wonderful thing that had ever happened to him.

And that he loved her.

But he could see by the expression on Brooke's face that she wouldn't believe him, wouldn't believe anything that came out of his mouth now. And he couldn't blame her. In her place, he knew he would feel the same way. Violated.

He backed away from her. Just before he opened the door, he said, "I'll send in your father."

"No," she ordered with so much feeling that the single word all but drained her. Her father had lied to her, too, had lied to her her entire life. "I don't want to see him, either." She pushed the button on the side of her bed that made the upper portion rise until her eyes were all but level with his. “I don’t want to see anyone, do you understand? I want to be left alone.”

He thought of the man waiting outside the room. Brooke was her father’s whole world. Mark deserved her censure, her father didn’t. *He’d* kept the truth from her to protect her.

“Brooke.” He tried again.

She drew herself up as much as she could, tethered the way she was to an IV on one side, a monitor on the other. “I said get out! Now!”

Afraid of what this was doing to her physically, Mark had no choice but to do what she said. With a nod of his head, he withdrew, closing the door behind him.

He didn’t hear her as she began to cry in the room. All he heard was the sound of his own heart, breaking.

Chapter Fifteen

"Mr. Walter Parks?"

Looking up from his desk, Walter Parks scowled. His secretary had selfishly taken the day off, leaving another woman to fill her place. Obviously, this woman didn't understand the ramifications of her job, since she had allowed some stranger to breach his inner office and annoy him. He hated incompetence.

"Yes?" he barked. In response, the young man stepped forward and thrust a thick envelope into his hand. Parks stared at it. There was only his name on the outside, nothing more. "What the hell is this?"

"A subpoena," the man said cheerfully, already retreating. "Consider yourself served, sir. Have a nice day."

Enraged, Parks threw the envelope after the man,

who was swift enough to make his exit and close the door behind him. The envelope landed with a loud thud against the door, then fell to the floor.

Cursing the stupidity of inept secretaries in particular and the universe in general, Parks walked over to where the envelope lay and picked it up. When he tore it open, he found the subpoena inside. A subpoena ordering him to show up at a local hospital in order to have his DNA tested.

This was that bastard's work, he thought. Tyler Carlton. Marla's young whelp had already been here once, claiming that he was his father, asking for recognition. As if that would ever happen. He'd thrown the money-grubber out, had security "escort" him out of the building. He'd screened his calls, making sure he had no contact with the pretender. If Carlton thought he was going to show up for testing, he was just as naive as his silly mother had been.

About to throw the subpoena in the trash, Parks saw that it had been issued with the backing of the D.A.'s office. Damn Jackson. The man had been looking for a way to come after him for years.

Furious, crumpling the offending document and throwing it to the floor, Parks stormed out of his office to go and fire his secretary's substitute.

Brooke smiled as her father gently helped ease her into the passenger side of his dark sedan. After three days in the hospital, she was more than ready to go home. The surgery to remove the bullet had gone well, and the surgeon who'd operated on her said that he'd never had a patient recover so rapidly. It was music to her ears.

"I won't break, Dad."

He'd almost lost her. He was taking nothing for granted again. Derek closed her door. "I don't know about that."

Brooke winced a little as she buckled up, but the pain was outweighed by the triumph of regaining her independence. "The doctor said I'd be good as new with a little rest. Better."

"Let me pamper you for a while," Derek said, getting behind the wheel. Starting up the car, he glanced at his daughter. Her color had returned, but there was a sadness to her now. A sadness that he knew had nothing to do with the terrible incident that could have cost Brooke her life and cost him everything. "You should forgive him, you know."

Brooke stared straight ahead at the road. She wasn't going to go there anymore, wasn't going to think about him, ache for him, silently rail at him. It was over, in the past, and she needed to move on. Her voice was hollow as she asked, "Who?"

Derek sighed quietly. She was stubborn, just like Marla had been. In so many ways, Brooke reminded him of his late sister. "You know who I'm talking about, Brooke. Mark."

There was no point in talking about Mark. He hadn't been to the hospital since she'd sent him away. If he'd cared, he would have tried again. In his place, she would have. Over and over. That he didn't just meant she was right. He was probably relieved to be out of the charade he was forced to play. "How do we even know that's his real name?"

"It is." Derek took a left turn at the light. "Brooke, he was just doing his job."

Her voice rose, emotion threatening to overwhelm her, but she managed to bank it down. "Don't defend him to me, Dad. He could have been up-front with you, told you who he was."

Derek shook his head. "Not the way I was in the beginning. I would have just denied everything and sent him away."

Sent him away. Then none of this would have happened. And her heart wouldn't be aching like this. "Would that have been so bad?"

"Yes." Surprised by his firm tone, Brooke turned to look quizzically at her father. "For one thing, he wouldn't have been there to save your life."

"He wouldn't have been there to mess it up, either." She couldn't keep the bitterness out of her voice.

He hated seeing her like this, hated seeing his daughter in pain. "Love can only mess up your life if you turn your back on it."

Her defenses immediately snapped into place. "Who's talking about love?"

"I am. You are." He glanced at her before looking back on the road. "You're in love with him."

"No, I'm not," she declared vehemently. Then, because she knew her father could see right through her, she relented. She'd never lied to him and she wasn't going to allow Mark-whoever-he-was make her start now. "All right, but it'll pass. Like the flu."

"No, it won't." His tone told her that he knew better. "Not your first one. Not if it's real."

"You're talking about Mom again, aren't you?" Right now she just wasn't in the mood for the old story. "Well, Dad—"

The time for secrecy was over. All secrecy. "No, I'm not. Jenna was a wonderful woman who tried to make me forget the pain I felt."

"Pain?"

He made up his mind. "What I'm going to tell you, I've never told anyone before. Not even your mother. But she knew without asking that there had been someone before her. Someone I could never forget. She accepted that and she was a remarkable woman." He spared Brooke a glance, trying to gauge how to tell her. "But she's not who I want to tell you about right now."

"More secrets?" Brooke felt her stomach quiver uneasily. How much more was there that she didn't know about her father? It seemed as if ever since Mark had come into her life, nothing was what it had been before.

"No, no more secrets," he promised. "I want to get everything out in the open." He took a breath, knowing this was going to shock her. "I fell in love with Walter Parks's wife."

She could only stare at him. Her father and another man's wife? Especially Walter Parks? It seemed too incredible to believe.

"What?"

"Yes, Anna Parks. She was a beautiful woman, full of life, full of energy. Walter sapped all that away." He could hardly keep the animosity out of his voice. "He treated her as if she was some lowly servant to be ordered around and then ignored. It was clear that he'd just married her for her father's money and connections. Once he had that, he stopped pretending that he had any interest in her whatsoever. He all but locked her up in that big house he insisted on buying."

She was trying to follow this. "If she was locked up, how did you—?"

"Twenty-five years ago, Walter threw an elaborate party on his yacht." He shivered as he recalled the events. But then, how was he to know that they would change his life so drastically? "He invited a lot of his so-called friends and business associates, among them my brother-in-law and his family. I was included. Walter had to be feeling particularly good about himself that day because he allowed Anna to come, too."

His voice grew soft as he recalled seeing the woman for the first time. "That's when I met her. That's when I fell in love with her. She didn't have to tell me how unhappy she was, I could see it in her eyes." Just as he could when he looked into Brooke's, he thought. The light turned red and he turned to look at his daughter. "You know how there are some people you can just look at and know everything about them instantly?"

Brooke sighed as she shook her head. "I would say

yes, except that in my case, it turned out that I didn't know anything."

He patted Brooke's hand. The light turned green again. "You knew the right things, honey. Mark's a decent man who loves you."

She didn't want to talk about Mark. Not now, perhaps not ever. "What about Anna?" she pressed. "What happened between you and her?"

He knew she was avoiding the subject, but he didn't mind. It had been years since he allowed himself to relive the events of that night, and he needed to. Needed to if he was going to be able to be of use to the D.A.

"Things got a little involved. The party went on for hours. Anna had a little too much to drink and was afraid that her husband would cause a scene if he saw her, so I took her downstairs to one of the cabins and sat with her. She fell asleep for a little while.

"I left her alone and came back on deck. That's when I found we'd gone back to the dock and everyone had left the party. Everyone except for Walter and Jeremy. They were topside, toasting something. I didn't hear what was said, but I saw Walter slip something into my brother-in-law's drink." His mouth became grim. "It had to be poison. Jeremy collapsed almost immediately, gasping and thrashing. Walter had this smug look on his face as he stood over him. When Jeremy finally stopped, Walter took his pulse. Then he put out to sea again. When we were out far enough, I saw Walter dispose of the body by throwing it overboard. He never saw me.

"I went back downstairs and hid with Anna. The second Walter turned the boat around and put into the harbor, Anna and I waited for our opportunity. We slipped out the first chance we got. Not knowing what else to do, I brought her to my house. We wound up spending the night together." He paused significantly, as if to relive those moments. "She was worried about her children, so in the morning, I took her home. Walter wasn't there. It was the last time I ever saw her," he concluded heavily.

Brooke's eyes were wide as she was reeled in. "Did he kill her, too?"

"Not literally, but he killed her spirit." And for that, more than any of the other offenses on Walter's' extensive list, he would always hate the man. "I heard that he sent her off to a sanitarium, convinced everyone that she'd had a nervous breakdown. No one contested it. I should have. But I didn't. I went to Marla and told her what I saw.

"She was afraid Walter would kill me if he knew what I had witnessed, so she told me to go as far away as I could. She did the same after the police told her the official verdict for Jeremy's death was drowning. She figured Walter had found someone to bribe. I wandered around for a little bit, but I discovered that I couldn't stay away from San Francisco."

He smiled ruefully at his daughter. "I guess I kept hoping Anna would come back. Then I met your mother and, well, you know the rest." Gripping the steering wheel, he made a sharp right before resuming his narrative. "My point is, I missed my chance because I allowed myself to get overwhelmed. Don't you do the same."

In this department, Brooke thought, she and her father were worlds apart. She didn't need that lying son of a gun, Mark, in her life. She would never know when he wasn't lying. "I appreciate what you're trying to do, Dad, but this is different."

"Every situation is different," he said, though he didn't see her point, "but he loves you."

Despite everything, she could feel her heart quickening inside her chest. "Did he tell you that?"

Derek would have liked to give her that added assurance, but there were to be no more lies between them, not even little white ones. "Some things don't need words."

And some things, she thought, shifting forward in her seat again and staring straight ahead, do.

"Hey, Maddy, hear the latest?"

Maddy Jones glanced up from her cluttered desk at the *Chronicle.* The as-yet-to-be-taken-seriously journalist looked at the man, Colin Woods, peering into her cubicle. As she did so, she eased a folder closed. Her desk was littered with things she had yet to get to. It was a display of chaos, in direct contrast to her mind, which kept a thousand things in their proper order.

"Which latest?"

The man moved in closer, lowering his voice, enjoying his moment. "My source at the D.A.'s says that it looks like there're more apples on the Walter Parks tree than the old man'd like us to know about."

"Oh?" She didn't even pretend to be above this kind of gossip. It was what got her blood moving. "Tell me more." And then a question struck her. "What's the D.A.'s office got to do with it?"

"They're the ones backing a subpoena. Robert Jackson handled it personally." The current D.A. was thought to be the darling of the tabloids because he made no secret of the fact that he was systematically bedding every attractive woman within a hundred-mile radius. "Seems he subpoenaed Old Man Parks to give a DNA sample to prove that this claim is legitimate."

She laughed shortly, picturing the uptight, condescending gem emperor. "Bet that makes Parks mad as hell."

"No bet."

"Thank you, Colin." She flashed a grin at him. "You just made my day."

Everything else in Maddy's well-organized head was pushed back. She could smell a media sensation in the offing.

He sat in his car, watching the house. Mark carefully rotated his neck and shoulders, trying to get rid of a nagging kink. He'd followed Derek and Brooke from the hospital. When they arrived home without incident, he'd positioned himself across the street, a silent, free-lancing guardian angel.

There was no way he was going to take a chance on

Parks sending out a second hit man to do the job right. Especially not after Tyler had convinced the D.A. to issue that subpoena asking for a sample of Parks's DNA.

The old bastard had to know the end was within sight. That the things he'd tried to keep buried all these years were finally beginning to surface. That had to make him desperate. Parks knew that once Derek talked, he would be facing a murder charge. They couldn't kill him twice. He had nothing to lose by killing Derek.

Unlike him, who had everything to lose.

Who was he kidding? He'd already lost it, Mark silently taunted himself. But lost it or not, there was no way he was going to take a chance on anything happening to Brooke or to her father. Not while he was alive.

He reached for the sandwich that was already growing stale on the seat next to him. It was going to be a long night.

"Are you sure you want to do this?" Brooke's voice seemed to echo up and down the long corridor as she looked at her father anxiously. "I mean, if you wanted to sell the store, pull up stakes and just move away, I'd go with you. There's no need to put yourself through this."

She knew it was the right thing to do, but after the incident with the gunman, she knew where her priorities were. She would never forgive herself if anything ever happened to her father because of this.

"I'm sure," he assured her. "Besides, there's not a box big enough to pack my conscience away in, Brooke." He patted her hand that rested on the wooden bench. "I've put this off for too long. Maybe if I'd come forward right away, a lot of people's lives would be different."

So now she knew what the pervading sadness in her father's eyes was all about. "You're thinking of Anna again, aren't you?"

"Among others." Anna might not have been shipped off to God only knew where, and Marla wouldn't have packed up the kids and disappeared. He looked now at his daughter, running a hand affectionately along her cheek. "About the only good thing that did come out of it, besides you, is that you met Mark."

She folded her hands primly before her. "Dad, let's not go through that again."

"I'll go through it as many times as it takes to make you come around." He felt he owed that to Mark. "He's been protecting us, you know."

Brooke blinked. She hadn't a clue what her father was talking about. "Who?"

"Mark." He was surprised she'd remained oblivious to it. Brooke was usually sharper than that. "I saw his car outside the house. He followed me to and from the bookstore while you were in the hospital. His car was two lengths back when we left for court this morning." He saw the frown forming on Brooke's face. "Whether you like it or not, the man's become our guardian angel. That says a great deal about a man when he doesn't think he stands a chance in hell of getting the woman he loves to ever forgive him."

Brooke pressed her lips together. But before she had a chance to say anything, the assistant D.A. was opening the outer office door. He stepped back as far as he could in order not to take up any room. "The D.A. is ready for you, Mr. Ross."

Mr. Ross.

That, Brooke thought as she rose to her feet, was going to take some getting used to.

Giving her father an encouraging smile, she hooked her arm through his. "Okay then, let's go, Dad. 'Second star to the right, straight on until morning.'"

Derek smiled. "I always did favor *Peter Pan.*"

Robert Jackson, the tall imposing D.A., dominated the small office the same way he did a courtroom, but Brooke's eyes were immediately drawn to the six-foot, dark-haired man sitting beside him.

The latter had the exact same coloring as she did, the same black hair, the same green eyes. He could have easily been her brother.

Or her cousin.

Which was exactly what he was, she quickly learned once the introductions were made.

Nothing could have pleased her more.

"You know," she confided as she shook his hand with her free one, "until this moment, I thought there was just my father and me. I always wanted to be part of a large family."

"Then," Tyler told her with a smile, "are you in for a treat." He glanced toward Jackson. "Okay if I show the others in?"

"Others?" Brooke asked as the D.A. nodded.

Rather than answer her, Tyler opened the door to an adjoining room. "Come on in," he said to his siblings, "it's time to let Brooke and Uncle Derek know what they're in for."

Stunned, Brooke exchanged looks with her father as four people entered the room, three in the front and one lagging slightly behind. The one male in the group looked like an exact carbon copy of the man she'd just been told was her cousin.

Tyler put his arm around the other man's shoulders. "This is Conrad, my twin brother. And these two lovely ladies—" he nodded at the two who had entered first "—are my sisters, Sara and Kathleen."

Brooke's attention was completely riveted to the latter. She instantly recognized the woman's face from the dust jacket of the book that was lying on her nightstand. "Kathleen," she echoed.

Kathleen, the oldest of the four, was the only one whose hair was blond and whose eyes were blue. It set her apart from the others as did, she felt, her talent. She couldn't help the slightly superior smile that nudged at her lips. "Yes."

"Kathleen Carlton," Brooke repeated, still unable to believe what her eyes were telling her. "Like the mystery writer."

It was obvious to everyone that this was one of the

things Kathleen loved best about what she did—the recognition. "I *am* the mystery writer."

Brooke's eyes were wide and sparkling. "I love your work."

Kathleen's smile grew larger. "I like her already," she told the woman at her side, the one who had yet to be introduced. Realizing the oversight, Kathleen magnanimously did the honors. She moved the tall, willowy redhead forward. "Oh, this is my friend, Carla Baker, librarian by day, scholar par excellence by night," she teased with uncustomary affection.

In deference to the moment, and to what he hoped to gain in the immediate future—fodder for his case—Jackson had stood by quietly much longer than usual. But it was obviously time to move things along.

He put one arm around Kathleen's waist and one around Sara's, ushering them toward the open door. "Why don't you all get to know each other while Mr. Ross tells me exactly how I can finally further my case against Walter Parks?" he suggested. He glanced over his shoulder at Derek. "You wouldn't know anything about this rumor about gem smuggling, would you?"

"Actually, yes, I do."

Derek saw the D.A.'s face light up. The smuggling had been something Marla had once confided to him. Something she'd said that Jeremy had on Walter. The same something that had brought about his brother-in-law's death. It was time to get this off his chest and finally begin living his life again, Derek thought. Perhaps, when all this came to its conclusion and was wrapped up, he could even discover what had really happened to Anna.

It gave him hope.

He watched his daughter disappear into the next room with the other young people, then settled back to tell Robert Jackson and Tyler Carlton his story. From the beginning.

Chapter Sixteen

"I'm afraid I made a mess of it," Brooke concluded, finishing up an abbreviated version of her aborted romance with Mark.

It had hit her with the speed of a lightning bolt when her father had told her that Mark was watching over them, to keep them safe from possibly another one of Walter Parks's hit men. Mark really did care about her. And, no matter what she'd tried to tell herself, she still loved him. Would always love him.

As for her pouring out her heart to Carla Baker in the room adjoining the D.A.'s office, there had been no incubation period. She had taken to these people—her cousins—immediately, especially to Kathleen and her friend, Carla.

She had always been crazy about the writer's

books and was more than a little in awe of the woman.

Her reaction to Carla was more of a case of finding a kindred soul. Carla was the same age as she was and embodied a combination of eagerness and shyness that Brooke felt defined her own approach to life. With very little encouragement, she found herself pouring out her heart to Carla, telling her all about Mark and the way she'd treated him once she'd discovered his deception.

She was having second thoughts, now that she had finally calmed down and started to think things through. Second thoughts about her reaction and second thoughts about what that reaction had cost her. When she'd discovered what he'd done, she'd honestly thought that Mark didn't care, that it had all been an act, because he hadn't attempted to make her change her mind.

But now that her father had told her Mark was keeping to the shadows, watching over them after the way she'd treated him, well, didn't that indicate something? Didn't that mean that maybe he really did have feelings for her? At least a little? She could go very far on just a little—but she'd destroyed everything by refusing to listen to him, by telling him to go away.

She didn't know how to make amends for that.

She looked at Carla, suddenly fighting back tears. "I was such an idiot. I've lost the one man I was meant to be with."

Granted, the words did come off a little dramatic, but Carla suspected that was because, as Brooke had confided in her, books had always been her best friends, always on call whenever she needed them, twenty-four/seven.

The pert redhead glanced around Brooke's head toward the other room, an idea beginning to form. "Don't be so sure."

Hope sprang up in the middle of a field of widening despair. Brooke placed her hand over Carla's, as if to tap into the other woman's idea. "Why?"

Carla grinned. "Because I think I might have an idea—offbeat for some, perfect for you—that I think just might do the trick."

Brooke knew she was willing to do practically anything to get another chance with Mark. "Don't just leave me hanging…"

Carla rose to her feet. By the expression on her face, the plan was clearly taking shape and gaining substance. "We're going to need help," Carla tossed over her shoulder as she went to see about recruiting Tyler to help his newfound cousin.

"This should cover it." Tyler tore the check out of his checkbook, holding it out to Mark. It was the fee they had agreed upon, plus a little more because Mark had done his job so swiftly. "Best money I ever spent."

Taking it, Mark didn't bother looking at the amount. He felt certain that Tyler had written down what they had agreed to. Tyler wasn't the kind of man to renege or cut corners. But what Mark didn't quite get was why Tyler had insisted on his coming to the D.A.'s house in order to give him the money when they could have just as easily met anywhere.

He folded the check and placed it in his pocket. The restlessness that had been part of his life for so long, that had only abated those short periods of time when he had been with Brooke, was urging him to move on. "Well, I'd better get going."

But as he turned to leave, Tyler hooked his arm through Mark's, stopping him.

"What's your hurry? Have a drink with us to celebrate." Tyler nodded toward the small bar that Robert kept behind his desk. Robert was already on his feet, getting three glasses and a bottle of champagne he'd kept on ice. Tyler grinned as the other man poured. "After the testimony my newfound uncle gave our illustrious D.A. here, I'd say we're well on our way to taking down the man who destroyed my mother's life."

Mark really didn't feel like celebrating, but he couldn't very well walk away, not when it was put that way. Not when he had been instrumental, in his own small way, in bringing this all about.

So he nodded at Tyler and accepted the glass that Jackson handed him.

"To the future," Jackson held his flute aloft. Tyler and then Mark raised theirs to form a small, bubbling circle. "And to the end of Walter Parks's rein as gem czar and smuggler."

"Amen to that," Tyler agreed. Taking a sip, he slid a covert glance at Mark. "Good company, good wine, but I have this feeling that something's still missing." He struggled to keep his expression innocent. Especially when Jackson had just rolled his eyes before turning away. "Oh, yes, good music. Or, in lieu of that, poetry." Setting down his glass on Jackson's desk, he looked at Mark. "How do you feel about poetry, Mark?" he asked as he stepped to the closed doors on the opposite side of the room.

The champagne he'd just swallowed went down the wrong pipe. Mark coughed, holding his hand up to temporarily pause the conversation. Clearing his throat, he could only ask, "What?"

"Poetry," Tyler repeated throwing open the doors to the next room.

The room was a library, with shelves lining three of the four walls. It reminded Mark a little of Brooke's bookstore.

Then, before he could ask his brother's best friend what the hell had come over him, he heard her.

Heard just her voice.

His heart quickened.

Brooke.

Looking around, he didn't see her. There were other people in the adjoining room. Tyler's brother and sisters and some woman he didn't recognize.

And her voice floating to him.

There was a wing chair facing a window on the far wall. Her voice was coming from there. He moved toward it.

"He has blue eyes,
This man who's won my heart.

I said some cruel words
That tore us both apart.
If he could forgive them,
I promise that I would be
Everything he ever hoped for
If he would only return to me."

Her heart pounding in her throat, Brooke finished the small peace offering she had composed. She was almost afraid to look up, afraid that the presence she sensed wasn't his.

But when she did look up, she saw him standing there. Looking at her. Her eyes stung. She wanted to throw herself into his arms. Wanted to cry.

Like someone in a dream, Brooke slowly rose to her feet. Suddenly her mind was filled with words, words that all rushed together, trying to charge out of her mouth. She selected the only ones that were truly pertinent.

"I'm sorry."

Unable to believe that she was real, Mark cupped her face between his hands. He never thought he'd be this close to her again. "No, I'm sorry."

Carla came forward, relieved that her plan had worked. "Okay, you're each one sorrier than the other. Now kiss and make up so we can move on with this."

Tyler decided that a measure of privacy was called for, and he came to the couple's rescue. "Moving on sounds like a good idea." With a wide wave of his arms, he ushered everyone else toward the open double doors. "Why don't we all move back into the study and let these two have some privacy?"

Brooke smiled her gratitude, but her eyes remained on Mark. "That's my cousin."

His hands still framing her face, Mark laughed softly. "Yes, I know."

She needed to apologize, really apologize before they could move on in what was hopefully still a relationship. "But I wouldn't know, if it hadn't been for you." She placed her hands on his shirt, absorbing the warmth she felt from his chest. So very happy to be here with him like this. She was never going to be able to repay Carla and Tyler. "I didn't mean what I said to you."

He didn't need her apology. Having her here like this was all he'd ever needed.

"You had every right to be angry." He looked into her eyes. "I never meant to hurt you or your father."

"I know." And she did. There wasn't a mean-spirited bone in the man's body. "This is a good thing you did." She wanted him to know that, know what a difference he'd made in her father's life in such a short time. "My father seems happier, freer, lighter than he has in years. And now we've found this big family—it means the world to him." And to her, but this wasn't about her, it was about her father. And Mark. "And it's all because of you. I'll always be grateful."

Mark shrugged off the thanks. Unlike Dana, he had never been comfortable assuming center stage. "I was just the middle man, Brooke. It was Tyler who initiated the search."

She laughed, shaking her head. She'd never known anyone like him. The man was unbelievably modest. All the other men she'd fancied herself in love with had egos higher than Mt. Everest, but Mark was entirely without one. Maybe that was why she loved him the way she did. He was real and he didn't need to feed on any outside reinforcements.

She touched his cheek. "Stop it, I'm trying to thank you."

He placed his hand over hers, bringing the palm of her hand to his lips. He pressed a kiss to the center. "There's no need."

Brooke caught her breath as a thrill undulated through her. "There's every need. I haven't been the same since you left."

"I know what you mean," he confessed. "I feel the same way." Afraid she might misunderstand, he quickly explained, "I mean, I haven't been the same, either."

He sounded about as suave as a chunk of cheese, he thought ruefully. This was his moment to make everything right and he was stumbling over his own tongue, having a hell of a hard time forming sentences. Nothing new there. But he needed to, needed to let her know exactly how he felt. And what he wanted.

He tried again, looking into her eyes, hoping she could see into his soul—which belonged to her exclusively. "Did you mean what you said, in the poem? About my having your heart?"

Brooke smiled, blinking back tears again. As if he had to ask. "Yes."

"That's good. Because you have mine." He knew his voice didn't carry enough inflection and that he probably sounded as if he was reading a laundry list. "Damn it, Brooke, I'm not any good at this." He took her hand in his. "I won't be writing poems for you, or even reading them. That's not my style."

"Okay," she uttered breathlessly, every fiber in her being coaxing him on.

"But I do love you."

Her heart was hammering so hard in her throat, she was surprised she could still squeeze out a word without having it squeak. "You do?"

"Yes," he told her solemnly. "You make me feel complete." As he spoke, he explored the sensation for the first time, thinking out loud. "I never felt whole before. I always felt as if there was something not right, something missing. I didn't think I was really capable of loving." His parents' violent death and the life that followed thereafter had left him feeling hollow. Even finding Dana hadn't done anything to plug the hole. "Because, a person who's really in love can sense when there's something wrong, and I didn't pick up on any of those vibrations with Dana.

"But with you, it's different." And he meant that from the bottom of his heart. "It's like there's a single soul that's both yours and mine." He paused, wondering if she thought he was some kind of babbling lunatic. "Is any of this making any sense to you?"

"Yes, oh, yes." It made sense, it made beautiful sense.

"Ask her to marry you, already, or do I have to put it on a teleprompter?" Carla prodded impatiently from the other side of the door.

Unable to help herself, an incurable romantic, Carla wanted to be sure everything had gone well. The others pretended not to be listening, but with the exception of Jackson, who had more than his fill of romance according to the tabloids, they were all milling around close to the vicinity of the double doors.

Mark frowned at the doors. Taking her hand, he drew Brooke further to the other side of the room, away from prying ears.

His courage flagging, he looked down at her. "Would you?"

The very air had stopped moving. It took the rest of the room with it. "Would I what?"

"You know." Helpless, Mark nodded back toward the double doors.

She wanted to jump to conclusions, wanted to shout "Yes," but this time she was taking it slow. If only for a minute. "No, I don't. You're going to have to spell it out for me."

Mark took a breath. "All right, here goes. W-i-l-l y-o-u—"

Laughing, she placed her fingertips against his lips. "What are you doing?"

His eyes danced. "Spelling it out for you, like you asked."

Still laughing, Brooke punched his arm with her good fist. "I had no idea you had a sense of humor."

The blow surprised him. Admiration entered his eyes. "And I had no idea you had such a left hook. For a little thing, you do pack a wallop. But then, I guess I kind of suspected that." He stopped rubbing where the blow had landed and took her in his arms, smiling into her eyes. Smiling with his whole soul. "All right, now the right way. Will you marry me?"

She released the breath she was holding. "I've been waiting my whole life to marry you."

He didn't want her entering into this with false illusions. "I'm no Prince Charming."

"That's what you think." She wrapped her one good arm around his neck, rising up on her toes. "You'll always be my Prince Charming. Even if you don't write me poetry."

His heart full, Mark brought his mouth down on hers to seal their bargain and their fate.

In the next room Carla looked at Tyler in frustration. "I don't hear anything."

Tyler laughed, drawing her away from the double doors. "I think this time that's a good sign."

And it was.

* * * * *

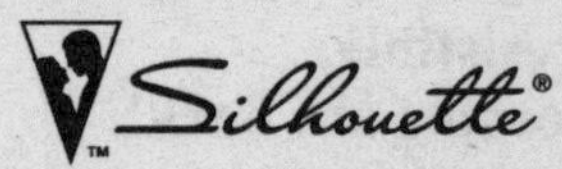

SPECIAL EDITION®

COMING NEXT MONTH

#1633 HOME ON THE RANCH—Allison Leigh
Men of the Double S
Rancher Cage Buchanan would do anything to help his child—even if it meant enlisting the aid of his enemy's daughter. Beautiful Belle Day could no more ignore Cage's plea for help than she could deny the passion that smoldered between them. But could a long-buried secret undermine the happiness they'd found in each other's arms?

#1634 THE RICH MAN'S SON—Judy Duarte
The Parks Empire
After prodigal heir Rowan Parks suffered a motorcycle accident, single mom Luanne Brown took him in and tended to his wounds. Bridled emotion soon led to unleashed love, but there was one hitch: he couldn't remember his past—and she couldn't forget hers….

#1635 THE BABY THEY BOTH LOVED—Nikki Benjamin
When writer Simon Gilmore discovered a son he never knew was his, he had to fight the child's legal guardian, green-eyed waitress Kit Davenport, for custody. Initially enemies, soon Simon and Kit started to see each other in a new light. Would the baby they both loved lead to one loving family?

#1636 A FATHER'S SACRIFICE—Karen Sandler
After years of battling his darkest demons, Jameson O'Connell discovered that Nina Russo had mothered his chid. The world-weary town outcast never forgot the passionate night that they shared and was determined to be a father to his son…but could his years of excruciating personal sacrifice finally earn him the love of his life?

#1637 A TEXAS TALE—Judith Lyons
Rancher Tate McCade's mission was to get Crissy Albreit back to the ranch her father wanted her to have. Not only did Tate's brown-eyed assurance tempt Crissy back to the ranch she so despised, but pretty soon he had her tempted into something more…to be in his arms forever.

#1638 HER KIND OF COWBOY—Pat Warren
Jesse Calder had left Abby Martin with a promise to return… but that had been five years ago. Now, the lies between them may be more than Abby can forgive—even with the spark still burning. Especially since this single mom is guarding a secret of her own: a little girl with eyes an all-too-familiar shade of Calder blue…

SSECNM0804

PRAISE FOR SANDRA HILL'S VIKING ROMANCES!

THE RELUCTANT VIKING

"I really enjoyed Ruby's story. Wouldn't it be wonderful if we could all have these sorts of second chances when we are at risk of losing something as precious as love."

—*Affaire de Coeur*

"*The Reluctant Viking* is a wonderfully in-depth, ambitious challenge for a first-time author, and Ms. Hill pulls it off with style!"

—*The Literary Times*

THE OUTLAW VIKING

"An entertaining battle-of-the-sexes romance that will keep readers laughing to the very end!"

—*Romantic Times*

"A well-told story, funny and heartwarming. Ms. Hill has created characters who will stay alive long after you close the book. This is a time-travel that shouldn't be missed."

—*The Paperback Forum*

"Ms. Hill transports not only the heroine but the reader back to the period in this fast-paced story."

—*Rendezvous*

THE LAST VIKING

"A fun, fast-paced page turner."

—*Romantic Times*

"The humor is delicious. Ms. Hill's Viking stories are always a thrill to read, and *The Last Viking* is no exception."

—*Rendezvous*

"Ms. Hill once again shows her talented, witty writing skills in narrative and character development . . . another winner for Ms. Hill!"

—*Old Book Barn Gazette*